Tom
Reynolds

THESE LOVERS
FLED AWAY

By the Same Author

Novels

SHABBY TIGER

RACHEL ROSING

MY SON, MY SON!

FAME IS THE SPUR

HARD FACTS

DUNKERLEY'S

THERE IS NO ARMOUR

THE HOUSES IN BETWEEN

A SUNSET TOUCH

THESE LOVERS FLED AWAY

For Children

DARKIE & CO.

SAMPSON'S CIRCUS

TUMBLEDOWN DICK

Autobiography

HEAVEN LIES ABOUT US

IN THE MEANTIME

AND ANOTHER THING. . . .

Criticism

BOOK PARADE

THESE LOVERS
FLED AWAY

****

BY
HOWARD SPRING

HARPER & BROTHERS PUBLISHERS
NEW YORK

Library of Congress catalog card number: 55-8049

Again for

MARION

And they are gone: aye, ages long ago
These lovers fled away into the storm.

John Keats, "The Eve of St. Agnes"

THESE LOVERS
FLED AWAY

CHAPTER ONE

I

S T. MICHAEL PENDEVEREL is a hamlet standing a mile inland.
North of it, across a few miles of intervening fields, you can see
the clay hills. When the sky is gray, they are gray, too. When the sun
shines, they blaze like a miniature range of snow-capped Sierras, cut
out sharply on heaven's blue.

South of the hamlet, when I was a child, were fields that I knew in
all their phases: the green of springtime, the colored riot of the ripening year, dog daisies, rusty spires of sorrel, and all this falling back to
green again when the haymakers had passed through. And there were
cornfields, likewise incessantly changing: brown ribs of corduroy, the
vivid green of young stalks, the wheat turning golden and then, in a
good summer, almost white, with splashes of poppy red and mustard
yellow. Southward of this lay the blue sea with the gulls lazing on the
air, adrift now over the water, now over this small sea of wheat that
had a liquid stir and ripple.

Where land and water met, there was not much rock. Here and
there, a hard spur ran out upon the beach, and the sand was yellow in
the small coves between these spurs; but for the most part the land was
soft, and there were falls of earth and loose stones. The blackthorn
hedge along the top was wind-slanted inward, a repellent barrier in
winter. In earliest spring it effervesced into white foam. It had been
breached in places, and plank bridges were thrown across the gaps.
There was the sense that we were being besieged, sapped and undermined; but don't let that worry you, my mother used to say: it'll last
our time.

Then there were the woods, damp and dripping except in prolonged
hot weather. The trees wore beards of moss, and ferns were everywhere:
on the earth and in the nooks and crannies of the trees themselves.
Primroses began to bloom before Christmas was on us, and then the
wood anemones came in patches of blue and white, and at last the
bluebells seeped and flooded everywhere, so that the burgeoning trees
were standing as far as the eye could see, knee-deep in a shadowed
blue tide. The songs of the birds swelled with the swelling year; in
May the place was a ringing choir, and restless with wings.

Everything—the pastures, the hamlet, the cornfields, the woods—belonged to Captain Orlop. In the heart of the woods you came on Captain Orlop's house. The chestnuts, the straggling Cornish elms, the beeches, sycamores and small scrub oaks gave place to rhododendrons and camellias, pittosporums, mimosas and brakes of bamboo. Within this circle of loveliness was a vast lawn. The house stood on the topmost edge of it, facing toward the sea. But you could not see the water. Beyond the lawn, the woods closed in again. All you saw was the entrance to a tunnel which was, in fact, a pathway through the woods, taking you down to steps built into the cliff and leading to the beach. At the bottom of the steps was a notice: PRIVATE.

It was difficult to conceive a greater privacy than Captain Orlop enjoyed: the circle of woods about him, and within that the circle of precious trees and shrubs, and within that the lawn, and upon the lawn the house. It was built of large blocks of honey-colored stone that did not belong to the district. Some eighteenth-century Orlop had brought them there and built them up to replace another house in which Orlops had lived for long before that. This house was a low, two-storied building. The oblong was broken by nothing but a charming portico, and the honey-colored stone was hidden by nothing but a wistaria that grew on the right-hand side of the entrance. I remember that it was in bloom that day when I came out of the woods and saw Rose Garland on the lawn, playing with a spaniel pup. It was 1901. I was twelve years old.

2

I have a rather odd, pretentious name—Chad. Chad Boothroyd. Some people think Chad is a contraction, but it isn't. I believe there was a saint named Chad. Perhaps I was named after him. Who knows? Boothroyd, anyway, was a queer name to find down there in the South of Cornwall. It belongs to the North of England.

I remember my father well. He was a handsome ingratiating rogue, always laughing, utterly without pride or shame. Even to me as a child, it was obvious that my mother adored him. She was a Bradford woman. Her father had a chemist's shop on Manningham Lane, and he was ambitious for his two children—this girl who was to become my mother, and a boy ten years older. When my mother was twenty and went for her holiday to Scarborough, her brother was already practicing as a solicitor. The Scarborough holiday seems to have been a sort of breaking out. Old Geldersome, the chemist, had kept a tight hand on the pair; if he had lived into old age, my mother would probably have become one of those sad dutiful spinsters tied to a deathbed that prolongs itself on and on through the years. Happily, he died, and the children found themselves with about a thousand pounds each. Off my mother went for a holiday of indefinite length at Scarborough.

Mr. Geldersome, strict in all things, had been especially strict about young men. In marriage, a girl should better herself. He saw the Geldersome line moving on an inclined plane, a bit higher in each generation, ending, I suppose, beneath gilded tombs encrusted with coats of arms and recumbent whippets. And so young men found no welcome in the rooms over the chemist's shop, for nothing more inspiring presented itself than the boys who sang with Edith Geldersome in the mixed choir of the Wesleyan chapel. To have a thousand pounds in the bank and to be able to talk to any young man who took her fancy must have seemed enchanting to Edith, and when the young man turned out to be Tom Boothroyd she was finished.

The man she met can't have been much different from the man I knew. He was of medium height, thin as a lath, brown as a berry, with blue laughing eyes and hair black as jet. Perhaps his utter irresponsibility was attractive after the calculating and cautious custom that had governed the Geldersome home. My mother once told me that the first words he ever spoke to her were: "Pardon me, madam. Could you lend me a shilling?"

She was alone in a teashop. She had noticed this handsome young man drinking tea at a neighboring table, had noticed, too, his fumblings in his pockets when the waitress brought him his bill. Then there he was, as cool as you like. "Could you lend me a shilling?"

She handed him half a crown, which was the smallest coin she had, and then, saying nothing of the eighteenpence which he could well have given back to her at once, he asked where they might meet on the morrow so that he could repay. She said it didn't matter; but I imagine she was hoping that he would not accept that dismissal; nor did he.

That was how it began, and, though she soon discovered that he had neither work nor money, it went on. Young men, as they had been presented to her through old Geldersome's conception, had been such industrious dutiful bores that Tom Boothroyd must have swept through her like a refreshing wind. I have watched him myself, when the rent collector called, turn that grumpy customer into such high humor that he went away laughing his head off, and without the rent.

The odd thing is that my mother never learned, never bothered to try to learn, anything about her husband's family. She told me that if he ever signed a document that required his "status" to be acknowledged, he would write "gentleman," explaining that that meant someone who lived without working. I know no more about him than she did. She took him for what he was, married him, and continued, as long as he lived, to adore him.

I should have thought Scarborough was all right for a honeymoon, but Tom Boothroyd, in his unpredictable way, whisked his bride to Bournemouth. Not till then did Edith write to tell her brother what had happened. There was a lot of Geldersome in my Uncle Arthur. He traveled south at once, chiefly concerned to find out what had happened to his sister's thousand pounds. She still had most of it, for Tom was not a luxurious liver. Give him bread and cheese to eat and no work to do, and he could be as happy as a king. My Uncle Arthur magnanimously said that he would make up what had been spent, and that the happy pair could consider this to be his wedding present. He asked permission to take charge of the re-established thousand pounds, so that he might invest it. This permission was given, and Uncle Arthur went home. Thus my mother was assured of a pound a week, and that is literally the only income the family could depend on throughout my childhood. You could not depend on what my father made. Sometimes he worked, more often he didn't. I have known him giving a hand at need in the harvest fields. I have known him as a groom, as a feller and sawyer of wood, as a poacher who would slip a hare or pheasant from under his coat. By the time I was born, he and my mother had settled in the cottage near Captain Orlop's place. That was the only country I had known up to this time of which I am writing. We had a sizable garden, and that was one thing my father looked after well. He was a grower of mighty vegetables, and did not neglect the flowers, either. Even throughout the winter you can find a flower of some sort down there. Every morning my father would lay one beside my mother's plate, even if it were only a wild head of winter heliotrope. "Better than Manningham Lane—eh?" he would ask lazily. And I am sure she thought it was, and regretted nothing. Why should she?

3

I was as handsome as my father, though not like him. I was fair, and where his black hair was straight my golden hair waved. I was a Reynolds angel. But I was not strong in those days; the winter weather, especially, down there did not suit me: day after day of warm "whispering" weather as they call it, when the woods are still and misty, jeweled with spiders' webs that had not a puff to tremble them. Day after day of soft south wind, and the sea coming lazily in with wide scallops of foamy lace trailing listlessly upon the sand. There were other days when the weather raged, and the trees in the woods seemed to be fighting like beasts, tearing off one another's arms, and the sea was a hissing chaos. Even then, it was not winter as I have since learned to know winter. It was never cold, as other places can be cold. Frost was rare, even a touch of it, and in my twelve years at Pendeverel I never saw snow.

4

We kept up roaring fires, all the same, for, if there was little cold, there was much mildew. It flowered on leather, mottled the pages of books, and the cardboard surrounds of the few engravings on the walls were spotted like Dalmatian dogs. Our fires were of wood. There was no lack of it. The tide washed it up and the woods dropped it all over the place. Wood was one of my father's manias. He didn't mind working so long as he wasn't working for someone else, and he loved working with wood. A shed in the garden was always overflowing with the sea's bounty of timber, and from this he made the chairs we sat on, the table we ate at, the bed I slept in, shelves, cupboards, and all sorts of things that we have learned to call gadgets. He even built himself a dinghy, and in this he would row out and drop the lobster pots he had made from withies cut by the streams. He made beehives. We never lacked lobsters, fish, honey, vegetables, eggs. Now and then one of the hens was killed, and rabbits were trapped.

When my father said he was a gentleman because he didn't work, he was maligning himself; and I have maligned him if I have given the impression that he was lazy. He would work as well as the next man on condition that he could throw down ax or spade whenever he felt like it. He would have these spasms when he would do nothing but the barely necessary things and loaf about for days on the beach or in the fields. And my mother would have to forget her careful Yorkshire housewifery and join him.

"But who's going to cook the dinner, Tom?"

"Nobody."

As easily as that he would dispose of it, and bread and cheese, with salad from the garden, did well enough.

Or he would say: "Bring a loaf of bread and a frying pan."

Then off we would go to the beach. He would take me out in his precarious-looking homemade dinghy, and we would trail lines for mackerel, and when we had a few we would light a fire on the sand, fry them, and eat them with bread. I remember those meals as paradisal.

I recall my father, after one such meal, lying on the sand, his long brown fingers playing with the warm grain of it, and my mother opening a workbag as she sat beside him and taking out socks to be darned. There was not a soul in sight. Our beaches were not then, as they are now, part of a publicized "Cornish Riviera," nor were the fields behind the blackthorn hedge full of caravans and gashed with the foundations of cement-block houses. The sea that day was silky and sun-splashed— "too bright for mackerel," but we had caught some!—and the gulls drifted about, too lazy and content to squawk. We might have been Adam and Eve, with an infant uncanonically begotten in Eden.

"For God's sake, Edie, put away that work. Take it easy for once."

"Someone's got to darn your socks."

5

"Why?"

He was full of unanswerable monosyllables like that. My mother rolled the pair of socks into a ball, dropped it into the bag, and lay down beside him in the sun. His hand took hers. "Better than Manningham Lane—eh?" It was a question he was always asking.

I had not at that time seen Manningham Lane: a lane to me was a narrow rutted leafy defile: and I had never seen a big town. I had seen nothing but woods and fields and sea. I was to see them all: the whole industrial, infernal setup; and then I was to understand my father better. Like my mother, he had been born to that sort of thing, had, as I see it now, weighed it up and rejected it. He was the aboriginal who took care to live clear of the straight Roman roads and the neat Roman cities and Roman Authority; who dodged the Normans and nibbled at their royal forests and took a pot shot now and then at their royal game. Such thoughts are clearer in my mind when I recall how, that afternoon of which I am writing, I myself awakened from a long sleep in the sun and saw him standing, looking at the cliff behind us where the brambles were touched with tints of gold and copper. "Blackberries coming on," he said to my mother. "I'll start picking next week. There'll be plenty of apples to go with 'em for jam." He was forever like that, on the lookout for God's plenty—blackberries, mushrooms, watercress—the incredible amount of stuff that there was, when you came to think of it, to be had for nothing more than the fun of picking it up in the fresh air. Almost everything he did, almost every word he spoke, now comes back to me as a big question: "Why, for heaven's sake, tie myself by the leg to someone else's machine in a black hole of a town, when I can live like a bird in the sun by the sea?"

4

Authority didn't trouble us much. So far as it existed, it was incarnate in Captain Orlop, R.N., retired, and manifested in his agent Mr. Tresooth. It touched us only insofar as Mr. Tresooth came now and then to collect the rent of our cottage. Like so many Cornish cottages, it was ugly beyond imagination: a square box painted a penitential gray, with a bit of mud color wherever someone had thought decoration appropriate. But you may be sure we didn't stand about looking at the outside; and inside it was comfortable. We had nothing of what are now called "conveniences." Our water had to be brought from a well a quarter of a mile away, and the cooking was done on an open fire in the kitchen which was also our sitting room. I need hardly say that for water transport my father had created a vehicle which made the job easy. It was an ancient perambulator with a tin bath fitted in where the babies should have been. A tap fixed at the bottom of one end passed through a hole in the perambulator, and there you had it. There was a slightly uphill path to the well, and that didn't matter as the tank was empty for the journey. The water supply came home under its own weight, bringing you with it. When my father had completed this masterpiece, he was so pleased that he spent a whole day given up to the joy of contemplating it; and on the next day he decreed a family picnic. We caught so many mackerel that day that he was visited by a new thought. He dug a pond in the garden and cemented it, announcing that it was for keeping fresh any unusual catch such as we then had. You occasionally renewed the sea water in the pond, and all you had to do was go out and take up your fish, alive and kicking. However, we were a mile from the sea, and the pond was never even filled, much less renewed.

We had about half an acre of garden, and altogether our cottage and small estate must have been a dead loss to Captain Orlop. The rent, I suppose, was not more than a few pounds a year. It was often unpaid, but all the same the little place was kept in perfect condition by Authority.

The only other matter in which Authority troubled us was that of education. Theoretically, I was a schoolboy. St. Michael Pendeverel was so small a place that it had no school, and the register on which I presume my name to have been included existed in a building a couple of miles away. I know that I was in that building from time to time, but the memory is, at first, of such vague and scattered attendances that I am sure my father, so great an expert in dodging any column he didn't see the point of joining, must have been helping me to dodge this one. I have said that I was not a strong child; and this must have been played up for all it was worth. I imagine that to the education authorities, such as they were in those old days and in that inconsiderable place, I was represented as being due any moment for churchyard mold.

I recall a gorgeous summer afternoon when I was feeling as well as I have ever felt in my life. I was in the garden, by the beehives, watching the come-and-go of the bees, when suddenly my father appeared, said: "Keep your mouth shut, Chad, and do as I tell you," and led me to a ladder that he had raised under my bedroom window. "Up you go!" he ordered. A moment later we were in my bedroom and he had hastily stripped me down to the shirt. "Into bed with you!" I got in, wondering what game he was playing now. "Whatever happens, don't say a word. Be asleep." Then he vanished through the window, and I saw the top of the ladder go as he pulled it down. A moment later my father came tiptoeing into the room, followed by a stranger. My mother was there, too. "Speak quietly," my father ordered. "Don't wake him up." They all three stood there looking down at me. My father sat on the bedside chair, reached for my wrist, and lifted my arm out gently. His fingers lay on my pulse. Through a slit of my eyelids, I saw him shake his head sadly at the other two. He put my hand back under the bed-clothes and a deep sigh rent him. "Pretty bad, I fear," he said. The stranger, a black-clad man, did not speak a word, but he looked very sorry for me. Only at the door, as they were trooping out, he said quietly: "Perhaps you should call a doctor." "A doctor!" said my father. "Well, we may have to. Not that it would be much good. Whatever is the matter with him, I fear it's Chronic and Constitutional."

He put in the capital letters magnificently, and the door closed.

This, I learned later, was a school attendance officer, in short, Authority; and the ancient Briton had dodged the invader again.

5

I learned as much at home as I should have learned in the village school. My mother taught me to read and to write, and I recall a small arithmetic primer which I romped through once figures had been explained to me.

I had not, then, met my Uncle Arthur. A photograph of him, in a pink plush frame with gilt metal corners, was on the mantelpiece in the parlor. After setting up in practice as a solicitor, he had decided that he wanted to be a barrister, and now he was a barrister. In the photograph, he wore a barrister's wig. My irreverent father was accustomed to call him Old Horsehair. Uncle Arthur was not now practicing as a barrister. He had become Town Clerk of Smurthwaite in Yorkshire. He had sent us another photograph, showing a civic procession through the Smurthwaite streets, with himself, horsehair and all, strutting along beside the robed mayor. This picture was an occasion of much joy to my father. He would stand before it and sing lustily: "See the mighty host advancing, Satan leading on."

Every child thinks of his mother as an old reliable sort of creature, and it is odd to realize now that she was then a beautiful girl just entering her thirties. Happily, I have a record of what she looked like, for it was at this time that Lucy Orlop painted her. At Chalk Hill I have a collection of modern pictures that I don't much care for but that I am told are the thing, and among them, startlingly incongruous, is this picture by Lucy Orlop. I picked it up in a saleroom not long ago.

Captain Orlop was a bachelor, and Lucy was his sister. She wasn't often at Pentyrch, which was the name of his house in the woods. She lived in London, and when she did come among us she startled us with her odd masculine appearance. Her hair was cropped, not closely, but so that she didn't need a bun or chignon or any of the other devices women use for taming their locks. It was a gray untidy halo, surmounting a face that was kind but had, at the same time, a no-nonsense-with-me-please sort of look. We would see her striding about the country, hatless in any weather, wearing a severe blouse with a stiff collar and a tie. Sometimes she would have a sketchbook with her, sometimes a painter's outfit, which she would set up and before which she would sit working under an enormous umbrella on a pointed stick that she dug into the ground. I once saw her thus engaged, and crept up, hoping to have a look at the picture. However, she gave me a hard glance and barked, "Go away, boy," and I fled as from a dragon.

You wouldn't think it to look at her, but Miss Orlop was a most sentimental painter and, I know now, a successful one financially. She was of the school of Marcus Stone, and she never failed to sell her annual picture or two exhibited at the Academy under titles that might have been those of novels. The one my mother appears in is called *Women Must Weep.* You can't be in any doubt as to the subject. There the fishing boats are, coming back after what has clearly been an exceptionally dirty night. On the distant jetty is a group of women, anxious and agitated, and in the foreground is the wall from which you look down on this scene. Sitting by the wall, on a lobster pot draped with nets, is the main figure. You know at a glance that she is too heart-stricken to join the others, that she is a young bride whose man has been out on his first trip after the wedding, and that in all probability she is now a widow. My young friends pause, look at it, and make vomiting noises. I don't mind. I do not tell them that the lovely distraught girl is my mother. And how lovely she was! It was from her that I got my looks. I have forgotten to mention the dog. He is a collie, and he lies there, looking up into the eyes of his mistress, clearly telling her that, even if the worst has happened, she can count on him to the end.

6

Away under the clay hills that were so white when the sun shone was the Town. We didn't go to the Town more often than we could help, and I knew it much less well than I knew every bole in the woods, every cleft in the cliffs. It wasn't much of a town, anyway. On a memorable autumn day, I had wandered halfway there, raiding the hedges for blackberries. The long school holiday was over, but the legend of my "delicacy" must have persisted, for there I was, a basket over one arm, a crooked stick for reaching the high fruits in my hand, my face smeared with blackberry juice, my shoes white with dust, hatless, as near a walking scarecrow as makes no difference.

It was past teatime and I was tired. I sat on a gate, a golden field behind me, and all about me the quiet mellow day. The white stream of the road flowed to right and left between banks of bracken, and in the sloe bushes, thick with purple fruit, flights of goldfinches whirred and flashed. It was an idyllic moment for meeting my Uncle Arthur, inappropriately so, for my Uncle Arthur had nothing to do with the sort of Arthurs who get into idylls.

Coming from the direction of the Town, puffs of white dust rising under his feet, was a fat white horse. I knew him, and I knew the dilapidated victoria that he was pulling and the driver, wearing a battered silk hat, who sat slumbering on the box. This historic contraption was to be found outside the railway station in the Town, and once, when we had been there shopping, my father, in a moment of costly bravado, had hired it to drive us home. So I did not need to be told that here were passengers from Town, and that they had probably arrived at the railway station. As the horse ambled nearer, I recognized two of the three people in the victoria. Facing forward, her dandelion puff of white hair proclaiming her from afar, was Miss Orlop. By her side sat a girl whom I did not know. She looked about my own age, and she contrasted strangely with gaunt, ill-dressed Miss Orlop, for she was all young curves, dark fascinating ringlets, and beautiful clothes. Then, as the victoria came abreast and disclosed the third passenger, whose back had been to me till now, I recognized Old Horsehair.

He was not so much in character as to be wearing his horsehair at that moment, but there was no mistaking the heavy, solemn face of the photographs. His unexpected appearance there in our Cornish lane, a family legend materialized before me, was so surprising—for I knew no one was expecting him—that I leapt in agitation from the gate, kicking over the basket of blackberries that I had put down on the grass verge. The fruits, as dark, luscious and glistening as the girl in the carriage, rolled out into the white dust, but the moment was so full of drama, of the Unexpected knocking me literally off my perch, that the minor disaster failed to affect me. I snatched up the more than half-empty basket and took to my heels. Walking, I could almost have kept pace with the fat white horse; running, I left him in the lurch. I was uplifted with the importance of a herald bearing great and unexpected tidings. My father and mother were in the garden, he in an apple tree, handing down the fruit that she was putting into a basket. "Old Horsehair!" I shouted madly. "Old Horsehair is coming! With Miss Orlop and a beautiful girl."

Of course, he did not come with Miss Orlop and the girl. They were decanted at Pentyrch, and then Uncle Arthur came on alone. He had decided on the hop to spend his annual holiday in our parts and so to assure himself that all was well with the sister whom he had not seen since her marriage. Journeying south from Smurthwaite, he had had to change trains at Plymouth, and there had got into the compartment in which Miss Orlop and Rose Garland had traveled from London. When they reached the Town, the old white horse's victoria was the only vehicle on the cab stand. They had agreed to share it; and there, twenty minutes or so after I had made my announcement, Uncle Arthur was, embracing his sister on our garden path, like a big bear affectionately hugging a gazelle.

7

My uncle Arthur Geldersome was forever telling me what an English Gentleman would do in any given circumstances. There were, of course, all the ordinary things like seeing women and children first off a sinking ship and then stepping into the boat unhurried, giving an example of calm that raised *morale*. It seemed to be expected that this was a situation in which any English Gentleman could find himself at any moment, and that he might as well be prepared, as also to burst into flaming buildings, carrying out women and children. These exigencies might cost a man his life, but an English Gentleman always died game. An English Gentleman was deeply soaked in the Team Spirit, if the other members of the team were English Gentlemen. Foreigners were Unaccountable, but if they were the Better Team, he was prepared to let them win. This, however, was a contingency he did not seem to entertain seriously. Coming down to humbler things, an English Gentleman dressed appropriately to all circumstances. It was this that struck me on that day when first I set eyes on Uncle Arthur: he was dressed for the country. He was wearing heavy brogue shoes, hairy stockings, knickerbocker trousers buckled at the knees, a Norfolk jacket of brown tweed, and a straw hat with a band of red and white. These were the colors of his tie, too. When he took off the hat to embrace his sister, I saw a baldness that made him look tonsured like a monk. His dark heavy face was clean-shaven.

My unceremonious announcement under the apple tree had given my parents a few moments for preparation.

"Don't speak of your uncle so rudely," my mother said. "Your manners are becoming shocking"; and my father asked, chewing a warm apple, "How do you know it's Horsehair? Where did you see him?"

"He was driving from the Town," I explained, "with Miss Orlop and a beautiful girl. I'm sure I'm not mistaken. I know it's him."

The proximity of Arthur seemed to be making my mother precise. "I know it's *he*," she corrected me.

"He or him," said my father, "if it's Horsehair, where's he going to sleep?" There were only two bedrooms in the cottage.

"He must have Chad's bed. Chad can sleep in the kitchen."

And so I did. A feature of the kitchen was an old settle standing at right angles to the fireplace. It was the very heart of our winter evenings. After our meal that night my mother made up my bed upon it and told me I could get into it as soon as I liked. "Your Uncle Arthur and I have a lot to discuss," she said. "We'd better have a fire in the parlor, Tom. The place smells rather damp."

It always did, for we rarely used it. Even when the fire was lit and the hanging paraffin lamp diffused its glow, I thought, as I loafed near the door watching the preparations, that the place didn't look a patch on the kitchen for comfort. "Now, off with you, Chad," my mother said. "To bed as soon as you like."

My father, who had been padding about in carpet slippers as he made the parlor comfortable, now came into the passage where I was standing and said: "I expect you and Arthur will have plenty to talk about, Edie. I'll take a turn outside, and Chad can come with me."

My mother looked up at him sharply. "Well," she said dubiously, "don't stay out too long, and mind what you're up to."

Father slipped on his clodhopper boots and took up a heavy-headed stick that stood in a corner. "Very well," he said. "We'll just take a turn in the moonlight."

What moonlight it was! The roads were white with it, and away on our left we could see its broad path shimmered by the gentle motion of the water. The woods looked black, but when we came to them we found the milky light filtered through and lying like vapor on boles and undergrowth.

I had never before been in the woods at night, or out at night with my father. It was a magical moment for me. I felt closer to him than I had ever done, for, just as some children are separated from their fathers by severity, pomposity or downright oppression, I was oddly separated from mine by jocular levity. This created an impalpable barrier between us, a sense in my heart of never being taken seriously, of being an adjunct of his life that amused him and that he used in such games as I had seen him play with the school attendance officer. All this, of course, was present as a vague fumble of emotion, rather than as anything you might call thought, or even acute feeling; but I was rarely with him, as always with my mother, in a condition of tranquil and unquestioned unity.

It was a sense of this unity that made magical our adventure into the moonlit woods. I knew what he was up to: he was after a pheasant. I had myself, when wandering in daylight through the woods, seen pheasants there, and I had seen pheasants appear in our kitchen. I was not such a fool that I didn't know how they got there. When that night we broke through into the woods, my father said: "We can't let Old

Horsehair starve, Chad. I should say the least we could do for a Town Clerk would be to put a bit of game on his plate." So there it was. He had told me. We were in something as partners.

There wasn't much risk about it. Captain Orlop didn't preserve pheasants and there was no gamekeeper. The birds were such as made use of the woods as the blackbirds and thrushes did. I had seen the Captain wandering about with a gun and a dog, taking a pot shot at any game that chanced along; but the woods of Pentyrch were by no means looked upon as sacred groves, and the days of Botany Bay were long past. When my father picked up a pheasant in the woods, I am sure he did so with no more either of fear or compunction than he would have felt if the bird had walked into the kitchen. However, it chanced that I had just read Captain Marryat's novel *The Poacher,* and the consequence was that that far-off moonlit night was full, for me, of danger and trembling apprehension. I stole along quietly at my father's side, uplifted with a sense of being, for once, *with* him in a tremendous moment.

Miss Orlop's appearance was a crushing anticlimax. She was strolling toward us down a ride, the moonlight silver on her hair. She could not have been more than fifty yards away when a bend of the path brought us face to face. It dates the time for me when I recall the shock with which I saw that she was smoking a cigarette. It made her at once a being from a world of incredible distance and complication. Instinctively, I moved to dash out of sight among the trees. My father seized my arm, and we continued to walk toward Miss Orlop.

"Well," she said as we met. "What are you two up to? Don't you know these woods are private?"

"Theoretically," said my father.

"You are Thomas Boothroyd, aren't you?"

"Yes, and this boy has the pleasure of being my son. His name is Chad."

"H'm." She looked at us, drawing on her cigarette, then extinguished it by squeezing the red end between her fingers. It made me wince.

"I've heard of you from Mr. Geldersome," she said. "He traveled with me from Plymouth today."

"May I ask what you heard from him?" my father inquired.

"Nothing good."

My father laughed aloud, and Miss Orlop smiled. This encounter between a poacher and the lawful owner of game seemed to me odd. Marryat had let me down.

"Well," said Miss Orlop. "I don't intend to stand here all night. Let us walk."

We walked, following the ride which curved back till we came to the mimosas and the camellias and the great house. Its honey-colored stone was lustrous in the moonlight. We stood silent for a moment looking at it. A tinny bell over the stables at the back struck ten.

It looked insubstantial: the lustrous stone, the white pillars of the porch with a lamp burning there, the moon-silvered slates of the roof, silhouetted against tall trees that, in that moment, by some trick of a small wind, lifted their shoulders and let them sink again in a sigh.

"It's very beautiful," said Miss Orlop.

"Yes," said my father.

Over the porch I saw the curtains at a window draw slightly back and a face appear. It was the face of the girl I had seen that afternoon with Miss Orlop.

"You'd better come in for a moment," Miss Orlop said. "My brother is in London."

The front door was open. We entered the house, which oppressed me with a sense of grandeur. A few oil lamps lit the hall. We didn't go farther than that.

"Sit down," Miss Orlop commanded. "I'll be back in a moment."

She disappeared through a door, and I sat uneasily in a huge chair, looking at a picture over the carved stone fireplace. Some old Orlop, I supposed. He was painted on the deck of a sailing ship, a telescope in his hand. There was a lot of smoke, and the sails hung in tatters.

Miss Orlop was soon back, carelessly swinging a dead pheasant by the neck. "Will you please give this to Mr. Geldersome with my compliments," she said. She looked my father hard in the eye, and he looked back hardily at her. Then they exchanged grins, as they had done in the wood. They understood each other.

"I have asked Mr. Geldersome to take tea with me tomorrow. If you can spare the boy, he may come, too."

"Thank you ma'am."

We began to move toward the door, and Miss Orlop came as far as the porch. "Forgive me for coming no farther," she said. "I expect you know your way through the woods?"

"Thank you, ma'am. Perfectly," said my father.

8

Using all the short cuts I knew so well, it would have taken me and Uncle Arthur about half an hour to get to Pentyrch. That, however, was not his idea of how an English Gentleman visited a lady. In the morning we had gone walking together. He wore the holiday clothes in which he had arrived and seemed to me a tremendous and impressive figure. Against my lean and volatile father, he was like a full-grown oak against a birch sapling.

"I suppose, Thomas," he said to my father at breakfast, "that we shall have time for a talk when you get home from work tonight."

"What work?" my father asked with a grin.

"Well, your customary avocation, whatever that may be."

"The happy thing about my avocation," my father answered, "is that it's never customary. It changes from day to day. I should loathe a customary avocation. Today I shall have plenty to do. There are spring cabbages to be planted out. I must earth up the leeks, and cut back the asparagus and top-dress the beds. I shall do that with seaweed, which I shall have to lug up from the beach. If there's any time left, there are still some apples to be stored, and maybe I'll go out and find a bit of fish for your supper."

My mother intervened. "Arthur, we had all this out last night. Tom will not work for anybody but himself, and we get along very well. He likes the way he's chosen to live, and it suits me. Why you should suddenly decide, after we've been married for a dozen years, that it doesn't suit *you*, I can't understand."

"For one thing, my dear Edie," Uncle Arthur said, "there's Somebody's future to be considered. Why is he not at school?"

My father moved out into the passage where his hobnailed gardening boots were kept, and shouted as he got into them: "Because his delicacy is Chronic and Constitutional. That's one thing."

"Is there any other?" Uncle Arthur asked, wiping his lips on a napkin which I had never seen used till it was produced for his service.

"Yes. If Edie and I can't teach him better than any village schoolmaster, I'll eat my hat."

We heard him go out, and Uncle Arthur, continuing the conversation with only my mother as auditor, said: "That still leaves the question of *esprit de corps*." And there, of course, he "had something," as they say now.

If there was one thing wrong with my bringing up, it was the isolation in which we lived. I had no friends, and my parents had none, either. There can hardly have been more than thirty families in our hamlet. We knew them all, of course, and passed the time of day with them, but I don't remember that we ever entered a house save our own; and my rare appearances in the distant school were like visits to a strange tribe.

I have pointed out how liberal the sea was in supplying us with wood, and there was a custom governing that. When this harvest was being washed in, you would see a number of men, my father among them, gathering the bits and pieces and lugging them beyond the high-tide mark. There each would make his own pile, for usually there was too much to be carried home at once, and the piles were sacred. It was one of those unwritten laws: you never touched another man's woodpile. I had gone down to the beach with my father one day to bring up some wood, and he paused before a pile that was not his, attracted by a door that lay upon it. He could not resist a bit of decent craftsmanship, and he took the door up to examine it. It was mahogany, a cabin door, with well-finished panels and brass fittings, and its presence there spoke eloquently, even to me, of some moment of terrible stress, perhaps of disaster. He was standing there, with the door on end, staying it with one hand, rejoicing in its details, when two men of the hamlet approached. One of them shouted: "Whose pile is that? Put that door down!" And the other said: "He wouldn't know. He's a foreigner."

My father put a foot against the door and slammed it down onto the pile. This lack of respect for a well-made job was so unusual that I looked up at him in surprise. A burning color of anger was spreading in his face, but he spoke quietly. "Who the hell would want to be a Cornishman?" he asked.

It was a foolish remark, a thoughtless remark, and I don't imagine it expressed what was in his mind. He didn't want to be a Cornishman any more than he wanted to be a Yorkshireman, a Hottentot or a Hindu. He wanted simply to be a man, living without interference from anybody—an aspiration that was to become increasingly quixotic in the world as it developed in my time. However, his words were never forgotten or forgiven.

That morning after Uncle Arthur's arrival, when I went walking with him, must have deepened the local opinion of us as foreigners, for nothing like Uncle Arthur can have been seen in those parts before. He strolled with me into the garden after breakfast, leaving my mother to deal with the pheasant, and my father, who was hard at work, said: "We're out of water, Chad. You'd better get some. Take your uncle along and show him the sights."

And there we were: uncle wearing the astonishing outfit in which he had arrived yesterday, and I, pushing the tank in the pram, wearing the next-to-nothing that was my customary clothing. That I appeared in this way even on Sundays when other boys and girls were fancifully clothed for service in the Wesleyan chapel, was another jot added to the total of the Boothroyds' foreignness. The combination of extremes —of me and my uncle—can but have deepened the feeling of our oddity.

I must give Old Horsehair the credit for admirable deportment. He cannot but have felt uneasy as he paced alongside the pram between the scattered cottages, but he gave no sign of this; his progress was as stately as in the photograph at home. If I had been a mayor in fur-trimmed scarlet gown, with a mace bearer before me, he could not have played the Town Clerk more proudly. He was not a conversational man. When in the mood, he talked, but he rarely conversed.

16

He always processed rather than walked, and as he processed his eye was fixed on space and his mind seemed withdrawn into the contemplation of abstruse municipalities. To walk with him, as I was so often thereafter to do, was like taking a gentle stroll with the Bank of England at a moment when a change in the bank rate was under review.

As I had been commanded that morning to show my uncle the sights, I left the perambulator near the well; and on we walked at his unchanging three-miles-an-hour pace. The sunshine fell out of the pale blue autumn sky, lighting up the clay hills beyond the Town. In my capacity of cicerone, I called his attention to them. "Those are the clay hills, Uncle Arthur."

He stopped, climbed onto a stile, and sat down facing the hills. "Tell me about them," he said.

"They are the clay hills," I repeated. "Some of the men from here work there."

"Yes. But tell me about the hills. What are they?"

"Clay. China is made from the clay."

"Ah! That is excellent. You have at last tried to give me a fact, Chad. But you are not right about that. China is not made from the clay, but from the clay plus a number of other things. And since you don't seem to know it, I must tell you that the clay is disintegrated granite. Dig out your facts, verify them, and then stick to them. Will you remember that, Chad?"

"Yes, sir."

"Good. Let me repeat it for your benefit. Dig out the facts, verify them, and then stick to them. Now, tin. Tell me about tin."

"What tin, sir?"

"Tin. Cornwall is full of tin. Tell me about it."

"I don't know anything about tin, sir."

"Now, copper. Cornwall is full of copper. Tell me about copper."

"I don't know anything about copper either, sir."

"Tell me about school. Where do you go to school, eh? Do you like going to school?"

"No, sir. I do go, but only when I can't help it."

"Perhaps if you went to school you would learn something about tin and copper?"

"No, sir. We were learning about Henry the Eighth."

"Ah. Henry the Eighth. Tell me about Henry the Eighth. Where in Cornwall did he build castles?"

"I don't know, sir."

"But I know. I am in Cornwall for but a week or two. Nevertheless, I decided I had better learn some facts about Cornwall. I learned some facts about china clay and tin and copper. I learned that Henry built the St. Mawes and Pendennis castles. I learned," he added with deep gravity, "that the nightingale has never been recorded so far west as this. Of course, the whole place is full of legends, too; but there's no need to go into things of that sort. Tennyson has done that for us, and has linked the legends up with sound moral teaching. You should read Tennyson, Chad."

"Yes, sir. I'm always reading. I want to read everything."

"That, I fear, betrays an excessive zeal, which time doubtless will qualify. We will continue our walk."

We did so; and, once on his legs, Old Horsehair became silent again. But I wasn't thinking of him as Old Horsehair. He was Uncle Arthur, and to my surprise I rather liked him. If my father had asked me questions that I couldn't answer, he would have laughed at my ignorance and said: "Why, any silly little fool ought to know a thing like that." Uncle Arthur's ponderous courtesy was soothing. And before we got back to our cottage he had endeared himself to me.

My father, in his mild way, was a rebel, even though, down there in Cornwall, he had little enough to rebel against. Still, he never went to church or chapel, he encouraged me to dress in rags, he helped me to dodge school, and, this moment of which I am writing being that of the Boer War, he loudly proclaimed himself a pro-Boer to anyone who would listen. Even in a remote hamlet like St. Michael Pendeverel, one could buy in the village shop the buttons decorated with the heads of British generals that were then all the go. Not a boy I met in the street was without one, and I bought one for myself. I remember that it was of an inoffensive-looking person named General Gatacre.

There was a terrific explosion when my father saw it. He snatched it from my lapel and shouted: "Have you nothing better to do with your money than to buy pictures of those hired butchers who are out there smashing up the homes of simple inoffensive people?"

I knew nothing about the Boer War, and cared less, and that was true of the other boys. But I wanted to be in the fashion, and, thinking the matter over in later years, I have often wondered how far a parent is wise in violently dragging his child outside the flock into which he has been born. Let him be his own rebel, if he wants to: that is another matter.

It wouldn't have been so bad if he had thrown the button into the fire and left it at that. But his principles were involved, and so I must be involved in them, too. He took me by the arm and marched me to the shop. It was a place for the gossips, and three or four of them were there when we arrived. My father threw the button onto the counter, treated the customers to a harangue on the sins of imperialism and Jewish financiers, charged the poor old soul who kept the shop with propagating hellish doctrines, and demanded the return of the penny

18

or tuppence or whatever it may have been that the thing cost me. I had no idea what the row was about, but I gathered that I had been corrupted, and I stood there burning with shame and confusion.

The old girl who kept the shop woke out of her daze when she understood that she was being asked to hand back the money. She refused to do it, and my father, with a few well-chosen words about commercial morality, marched me out.

This was another of those things that branded us as "foreigners." You may be sure it lost nothing in the telling throughout the hamlet.

That storm blew over, but there was one thing that did not blow over—nothing so dramatic as this, but continuous like an aching tooth. This was the matter of the perambulator-watercart. It was characteristic of my father: practical, sensible, yet not without its comic and unconventional side. The boys could not get over it as they soon got over the affair of General Gatacre. It was constantly there to arouse their mirth. On my journeys to and from the well I would be greeted by their cries: " 'Ow's the baby, Chad?" "A wet 'un that be." "Better change the napkins, Chad."

It was a torment, and I came to loathe the journey to the well; and that day when Old Horsehair and I began the walk home I knew that morning school would be over and that the boys would be drifting down the street. I trembled as I filled the tank. The thought of Uncle Arthur exposed to the ribaldry of the young villains was more than I could bear.

There they were, sure enough, outside the village shop, their cheeks distended with gob-stoppers, their lapels all that the most patriotic could desire. This time they had thought out a new angle.

"Let's 'ave a look at the mermaid, Chad."

"What do 'ee feed 'un on, Chad—pap or fish?"

Oh, I thought, how Uncle Arthur will hate me for letting him in for this! And then I was aware of two things. My uncle, sizing up the situation, had elbowed me aside and taken the shafts himself, and Miss Orlop was coming out of the village shop.

With incomparable dignity, as if he were propelling the whole scientific and up-to-date water department of his municipality, Uncle Arthur rolled majestically upon my persecutors, who shrank back, dumb with amazement. Then he dropped the shafts, bringing the contraption to a standstill, in order to raise his straw hat to Miss Orlop.

"That looks to me a surprisingly useful idea, Mr. Geldersome," Miss Orlop said in her clear regimental voice.

"Yes, ma'am. It was invented by my brother-in-law, with whom I am staying and who has a turn for such things."

"Indeed! Very clever. Very clever. Well, don't forget. I'm expecting you and this boy to tea at four o'clock. Clean him up a bit."

Off she went, and Uncle Arthur took the shafts again. We moved on our way, victorious. It would be known everywhere. Pentyrch, the unapproachable, had invited us to tea! Pentyrch had called the water-cart very clever! I wished Miss Orlop hadn't said that bit about cleaning me up. But you can't have everything. In a silence that was almost of awe, the boys stepped aside as we passed among them.

9

If this was surprising, it was not the end of Uncle Arthur's surprises for that day. We reached the cottage just as the ancient victoria from the Town stopped at the gate. It contained a large leather trunk which, my uncle explained, he had been obliged, for lack of space in the vehicle, to leave in the luggage office at the station. "And if you will be so kind as to be here this afternoon at twenty minutes to four—twenty minutes to four *precisely*—I shall be vastly obliged to you," he said to the driver.

Luggage was luggage in those days: none of your cane and fiber. It was of hide that a bullet could hardly penetrate. Of this perdurable material was a small box, of a shape I had not seen before, that was handed out after the trunk. Uncle Arthur took it up affectionately. "My Hat," he explained.

My father had come in from the garden. "You haven't brought a silk hat!" he exploded.

Uncle Arthur opened the hatbox, took out the gleaming topper, and smoothed the nap with his cuff. "As you see," he said with satisfaction. He held the hat away, twisting it in his hand and looking at it with pleasure, as though it were a trophy he had just been awarded for an exceptionally fine piece of town clerking. "You never know," he said. "A man and his Hat cannot be parted with impunity."

The smell of the cooked pheasant brought us back to matters on which all could agree. My father and my uncle humped the big trunk upstairs, and I followed, bearing the case that contained the Hat. Then we went down to the kitchen and fell to. My uncle ate with a will, and my mother said to him: "I hope you are well looked after, Arthur? I remember that you were always a one for your dinner."

"My housekeeper, Mrs. Ramsden, is adequate, if hardly more."

"Why don't you get a wife to look after you? Haven't you ever thought of marrying?"

"I have thought of it, my dear Edie, full many a time and oft. But always I have decided against it. To begin with, there was my Career to be considered, and now there is my Municipality. Mayors may come and mayors may go, but I go on forever. I am the continuing factor in constant flux. My Municipality leaves me little time for domestic bliss."

"Down here," said my father, "you can keep a wife and family on the sea and the hedges. What sort of existence do you call that—tied up in red tape till you can't move hand or foot or find a moment for the life God intended a man to live?"

"What life God intended a man to live is a moot point," my uncle said equably. "I cannot profess to be so deeply in His counsels as you, no doubt, are, my dear Tom. And somehow I cannot—quite definitely I cannot—imagine myself browsing upon the hedges like a goat or gathering the harvest of the tide like a sanderling. In my office we use remarkably little red tape, and I never allow myself to be Tied Up in it. Ill fares the Municipality, to hast'ning ills a prey, where red tape accumulates and Town Clerks decay."

With this conclusive pronouncement, the dinner being finished, he wiped his lips upon his napkin, rose, and said: "Now for an hour in the arms of Morpheus—an indulgence I always grant myself after my midday meal during holidaytimes." We heard the stairs creak under his heavy tread, and then, over our heads, the groaning of the bed as he lost no time in casting himself upon it.

At twenty minutes to four, as ordered, the victoria arrived at our gate and Uncle Arthur, watch in hand to check the time, descended the stairs. If he had come wearing his gown and horsehair he could not have surprised me more. I was waiting impatiently for him, scrubbed and wearing what passed for my best clothes, when the apparition burst upon my sight: the frock coat with its silk lapels, the double-breasted lavender waistcoat, the striped trousers and the gleaming black buttoned boots. He carried the Hat in his hand and put it on as he took his seat facing the rump of the old white horse. Speechless, I climbed in after him. Speechless, my father raised the battered black felt hat, with several holes in the crown, that was the only hat he had. With the ferrule of a silver-headed Malacca cane my uncle prodded the driver in the back. "To Pentyrch," he said, and we were off.

10

Pentyrch is still there—the name and the house are still there—but where is the Pentyrch I saw that day? Men talk of moments of creation, and there are such times. They do not always bring forth pictures and poems and music. Sometimes they create a masterpiece in the mind, a private possession, born of a mood and a moment and the way the light fell and a bird sang. If I go back to Pentyrch now, I shall see most of what I saw that day when I rode with Uncle Arthur behind the old white horse, but I shall not see what I mean when I say Pentyrch.

All day the weather had been still; the sun had shone out of a sky of autumn blue. We bowled slowly along between hedges gray with old-man's-beard, jeweled with berries of bryony, and the sun, sloping west, turned the blackberry leaves and fading hawthorns into golden patterns. A soft milky dust rose up under the wheels. Chaffinches were flashing everywhere, and the small songs of robins, so intimate and confidential, could just be heard. The fields were either green, with a lapwing or two falling about as if on broken wings and uttering desolate cries, or stubble dotted with chattering hosts of starlings that now and then regimentally whirred up, and wheeled, and settled again. Of human beings, there was not a soul save ourselves. I was aware, as I had never been before, of the solemnity of beautiful things. All through the short journey Uncle Arthur did not speak a word, but as we turned off the road, between the granite gate pillars, crowned with large granite balls, he rested a hand briefly on my knee and squeezed it.

Now we were in the long drive that twisted through the woods in which Pentyrch lay buried. Though all the leaves were sere and ready to fall, few had fallen yet, and so we were in a sudden gloom. Now and then, a beech leaf, like a thin-beaten arrowhead of gold, spun silently down, and to this silence was added the silence of the horse's hoofs, for the ground beneath us was thick with the rot of many years. When the silence was broken at all, it was by the harsh violence of magpies and jays. Their butchering cries threaded a menace into the peace, and this, too, was part of the beauty of the moment.

Rose Garland was standing in the dusk of the woods where the drive made a turn to the right. I remember that, as when I first saw her driving from the Town, she was wearing beautiful clothes, but, beyond that, I cannot remember anything about her clothes except a crimson richness. What I do remember is that round her forehead was twined a wreath of broad leaves and berries, so that, standing on the edge of the woods, she seemed, despite her rich clothes, to belong to them, the more so as she did not await our coming, but suddenly was gone, vanished among the boles, as a deer might have been. When the old horse stopped at the front door a moment or two later she was there, with no wreath upon her brow, holding Miss Orlop's hand, politely waiting to receive us. And so, within a few seconds almost, there was printed into my mind the sense of two Rose Garlands, one of the woods and the vine-wreathed hair, and the other of the hostess on the doorstep.

Miss Orlop had not followed Uncle Arthur's example: she was not got up for the occasion. She was, indeed, looking odder than ever, for she was wearing a green linen overall, smeared with paint, that reached almost to her feet. "Come in, come in," she cried; and as she went before us into the house she took hold of this garment with both hands, heaved it up over her head, and threw it, crumpled, onto an oak chest in the hall. And there she was, the same Miss Orlop as ever, except that the overall's swoop had made her halo more than usually sensational.

It was four o'clock, and Pentyrch was a house where night came early. The westering sun, and an autumn sun at that, had no power against the trees that besieged the place. Outside the front door it was already dusky; in the hall it was almost dark; in the drawing room, to which Miss Orlop preceded us, the curtains of heavy brocade had been drawn, a fire of logs was blazing on the hearth, a few rose-shaded oil lamps on tall wrought-iron stands burned here and there, and on a little round table near the fire a candelabrum upheld six lighted candles. A silver-gray Persian cat, with copper eyes, was stretched luxuriously upon the hearth. Rose Garland, in one sinewy movement, undulated down to the rug alongside the cat, began to murmur nonsense to it, to scratch its ears. The cat was all for it. He rolled over, offering a stomach whose heavy fur the girl massaged softly. The leaping flame of the logs put gleams into her black hair and upon the crimson silk of her clothes.

Many a time, an intruder through the woods, I had come within sight of the house, and I had wondered what sort of life was lived within it. I had tried to picture the rooms, but, knowing no rooms save our own, I had achieved nothing but a vague grandeur. The reality exalted and intimidated me. It all fitted in to the mood that had been upon me during the drive: the mood of one of those rare days which, for whatever reason, are not ephemeral like other days, but are destined, in their general sense and in all their particulars, to be inextinguishable. I knew that I should never forget any of this: the old white horse, the golden dying of the autumn day, my uncle's hand pressed reassuringly upon my knee, the girl with the vine leaves in her hair, this room in whose dimness the pictures were glows of indeterminate color, and the firelight dancing in ruddy flecks upon silver and mahogany and the girl's crimson silk. But I was afraid. I felt like someone who, by a clumsy movement, could smash what enchanted him; and I stood there, in what seemed a long, long suspense, listening to the only sounds: the whickering of the flames, the girl's murmured endearments, and the crescendo rapture of the cat's purring.

But it can't have been as long as all that. Miss Orlop, passing her hand so vigorously through her halo that I expected to see it dissipate like a roughly handled dandelion clock, leaving her as bald as a coot, said briskly: "So this is the Chad Boothroyd you were telling me about, Mr. Geldersome. Rose, you'd better shake hands with Chad Boothroyd."

The girl got up, and we shook hands. Her hand was warm with fur and firelight and its own young life. She gave my fingers but a perfunctory pressure, and then subsided again beside the cat, as though she preferred his company to mine.

"Rose," Miss Orlop explained to Uncle Arthur, "is the daughter of an old friend of mine, stationed in India. India's no place for a girl —all snakes and climate and natives; so Rose stays with me. Well, we'd better have some tea."

She hauled on a silken cord, and presently a parlor maid came in with the tea tray; and this, when it was put down on the table near the fire, was something else for the flames to play with, for the tray itself and the jugs and teapot were all of silver.

Rose Garland and I were silent during the meal, but Miss Orlop chattered endlessly to Uncle Arthur. She was a woman of boundless curiosity: she could not meet a stranger without wanting to pump him of all the information he could impart. Chance had thrown Uncle Arthur in her way, and when she found that he would be staying for a fortnight on her doorstep she could not resist asking him to Pentyrch. That is how I see it now, with my fuller knowledge of Miss Orlop; and that afternoon I sat and listened to my uncle being cross-examined more thoroughly than he can ever have cross-examined a witness when he was a practicing barrister. How big a place was Smurthwaite—what was the principal industry—was there a great house—who lived in it? How did one become a Town Clerk and what did a Town Clerk do? What was the climate of Smurthwaite? Did they have much snow in winter? Had he ever seen shepherds digging lambs out of snowdrifts?

I felt as though our whole family were on trial, and was glad that Uncle Arthur turned out to be a cool witness, ready and concise with his answers.

Miss Orlop rang the bell, the tea things were taken away, and she fitted a cigarette carefully into a holder. The conversation went on, now round the fire, and switched from Smurthwaite to general matters. I discovered a number of things about Miss Orlop that surprised me— and seemed to surprise Uncle Arthur, too; and none more than this —that she shared my father's views about the war in South Africa.

"Of course," she said, "Alaric"—by whom I supposed her brother was meant—"is furious when I express such opinions. The Orlops have been Service people for generations. You'll see one of them hanging in the hall—the smug-looking eighteenth-century customer who built this house. He did it all out of prize money. Never attacked a man-of-war in his life. Always went for the fat merchantmen. And there you see him, with the smoke of battle rolling round him. Incidentally," she added with a harsh laugh, "it's a damned bad picture."

"That is a matter, madam, on which I would not care to express an opinion," Uncle Arthur replied.

"Well, you can take it from me," said Miss Orlop. "I know a bad picture when I see one. I've painted plenty."

She looked at me and Rose Garland and said: "I fear these children are finding us bores, Mr. Geldersome. Rose, take Chad Boothroyd and show him something of the house."

The girl got up from the hearthrug, where she had been feeding bits of cake to the cat, and, with hardly a look at me, began to walk out of the room. I followed into the hall, where now a few candles were lit. Rose took up one and said brusquely: "You'd better bring one, too. This place is miserably dark. In London we have gas."

She crossed the hall and opened a paneled mahogany door. "This is the library," she said.

We stood in the doorway, and our points of light hardly disturbed the gloom in which I dimly saw row upon row of books, with a portrait hanging here and there.

"Well, that is that. No one reads them," Rose Garland said, and turned into the hall again, shutting the library door behind her. "This is the dining room. Do you want to see anything else?"

She didn't look at me; she spoke with a cold rudeness. I was annoyed with her, and I said: "Please yourself. I didn't ask to see anything. I didn't ask to come here at all." Warmed by my own daring in speaking to her like that, I asked: "Who do you think you are?" and, putting my candlestick down on a table just inside the door, I began to retreat toward the comforting presence of Uncle Arthur.

At once she put down her own candle, came swiftly after me, and took me by the arm. We were of a height, and, my eyes level with hers, I saw a tear upon her long dark lashes. I saw, too, that her eyes were of an incredible dark blue—a blue darker than any even in those Cornish seas. I was so surprised by this sudden change from rudeness, by the pleading look she directed upon me, that I allowed her to draw me into the dining room. We took up our candles and walked to the fireplace, where a fire was burning. Following her example, I put my candle on the mantelpiece. She made her sinuous slide to the rug and patted it, inviting me to join her there.

"I'm so unhappy," she said. "I'm always rude when I'm unhappy, and I hate being unhappy and I hate being rude."

The silken fringe of her long lashes was now wet all over. The firelight sparkled on her tears.

"I don't see what you've got to be unhappy about," I said unfeelingly, thinking of Pentyrch and its splendor as a solace to all earthly woe.

25

"It's because I don't know who I am," she cried desperately. "Wouldn't you be unhappy if you didn't know who you were?"

Not knowing who I was seemed to me so incredible that I could only stare at her in amazement.

"Why does she talk about India?" Rose demanded, beating her stout little fists into the rug. "Whenever she tells that old story I become desperately, desperately unhappy."

She produced a handkerchief and dried her eyes. The tears had ceased to flow. "I believed it all once," she said, "but I don't believe it any more. I'm getting too old."

She stood up in a crackle of silk as voices were heard in the hall. We took our candles from the mantelpiece and walked out of the room. "Well," said Rose, "that is the dining room." I was amazed by her self-possession and duplicity.

Uncle Arthur was lifting his topper down from a peg in a little clothes closet opening off the hall. "I wonder," Miss Orlop speculated aloud, "whether Solomon in all his glory ever reflected, when he walked under the stars, that they were rather aloof and uncaring? I hope you'll call again, Mr. Geldersome. Come incognito. Not as the Town Clerk."

Uncle Arthur did call again, arrayed as on that occasion. "An English Gentleman," he explained to me, "does not make a social call in rags."

II

Child though I was, I was aware that what had happened between me and Rose in the dining room was not a thing to be revealed, much less discussed. Her strange outburst occupied part of my mind as Uncle Arthur and I began to walk home. But the greater part was occupied by pride as Billy Pascoe walked before us with a lantern. Billy Pascoe was one of the Pendeverel boys who delighted to tease me about my perambulator-watercart. He had been of the group whom Uncle Arthur's dignity had routed that morning. In his spare time he did odd jobs at Pentyrch, cleaning the boots and the knives and so forth; and just as we were about to leave, Miss Orlop shouted for him and he appeared in the hall, wearing a green baize apron.

"Pascoe," Miss Orlop said, "get a lantern and see Mr. Geldersome as far as the gates."

And there Billy was, lighting us through the darkness that was now absolute among the trees. When we reached the gates Uncle Arthur gave him sixpence. "Thank you, Pascoe," I said with satisfaction, but envying him all the same. I should have liked the sixpence myself.

Uncle Arthur improved the moment, giving me a homily on the dangers of dead-end occupation. "Now what will become of that boy, Chad? Here is the world and all that therein is. Here is trade, here is commerce, here are the learned professions, the investigations of science, the speculations of philosophy. And there, on the other hand, is the village school, which I regret to say you do not regularly attend. In this happy realm the world is all before you where to choose. The village school is the humble starting point. The grammar school, the university, lie ahead. And what does young Pascoe choose to do? He cleans boots and knives. With luck, he will become a footman, and with better luck in time a butler; but he will always remain a menial, serving the needs of others. It is not for me, Chad," he said oratorically, leaving me in no doubt that it was indeed for him, "to question whatever, in the wisdom of your father's heart, may seem to him the desirable direction of your infant footsteps. But consider the Ladder, Chad. It is planted in the village school, and there's always room at the top."

As was his way after such an oration, he became silent and plodded steadily on. He liked to hand you these large platefuls of pudding, and leave you to chew and digest them.

When we got back to the cottage, he went straight to his bedroom and changed into what my father called his deerstalking outfit. He joined us in the kitchen at supper, and it was during this meal that he told my mother Miss Orlop would like to paint her. "She has observed you, my dear Edie, and thinks you have just the face for the main character in a canvas she is engaged upon."

My mother didn't mind, and my father regarded it as a lark; and so it came about that during the next week Miss Orlop was at our house every day, and my mother was planted on a lobster pot by the wall at the end of our garden, and the figure was painted into the already almost finished picture.

Sometimes Rose Garland came with Miss Orlop and sometimes she didn't. She was always dressed in finery, new finery every time she appeared, a startling contrast, a dark fairy, looking the odder for the unvarying frumpishness of the old griffin. My father was enormously taken with her, and was forever finding her a few raspberries that had unseasonably postponed their appearance, or a handful of mushrooms, or a posy of primroses that are capable in that climate of pretending that late autumn is early spring. She would receive his gifts with a cold politeness. She never, as they say, gave him an inch. Nor had she much to say to me. It was as though, by her aloofness, she wished to unsay all that she had said when she wept by the dining room fire.

That was a week of wonderful weather, cloudless, warm at midday, cold at nights. On the day when, Miss Orlop had told us, she would be finishing the portrait, my father was waiting as usual, watching the setting up of the easel, and then turned to Rose. "What's my little blackberry going to do today?"

It sounded an absurd form of endearment, but it fitted her: dark, luscious, dew-sparkling. She turned away with a shrug, and Miss Orlop said over her shoulder: "Leave the girl alone, Mr. Boothroyd. Chad, take the girl out in that boat of yours. There's no need for her to mooch about all the afternoon."

It was a command, like the command, "Take Chad Boothroyd and show him something of the house." Rose looked at me, and I said: "If you would like . . . ?" Without a word she followed me out of the garden.

We went through the fields toward the beach, her dark blue silk swishing as she walked. "I shall be sick," she said.

I laughed. We had come within sight of the water that reached away without a ripple into the horizon's haze. "On that?" I asked, waving a hand toward it.

"I shall be sick," she repeated with determination.

We clambered down the steps roughly scored into the cliff face. She was awkward about it, but disdained my offered hand.

"My shoes will become full of sand," she said.

"Then take them off." I sat down and pulled off my own and threw them into the dinghy. She kept hers on.

The tide was low, which meant that the dinghy had to be pulled a long way. The old homemade boat was heavy and rather clumsy. I strained my guts over the job, but she made no helping gesture. She lifted her skirt an inch or two and stepped delicately in when the stern was in the water. She remained standing, and I was so annoyed with her that I pushed the boat out without a word and leapt in over the bows when we were in deep water. She flopped down suddenly onto the stern thwart, gripped the gunwale on either side, and looked daggers at me.

"You did that deliberately," she said.

"Don't you know that you should sit down in a boat?" I demanded, taking up the oars. I swung her round and headed out to sea.

"I know nothing whatever about boats," she said. And added: "Except that they make me sick."

"You *can't* be sick in this thing and on this water," I said, almost angrily.

She didn't answer, but after a time said: "I can see nothing but the sea. I want to see the land."

"You can see it if you screw your neck round."

But instead of doing that she stood up, rocking the boat violently, turned round, and sat with her back to me, looking at the shore. I rowed

28

for a time in silence, and when we were a few hundred yards out she said: "I am about to be sick." And promptly was. She knelt on the thwart, and I could see the convulsions shaking her silken back. When she had done, she scooped up a handful of salt water and washed her mouth. She turned round and seated herself again, facing me this time. "You see?" she said with satisfaction. "Now please take me back."

I took her back, and nearly killed myself by laboriously hauling the boat up beyond the high-water mark. Then we walked home in a silence broken only by her saying: "I am sorry to have given you so much trouble." It was said in a tone matching the gesture with which Uncle Arthur had given Pascoe sixpence.

The pony trap in which Miss Orlop came and went each day had arrived by the time we reached the cottage. Miss Orlop was ready to go. "Well, Rose, did you have a good time?" she asked.

Rose got into the trap. "A lovely time, except for being violently sick."

"Oh, well," Miss Orlop said absent-mindedly.

12

About a week later, Miss Orlop and Rose Garland returned to London. I did not see either of them again on that occasion, but there was a reminder of them always before me in a water-color sketch that Miss Orlop sent to my mother with a note of thanks to her for sitting. As is often the case, it was (as I see now, though I wasn't able to think of such things then) a more attractive piece of work than many of the finished pictures that came from the same brush; and it had a great interest for me because it was a picture of a girl wearing vine leaves round her brow, poised like a wild animal ready for flight on the fringes of an autumn wood. Although no pretense had been made that the girl was strikingly like Rose Garland, there was a suggestion of her, and I guessed that it had been sketched that day when she wept as she told me that she didn't know who she was.

Uncle Arthur went, too. The vehicle of the old white horse turned up; the luggage went aboard; and my mother and I got in to accompany Uncle Arthur as far as the Town. I was impressed to notice that he traveled first class. There were a few moments to wait before the train pulled out, and he walked majestically up and down against the station's background of fading hydrangeas and vast dahlias of vivid burgundy red. "Now, Edie," he said, "bear in mind what I have told you. Don't let Tom have the last word in everything. Remember the ants and the grasshopper. Futurity for you," he said, laying a hand upon my head, "is bounded in this mortal boy. As a man sows, so shall he also reap. It's time Chad started a bit of sowing."

29

He made a sweeping gesture as though casting seed upon the warm asphalt of the platform and then the porters began running along the train and banging the doors. He kissed my mother, shook my hand; and off we went, it being my mother's opinion that it was unlucky to watch traveling friends or loved ones out of sight.

We were not to see him in St. Michael Pendeverel again, save for a brief visit of which I shall tell you, but his visit bore fruit. I was aware that my father's references to Old Horsehair were not, after this, so well received; even I didn't much like them, for I was aware that Uncle Arthur had opened, however briefly, a door that, but for him, would have remained shut. The village boys were not so saucy, and, anyhow, I now began to know them as I had not done before, for I became a regular pupil with them at the village school. They pulled my leg; they called me Angel-face, which I suppose I was; and once, when our schoolmaster produced Gregory's celebrated chestnut—"Not Angles but Angels"—a gust of laughter filled the schoolroom. I was dispassionate enough to be able to observe with satisfaction that both I and our master joined in. From that day he himself began to use the nickname. "Come on, Angel-face. Clean the blackboard."

I enjoyed it all as I had never expected to do. I found that I was a good scholar, and on an awful occasion when one of His Majesty's Inspectors visited the school I was commanded by the headmaster to read aloud an essay I had written on Sir Walter Raleigh. For it was His Majesty's now. The Queen was dead. We were in a new century and a new reign. It was the spring of 1901.

In these few months I learned a lot about St. Michael Pendeverel that I had not suspected. I learned a lot, for one thing, about Billy Pascoe, who had lighted me and Uncle Arthur through the wood. He was of my own age, and, if I was a good scholar, I was never within miles of Billy. One evening, having returned from school, I was pushing the odious watercart uphill when Billy came along and said: "Let me give you a hand, Chad." We became friends from that moment, and there were no more jokes about the watercart after that. Billy was too much respected. He was the only child of a widow living in the hamlet's smallest and most ramshackle cottage, a dark, wiry boy, with eyes that sparkled with both fun and intelligence. How the pair lived was best known to themselves. Mrs. Pascoe had an antiquated hand-driven sewing machine, and out of charity neighbors would send her bits of work to be done. I began to understand why Billy spent his spare time at Pentyrch. One day, as delicately as I could, I put before him Uncle Arthur's homily on dead-end occupations. I asked him if he thought there was a chance of his ending up a butler.

It was a Saturday in May. We had wandered off together, as had become our custom, and were on the beach, gathering driftwood. I can see Billy now, standing there with a spar in his hand, the gulls and the blue sky above him, looking at me with incredulity in his dark intelligent monkey eyes. Then, seeing that I was serious, he burst into wild laughter. "Me!" he shouted. "Me! A butler?" When he could control his mirth, he said with a seriousness that often suddenly overcame him: "No, Chad. What William Pascoe is going to be doth not yet appear, as the parson said in church last Sunday."

His mania was science; his heroes were the two Cornishmen Trevithick and Sir Humphry Davy. "Poor old Davy," he said to me once. "D'you know, Chad, he married a wealthy dame named Mrs. Apreece, and soon after that he went on a continental tour with her and took young Michael Faraday along. The dame didn't think Faraday was quite the thing, treated him like a servant, didn't see why Faraday should sit at table with them. All that sort of thing. Fancy that, Chad! Faraday! Silly old bitch!" I can hear now the note of passionate outrage in Billy's voice, see his hands unconsciously closing on the spar he was holding, as if about a throat. Whenever he had done anything for me, he would command: "Say it. Go on, Chad. Say it." I knew what he wanted, and sheepishly I would repeat the foolish words I had spoken when he lighted us through the wood. "Thank you, Pascoe." He would shake with laughter. "God, Chad," he said, for he was a profane boy, "how I laughed as I walked back to Pentyrch that night. And d'you know, Chad, all of a sudden, as I was cleaning the knives with powdered bath-brick, it came over me that you'd said more than you knew. 'By God,' I said to myself—I kept on saying it all the way home—'I'll light some of 'em through the wood yet, and they'll go on their knees and say "Thank you, Pascoe." ' "

13

And now, although I didn't know it, I was nearly done with Pendeverel. It was toward the end of that same May month in which I asked Billy whether he could climb up to being a butler. My father, as I have said, would now and then take on some job so long as he could soon be done with it; and he had taken on a job at Pentyrch. I have told you that as one stood on the lawn, with one's back to the house, an opening in the trees could be seen: the entry to a path leading to the beach. It was a downhill path, and a twisting path, and a sunken path, with the trees growing to the edges up above and sometimes meeting overhead. Captain Orlop was very particular about it. Pentyrch was well kept up in those days: not a detail was neglected. The middle of the path was cobbled and cambered, so that water would flow off into

31

gutters on either side. These were of large stones laid edge to edge in a shallow **V**. One way and another, a lot of water ran down that path in the winter months, especially when the springs rose in the woods. I have seen the place a proper little boiling torrent, shooting a cascade down the steps at the bottom and onto the beach. Stones would be prized out and borne along, and every spring someone would be given the job of hauling them back from the beach and making good the damage to pathway and gutters. No one bothers about this any more. The path is still there: a deeply rutted choke of rotted leaves and loosened stones.

In that May of 1901, my father was working on this job of annual repair. It was the sort of job he liked: he was alone; he could do it in his own time and in his own way. If he wanted to stop and smoke his pipe and listen to the birds that were rioting in the woods at that season, there was no one to say, "Get on with it."

Usually, my mother wrapped some food for him to eat at noon, but that day he got up rather late, snatched a cup of tea and hurried off. When I had finished my own midday meal, my mother said: "Here, Chad, take this along to your father. You know where to find him."

Times had changed so drastically that I did not like this. I wanted to run back to school, and said so. My mother said: "Do as I tell you. It won't matter if you're a bit late at school, or even if you miss it for an afternoon. I'm not going to have your father starving."

So off I went, reluctantly enough, not knowing that I should never see the school again. I plunged through the woods on the most direct line I knew, and came out to the fringes of the Pentyrch lawn. Rose Garland was on the lawn, playing with a spaniel pup.

I hadn't known she was in the district again, and I stood there watching her, watching the pup, admiring the wistaria whose flowers hung on the honey-colored stone like long bunches of mauve grapes. The sun was at its height.

The pup kept on running away. Rose would chase it, bring it back to where some scarlet cushions were spread, and lie down there, hugging it, fondling its ears. But it didn't want this play. Again and again it struggled free, ran to the mouth of the tunnel path, and stood there barking.

I walked across the lawn, and said: "That dog is trying to take you somewhere."

Rose looked up lazily and said: "Oh, it's you. What do you want?"

"I'm bringing my father's dinner. He's mending the gutters."

The pup had slipped from her arms again and was once more barking at the head of the path. She took no further notice of me but called: "Wogs! Come here. Come here, you disobedient dog."

I left her and walked toward the dog, who immediately shot off along the path. Then Rose Garland got up and followed.

It did not take us long to find what it was the dog wanted to show us. Two or three sharp twists of the path brought us to a more open stretch, and halfway along this was a fallen tree, a small pine. Looking up, I could see how it had been growing on the very edge of the cutting. The earth was torn away there, and the roots hung on, uncovered. The head of the tree had crashed down, and a protrusion from the trunk, about a foot long, where at some time or other a small branch had been cut off, had struck my father in the back of the neck, and penetrated. It must have been like a sudden dagger blow in a vital spot. He was alive. We could see him, prone beneath the canopy of needled branches, and we could hear him groaning faintly. The dog was barking with furious satisfaction at having done his job, and the woods were full of the cooing of pigeons.

I said to Rose: "Go and get someone, and tell them to bring saws." She ran off.

I knelt down, putting my face as near as I could to my father's, which was pinned to the stones of the path. He had heard my voice, and he said faintly: "Chad." Then: "This is a bad do, Chad." I could just hear the words, which were the last he spoke.

Having brought us there, the pup considered his work done. He stopped barking, smelled the lunch basket, tore off the napkin, and began to eat my father's dinner.

I had been calm enough till then, but this brought tears to my eyes. I was weeping without restraint when Captain Orlop and two estate workers came running down the path, Rose Garland at their heels. Seeing me thus, apparently useless, Captain Orlop said brusquely to Rose: "Take this boy away, and stay away yourself."

The girl took my arm and led me back to the lawn. "Lie down there," she commanded, and I lay down on the red cushions. She went into the house and was soon out again with a blanket that she spread over me. "You don't feel sick?" she asked maternally. I shook my head. "I don't think you should go back to your mother yet," she said. "Goodness knows what nonsense you'd babble. I expect your father'll be all right. Go to sleep now."

Strangely enough, I did go to sleep. I saw nothing of the procession, carrying my father into the house on a hurdle of pine branches, knew nothing of the doctor for whom Captain Orlop had sent a man with the pony trap as soon as Rose had told her story. There was nothing the doctor could do. Before I was awake, Captain Orlop himself had ridden off to tell my mother the news.

Uncle Arthur came down for the funeral, and when he returned to

33

Smurthwaite my mother and I went with him. Billy Pascoe walked all the way to the Town to say good-by. "Write to us, Chad," he said.

I swore that I would, but you know what boys are. I never did.

CHAPTER TWO

I

WE WENT to Smurthwaite by lazy stages, as befitted my uncle's habit. Not that he was thinking only of himself. "Edie," he said to my mother, "you must consider yourself and Chad to be under my Wing," and under Uncle Arthur's wing there was a sense of ease and space and of taking things quietly.

I hardly knew my mother. She was all in black and wore a black veil. She can hardly have known me, for I was in black, too. My accouterments included a handkerchief with a thin black edge that I was furtively proud of. Our trappings of woe had been bought in the Town, whither Uncle Arthur had taken us and paid for everything. He had even had mourning cards printed. These, like my handkerchief, were black-edged. A tomb with weeping willows was die-sunk at the top. Beneath this was my father's name, with the dates of his birth and death, and beneath that again the line "In the midst of life we are in death." These were all things that an English Gentleman did on such as occasion; and when my mother protested against the expense, Uncle Arthur said: "It would be a poor thing, Edie, if I allowed the expense to bow your frail shoulders. Believe me, your Little Fortune will not suffer. I am Nursing your Little Fortune," so that I had a vision of Uncle Arthur, by his bachelor fireside, nursing the Little Fortune night after night.

Well, there we were, on the way to London, which was to be our first stop; and if I was already aware of a comic side to my uncle's character, I was also aware that my mother and I were lucky to have him about. You will remember that he had commanded me, during his first visit, to read Tennyson. He had followed this up by sending to me from Smurthwaite a copy of *Idylls of the King*; and now he appeared to me like a heavy knight on a cumbersome charger who had taken over the responsibility for a lady in distress and was doing his job in careful compliance with the code of chivalry. We made the journey in a first-class carriage and with every convenience. Uncle Arthur had provided magazines for my mother, which the poor dear made a pretense of reading with her tear-reddened eyes, the *Times* for himself, and Sir Walter Scott's *Ivanhoe* for me. At midday, he opened a basket that contained cold chicken, rolls and butter, fruit, and a bottle of wine. "Let us fortify our somber spirits," he said, and ate with gusto.

So did I. I could not conceal that I was excited, more stirred by what was to come than depressed by what was finished. This was my first journey in a railway train, and it was to end in fabulous London! Everything was marvelous, and it was Maytime. The Cornish fields were a vivid green; the Devonshire cliffs were a vivid red; the sea was a vivid blue; and the White Horse of Wiltshire a shining white. So were the leaping lambs, and here and there brooks twinkled and sparkled or canals lay sleepy, thick with cresses and opening flowers and lively with coots and moorhens. Swans sailed majestically by, seeming to tow their following trains of cygnets, almost within smell of my nose pressed against the window. I forget where it was that the train stopped in the late afternoon, and we got out and drank tea on the platform; and Uncle Arthur took my arm, led me away ostentatiously to study a bookstall, murmuring: "An English Gentleman, Chad, withdraws on certain occasions," and my mother wandered off on her own. Then he and I wandered in another direction.

I remember the London dusk—the bloomy dusk of a great waterside city—that I saw then for the first time; and it was full of flowering trees, and shouts, and men and women, and horses without number, as we three bowled sedately from Paddington in a four-wheeled cab. I don't know where we stayed, except that it was in a small hotel in a backwater. There was a room for my mother, and one that Uncle Arthur and I were to share. I remember throwing myself at once upon the bed, suddenly worn out by the excitements of the day, and Uncle Arthur saying: "Leave him there to rest for a bit." They went out, and I must have slept for hours. It was dark when I was awakened by the slight sound of the door opening and the small light of a candle. I was aware that someone, in the course of my sleep, had drawn off my shoes and thrown blankets over me. Uncle Arthur was coming into the room. I was in that state of being half-asleep and half-awake when one is not quite sure which one is. I must have dozed a bit, for the next thing I knew was that Uncle Arthur, wearing an enormous white nightshirt, was kneeling down by the bed near mine. I couldn't make out what he was up to. His lips were moving without sound. Suddenly I knew that he was saying his prayers, as I had never said mine. It gave me a spying feeling, and I shut my eyes tight. Then Uncle Arthur came across and kissed me on the forehead. I heard him climb heavily into bed, creaking the springs. He blew out the candle, and in the darkness his snores soon arose, mingling with the unending noises of the great city that were not so much heard as sensed, as you could sense the breathing of the sea while lying snug in our cottage at Pendeverel.

2

We were in London for three days. Municipalities, I gathered, didn't do exactly as they pleased. There were certain strings tying them to Government, and Uncle Arthur, wearing the Hat and its appropriate garments, had several calls to make in Government quarters. It was impressive to see him set off from our hotel in a hansom cab, fitting it as closely as an outsize sardine that needed a whole tin to himself. There came to him several times large envelopes marked O.H.M.S., and no boy could fail to be impressed when told what those letters meant. It seemed to me incredible that His Majesty, so soon after becoming King, should be corresponding with Uncle Arthur, who continued to say his prayers at night as humbly as though he knew no one of more consequence than God. While he was away on these expeditions, my mother and I would explore the shopping streets and wander in the parks which were radiant with May weather, and the houses that edged them seemed all to have been newly painted and decorated with flowering window boxes and striped awnings. My mother, like me, had never been in London before and often expressed her fear that we would be lost. "You need not worry about that, my dear Edie," Uncle Arthur said. "You simply call a cab and give the cabby your address. But *not a hansom cab*. It must be a four-wheeler."

"You always use a hansom cab, Uncle Arthur," I ventured to say; and he said: "I'd like to see the hansom cab that tried to take liberties with me."

It was in a four-wheeler that he took us to see the Royal Academy exhibition, but not before he had seriously debated with my mother the propriety of a widow, in so early a stage of her mourning, being seen at a place of entertainment. "I don't think you need have any qualms," he finally decided. "The exhibition is in the realm of Art, and I don't see how that can be considered entertaining."

So we went, and we saw Miss Orlop's picture *Women Must Weep*, and were surprised at the number of people standing before it. They made quite a crowd. The *Daily Mail* that morning had contained an article headed *"Why?"* and had asked *"Why Must Women Weep?"* Would so many fishermen's women weep if we had a better lifeboat service? And so Miss Orlop's picture was talked about as the Picture of the Year, and was eventually bought by an insurance company. It was reproduced as the cover of a booklet which the company issued called, "You Know Not What a Day May Bring Forth."

36

However, this had not happened on that day when we stood before the canvas and I was full of pride, thinking how beautiful my pictured mother looked. Uncle Arthur, with the *Daily Mail* article in mind, said: "Art in the service of Humanity. That is a noble thing, Chad." He placed his large bulk between my infant eyes and a nude on a tiger skin, and soon afterward we left. We had seen my mother's portrait, and that was all we had gone to see.

That was not a successful visit. As soon as we were in the street, it was evident that my mother was overcome. The picture showed her as a young widow, and now she *was* a widow. None of us had thought of that. It had been too much for her. She went to bed without any lunch, and Uncle Arthur and I ate a gloomy if plentiful meal. He enlarged to me on the importance of eating well in times of depression. It was a duty we owed to ourselves and to those about us, he said, calling for another cut of the excellent saddle of mutton. "When a blow is struck, Chad, a man does not sit down under it like a craven. He asks himself what he can do about it, and the least—the very least—is to sustain his body to endure it."

After lunch he went up to my mother's room and returned with the news that she intended to stay in bed till dinnertime. "My official *pourparlers* are now ended, Chad," he said. "Tomorrow we leave London early. Tonight I shall be busy preparing a Report. We have this afternoon to ourselves. I have spoken on the telephone to Miss Orlop. She invites us to tea."

We walked for an hour in Hyde Park, and then struck across to the Bayswater Road where Miss Orlop had her house, with a studio in the garden. I don't remember much about that occasion except that Miss Orlop in town was dressed exactly like Miss Orlop in the country— the same severe collar and tie, blouse and skirt—and that we took tea in a room on the first floor, overlooking the park, in the company of a throng of statues whose qualification for admission seemed to be maiming. There was a lady with one arm and a gentleman without any nose to speak of and an angel who must have had a violent set-to with another angel in mid-air and snapped off a piece of wing. There were some unfortunates so far gone that they had lost not only all four limbs but their heads as well, and stood with their thighs chunkily planted on wooden stands. Some who were lucky enough to have otherwise complete faces were obviously without the faculty of sight, staring out of eyes that lacked pupils. Miss Orlop sat like an efficient surgeon, amid patients awaiting treatment, with a side hint also of being a tailor who would presently measure them all for clothes.

I remember that, and I remember that as I was eating seed cake Miss Orlop pounced on me suddenly with a question about my father's fatal accident. She had not been at Pentyrch when it happened. She

37

had sent Rose Garland down there alone. I told her how the spaniel pup had led me and Rose to the fallen tree.

"Is the child still in Cornwall?" Uncle Arthur asked.

"Yes."

"Will she be joining you in town soon?"

"I don't know," Miss Orlop said. "I don't know what to do for the best. Please don't ask me about her."

3

We set off so early the next morning that we were able to eat lunch in the Midland Hotel, Bradford. Now I was in the North. To my mother and my uncle this was accustomed ground. Their infant feet had trodden these stones, as mine had trodden the turf and the beaches of Pendeverel. And how stony it was! That was the impression that dominated all others in my mind. The start of the journey had been fair enough. Once the drab excrescences of London had been shed, there had been at least trees and fields, if none as satisfying as those through which we had come to London. But long before we reached Bradford itself we seemed to be in a world of stone: stone that served for hedges in starved-looking fields; stone that sprawled upon the ground in mills covering acre upon acre; stone that lifted into the air the tall monitory fingers of the chimneys; and even in the voices of the people there seemed an uncompromising stony hardness, so different from the soft slur of Pendeverel.

It was as we were within the last mile of the journey, rushing through cuttings that were black stony acclivities, and finally through a tunnel that stank of stone saturated with soot and moisture, that I shouted to Uncle Arthur, above the shriek of the wheels, voicing as I did so the deep troubled thought of my heart: "How far are we from the sea?"

Uncle Arthur replied: "As far as we can be in this sceptered isle."

I had feared as much.

It was at the Great Northern station that we arrived, and the Midland Hotel was no distance away, but we took a four-wheeler because of the luggage. It was a journey through canyons of stone, impregnated with the smell, that came to me then for the first time, of oily wool. The very road was of stone setts over which the iron tires jarred and jolted.

We could easily have reached Smurthwaite that day if we had taken a train after lunch; but Uncle Arthur had decided that it was best for my mother to travel by easy stages. "Besides, Edie, now that you are back on your native heath, I expect you'd like to have a look around."

"Better than Manningham Lane—eh?" my father had been used to saying; and I thought of the words as we three walked along Manningham Lane after dinner that night. The middle of the town is a bowl into which streets pour down like streams into a lake. We climbed one of these streets and came out into Manningham Lane, a long road cut along the side of a valley. On the left, streets fell down into it; on the right, more streets fell out of it, ending up in the valley bottom, a valley full of railway lines, beyond which the land rose again.

The lane itself was not my sort of lane: all shops and houses, with a grimy shrub or two in the front gardens. We paused before one shop, a chemist's, and on the fascia board I read: "BRIGGS, LATE GELDERSOME." My mother and my uncle looked at the shop and at the windows of the living room over it; and what their thoughts were I do not know. After a moment Uncle Arthur said: "Well, there it is," and on we went.

Looking at the streets rushing down into the valley, Uncle Arthur said: "A wonderful place this in the winter, Chad. There's always snow, and those streets are perfect toboggan runs. I remember it. The street lamps on, and everything dumb with the snow, and we boys whizzing down and hauling up. Girls, too. Do you remember, Edie?"

I found it difficult to imagine my uncle as a boy active enough to whizz about on a toboggan. My mother said: "I remember you breaking your leg, if that's anything."

"Well, well," said Uncle Arthur rather proudly. "Everything has its price. It was worth it."

The dusk was settling upon the town, the lights were coming on in streets and houses; and we turned to the left and climbed higher, coming out in Heaton. Here we leaned on a rough unmortared stone wall and a vast prospect rolled before us. There was still just light enough to see fold upon fold of hills melting and merging into the west. The nearer prospect, where the roads of the chaotic town ran up hill and down dale, was a fantasia of lights swooping and looping, gathering here in tiaras, there stringing out into necklaces. But it was upon the further prospect of the darkening moors and dales that Uncle Arthur's eyes were fixed. "Smurthwaite," he said. "Smurthwaite tomorrow."

4

My infant mind had formed no clear picture of Smurthwaite, and the little town came upon me with a shock of pleasure. Traveling west from Bradford, we took about an hour to reach it, and in that hour we increasingly shed the smirch of the industrial West Riding and came out into clear skies and sharp winy air and green fellsides terraced with limestone that shone as whitely as the clay hills I had been able to see from Pendeverel. The exciting new experiences of the last few days had overlain but not extinguished a fear in my heart: a fear that I had not formulated, but that was concerned with the disappearance of everything I had known till then and with the need to adjust myself to an environment I could not imagine. The second half of our journey north had deepened the fear, but now it seemed to be blown away by the drafts of vigorous air that came through the window. Uncle Arthur was obviously aware of my pleasurable excitement. He sat opposite me, looking at me with a smile upon his broad placid face, the rather smug smile of a conjuror about to work the trick.

"Edie," he said, "you were exactly fifteen when you were last in Smurthwaite. Do you remember?"

My mother said that she did.

"It was your fifteenth birthday. I was twenty-five. You seemed nothing but a slip of a child to me, and for your birthday present I gave you a day's outing. We took train to Smurthwaite and walked all round the place: Grassington and Linton-in-Craven—oh, everywhere. It was a happy day. Did you find it a happy day, Edie?"

"Very."

"Well, then. Here we are again. Many happy days to you at Smurthwaite."

He had timed his little speech well. The train pulled up in Smurthwaite station. We climbed down onto the platform, into the air that had a clear taste like the cold water of a tarn, something altogether different from the languorous air that loitered, warm and moist, among the trees of the woods around Pentyrch. This was not air that would make ferns grow in the crotches of the elms.

There was no cab at the station. My uncle hailed a man with a handcart, the trunks were put on, and the man set off, not needing to be told where Mr. Geldersome lived.

"We shall walk," Uncle Arthur announced. This clearly was his moment. In decent leisure we should be conducted through his Municipality. He tucked my mother's arm through his and off we went, he taking care, whenever we crossed the road to look at this and that, to transfer to the other arm, keeping her on the inside of the pavement, as an English Gentleman should.

It was a little place. It was not so big as our Town. It was one of those small country townships that somehow or other once achieved the status of a borough and had hung on to it ever since. It looked a place that had neither grown nor declined through the centuries. It looked as if long long ago it had been built to last and had lasted magnificently. There was no wattle and daub in Smurthwaite as there was in so many of the cottages I had known, and no thatch, either. It was all gray weathered stone, even to the roofs, which were not of slate but of thin stone. It was what I should call a solid, respectable, handsome little town.

Uncle Arthur's Municipality, I thought, suited him perfectly. It was the sort of municipality he would have made if he had been given the job.

The two main streets made a cross, and each of these streets was wide and planted with sycamores. They were so wide that, at their intersection, a handsome building stood with the crossroads flowing round it, giving no sense of causing an obstruction and needing to be moved on. It looked like the focus of everything at Smurthwaite, and so it was: it was the Town Hall.

Uncle Arthur drew us to the Town Hall, almost tiptoeing with reverence. I expected him, as we stood there looking up the broad flight of stone steps, to raise his Hat. Not a word was spoken. We just looked, till at last he said: "I'll show you round some other day." For the moment he contented himself with walking us round the outside. In one angle of wall I saw a notice: "COMMIT NO PUBLIC NUISANCE HERE. BY ORDER. ARTHUR J. GELDERSOME, TOWN CLERK." I looked at my uncle with enhanced respect. That his name should appear, enforcing a public admonition, seemed to me a matter of immense prestige. He observed the direction of my glance, and I thought a modest blush tinged his countenance, but he said nothing about it and called our attention to the magnificent parish church standing amid its gravestones on a corner of the intersection. "Some day," he said, "you may meet the Rector, Mr. Hawke."

On another corner, facing the church, was the Grammar School, solid like everything else in Smurthwaite, stone mullioned, having the feeling that pervaded the whole small town of combined homeliness and strength. "Some day," said my uncle, "you will undoubtedly meet the Headmaster, Mr. Ashmole. He conducts the school on the principle that to spare the rod is to spoil the child. A sound principle. Why, Chad, at school I was again and again thrashed within an inch of my life. And look at me."

"No one had better thrash Chad within an inch of his life—or within a yard, for that matter," said my mother.

"Oh, I don't know," my uncle answered easily. "It would brighten his ideas no end. I expect Ashmole will beat some sense into him yet."

I looked apprehensively into his face, and was rewarded with a heavy wink.

With the Town Hall at our backs, and with the Parish Church on one hand and the Grammar School on the other, we looked up the top arm of the cross. The ground here rose sharply as if to call the eye to what closed the view. This was an enormous battlemented wall pierced by a gate between whose wrought-iron intricacies could be seen the façade of a castle. Unlike everything else in Smurthwaite, it was not of gray stone. It was of red sandstone. Under the midday sun it seemed to burn. Uncle Arthur looked toward it with a reverence second only to that which he had accorded to the Town Hall. "The home of the Newtes," he said. "Newtes have lived there for centuries. They have never been ennobled, but it's a most ancient baronetage. Some day, perhaps," he said, "you will meet the present baronet, Sir Titus Newte."

5

If you think of the layout of Smurthwaite as being like that of a church, with the rood screen at the Town Hall and the castle as the high altar, then you may say that we now turned into the north transept. It was a shortish street, and, like the others, planted with sycamores, now wearing their springtime green. On both sides of the street at the Town Hall end were shops, and they were not your blatant shops of today with plate-glass windows and chromium fittings and neon lighting on the fascias. They were modest and retiring shops that seemed to know that people wanted what they had to sell and would come for it without any need to shout for them. The shopkeepers lived over the shops. There were private houses at the farther end of the street, and the last of all, on the right-hand side, was Uncle Arthur's. It was a three-storied, flat-windowed building, standing flush to the pavement, and as we moved through the dark green brass-gleaming doorway a most satisfying smell of cooking came to meet us. My uncle's nostrils dilated. "Ah!" he said. "Roast duck and green peas. As ordered."

We found in the course of the next few moments that, though he had said nothing to us, he had done a good deal of ordering. His housekeeper, Mrs. Ramsden, came through from the kitchen. I didn't like the look of her. Everything about Smurthwaite thus far had suggested coziness and comfort and, so to speak, rotundity. Mrs. Ramsden, though not tall—indeed she was on the short side—was angular. Her nose was sharp and her eyes were sharp and her voice was sharp as she exclaimed, looking me and my mother up and down: "So these is them." I knew all about hedgehogs, and I seemed to feel spines shooting out of her voice.

"Yes," said my uncle, "these are they, Mrs. Ramsden—my widowed sister Mrs. Boothroyd and her Orphan Child."

Mrs. Ramsden contemplated the Orphan Child with no notable enthusiasm. "I hope," she said, "we're not going to start having dirt trampled into t'house."

It looked, indeed, as though this would be a profanity on Uncle Arthur's premises. The floor boards and the hall table gleamed, and mingling with kitchen smells was the smell of furniture polish. I was

42

to hear Mrs. Ramsden later speak of feeding the furniture—which was not surprising seeing how well fed everything in that house was —and certainly, as I stood there hesitant, twisting my cap in my hand on that May morning, the table and the chair alongside it had an opulent look as though every pore oozed an oily nourishment. The only thing that looked half-starved was a silver-gray whippet: a tiny creature all sinew and bright intelligent eyes that now came bounding from the kitchen and stood before Uncle Arthur trembling with the ecstasy of a saint before his god.

Uncle Arthur was not built for stooping. He laced the fingers of his hands together, making a cradle, and the whippet, leaping upon them, was lifted to his face which she proceeded to lick, shivering mightily. "Madeleine!" my uncle murmured. "My little Madeleine! Uncle's back. Uncle's back again. It's all right."

He put his vast paws around her—I feared they would crack the frail visible cage of her ribs—and handed her to Mrs. Ramsden. She received the small bitch with an affection I had not felt flowing toward me, and disappeared toward the kitchen. We followed Uncle Arthur's heavy tread up the solid crimson-carpeted stairs. "Mrs. Ramsden is very kind to Madeleine," he said, as though that covered everything.

We went up two flights to the top story of the house, and Uncle Arthur opened doors and peeped into the three rooms. He rubbed his hands with satisfaction. "All as ordered," he announced. "Now, my dear Edie, all this house is your home. I shall be happy to see you and Chad in any part of it. But these rooms up here are your Private Quarters, where you can be alone if you want to be."

Two of the rooms were small, and these were bedrooms. The third was sizable, furnished as a sitting room. There were two easy chairs and a settee covered with rosy chintz, a well-fed looking mahogany bureau, a table with a few women's magazines on it, more rosy chintz at the window. The fire was laid, and the fender and fire irons gleamed. Uncle Arthur began to tiptoe out. "Come down as soon as you are ready," he said. "Luncheon will be on the table."

My mother sat in one of the chintz chairs and began to blubber. "Why d-don't you get married?" she asked. "Y-you and y-your whippet!"

"Now, now!" he said, holding up a stout finger. "Not a word against Madeleine."

6

I left my mother there and went into my small bedroom. From the smell of it I could tell that it was newly decorated. Looking at the walls painted in pale pink, and the gleaming white of the woodwork, and the

43

chintz mainly black but with pink rosebuds scattered upon it that draped the windows and formed the bedspread, I realized that it had all cost Uncle Arthur a pretty penny, and I humbly resolved that Mrs. Ramsden should never have reason to complain of my bringing dirt into this spotless retreat. The room had a bow window with a seat running round it, and standing there, looking out on the fresh green of the fields that rose into gentle hills ribbed with the outcropping white of limestone, I fancied these outcrops to be the foaming crests of waves on a green sea and myself a captain gazing astern from his poop cabin. A few Pendeverel gulls were all the illusion wanted, but I was not thinking of Pendeverel in that moment. The present, the immediate, was too rapturous.

My mother came in, and I wanted to show her all that had entranced me, but she said: "We'd better get down, Chad. We mustn't keep your uncle waiting."

If the rest of the furniture had been well fed, that in the dining room looked the most fatly nourished of all, as though it used its privileged position to imbibe the very essence of festive moments. All was of mahogany and the gleam of it, even on that fireless day, positively chuckled. Had the fire and lamps been lit, it would have winked and twinkled with well-being. The food was carved and waiting on the plates, and Uncle Arthur, with his back to the fireplace, had the look of a hungry boy at a Sunday school outing, standing impatient at the groaning board while a long grace is being unnecessarily said. He lost no time in seating my mother and dropping heavily into his own chair. As if it were the only grace needed, he said: "Fall to, Edie. Lay into it, Chad." He set us a good example.

Alongside his chair on the floor was a pink satin cushion on which Madeleine awaited her meal. I must say she was a good-mannered little bitch. When Uncle Arthur had taken the edge from his own pangs, he carved a meal for her, put the plate containing it down by the cushion, and she ate her dinner with a high-bred finicky particularity. Then she lay down quietly again.

We were halfway through our sweet before my uncle felt at liberty to give his attention to anything other than his plate. Then he said: "I am a little disappointed, Edie."

"Why, Arthur," my mother asked. "What is wrong?"

"Unremitting attention, loving attention, and attention informed by knowledge, is necessary throughout the twelve mortal months of the year," Uncle Arthur said, "to produce a display which has been accepted without a word of comment."

His gaze rested upon the enormous wire contraption that stood upon the table. The wire, white painted, was elegantly twisted to form containers for flower pots. There were four tiers: five pots, four pots, three pots, and one crowning all. In each pot was an auricula in flower.

"They look very nice, Arthur," my mother conceded.

Uncle Arthur laid down his spoon. "My dear Edie," he said, "if a well-balanced life like mine, a life dominated by the cold particularities of municipal administration, may be said to have a dominating passion, that passion is The Auricula."

He placed a hand on Madeleine's head. "Madeleine is aware that even she," he said, "holds a second place. Before you, you behold a display which at the annual exhibition of the West Riding Auricula Society in Leeds was awarded first place and a Certificate of Merit. You tell me this display looks *very nice*. One of the glories of God's creation looks *very nice*. Lovely Ann, Cheetham's Lancashire Hero, Bolivar, Lord Lynedoch, True Briton, Ne Plus Ultra, the whole crowned with the monarch of the auricula world, that is Geldersome Green, looks *very nice*."

It was the measure of his agitation that he did not finish the pudding on his plate. He rose and opened the door. "Kitchen, Madeleine," he said. And to us: "I must see what is happening in my Town Hall. I shall be back at about six."

The door closed but a moment later it opened again, and Uncle Arthur stood there holding the Hat. "Dull would he be of soul," he said, "who could pass by a sight so touching in its majesty." He put the Hat on and went. My mother sighed. "Well, there it is, Chad. Whether by keeping your mouth shut or opening it, you never know when you'll step on a corn."

That seemed a mixed sentiment to me, but I let it go.

7

"I was, perhaps, my dear Edie, a trifle impetuous at the luncheon table," Uncle Arthur said that evening.

He had returned, as he had promised, at six—at six to the dot. Meanwhile, Mrs. Ramsden was gone. She did not live in. "A Town Clerk," Uncle Arthur once explained to my mother, "has the rectitude of his Municipality in his hand. He must be circumspect, and give no occasion for his own rectitude to be aspersed." This was why Mrs. Ramsden did not live in.

"You needn't bother about Mr. Geldersome's supper," my mother said to Mrs. Ramsden that afternoon. "I can see to that."

" 'Igh tea, that's what he has, not supper," Mrs. Ramsden answered, "and I can see to that like I've always done."

"Like I've always done" must have been a sore point with Mrs. Ramsden. She had been with my uncle ever since he came to Smurthwaite. She had given him his breakfast and seen him off. She had cooked his dinner, and left his high tea ready; and, above all, apart

45

from mealtimes, she had had the house to herself and had been able to get on with feeding the furniture and Madeleine and doing whatever else needed to be done. Changes gradually came. For one thing, my mother did all the cooking and looked after the three rooms on our floor. Mrs. Ramsden took it well; and when I once apologized to her because the prints of my shoes were clearly visible on "me polished floors," she tried to look severe for a moment, then grinned, and said: "Ah, well. Tha's not bad as lads go." And after that, as though we had exchanged some Freemason sign, things went smoothly between us.

Well, when Uncle Arthur got back that night, the high tea was on the dining room table—my first experience of this meal which consists of plenty of cold meat and bread-and-butter and cake and jam, with tea to wash it down. And there was Uncle Arthur reporting that in his absence things had gone as well as could be expected at the Town Hall and apologizing to my mother for his words at the luncheon table.

"Concerning The Auricula," he said, masterfully whipping a knife up and down the steel at the sideboard, before carving generous helpings of beef, "I can become heated. I deplore the illogicality of this attitude, for the beauty and refinement of these flowers should enter into the soul of the man who cultivates them. The auricula growers of Britain normally reach a great old age, and as year succeeds year you will see in their faces a deepening serenity and grace. I have known a rose grower, awarded a second place when expecting a first, sweep his exhibit to the ground and trample upon it in rage. An auricula grower would merely ask himself where he had gone wrong and resolve to do better in future."

"They sound to me," said my mother, pouring the tea, "more like the communion of saints than normal men."

"I had not thought of it in that light before," said Uncle Arthur, putting Madeleine's plate down by her cushion, "but you have hit the nail on the head, Edie. An auricula grower will have little to learn in the great forever. He will know how to make it, in Kingsley's words, one grand sweet song."

There was no fear of getting lost in Smurthwaite, and so the next morning, after Uncle Arthur had departed for the Town Hall, my mother turned me loose to explore. I became impressed by Uncle Arthur's iron grip upon the town. Smuthwaite had most things, but on a small scale. There was even a small public park, though why that was necessary with the dales of Yorkshire striding about us in all directions goodness knows. I wandered through the gates and read a notice posted up inside them, telling the public when they could come in and when they must stay out, that they must place their litter in the receptacles provided, that dogs must be kept on a leash, that any infringement of these by-laws would be visited with appropriate penalties, the whole stern concatenation ending: "By Order. Arthur J. Geldersome, Town Clerk."

As I strolled here and there through the town, I found warnings about the times when dustbins should be removed from the public pavements, about riding bicycles on foot paths, about the licensing of vehicles and the muzzling of dogs, and, near the spot where the weekly cattle market was held, an injunction that "beasts must on no account obstruct the public thoroughfare at this point." And all these warnings and instructions were signed: "By Order. Arthur J. Geldersome, Town Clerk."

My small chest began to swell with pride at my association with so much authority. It seemed to me that no one in Smurthwaite could be more powerful than Uncle Arthur, that anyone who kept on the right side of him was on carpet, and that those who didn't had better look out. There was no place in his municipality where you were free from his all-seeing eye. I went into Smurthwaite's small public urinal, and Arthur J. Geldersome commanded me to adjust my dress before leaving. I happily obeyed, and walked about in smug satisfaction, feeling as though there were written all over me in glowing letters: "This is my nephew, Chad. Give him the respect he deserves. By Order, Arthur J. Geldersome, Town Clerk.

So it was perhaps with not so much surprise as I should otherwise have felt that I heard myself addressed by name. "Well, Chad, what do you think of your new home?"

I turned from the shop window and looked at a stranger: a tall man in gray, wearing a parson's collar. "I know you're Chad Boothroyd," he said. "I saw you and your mother walking through the town yesterday with my friend Geldersome. He told me he would be bringing you both to live with him. My name is Hawke. I'm the Rector here."

He held out his hand and I shook it. "What do you think of those buns, eh?" he asked; for it was before a bun shop that I had paused. "Time for my morning coffee. We'd better go in and sample them."

So we went in and sampled the buns and drank coffee, and Mr. Hawke talked to me as if I were a grown-up person, inviting me to call on him at the Rectory and see what he called his "collections," telling me about his son Eustace—"He's just gone off to Shrewsbury. You must meet him in the holidays"—and his daughter Phoebe. "We're the only two there now—Phoebe and I. My wife's dead. A housekeeper looks after the place."

Like all children, I thought anybody over twenty was on the brink

47

of eternity. I suppose Mr. Hawke then could not have been more than forty. His thin face was fair, blue-eyed and clean-shaven. It had what I can only call a stern kindliness.

"Well, now," he said, rising at last, "don't forget that I shall expect to see you at the Rectory. And in church! Can you sing?"

I said I didn't know, sir; nor did I, for though I sang like a lark when in the mood, I had never thought about such outpourings as singing in the sense which Mr. Hawke now clearly intended.

"Well, well. We shall see," he said. "We could make use of you in the choir."

I walked home pondering this. It fitted in with my complacent mood as a person of consequence in Smurthwaite: a nephew of Arthur J. Geldersome, a friend of the Rector. I saw myself with a pie frill round my neck, melting the hearts of the congregation in the dusk of a summer evening. Angel face with the angel voice. As I turned left at the Town Hall toward Uncle Arthur's house, I cleared my throat and tried a stave or two of "Soldiers of the Queen." The boys were just coming out of the Grammar School. Some were pushing bicycles, some were taking swings at one another with satchels of books. They gathered round as I caroled, grinning and cheering. I stopped, overcome with confusion. "Go on!" "Keep it up!" they shouted. One said: "It's Jenny Lind, the Swedish nightingale. Pipe up, Jenny." I glared at him, not feeling so important now. He gave me a kick in the seat of the pants, hopped onto a bicycle, and rode away. That was my first meeting with Gregory Appleby.

9

There never was such a boy as Gregory Appleby for knowing odd, possibly unimportant, but always amusing or exciting things. How on earth should he, living on a small Yorkshire farm, know that in exalted circles mutton chops were served with frills round the knuckle? And so, when at last I did join the choir and wear a frill, it was he who began to call me mutton chop, or mutton, or muttonhead, as the fancy took him. It was a come-down from my fanciful notion of the angel face with the angel voice. Gregory seemed born to keep people right, to keep their feet on the earth. He was the only boy I ever knew with the hardihood to correct Mr. Ashmole. It was at the end of a school term and Mr. Ashmole was in a good mood. "Well, off you go," he said. "Thank God I'm seeing the last of you barbarians for a few weeks. Off with you to fresh fields and pastures new."

"Woods, surely," Greg murmured.

"What did you say, Appleby? Don't mutter. Speak up."

"I said fresh woods, sir. Surely it is fresh *woods* and pastures new. Fields and pastures are the same thing. A poet of Milton's size wouldn't repeat himself like that."

Mr. Ashmole checked the passage. "I award you six marks for accuracy, Appleby, and six cuts for a public impertinence. Which will you take first?"

"Would it be reasonable to let them cancel one another out, sir?"

It was left like that. Greg knew that Mr. Ashmole was fond of him.

However, all this was in the future. That morning when I first met Mr. Hawke I went home pondering a side of my new life that I would have to reckon with—the boys of Smurthwaite. Uncle Arthur, I was sure, would not let things go on as my father had done at Pendeverel.

The next day was a Saturday, and uncle did not return to the Town Hall after lunch. "Chad," he said as we sat at the table, "make the most of this week end, for on Monday life will begin for you in earnest."

I was to present myself at the board school, as the council school was called in those days, "and in due course," said my uncle, "you will proceed to the Grammar School. At least, I hope you will. Far be it from me to hold up my humble self as an example, but your mother will be able to tell you that, beginning in a board school, I carved my career with my own unaided hands. So it must be with you, Chad. A scholarship will take you into the Grammar School: therefore, you must say to yourself, I will win a scholarship. From the Grammar School there are scholarships to Oxford. Therefore, say to yourself: I shall win a scholarship to Oxford. As with the cultivation of the auricula, the final prize must be in view from the beginning and must be *worked* for from the beginning. Here we are in May. Since June of last year I have been working to produce the results displayed on this table. There are those who will tell you that May is a dead month in the cultivation of the auricula: a month with nothing to be done. On the contrary, it is the month when one can do the main thing, and that is indulge in prolonged admiration of nature's outstanding floral treasure. Take some cheese with your apple pie, Chad. It is a Yorkshire specialty. We must build you up for the battle of life. We must tighten the girth, look to the bit and bridle."

"For goodness sake, Arthur," said my mother, "leave the boy alone. What are you trying to make of him—an auricula or a warhorse? You get out for a long walk, Chad. It's a beautiful day. I'll put you up some sandwiches."

That was something I understood, the old Pendeverel proposition: food in the pocket and the world to roam in. So, while Uncle Arthur, who had appeared now in a disreputable suit, went off to his green-house with Madeleine snuggling in his arms, I took to the road. There was no languor in this air: there was a heartiness that made me feel I could go on forever. The trees were fewer and harder than I had been accustomed to; but there were fellsides to climb, with cloud shadows running on them like greyhounds, and from their tops wide views opened of dales and streams, sheep in the pastures and growing corn, scattered farms looking snug among trees. I did not want to lie down and sleep in the sun as I so often did in Cornwall. After I had eaten my sandwiches I walked on and on, cross country, over the stone-piled walls, through gates, wherever my fancy took me. The sun was setting, and I was tired at last, and I rested on a gate. On the other side of this narrow road there was another gate, and behind me a path-way led to a farm. A herd of milch cows, with heavy udders, was com-ing through the fields toward the gate facing me, and, guessing that they were being driven for milking to the farm, I got down and threw both the gates open. They knew their way, and lolloped across the road. A boy walking behind them with a hazel switch in his hand grinned at me and said: "Thank you, Jenny Lind." I recognized the boy who had come out of the Grammar School and kicked me in the pants. He shut the gates and let the cows find their accustomed way home. He was a sturdy, ruddy boy. "You're a long way off your beat, aren't you?" he asked.

I told him I'd been walking all the afternoon and was about to walk back to Smurthwaite.

"You've got all of eight miles to go," he said. "Come and have a drink."

It sounded a sophisticated invitation, but the drink was only a glass of warm milk at the farm. He came out from the house carrying it in his hand, his lip pearled with a drink he had taken himself. "I've got to go in to Smurthwaite," he said. "I'll give you a lift."

He wheeled his bicycle out from a shed, and I walked alongside him as far as the road. "Hop on the step," he said, "and grab me round the waist."

I don't see these steps on bicycles nowadays. They were useful things. Up to a point. Eight miles with one foot precarious and the other flying loose, over a road that was nothing to write home about, was no joke. It didn't leave the attention free for much conversation. However, he shouted over his shoulder: "My name's Gregory Appleby. What's yours?"

"Chad Boothroyd. I've just come to live with my uncle." I added proudly: "He's the Town Clerk."

"Oh—old Geldersome," said Gregory Appleby.

Somehow, that didn't seem right, but there was nothing I could say about it.

"Well," Gregory said, dropping one foot to the road outside our front door, "here we are. I'm on my way to do a bit of Latin with Mr. Hawke. Good night."

I watched him go with mixed feelings.

10

This, as I say, was a Saturday, and Saturday night was Uncle Arthur's time for smoking a pipe. There was, with him, a time for everything, and a place for everything. The place for smoking was his "den"—a small room behind the dining room. It had the advantage that you could look down the garden to the greenhouse where the auriculas were cultivated. "Not grown, my dear Chad. An auricula will grow, yes. But an auricula that has merely grown is one thing. An auricula that has been cultivated is another." There was also a dress, if not for everything, at any rate for most things; and the dress for smoking in the den included a black velvet jacket and a smoking cap. I believe this headgear was common enough at one time. Uncle Arthur was the only man I ever saw wearing it, and he wore it with an air: the black velvet pie squatting on his crown, the maroon silk tassel drooping toward his left ear. He reclined in a chair upholstered in worn green plush. His feet, embellished with scarlet slippers, were thrust out on the hearth mat. Occasionally his hand fondled the transparent membrane that was Madeleine's ear. She lay at bliss in his lap. I was on a footstool on the hearth. It was a snug, rather shabby, room, with something of the air of an office. On the walls were engravings of Lord Chancellors; there were pigeonholes full of bundled documents, and a few black japanned tin boxes.

"So you have been out and about in our little town," said Uncle Arthur. "Tell me. What did you think of our little town's general deportment—eh?"

I said I thought the buns in Mrs. Cunliffe's shop were very good.

"Ah, then you met Hawke! And Hawke, I suppose, invited you to see his 'collections.'"

"Yes, sir."

"There will be occasions, Chad, when formality calls upon you to address me as 'sir.' In the informal atmosphere of this snuggery 'uncle' or 'Uncle Arthur' will do well enough. Well, as a matter of politeness, you had better accept Hawke's invitation. But don't expect any great enlightenment. Hawke is a good fellow, but he has never learned the importance of cultivation. There is no one subject that he has

51

pursued to the end. I hesitate to call him scatterbrained, though my hesitation does me no credit."

"He teaches Latin," I said. "I came home on a bike with a boy named Gregory Appleby who was going to learn Latin with Mr. Hawke."

"I know Gregory Appleby," said my uncle, "and I have no doubt that in a few years' time, if there is still any question of teaching, it is he who will be teaching Mr. Hawke."

It sounded like a compliment, but there was a tone behind the words which made me feel that my uncle did not like Gregory.

"Don't you like Gregory Appleby?" I asked boldly.

"I have watched young Appleby grow from a child in the board school to a boy in the Grammar School. As a governor of the Grammar School I had a hand in encouraging him to sit for his scholarship, which he won hands down. I have a great admiration for Gregory's talents."

I felt rather hurt. Uncle Arthur had dodged the question.

"Now, Chad," he said, "I think it would be a pleasant thing for your poor mother if you joined her for a few moments in her boudoir before going to bed. Go up and cherish her, my dear boy."

11

In the middle of the following week, leaving the board school at midday, I met Greg coming out of the Grammar School. We stood talking where the Town Hall was islanded at the intersection of the main streets. I told him that Mr. Hawke had called at our house and formally invited me to tea on the following Saturday.

"Oh—old Hawke," Greg said. It was the same tone in which he had said: "Oh—old Geldersome." One didn't get the impression that Gregory Appleby was bursting with reverence for his elders. As the years went by, and I got to know him well, I found he was not bursting with reverence for anyone or anything except what he called "the facts of the matter." He was not easy to talk to, because, whatever you said, he was apt to answer: "Oh, you think so?" or, more disconcertingly: "Tell me, what makes you think so?" And, if you couldn't tell him, he would say impatiently: "You're not thinking at all. You're wambling."

However, a long time was to pass before we reached that stage. When the stage was reached, we were contemporaries. A few years' difference in age doesn't matter in the twenties or thereafter; but, when you are twelve, a boy of fifteen, especially such a boy as Greg, seems almost an elder statesman. I was proud to be seen talking to him, not least because he wore the Grammar School cap of dark blue cloth with light blue rings. He was friendly, but didn't seem to have much time to waste on small fry. He hopped on to his bike and rode away.

The Rectory was halfway between the church and Sir Titus Newte's castle. As I swung open the wrought-iron gate on the Saturday afternoon I saw Mr. Hawke, with spectacles clinging to the end of his nose and a wide-awake hat on his head, mowing the lawn. He was in his shirt sleeves. It was a lovely garden, enclosed in gray stone walls. A circular pond was in the middle of the large lawn, and the paths were wide enough for a carriage to drive up to the porch. Roses clambered over the front of the house, and under the enclosing walls, on which more roses grew, flowers of all sorts rioted. At the back, I discovered later, was an orchard and paddock with a white pony browsing in it. The clang of the gate behind me roused the attention of a girl who was kneeling by the pond, gazing at the fish that swam there. It was altogether a charming first impression that I had of Smurthwaite Rectory, for the late May sun was unclouded. Light and color, the smell of the mown grass.

The girl got to her feet. She looked a bit above my own age, and she wasn't fantastically enclosed in silks, as Rose Garland always was. She wore some plain stuff that reached only to her knees, revealing fat calves in black woolen stockings. Mr. Hawke walked over to the pond to pick up the coat that he had thrown there, and Phoebe with a forefinger pushed the spectacles from the tip of his nose to the bridge—a gesture that looked accustomed.

"Phoebe," Mr. Hawke said, wrestling his thin arms into his coat sleeves, and shooting the spectacles down in the process, "this is Mr. Geldersome's nephew, Chad Boothroyd. This is Phoebe, Chad. I told you about her."

Phoebe had formal unembarrassed manners. She shook hands, almost sketched a curtsy, and said: "How do you do?" Then, turning at once, she said: "I'll make sure tea's on the way, Father." And off she went.

"I'll finish this some other time," Mr. Hawke said, and put the lawnmower away in a shed tucked into an angle of the walls. We walked round the garden, where everything grew cheek-by-jowl, and he said: "I'm afraid your uncle doesn't approve of this at all. I just stick the stuff in, and somehow it always grows for me, but I never reach show standard with anything. Still, there it is. I'm no specialist, Chad. I'm the perfect potterer." He bent to smell some blooms, rescued his spectacles that precipitated themselves into the flowers, and said: "Why should I dragoon them, eh? They're happy enough as they are."

We took tea at a table in the bow of the drawing room window, which was open, and from here we could see the church tower, with the tall pinnacle on each corner, rising over the elms, newly green. We could see the paddock and the pony, and beyond that the orchard, a pink

53

and white cloud in the blue sky. The paddock reached right to the window, and, seeing us there, the pony came trotting up and impudently put his head into the room, rolling his moist black eyes at us. Phoebe gave him cake and bread-and-butter, and then slapped him on the rump and shooed him off. He went with a great display of *joie de vivre*, kicking up his heels and generally cavorting.

Mr. Hawke said: "I hope Eustace is having as good a tea as this. When I was a boy at school we were half-starved. I don't know what things are like now."

"You could ask," Phoebe said practically. "You could ask the matron what the boys have to eat, or you could ask Eustace himself."

"No, no. It's not so easy as that."

"But it is," Phoebe insisted. "A lot of things are easier than you think."

"Ah, my dear, you have been reading your *Pilgrim's Progress*. You imagine that one has only to advance and the lions disappear from the path."

Phoebe laughed. "I haven't been reading *Pilgrim's Progress*," she said. "You know very well that I never read anything. It was from one of your own sermons that I heard that. And what a way to talk! Lions in the path, when all you have to do is ask: Is that boy getting enough to eat?" She was like a rather severe elder sister chiding a timid brother.

"Alas, my dear," said Mr. Hawke, picking up the spectacles from his lap, "if I were the man that my sermons urge other men to be, I'd be a saint of God, a knight in armor, a brother to all in distress, a fearless fellow pulling lions by their beards all over the place. And you know I am none of these things. I positively cannot ask the matron what the boys have to eat."

"Then ask Eustace."

"I am sure Eustace would dislike the suggestion that I was inviting him to complain behind people's backs."

Phoebe looked at him with exasperated affection. "You *create* lions," she said briefly. After a moment she added: "So does Eustace. That poem he sent you is just creating lions. I don't suppose things are as bad as he makes out."

"Chad has not heard the poem," Mr. Hawke said. He rummaged in several pockets. Phoebe got up and brought an envelope from the mantelpiece. "This is it."

Mr. Hawke said: "This was enclosed with Eustace's last letter." He read:

> *Here on the Severn I think of the Aire;*
> *Here where the salmon leap I think of the trout.*
> *Give me little things: the fells for the mountains.*
> *Our parish church for the abbey, our old white pony*

> *For the great shire breeds; give me our evening bell*
> *For the strong carillion.*
> *Give me the doves for the eagles.*

"I don't know whether that is poetry," Mr. Hawke said. "It doesn't rhyme, and I doubt whether there is such a word as *carillion*. But it doesn't sound as though Eustace is happy."

"If he's unhappy," Phoebe said, "it's not for bread and butter. And of course it's poetry. You ought to know by now that Eustace is a poet. He's given me lots of things. May I have that one?"

Mr. Hawke handed her the paper. "I'll paste it up in Eustace's book," she promised. "And don't let it make you unhappy," she added. "It's all very well for poets. They like to be unhappy. When men are comfortable they call on them to fight. When they're fighting, they call on them to taste the blessings of peace."

I listened, fascinated. Phoebe seemed an extraordinarily mature person. "I'll bet you," she said to her father, "that once Eustace is back here he'll be writing about the great mountains of Wales. 'Give me the big things, the mountains for the fells, the eagles for the doves.' Poets always want what they haven't got. Now I expect you'd like to show Chad your collections."

She sounded like a wise old nanny sending a pair of children off to their toys. As we went out of the room she gave a parting shot. "Of course, you know, you *want* him back." She was already assembling the tea things on a tray.

The Rectory was a large house, three-storied like our own. The top floor had at some time or other had walls removed, so that what had been a number of small rooms was now one large room, lighted by dormers on two sides. I should imagine that some rector with a big family had done this to make a spacious playroom. Now it was Mr. Hawke's playroom.

I dutifully trailed about with him as he told me this and that. I dutifully looked through the microscope and saw things squiggling about. I gave my admiration to Mr. Gladstone's autograph and to chunks of wood and stone. At last, a little tired of the perambulation and exposition, I left him peering through the microscope at a new slide and walked to one of the dormers. Standing on a box beneath it, I could see, through the open window, the church tower rising out of the elms, and the rooks rising out of their nests in the elms, objecting strongly, as they always did, when the bells were rung; and I could see, looking straight down, the paddock where Phoebe and Greg Appleby were chasing the white pony. They caught him, and Greg leapt onto his back, and Phoebe leapt after, clinging round Greg's waist. Greg kicked the pony with his heels, and off they went, without saddle or bridle, round and round the field.

"We must be getting down, Chad. Gregory Appleby is due any minute for a Latin lesson," Mr. Hawke said. "Give my respects to your mother. And come another day."

CHAPTER THREE

I

IT WAS a year after this—the fruit trees in Mr. Hawke's orchard were in bloom again—when something happened that shook me deeply. Greg no longer needed Mr. Hawke's tuition, and I had been taken on instead. "Of course, Muttonhead, you're the old man's white-headed boy," Greg said. "Guess why."

I couldn't guess why, and Greg laughed. "You'll find out soon enough," he said.

I knew that Mr. Hawke liked me. I was in the choir; I was often in his house; he was often at ours, usually when Uncle Arthur was at the Town Hall. Two or three times a week Mr. Hawke would find himself passing by at teatime and would look in and be invited to tea. It was at the moment when I got in from afternoon school. I would see him lingering in the street as though on the lookout for me, and we would go in together. After a time he lost his shyness, and I would find when I arrived that he had been there for some time talking to my mother. I did not doubt that I was a sufficient reason for these visits. Mr. Hawke had taken me in hand. I was being coached for a Grammar School scholarship. With so important a person in question, there would be plenty for them to talk about.

In the meantime, Eustace Hawke had come home, and stayed home. He was a thin, blue-eyed gangling boy of sixteen or so, to whom I was introduced but with whom I seemed to establish no sort of contact. I would find him loitering in the church, or turning over books in the secondhand department of the bookshop near the Town Hall, or moving off, with his long loping stride, on one of the walks that took up a lot of his time. He would speak to me with great politeness, even with a smile that made his blue eyes, I thought, very beautiful, but then he would be gone, like a thoroughbred greyhound that had small time to spare for an ill-conditioned pup. Gregory's nicknames and occasional kicks in the pants or clouts across the head never disturbed me, for Greg, in most of his moods, was an overflowing well of benevolence; but Eustace's courtesy of itself established a distance between us and sometimes annoyed me deeply, seeing that I was so often in and out of the Rectory, so cordially welcomed by Mr. Hawke and Phoebe.

It was when I had received one of these cold courteous cuts on the way home from school at midday that I burst out: "Who does Eustace Hawke think he is? He goes by me as if I were dirt."

"You needn't worry about *'im*," said Mrs. Ramsden, who never denied us the privilege of having our conversation embellished. She had come in for her plate, to bear it away to the kitchen. "The 'Oly Ghost we always calls 'im. Old Hawke's all right. It was his Late that gave all the airs and graces to Master Eustace."

My mother did not as a rule encourage Mrs. Ramsden's irruptions, but now she asked: "What was Mr. Hawke's first wife like, Mrs. Ramsden?"

"Thank you, Mrs. Ramsden," Uncle Arthur interposed with dignity; and when she had closed the door he said: "I can answer your question, Edie. Mrs. Hawke was still alive when I came to Smurthwaite. She has been dead now for three years. She was what is commonly called not a good mixer. Why she should be, if she didn't want to be, I don't know. She was a beautiful woman, and in my opinion an admirable woman. But there it is. She just didn't fit in—made no effort to do so. Eustace seems to exaggerate all her qualities."

"I rather like Eustace," my mother said.

But his off-hand manner had touched me that morning more sharply than usual on the raw. "Well, I don't," I declared.

"I'm not suggesting that you should, Chad," my mother said reasonably. "I am giving you my opinion, not asking for yours."

"Well, I think it's a rotten opinion," I said heatedly.

My uncle rose from the table, and walked to the sideboard where a writing pad was kept for jotting down things needed in the house. He wrote upon it, and placed the sheet alongside my plate. I read: "Do not be impertinent to your Mother. By order. Arthur J. Geldersome, Town Clerk."

I looked at him in surprise. He gave me a wink, which clearly said: "Cheese it, Chad."

"A little more silverside, Edie?" he invited; and my mother answered irrelevantly: "I think they're a very nice family."

So we came to my second Maytime in Smurthwaite. It was a Saturday afternoon, mild and full of bloom as on the day of my first call at the Rectory. I had come for my Latin lesson. Eustace and Phoebe were away on one of their long walks and Mr. Hawke and I worked in his study. He gave me a passage to translate. "Now, Chad. You should manage that in an hour. Get on with it. No one will disturb you here. We'll go through it together when you're done."

It was a short passage and easy enough. It didn't take me an hour. I was so much at home in the Rectory now, so used to wandering where I liked, that, when I had looked about and found Mr. Hawke nowhere in sight, I decided to go up to the collections room and see if there were any new slides to push under the microscope. There weren't, and I climbed onto the stool by the dormer window to see if the Rector were in the paddock. He was not there; and I remained at the window with its view, so pleasing at that time of the year, of the green foreground and the apple blossom beyond that, and the blue sky over all. As I stood there watching, I was surprised to see my mother come from among the apple trees with the Rector. His arm was round her waist. He pulled her to him and kissed her. She broke from him and walked rapidly toward the house, he following more slowly. I dropped from the box as though I had been shot and was in the study before they reached the house. My burning face was studiously bent over my translation when Mr. Hawke entered. "Oh, Chad," he said. "We'll leave this now, shall we? I'm afraid we'll have to go through it some other time. Your mother's called to take you home."

His hands and his voice were trembling. He tried to push up his spectacles and knocked them right off his face.

2

The wedding didn't take place till the late autumn, but the engagement was announced at once. That summer Eustace Hawke went right off the rails. Though Smurthwaite was mainly a country town, there were a few industrial establishments on the outskirts. For one thing, it was difficult for any sizable place in the West Riding to be without a woolen mill. Our mill was old, the customary huge box of gray stone punctuated with window glass. It had the advantage, denied to so many mills, that air flowed round it and through it, and from the windows you looked out upon the fellsides.

If you want to know who the Amanda was, who figures in Eustace Hawke's first published book of poems, I can tell you. She was Eileen Waddilove, one of the mill girls. I suppose Eustace was in his early twenties when he wrote the poems. He had had time to assimilate the experience, and the writing finally cleared Eileen out of his system. Something of the sort was bound to happen; but it is odd to think that the embrace of my mother and Mr. Hawke, which I watched as I leaned out of the dormer window that May afternoon, was, in fact, the fulcrum that precipitated the career of a poet.

Eustace had been miserable at Shrewsbury. He had dreamed of home because he had longed to be back in the place where he had been under his mother's wing. For a month or so he had been happy in his way, and then my mother, a stranger whom he had never heard of, caused the dream to crumble. My mother was about the Rectory a good deal that summer, and Eustace would not stay in the house. He began to develop a conscience. He said he could not be a burden on his father's bounty: he must work for his living. Mr. Hawke's idea was to take Eustace in hand himself and coach him for an Oxford scholarship; but something had snapped between Eustace and his father. The boy kept as far from the man as he could. He found a job for himself as some sort of minor clerk in the mill office, and there he met Eileen Waddilove, who was the daughter of our Mrs. Ramsden's brother.

As a child, I was aware, of course, of nothing but the *aura* of all these goings-on, oddly mixed with the wedding preparations. My later knowledge tells me what a fine lot of chitchat it must have provided for so small a place. It all blew over before the year was out, and it is not surprising that Uncle Arthur was the efficient manager of the thing. He took it in hand as though he had discovered some impropriety smirching his municipal affairs.

"A wily old bird," Eustace said to me years later, when the very thought of Eileen Waddilove was buried beneath layers of experience. "I didn't realize at the time that it was he who had Eileen bundled out of the town. He worked it through Mrs. Ramsden, who adored him and had a great sense of propriety. So Eileen was packed off to an uncle and aunt in Bradford, where there were plenty of mills for her to play about in. She used to write to me at first, and of course that soon cured me. Eileen was one thing; Eileen's letters were another. You can imagine. . . ." He gave a fastidious shudder. "I soon stopped writing. She was back for a holiday once, and I passed her by in the street. She spat on the pavement." He laughed.

And yet, there are those poems. Shall I ever understand Eustace?

"Your uncle, you know, had a great respect for my mother," Eustace said. "A lot of people thought she was stuck up. He understood her."

And, of course, that would count with Eustace, emotionally at sea as he then was. It permitted him to consent to the odd arrangement that was finally made. In a lesser degree than Eustace, I was upset and unhappy by what was going on, and Uncle Arthur, who had a strong domestic sense, bachelor though he was, did not take kindly to the thought of retreating upon the isolation he had known before my mother and I came to live with him. "You don't need to disturb Chad all over again," he said. "Let him stay where he is, for the time being. And if Eustace cares to lodge here, he can do so, too. You'll be just round the corner. The boys can be in and out as much as they like, and you can be in and out here, if you want to."

Mr. Hawke, I am sure, accepted this arrangement with gladness, my mother more reluctantly. What surprises me is that Eustace accepted it at all. I had never thought that I was one with whom he would on any terms consort. But there it was. After the wedding he and I had the top floor of Uncle Arthur's house to ourselves: a bedroom each, and a sitting room from whose windows, as the winter drew on, we now and then looked out on the cold white shoulders of the fells sloping below the blue of a sunny sky.

3

My mother and Mr. Hawke went off to the South of France. That was in October. They were back in November, and by then Smurthwaite had already had a few light falls of snow. Small things—or things that seem small at the time—may prove decisive. There we were, what Mrs. Ramsden called "my three men," living separate lives under one roof. Plentiful coal made this possible. It would have been difficult today. Eustace would not use the sitting room on the top floor. He was a savage recluse, coldly polite to my uncle when we all three came together for meals, but with hardly a word for me. He made it plain that nothing would induce him to spend the long evenings in my company. He had thrown up his job at the mill. In the daytime he took prodigious walks, often not coming in for the midday meal, and at night he lit the fire in his bedroom and stayed there. Next door to him, I had a fire blazing in the sitting room. Downstairs, Uncle Arthur had a fire in his snuggery. Without this plentiful supply of coal, permitting him to live his life comfortably and alone, I am sure Eustace would never have stayed with us during this time when he was licking his earliest wounds.

For myself, I had plenty to do. Uncle Arthur believed in lives organized like a municipal tram service, with a start, a destination, and smooth rails under all. I was to sit for a Grammar School scholarship, and I was instructed that there were to be no fits and starts, no hare one day and tortoise the next, but a steady and perpetual movement. "Like a moke in a cider mill," Eustace said with one of his frosty grins when Uncle Arthur was out of hearing. His own life was being conducted then, and was ever to be conducted, on the opposite principle.

If I wanted an example to stimulate my efforts during that November, I had but to pull the curtains of my sitting room. Then I could look down the garden to the greenhouse where Uncle Arthur was working among his auriculas. He had already begun to talk of the annual show which was to be held six months hence. "It gives me plenty to do, my dear boys," he said to us one breakfasttime. "They are hardy chaps, these auriculas. As you see, the greenhouse needs no heat—indeed it needs ventilation —but they mustn't be left to themselves. A loving eye must be perpetually bent upon them. We must shut the ventilators when frost threatens. We must clear decaying leaves and stir the surface soil of the pots. And then we must provide umbrellas."

Eustace, with a Virgil propped against the marmalade pot, did not

60

raise his head. "Virgil, my dear Eustace," Uncle Arthur said firmly, bringing the head up at last, "Virgil wrote much of crops and bees and flowers. A word from a contemporary practitioner may add to your knowledge. I doubt whether Virgil has anything to say about umbrellas for auriculas. Has he?"

"I have not come across anything, sir."

"Very well, then. You come across it now. Mrs. Ramsden, will you have the kindness to bring one of the auricula umbrellas. You will find them in the snuggery."

They were cones of paper balanced on sticks. "I had the supreme pleasure of making these last night," said Uncle Arthur, helping himself to three more sausages, "and, as you see, the cones are pleated. The pleating is unnecessary, a mere refinement, a *je ne sais quoi*. I think it adds something. The Auricula, I believe, is a plant aware of tenderness and responsive to it. So why should I not express my tenderness with what, I admit, is an elfin touch? The umbrella gives protection: the pleating says, 'I am thinking of you.' Give Mr. Eustace some more coffee, Mrs. Ramsden. Virgil, my dear Eustace, living in the first century B.C., was one thing. A town clerk in the dawn of the twentieth century A.D. is manifestly another. Yet each may have the soul of a yeoman, though the methods of expression differ. Each may cry, '*O fortunatos nimium*.' You may learn something from the practitioner of today that you cannot learn from the recorder of two thousand years ago. Now supposing, in a cold greenhouse, you have an auricula that needed a little extra warmth. Does Virgil tell you how to set about the job?"

"I'm afraid not, sir."

"You simply place the pot containing the plant in a larger pot and stuff peat between the two. Mrs. Ramsden," Uncle Arthur concluded, wiping his lips as he rose, "Madeleine has spotted her coat with sausage gravy. Will you please put a clean one onto her?"

He joined his hands for Madeleine to leap upon them, snuggled her into his face, and handed her to Mrs. Ramsden. "Perhaps the yellow one today," he said. "I think she always looks well in yellow."

Madeleine had gone into coats as soon as the weather took a wintry turn. They were of many colors. There were thin ones which she wore indoors and thicker ones for the open air. All were emblazoned with the monogram "A.J.G."

And so, if I wished for a lesson in diligence, I had, as I say, but to draw my curtains, and I would see Uncle Arthur in the greenhouse, wrapped in an overcoat, lighted by a lantern, stuffing the peat between the pots, setting up the umbrellas, or with a bit of stick stirring the hard soil of the surface; or, just standing there, with Madeleine in blue or red or yellow in his arms, dreaming of some May day when judges would stand struck dumb, recovering at last to write: "First Prize, Arthur J. Geldersome."

4

To win a scholarship, I should have to know something about English literature, and one night I was in my sitting room reading Keats. All day long the snow had been falling. Beyond my window was the dumb countryside. In the morning I should awake to a room full of white light and white silence. At the moment, Mrs. Ramsden's three men had the place to themselves. Here was I. Downstairs, with Madeleine for company, Uncle Arthur was engaged on an enterprise whose intricacies he had explained over the midday meal: he was making an auricula theater. Next door, Eustace was doing whatever it might be that he did in his solitary evenings. The little town was blanketed, quiet as the grave. I could hear nothing but the pennons of flame flapping in the fireplace. I put down my book and thought of the white streets and the white roofs and the sky colored like a damson, and the blotches of red and yellow staining the pavements outside the pubs and shops. It was nine o'clock, and a hymn began to drop into the stillness from the church tower. The church was locked, and I thought of the cold stone floors and the frozen effigies, and warm though my room was I gave a mental shiver. I took up my book and began to read again:

> St. Agnes' Eve! Ah, bitter chill it was!
> The owl, for all his feathers, was a-cold.

My mind had been dithering for half an hour, and everything it had vaguely thought of, every picture it had been calling up, was there in those two lines, condensed like a whole snowstorm represented in one crystal of snow. I didn't think of it in those terms. I was simply flabbergasted. For the first time in my life, a poem had knocked me endways, as they say. I read on, and couldn't get over the miracle of it. I had found such treasure that I had to share it with someone. Whether he wanted to see me or not, I must tell Eustace about it. I crossed the passage and, without knocking, entered his room.

There was no light but firelight. Eustace was sitting before the hearth in a long low wicker chair, which, with his books, was all that he had brought from the rectory. His thin legs were extended to the blaze; his hands were behind his head; he was smoking a pipe. He hardly looked at me as I burst out, as soon as I had crossed the threshold: "Have you ever come across a poem called 'The Eve of St. Agnes'? It's by John Keats."

The convex roof of the fire fell in; flames shot up and lighted his face.

I saw that he was smiling. How fatuous he must have thought my question! It was like asking a well-nourished child if it knew anything about milk that came from its mother's breast.

He didn't shift his position or take the brier from his mouth. "Yes," he said.

I had wanted to read some bits to him, but he was as unresponsive as the figures I had been thinking about, lying on the tombs in the church —what Gregory Appleby called "The glorious company of Marmoreal Newtes."

After a while, he said: "If you're working for that scholarship, you're on the wrong track. Don't waste your time reading English literature. Read what someone else has said about it and pass it off as your own."

I must have looked surprised and deflated. He blew a smoke cloud into the air, and went on: "Don't think I'm trying to be funny, Chad" —and this was the first time he ever used my Christian name. "You'll never get through the stuff you're supposed to know if you try to read it for yourself. Look—top bookshelf, third book to the right."

I pulled it out—Stopford Brooke's *Primer of English Literature*. "Take that and read it," he said. "Later, we'll get you on to Taine."

I felt that he didn't want me to stay, and I was going out when he said: "What do you think is the best line in 'The Eve of St. Agnes'?"

"I wouldn't like to say."

"Neither would I," he said, and this time he laughed frankly, the firelight glinting his tousled tawny hair and the blue eyes in his thin face. "But I have a fancy for 'And the long carpets rose along the gusty floor,' which is the finest *visual* line I know, or for:

> *And they are gone: aye, ages long ago*
> *These lovers fled away into the storm,*

which is a perfect condensation of sentiment. Well, good night. Sleep well."

I did. I positively glowed with happiness under the bedclothes that night, and, being down before Eustace in the morning, I said to Uncle Arthur: "I'm fond of Eustace." Uncle Arthur answered, with decision: "Eustace would grace an Athenian thoroughfare."

5

I was singing in the church choir by now. How much, I was beginning to think, my father had caused me to miss! The beautiful old building, the beautiful words, the beautiful singing, and especially my own singing, enchanted me. I dreamed the services away. "Who is that angelic child with the wonderful voice?" "Don't you know? That's little Chad Boothroyd. That lovely woman is his mother. She was painted by the famous artist, Lucy Orlop. The picture caused quite a stir. Now she's married to the Rector. That dignified-looking gentleman is Chad's uncle, Mr. Arthur Geldersome, our Town Clerk, and celebrated as a cultivator of auriculas. They tell me the boy is promising as a scholar. He'll almost certainly get a scholarship to the Grammar School, and later to Oxford. Singing is just a side line with him."

In short, I was as smug a little snotty as you'd find in a long day's march.

"Come and eat lunch with us, Arthur," my mother said after the service, "and you, Chad." My pie frill and all the etceteras were gone. I was wearing, God help me, a nice little Eton suit—what Greg inevitably called my bum-freezer—and a nice little Eton collar. Phoebe joined us on the path leading through the churchyard to the Rectory. "You sang beautifully today, Chad," she said.

"Oh, I don't know. I've got a lot to learn yet," I conceded generously.

"What have you for luncheon, Edie?" Uncle Arthur intervened.

Phoebe answered for her. "Good thick soup, pheasant, straw potatoes, Brussels sprouts, a soufflé, cheese and biscuits, coffee."

Uncle Arthur's eyes lit up. "Then perhaps I shall permit myself to venture," he said. "If you will excuse me, I'll go along and bring Madeleine. She is lonely. Lay a cover for her, Edie, alongside my chair."

Sunday was a difficult day for Uncle Arthur. Mrs. Ramsden did not appear, and unless he had an invitation like this he had to subsist on half a dozen sorts of cold meat and game, cold fruit pies and cheese. He was soon back, and in the hall changed Madeleine from her dark green outdoor coat to his favorite indoor yellow. With all this snow about, it was rather surprising that she didn't have four little galoshes.

Mr. Hawke came in, rubbing his cold thin hands. "How is Eustace?" he asked. "We never see him in church nowadays."

We certainly never did. We did not see Eustace where he was likely to meet my mother. That morning, he had stuffed half a cold chicken and half a loaf into a haversack, and with this on his shoulder, a pair of skates in his hand, and a violent-looking scarlet muffler flung round his neck, had announced: "I'm off to see if I can find some ice."

He wore no hat or overcoat, but we were used to that. The absence did not cause comment. The muffler was another matter. Uncle Arthur trembled as he looked at it, clearly of the opinion that no one wearing it would grace an Athenian thoroughfare. "A happy gift, my dear Eustace, that the Auricula bestows upon its lovers is a restrained color sense," he said. "The delicacy of the meal, the green that is never flamboyantly green, the purple that is as chaste as the obsequies of kings, these restrain such color outbursts as may be expected of the unredeemed. I cannot, Eustace, with the best will in the world I *cannot* see Madeleine in that muffler."

The thought of those few ounces of prancing nerve and sinew submerged in Eustace's muffler set me into a roar of laughter, and Eustace joined in. I felt happy to see and to hear that laugh.

"You'd better not let *me* catch her in my muffler," he said.

"I should die of shame," Uncle Arthur said, "if her taste went so far astray."

After luncheon at the Rectory, Uncle Arthur went to sleep in the drawing room. Phoebe and I walked in the snow till teatime. We went all together to the evening service, and then my uncle and I walked home, he carrying Madeleine tucked inside his overcoat. The light of a bicycle lamp coming from the direction of the open country was visible as we approached our door. We saw that Eustace was riding and Gregory Appleby standing on the step. Eustace had found his ice near Greg's father's farm. They had spent the day on it together, breaking off for a farmhouse tea, and now here they were. I was alarmed, for I was wearing my bum-freezer; but Greg seemed in an exceptionally polite mood. "Eustace invited me to come and spend the the night, sir," he said to Uncle Arthur. "I can go straight on to school in the morning. That is, with your permission. That's a lovely whippet, sir," he concluded diplomatically.

"Madeleine, shake hands with Gregory Appleby," my uncle commanded. Madeleine extruded a paw from his coat and Greg shook it. That put the matter in order. Uncle Arthur produced his key and we all went into the house. I rushed to my bedroom and changed into clothes that would not excite derision. Soon the fires had been poked into cheerfulness, the kettle was singing in the kitchen, and in the dining room Uncle Arthur was surveying the sideboard, carving knife in hand. "Chicken, ham, tongue, beef," he intoned with more fervor than he imparted to the psalms in church. "Chad, see to the teapot. Warm it well. Then put in five level spoonfuls. Pour on the water within three seconds. Eustace, Mrs. Ramsden has forgotten the pickled walnuts. You'll find them in the pantry. Bring them along with the apple pie and the Gorgonzola. Gregory, cut some bread. Let us all get busy, and we'll finish up this side of starvation yet. Chad, halt!"

I was halfway to the kitchen. Uncle Arthur shouted: "Take off the kettle and leave the tea alone. Dammit, we'll crack a bottle. It is not often," he went on, as we stood around him, "that I can play host to three young men entering upon the rich inheritance of the twentieth century. Tea, forsooth!" he cried with a reckless laugh. "Nay, this occasion calls for Chambertin. We will violate it by drinking it straight from the cellar. It should be *chambré*, but there is no time for that, and we shall not insult it by warming it at the fire as if we were thawing out chilblains instead of subtly releasing the essence of wine. Chad, alas," he said with a grin at Eustace and Gregory, "is not in the class of us old soaks. He must have very little, and it must be watered. God forgive the sin."

Certainly, on this occasion of the first visit he made to us, Greg had no reason to complain of his welcome. Uncle Arthur drank the best part of the bottle and became loquacious. "A Sunday night in the winter, in times past, my dear boys," he said, "before my widowed sister and her child arrived, was no joke for Arthur Geldersome. To many his lot might seem enviable, the Permanent Undersecretary, so to speak, of a virtuous little Government. But there he would be, with nothing but a whippet for company—admittedly, my dear Madeleine, the most intelligent and attractive whippet in the West Riding—pecking among his cold meats like an orphaned sparrow on a cab rank, with the snow falling."

He twirled his glass beneath his nose, enormously enjoying this gloomy retrospect. "There was one consolation and resource," he said, "upon which I could happily fall back, and that was to review the banquets I have in my time been privileged to attend."

Though there would seem to be no call for it on this present occasion, he fell back again on this resource and wandered through an enormous gastronomical discourse. "And then, my dear boys, comes the *sorbet*. A moment arrives when you must ask yourself, 'Can I face the roast?' With the best will in the world, the answer is often 'No.' The soup, the pheasant, the fish, the *mousse de jambon* maybe, lie pleasantly on the memory, and discretion may say, 'Onward to the coffee and be done.' But the true Gastronome is not so easily defeated. The will to endure is strong in him, and the *sorbet* is called in aid. Fortified by a Russian cigarette, it cools and settles the stomach and when the roast appears, the will cries, 'Tally-ho,' and the chase is on again. The roast turkey, the *haricots verts sautés*, the sprouts, the chocolate ice, the savory, all become possible, with a glance, maybe, at the side table. Then to the coffee and cigars, accompanied, alas, by oratory which seemed always, to me, to lie within the realm of salutary retribution."

"Quite so, sir," Greg said, and if there was a quirk in that Uncle Arthur did not see it. "Off with you now," he said, "to the upper deck. Let this be but the beginning of many such occasions. It is good for youth to meet and talk. Off with you. Madeleine and I will to our snuggery."

That was the first time Eustace used the sitting room on our top floor. How they talked that night, he and Greg! I don't remember a word of it, but I remember my joy in sitting there and listening and feeling at one with them till Greg said: "Well, I'd better curl up on the sofa," and he did so, fully dressed, and Eustace brought a blanket and threw it over him before we two went to our own beds.

6

Not much happened in Smurthwaite without the approval and patronage of Sir Titus Newte. He had been chairman of the county council and of the Smurthwaite bench of magistrates. He had been mayor of the borough, and Mr. Hawke's living was in his gift. I was working to obtain a Titus Newte scholarship to the Grammar School, of which he was chairman of governors, and Greg hoped for a Titus Newte scholarship to Balliol. There was not a cricket club or football team or ramblers' association in our district that did not invite Sir Titus Newte to be president; and at the annual feast in the Assembly Rooms, when the poor children of Smurthwaite were given their one opportunity in the year to eat more than was good for them, Sir Titus carved the turkeys. He had been, time out of mind, Conservative member for Smurthwaite, master of the local hunt, and a member of the Layman's House of the Convocation of York.

I speak of him in the past tense, because when I arrived in Smurthwaite Sir Titus was in the United States of America. He had called in the new world to redress the bank balance of the old by marrying an American lady of great wealth. He had gone with her on one of their periodical visits to her country, and there she had suddenly died. Sir Titus, now a childless widower, remained for a long time across the Atlantic. Indeed, more than two years had passed and I was in my first term at the Grammar School as a Titus Newte scholar before I set eyes on him.

It was a beautiful late September day. Our little town was slumberous. All its sycamores were golden, and up and down the streets cattle were lowing and sheep were bleating and farmers were gossiping, for it was the weekly market day. On the telegraph wires the swallows, making ready to fly, were thick like notes of music on a score.

Uncle Arthur came down the steps from the Town Hall, adjusting his Hat, as I rushed out of school. I joined him and we were walking home together when a shabby little oddity who had been talking to a group of farmers turned and, seeing my uncle, cried: "Ah, Mr. Geldersome, we must have a talk."

My uncle raised his hat. "We are all glad to see you back, Sir Titus," he said. "My poor services are at your disposal any time you wish."

You could have knocked me down with a feather. Sir Titus's face was thin and mouselike, but a mouse's shrewd little eyes peered through the spectacles that were perched on a nose as sharp and peaked as Mrs. Ramsden's. A straggling mustache adorned his lip, and what I could see of his hair was sparse and straggling, too, like a crop doing its best on ill-nourished soil. But I couldn't see much of it, for Sir Titus was crowned by a shapeless tweed hat. He wore a Norfolk jacket and knickerbockers that revealed thin shanks. His ash stick was innocent of ferrule and the end had frayed into wooden whiskers. By a leash he held a superb golden retriever, that was now squatting on the pavement, looking adoringly at the last of the Newtes, the end product of centuries of privilege. The hand that held the leash was thin and as blue as though this lovely day were blustering with a blizzard.

"Will you allow me, Sir Titus," Uncle Arthur said, "to present young Chad Boothroyd, my nephew, who is relieving the solitude of my bachelor quarters?"

Sir Titus gave me a bony hand, and I removed the cap which proclaimed me a scholar of the school some Newte had founded in the fifteenth century. He must have observed the cap, for he said: "Try to do us credit, boy. We've produced many good scholars and five famous men. I suppose you've seen their portraits in the school hall?"

"Yes, sir."

"Portraits. That's what I want to discuss with you, Mr. Geldersome. The mayor's worrying me about this portrait for the Town Hall. I'd like your advice."

"I think I can help, Sir Titus."

"Very well, then. If it suits you, I'll be at the Town Hall at three this afternoon."

"That will do excellently."

We were alone at luncheon. This perfect September weather was too much for Eustace. The house couldn't hold him. He was tramping the fells almost from dawn to dusk.

"I must say," I exclaimed frankly, "that Sir Titus Newte surprises me. I thought he was an aristocrat?"

"When you have been a little longer at school," said Uncle Arthur, "you will be, I hope, better acquainted with the meaning of words. What do you suppose the word aristocrat means?"

"Well—a topnotcher."

"Not a bad definition, Chad. Literally, it means one of the best, and you will go sadly astray if you think you can tell one of the best from the cut of his coat or the cut of his jib. However, enough of that. I have no doubt Sir Titus will grow upon you. Now this portrait that he mentioned. For the moment, not a word. But a vision opens before my mind. Positively Pisgah."

From time to time since I had been living in Smurthwaite Uncle Arthur had been up to London on the affairs of his Municipality, and he had not failed during these visits to improve his acquaintance with Lucy Orlop. Indeed, you could say that they were now friends. They wrote often to one another, and I think something odd and idiosyncratic in the character of each attracted the other. For one thing, I learned after one of the visits, Lucy Orlop was as fond of a good dinner as Uncle Arthur was. He would take her out to dine and to a theater as the highlight of his London call. Rose Garland was no hindrance to these festivities. She was now at a boarding school. "Her people in India," Uncle Arthur said, "feel that they have imposed on Miss Orlop long enough. Of course, Rose is still with her during holidays."

Recently, Miss Orlop had been attracted to portrait painting. Even the young friends I have in these days in which I write, after they have laughed at her "every picture tells a story" painting, may sometimes say: 'Still, the old girl *did* do a decent portrait or two. Perhaps rather heavily influenced by Raeburn, but good enough all the same."

It was the custom in Smurthwaite, as in so many other places, to have the mayor's portrait painted when his term of office ended. The Town Hall was full of these worthies, and Sir Titus Newte's was to be added to the number. He had been for four successive years mayor of the borough before leaving for the United States; and now that he was back the work must be put in hand. Uncle Arthur's Pisgah vision was of Lucy Orlop visiting Smurthwaite to paint the portrait of Sir Titus Newte.

8

Miss Orlop came, but not at once. To begin with, she had a number of commissions on hand that occupied her till the end of the year, and then, just when arrangements had been made for her arrival, Captain Orlop died. That was in January of 1904. Miss Orlop inherited the estate and went down to Pentyrch to tie up the ends. It was from there, in March of that year, that one of her frequent letters reached Uncle Arthur. He was reading it at breakfasttime, and gave a chuckle. "Would you like to change your name to Orlop, Chad?" he asked, and went on at once: "If so, you have only to marry Miss Orlop and the deed's done. She's the last of 'em, you know, and it's unalterable law in that family that, if an Orlop woman inherits, then, whoever marries her, becomes an Orlop, too. It's happened often enough in the past, but I think the game's up now. I can't see Lucy wanting to marry anyone, or, for that matter, anyone wanting to marry her."

"Why not?" asked Eustace. He had heard plenty about Lucy Orlop of late. "Is she a gorgon?"

"No, indeed," Uncle Arthur said severely. "At any rate, not to my way of thinking. But she has an independent mind, and that is something men are not inclined to tolerate in a wife."

He read further into the letter, and exclaimed: "Ha! Here is an example of what I mean. Now would a husband put up with this?"

He read aloud from the pages in his hand:

So there it is. Things are more or less straight here now. Frankly, I don't want the place. I like coming down here from time to time, but the gardener's cottage would give me all I need, or I could turn the stables into a splendid little house. However, some fag end of Orlop sentiment for the place hangs on in me, and so I shall keep it up just as it always was, but Mr. Tresooth, our agent, must have a sharper eye on it in future, for it's certain I shan't allow it to bother *me*. But I've had a bright thought that pleases me immensely. Do you, by any chance, recall a boy named Pascoe?

Uncle Arthur looked at me over the letter. "I do not," he said. "Do you, Chad?"

"Yes, indeed," I said. "You met Billy Pascoe. Don't you remember? It was the afternoon you first took tea with Miss Orlop. Billy was working in the kitchen, wearing a green baize apron. He carried a lantern before us in the woods."

"Yes. I dimly recall the urchin. Well, well. The said Billy Pascoe is to have a startling change of fortune. How old is the boy?"

"He's just my age—fifteen."

"Well, let Miss Orlop tell you what has happened to him."

He continued to read from the letter:

Pascoe has been about the place here doing odd jobs for some time. I always thought him an exceptionally intelligent boy, and I was not surprised when he won a scholarship to the Grammar School in our neighboring town. He walked into town every morning and back every evening, and that did him no harm—I loathe coddled kids—but I *was* surprised when he continued to turn up here in the evenings to do his odd jobs. Sometimes he would be here till nine at night. I asked him whether the school didn't set homework for him to do, and he said it did. I asked him when he did it, and he said confidently, "I do it on my head when I get back." There was no self-pity about young Pascoe. "We've got to have the money," he said. I didn't want to interfere with a spirit like that, so I let him go on. Then his mother, a poor gutless creature if ever there was one, decided that life was too much for her—with a son like that!—and drowned herself. At the bottom of our garden, too, of all the impudence! My brother was furious! It was a sorry lookout for the boy then: no home, no one to cook his meals. I offered to grubstake him, but the independent little devil wouldn't have it at any price. He said so long as he could work for us he could pay for lodgings in Pendeverel. He did it, too. I had taken an enormous fancy to young Billy, and the thought that visited me when I was settling things here was that this empty barrack would be all the better for housing a spirit like that. I put it to him frankly that he could live at Pentyrch—all the time, whether I was there or not—that he *ought* to live there, because the place had so much to give him—books and space and quiet. Well, he took a long time to think it out, and he's here now, but on his own independent terms. Nothing will induce him to share my meals or to sleep in the bedroom I had prepared. He eats in the kitchen with the others and sleeps in the servants' quarters. But I *have* managed to stop the scullion work, and he spends his evening hours in the library. I hope in time to wean him into a proper understanding of what people like us owe to people like him; but, for the moment, he's still as ready to fly from me as a young deer. Forgive all this, but Billy fills my mind, and perhaps, *when* I come to do that much-post-poned portrait, I shall bring him with me. A bit of getting about would broaden his outlook.

I thought a lot that day about Billy Pascoe. I didn't remind Uncle Arthur that he had used Billy as an illustration of the dangers of dead-end work. It looked as if he was out of the dead end now, and I wondered whether—if Miss Orlop succeeded in luring him to Smurth-waite—he and I would get on as well as we had done at Pendervel. I remembered that when, after my father's death, we had set out for London, Billy had walked all the way to the Town to say good-by. "Write to us, Chad," he had said; and I had never written or given him an address at which he could write to me. We should have to start all over again, I thought; and when Miss Orlop wrote saying that she would be in Smurthwaite at Eastertime, it looked as though this new beginning would be complicated, for the letter said: "I have persuaded Billy to come, and Rose Garland will be with me, too."

It became a widely separated party. During the negotiations about the painting of the portrait, Sir Titus Newte had asked: "Orlop—Orlop? Wasn't there an Orlop in the House some years ago?" And it appeared that Captain Orlop had indeed, for a short time, represented a Cornish division in the House of Commons and that he had known Sir Titus, who now, finding that this painter, whom he had been inclined to look upon with suspicion, belonged to a family almost as worm-eaten with antiquity as his own, invited Miss Orlop to be his guest at the castle. Rose Garland stayed at the Rectory, and Billy at Uncle Arthur's. There was plenty of room for him. Eustace had sud-denly vanished. After his long pottering interlude, he had put a few things into a haversack, walked down to the station, and taken a train. We thought he was off on one of his usual walks. A week later Uncle

Arthur received a letter with a Bloomsbury address. It was brief. Eustace said he had a "job of sorts" in a publisher's office, but he didn't tell us what publisher. "Let them know at the Rectory that I am all right." That was about all it came to.

9

Gregory Appleby was near the top of the Grammar School when I went in at the lower end. His attitude to me was avuncular. During his visits to Uncle Arthur's, which had become frequent while Eustace was still there, the two of them would argue for hours on end about everything under the sun. Greg was impressed by Eustace's pipe, and took to smoking one himself; and there seemed to me, sitting there with them, something tremendously man-of-the-world in the way one would throw a tobacco pouch or a box of matches to the other without pausing in some furious tirade. Neither would argue with *me*. I was a kid to whom the law was laid down.

Now that Eustace was gone, Greg came no more to the house, but he continued to give me his patronage. I was proud of this, and especially of our Saturday morning sessions in Mrs. Cunliffe's coffee shop. Smoking his pipe, and watching the pageant of the street through the small window panes, Greg would improve my mind with his comments on Smurthwaite life and on the world in general. We were sitting there one morning after Miss Orlop's arrival when she and Sir Titus Newte passed along the street together. I told Greg who the lady was, and he looked at her with a broad grin on his deceptively homely face. I could not blame him for the smile. I had known Miss Orlop a long time. Ever since I was a child she had appeared now and then at Pendeverel, and I had become acclimatized to her oddities. To see her for the first time was another matter. There was not a passer-by who did not turn to stare at that hatless head surrounded by its halo, at the tall gaunt length of the woman and her abrupt masculine air. Sir Titus seemed to be positively *trotting* at her side; and Greg said: "She'll pat him in a moment and say, 'Good dog.'"

We strolled into the street, and Greg got some further amusement out of another trick well known to me. Something would catch Miss Orlop's attention; she would pause abruptly, make a ring of her thumb and forefinger, and, holding this to her eye like a spyglass, peer through it. I imagine a good many artists have this trick, but it was something new to Smurthwaite—most things on earth would have been new to Smurthwaite—and it tickled Greg immensely. It mightn't have been so funny if she hadn't suddenly laid a hand on Sir Titus's shoulder and commanded: "Now stand steady a minute." Then, moving off a little way, she subjected the poor man's face to this spyglass scrutiny, exclaiming in her loud voice: "It's the nose. I'm not at all pleased with it."

"Sacrilege," Greg said between his gusts of laughter. Even he would not have dared to laugh publicly at something that concerned Sir Titus, and he had drawn me back into Mrs. Cunliffe's shop, where he manfully stuffed his pipe and ordered more coffee. "Never," he said, "has a Newte on its native heath—if Newtes live on heaths—been so ignominiously treated in the public eye."

"But you may have noticed," I said, "that Sir Titus didn't seem to mind a bit. He seemed to be enjoying himself."

"True enough," Greg agreed. "That is one of the odd things about a Newte. It can do what it likes and not give a damn for anyone's opinion. Still, Chad, it was very funny."

I was to wish that the funniness of it had not remained in his mind.

The school holidays were on; we all had a lot of time on our hands; and Phoebe Hawke, in her practical way, took to organizing our leisure. Phoebe was less surprised than either her father or Uncle Arthur when Eustace calmly took himself to London. "What did you expect him to do—loaf around in Smurthwaite for the rest of his life?" she asked.

"Well," said Mr. Hawke, aggrieved, "he might have told me what he was up to."

Phoebe laughed at that. "Oh, dear," she said. "I wonder am I the only person on earth who understands Eustace?"

Mr. Hawke said plaintively: "I don't want any harm to come to the boy—that's all."

"Whatever's coming to Eustace is coming," Phoebe said. "There's not much any of us can do about it."

The long day's outing that she organized took place a few days after Greg and I had watched Miss Orlop and Sir Titus. Uncle Arthur had no sooner left for the Town Hall that day than there she was at the front door with her pony harnessed to a trap. As commanded, Billy Pascoe and I were ready. Rose Garland was in the trap with Phoebe.

I had got on well enough with Billy Pascoe since his arrival at Smurthwaite; and well enough about covers it. We had not taken up our old friendship where it was left off at Pendeverel. There is no doubt about that. The dark little ragamuffin had shot up into a dark, tall, skinny boy who seemed to be outgrowing his strength and his clothes, and was wrapped away from me in contemplation of his own things, whatever they might be. Nothing could have been more different from Greg's overt buoyancy than Billy's brooding silences. He was polite to me, and that was the awful thing about it. Among boys, politeness is freezing. I had suffered it, at first, from Eustace. Billy told me all I wanted to know about Pendeverel; and when that had been said there

73

seemed little more to say. Smurthwaite didn't interest him. He had brought masses of books with him and preferred their company to mine. Some of them, I noticed, were handsome leather-bound things with the Orlop crest embossed on the covers.

I hadn't seen much of Rose Garland during this visit, but I liked what I had seen. She was not so much wrapped up in herself as she had been at Pentyrch. She didn't wear stylish silk clothes. Her eyes of that incredible blue were readier to smile. She seemed to have learned a lot about the small change of human intercourse. She was a friendly girl.

Well, there they were, that far-off May morning, waiting in the trap, with a hamper of food on the floor, and Billy Pascoe and I went out and joined them. At the last moment Billy stuffed a book into his pocket. The trap seemed crowded. "Where on earth Greg's going to fit in I don't know," Phoebe cried gaily. We were to pick Greg up at his father's farm.

"Well," said Rose, "if there's any difficulty about *that,* I've no doubt you'll drop one or other of us."

Phoebe blushed—a furious blush that spread all over her face; and, as if annoyed with herself for that, she took the whip and gave the pony a sharp lash. And off we went, spanking past the outlying cottages that flashed to us their glimpses of laburnum and lilac, hawthorn and flowering cherry. Lambs were at play in the stone-hedged fields. Their bleating cries rose up, and the skylarks' songs showered down, and every bush was lively with thrush and blackbird, fluttering and singing. There wasn't a cloud on the blue.

We met Greg before we reached his father's farm. He had tramped a mile or so along the road to meet us, and was sitting on a gate, smoking his pipe, with a basket at his feet. "Ah've brought a stay-bit," he explained, lapsing into the dialect, as he was pleased to do at times.

Phoebe gave the reins to Rose and got out of the trap. She pulled the linen cover off the basket, revealing sandwiches and bottles of milk, a large cheese, a cake and bars of chocolate. "Good lord, man, what are we going to do with all this stuff?" she asked. "I told you I was bringing the food."

"We'll manage," Greg said. "It'll be the miracle of feeding the five thousand in reverse."

"It'll certainly be a miracle if we eat this lot."

"We'll eat it," Greg promised confidently, "and come home ravening with hunger. We'd better start right away with our midmornings."

And we did. We stuffed ourselves with sandwiches and drank milk and finished off with chocolate, and then Greg took charge of the day. "We'll go to the tarn," he said. "We'll show these southerners what a bit of real scenery is."

I had never been to the tarn, but I had heard plenty about it. It was one of Eustace's favorite places when he was walking. "The Tarn's white-stallion mane wild-blowing in the March wind," was a line he was to write.

It took us a long time to get there, and Greg, Billy and I walked a good part of the way. Greg had a farmer's consideration for horses. He would not allow more than three to be in the trap at once, and the pony jogged along as comfortably as it pleased. Half a mile from the tarn the cavalcade halted. This was as far as we could go by road. The baskets were taken from the trap, the pony's harness was removed and piled into it, and off we went, pony and all. A gate led into scrubby land, heather and gorse and rough stone. The heather would have its glory later. Now was the time of the gorse, burning bushes of gold as far as we could look, beneath a sun unusually hot for May. On our right the limestone rose steeply, forming a ridge of shining white dappled with shrubs. Rabbits flirted their scuts and vanished. A hawk lay high up on the air, sustained by nothing more than an occasional tremor of the wings.

It was no wonder, I thought, that Eustace loved this place, and the waterfall was the last touch of the enchantment. We could hear it long before we saw it, and when we saw it we all stood still: Greg and Phoebe, who had seen it often; Rose, Billy Pascoe and I, who were seeing it for the first time. It was like that: it had the power to stop you in your tracks.

The limestone cliff here reached a height of about fifty feet. Beyond it, unseen, were miles of watery moorland where the bog cotton grew and the curlew piped and an infinity of small streams seeped through the peat and at last, by the lay of the land, we were persuaded together into the stream that reached the limestone lip and made the great leap. The ridge that had been on our right as we walked was scooped out into a semicircle of white walls embracing the tarn. Now, with the sun of this perfect spring day nearing its height and pouring a gentle light on the fall and the tarn, one's only thought was that the place was beautiful. In winter, with the wind up, and the clouds racing, and the darkness coming on, it could be frightening, especially as, with all this water falling everlastingly, none was flowing out.

The rocky land we walked on shelved gently upward toward the tarn. The edge of this shelf was over the water. Thence we looked down upon it, eight or nine feet below: the froth and dither at the point of impact, the ripples diminishing to nothing at the edges. Phoebe had an arm round Rose's waist. At their feet Greg was sitting with his shoes dangling over the water. Billy and I lay flat, looking into the peat-brown color which the water took at the sides.

"Seems to be an underground outflow," Billy said.

"Obviously," Greg answered.

"How deep is it?" Billy asked.

"It is without depth," said Greg; and added with a laugh: "That is, if you believe what you are told. However, I decided to see for myself, so I brought a plumb line and dropped it over just where you're kneeling. At that point, I made it, as near as makes no difference, thirty-five and a half feet."

"Good man," Billy approved.

"You believe in scientific accuracy?"

"Who doesn't?" asked Billy.

Greg laughed. "My old man for one," he said. "When I told him what I'd done he was quite annoyed. He flatly rejected the evidence. 'That tarn is bottomless, lad,' he said. 'There's no call to go interferin' there.' So I shut up about it, because, when he gets annoyed, I soon find that, whatever the tarn may be, *I'm* not bottomless."

"Oh, you liar, Greg," Phoebe said. "I don't suppose your father has laid a hand on you in his life. He worships you."

"Quite rightly," said Greg.

"And so you just made that up for the sake of a joke."

"So I did, Phoebe. You're a woman of great insight. You're the only woman who understands me."

Phoebe swiftly backed away from this. "Come along," she said. "It's time we started to gather fuel. Rose, get the kettle out of that basket, and mind you don't spill it. It's all the drinking water we have."

Soon she had chivied us into practicalities. A fire of heather roots was started and a cloth spread on the rabbit-bitten turf. We fed royally, with the pony now coming up for his share, now moving off to nibble the turf. For the fun of it, when we needed it no longer, we kept the fire going, rejoicing in gypsy freedom. We washed up with water from the tarn. Greg lit his pipe and sat leaning against a warm rock, and Phoebe sat near by, admiring his young manliness. Looking at them, I thought incongruously of my father and mother lying on the sand at Pendeverel. She didn't lie on the sand or on turf any more. Mr. Hawke was not the man for shedding earthly cares in a bout of voluptuous idleness. Greg might well be, I thought; but only for a time; he would soon be up and doing again.

Rose Garland had wandered away and was gathering the small flowers that grew on that tough land, and Billy had taken out the book that I had seen him stuff into his pocket that morning. I felt aloof and outside them all, considering them, and especially considering Rose Garland. I hadn't seen her since a day like this, a May day, when she had told me to lie down on the cushions on the Pentyrch lawn and had spread a blanket over me. I had gone to sleep, and, so far as she was concerned, I had remained asleep from that moment to this, and had now awakened to find so different a girl. I wondered about her people in India. Would she soon be rejoining them, or they coming home to take her to some life away from mine?

I hoped not, for a reminder had kept her image before me during the years at Smurthwaite. This was the sketch of the garlanded girl that Miss Orlop had given my mother. It was hanging now in my sitting room at Uncle Arthur's; absurdly, I allowed it to make Rose "belong" to me.

Sure enough, Greg, unlike my father, was soon on his feet, calling for action. "Come on, Phoebe, let's have a ride."

They caught the pony; Greg leapt onto him as I had seen him do in the Rectory paddock, and Phoebe climbed up behind him, clinging to his waist as he hung to the pony's mane. "You look out for rabbit-holes," Rose warned them, coming up. She threw some heather roots onto the fire and sat down between me and Billy. The flame spurted, almost invisible in the bright light. The blue smoke corkscrewed up, unwavering, smelling delicious. "What's that you've got there, Billy?" Rose asked.

Billy shut the book and put it back into his pocket. "Oh, some old thing Miss Orlop thought I should read. Not much in my line, though."

"Don't be rude, Billy," Rose reproved him. "I asked you what you were reading."

"It's called *King Solomon's Mines.*"

"Well, then, I'm sure Miss Orlop didn't think you *ought* to read it. She thought you'd *enjoy* reading it as a bit of a change."

"I don't get anything *out* of it," Billy complained. "Have you read it?"

"Yes. I thought it was a very good yarn. And when you're asked a question, you must answer. Don't try to give yourself an air of superiority."

"I'm sorry," Billy said humbly, and I felt a stir of my old friendship for him, for I was sure he had not been trying on superior airs. The book meant nothing to him and he had said so. That was all.

"Look at that boy Appleby," Rose said. "Phoebe's mad about him, as you can see. And he certainly seems to be a most unusual boy. All the same, he's full of fun, and I'll bet you if a good yarn came his way he wouldn't be so superior as to pretend he didn't like it."

And then I was aware of the dangerous underlying violence in Billy. I had noticed it on the beach at Pendeverel when he spoke of Mrs. Apreece insulting Michael Faraday, and his hands had clenched as if they had hold of her. So now, when Rose thoughtlessly praised Greg Appleby, Billy's fingers dug into the heather and his face went white. He got up and said: "I may be superior, but I am *not* pretending." He walked the few paces to the fire and began moodily kicking the embers apart.

Rose said to me, dismissing Billy: "Look at those two lunatics."

The pony was flying; Phoebe's hair was flying; and Greg, having let go the pony's mane, was waving his hands in the air and singing. They came thudding up, made a wide circle round us, and were off again, whooping as they went by. Billy strolled away by himself.

I said to Rose: "Have your people come back from India?"

Her blue eyes gave me a long look. At last she said: "I'd forgotten you had heard that story."

"I heard it the first night I was at Pentyrch. Miss Orlop told my uncle. And then you showed me over the house—or rather," I twitted her, "you were supposed to." I became bold, and added: "You're a nice one to talk about manners to poor old Billy. Your manners to me were abominable that night."

She looked surprised by this sudden attack and her face slowly reddened. "I'm very sorry," she said. "I had forgotten all about that, but I remember it now."

"Well, you said it made you furious when Miss Orlop told that story about your people in India; and then you began to cry and said you didn't know who you were."

She recovered her composure and said: "Well, I know now, and I'm quite happy about it, thank you."

I waited for her to continue, but she had nothing more to say. Greg and Phoebe cantered toward us, leapt to the ground, and shooed the pony away. Billy came up, hands in pockets. Greg was excited by that whooping ride. He said to Rose: "Would you call Phoebe good-looking?"

Rose was not to be caught into seriousness. "Oh, she'd pass with a push."

Greg switched his question into a joke. "I'm not quite satisfied that she passes the highest tests. It's the nose," he said. Guying the gesture we had observed in Miss Orlop, he made a circle of thumb and forefinger, and, quizzing Phoebe through this, said: "I am not at all satisfied with the nose."

Billy, standing by with his hands still in his pockets, said in a deadly serious tone that chilled us all: "That's a gesture of Miss Orlop's."

"Yes," said Greg. "I noticed it the other day."

"And you think it amusing to make fun of a lady's small idiosyncrasies?"

Greg was so taken aback that he could only say: "Well, for heaven's sake, Billy—" but he got no further. Billy took a hand from his pocket, clenched his fist, and gave Greg an uppercut to the chin.

It was so unexpected that Greg, stepping backward, slipped on a jut of rock, fell to the ground, and landed with his hand in the fire. But for that, his profound good temper would perhaps have triumphed even over Billy's insulting blow; but the burn—nothing much in itself, for his hand was no sooner in the fire than it was out again-

stung him to retaliation, and as soon as he was on his feet he sent Billy reeling with a blow to the chest.

I was not surprised that Billy felt as he did about Miss Orlop, and that he resented what he took, however thoughtlessly, to be a gesture of insult. But, even then, I was aware that this was not the root of the matter. What had infuriated him was Rose Garland's praise of Greg. Everything else was pretext.

What followed was neither boxing nor wrestling. They knew nothing of either. They just went for one another like two furious tomcats, trying to knock down, trying to throw down, trying in every possible way to hurt one another. They looked ill-matched, for, though they were much of a height, Greg had a life of good feeding behind him, and Billy had been more or less starved from birth. But they were not so ill-matched in fact, for Billy had the agility of whipcord. And so they most unscientifically went at it for no more, I suppose, than five minutes. By then, Greg had a black eye, and a thread of blood trickled from a corner of Billy's mouth down his chin. His tongue kept snaking at it.

The affair ended by Greg simply dropping his arms and standing back. "Oh, this is fair daft!" he said. "What are we up to?"

Billy tried to come on once more, and indeed landed a blow or two on Greg's undefended body; but Greg was not to be enraged again. "Stop it, you bloody little fool," he said, almost good-naturedly.

Billy was panting hard. His blows stopped. "You didn't beat me," he said.

The girls had been standing by, helpless, near to tears. In relief at the sudden end to the fight, they broke into indignation. "Beat you!" Rose cried. "You stupid little creature! It's a pity you haven't a mother to beat you!"

Billy went white, and rigid with fury. "Yes," he said. "It is a pity, isn't it? It's a pity she was starved till she couldn't stand her life any longer. It's a pity one half of the world lives as you do, and the other half as she did."

All that was stark and violent in Billy glared at poor Rose, who hadn't a word to say in reply. Phoebe said forlornly: "We'd better be getting home. Everything's been spoiled."

"Everything is spoiled all the time," Billy said relentlessly. "The whole social setup . . ."

Greg intervened, his good humor impregnably re-established. "I'm with you, Billy, in all that. But let's postpone the reform of the world for the next half-hour. What we'd better do now is wash your mouth and my eye."

He took Billy by the arm and led him toward the tarn. When they were gone, Phoebe picked up a stick and angrily dispersed the fire, stamping out the embers. She whistled, and the pony came trotting up. She caught him by the mane and began to lead him off to the place where we had left the trap. "You two pack the baskets and follow," she said. "I'll get harnessed up."

Greg and Billy were a long time by the tarn. When they had washed, they stayed there talking. Everything was ready for departure when they strolled over to where Rose and I were waiting. "You push off," Greg ordered. "Three of you will be enough in the trap. Billy's going to walk with me to my old man's place. We'll have tea there. I'll bring him back on my bike."

Billy's cut lip had ceased to bleed. He looked calmer, and some color had come back to his face. Greg was stuffing his pipe. They sat down together on the ling; and Rose and I, feeling unwanted, moved off with the baskets. The larks were still singing, and the gorse was gay with butterflies, and, knowing something of both Billy and Greg, I felt happy about the way this affair had ended. But Rose was not happy. "How did I make him so angry?" she asked.

"You shouldn't have dragged his mother in."

"But mothers do die," she said reasonably.

"Yes. But not many die as Billy's mother died."

"Why? How did she die?"

"Don't you know? Didn't Miss Orlop tell you?"

"No."

So I told her. She said nothing, and remained in the deepest gloom. So did Phoebe. It was a miserable drive home for the two of them. They uttered hardly a word. For me, I was not depressed. I felt that in some odd way the outing had been a success.

10

There was no banquet, great or small, in Smurthwaite to which the Town Clerk was not invited, and no invitation that he refused. On the night of this day when we picnicked at the Tarn there was some jamboree or other at the Assembly Rooms, and I was standing in the doorway, watching a resplendent Uncle Arthur setting out, like a new stately steam roller, to the appointment, when the ringing of Greg's bicycle bell caught my attention. Billy, not Greg, was riding. Greg was standing on the step. I noticed that his right hand was bandaged. This was the hand that had landed in the fire when Billy knocked him down. A teapot containing the cold dregs of our tea had been there handy, and during our dreary drive home Phoebe had kept up a lament about not having poured this onto the burn. I got quite fed up with listening to her housewifely exposition of the virtues of tannic acid and her self-reproaches at having failed to apply it. But the fight had put it all out of her mind, and the fight had, too, exacerbated what would otherwise have been negligible scorching. Greg's skin had burst and become inflamed. His mother had dressed and bandaged it, and here they were. "I didn't want to ride both ways," Greg explained. "I can't get much of a grip, swathed up like a mummy; but I'll manage return trip all right."

This fight and the burned hand were altogether a small matter; but it had big consequences for these two. They came in, and we carried our supper to the top-floor sitting room, and lit the fire, though we didn't need it, and we ate and drank sitting on the rug. Greg was a wonderful boy at pacifying tempests, whether among many or in one human soul. What he and Billy had talked about during the few hours they had spent together I don't know, but Billy was calm, and a quiet happiness had replaced the brooding self-defensive line he had been taking with me during this visit. It is possible that during the years since I had parted from him at Pendeverel he had remembered his impulsive invitation, "Write to us, Chad," and had been aggrieved that I had never done so.

It was quite dark when Greg set off for home that night. I recall one remark he made during the couple of hours we sat there talking in the little room that I shall always remember because there, when we were all young and the world seemed a safe place to live in, I first knew well the three men who were to be so influential in my life: the three men who were the three boys Greg, Billy and Eustace. "About Miss Orlop," Greg said, "don't go about turning your gratitude into a morbid disease. She'd be the last to want it. You make me sick, Billy, talking about what you *owe* to the people who granted you a scholarship down there in Cornwall, and what you *owe* to Miss Orlop. Try to think of what people owe to *you*. The thing cuts both ways. Now I'm not saying this savagely or with any sort of resentment, but I *do* say, as a simple matter of historical fact, that the rich have done damn well out of the poor for a good many centuries. It's time they began to realize what they owe to *us*. And if they don't, we shall have to realize what we owe to ourselves."

11

A solemn little farce was played each year at the May meeting of the Grammar School governors. It had been in abeyance during Sir Titus Newte's long absence in America, but this year it was revived. Uncle Arthur, one of the governors (because his legal knowledge as a barrister was useful, I suppose), told me how it went. When all other business had been disposed of, Sir Titus would say from the chair: "I venture very deferentially to suggest, gentlemen, that as Mr. Ashmole has well maintained the standard of scholarship among the boys, they might be persuaded, just for one day, to tear themselves away from their books. I propose, therefore, a whole day's holiday for the last Friday of the month. All those in favor?" Every hand would go up; but, nevertheless, peering over his steel spectacles, Sir Titus would ask: "Against?" No hand would go up, and with a beam of satisfaction he would say: "I *believe* the Ayes have it. Mr. Ashmole, will you have the kindness to communicate the board's decision to the boys? If any considerable number of them wish to remain at school, we will, of course, rescind this resolution. Thank you, gentlemen. That is all."

This was the preliminary to Sir Titus's annual reception of the school at the castle. It was always on the last Friday in May, and, traditionally, the weather on that day was fine. The boys were permitted to take their parents, brothers and sisters with them; and there was such a shining of shoes, brushing of clothes, wiping of noses and washing of necks on that day as nothing else called forth in Smurthwaite. The very town seemed to polish itself up for the occasion. The sycamores that lined all the main streets shone in their loveliest green; the clouds had been scrubbed till every trace of gray was gone from them and they were turned out to frisk like lambs on a blue field; the winds that might have raised a dust were under lock and key for the day; and some celestial choirmaster had the birds piping from peep of dawn. After lunch, when the birds were enjoying a well-earned siesta, the Smurthwaite Silver Band took over the musical side of the occasion, and paraded through the town in their blue uniforms piped with scarlet, headed by a majestic figure in white gantlets who recklessly threw about a baton as long as a barber's pole, twirling it, hurling it, and generally punishing it in so fantastic and extravagant a manner that it was difficult to recognize in him the humblest employee of Uncle Arthur's Street Cleansing Committee.

As soon as the church clock pointed to two the drift toward the castle began. There were only about two hundred boys in our school, but each boy, like a flowing stream, gathered to himself tributary sisters and brothers, all looking as though they had been delivered on an endless belt from the hairdresser's and drycleaner's, and parents whose aroma as they passed suggested that the carnage among moths at Smurthwaite must be frightful. Indeed, some of them had outdone Lot's wife, becoming not static pillars of salt but ambulating pillars of camphor, so that an observant eye might see the butterflies of our borough prudently betaking themselves in clouds to the outskirts for the day.

We at the Rectory were in no hurry. Rose Garland had gone to the castle to take luncheon with Sir Titus and Miss Orlop. Uncle Arthur, Billy Pascoe and I joined my mother, Mr. Hawke and Phoebe. Uncle

Arthur understood what was due to a gala day. He was in white flannels, white shoes, with a red and white tie. A scarlet cummerbund encircled him like the equatorial tidal bulge. Phoebe, I remember, had her hair up for the first time and was wearing some flowing garment of lilac silk. On a peg in the hall was uncle's panama hat. Madeleine was there guarding it, having survived the fearful ordeal of being bathed. This had taken place last night, in a tub by the kitchen fire. I had been commanded to stand by in order to hand the soap, the brush, the towels, to Uncle Arthur, who, with his coat off and his sleeves rolled up and one of Mrs. Ramsden's sacking aprons girded on, had knelt upon a bathmat and crooned demands for forgiveness of his darling as he soaped and lathered. She loathed it, and, by the time it was ended, it was difficult to say whether she had bathed Uncle Arthur or he her. She terrified him by putting up a tremendous show of shivering. From her toes to the tip of her downhung tail and to the point of her nose she vibrated and trembled as though about to fall apart in a hundred pieces, and her eyes were all whites, demanding how he could so cruelly ill-treat her. I was sent scurrying for her thickest winter coat and commanded to warm it at the fire. Then I had to bring the lambskin hearthrug from the dining room, and in this Madeleine, coat and all, was wrapped like a parcel ready for the post, and laid on a chair by the kitchen fire. When I told Greg about it, he said: "You should have tied her up by t'tail in front o' the fire and let her turn like a joint, basting with hair oil meantime. She'd have made a tasty snack for a tomtit."

It didn't come to that, but I was commanded to sit there and keep an eye on her while Uncle Arthur went upstairs to change. Then he took over guard duty. Whether he sat up all night with her I don't know. He was certainly there when I went to bed. All was well in the morning, and, rewarded with a bow of blue ribbon round her neck, Madeleine accompanied us to the luncheon party at the Rectory the next day.

We didn't arrive at the castle till three o'clock, and Gregory Appleby, who had been there already for an hour with his parents, detached himself from them and me and Billy from our party and made himself our unofficial guide. What I had seen, looking in through the great wrought-iron gates on the street, was nothing but a long façade standing behind a lawn and pierced by an archway. Greg led us through the archway, and immediately we saw that such a house as Pentyrch, hitherto the sum and masterpiece of grandeur to me and Billy, was hardly more than a chicken coop compared with this place. We found ourselves in a vast quadrangle of red sandstone, one side shining bloodily in the afternoon sun. It was turfed, and the graveled path running round it was as wide as Smurthwaite's main street. In the middle of the lawn, on which three or four games of cricket might simultaneously have been played, a stone fountain housed an elaborate group of bronze statuary. Water spouted and sparkled about a Triton and the well-developed ladies who were according him their broad-minded sportive company. There were no flowers, and that seemed as it should be. The great expanse of green, the shining bronze figures and the water, the square of the red buildings: these were enough. On a corner of the lawn, looking remote and toylike, Sir Titus Newte, Miss Orlop, Rose Garland dressed in the elaborate silks I remembered so well, and a boy I did not know, were knocking balls through croquet hoops.

We did not approach them. Greg led us right through the quadrangle, out through an archway at the other end, and into the gardens. We had them more or less to ourselves, and here were flowers enough, growing in the beds, ramping on the red walls, spilling in cascades about the rockeries, and floating on the surface of ponds. There was statuary, there were entrancing stone bowers, there was a maze of clipped yew from which came the shouts of lost souls imprisoned there.

But most of the shouting came from the meadow beyond the gardens where the proletariat was taking its pleasure. A boys *versus* old boys cricket match was going forward. There were races and three-legged races, and egg-and-spoon races, and greasy poles to climb, and long jumps and high jumps and all the fun of the fair. The Smurthwaite Silver Band, wiping their lips with their blue cuffs, were climbing a dais, and soon the airs of Leslie Stuart and Sullivan were soothing the elders in a semicircle of deck chairs.

It was, Greg assured us, well up to the standard of these occasions, and the great moment of the day was yet to come when the "over-fifties" hundred-yard race was to be run, in which Sir Titus always competed. "It's a fair scream," Greg said, "to see him trying to lose, and everybody else trying to make him win. Give him his due, he's not a bad old cock, but when you come to think of it—"

What Greg thought of it he did not say, but his fresh young country face creased in a frown, and he waved his hand toward where, beyond the meadow, the land climbed away toward the moors. "A thousand acres and more up there," he said, "of the best grouse shooting in Yorkshire. All his."

And now the fabulous creature who owned the castle and the gardens and the meadows and the moors came strolling down from his croquet game, with Miss Orlop and Rose, peering about through his steel-rimmed spectacles. smiling and bowing and crying: "Come on, now. Who's racing me this year?" and the customary pleasant farce was played out and a silver cup, as big as an egg cup, was presented to Sir Titus, amid cheers, by Mr. Ashmole. The cheers continued for the farm cart which was now trundling through the field laden with tea urns and crockery, cakes and bread-and-butter and buns. The crowd ate and drank sitting on the grass, Sir Titus among them, Mr. Hawke having first said grace; and then Mr. Ashmole called on our well-known and respected Town Clerk to say a few words. Uncle Arthur, who had been preparing his few words for the last week, protested against being taken unawares before rolling out his measured and majestic lines. Then the Smurthwaite Silver Band played "He's a Jolly Good Fellow," everybody cheered, Sir Titus beamed, and the straggle home began.

We three loitered for a time in the meadow whose scents were all released by so many trampling feet, and Greg, as if trying to put to sleep a puzzling thought, repeated: "No, say what you will, he's not a bad old cock. I heard of a duke the other day who was interviewing a parson about a living vacant on the estate. He had only two questions to ask: Are you against all this Radical nonsense? Are you *not* against fox hunting? The parson gave satisfactory assurances and got the job. I don't think old Titus could do a thing like that."

"And I don't think," I said, "Mr. Hawke would have given such easy answers."

"Oh, I don't know," Greg said. "Poor old Hawke. I don't suppose he really believes or disbelieves anything."

Billy said, rather surprisingly: "Oh, shut up, Greg. You don't know what you're talking about. You can't always tell what a man believes by what he does. I don't believe in charity, but I'm taking it. When you're as old as Mr. Hawke you'll know something about life and then you can begin to spout. Compared with some, you've been brought up with a silver spoon in your big mug."

Greg exploded at that. "What!" he shouted. "Me! You're daft, Billy. Why, I've heard my father say that his old man worked all the hours God sends for twelve-and-six a week."

"Who's talking about your grandfather?" Billy asked. "I'm talking about you, and I'm telling you—"

They were both getting heated, and I was expecting another collision when Phoebe came hurrying along. "Well," she said, "you're an exclusive lot, aren't you? Where have you been keeping yourselves all day?"

But it was not to me and Billy that she was speaking, and soon she and Greg had moved on ahead of us, talking twenty to the dozen.

12

It was Greg who kept me in touch with Billy's doings. The letters began from this time to flow between them. When the summer holidays came, Greg asked: "Have you heard about Billy's grand tour?"

"No," I said. "If he's having a holiday it'll be the first in his life, I imagine."

"Oh, he's having a holiday, all right. I wish one of the nobs would decide to take *me* in hand and lavish some ill-gotten gains upon me."

He gave me Billy's letter to read. From it I gathered that he was making his first visit to London, staying at Miss Orlop's house in Bayswater, and that she and he, with Rose Garland, would be starting off in a few days' time for Paris. They were to dawdle down to Marseilles, take a ship to the south of Italy, move up through the country to Germany, pass over into Belgium, and thence return home. It would be an eye opener, I thought, for a boy who had never seen more than a bit of Cornwall and a bit of the West Riding of Yorkshire. A boy like myself, in fact. It made me feel envious of Billy.

"Well," Greg asked. "What about it, Chad? D'you know anyone who wants to invest in a promising lad? Here I am at a loose end. Nothing to do but look after the pony for Phoebe."

Phoebe was away, too. With her father and my mother she was spending a fortnight in Bridlington. I myself would be moving off soon with Uncle Arthur, who intended to pass his holiday in London. I told Greg so.

"Well, I'm not looking after Mistress Madeleine," he said firmly.

"My uncle would never trust you with her," I assured him. "I walked out with him to Holroyd's, the vet's. We inspected every yard of the premises and left a memorandum as long as my arm concerning diet, hours of exercise, and so forth. What are you going to do, Greg?"

"I'm waiting for the glorious twelfth," he said. "I'm told the grouse are strong on the wing this year." He grinned at me. "I dare you to join me in making a day of it."

I was staggered by the audacity of his proposal. It was one thing to knock a pheasant over in the woods of Pentyrch where you hardly ever met a soul and shooting was not a serious pursuit. To go for the grouse on Sir Titus Newte's moors was another matter. His shooting parties were famous. The castle would be full of guests.

"But, Greg, there'll be guns all over the moors."

"There's over a thousand acres," he said. "If we can't get away with a grouse or two up there we're a poor couple."

"Have you a gun?"

"Yes—of sorts."

"What would your father say?"

"He'd baste the living lights out of me," Greg said with relish.

"What would you do with the grouse then, if we get any? You can't take 'em home."

"Give 'em away. I don't want to eat 'em. I want to shoot 'em—just for the hell of getting some of old Titus's birds."

86

He talked me into it, and on the twelfth, which was three days later, I was out of the house before dawn. I had got into the habit of all-day walks, and to be away at so early an hour was not unusual. Uncle Arthur would suspect nothing, I told myself, and with food in my pocket I joined Greg who had come on his bicycle to the out-skirts of the town. I hopped onto the step and off we went between hedges dripping with the mists of the night, amid the first stirrings of the birds and the first gleams of day.

"How're you feeling, Mutton-chops?" Greg asked.

"Fine," I assured him, wishing it were true.

"There'll be no fine about it," he said. "If we're nobbled it'll be quod without the option. I can see the headlines in the Smurthwaite, *Sentinel*. 'Mutton-chops, the Choirboy Criminal. Taken Red-handed. Unknown Confederate Cleverly Escapes.' "

"Oh, shut up," I said, feeling that we were a pair of foolhardy lunatics. "Where's the gun?"

"What d'you take me for?" he asked. "You'll see the gun soon enough."

We had met nobody when we reached the outskirts of the moors. There, in a ditch grown full of bracken, Greg buried the bicycle and we began to climb the acclivity that led to Sir Titus Newte's thousand acres. I was glad to be walking. The cold of the morning had set my teeth chattering, and, seeing this, Greg said: "What you want is a nice hot cup of tea."

A fat chance there is of that, I thought; and then we were on the moor and making our way down into a gulley that scored its face. Greg pulled away a pile of bracken and revealed beneath it a kettle, dry wood, and two tin mugs.

"A good general thinks of his troops," he said. "There's time to boil the kettle and have the fire out again before this mist clears. Things should always be thought out beforehand, Mr. Mutton."

He worked quickly; the kettle soon boiled, and he threw tea and sugar into it. "You'll have to do without milk," he said.

This was better. The fire with its telltale smoke had been trampled out. We were eating beef sandwiches and drinking scalding tea, and the mist was breaking up into floating scarves and wavering curtains as the larks rose to greet the sun of a perfect morning.

"Where's the gun?" I asked again.

"All in due season," he said. He lit his pipe, and for some time neither of us thought of guns or grouse or anything but the beatitude of the day's first sunshine. "When you can sit here like this," Greg said, "it seems fair daft to waste time and energy banging away at inoffensive birds."

"Then why have we come?"

"To establish a point. I don't know whether you have ever considered the economics and ethics of preserving game, my dear Mutton-chops, but I was reading something on the subject the other day. I found this lovely sentence. 'Much legislation was framed for the preservation of deer and game for the recreation and amusement of persons of fortune, and to prevent persons of inferior rank from squandering in the pursuit of game time which their station in life required to be more profitably employed.' Our friend Eustace loves to learn long passages of poetry. I prefer to stuff my head with passages like that. They enchant me, Chad. So now this person of inferior station will produce his gun."

A little way off from where we had lit the fire a long flat stone was lying on the ground. "I took the precaution of bringing the gun privily the other night, wrapped in oilskin," Greg explained. "*If* we'd been seen approaching this place this morning, it wouldn't have done to be seen carrying a gun."

He heaved up the stone, revealing a scooped-out hollow, and gave a cry. "Why, t'damned thing's gone!"

There was, indeed, no gun, but there was a sealed envelope. I took it up and opened it, and saw to my amazement that what was written inside was in my Uncle Arthur's handwriting:

Gregory Appleby to report home at once to milk the cows. Chad Booth-royd to report home at once to exercise Madeleine. By Order, Arthur J. Geldersome, Town Clerk.

Greg dropped with a bump into his broadest accent. Livid with rage, he shouted: "Well, of all t'interfering bloody old busybodies!"

I couldn't share his anger. Indeed, Uncle Arthur's note filled me with joyous release. I began to laugh.

"If he's pinched that gun, I'll sue him," Greg threatened. "Great big damned old fat-belly, pandering to the leisured classes. Sittin' there in t' Town Hall waiting for Sir Titus to have the condescension to send him a brace of grouse."

The sun was well up now, warming me to the bone, and I felt good. "Cheese it, Greg," I said. "If you talk like that about my uncle I'll smack you in the snout."

It was the first time I had asserted myself against Greg, and he looked as surprised as I was. For a moment his face darkened and I thought he was going to charge at me like a young bull. Then he laughed, and said: "So Angel-face has got some guts after all. Well, well, to hell with the grouse. Let's see if there's some more tea in t'kettle."

There was, and we carried our steaming mugs higher up the flank of the moor. In front of us the heather flowed away like a purple sea, lapping here and there against the outcropping rocks whose gray was livened with lichen golden in the morning light. Turning about, we could see the valley out of which we had climbed: the white road and the river, the woods, the stone hedges, the smoke rising from the farm chimneys, the sheep and cattle moving in the fields. The sound of a reaper down there far beneath our feet mingled with the songs of the larks high above our heads.

As it turned out, we made a random day of it, up and down Wharfe-dale as the fancy took us, riding the bike, walking, bathing in the river, climbing the fellsides, taking meals in cottages. The sun shone from morning to night; and when the light was gone and we had eaten in Greg's vast gleaming kitchen, the glory of the perfect day was in us yet. It was one of those days you want never to end, and we were still about when the full moon breathlessly rose, and bats weaved and flickered, and in the stillness the faintest imaginable footfall of autumn could be heard, overtaking the too ripe summer.

It was such a night as that on which Billy had lighted the lantern and gone before me and Uncle Arthur through the wood, and, think-ing of this, I said to Greg: "I hope Billy'll have a good time."

Greg, as I have told you, was a few years older than I. He was at the point when his boyhood was still about him, but moments almost mature would intrude. The grave beauty of this night made him grave, too; and the answer didn't come from the harum-scarum Greg who had been abusing my uncle that morning. "Billy'll never have a good time," he said. "He wants to know too much."

I didn't see then what Greg meant, but often in the years ahead of us I thought how true of Billy that remark was, and how much more subtle than mine Greg's mind was that he had seen it so soon.

The moon was smaller and whiter when, at ten o'clock, I dropped off the step of Greg's bike and he turned about and started to pedal home. Uncle Arthur was standing on the doorstep, looking at the light striping the street like a pale tiger. "Ah, Chad!" he said, and took my arm and began to walk me up and down, as though he, like me, were unwilling to admit the end of a magical day. Madeleine trotted at his heels.

"I have bought you a bicycle, Chad," he said. "You seem to be forever hopping off Gregory Appleby's back step and thus involving him in a long return journey."

I gave him my thanks, glad that I had stood up for him against Greg.

"Besides," he said, "in a year or so I suppose Greg will be off to Oxford."

It was true. Only at that moment did I realize that I had been thrusting the thought out of my mind, unable to admit how much I was going to miss Greg. Eustace was gone; Billy was gone; and when Greg was gone, too, I was going to be very lonely.

"Madeleine, my darling," said Uncle Arthur, "not *every* lamp post, please. I am sure it is unnecessary. Did you get any grouse, Chad?"

"No, sir. The gun was gone."

Uncle Arthur looked up at the few pale stars that managed to show themselves. "Our police are wonderful," he said.

"Yes, sir."

"You have perhaps noticed that dull-looking dog—I beg your pardon, Madeleine—that dull-looking fellow Ockenshaw of the county force? Nothing escapes his eye. Unseen himself, he observed Master Appleby journeying to the same spot late on successive evenings, and returning each time without a parcel he had been carrying. Investigation revealed the gun. Happily, Ockenshaw does not revel in police courts, so he took the gun to Greg's father, and he, meeting me, told me the story."

"My name was in your letter, sir. How did you know I would be there?"

"Cerebral ratiocination, Chad, which is to say the gentle art of putting two and two together. Or rather one and one. I have noticed that where Greg is Chad is apt to be. And when you told me you would be off at crack of dawn—well. Ockenshaw delivered the note. He observed the recipients perusing it, and so informed me by telephone as soon as I was at the Town Hall. By the way, grouse for luncheon tomorrow. A couple of brace were sent round from Sir Titus this evening. Come, Madeleine, that is *really* enough."

13

Looking through what I have written, I find that I have given the impression of a break between me and my mother after her marriage to Mr. Hawke. I must put this right. She was well aware of the value of what her brother Arthur had done when my father died. He was at that time nearing his middle forties and was set in comfortable and rather self-indulgent bachelor ways. To alter his fashion of life so completely as he did was not a light thing. It might have turned out badly for him. That it did not, that it, indeed, turned out well, didn't alter the fineness of what he had done. To bring it all to nothing by taking me with her when she married Mr. Hawke—which is what my stepfather wished her to do—would have been a poor return; and so it came about that I had virtually two homes. Five minutes' walking would take me from Uncle Arthur's to the Rectory, and I wandered in and out of the two houses as I chose. Uncle Arthur and Mr. Hawke, each with a job to do, and each of set habits, didn't worry one another much; but my mother, Phoebe and I were constantly in and out of the two houses. If I wanted to read on the Rectory lawn, or ride Phoebe's pony round the paddock, or take some fruit from the orchard, I had no need to ask anybody's permission.

In the spring of the year following our abortive venture after the grouse I was, in this way, sitting in the Rectory garden with a book in my hand one Saturday afternoon. I was at a loose end, for some municipal affairs had taken Uncle Arthur to a conference in Leeds, and Greg was at Oxford. In the following autumn he would be going up to Balliol College. No one doubted that, though he had not yet sat for the scholarship examination. That week end he was on a visit. An old boy of our school, up at the college, had invited him to come and inspect the fields he was to conquer.

I wandered round to the Rectory and found that the Rector with my mother and Phoebe had gone out. One of the maids said they would be back to tea, so I sat down with my book to wait for them. I had not been there long when a youngish-looking man came striding energetically through the gate and across the lawn. He was dressed in tweeds, carried an ash stick and had a rucksack on his back.

"Hello!" he greeted me. "D'you know whether Mr. Hawke is at home?"

I said that he wasn't, but that he'd be back by teatime.

"Oh. Then I'll be looking up a few people in the town. Will you tell him I'll pop in about four? Whitworth Rhodes the name is."

He strode away as though to sit down and wait for an hour were unthinkable.

As it happened, the Rectory party arrived back just as Whitworth Rhodes was returning. He positively ran to overtake them, shouting: "Hello, Hawke! Hello, Phoebe!"

Mr. Hawke seemed pleased to see him. "My dear Whitty!" he cried. "Well, well—this is a happy surprise! How are you, my dear boy? And what are you doing in our dead-alive little town?"

"Hush, hush!" Mr. Rhodes warned him. "I heard of your marriage to Arthur Geldersome's sister. This, I take it, is she," he said, shaking hands with my mother. "Madam, not a word to your brother, I pray you, of what Mr. Hawke has said. Mr. Geldersome would certainly consider dead-alive to be a treasonable expression."

"So you know my brother?"

"Very well, madam."

"Whitty was Daddy's curate," Phoebe explained.

"Don't be impertinent, miss," he reproved her. "Whitty, indeed. I am Doctor Whitworth Rhodes."

"Everybody in the town called you Whitty," Phoebe said. "Of course, I hardly remember you. I was only a child when you left."

"And now, if I may say so, you are a most personable young lady. I can't hope to have equally improved."

Phoebe went in to see whether tea was ready. She knew very well that it would be seen to without her, but Phoebe was like that. My mother introduced me to Whitworth Rhodes, and we all sat in deck chairs on the lawn.

"One often hears of men throwing up other professions to take Orders," said Mr. Hawke. "Whitty is one of the few I have known to give up Orders for another job. He is a general practitioner in Manchester."

"On trial, Mrs. Hawke, I couldn't stand the Church," Mr. Rhodes said. "It seemed a dead-alive little institution. All right for a scholar like your husband. No good for me. Too much energy to work off. I work it off in Manchester, I can tell you. Why don't you visit me there some time, Hawke?"

"Oh, dear, I really could not do that, my dear fellow," said the Rector. "I was once induced to spend a week end there with my old friend the Dean. He has since become a bishop, and I suppose a deanery in Manchester would be tolerable if one could be certain that it would speedily lead to a pleasant bishopric. Say Wells or Lichfield. But not on any other terms. It has a splendid newspaper, a tolerable university—if one can call these nonresidential places universities —a fine grammar school, older than Eton, first-rate music, good theaters for those who want them, and a lively civic life. On the other hand, it is as flat as a blackboard and as black as a blackboard. Smuts. They rain down. I cannot stand smuts."

Whitworth Rhodes laughed heartily. "You hear that, Mrs. Hawke?" he demanded. "And the best sermon I ever heard your husband preach was on the text: 'The Kingdom of Heaven is within you.' I remember he quoted that old Milton tag

The mind is its own place, and of itself
Can make a Hell of Heaven, a Heaven of Hell.

It converted me, that sermon. Till then I was a heathen in holy Orders. But Hawke made me see that all this pleasant doodling didn't come to anything and that I'd better get out and do a job where it was wanted. Anyway, it was a doting mother who fancied me as a parson. I always wanted to be a doctor."

"You could have been a medical missionary," said Mr. Hawke.

"I *am* a medical missionary, in darkest Manchester."

"Well, I'm glad Wharfedale has called you back for a moment," said Mr. Hawke.

"Just a few days' tramping," Rhodes said. "Away from the smuts."

"You must stay here for the night."

"I'm sorry, but on these occasions I have a leaning to pubs. I've already booked at the Dragon. Tell you what, though. I'll come round after dinner and beat you at chess."

"You can at least eat your dinner here."

"No. I've invited Frank Lidgett to join me at the Dragon."

"The policeman?"

"Yes. I ran into him in the street. I was always fond of Frank."

"Very well, then," Mr. Hawke said with resignation. "After dinner."

And after dinner Whitworth Rhodes came round and, as he had promised, beat Mr. Hawke at chess.

14

Oxford in those days was not the stinking horror it has now become. It was as peaceful as Smurthwaite itself; "and, of course," Greg said, "it has one or two things that Smurthwaite hasn't." He came back talking as some sinner might talk who had been given a week end in heaven. If anything had been needed to stiffen his resolve to win the scholarship, this week end was it. "And old Eustace turned up. Charlie Briggs had invited him at the same time as me. I wouldn't have known him. You'll see for yourself. He promised to be round here this evening."

We were in my room upstairs—"Mr. Chad's study" Uncle Arthur now called it when speaking to Mrs. Ramsden, and this was a tribute to the changed status of me and the room. I was shooting up into a lanky hobbledehoy, one of Mr. Ashmole's prefects, and the room reflected my changing tastes. Dear Uncle Arthur was ever ready to pamper my whims. There were long wicker chairs, sectional bookcases eating up more and more wall space, prints of sentimental Pre-Raphaelite pictures above them, Lucy Orlop's sketch of Rose Garland over the mantelpiece, and—what gave me a ridiculous grown-up feeling, though I didn't smoke myself—ashtrays lavishly scattered about. I was in a turmoil of growing up, as eager to be a man as any disillusioned man could be to return to his childish innocence. My voice had broken. I wore the pie frill no more.

"Eustace!" I cried. "Is he in Smurthwaite?"

"Yes, for a day or two. Staying at the Rectory."

Greg was a traveler back from a strange world. He had so much to tell me that we forgot the time, and it was not till Uncle Arthur came up at nine o'clock bringing a tray of coffee as humbly as a college scout might do that he looked at his watch and said: "Eustace seems to have decided against us after all." He swigged his coffee. "I must put this down and be off. I promised to be home by ten."

I said I'd ride part of the way with him, and we wheeled the bicycles out into the street. The night was moonless, but we knew every inch of the road, and in those days there was no traffic to worry us. There was only one part of the road where the gradient was too much for us. We used to struggle on till our calves could push the pedals down no more and then jump off, our legs trembling. The annoying thing was that after that there were only a hundred yards to go, but that hundred yards we always had to walk.

We were walking it that night when the light of the bicycle lamps fell upon a huddled figure in the hedge, and we stopped to see who this could be. It was Eustace. He looked comfortable enough, slumped down there with his head in the grass and snores bubbling from his mouth. We laid the bikes against the hedge, and Greg said: "Eh! This is a bad do!"

"Is he hurt?" I asked in alarm.

"Nay, he's tight. He was drinking too much at Oxford."

We considered him for a moment, and then Greg said: "Look here, young Chad, keep your mouth shut about this. Not a word at the Rectory. Understand?"

I nodded.

"If anything of this gets to Phoebe's ears, I'll—I'll take action."

He glared at me fiercely, and I said: "I know when to keep my mouth shut. You needn't worry. But what a fool!"

"That'll do!" Greg said sharply. "We don't want any self-righteous Pharisee act from you." He was deeply upset.

We were on land that Greg's father farmed. Near by, a gate led into a field. "We'll get him through and into that shed," Greg said. "Take hold of his legs."

I did so. Greg took his shoulders, and we bundled him into the shed.

"Stay here till I'm back," Greg ordered. "It won't take me ten minutes to get home."

I sat down in the straw near Eustace, who tossed and muttered. The time seemed long before Greg was back, carrying two horse blankets. "We don't want the old devil to get clemmed," he said, and rolled Eustace up as Uncle Arthur had rolled Madeleine in the hearth-rug after her bath.

"I nobbled these blankets on the sly," he said, "so nobody at home knows a thing. I'll be along here first crack in the morning, and I'll take him home to breakfast. I'll say we arranged tonight for him to walk out. That'll be in character for Eustace. You get back now, and call at the Rectory. Tell 'em I persuaded Eustace to come home with me and spend the night. That'll be in character, too. He's done it before."

Greg had got it all worked out. We drew the straw thickly together into a corner, working by the light of a bicycle lamp, and dumped upon it the bundle that was Eustace. Greg shut the door and dropped the wooden bar that fastened it. "That'll keep him in till I come for him," he said.

We went down to the road, both of us feeling subdued now that the job was done. I stood ready for my return journey. Greg took my arm. "Sorry, Chad," he said, "if I was a shade brusque. This thing worked me up a bit. You see, I'm fond of the old fool; and then there's Phoebe."

It was the first time he had ever said anything serious to me about Phoebe.

"Tomorrow's Saturday," he said. "Ride over and join us at breakfast. Eight o'clock."

I promised to do so. Then I rode back to Smurthwaite and told my lie at the Rectory.

15

Eustace needed a shave and his eyes looked tired. He ate little and drank a lot of tea. We three were alone in the kitchen. Greg's father had long been up and out on the work of the farm, and Mrs. Appleby had breakfasted with him. Not a word was said by any of us about last night's affair. I learned later that Eustace didn't even know that I had been concerned in it. Much later still I learned that he had by now written his first book of poems, though some years went by before it was published, and had in this way ejected Eileen Waddilove from his system. To read that book, you would think it the outcome of a tremendous carnal adventure, whereas all that had happened amounted to a few kisses in doorways and futile tumblings in hedges. His second book was as pure as snow on the fells. A long time was to pass before that one appeared, but Eustace was now in the grip of the emotions that begot it. I am going ahead and telling of what I didn't know on that Saturday morning when we breakfasted in the farm kitchen. This second affair, to be expressed in such Blessed Damosel terms, was the real thing. His lady had surrendered, and then, being married, had taken alarm and sent him marching. Hence the too much drinking that Greg had noticed at Oxford. Hence the flight to Smurthwaite, the long hours in a country pub, and the boozy passing out in the ditch.

However, sitting there that morning, with the sunlight pouring in upon the scrubbed red brick floor of the kitchen, with Greg lavishly

95

helping himself and me to toast and eggs and ham fried to a rich brown, with a laburnum outside the window dangling its golden chains against the blue, I was too uninstructed, too naïve, to be aware of young manhood in torment. I saw only that Eustace had sprung up to a rakish six foot, that his ascetic face was thinner than ever, and that his blue eyes looked intolerably tired. I was fascinated by a tic in his cheek.

I think he considered not only me but even Greg to be an unsophisticated rural pup, though a well-meaning one, and he did his best to be courteous and considerate. Greg, for his part, was careful to keep the conversation on neutral ground. He talked at large of Oxford and regretted that Eustace would not be there to share its joys with him. Eustace turned his sad gaze upon him. (I do not remember that once that morning he smiled.) "It wouldn't have been any good, Greg," he said. "There was never a less academic mind than mine. I should have just upset everybody by walking out in a year or so. I couldn't stick Shrewsbury, and I'm sure I couldn't stick Oxford."

"Well," said Greg. "I hope you find this job you have in London congenial enough to stick that."

Eustace passed his cup over for more tea, and asked: "Does your mother object to smoking in the kitchen?"

"Good lord, no! The old man and I are at it all the hours God sends," Greg said in his best grown-up fashion.

Eustace filled and lit his pipe. "You're wrong about that job in London," he said. "I'm *not* sticking it. I've thrown it up."

This, too, belonged to considerations about which neither Greg nor I knew anything. Greg said: "Oh, damn it all, old boy, that's too bad. They'll be right fed up at the Rectory. Phoebe thinks you're settled down."

"Does she? You've got a lot to learn about Phoebe, Greg. I do *not* think Phoebe sees me what you call settled down. What d'you take me for—a pinch of sediment?"

He asked the question with some asperity. Greg was nearer a raw nerve than he knew.

"Well, what are you going to do now?"

"I'm going to Germany."

"Well, of all the— Why Germany?"

"Why not Germany? I've got to go somewhere."

He looked miserable, lost. The bright morning dimmed. Greg had pushed us up against something he hadn't intended.

Mrs. Appleby came bustling into the kitchen. "Greg," she cried, "get outside with that pipe. Your father'll baste you if he catches you smoking in the kitchen—or anywhere else for that matter."

Eustace apologized to Mrs. Appleby for his pipe, and we all went out to the sunshine and the white clouds of hawthorn and the swifts skating in swooping arcs upon the bright air. But we didn't see much of it, troubled as we were by a sense of crisis.

"Look," said Eustace, "don't say anything at the Rectory. I'm going back to London. That's all they need know. I'll write to them from Germany. I loathe family arguments and explanations."

We loitered down the lane to the highroad, and there Eustace held out his hand to Greg and said: "Well—till sometime, Greg."

"Oh, I'll be seeing you before you go."

"No. I've just decided. I shall take a train this afternoon."

"Well, at all events let me run you in to Smurthwaite on the back of my bike."

"Thank you, Greg. I'd like to walk."

He set off at once. We watched him round a bend of the road.

It was a wonderful day. Greg and I spent it as we had spent many another, wandering wherever fancy took us and not getting back till the evening was closing in. But somehow it was not as good a day as the flowering trees and the birds and the sunshine should have made it. I think Greg and I, unconsciously, were aware for the first time that boyhood ends.

CHAPTER FOUR

I

IN JANUARY of 1906, when I was within a month of my seventeenth birthday, Smurthwaite and its ancient grammar school were shaken to the roots. At breakfast one morning in that month Uncle Arthur said to me: "I hope you will be able to dine with me tonight at the Dragon, Chad, and then go on to the meeting."

I said that I would, and I must explain why we were to dine out. Mrs. Ramsden had left us. Young people take it for granted that life will go on and on more or less in the same way; and I certainly, once I had got over the sharp upset of my father's death, saw no reason to fear disruption in Uncle Arthur's comfortable household. He himself, ironically, blew his own smooth arrangements sky-high.

The oddest rumor had lately been gaining ground, and at last could no longer be ignored: Mrs. Ramsden was living in sin. Her paramour was a sturdy old rogue named Henry Jennison, an odd-job man whom you would see about the town, bursting with bonhomie and good humor which were the more incongruous because, among his other bits and pieces of work, he was a gravedigger. That Mrs. Ramsden, who had been so sharp on her niece Eileen Waddilove, and who had been considered a model of propriety, should become anyone's mistress was a hair-raising thought: that she should become mistress to a grave-digger gave a touch of macabre comedy that pleased me.

This was not a situation that Uncle Arthur discussed with me, but he took his own steps to end it. In the municipal politics of Smurth-waite, the question of a graveyard had been agitated for some time. There was a graveyard round the church, but that had been full long since, and an adjacent field into which it had been extended would soon be full, too. Our small municipal park was under the charge of a Parks Committee, and it was well known that Uncle Arthur wished to extend its functions so that it should become the Parks and Cemetery Committee. This had now been done; the municipal cemetery was in being; a field had been leveled and surrounded with walls and given an ornate entrance with the inscription above it: "O Rest in the Lord." Paths were laid out; flowering trees and shrubs were planted, and, in contradistinction to God's Acre round the church, it was known to the more ribald spirits such as Greg Appleby as Geldersome's Four Acre. I took Greg to see it during one of his vacations from Oxford, and he looked about for a while and then said: "It's old Geldersome's perfect memorial. *Si monumentum requiris, circumspice.* Dust and ashes." We were coming out, and Greg read aloud the inscription over the entrance: "O Rest in the Lord," adding, "By Order, Arthur J. Geldersome, Town Clerk."

Well, there it was; and when the place was ready for receiving guests the question of a cemetery keeper arose: someone to mow the grass and rake the paths and trim the trees and now and then dig a grave. Uncle Arthur wangled the job for Henry Jennison. He reckoned —so he told me when he was able much later to look back on the affair with amusement—that a regular wage would turn Henry's thoughts to marriage and so he would not be embarrassed by having a notorious sinner as a housekeeper. He was right, up to a point. Henry and Mrs. Ramsden married, and Henry showed a sense of his new respectable status as a municipal employee by buying a plot in which he and Mrs. Ramsden would at last continue to lie side by side beyond the reach of censure; but, alas! his respectability was absolute and did not permit him to tolerate the thought of a wife who went out to work. He said he would knock her teeth down her throat if he caught her at it, and so Uncle Arthur found his ace trumped. That is why we were now scrambling together our own breakfasts and taking lunch each day at the Rectory; and that is why, on that January night in 1906, we dined at the Dragon before going to Sir Titus Newte's meeting in the Assembly Rooms.

Mr. Balfour had handed in his chips; Sir Henry Campbell-Bannerman had formed a government and was "going to the country." So far as Smurthwaite was concerned, he might have saved himself the trouble —or so, at any rate, most people in Smurthwaite thought. What shook them to the foundations was that Sir Titus was to be opposed. He, and a line of Newtes before him, had been hereditary unopposed representatives of Smurthwaite in the House of Commons time out of mind. It is true that not one of them had been known to introduce a bill, or make a speech of note, or even to attend regularly in the House. The Smurthwaite *Sentinel* had once interviewed Sir Titus about an agitator's speech charging him with being a notorious absentee, and Sir Titus had replied with what was considered admirable pith: "What are the Lords for? Can't they look after us?" And now things had reached the pass that Sir Titus was to be opposed by a Liberal candidate, and the Liberal candidate was Mr. Ashmole! No wonder that Smurthwaite felt as though the earth's foundations themselves could not be trusted. There were those who asked how Mr. Ashmole was going to combine the duties of schoolmaster and M.P., supposing him to be elected. There were those who said it was a scandal that the headmaster should oppose the chairman of the governors, and that Mr. Ashmole ought to be sacked. There were even one or two who removed their sons from the school and its pernicious Radical influence. The only person in no way disturbed was Sir Titus Newte, who said to Uncle Arthur: "Well, well, fancy Mr. Ashmole doing a thing like this! It looks as though I shall have to make speeches, and I'm not used to that. A damn nuisance starting that sort of thing at my time of life."

And so for the first time in living memory preparations were made for a party fight in Smurthwaite. Rosettes appeared in buttonholes in the streets and even in our school; and, seeing the formidable predominance of Sir Titus's color in classrooms and corridors, I was surprised that Mr. Ashmole could maintain a stomach for the fight. However, he appeared undismayed, and at morning assembly for prayers in the great hall, from whose walls Newtes innumerable gazed down, there was nothing lacking in the fervor of his thanksgiving for our Founders.

The meeting in the Assembly Rooms was to be Sir Titus's only public appearance. He had published an election address in which he assured the voters that he stood for England, God and the Crown, that, as he knew them and they knew him, he thought it superfluous to waste their time and his with a lot of public talk, but that he would hold one meeting for the statements of his views and for the answering of questions. There was no doubt that Sir Titus had written his own address. "Let us get this thing over as quietly as possible," he ended, "and settle down again to be the happy family that Smurthwaite has always been, and so a good example to more restless and turbulent parts of the country."

3

Before the meeting we fed well at the Dragon, an ancient inn that had been learning the arts of hospitality for some centuries. Nowhere had fires mastered their business of looking like welcoming spirits more thoroughly than at the Dragon. Nowhere was napery whiter or cutlery more polished or crystal more sparkling, or food more wholesome. Any "occasion," to Uncle Arthur, called for celebration, and Sir Titus's meeting was decreed an occasion. Standing in the lounge, with his legs well apart before the fender, he gave to the fire the appearance of a distant conflagration seen through a triumphal arch. He held a glass of sherry to his nose, sniffed it, drank it. "It is a pity, my dear Chad," he said, "that youth precludes your joining me in this excellent Bristol Milk. But there is a good Pommery to be had here, and I have ordered it to see us over the sirloin. I think you might venture on a slight acquaintance with it."

"I am glad to see," he said later, as he scooped into the port-enriched Stilton that lay before us, "that Mr. Ashmole understands the code of an English Gentleman. An English Gentleman has a high regard for Fair Play, and in canceling his meeting Mr. Ashmole has shown that he understands this."

Mr. Ashmole's meeting for tonight had been arranged before Sir Titus announced his; and Mr. Ashmole had decided to let the old buffer have the field to himself, seeing that this meeting was a one and only. However, I could not refrain from asking why Sir Titus had not canceled or postponed his.

Uncle Arthur had decided that there was not time for a full-blooded cigar, but that he might treat himself to a light Panatella with his coffee. He looked at me reproachfully through the smoke of the first whiff. "My dear Chad," he said, "the Collect for the day of St. Michael and All Angels begins with the words: 'O Everlasting God, Who hast ordained and constituted the services of Angels and men in a wonderful order . . .' Among men, Chad, as among Angels, Order is Ordained, and it behooves us to recognize our place in the Order and act accordingly. This, I am delighted to say, Mr. Ashmole has done. Let us adjourn."

We adjourned, drank our coffee in deep leather chairs by the lounge fire, and then went next door to the Assembly Rooms. Snow was falling, but despite the weather, a crowded audience had come to hear Sir Titus who had his own ideas about how a meeting should be conducted. He didn't bother to have a chairman or a supporting bench of notable nobodies. He was Sir Titus and could do all that was necessary for himself. So on the stroke of eight he walked out of the anteroom and plunged right into it. "Good evening to you all. Well, here we are—goodness knows why. But I suppose I'd better say a few words to explain why I think you ought to vote for me and not for this excellent feller Mr. Ashmole."

The excellent feller, a hand cupped to his ear, was sitting in the front row with Greg alongside him. I was rather surprised to find that, in a racy idiosyncratic way, Sir Titus could talk fluently enough; but whether what he talked was political sense I was in no position to understand. It was certainly well received, and when, at the end, he said: "Well, that's all I have to say, and if any of you want to fire questions at me, now's your chance," no one seemed to think that clarification was necessary. "Well, then," said Sir Titus, "if I've convinced you all—" when Greg rose to his feet. He said in a clear voice: "Sir, in the almost certain event of your being returned for Smurthwaite"—cheers—"may I ask whether, in the almost equally certain event of a Liberal Government's being returned, you will support them in their announced intention of curbing the destructive powers of the House of Lords?" (Gasps—notably from Uncle Arthur.)

Sir Titus was not gasping. He looked amused, and he answered promptly. "Our young questioner—too young, I imagine, to have a vote and a sense of the responsibility that goes with it—can surely expect no other answer than the one I must give. I do not accept that the powers of the Upper House are destructive, and, if elected, I should certainly do my best to give a Liberal Government hell."

Loud cheers, amid which Mr. Ashmole rose and asked: "Does Sir Titus realize that to give the Government hell he will have to attend at Westminster? And can he endure the thought of such a break in his customary habits?"

"Shame!" from Uncle Arthur.

Sir Titus said: "My habits, like myself, are well known in this constituency, whose electors must make their decision." There the matter ended, and we began to shuffle out to the snowy night. Walking beside me, Uncle Arthur was stiff with outrage. Our Assembly Rooms were a handsome building with a fine flight of steps leading down to the street where, under the steady fall of the snow, we could see Sir Titus's carriage waiting, the cockaded coachman huddled under a whitened cape, the lamps throwing their rays into the welter. Though we had so short a way to go, Uncle Arthur and I stood there at the top of the steps, hesitating to take the plunge. Greg joined us. "What a night!" he said. "I'm counting on an invitation to stay at your place, sir."

"I regret, sir," said Uncle Arthur stiffly, "that I do not see my way to invite you."

Poor Greg looked thunderstruck, and I felt ashamed. Mr. Ashmole and Sir Titus at that moment came up together.

"May I have a shake-down at your place tonight?" Greg asked Mr. Ashmole. "I was hoping to stay with Mr. Geldersome, but find myself unwelcome."

"Unwelcome?" cried Sir Titus. "For God's sake why? You're Bart Appleby's boy, aren't you?"

"Yes, sir."

"How are you liking it up at Balliol?"

"Very well, sir, thank you."

"I was there myself. Look—you'd better come and take pot luck with me."

Greg grinned, knocked out of gravity by the implications of this. He gave me a wink. "That's kind of you, sir," he said. "I should be delighted."

"Come on, then. Mustn't keep the horse standing about in this."

We watched the pair of them climb into the carriage and Greg drive off to take pot luck at the castle. Uncle Arthur looked deeply disconcerted. The odd things that could happen in Smurthwaite seemed beyond even his reckoning.

4

There was no domestic servant problem in those days, and Uncle Arthur could have ended his household embarrassments any time he cared to. But there were two obstacles to be overcome. One was his feeling that Henry Jennison had got the better of him, coupled with his hope that Mrs. Ramsden would feel that to serve the Town Clerk was worth the displeasure of her husband—worth, almost, having her teeth knocked down her throat. The other was his addiction to social tram lines. As things had been, they should, in a well-organized world, remain. The idea of a change, of having to instruct a newcomer in the feeding of the furniture and the care of Madeleine appalled him; but at last, as Mrs. Ramsden continued to show a liking for keeping her teeth intact and the furniture took on the bloom of neglect instead of the shine of affectionate care, something had to be done about it.

When Uncle Arthur had gone to the Town Hall on the morning after the meeting, Greg called on me, and we sat before the fire in my study, as he expanded the saga of his night at the castle. The snow had ceased to fall. Through the window we looked out on a tranced landscape of blue and white. Greg had got on famously with Sir Titus. They had sat up till midnight. "We talked about everything. That funny-looking little noddle of his is damned intelligent, believe you me. He led me on and made me challenge everything he stands for. And he gave me all the perfect answers—that is, according to his way of looking at things. But there's not two pennorth of animosity in him. He admires old Ashmole, and," added Greg complacently, "me. And he thinks my old man is the best farmer hereabouts, which is true. I was amazed. There's not an acre within miles that he doesn't personally know, and who's farming it well or badly. But the servants! My God, Chad, you should have seen 'em! They bobbed up all over the place like rabbits out of a warren. All old and all fat, padding round Sir Titus like damn great St. Bernards and mastiffs round a whippet."

Clearly, Greg had had the night of his life. When he had exhausted his material, I gave him mine—the plight of this house where two hard-working men had to deal with their own domestic cares. "You'd better have a word with Phoebe," he said.

And, of course, the practical Phoebe was the person we should have turned to long ago. We turned to her that very day when we were lunching at the Rectory. "Of course I'll come and look after you," she said. "I've only been waiting to be asked. I thought you'd soon be in a mess."

"We are not in a mess," Uncle Arthur protested. "But the need to keep out of a mess is causing me to neglect my auriculas."

My mother said: "I'm afraid you've come too late, Arthur. Phoebe, you must forgive me and your father for not telling you this before. It's only just settled, and we had decided to break the news today. The fact is, we—well, you'd better tell them, my dear."

So Mr. Hawke told us, and what it came to was that he had been offered and had accepted a living in the Home Counties. "I feel Smurthwaite is a bit too much for me," he said. "Why, bless me, Arthur, the place is becoming almost metropolitan! Crossgates is little more than a hamlet. And, as it happens, I was born there. All very sentimental, I'm afraid. My father was the village doctor."

This news was so surprising that we forgot the question that had caused it to be imparted till Phoebe said: "All the same, I don't see why I shouldn't stay here if Uncle Arthur would like me to." She had called him that since her father's marriage to my mother, though he was no uncle of hers—only a stepuncle, if there is such a thing.

I suppose Phoebe was nineteen at that time. With her hair up, and wearing a woman's clothes, she was a person difficult to imagine as the harum-scarum whom I had seen riding the pony with Greg on the day, which now seemed far off, when I first called at the Rectory. I was to know Phoebe for a lifetime, and, though her qualities developed, they never changed. If some people called her obstinate, I could never call her anything but resolute. It was clear now, at this lunchtime gathering, that the moment her father's announcement was made she had decided on her own action and would stick to her decision.

"There's nothing for me to do here," she said. "The servants do it all. And there'll be less in a small country vicarage."

"I suppose," said Mr. Hawke, "you're thinking of young Appleby."

"But naturally," said Phoebe. "That among other things. Greg will be coming down here for his vacations and I'll want to see him."

Uncle Arthur, as if intent on cooking his own goose, said: "That boy's a political hothead."

Phoebe answered briefly: "Nonsense. He's awake to what's happening in the world."

"I must frankly say," said Uncle Arthur, "that his remarks about the Upper House shocked me."

"Why shouldn't he say what he thinks?"

"What! About Peers of the Realm!"

Phoebe laughed. "If what Greg tells me is true, we shall all live to see some odd Peers of the Realm."

"The Upper House, paradoxically, underpins the Constitution," Uncle Arthur declared; but Mr. Hawke, for once sticking to a point, brought the matter back to Greg.

"But all the same," he said, "you're not engaged to be married, and if you remain here you'll give the impression that you're hanging round for him."

Phoebe brushed that aside. "That won't worry me. Of course I'm hanging round for him."

My mother perhaps remembered a youngster named Boothroyd sweeping her off her feet in Scarborough. "I'm very, very fond of Greg," she said. "I have no doubt whatever that he wants to marry Phoebe and that he'll raise the question as soon as he feels justified in doing so. If she came with us to Crossgates, it would make no difference to him; but if she'd rather stay here I don't see why she shouldn't. I suppose Chad will have to stay, anyhow. It would be a great pity to break up his schooling at this stage. That is, Arthur, if you'll be kind enough to keep him."

"My dear Edie," said Uncle Arthur, "in the autumn of next year Chad will be going up to the University. I sincerely trust that for that brief time I shall continue to have the pleasure of his company."

And that is how it was settled. My mother and Mr. Hawke went to Crossgates in Buckinghamshire. Phoebe came to live with us and a "daily" girl came in to "help with the rough," as they called it. And, to end the account of this stage of my life, Sir Titus was elected with a majority of 5,673 votes, which was astounding for a Conservative candidate in that election. Mr. Ashmole retired and went to live in an Oxfordshire village, and thence "nursed" a country seat as a prospective Liberal candidate. The months passed by, and the moment came when Oxford for me and for Billy Pascoe, who went up at the same time, was just ahead. And then I met Rose Garland again.

5

"Chad," said Uncle Arthur in that summer of 1907 when I was working my last term in the Grammar School, "upon the death of your father I put my hand to the plow. The furrow is now all but completed."

I had been reading in my study, and he had come up and knocked at the door, as he always did. From the moment when I and my grief-shaken mother had arrived in this house and he had taken us up to the top floor and told us that that was ours, safe from intrusion, he had kept his word and never entered without asking permission. He had, in all things, kept his word. I was old enough now to realize, and I am glad to say that I did realize, what I owed to my Uncle Arthur. I did my best to let him understand this. That day, I called to him gladly to come in. We were alone in the house. The long Oxford vacation had begun, and Phoebe was off somewhere with Greg. I realized that Uncle Arthur was in for a long loneliness. My mother was gone, and I would soon be gone, too. Perhaps I would come back in the vacations, perhaps not. Phoebe would be gone. My first year at the University would be Greg's last, and he and Phoebe would be married when the year was ended. Uncle Arthur would be lonelier than before we came, for his cronies Mr. Hawke and Mr. Ashmole were there no longer. This morning, when I had come down to breakfast, he did not hear my coming, and from the dining room door I saw him walk to the hearthrug where Madeleine was lying. She got up and flagged her morning welcome, and Uncle Arthur went through his old gesture of joining his hands so that she might jump upon them to be lifted to his face. She raised her sharp intelligent little face to his, and I could almost have sworn that she shook her head sadly. The moment had to come, and it had come now. Madeleine found the jump, small though it was, beyond her. Stooping was no easy matter for Uncle Arthur, but he creaked down and gathered her into his arms and they exchanged their morning salute. He did not then put her down again, as he usually did. He remained holding her close to his face. His back was to me, and I did not want to see his face, so I went upstairs and came down again, slowly and noisily, whistling. He was seated at the table, and Madeleine was on her cushion, eating her breakfast.

So when Uncle Arthur came and knocked at my door that evening, I did not shout, "Come in," but I jumped from my chair and ran to the door and opened it, and said: "Come in, Uncle Arthur. How nice to see you."

He came in, carrying Madeleine. He lowered himself stiffly into a chair. It was his smoking night, and he was wearing his smoking cap and jacket. "Do you mind if I smoke here, Chad?" he asked punctiliously.

I knew what Greg thought of him: an out-of-date old stick-in-the-mud, to be joked about in his absence, and, in his presence, to be treated with ironic deference that the young can afford to spare for those they have left far behind. And, of course, he was all that; yet which of us is worth tuppence but for his saving graces?

It was of nothing but Uncle Arthur's saving graces that I was aware that night. With the absurd silken tassel hanging over his ear, with Madeleine in his lap, with his chair carefully placed so that he could look through the window toward the auricula house, he was an endearing figure. An irresistible compulsion was on me to tell him that I was aware how he had been a rock of shelter. It was difficult to say. What, I wondered, would have become of me and my all but penniless mother if Uncle Arthur hadn't intervened? So I said just that.

"Uncle Arthur," I said, "I often wonder what would have become of me and my mother but for you."

He looked taken aback. In his own absurd way, he would have said, if he had wanted to speak about the matter at all, that an English Gentleman did his duty, and his duty had been plain to see. But, equally obviously, an English Gentleman did not talk about his duty. He did it. So, when he had recovered from my unexpected plaudits, he used the cliché that would have made Greg laugh. "I put my hand to the plow."

"I hope," I said, "that you are not going to be disappointed with the harvest."

"I don't think I shall be, Chad. What do you think? You should know more about that than I do. What are you aiming at?"

I was afraid that some day I should be asked that question. I often put it to myself, and I didn't know the answer. The world seemed to be full of people who, almost from infancy, knew what they wanted to do with their lives. There was Billy Pascoe. As long as I had known him he had been eaten by a fierce flame of desire to shine as a scientist. There was Greg. "What makes men tick, Angel-face? Believe me, it's the desire to get hold of a bit more wealth. And don't chip in and tell me that that's a low unworthy ambition. I'm not talking about money, though money comes into it. I'm talking about wealth—well-being—which is what money can buy. *The Wealth of Nations*. What a title! And what a thing to aim at: giving well-being to the nations. That's why I think being an economist is the most important thing on earth. For the moment, anyhow. When that's all been sorted out—the framework of living, so to speak—then men will have a roof over their heads beneath which they can settle down to other matters."

That was Greg, in one of those outbursts that followed our silences as we lay by a summer stream, or sat on a tor of the fellsides, looking down into the valley.

"Happily," I said, "the arts and sciences, philosophies and religions, haven't waited for your roof—your economic New Jerusalem. They've gone ahead somehow. Perhaps they're born out of trying to get somewhere, and will wilt when they get there."

"Are you satisfied to see men pigging along, mucking up the world as they've always done?"

"I didn't say I was satisfied. But perhaps Housman's right:

> The troubles of our proud and angry dust
> Are from eternity, and shall not fail."

"Never mind Housman. Think for yourself. If you're not satisfied, what's your prescription?"

And that's what Uncle Arthur was asking now. "What's your prescription?" "What are you aiming at?"

"Frankly, Uncle Arthur," I said, "I don't know. I can't pretend that I have any particular aim or ambition in my life."

"Well," he admitted handsomely, "life can't be run like a municipality, with blueprints for everything. The oddest things happen." He was silent for a moment, as though his mind was occupied by some train of thought and he was wondering whether I was a person in whose presence it could be developed. At last he seemed to decide, and said: "Now take me. I look a solid enough person, I hope. You would not expect a rash romantic impulse to come my way, would you?"

It was hardly a question I could be expected to answer, so I said nothing. "Here I am," he said, "middle-aged, set in my ways, the responsible prop of my Municipality. And yet, I recently proposed marriage to Miss Orlop."

This was so staggering a revelation, and that Uncle Arthur should confide such a matter to me was so unexpected, that I still said nothing.

"What would have happened had the marriage been possible," he said, "I don't know. But it was not possible. She is already married. Rose Garland is her daughter."

He told me a little of the matter that night, and years later, when I was one of the executors of Miss Orlop's estate and her papers came into my hands, I read her own account of the matter. Rose has given me permission to use it here in her mother's own words.

6

May the Second, 1904.—Yesterday was Rose's birthday. She is sixteen. I thought she was old enough to know the truth, and I told her that she was my daughter. The nicest thing of my life happened. She hugged me, gave me a kiss, and said: "I don't know *why*, but I've *believed* I was for some time. How lovely that it's true."

The darling meant it, and I cried. A pretty sight I must have been. God knows I was never a beauty, and now—!

Well, it was a good birthday. I gave the child the gold and turquoise brooch that had been my mother's. We went to Daly's at night and afterward took supper at Rule's, where Rose was fascinated by the gay theatrical trash that uses the place. All through the day there was a sense of release between us, as though a bank had been dug away that had separated two streams, now flowing happily together. Thank God this moment which I have long dreaded is so satisfactorily past. I had feared I know not what—anger, sullenness, or endless questions. But the darling only said: "You'll want to tell me all about it some day. Don't bother now. When you like." Could anyone have been more thoughtful and understanding? I feel, emotionally, a dry old stick, unable to make clear what is in my heart—I, who was once so madly impulsive! I hope Rose feels how I adore her. She is growing up so beautiful.

I had been able to wangle a day's holiday from school for her, and how she enjoyed putting off the uniform, dressing in a new frock for the theater. She looked a woman, God help her.

This morning I saw her off at the station, a schoolgirl again. She said: "Thank you, darling. That was my loveliest birthday. I'm so proud."

Well, this damned old dusty house of mine has always been dreary enough. Without her, now that the current is released between us, it seems unendurable. So I decide to spend it writing down what Rose will have to know some day. Here goes.

I had a lonely enough upbringing at Pentyrch. I didn't see much of my brother Alaric once we were out of the schoolroom. After that he was at Dartmouth and, as often as not, spent his holidays with what I thought of as his jolly old messmates. Once he was in ships, he hardly seemed to count in my life at all except as a provider of foreign stamps from the China station and such places. My father didn't trouble us much, either. Like so many Orlops, he was a naval man. He was now ashore, a rear admiral with a job at the Admiralty. When he visited us at Pentyrch—from the beginning I thought of him as a visitor—the days darkened. He was a hectoring type, and our large staff, indoors and out, was treated to quarter-deck manners. From my mother and me down to the bootboy, we might have been pressed men caught in a mutiny for all the grace he showed us. We were always glad to see the back of him, damn his eyes. At least, he taught me to swear from infancy.

My mother was a very gentle woman. I don't know whether he ever loved her, or whether he married her for her money. She had a lot. Even as a girl, I was aware that he frightened her. She was physically afraid of him, and, as I adored her as blindly as I adore Rose, I detested him. But I never feared him, and I am glad to remember occasions when I defied him. In my middle teens I had a mastiff that terrified everybody else but was abjectly obedient to me. I trained it, consciously encouraging its fierceness. One day my father said I was to go with him on a call he was making upon a neighbor. I had arranged to walk that afternoon with my mother and said so.

"You will come with me," he said.

"I shall do nothing of the sort," I answered.

Such flat mutiny roused him to fury. We were in the hall. He snatched a walking stick out of the stand and came threateningly toward me. I ran out, calling the dog. Side by side, we rushed toward the woods, with my father in pursuit. When we had a good lead I turned in one of the rides, waiting for him, my hand on the dog's collar. He knew that dog; he knew it would attack if I told it to do so; and he knew that I was capable of telling it. He had once kicked the creature, and only my command had saved him from being savaged. So there he stood, and it was one of the happy moments of my life, for he knew that I knew that he was afraid. He turned and walked back to the house. The next day he shot the dog.

During his long and unlamented absences in London my mother and I had beautiful times. Occasionally, we would drive forth on some stupid ceremonial call, to sip tea at a neighboring house, but the less we had of that the more we liked it. For the most part, we hardly left our own estate, where she taught me all I know about birds and beasts and flowers, which is a lot. In the winter we loved our indoor life, regretting only Christmas which brought Black Jack home, full of seasonable noise and carousing. His jolliness was unbearable, and usually ended in his damning and blasting us as a pair of mice who didn't know the meaning of enjoyment. Happily, we soon nauseated him, and he would flame away to metropolitan delights.

My mother was one of the best amateur painters I have known, whether in oil or water color. It was she who set me on my way. The only lessons I ever had were from her, and they could not have been bettered. From the time I was toddling till she died when I was twenty, painting together was our chief occupation and delight.

She was small as well as gentle. I grew up a great ungainly creature who could have carried her about, and I developed a protective feeling for her that made me suffer abominably if anything hurt her. I remember that once she was sharpening a drawing pencil, and the penknife sliced her finger. I winced and gave a cry, and, looking down, saw that a spot of blood had oozed from my own finger. Now, believe that or not. It happened.

But I had more than this to suffer on her behalf. She was aware, I am sure, of my father's infidelities, and so by this time was I. So long as he kept them out of the house we said nothing; but in the spring of the year when she died he brought them home.

I can see Mrs. Elton now: a man-eating merry widow if ever there was one. She was handsome in her way, big-built, with piles of ginger hair and blue eyes and a fine complexion. She was hale and hearty, loud-mouthed and dashing. A dem fine woman in fact, God rot her. The only thing I can say in her favor is that she had Black Jack crawling, and I was glad to see him crawl.

She loved horses and rode like an Amazon. I don't think he loved horses or any living thing, but he liked to ride, though he rode badly. There was one good thing about it: it kept them out of the house for most of the day—that is, till she took a toss and sprained an ankle. Then she was quartered on us all day, and he was about the place from morning to night, putting on an air of solicitude that made me laugh. As I say, I was twenty then, and less afraid of him than ever. I despised him, and he knew it.

Having that woman quartered on her so closely made my mother a quivering bundle of misery, for all the household was aware of what was up. My mother took to her bed, with her nerves torn to pieces, and I spent all my time with her, even ordering my meals to be served in her room. He made a pretense of sympathy, asking me one day how my mother was.

"In hell," I said, "and there she'll remain so long as Mrs. Elton is in the house. The woman is capable of walking with a stick as far as the front door, and from there a carriage can take her to the railway station."

That was plain enough, so plain that his veins congested with anger and he was on the point of another of his celebrated explosions. I said to him: "Get hold of yourself like a sane being. One of these days you'll have a stroke."

I was glad to see fear in his eyes again, and I made a guess that some doctor had told him the same thing—perhaps that some mild shocks of the blood had already given him a warning. "You hate me, you little bitch. Don't you?" he said.

"With all my heart, with all my mind, and with all my strength," I said.

The next day they were gone.

To my mother their going was like the rising of the sun. She got up that very day, and our old style of life went on, but it was clear to me that even her little strength was not what it had been. There were days when our ever shorter and shorter walks would so tire her that I would literally carry her back to the house, terrified by the fragility of what my arms cherished and enclosed. Then there were no more walks, and she died in the winter.

I remained alone at Pentyrch till the following May, when I received a letter from my father. He told me that he would soon be marrying Mrs. Elton, leaving the service, and coming to live permanently at Pentyrch. There were changes he would have to make in the establishment. Most of them he would see to himself when it was convenient for him to come down, but in the meantime there were certain matters that could be put in hand. Would I therefore see that this, that, and the other was done at once.

The idea of putting myself out in order to turn Pentyrch into a love nest for Black Jack and his ginger Amazon seemed to me so funny that I had my first laugh since my mother died. My mother's will had left me very well off indeed. I didn't answer the letter. I packed a few things in a suitcase, knowing that I could buy all I wanted when I reached London, and the next day I had myself driven to the station. I told the coachman that I was going to visit friends in Plymouth and that I'd write saying when the carriage was to be at the station to meet me on my return. However, it was at Paddington, not Plymouth, that I alighted.

I never saw my father again, and neither he nor Mrs. Elton saw Pentyrch again. I read of his death in a newspaper a week later. It was caused, as I had expected it would be, by an apoplectic stroke. Pentyrch remained empty, looked after by our agent, till my brother Alaric left the service and went to live there many years later.

I bought this house in Bayswater, where I have lived ever since, built a studio in the garden, and began to exhibit and sell my pictures. I thought often of my martyred mother, but I must not be sentimental enough to pretend that that weighed against the things that made for my happiness. I *was* happy. The clouds that had darkened my childhood and girlhood were lifted. I was an independent being, and, in the one direction in which I wished to expand, I was successful— though then only in a small way. And I was in my earliest twenties. It is not surprising that then, if never before or since, I had the outlines of some physical attractiveness.

My picture framer had a shop in a lane between Oxford Street and Cavendish Square. It was there that I met Willy Lancaster, and since this is merely a sketch of what happened to me, and not a psychological analysis, I shall say simply that I was infatuated with Willy from the moment I set eyes on him. He was twenty-five, handsome, and good at his work. He would often dissent from his employer's opinions, and he was usually right. I sometimes wondered what Black Jack—or my mother for that matter—would say to the idea of an Orlop shamelessly making eyes at an assistant picture framer! But I *was* shameless. I couldn't get the man out of my mind: he was physically so perfect, and he was bold and on-coming, realizing my infatuation.

I arrived in the shop one day just before one o'clock. Only Willy was there, and he was locking the door. "The boss is gone to lunch," he said, "and I'm just off. We shut from one to two. Care to join me?"

He was both casual and confident. None of the deference of trades-man to client. He knew me, alas! all too well.

He took me to a miserable place, so that, when we lunched together after that, which we often did, it was at my invitation and in the sort of restaurant I liked. Though he was bold to meet every advance I made, he left all the advancing to me.

Looking back, it is easy enough to see what a fool I was and to acknowledge that ninety per cent of the blame for the disaster rested with me, not Willy. But there it was. I had never been presented at Court, never had a "season" which would have permitted me to meet young men. The few I had met in Cornwall had not interested me, and I am sure I had not interested them. I was an awakened virgin who had met a male of exceptional physical attractions. I was overcome by the vehemence of my own physical response, and there was no one to interfere with any folly I cared to hurl myself into. Thinking it over in my sterile middle years, it seems no more than that. At the time, I was sure that Héloise had never felt for Abelard what I felt for Willy Lancaster.

A trivial affair brought matters to a head. It is not easy to enjoy a luncheon occasion that is rigidly guillotined to one hour. Willy began to return to the shop five minutes, ten minutes late; and then there came a day when he overstayed his time by half an hour. He was very self-indulgent, and I loved to indulge him. I would urge him to have another expensive dish, another glass of wine, and that day even I was aware that the wine had taken the fine edge off his perceptions. He didn't even think about the time, but sat there enjoying a cigar till I had to remind him gently that duty called. When he got back to the shop, he found his employer rattled. A Royal Academician had been in creating hell's delight about delay in delivery of work, and it was clear that Willy, whose late returns had already caused comment, would not do much work that day. Moreover, his employer was a teetotaler. In a burst of anger, he dismissed Willy on the spot.

Willy came round to my house that night and told me about it. And for the first time he told me something about himself, though to this day I don't know how much of a liar he was. He claimed to be the only son of a country doctor, a widower, who had skinned himself to the bone to send him to a public school and to Cambridge. "I had just scraped through with a wretched degree when my father died. And that was that. He left hardly a penny." Willy said he had tried schoolmastering and acting and many other things; and I can now well believe that he had, if the word "tried" isn't too seriously stressed. I soon learned, to my sorrow, to place him in Browning's category of "finished and finite clods, unlighted by a spark."

I had never been abroad, but since independence had come to me I had been planning to spend a year visiting the European galleries. That night I persuaded Willy to marry me. We were married in Paris, and we lived together for exactly a year, wandering hither and thither. In about three months my physical appetite was assuaged. In six months I was seeing him as he was, and in twelve months I could stand him no longer. He was so utterly nothing but a body that was being pampered at my expense. He was good-tempered, lazy, greedy and self-indulgent. He was after every pretty girl who looked at him, and plenty did. I saw with disillusioned eyes how he had never been after me; and one night in bed I realized with a shock that he was not enjoying me: he was good-humoredly indulging me. Thereafter I shuddered at the thought of his touching me, and he never did again.

A life of sorts would have been possible with him, and he was willing enough to go on with it. But carrying a handsome carcass around was not my idea of living, and I told him so. "Well," he asked lazily, "what do you propose?"

We had reached the point where we could discuss our relationship in terms of a business deal. "You could live on five hundred pounds a year," I said.

He was sitting under an awning on a hotel veranda looking over the Mediterranean. "I could *exist* on it," he said. "I could hardly *live* on anything under a thousand. I'll give you grounds for divorce if you'll agree to that."

"I have plenty of grounds for divorce," I said, "but there will be no divorce, for this reason. No one knows of our marriage and no one shall know, because I cannot bear the thought of my idiocy becoming public property. I left England as Miss Orlop, and so I shall return."

"And what if I return too, and blow the gaff?"

"Then you will have to work, and you won't like that, for I shouldn't allow you a penny. I bought you. I admit it. And now I want to sell

113

you. You're a born remittance man. You shall have seven hundred and fifty pounds a year so long as you remain abroad. If you show your face in England, not a penny."

He took a long cool drink and smiled. "That sounds fair enough to me," he said.

We parted the very next day. He remained in Italy; I went to the South of France. I knew a child was on the way, but I didn't tell him that. As I was determined never, *never,* to acknowledge a marriage which now outraged my sense of all that a marriage should be, I had to choose between returning with an apparent bastard, or leaving Rose in France. I left her in France with excellent foster parents till she was five years old, and then had her sent to me, devising the story of friends in India who wished me to look after her. It was an awkward trick, but it worked well enough. Even my brother Alaric believed in it, or magnanimously pretended to. One thing I couldn't face was that the child should have her father's name. That is why she is called Rose Garland.

Well, put down in this bleak outline, it seems an odd story. I haven't either the heart or the skill to embroider it with the passion that went to its beginning or the boredom and disgust that marked its close.

7

It was to be a long time before I read this account of Lucy Orlop's marriage, but already in 1907, as I say, I learned from Uncle Arthur that she was Rose Garland's mother. Rose would no longer need to weep, as she had once wept on my shoulder at Pentyrch, because she didn't know who she was. My contacts with Rose had been so few and far between that she would perhaps have disappeared from my mind altogether, or remained as little more than a name, but for the sketch Miss Orlop had given my mother and that now hung in my room. It could always bring her back freshly to my imagination, always make me think of that day of many memories: the day when Uncle Arthur took me to tea at Pentyrch, and the year was gently dying, and Rose appeared, wearing a vine in her hair, as we rolled behind the fat horse through the woods, and, later, Billy Pascoe lighted us to the highroad. "Thank you, Pascoe."

I looked at the sketch that night with new interest, and for the first time I felt a pang of jealousy. How much, since the change in Billy's fortunes, had he been seeing of Rose? What did she mean to him?

I knew that Billy had won his scholarship, as I had now won mine. We would be going up to Oxford together. Years later, I ran by chance into a man who had sat with Billy for the scholarship. He told me that there had been half a dozen of them, and when the examination was over they had gone together to a tearoom. "We were all more or less trembling wrecks," he said, "except Billy. He ate a hearty tea while the rest of us nibbled miserably at our buns. Then he said: 'I can't understand why you chaps wasted your time coming here, when you knew I was competing.' And the devil of it is, we all knew that he was right."

That, indeed, would be the devil of it. I could hear Billy's calm, almost disinterested voice, speaking those words not as a boast but as a statement of fact. And that afternoon in 1907, looking at the picture of Rose Garland, the idea that Billy Pascoe usually got what he wanted was overpoweringly present in my mind.

With the examination safely behind me, and some empty months ahead, I was living a vague loose-ended life, walking a lot, reading for fun; and it was during one of my solitary walks that I encountered a man I had not expected to meet again. On the moors there is a pub that I shall ever remember with affection: gray-walled, stone-roofed, sheltered by sycamores, cool in the summer heats, fire-warmed in winter. Tired by walking, I had turned in there to eat one of the mammoth teas that they provided in those days and that my young stomach could take in as easily as my legs could take in another mile of the road: an affair of grilled ham and two or three eggs, with lashings of bread and butter, stewed fruit and a big earthenware pot of tea. I had got outside this lot and was sitting back with a satisfying feeling of being well and truly stoked for the return journey, when a man whose back had been to me as he ate at another table got up and came across the stone-flagged floor. "Well, Adonis," he said, "you've done yourself proud, I must say. I've been watching you in the mirror."

He was trailing a heavy rucksack in one hand. The face stirred a memory. "Rhodes," he said. "Whitworth Rhodes. Ex-curate. I called on Mr. Hawke once, soon after he'd married your mother. Remember?"

That placed him. I got up and we shook hands. "If you're going back to Smurthwaite," he said, "let's walk together. I shall be staying there tonight. I always take the place in when I'm walking in these parts."

He paid for his tea and mine, and off we went. I was glowing with sun and exercise. My years in the Yorkshire air had been what I needed. No one would think now that I had ever suffered from that Chronic and Constitutional weakness that had delighted my father. The breeze stirred my hatless hair. The Reynolds angel of childhood had grown into the tanned Adonis that I forgave Whitworth Rhodes for calling me. Indeed, I liked it. I was aware of it. I hoped it was something to set against Billy Pascoe's way of getting what he wanted. What a fool I was in those days!

I found Whitworth Rhodes easy to talk to. We climbed the path to the crest of the moor, with the beaten springy peat beneath our boots, the contours flowing in bare beauty round us, a scutter of grouse rising now and then, and invisible larks everywhere in song.

"So you're going up to Oxford," Rhodes said; and when I showed surprise that he should know this, he said: "I have it from Mr. Hawke. I write to him now and then. I imagine he's heartbroken that Eustace isn't there. He never tells me anything about Eustace. How is the boy?"

There wasn't much to be said. Since that night when Greg and I had found Eustace drunk in a ditch, followed at once by his departure for Germany, I had heard nothing from him. Greg and Phoebe had received a letter or two, at long intervals, but they were not enlightening. He was in Munich. That was literally all I knew.

"A rum household that was," Whitworth Rhodes said. "There was never a more sensible practical little creature than Phoebe or a more unpredictable meteor than Eustace. I imagine that to old Hawke Eustace is the sort of pain in the neck that Branwell Brontë was to his father. Eustace adored his mother."

"I have never heard him speak of her," I said.

"No, you wouldn't. That's the last thing I'd expect him to do. It might be a good thing if he *could* speak of her. As it is, he'll just go on looking for her all over the world. And he won't find her. However, forgive me. I'm too grave."

"What was she like?" I asked.

Rhodes sat down on a boulder that thrust up out of the heather and lit his pipe. He thought for a long time, and then said: "Nobody's ever asked me a more difficult question, Chad. She took no part in any sort of affairs. All her life was inside herself, and there was so much of it, and it was so beautiful, that it spilled over without her doing anything about it. Do you see what I mean? To be with her was peace."

We walked on then, and I said good-by to Whitworth Rhodes an hour or two later outside the Dragon in Smurthwaite, where he was to spend the night. "By the way," he said, "when you get up to Oxford look in on my brother Bob. He's much younger than I am. I've more or less brought him up. He's at Balliol on a Manchester Grammar School scholarship."

8

Mr. Hawke's successor at the Rectory was an energetic person who got about on a bicycle. He had no use for a paddock, and he permitted Phoebe to keep her pony there. She didn't ride him now, or drive him.

He was already well on in years when I first saw him, and now he was turned out to grass.

Mr. Hawke himself, I thought, when I saw him at Crossgates, was rather like an old horse turned out to grass. Not that he was as old as all that, but he was a constitutional browser, and Crossgates, his parish in Buckinghamshire, was a quiet paddock.

Phoebe and I traveled down there together. Greg, with a man from his college, was walking in Germany. He intended to "look up old Eustace." Uncle Arthur had gone to Cornwall to spend his holiday at Pentyrch with Miss Orlop and Billy Pascoe. I was glad to hear that Rose Garland was not with them; but I was unprepared for Phoebe's announcement, when we had changed from a main line train and were doodling across country toward Crossgates: "Your mother's asked Rose to join us."

I didn't know whether I was glad or sorry. My mind was disrupted by the knowledge of impending change. I should not be going back to Smurthwaite. This was the first day of October, and within the fortnight I must present myself at Exeter College. All my gear and books were with me, and I had said good-by to Uncle Arthur. He took the occasion rather heavily, for once forgetting how an English Gentleman would behave in these circumstances. The moment called for a sticking out of the chin, an absence of emotion, and a hearty slap on the back, but he couldn't rise to any of this. There was a large wicker basket in the hall, and I knew that this had been made for Madeleine's journey to Pentyrch. Madeleine had never before accompanied Uncle Arthur on a holiday, and I asked him nothing about this change of custom, knowing that Madeleine was on her last legs and that he did not intend that she should lose a moment of his company, or he of hers. Even now, I cannot think any of this absurd. My uncle was a good man. If his affections were oddly distributed, that was his affair. Now the objects of his affection were leaving him, and he made no pretense of being unaffected. He would not even walk as far as the railway station to see me and Phoebe set off. Without a word, he shook our hands as soon as breakfast was over and hurried to the Town Hall.

So on that October day, as Phoebe and I journeyed toward Crossgates, I knew that whoever went back to Smurthwaite would not be the Chad Boothroyd who had grown up there, and who didn't feel especially grown up as he contemplated the new world ahead of him, in which he expected to be of as little consequence as the small boy Gregory Appleby had kicked in the behind outside the Grammar School years ago. I would have liked these last few days of my boyhood to be spent peaceably with my mother. I could have done without even Phoebe, equable though she was; and now came this news of Rose Garland to enchant and disturb me.

The railway does not touch Crossgates. There were three miles to go, and Rose was waiting at the station to meet us. How extraordinary women looked at that time! And Rose was a woman. I remember a horse trough outside the little station where at last we drew almost casually to a standstill, and the great iron-gray bole of a beech tree unfurling into an umber cloud of leaves. There were Michaelmas daisies and scarlet dahlias and a flawless autumn sky, and there was Rose Garland with her hair in a bun, and a flat straw hat on her head, and her sleeves puffed out above the elbows in what was called the leg-of-mutton style, and her white muslin skirt reaching the white chalk dust. And her eyes, as she kissed Phoebe and shook my hand, had the deep disturbing blue that I remembered from the first time I saw her. She said: "Isn't it heavenly weather! I do hope they're having it like this at Pentyrch. Billy has been working so hard and can do with a rest."

I thought, "Damn Billy," and turned aside to see that the luggage was being brought out of the van.

It was uphill all the way from the station to Crossgates, and, then, a horse-drawn brake made the journey. We got in with one or two other passengers and began the crawl. The hedges were flaming. Looking over them, I could see the white unmoving corn, and the cattle dozing in the shade of trees that dotted the pasture; and for some reason I remember the small golden domes of straw beehives in a cottage garden, with minarets of hollyhocks rising round them. The hill flattened, and our crawling horse made a brief pretense at a trot, and then intelligently settled down again to finish the journey in accord with the serenity of that autumn day.

There was not far to go on this flat road; soon we were at Crossgates. Four roads met there. I have motored that way of late, slowing down to take the "roundabout" that stands now at those crossroads, widened to racing tracks, with cement sills all over the place, an A.A. hut, and a tin garage. I didn't stop. I shall never stop there again.

That day the crossroads were narrow and dusty, ancient stocks stood at the meeting place, and beech trees shaded a pond to one side. Mr. Hawke was sitting on the bench of the stocks, a straw hat, the color of a speckled hen, perched on his head, a book in his hand. He got up and brought forward a wheelbarrow from the side of the road. While he was welcoming his daughter, I piled the luggage into it. Then I shook his thin brown hand, took up the shafts, and off we went.

It was a short trundle: a few hundred yards along one of the roads, where, on both sides, the cottages, the small post office–shop, the local policeman's house, the pub, were scattered, all thatched and color-washed; and then down a lane that led to the homely-looking flint church with the vicarage alongside it. A lich gate led into the church-yard. There were seats under its arch, and on one of these seats my mother was sitting. With the absurdity of youth, which imagines everything aging except itself, I had been wondering how she would look. She looked the same as ever.

The vicarage was a modest house, its walls smothered in a tangle of growing things. In front, there was no garden to speak of, but there was an acre at the back, hanging over the prospect through which we had come. Telling me to leave the luggage by the front door, Mr. Hawke hustled us all at once to the low gray wall that edged this acre, whence, as from battlements, we looked down on the scene that he had known as a child and to which he had gladly returned. It was beautiful, that wide valley enriched with the beeches that everywhere in those parts grow so magnificently, and, in the far distance, a blue smudge under the autumn light, the land rising to another chalky down like the one we stood upon. It was worth coming to; but, all the same, I could imagine Greg Appleby saying: "Poor old Hawke! Back where he began. Can you beat it for sheer futility?" And thinking of impatient Greg, my mind wandered to Eustace whom he hoped to see in Germany; and then I looked at Mr. Hawke, his thin hands on the parapet, his beaked head thrust like a wistful gargoyle over the abyss, and seeing how he seemed to be unaware of us, caught up in his own imaginations, I wondered whether he, too, was thinking of that so disappointing son of his. If not at this immediate moment, I thought, then at any rate so often that Eustace must be a sad undercurrent to all his days. It was the first time that any understanding had come to me of the chafe of lives one upon another; and I knew that not any intrinsic fear of life's battle had driven Mr. Hawke back here, but an intense sadness, a sense of there being no need to battle now, for he had lost what he would gladly have battled for. I hoped to God that Eustace would do something, some day, to—well, how banal the thought seemed, but, still, there it was—to make his father proud of him. It is terrible when the object of your love withdraws from what you ache to give it; yet long ago prosaic Phoebe had seen that the only thing you could give to Eustace was to stand out of his light.

I suppose it was a reflex of these thoughts that made me look at my mother. She smiled at me, and I went to her and put my arm round her and kissed her. "It's good to be with you again," I said. She laughed and said: "Whatever's coming over the boy?" But I knew she was pleased.

She and Phoebe and Mr. Hawke drifted back to the house, but for a moment or two Rose and I remained there, and I was terribly aware of her and of the faint scent of her and of the rustling of her muslin clothes as she stirred from one position to another on the wall. I longed to be able to say something to her that would be significant, but I could think of nothing, and so what had been passing in my mind echoed in my words.

"You've never met Eustace, have you—Phoebe's brother?"

She got up, and we began to move after the others. "No," she said. "I've never met him."

Well, little though we thought of it then, the years were to put that right.

9

The autumn dusk was already closing in when we had finished supper. Rose asked Phoebe and me if we would like to walk. "No," Phoebe said, "you two go. I must write to Greg."

How fortunate, I thought; but Rose looked a little doubtful. "I ought to write, too," she said. "I owe my mother a letter."

I was glad she had said it. It told me that she now spoke openly of Miss Orlop as her mother, and so I knew where I stood in that matter.

I said boldly: "I'd love to go. Can't your letter wait, Rose? After being mewed up in a train all day, my legs need stretching."

She didn't jump at it; she looked at me, unsmiling, considering, and said: "Very well. Let's go."

So we went out into the bat light, and I followed the rustle of her white clothes down the path. In the church there was a rumble of organ music and a crying of young voices. The choir was at practice. I thought of Smurthwaite church and the marmoreal Newtes and my pie frill, and felt infinitely old and emancipated and removed from my youth.

"Why does it always make me feel sad?" Rose asked, "the sound of boys' voices in a church. Especially when you're listening, on an evening like this, from the outside? You feel that there's some beautiful secret in there that you're not sharing."

"There's not really," I said. "There's just a dissatisfied choirmaster giving you hell. 'Chad Boothroyd, we'll have that again. Your voice is as flat as a duck's webs.'"

"You mustn't destroy my illusions," she said. "Illusions shouldn't be destroyed: they should be made true."

"You can't make an illusion true. A thing is true or it's an illusion. One can't become the other."

Oh, this was all wrong. This wasn't the sort of thing I wanted to say to her. I didn't especially want to say anything. I wanted to be with her and to feel that she was with me, and contented to be so.

She sighed. "You talk like Gregory Appleby," she said.

We hadn't been standing still. We walked as we talked, and we had

120

come to the end of the lane the church stood in. The hedges fell away; the path strode on before us, glimmering on the shoulder of the downs. To our left was the valley, wide enough in its bottom to be called a plain, but you couldn't see much of it now beyond an indigo sea with clumps of trees standing over the water, vague immensities, tranced and still. This was what I wanted: that Rose and I should feel all these beauties of the night, two of us at one before them.

I said: "What's wrong with Greg then?"

"I didn't say there was anything wrong with him," she answered. "I'm not all that sure of knowing what's right and what's wrong. I only said you were talking like him."

We came to a halt, and she said: "Let's sit down here."

It was a chalky upthrust, cushioned with turf. We sat and for a time said nothing. A few gleams were coming on in the valley, as though ships lying there had run up their riding lights, and presently a train rushed along, glowing from end to end like a liner racing through the night.

"What about Billy Pascoe?" I said. "He's not likely to be fobbed off with illusions."

Rose stirred impatiently. I could feel the movement of her shoulder warm against mine. We had almost to nestle together on that small seat.

"You don't seem to know much about Billy," she said.

"What—me?" I cried. "Why I've known Billy all my life. We were born in the same village. We grew up together."

"You don't know how humble he is."

"Billy humble! Good lord!"

"Oh, I'm not talking of Uriah Heep's sort of smarmy humbleness. I don't mean humbleness at all. I mean humility. They're different things. Billy worships knowledge, and worshipers are humble before what they worship. You'll see. Billy won't go at things like a bull at a gate."

"Poor old Greg!" I twitted her.

"Oh, you needn't misunderstand me. I like Greg. But he's concrete. He hasn't got any feeling—" She hesitated for a word, then said: "He hasn't got any feeling for immensities."

"And Billy has?"

"Yes," she said simply. "That is the main thing about Billy."

So it had all come back to Billy, and I had done it myself. It was too late to undo it. Rose got up and said: "I feel it a bit chilly. Let's go back."

So we walked back, and as we went she said in a friendly way: "I suppose Oxford's a big adventure for you. I hope you have a happy time there."

"I shall be wondering," I said, "how you and your mother are getting on. Will you write to me now and then?"

"I don't think that will be necessary. We shall be seeing one another. I shall run down now and then from town."

"To see me?"

"Oh," she said lightly. "I shall take you in with the others. Greg will be up for another year, and there'll be Billy."

CHAPTER FIVE

I

I HAD not thought that I should ever have to thank old Geldersome, who had kept the chemist's shop in Bradford and was the father of Uncle Arthur and my mother. But soon after I had settled into Exeter College a letter reached me from my uncle, containing an efficient-looking sheet of figures headed "Mrs. Hawke's Fortune. A Statement of Accounts." Knowing Uncle Arthur as I did, I had no doubt that this was a miracle of lucid exposition, but I wasn't good at reading that sort of thing and turned at once to the letter. What this came to was that ever since my mother's first marriage Uncle Arthur had been nursing her little fortune expertly enough to produce five per cent interest a year. This had given her a pound a week as long as my father lived. Once we had moved to Smurthwaite Uncle Arthur had borne all our expenses and the fifty pounds of interest each year had now piled up to add three hundred and fifty pounds to the thousand that old Geldersome had bequeathed.

"Your mother," Uncle Arthur wrote,

has decided to make this little fortune over to you, and if you so wish I will continue to administer it. As you know, your scholarship is not financially a very handsome one. It does not fully meet even your scholastic expenses at the University. What I propose, my dear Chad, is that I should be permitted to make up the difference, and that out of your mother's fortune, which now becomes yours, I should allow you £250 a year for extracurricular disbursement. Thus £750 of the capital will be dissipated during your three years at the University, a regrettable but necessary inroad. However, this will leave £250 of the original thousand pounds, plus the £350 of interest so far accrued, and a little more interest will come along in the course of the three years. So, when you take up the burden of life, you will not be altogether penniless. Let me know if these proposals meet with your approval. I must have official Authority.

P.S.—Madeleine would send her love if she could speak, but speech is a human quality she lacks—perhaps fortunately. She is far from well, and I look forward to the coming winter with apprehension. I am having new coats made for her of warm felt.

Those first weeks at Oxford were very exciting—so exciting that to receive even such a letter was a mere incident, and my thanks to my mother and Uncle Arthur were more formal than I care to remember. I confess that the chief impact upon my mind was one of relish for that delicious phrase *extracurricular disbursement* and of joy that I had a fiver a week to do what I liked with. I had a mild outburst of spending: Pre-Raphaelite prints for my walls, rather delirious cushions for my chairs, a rug that looked like an enormous bison mane to go in front of my fire. But my long association with Uncle Arthur had unconsciously infused my mind with northern caution. I was not likely to break out financially and end my years at Oxford with ruinous bills owing to tradesmen.

I was comfortable enough—even very comfortable, I thought, as I sat at the fireside on an afternoon when that first term was drawing to an end. I had been on my legs for two hours, and had come back to a town enchanted with the mists of early winter. I was relaxed in a long wicker chair, with tea and muffins beside me, when Greg Appleby came in. I had got over my awe of Greg as a man in his last year. He was Greg Appleby again. We ate tea together and filled our pipes. In here, like this, we were near enough to the boys we had been in my room at Uncle Arthur's. I could forget that he was president of the Union and that his speeches had twice been reported in the *Times*. One of them had been castigated in a short leader. In this speech Greg had weighed into those members of Parliament known as Lib-Labs—"that contemporary hybrid with neither pride of ancestry nor a dog's chance of posterity, as useful to the march of mankind as a signpost with its one arm on a swivel, pointing now backward, now forward, as the wind blows. I know the wind is against Labour at the moment. Well, there's only one thing to do—march into the teeth of it."

"It is ironical," the *Times* said, "that this hot-headed stuff is talked by a youth up at the university on a scholarship endowed by a family whose adherence to the cause of Conservatism has been unshaken for generations."

"What d'you think of this?" Greg said that day, as we sat with our feet embedded in the bison's mane. He pulled a letter out of his pocket and handed it to me.

Dear Mr. Appleby:
I see that you and I have been getting into the bad books of a London newspaper called the *Times*—you for saying what you think, I for giving you the opportunity to think. I don't give a damn what the *Times* thinks, and I hope you don't. Though you talk a lot of poppycock in most matters, I'm with you at least in damning Lib-Labbery. Let's know where we are and go at one another straight. I don't mind paying to produce someone who

thinks differently from myself, because I believe that what I stand for is strong enough to deal with opposition. I saw your father the other day. He is very well.

Yours sincerely,
TITUS NEWTE

"Vive Smurthwaite!" Greg said as I handed him back the letter. "Live and let live. By Order, Arthur J. Geldersome, Town Clerk."

"You'd better let Phoebe have that letter," I said. "She already has a Eustace scrapbook. I'm sure she'll want to start one for you. A word of encouragement from an antediluvian Tory must be most flattering."

"Oh, Titus isn't the only one," he assured me. "I had a line from Keir Hardie. I know what *he's* after. Thinks I'd make a useful Labour candidate. But I don't want it. Parliament's not my line. Not for a long time anyway. I want to write—to educate the blokes that go there. Too many boilermakers at the moment, who think there's something sacred in horny hands as such. There isn't. By the way, you've been elected to the Cloggers. Strictly speaking, you're not eligible. But I proposed you, and you were seconded by a chap called Bob Rhodes. I knew his brother long ago. He was old Hawke's curate in Smurthwaite."

Greg had a mania for founding societies. He had started the Cloggers in his first year up. Clogs are—or were then—northern wear, and the Cloggers were elected from undergraduates who had been born north of the Trent but south of the Tweed. I doubt if any of the Cloggers had ever worn clogs. Several of them were titled. One hailed from a vast and notable mansion with which Vanbrugh had burdened the Yorkshire soil.

"You'll have to behave yourself," Greg said, "and try to live down Cornwall. I've pointed out that, though you had the misfortune to be born there, both your parents were reight Yorkshire and that you've had the advantage of living in the West Riding for years. It'll cost you a fiver entrance fee and a fiver a year. You'd better pay me now. I'll hand it over to the treasurer."

I paid him and he got up to go, reserving his bombshell for the last. "If you've nothing better to do, you can come along tonight," he said. "We're having the monthly address. It's by Eustace Hawke."

2

Eustace had become for me almost mythical. Greg, I knew, heard from him occasionally, and so did Phoebe, but even they had nothing to tell me beyond news of his movements, for that was all they knew themselves. His last brief letter had come from Sweden. A month before this night, his first volume of poems had been published by Sidgwick and Jackson. I had read it, and thought it a piece of Swinburne and honey, but in those days poetry was written about, and a good deal of ink had been devoted to Eustace. He was the sort of man the Cloggers liked to get hold of. Their speakers, like their members, had to be northern.

But anything less like the "hard-headed northerner" of tradition than Eustace was that night could not be imagined. The Cloggers filled the small room in which they met. The membership was restricted to fifty. I had been elected in place of a man named Metcalfe, sent down for winning a wager that he would run round the quad of Christ's Church naked at noon. He nearly lost, for halfway round a don seized and almost held him, but he got clear, having taken the precaution to lubricate his body with cod liver oil. He afterward gained admission to Jesus, Cambridge, and repeated his performance there. His parents then took the precaution of sending him to St. Andrews. History has no further record of him, but at all events he permitted me to be present when Eustace spoke that night.

The door leading from a cupboard called the anteroom opened, and Greg, as president, led in the guest. But they were not alone. Greta Lund was with them. I shall not forget the gasp of admiration and surprise that went up as those three seated themselves behind the table. A pair of clogs, the club's symbol, lay in front of Greg, and taking one up, he rose and banged the table with its iron shoe. But there was no need to ask for quiet.

However, a Clogger rose at the back of the room and said: "Mr. President, may I ask a question?"

Greg nodded and sat down.

"May I ask, sir, whether you are aware of Rule Six of this club: That women are not admitted, whether as members or guests'?"

Greg got up, and with the friendly grin that no one could resist, said: "Yes, sir. I am aware of Rule Six. I had it in mind when Mr. Hawke arrived tonight, bringing Miss Greta Lund with him; and I decided that a rule framed to exclude women did not apply to celestial apparitions."

Miss Lund rose, and said: "For that, I kiss you." And did so.

Amid the tumultuous applause that greeted Greg's blush as much as Miss Lund's spontaneous action, the Clogger at the back rose again, making himself heard with difficulty.

"Sir, your remark is courteous, but your conduct is *ultra vires*."

"I put it to the meeting," said Greg, toying with the clog as though he would gladly bash the objector with it, "that, for the duration of the present assembly Rule Six be in abeyance. All those in favor?"

There was a shout of "Aye!"

"Those against?"

The Clogger at the back squeaked: "No. Rule Fourteen reads: 'Any alteration of these Rules shall take place only by majority decision at the Annual Meeting, which shall be the first meeting in the Michaelmas Term.'"

Greg said: "The Honorable Clogger at the back of the room is well up in the rules. Well, damn the rules. Let's take what the gods have so fortunately provided and get on with the meeting."

"As President of the Union, sir," insisted the Honorable Clogger at the back, "do you dare to say, 'Damn the Rules'? Any rules, of any democratically organized body? I protest that you are acting tyrannically, playing fast and loose with the very foundations of our existence. I beg to resign."

Greg had a sure sense of his audience. "The Honorable Clogger at the back," he said, "whose name I have not the pleasure of recalling, offers his resignation. Does anybody second that?"

There was a full-throated yell of "Aye!" amid which the protester noisily withdrew.

What had interested me throughout this absurd, noisy, hilarious incident, was the attitude of Eustace. It might not have concerned him or his companion. His look of weary indifference to us all, to what we were saying and doing, was backed by his physical attitude: his body slumped in his chair, his hands thrust into his trouser pockets, his eyes fixed on the far wall over the heads of his audience. Another thing was this. There was a certain punctilio about dress in those days, and the Cloggers wore dinner jackets and black ties for their assemblies. Eustace had no tie. His blue shirt was open at the neck and his foxy-red tweeds were shapeless on him and frayed at the cuffs. All the same, he made me think of Uncle Arthur's remark that he would grace an Athenian thoroughfare, though perhaps he would have been more at home in Sparta than in Athens, for he was as lean and hungry-looking as a wolf.

When the Honorable Clogger had removed his presence from the back, Greg said: "Gentlemen, our late lamented Clogger Metcalfe, 'with native honor clad in naked majesty,' has been thrust forth, like his forerunner, from this Eden. Well oiled, though not more so than was his custom, he displayed his—er—talents not wisely but too well. It is perhaps regrettable that those who administer the affairs of this seat of learning should quail before the naked truth, but we must admit that their wish to draw a veil over Clogger Metcalfe is not without reason. Had his infection spread, the fauns and satyrs of Parson's Pleasure might even now be prancing and prinking along the Broad and the High, to the undoing of virtue. However, the departure of Metcalfe opens the gate to a Clogger I am especially pleased to see with us."

Greg went on, with raillery and affection, to introduce me to the meeting, and then called on me to sign the vellum roll that contained the names of the members. I didn't know many of the Cloggers, but Greg's introduction earned me a cheer as I went up to the table to shake his hand and sign my name—a cheer in which even Greta Lund joined, but not Eustace. He remained, as before, with his hands in his pockets. His eyes went over my head.

I am not given to flaring into anger, and I had, then, all the nervous-ness of a freshman; but within, I was boiling with resentment. My mind was calling Eustace every evil name I could think of: a bloody poseur, a bogus Swinburne, and a few other things worse than these. He had been hospitably received in Uncle Arthur's house; he had shared my quarters; I had picked him, stinking drunk, out of a ditch; and that he should now sit there like a blue-eyed angel whose very glance could not contaminate itself by contemplating a clod like me: well, it set my insides sizzling.

Nor was I reconciled when he got up to speak. His subject was Swedish poetry, with especial reference to what he called Strindberg's symbolic cycle *The Road to Damascus*. There were not many intellec-tuals among the Cloggers. They listened with restless courtesy for an hour. Before sitting down, Eustace said: "The translations I have given you from these great poems are my own, and I fear they amount only to feeble gleams caught from that great fire. So I think, if the chairman will permit, it would be beneficial if Miss Lund spoke some of the poems in their original tongue."

For another quarter of an hour we listened to Miss Lund. I imagine that most of the men were looking at her rather than listening to her. Certainly I was. The girl's beauty, which had startled us when she first appeared, was static, like that of a motionless slender tree. Now, as the emotions of the poems passed through her spirit—sad, heroic, romantic— she was the same tree with the wind in its branches, stirring and swaying them. We didn't understand a word of it, but we didn't need to. It was all there. She was an actress. The Cloggers gave her an ovation as she sat down, looking exhausted.

Then there was the noise of the meeting breaking up, and I was pushing out with the rest when Greg leapt down from the platform, elbowed his way to me, and took my arm. "Don't go, Chad. Eustace is expecting to meet you. Come to my rooms."

3

Greg was not living in college. He was in rooms in a narrow lane with houses on one side and on the other a crumbling college wall whose top was as frayed as Eustace's cuffs, whiskered with fern and valerian. It was a raw night. Greg and I pulled overcoats over our dinner jackets, and Eustace helped Greta into a fur coat. He himself loped along coat-less, hatless, his hands in his pockets. He had seemed glad to meet me when Greg took me into the small room at the back of the hall where the secretary of the club, with an absurd solicitude, was locking up the pair of clogs and the vellum roll. Soon he went, and we four were left together.

However well I may have managed to wear a man-of-the-world veneer, I can't pretend that inwardly I felt the calm I assumed. I don't suppose there had been a Clogger present that night who was not excited by the thought that this beautiful girl was the speaker's mistress. She hasn't much to do with this book. I never saw her after that night. She was with Eustace for about two years. Then her yearnings for the theater, from which he had snatched her, became too strong. She went back to Sweden and had a middling success as an actress. However, nothing of this was apparent to me then. My only thought was that here was Eustace with a wonderful mistress and that I was a wonderful fellow to be in such company.

Outside in the cold night, Greta took Greg's arm and they went ahead. I was, I confess, a bit apprehensive, following with Eustace. It was so long since I had seen him: he had laid hold of the beginnings of fame: his world, as this girl demonstrated, was so different from mine. He had always been able to make me feel small, and I wondered if I should be able to hold my own with him. After all, only a few months ago I was a schoolboy in Smurthwaite. But it was all right. He slipped an arm into mine and said: "Well, Chad, how is Mr. Geldersome?"

I told him and he said: "I must write to him." (But of course he never did.) "I owe him a lot."

It took us a quarter of an hour to reach Greg's rooms, and all the time Eustace kept the conversation like that. How was I settling into Oxford life? Did I miss Smurthwaite? What was I hoping to do when I went down? Didn't I find the country damned flat and uninspiring after the Yorkshire hills? It was there that I put in a question about Sweden. I supposed *that* had hills to his taste? He merely said: "I loved Lapland. That was flat enough," and then came straight back to the commonplace. Greg had told him that I had recently seen his father. How was the old man looking?

So I was to learn nothing about Eustace: about his thoughts, his travels, his work, his girl. I was the boy who had been accidentally thrown across his path for a moment of youth. I didn't matter to him one way or another. He made no inquiries about my mother. "My mother was looking very well when I was at Crossgates," I said doggedly. "Good. Good," he said. "Ah! We have arrived."

There was a welcoming fire in Greg's room, and sandwiches and glasses were on a table in front of it. Greta Lund threw her coat across a chair, sat down and kicked off her shoes, stretched her toes to the blaze. "Now we eat," she said expectantly.

"Now we drink," Eustace amended.

"You can do both," Greg laughed.

"No, thank you," said Eustace. "Have you any whisky?"

Greg brought bottles of lager beer and a bottle of whisky from a cupboard. "Help yourselves," he invited.

Eustace poured a large whisky and added a thimbleful of water. Greta got up and took it from him. "You will eat first," she said. "You will eat first or with." She held a plate of sandwiches to him.

"I do not want to eat either first or with," he said. "You eat far too much. You eat like a horse. You had a good dinner tonight."

"Yes, for once I had a good dinner, thanks to Mr. Appleby. I do not get many good dinners thanks to you. And that is because you drink too much. You drink my dinners." She turned to me and Greg. "Do I look as if I eat too many good dinners?" she appealed. "I starve. I am bone where body should be."

She didn't look it.

The old familiar tic was working in Eustace's jaw. He left her in possession of the glass and poured whisky into another, not bothering to add water. He swigged it down like milk. Then he took up her coat and held it for her to slip her arms into. "Now we'd better go," he said. "You are not fit to be in decent company.'"

"It is you who are not fit, you drunk bully," she said.

Then she began to cry, still holding the glass of whisky. Greg took it from her hand, added a lot of water, and took a sip.

"Now," he said placatingly, "let's sit down and act sensibly. Miss Lund, would you like beer with your sandwiches?"

She said she would, and she ate mightily. She cleared up the sandwiches that had been prepared for four. So occupied, she had no time for speech, and Eustace was in no mood for it. He walked about the room, his hands in his pockets, his cheeks tic-ing.

"Do eat something: Sit down, old man, and eat something," Greg urged him.

"No, Greg, really, thanks very much," he said with his deadly politeness. "I am merely waiting for Greta to take the edge off her hunger. Then we must go."

"Why go? I was looking forward to a long crack."

"Sorry, Greg. We really must be off. It's getting late."

"Late! Don't talk daft, man. Sit down. We'll see the dawn in."

But we didn't see the dawn in. Eustace had made up his mind. When Greta had finally wiped her fingers, he held out her coat again. "Another drink before you go?" Greg invited.

"No, thank you."

"Just a little one?"

"No, thank you. I drink too much."

"I will cure you," said Greta, all smiles again.

"You will not cure me. You are more likely to drive me mad. Are you ready?"

"Yes, darling. It is time for bed."

When they were gone, Greg said: "I don't often drink two whiskies one after another, Chad, but I'm having another now." He renewed his glass and lit his pipe. I poured myself a glass of lager beer and settled on the other side of the fire.

"What's the *matter* with Eustace?" Greg demanded. He was very fond of him, in a way I was not. "Damn and blast it, Chad, what's the *matter* with him?"

We talked for a long time, but found no answer to that question.

4

At the Cloggers' meeting Whitworth Rhodes's brother Bob had edged up to me and introduced himself, but there hadn't been much time for talk. He was a dark, robust-looking youth, with flaring nostrils and pebble spectacles. His blue chin had the appearance of already needing to be shaved twice a day. I saw him once or twice after that; we had tea in one another's rooms; but it wasn't till Commemoration in the following year that I had any reason to remember him. There was, indeed, a lot to remember about that Commemoration. It was the end of Greg's time at Oxford. He and Phoebe were to be married in the autumn, and it was Greg's own idea that we should make what he called a "reight do" of his farewell to the university. "Let's talk it over with Billy Pascoe," he said to me. "I'm just going to have tea with him. Come and make a third."

I was not overanxious to go. For one thing, Billy was up to the neck in mathematics and physics, subjects about which I knew nothing. I was a modern languages man. Our studies didn't give us much contact. Another thing was this. One day in that summer I had taken a punt up the river, as I often did, and poled myself into a favorite spot where willows curtained me into a green privacy. I liked to lie there on the cushions, smoking and reading, lulled by the water chuckling under the passing punts, never disturbed but rather soothed by young voices laughing, singing, arguing, as today's detachment went by of youth that had gone that way through so many centuries of summers. It was a thought that fascinated me, and sometimes I turned over the idea of a play, that would be more a pageant, a cavalcade, than a play, with so much famous dust reanimated for a moment, drifting by with girls, with friends, but all with young hopes whose statement could be made ironical against the knowledge of what, in fact, happened to them. No mile or two of water in the world was hovered over more thickly than this by illustrious ghosts ready to answer my call. My own ghost, I thought, when its time came, would be drawn back to earth more swiftly by this smell of river rottenness and mint than by anything else I could then imagine. At last the question "What do you want to *do*?" that so many people had put to me, was finding the shadow of an answer. I wanted to write plays, and I was reading little but plays, from the Big Three of the Greeks to Mr. John Galsworthy.

That day, my preoccupation with a procession of ghosts was sharply brought down to a consideration of two living beings. Unseen myself, I could see through the green curtains of my lair all that passed on the water. It was the voices that brought my head up from the book. I heard Billy Pascoe say: "It's all kickshaws and nonsense. Give me a solid Cornish pasty."

I looked through the leaves, and they were going slowly by, Billy in white flannels managing the pole, Rose Garland bending over an open tea basket, whose treasures she had evidently been displaying. "But, Billy," she said. "Meringues! Chocolate éclairs! And to talk to me of a horrid dollop of chopped meat and onion blanketed in dough!"

"The point is not what I'm talking to you *about*," Billy answered, "but simply that I'm talking to you."

Then they were out of sight, and a youth with a Magdalen blazer and a guitar soon put them out of hearing.

But they remained on my vision, looking happy. Well, had I but known it, this was something else on which time was to make an ironical comment; but I didn't know it, and suddenly the bright day was dark.

Over the mantelpiece in my rooms was Lucy Orlop's sketch of the child Rose. Rose was a child no longer. How beautiful she had looked, kneeling in the punt, the wide white hat shading her face, the curve of her back over the basket so lovely an arc! I looked at the sketch that night. What was all this about Rose Garland? Was it a self-induced obsession, arising from nothing but the propinquity of a picture? I thought of all the years I had known her, of the few times I had met her. She had never given me any reason to think that I was more than another acquaintance, casually met. At times she had been rude; never had she been more than friendly. Well, then, I asked myself, what's the matter with you? Do you *really* have any feeling for her, or is it only that this picture makes her the conveniently placed focus for the vague dreams of women—any women—that encompass young men at your time of life?

Yesterday, I should have found it difficult to answer. Now the answer had come, as the most important answers often do, without seeking.

What I had seen that afternoon convinced me that Rose and Billy were in a relationship from which I was shut out; and I suffered in the hell of that exclusion.

For a day or two I allowed myself to hope that Rose would call on me. I remembered asking her to write when I said good-by to her at Crossgates. "Oh," she had replied lightly, "I shall run down from town now and then. I shall take you in with the others." But when a week had gone by and I had not heard from her, I decided that nothing was to be expected. I kept off the river throughout that week.

5

So, when Greg suggested to me that I should join him and Billy at tea, I was not anxious to go, but I went. I had not been in Billy's rooms before, and was surprised at their splendor. The carpet on the floor, the silken curtains that a summer breeze was stirring at the windows, the porcelain of the tea service spread out for us: all had quality. The Minty wicker chairs were new, and in the bookcases rows of beautifully bound volumes made bands of color. On the mantelpiece was a contemporary photograph of Rose Garland in a silver frame. I thought of the cottage at St. Michael Pendeverel that Billy had shared with his feckless mother. I thought of Billy lighting us through the wood and of Uncle Arthur's pessimistic speculations concerning his future. I thought of a lot of things, and I said: "You do yourself proud, Billy."

"Oh, no," he said. "I don't do it. It's all done for me. The curtains and the carpet are new. This china and a lot of other stuff, including the books, come from Pentyrch. Have a look at 'em. I didn't want 'em."

I glanced at the books resplendent in many colors of leather: sets of *The Tatler* and *The Spectator*, the complete works of Thackeray and Scott, masses of stuff that one is supposed to read and rarely does.

"It was all in the library the night Rose took you there. D'you remember? The 'Thank you, Pascoe' night. Rose just took a peep and said that nobody read the things."

"How do you know?" I foolishly asked, for how could he know save in one way?

"Oh, there's not much Rose doesn't tell me," he said.

"Do you see much of her?"

"She and Miss Orlop come along now and then. The old girl *will* do this to me," he said, waving his hand round the room. "I don't want it."

"I wouldn't complain if I were you," Greg said. "I saw you on the river the other day. I envied you your flannels."

"That's another thing." He began to pour out the tea. "I don't want to be smothered."

Greg, who, I knew, had to watch his extracurricular disbursements, began to laugh. "Well, I'm nearly through here now," he said, "but I can tell you, Billy, there have been times when a bit of this sort of smothering would have had me singing the Hallelujah Chorus."

"It's all right up to a point," Billy conceded. "But with me the point's soon reached. Leave it, shall we?"

But Greg wouldn't. He whistled when Billy put two plates of gorgeous pastry onto the table. "Even the eats are ambrosia," he laughed.

Billy went red. "What the hell do you expect me to provide?" he asked. "Dollops of chopped meat and onion blanketed in dough? Yorkshire pudding and Eccles cakes?"

My cup and Greg's were filled. Billy had not yet filled his own. He picked up the delicate Rockingham shell, and I wondered for a moment whether he was about to smash it against the wall or crush it with the sort of convulsive gesture I had seen on the beach at Pendeverel when he talked of Mrs. Apreece and Michael Faraday. He was wearing flannels and a new blazer, but they didn't make any difference. I saw clearly the *farouche* boy I had known, standing on the beach, barefoot and in rags. Then his eye fell on the photograph of Rose. His whole being slowly relaxed. He put down the cup quietly and filled it. He even laughed.

"Don't tease me, Greg," he said. "I know what a fool I am and what gratitude I owe. I must get used to lovely things and thank God for them. But I tell you this"—a slight heat again touching his voice—"when Rose and I are married, we'll live on what I make *and on nothing else.*"

Greg and I looked at him in surprise. It was Greg who spoke. "Married?" he said. "Why, what's all this about, you cagey old devil? I didn't know you were engaged."

"We're not," Billy said. "But I suppose it's only a matter of time."

I had known it would happen, but that didn't make it any easier. "Congratulations, Billy," I said.

"Hardly yet," he laughed. "Greg rushed me into a most unscientific announcement. I shouldn't go into publication till the case is proved."

"What about Miss Orlop?" Greg asked. "Is the old warhorse pawing the ground and crying, 'Ha, ha! I told you so'?"

Billy said: "If she's not all for it, I'm greatly mistaken. Though, mind you," he added, "that's got nothing to do with it. This is something between me and Rose."

6

It was about a fortnight after this that I stood Greg a lunch at the Mitre. He had news for me. "Well, Eustace is on his own again."

A letter from Eustace had reached him from Italy, saying that Greta Lund had departed for Sweden. "I am not altogether sorry," Eustace wrote. "She became tiresomely anxious to see me both teetotal and famous."

"What on earth does Eustace live on?" I asked. "He hasn't a penny, has he? His few little books can't keep him."

Greg said: "Eustace's theory, which has worked all right so far, is that any man can live abroad on the strength of his native language. He moves from country to country, teaching English, doing a bit of lecturing, and so on. One thing, now he's unattached, I may be able to lure him home for my wedding. After all, I'm marrying his sister."

When Greg was gone, I took a few books and wandered down to Magdalen bridge to find a punt. It was the first time I had been able to face the river since seeing Billy Pascoe and Rose in the punt together. With a good deal of a shock, I saw that Rose herself, with Miss Orlop, was standing on the stage. I would have retreated, but Miss Orlop saw me and called to me. "Well, Chad! This is a surprise. Why is it we never see you when we come to Oxford?"

I could have answered that rudely enough; but I let it go, shook hands with her and Rose, and asked if she wished to hire a punt.

"I can't manage a punt," she said. "Neither can Rose. I was going to hire a rowing boat. I think I could manage that. But if you're going in a punt, would you be a dear and take Rose? I'll rest in our rooms. It's so hot."

"Why, where's Billy?'" I couldn't help asking.

"We expected Billy at half-past two," Miss Orlop said. "It's now a quarter to three. I must have a word with Billy about this."

I didn't like the sound of that. "He'd have been here if he could," I said. "He's working very hard. All sorts of things could have cropped up to detain him. He's not a loafer like me, you know."

"Well, if you will be so kind," she said.

Rose was wearing the flimsy-textured clothes of that time, flowing and airy. The dress was dusky red, the wide hat white with crimson roses. I didn't feel that I was being kind to anyone but myself. I hired a rowing boat and helped her in.

We had pushed off and I had taken a dozen strokes with the oars when I saw Billy Pascoe run down to the landing stage and join Miss Orlop. Rose, with the rudder lines in her hands, had her back to him. I stopped the way on the boat, and said: "There's Billy. Shall I go back?"

Rose did not look round. "If you keep on rowing," she said, "I can steer. Otherwise, I can't. Don't let's be a nuisance on the river."

Billy was too far away for me to see his face clearly, but I could imagine it. "Miss Orlop is standing there with Billy," I said. "I'm sure she is expecting us to turn back. She must know that I've seen Billy arrive."

"Please go on," Rose said; and as I dipped the oars again, she added, as if to give the conversation another line: "Why did you choose a rowing boat instead of a punt? We have always used a punt."

Nevertheless, she was skillful enough in a boat. She took me smoothly through the traffic that was thick on that part of the river.

"I had an idea," I said, "that I'd like to recreate a moment of the past."

"Well, you can't do it," she said pedantically. "The past is the past and how can you recreate it? You can only try to make a moment of the present resemble something you have known. And if you're thinking of the moment when you took me out in a boat at St. Michael Pendeverel, this moment is no more like that than chalk is like cheese."

If she had wanted to take my thoughts off Billy, she had succeeded. Anyway, he was now out of sight.

"Oh, that was a dreadful old tub my father built," I said, "and this is a nice little boat. We were on the sea, and now we are on the river. You were in a bad temper and you were sick just because you had decided to be. Now you seem good-tempered enough and you will not be sick. But a point of resemblance remains. We are in a boat together."

I had nothing to do but row. All the important work was hers. So I could sit there, as I could not have done in a punt, and take my fill of looking at her. Presently, she dropped her eyes under my impolite stare. A light blush stained her cheeks.

"When we went out at Pendeverel," I said, "you insisted on looking at the shore. That meant that you had your back to me. This is much more agreeable."

"Please don't keep on reminding me of that beastly child," she commanded.

"Did you ever tell Billy of our disastrous voyage?"

"Why should I?"

"Well, you told him of the night when you were my guide to the splendors of Pentyrch."

It had rankled—the thought of her and Billy Pascoe turning over the memories of that unfortunate night.

"When I'm with Billy," she said, "I must talk about something. I can't sit like a deaf-mute. Naturally, we occasionally speak of the places and people we have in common. Why he should pass our remarks on to a third person I don't understand."

This is one of the moments I remember forever. The blush of slight embarrassment that had touched her cheeks darkened to a red of anger. A punt which I could not see, but could hear, was approaching us, and to avoid it she gave the rudder lines a violent jerk. The boat swerved almost into the bank before settling to its course again. Her moment of agitation passed; she was in control of herself, as of the boat; and she said: "I'm sorry. That was a shocking exhibition." A most revealing one, anyway, I thought. In that moment I was certain in my bones that she no more cared for Billy Pascoe than for the man in the moon.

I was happy. I said nothing. I rowed lazily along, on water that now had little traffic. The sun of the late summer afternoon blazed down, dancing on the ripples that the oars created. I watched the voles swimming, and the cows that spraddled down inclines of broken bank to stand knee-deep in the water, their tails swishing at the plaguy flies. The swallows flew low, and the smell of the mint was loosed by the day's heat. Rose dangled a hand overboard, drawing her fingers through the water. She seemed to have forgotten the small significant explosion. Presently she said: "Chad, I've never enjoyed the river more. How far are we going?"

"As far as you will," I said.

"I should like some tea. Do you mind?"

"I should like some too. When are you due back?"

"Why should I be due back? *Du*, past participle of the verb *devoir*. Don't you ever get tired of doing what is laid down, Chad?"

"Often and often and often."

"Find me a nice tea place. I'll go back for once when I feel like it."

What is the matter with you, I wondered? Has something suddenly opened your eyes, as well as mine?

There was no one else in the tea garden. It was the simple lawn of a cottage. From the table we could look down at the water sliding by, and at our boat tied to a willow whose green hair drooped upon the seats. I knew the place. "You can get honeycombs here," I told her.

"Bring me a honeycomb."

I brought her a honeycomb, and one for myself, and I watched her white teeth crunch the drenched wax. We ate bread and butter and drank tea. On two sides of the table mauve asters were blooming.

> I am come into the garden, my sister, my bride;
> I have eaten my honeycomb with my honey.

The peace could not have been deeper. The words of the Song of Songs droned in my head and I thought of the choirboy in Smurthwaite church and of Mr. Hawke and Phoebe.

"Are you going to Greg's wedding?"

"Oh, yes," she said with a laugh. "I'm cast for an important role. Phoebe has asked me to be a bridesmaid."

She pulled off her white rose-trimmed hat and threw it to the ground. Her dark hair was in tendrils round her ears.

"Perhaps you will at last meet Eustace. Greg is inviting him to come."

She sat with her hands folded in her lap, looking at the river, where the swallows seemed to be feeding by suction, flying open-mouthed among the midges. She said:

> And the hiss of the kiss of the whetted scythe,
> The kiss of death for the swathe betrayed,
> Falling with coronet disarrayed
> Of marguerite, poppy, sorrel and clover.

They were Eustace's lines. "You like that?" I asked.

"I feel I know a lot about him."

"But really you know very little about him."

She looked at me oddly. "Are you hoping I'll dislike the rest?"

"Well," I said, "Eustace is a strange person. Never happy. Never satisfied. New countries. New women." I told her about Greta Lund.

"Light your pipe, Chad," she said. "The midges are a nuisance."

I lit my pipe. "Now let's go," she said. "Thank you for my honeycomb."

I paid the bill, helped her into the boat, and began to turn the bows back toward Oxford.

"No," she said. "Let's go on."

"We shall be late back."

"Let's go on."

So we went on, into less and less frequented water; and after a time she said: "I know all about Greta Lund. Billy told me."

"So you see," I said with a laugh. "Eustace is a danger to all virgins."

"Men can't help what they seek," she said. "Billy Pascoe, confronted with a chunk of matter, thinks that everything worth knowing is somehow mysteriously contained within it. He'll spend his life smashing it to bits, and the bits to bits, and God knows what specters he'll start up out of it at last. From what I know of Eustace Hawke, I'd say he was the other way about—that he must range out, not in. I don't suppose he'll ever find what he wants, and I don't suppose either that you'll ever stop him looking for it, not if a score of Greta Lunds are picked up, weighed, and found wanting."

I laughed. "I'm fortunate that I don't come within the scope of your analysis," I said.

"How could you, Chad?" she asked. "I know nothing about you. Except," she added magnanimously after a pause, "that I have found you this afternoon better company than I expected. Very soothing."

"Thank you. You seem to be cutting the teeth of experience. To be accepted as a soothing powder is something."

A light mist was spreading on the fields and the river, and a curl of new moon was following the sun toward its setting.

"Please, Chad," she said, "don't speak as though you were hurt. It's true, isn't it, that we know next to nothing about one another?"

It didn't seem to be my own voice that said: "You may know very little about me, but I know this about you—I would die for you."

"Oh, Chad!"

It was spoken in a voice of such pity and surprise that I knew her mind had never before even glimpsed the thought of me as a lover. I stopped rowing. She let go the rudder lines, and the boat drifted in toward the bank. She leaned forward and laid a hand on mine. "I'm so sorry, Chad," she said.

I took the hand and would have held it, but she drew it back. "No. Please no," she said.

We were quite alone on the river. It was so quiet that you could hear the minute slap of the water on the bows and the breathing of cattle beyond a hedge. How long our silence lasted I don't know, but there we sat with all the distance of the world between us in the length of the boat, till I said: "You don't want Billy Pascoe. I know that."

She pardoned it. She looked at me and sighed. "No," she said. "You're right about that."

Unreasonably, I said: "Billy deserves better treatment. I wonder if you know how sensitive he is?"

To my horror, tears gathered in her eyes and began to roll down her cheeks, as I had watched them so long ago as we knelt by the fireplace at Pentyrch. "Let's go back," she said. "I'm feeling rather cold." She began to shiver a little. I shook out a folded rug that I had been sitting on and put it round her shoulders. She thanked me, and I began to row quickly home. "This isn't the trial eights," she said. "Go slowly, Chad. I've got a lot to think about."

I fought down my angry ardor and slowed the boat.

"What should I do about Billy?" she asked. "I don't need to be told how sensitive he is."

There was nothing I could say to that; and presently she went on, not so much speaking to me as seeming to analyze the situation for her own clear thinking: "Really, you know nothing about it. How could you? We've met, you and I, off and on, for years. In all those years Billy has been there: at Pentyrch, in London, during holidays on the Continent. You don't know Billy as I do. When you knew him day by day you were nothing but children. All the time when he was becoming a man and I was becoming a woman we were together. I've never known any other man so well, or he any other woman. We never liked the same things. I remember a day in Italy. My mother had taken us through a gallery in the morning, and she proposed to take us through another in the afternoon. Billy came all right: he is very obedient; but he said to me aside: 'Well—for Christ's sake! More madonnas!' "

I was glad to see that the reminiscence permitted her a smile. "Now Greg Appleby isn't like that," she said. "I know that economics and what he calls political science are his thing. But one day, when Phoebe was down here, he took us both on the river, and he spouted reams of Homer in Greek. We didn't understand a word of it, but we loved it. And so did he. Of course, Phoebe would have loved it if he'd been talking Hottentot, but then she loves Greg. Do you see?"

I saw clearly enough; and I noted, too, that she seemed to have been often in Oxford without my knowing of it.

The swallows were gone. The sun with its attendant slip of moon had disappeared. The western sky was a fudge of pearl gray and smoky red, and in the fields the mist thickened. I could have wept for her when she said: "You see how it is, Chad. It's not that he despises everything that makes life interesting and significant and purposeful for me. He doesn't consider such things long enough or deeply enough even to despise them. They just don't exist for him. If his studies make it necessary for him to learn Greek, or anything else, he'll learn it, but only as he'd learn to ride a bicycle in order to get somewhere. He'd never want to spout it to a girl in a boat."

I thought of her bending over the basket in the punt—the basket full of dainties—and of Billy standing upright, watching her with the dripping pole in his hands. "All nonsense and kickshaws," I said aloud.

"Yes, that's it," she said; and then looked at me, startled.

"I couldn't help overhearing. I was in a punt when you and Billy went by. I am on the river occasionally, you know," I said, reproaching her for the first time for that broken promise. "Usually alone."

"You would have been alone today," she said, "if Billy had been a few moments earlier."

I fished shamelessly. "Are you glad you didn't turn back?"

She took it lightly. "Chad, you're a great dear, and I loved eating honeycomb with the handsomest man in Oxford."

"You must do it again."

"Perhaps I shall."

"And now you must face your mother. She waved to us to return. She will be annoyed that we did not."

"I didn't see her. My back was to her."

"But I saw her."

"Yes. And said nothing to me about it. You wanted me to yourself."

"That's your story?"

"Yes."

We were nearing Oxford, and there was one more thing I wanted to say to her. "Seriously, will your mother be annoyed?"

"A little, I expect. But I'll get round it. She looks pretty formidable to outsiders, but she's never very heavy with me."

"Is she pushing Billy down your throat?"

She looked at me aghast. But I had been determined to say it the most brutal and unmistakable way.

It was a long time before she said: "I don't think that's putting it very fairly. My mother loves me."

"I shouldn't call that an answer," I said ruthlessly.

The trees were closing in on the water. It was quite dark. Again after a long considering pause, she said: "My mother thinks a lot of Billy, you know. It's a very odd relationship. She almost looks on him as something she created out of nothing."

"She didn't do that," I said firmly, "and Billy would be the last man to believe that she did."

"She certainly likes us to be together, and creates occasions for it," Rose said.

I was almost overwhelmed by a sense of danger, of impending disaster. That Billy wanted to marry Rose I had no doubt. What his feeling would be if he sensed any pressure I wondered. I recalled his words to me and Greg: "When Rose and I are married, we'll live on what I make, *and on nothing else*." Already that suggested a sense of meshes that he wanted to cut.

We were approaching the landing stage at Magdalen bridge, and Rose threw off the whole discussion. "For heaven's sake," she said, "remove these cerements. I must look like a black widow."

I took the rug from her shoulders, recalling the day when my father had died, and it was she who put rugs about me, lying on cushions on the Pentyrch lawn. But the night was chill, and I insisted after all that she should keep it on. I tipped the boatman heavily and told him I'd bring the rug back first thing in the morning. I hurried her through the streets to the rooms where she and her mother were staying, and we had nothing more to say beyond the politeness of good-night.

7

I met May Ingleby on the night of the Commemoration Ball. Bob Rhodes brought her up to me and said: "Boothroyd, will you look after a Lancashire lass for a moment or two? May Ingleby—Chad Boothroyd." Then off he went toward a girl in orange silk. It was pretty impudent, I thought. What made me dislike May Ingleby at sight was that she was so much like Rose Garland. She had no right to be. She had the same dark hair, and skin that gave the sense of full-blooded life, and eyes of deep blue. But at the same time, everything that was Rose Garland was missing. Miss Ingleby was like an art student's copy of a masterpiece. Everything was there: everything except something that could never be copied, never repeated. For me, anyhow. You fake, I thought, looking at May Ingleby. I felt like suicide. The wind that had been increasing all the evening shook the vast marquee. The candlelit lanterns swayed, and rain swished across the canvas like a rushing wing.

"Isn't it an awful night?" Miss Ingleby said; and her voice was not like Rose Garland's. It was thin, complaining.

You will never know, I thought, how awful this night is.

I could see Greg and Phoebe dancing. The red carnation he was wearing was crushed between their breasts, and I was sure they knew nothing of the storm, that they didn't hear the rain. Their eyes were eating one another. Should I break into their world apart, tell them what I had seen? No.

"You seem very moody, Mr. Boothroyd," Miss Ingleby said. "Can I help to amuse you?"

It was something a tart had once said to me, trying to pick me up in Hyde Park. I looked at this simulacrum with horror. But I was sure she was innocent of any meaning. Still, I thought, *you* amuse me? Tonight of all nights? I gave a harsh laugh and said: "Shall we see if I can find you a drink?"

It was all very pretty; no expense or effort had been spared. Round the dancing floor streams flowed in troughs of lead, and here and there fountains leapt. The musicians were playing "The Blue Danube" in a bower of blossom. A good enough effort at a night's fairyland.

"Actually," Miss Ingleby said, "a drink is what I've set my heart on."

Well, well, we mustn't break your important heart. Let us drink. She was wearing crimson silk and gold shoes, and had a crimson rose pinned above her ear.

We went through the canvas corridor to the supper marquee. It was crowded with girls and youths, a lot of them pretty well lit up by now, and Billy Pascoe was standing by himself with a glass in his hand. It was the first time I had seen Billy in full-fig evening clothes. He looked distinguished: dark and lean, and, even in that crowd, he wore his habitual isolation. I brushed past him, and asked: "Not dancing, Billy?"

"You know I don't dance," he said. "Seen anything of Rose?"

"Not for some time."

I was tempted to tell him what I had seen; but what the hell, I thought. There's nothing to be done about it now. Let them go. Give them time.

Billy put down his glass. "I'll see if she's dancing," he said.

I went back to Miss Ingleby, carrying a tray laden with jellies and trifles and amber wine. We sat at a small table, our knees touching. She did not try to take her knees away. "They do you well here, don't they?" she asked, as though we were patronizing Lyons or the A.B.C.

"Yes," I said. "Here, Miss Ingleby, you may have

> *Jellies soother than the creamy curd,*
> *And lucent syrops, tinct with cinnamon;*
> *Manna and dates, in argosy transferr'd*
> *From Fez; and spiced dainties, every one,*
> *From silken Samarcand to cedar'd Lebanon."*

"You are a funny one, Mr. Boothroyd," she said. "Are you a little bit tight?"

I took a swig of wine and said: "Don't you know your Keats, Miss Ingleby? Years ago, on a snowy night in Yorkshire, I read that poem, and I rushed to the next room to share it with a friend. A most peculiar friend, Miss Ingleby. He knew the poem, and loved it, and talked to me about it, and he recited some lines from the last stanza:

> *And they are gone: aye, ages long ago*
> *These lovers fled away into the storm.*

What would you do, Miss Ingleby, if you saw a pair of lovers flee away into the storm?"

She giggled. "You *are* tight." Her knees pressed mine.

"Your kneecaps tell me that you're a woman of the world," I said. "What would you do?"

"Well, actually, what can you do," she asked, "except hope they don't get too wet?"

"Yes, indeed. What more than that can one hope? One couldn't hope, I suppose, that they'd be very, very happy?"

"Well, that's up to them, isn't it?" Miss Ingleby said.

Greg and Phoebe came in. Phoebe looked almost beautiful. "Seen anything of Rose?" Greg asked. "Billy's looking for her."

"No."

While Greg went to the buffet Phoebe sat with us. "This is May Ingleby, Phoebe, a Lancashire lass. This is Phoebe Hawke."

Phoebe was seeing visions that night. She didn't seem to notice Miss Ingleby. "Isn't it being a wonderful night, Chad?" she said.

"It is a night that will be ever memorable. I must dance with you, Phoebe. Now, at once, before Greg comes back. I wouldn't dare to ask him to spare you for five minutes."

Phoebe got up, laughing. "All right," she said. "But don't expect much. I'm nearly dead on my feet already."

I bowed to Miss Ingleby. "You will excuse me for a few moments? If the robust young economist returns from the buffet, entertain him with your dark enigmatic conversation."

Miss Ingleby giggled and Phoebe laughed. "Why have you gone and got tight, Chad?" she asked as we moved toward the dance floor.

"Because two young lovers have fled into the storm."

"I know," Phoebe said.

"You *know!*"

"Yes."

That shocked me cold sober.

There was no dancing. A maniac from Merton had thrown some celluloid balls onto the jet of one of the fountains. They were tossing and falling, and he was shooting at them with an airgun. A moment ago the spectacle of the dancers running for cover would have amused me; but I was so sober that I walked up to the man and knocked him flat. Three friends bore him out. "*Mesdames, Messieurs,*" I invited, "*reprenez la danse.*" The band began to play.

"So you knew?" I said to Phoebe.

"Yes. After all, haven't you been expecting it?"

8

I suppose I had. The answer that Greg received to his letter inviting Eustace to the wedding was Eustace himself. He arrived in Oxford a week before the Commemoration Ball. He had grown a small fair mustache and an imperial. I decided that he was trying to look like Strindberg. But he didn't look mad, as Strindberg does in all his pictures. He looked, to me, intolerably attractive. He put up in Greg's rooms. It was to be a glorious time, a time, we told ourselves, we would all remember—these last few days before the ball, that was to be followed so soon by Phoebe's marriage to Greg. For once, Miss Orlop's vigilance was relaxed. Not that she intended it. She was to have stayed with Rose and Phoebe at the Mitre, but an attack of pleurisy kept her in Bayswater.

Now, when it seems to be literally "ages long ago" since those lovers fled into the storm—even now there is much that I can only guess at about those few days. The weather was wonderful, and none of us except Billy Pascoe did a stroke of work. I imagine he rejoiced at Miss Orlop's absence. There was no one to bid him relax, take it easy for once, get on the river with Rose. He was not with us on our joint outings. The five of us would take a punt and be out all day. I don't remember Eustace ever being so lighthearted as he was then. He left all the work with the pole to me and Greg, and he would sit on a pile of cushions strumming a gaily ribboned guitar and singing old songs. We would land, and eat in the autumn fields, and someone would speak a poem, and someone another, and it was while we were doing that one day and Eustace was speaking the "Ode to Autumn," that he came to the words "Thy hair soft-lifted by the winnowing wind," and his hand reached out and lifted Rose's hair. We were all lying, staring up into the milky blue sky, and with a look askance, I saw that his hand remained in Rose's hair and that they had both closed their eyes and, without sight, were together, the hand and arm an isthmus between gladly connected territories.

And on one of those excursions we came to the garden where Rose and I had eaten honeycomb, and she cried: "Let us stop here. They have wonderful honey," and my face must have given a wince of pain. Cannot even that, I thought, be something between her and me, unshared? She must have seen and understood, for at once she said: "No, no. Let's go on. It's far too early for tea." And that evening, when Greg and Eustace had left us, and I walked the two girls back to the Mitre, she said: "I'll always remember the day we ate honeycomb, Chad," and kissed me.

Well, that is the sort of week it was, with me feeling more and more the unwanted odd man out, and Billy Pascoe blindly pegging away in his labyrinth. I felt badly about Billy, and one day looked him up and said: "Why don't you chuck it for a day, Billy? Come on the river this afternoon."

"No, Chad. There's so much I must do before this term ends. Once the vacation's on us I shan't be able to do much. Miss Orlop's set on trotting me and Rose round the Continent again. Tell you something, Chad. I hate the bloody Continent—every rod, pole or perch of it."

He was as unsuspecting as a nest of field mice with the scythe bearing down. "For God's sake wake up, you fool," I wanted to shout; but I didn't. I went to the pastry cook's to buy my contribution to the afternoon's feast. That was the day when we were out so late that we saw the great copper gong of the moon suspended over the misty meadows. Greg and Phoebe had wandered off, leaving the three of us in the punt; and then, without a word, Eustace and Rose got out and went another way. The punt was tied to a tree, and I lay full length in it, miserable to the marrow, looking up through the leaves at the sky washed with the light of that great moon. I must have lain there for an hour before Rose and Eustace came back. He had tangled a wreath of bryony in her hair. She was wearing such a wreath when first I saw her as a child. But she was no child now. They walked as though they were drunk, holding one another up.

Well, I knew all this about those few days, but it was not till later that I learned something of what happened on the night of the ball.

Why did they bother to come at all? Since Eustace wanted to take her away, why didn't they go and have done with it? I suppose he loved to heighten an occasion with drama; and so, though she must have known they would go, she did not know it was to be then. But that is how he had arranged it. The first-class tickets for London were in his pocket. The cab was waiting in a dark lane. All I saw was a dance end, and Rose stand almost fainting in his arms. He must have said: "Now! Now!" or some such words, and they stumbled away together. They parted for a moment, and presently I saw her return with her cloak, and stand waiting, looking about her with a wild rapture on her face. Red rosebuds lay across her head from ear to ear. Then Eustace came striding swiftly, wearing a black cloak that had silver lionheads for a clasp. She ran toward him, holding out her hands as though they had been parted for an eternity. The canvas shuddered under a buffet of the wind, and you could hear the rain hissing down and the dance music wailing. Eustace tore the cloak from his shoulders, the scarlet lining flashing, and those wings of black and red, falling upon the roses she wore, was the last I saw. Eustace lifted a flap of canvas, and they ran through.

The swift event paralyzed me. I stood rooted there for moments, and then I followed, lifting the canvas and shouting: "Rose! Eustace!"

The rain was falling; the wind was blowing; and, looking up, I saw the moon being bandied about like a slut among the ragged cohorts of the clouds.

9

"So you know?" I said to Phoebe.

She took my arm and led me to the chairs on the edge of the dance floor. We sat down, isolated by our thoughts from the music and the laughter and the swish of colored silks. What her thoughts were, God knows. I told myself again that she looked, tonight, almost beautiful, and she looked, too, full of feminine wisdom.

"You mustn't say that I saw it," she said, "and I shall not say that you saw it. After all, Chad, anybody with an eye in his head must have seen it all through the last few days. There was nothing whatever that anyone could have done about it. If it hadn't been now, it would have been soon."

"For you," I said, "Eustace can do no wrong."

She considered that for a moment, turning round and round the ring that Greg had given her. She had drawn off her long white gloves. As if arriving at the end of a process of thought, she said: "I don't think that is so. But I don't think he has done wrong tonight."

"What about Billy? Hasn't *he* been wronged?"

She looked at me with her disturbing wise eyes. "Would *you* have bothered about Billy?"

"What have I to do with it?"

She laid her hand on my sleeve. I looked down at the white skin, the flashing diamond, on the black cloth. "Don't pretend," she said quietly.

I was aware of tears in my eyes. "Oh, Chad!" she said. "Dear Chad! I'm so sorry."

After a while she said: "Try not to think too hardly of Eustace. Or of Rose. I'd have done it myself for Greg. Not," she added, with a smile, "that Greg is a Lochinvar. He doesn't rush through the night. He stands rooted in it like an oak. I'm so lucky," she ended simply, "because that's how I like it. But everybody's not like me."

Then Greg came toward us. "What are you two up to? Your drinks are waiting. And Miss Ingleby is asking: 'What's happened to my young man?'"

"You see, Chad," Phoebe said with a hint of mockery, "life is full of compensations."

We went back to the buffet, and presently Greg and Phoebe returned to the dance floor, leaving me alone with Miss Ingleby.

"I'd have been so lonely without you," she said. "Actually, a man from Worcester invited me, and then he introduced me to Mr. Rhodes, and then Mr. Rhodes introduced me to you."

"What college are you at?" I asked.

"Oh, I'm not at any college. I'm at a commercial school. And then I met this man from Worcester."

It sounded a familiar story.

"Let's dance."

"Now that's something I *can* do," she said.

She was right. That was something she could do. She danced divinely. We danced the dawn in. I remember seeing Billy Pascoe's searching eye on the edge of the dance and then I saw him no more. I remember Greg taking Phoebe away, and the dancers thinning, and someone announcing that it was a beautiful morning. I had not noticed that the wind had dropped, the rain ceased. I stood there with my arms round May Ingleby and smiled at her. I was grateful to her. She had danced me through the horror of the night. Dancing, she was not talkative. She gave herself to the business with a total absorption, carrying me with her into the world of physical rhythm that she inhabited like a native.

And so I smiled my gratitude, and she smiled back, and said a little ruefully: "Well, Mr. Boothroyd, I suppose that's that. Thank you for a lovely time."

"Thank *you*, Miss Ingleby," I said. "I had better see you home."

Like an obedient child, she went off, as in response to a command, to find her cloak. She looked tired now, and forlorn; and damn it all, I thought, you can't let the girl go like that, as though you had battened all night on her youth and vitality, using them to cushion the blow, to help you down the steps to Lethe, and then throw her out like something that has served its casual turn. So I got my coat and was waiting for her, and I said, when we were in the open air: "How lovely it is now, after that dreadful night. Would you like to come on the river?"

"I'd love that, Mr. Boothroyd," she said, "but, O-o I *am* hungry!"

I ran back and salved a couple of sandwiches, wan survivors of the night's siege. "Eat these," I said, "for a stay-bit. I shall find you a decent breakfast presently."

She laughed at that northern "stay-bit," and began at once to munch contentedly. "Doesn't everything always seem strange and quiet," she said, "when everything's all over?"

You don't know what you're saying, I thought. You don't know how spectral-strange and quiet this morning light looks to me on these old tufted walls and gray buildings and rain-glistered pavements now that everything's all over. I wondered what Billy was doing, what Greg was about now that he had discovered that Rose and Eustace were missing.

"Shan't we look an odd pair on the river at this time of morning in these?" May giggled, indicating her trailing clothes.

"We're not on the river yet," I told her, "and after a Commem Ball the river will see odder sights than we shall afford. We shall be lucky if we find a punt."

But we did. She looked tired, and I made her lie down on the cushions. I put a cushion under her head and wrapped rugs round her. "Now take it easy," I said. "Go to sleep, if you want to."

And go to sleep she did, almost as soon as she was stretched there. I looked back at her now and then, at the dark lashes on her cheeks, her mouth a little open, her small white teeth. I wondered if Rose, sleeping, looked like that? I wondered if Rose was sleeping now, and then I was stabbed by a horrid vision of two faces on a pillow: Rose's dark and flushed, Eustace's pale and fair, both satiated. I dug the pole fiercely into the ooze, and did not look back again.

There were, indeed, odd sights on the river that morning, and untimely music, and squeals from behind willow curtains; and I poled through it all to quiet water flowing among the fields that smoked gently under the warmth of the strengthening sun; and the cattle were lumbering to their feet and looking dazed to the miracle in the east, and the skylarks were high and clear. It was the redemptive end of a symphony that had been violence and disaster.

May Ingleby woke as the punt grated against the homemade landing stage of the tea garden where I had given Rose Garland a honey-comb. "Hello, Mr. Boothroyd," she said, sitting up and rubbing her eyes like a child. She didn't look tired any more. She looked rosy, as dewy as the morning.

"Would it be rude of me to ask how old you are?"

"Eighteen last week," she said. "I've been having such wonderful dreams."

I didn't ask what her dreams had been. I tied up the punt and helped her out. They were just stirring in the cottage whose chimney was sending up a wavering curl of blue. They didn't seem too glad to see me, but I used the Boothroyd charm, and that, with a call upon extra-curricular disbursements, brought us tea and toast, thick rashers of fried ham and eggs. We ate at the table overlooking the river. The mauve asters had their drenched and battered heads spotted with dirt.

"This is the first time I've ever been up all night with a young gentleman and had breakfast with him," Miss Ingleby said.

"Now you know," I said, "through what perils a girl can come unscathed."

"It's not as if I was at a college. Young gentlemen don't seem to think the same of you if you're not at a college. My mother likes to say I'm at Oxford, and in a sense I am, but not actually, am I?"

She had a prattling innocence that stirred my pity.

"Never mind all that," I said. "Just enjoy your breakfast."

"Oh, I shall do that, I promise you."

And now, I thought, as we got into the punt once more, back to Oxford, where by now the bomb has surely burst; back to the feigned innocence and ignorance, back to abetting Phoebe in knowing nothing —nothing whatever.

I parted from May at Magdalen bridge. "Thank you ever so much, Mr. Boothroyd," she said, tendering me her hand very prettily. "You've been ever so considerate."

10

And so the marriage of Greg and Phoebe was a quiet family affair. Miss Orlop, as one would expect, did not come, though it had been arranged that she should accompany the bridesmaid Rose. I don't remember what she did that autumn, but she didn't go abroad with Billy Pascoe. As soon as term was over, Billy disappeared as completely as Rose and Eustace had done. I had sounded him on his intentions, hoping I might persuade him to come to Smurthwaite with me, for I knew he was desperately poor. He was in his most *farouche* mood. "I've cleaned boots for a living before now, and I can do it again if necessary." Perhaps he did. I don't know.

I forget who the bridesmaid was, but I was Greg's best man, and old Hawke took the service. It was a decorous occasion, passing off more or less in accordance with instructions handed to me by Greg:

Nuptials of Phoebe Hawke, Spinster of this Parish, and Gregory Appleby, Lecturer in Economics at the University of Manchester.

At the wedding feast no one shall say, "May all your troubles be little ones."

No confetti shall be thrown; no hailstorms of rice shall descend; no boots and/or shoes shall be attached to any vehicle; nor shall a placard bearing the words "Just Married" be publicly displayed.

Tears shall not be shed, nor shall the married couple be treated in any other way than as fully reasonable people taking a fully reasonable step.

It is forbidden that the organist shall play "The Wedding March" or that the congregation shall sing "The Voice That Breathed o'er Eden."

By Order, ARTHUR J. GELDERSOME, *Town Clerk*

Arthur J. Geldersome was present, and I remember that he and I, while the few others were still at the marriage feast, walked down the long hill to the railway station and there awaited Mr. and Mrs. Gregory Appleby who were to spend a night in London and then go on to the Lake District. Almost as soon as we were there, they arrived in a trap driven by a friendly farmer. It was all nicely timed to avoid the fuss of farewells. The train pulled in as they reached the station; they hopped aboard with their few bits of luggage, and before I could wink the tail of the train was disappearing round a bend. I felt suddenly desolate and forlorn. Greg, Phoebe, Rose, Eustace. Who could believe that a few weeks ago we were all together, gay, careless— But I broke off that line of thought, knowing that I alone of the five of us had chosen to shut his eyes, to ignore what was written large as life.

The farmer who had brought Phoebe and Greg to the station gave me and Uncle Arthur a lift up the hill as far as the duckpond at the crossroads. We walked the short distance to the rectory. We did not go in at once but strolled through the garden to the bastion that overlooked the noble sweep of country below, blue with the haze of autumn. Uncle Arthur took off his silk hat and laid it reverently on the wall—the same hat, I was sure, that I had with wonder seen him produce so long ago at Pendeverel.

"Well, Chad," he said, *"fugaces labuntur anni.* One year of your university course is run."

Yes, indeed, I thought. A year ago I was standing here, with the strange, exciting experience all before me, and I asked Rose Garland if she would write to me.

"It's been a strange year," I said. "A lot has changed."

"Yes," he said, reading what seemed my meaning. "Phoebe and young Appleby. I've watched them both grow from children. Now fullness of life comes for them. That's how it is, Chad. Life comes and life goes. On the morning I left home to come here, my dear Madeleine died in my arms. I haven't mentioned this before. I didn't want to cast a gloom over the happy occasion."

It sounded so disproportionate to all that was in my heart that I turned sharply to see if he was joking. But his eyes were misted with tears. "Stay here," he said, "while I break the news to your mother. Perhaps I should tell Hawke, too. He knew Madeleine well."

CHAPTER SIX

I

I WAS twenty-two when I left Oxford in 1911. I had been there for four years. It was neither a mania nor an aptitude for scholarship that kept me there for the extra year. I stayed because I was lazily content and afraid of getting outside the enchanted groove in which I found myself. Without Greg and Billy Pascoe I was lonely enough, but I got hold of some good rooms when I moved out of college, and I made myself comfortable. Greg had settled down to his lectureship in Manchester and Billy was at Cambridge. I don't know to this day how Billy spent the long vacation following Rose's disappearance, but he at last turned up at Miss Orlop's place in Bayswater, cried on her bosom, I suppose, and became once more tucked under her wing. I knew that he had for a long time thought Oxford not the place for a physics man; and now he was at Cambridge. This meant that he had given up his scholarship and that someone was paying his fees in full. I didn't need to be told who that was. But Billy didn't write to me, and I had not seen Miss Orlop since the day she asked me to take Rose on the river.

I seem to date everything from the night of Rose's disappearance. And how could it reasonably be otherwise? That was the first event in my life that had seized me and shaken me to the roots; nothing that has happened to me since has had so disintegrating an effect. And so here I am writing that it was a year after Rose's disappearance that my mother rejoined Uncle Arthur at Smurthwaite. I was spending my holiday with him, and it was almost possible to imagine that old times had come back, for Greg and Phoebe were staying at Appleby's farm. But they were not riding bareback ponies now: Phoebe was swollen with their first child. Greg and I did a lot of walking together; and it was on a late September afternoon, when we had walked into Smurthwaite from the farm, that we heard of Mr. Hawke's death. Uncle Arthur was standing in the hall, holding the receiver of the telephone that he had lately had installed. He was staring stupidly before him, and I got the impression that he had finished talking for some time and was unaware that he had not put down the instrument. When we entered, he dropped it onto its hook alongside the glass case that contained the mummified remains of poor Madeleine. There she was, ghastly and glassy-eyed, one slender paw upraised, wearing a coat of the yellow that in life had so become her. Uncle Arthur was as glassy-eyed as she.

"Why, Mr. Geldersome—anything wrong?" Greg asked with understandable alarm.

"Phoebe's father—suicide," Uncle Arthur whispered.

"My God!" Greg said, his first thought for his wife. "Phoebe mustn't know—not now."

Uncle Arthur's account was incoherent, and that, I guessed, was because my mother's had been. As though his presence with Phoebe could prevent this and any other ill from touching her, Greg went back home at once. Uncle Arthur, too, reacted characteristically. As, when my father had died, he had preached the importance of sustaining the body in order to support the blows that fell upon the spirit, so now, when the shock of the announcement had passed off a little and a journey to Crossgates lay before him, he said: "We must dine at the Dragon."

We did, and this time he did not deny me the Bristol Milk. With our hearty meal we shared a bottle of Chambertin, and we had cognac with our coffee. "Now," he said, lighting a cigar as we started on our homeward way, "that's better. We can't expect a good head of spiritual steam, Chad, till we've stoked the fires of the body. The fakirs and anchorites may tell you a different tale. But don't believe 'em, my boy. Your Uncle Arthur knows what he's talking about."

2

What had happened at Crossgates was simple enough. I had seen, when I was there for the wedding, how hardly Mr. Hawke had taken his son's defection. It would have been better if there had never been a question of Eustace's coming. The expectation of seeing his son after so long and so obviously deliberate an absence had raised the old man's spirits high, and the bump, when it came, was proportionately severe. Neither he nor my mother knew that Rose Garland was concerned; and it was Phoebe, managing matters as usual, who drilled it into me and Greg that they must not know. To them, it was just another of

151

Eustace's vagaries. There was an extraordinary moment during the wedding service when Greg and Phoebe stood with joined hands and Mr. Hawke said to Greg: "Repeat after me. I, Eustace, take . . ." He recovered himself quickly and began again: "I, Gregory, take thee Phoebe . . ." but the small symptomatic slip flooded me with an apprehension of the chaos in the old man's mind.

When everyone else was gone away and my mother and Mr. Hawke were left alone he fell into a melancholy that never lifted, but rather deepened. He would spend hour after hour sitting on a seat that overlooked the vast view from his garden or, in the winter, alone in his study. It was a bad time for my mother, for she knew that before she married Mr. Hawke there had been understanding and friendship between him and Eustace. She could only hope that this aspect of the matter was not too clear to Mr. Hawke, but her hope was cruelly crushed. One winter night she was reading in the small sitting room and her husband was in his study as usual. Presently, he came into the sitting room and said in a conversational way: "Eustace is quite right, you know, my dear. We should never have married."

She was not surprised. It was one more sorrow, and she was ready to carry it. That night, and thereafter till his death, old Hawke slept in the visitor's bedroom.

This change of affairs, by bringing the matter into the open, seemed to ease it. Mr. Hawke became lighter-hearted, as though he had purged some guilt. My mother dutifully performed her tasks as his companion-cook-housekeeper. A way of life, of a sort, worked itself out, and became a pattern that was at least tolerable. I have sometimes wondered what my mother felt about Mr. Hawke. Never, I should say, anything like what she felt for that charming rogue who was my father, whose fingers I had so often seen twined with hers as they lay beneath the blue sky and the seabirds' flashing wings on the beach at Pendeverel.

The winter went through in this way, with occasional lapses into gloom on Mr. Hawke's part; and when the spring was well advanced she looked forward to taking him away, as she had done each year, hoping that a change would cure the lingering traces of his melancholy. But there was another shock for her when she raised the question of the summer holiday.

"I think, my dear," he said with his unfailing courtesy, "that it would be better this year if you took your holiday alone. Do you think you could manage that?"

She asked him what the idea was, and he said: "I have a notion that Eustace will come to England this summer. He would be more likely to visit me if he knew I was alone. My idea is that we should wait till his letter comes, and that then you should go off on your holiday. That would leave me free to invite him. You see, with Phoebe married, I am very lonely."

My mother agreed even to this. Perhaps she welcomed it. Who knows?

But the summer went by, and the expected letter did not come, and, said my mother, when she told me all this later, "I could have cried to see the way he took to walking down the lane, day after day, to meet the postman. He would come back and throw his hat onto the chest in the hall and say, 'Tomorrow, perhaps. Well, good news will keep, my dear.' "

What did come, toward the end of the summer, was the letter from Rose. It is easy to say what a fool Phoebe had been, how much better things might have turned out if we had told my mother and Mr. Hawke about Rose in the first place. A catastrophe is better borne when its full extent is seen at once, and you can measure it and deal with it. But the effect of Rose's letter on those two, who had been told that her absence from the wedding was due to Miss Orlop's illness in London, can be imagined. When the landslide was stabilizing, it shifted another stone, and everything crashed down.

The letter was from Munich, and was addressed to my mother. It was written in the belief that my mother and Mr. Hawke had been told of the elopement. It was a gossipy friendly letter, and ended with the news that Rose was expecting a child.

My mother had gone that morning to the village shop which was also the post office, and the letter was handed to her there. She read it before she got back to the vicarage, and though there was nothing in it which said that Rose and Eustace were not married, she had a presentiment that this was so. She knew more about Eustace than his father did. For one thing, I had myself told her about Miss Lund at the meeting of the Cloggers, and that was not the sort of thing she would pass on to her husband.

In any event, she decided not to show the letter to Mr. Hawke. But he soon found out. He met the postman in the lane as usual. "That'll be what you're expecting, Mr. Hawke—the one Mrs. Hawke picked up at the post office. Foreign stamps on it."

He came bursting back into the house and shouted: "Has Eustace written?"

"I have seen nothing from him," my mother answered.

"But the letter from abroad. The postman says you have one."

"Oh, that was addressed to me. It was from a friend of mine."

He looked at her with suspicion. She saw not only suspicion but what she called "almost a gleam of hate in his eyes."

"Show me your letter," he commanded.

"Very well." She handed it to him. His face lit with joy as he read.

When he had finished, he said: "Did I speak roughly, my dear? I beg your pardon."

He read the letter again, and said: "So Eustace is married. Why did he not tell me? I always intended to give him his mother's writing desk when he married."

"How do you know he's married?" she asked.

He looked at her, livid. The letter fell from his fingers. "What!" he shouted. "How do you dare to make such a suggestion? You hate the boy."

"Then he went terribly pale," she said "and looked frightened."

She picked up the letter and handed it to him. "The address is there," she said. "Perhaps you'd better write to Eustace."

He did so. "And what was so terrible," she said, "was that he did not go any more to meet the postman. It was as though he was afraid of what the answer would be."

She never saw the answer. When it came, he took it to his study. After he had hanged himself she found the ashes of the burnt letter in the study fireplace.

3

When I had seen Uncle Arthur off on his journey I cycled out to Greg's place. I was to stay on the farm till my uncle and my mother returned.

Greg and I walked to the tarn that afternoon and dived into its icy water. Then we lay naked in the sun as though he were at Parson's Pleasure.

"It'll be a rum thing, Chad, about this kid of mine," he said. "Did you know that old Hawke was the son of an earl's younger son?"

That was something I hadn't known, and Greg said: "The parsonry and the army used to be full of people like that. Well, this young Ronald of ours"—they had already arranged the name and the sex—"will have this aristocrat for one grandfather and my old man for another. And my old man's father was a laborer at twelve-and-six a week."

"Well, what about it?" I asked lazily. "It's happening all the time, isn't it?"

"Of course it is," Greg said. "Look at Catherine Swynford."

"I'd better not, at the moment. I don't want to be arrested."

He sat up and began rummaging in his coat pockets for his smoking things. I looked at his tough sunburnt body. He was as strong as a young shire horse.

"I don't think you've ever heard of Catherine."

"No."

"What the heck do you *do* with yourself at Oxford, Chad?"

"Preside over the Cloggers."

"That's a life's work, I must say." He was sitting up, puffing furiously, his dark hair tousled. "Where are you trying to *get to?*"

There it was again. Where was I trying to get to. "Tell me about Catherine."

"Well, she was governess to John of Gaunt's kids, and *sub rosa* she was the mother of a few of his bastards, and in the long run he married her, and several of the descendants of those now legitimate bastards sat on the English throne."

"Well, there's a life's work for you," I chaffed him. "But I don't see any opening in it for me."

"What I'm getting at," he said, "is the bloody awful delicious mess-up that English society is. I'm going to call my book *Cook's Son, Duke's Son.*"

It was from "The Absent-minded Beggar," Kipling's bit of Boer War bunk. We used to sing it in Pendeverel. I recalled the day when I bought the button of poor General Gatacre for my lapel, and my father raised holy hell in the village shop.

"What are you wool-gathering about now?" Greg asked.

I told him, and he said: "You can never keep your mind on a subject. You'll end up a bloody novelist or something."

"That's an idea. I must do that. Better than being John of Gaunt's mistress. Anyway, this is the first I've heard of your book."

Then he was off again on what he called the social significance of vertical structure in society.

"It's been our salvation again and again. We must have more of it," he declared, warming up.

"I don't mind," I agreed. "You'd better fix it up with the editors of Debrett and of the Houndsditch Street Directory."

At that, he began laughing heartily, and fell upon me and pounded me; and then we dressed and ate some sandwiches and started to walk back to the farm. We were young and heartless. All thought had gone from our minds of Uncle Arthur, chugging along on his lugubrious errand, and of my mother in the vicarage where her only company was that sad self-made corpse. We leaned over a gate and watched Greg's father, a brown muscular giant, heaving ripe sheaves of corn onto a wain. "Look at him," Gregg said. "It fair beats me how he ever came to be grandfather of my son."

"How do you know your son's going to be all that special?" I asked.

He looked at me in genuine surprise, and said briefly, with his strongest northern intonation: "Don't talk bloody rubbish."

We went to Manchester the next morning. Greg was not, like me, frittering away the long vacation. He was up in time to be working on his book—the first of his long line of books—at six in the morning. He and Phoebe and I breakfasted at nine, and thereafter he shared the day between pottering about with her near the farm and walking enormous distances with me. But now he had to visit the small house they had taken in Manchester in order to pick up some notes he had forgotten to bring. I had never seen Manchester and was glad to go with him. We were to spend the night there. We set off early from Smurthwaite, and walked across Bradford to the Lancashire and Yorkshire Railway station. Our train took us through the Yorkshire hills, clothed with trees whose leaves, at that time of year, seemed to have a rusty shrivel rather than the gentle and pleasing tones of autumn. As we rushed through one small station, Greg said: "That's where Branwell Brontë use to work. Ticket collector. Fancy that, Chad. Emily Brontë's brother a ticket collector!"

"What would the young waster be in your vertical society?" I asked.

He didn't answer that. "There was a lass for you!" he said. "Worth all the rest of 'em rolled into one."

Soon we roared through the long stinking tunnel at Todmorden and shot out on to the Lancashire plain. Passing thus under the spine of the Pennines had given us a change even in the weather. The day was suddenly gray and desolate, the prospect flat and infinitely sad. "No wonder Lancashire produces the world's best comedians," Greg said. "They need something to laugh about in this place."

It was lunchtime when we walked out of Victoria Station. "Let's eat before we go out to Didsbury," Greg said.

I was suddenly depressed. London and Bradford were the only big cities I had seen till now. London was something in those days. It was still possible to say with Dr. Johnson that a man who was tired of London was tired of life. The guidebooks quote it still, but I wonder what Johnson would say of the abominable place now? Bradford had an agreeable up-and-downity. You could see hills wherever you looked, and there was a taste of vigor in the air. But Manchester, flat as a table, with nothing for the eye to fall on save more and yet more unattractive building on more flatness, with the Irwell flowing dirtily past dirty warehouse walls, and, on that day, a gray flatness overhead to match the flatness on earth: Manchester, with its roaring trams and hurrying thousands, seemed to me abominable. I said so, and Greg said: "Aye, it's bloody awful, but tha gets used to it."

We walked to Cross Street, and Greg said: "That's the *Manchester*

Guardian office. Take off your hat. That is Sinai. The voice of God dwells there." We went through Cross Street and into Albert Square, where we ate our meal in a Lyons teashop. It was crowded. People kept coming in and standing round, waiting for someone to leave a table free. Pointing to this knot hovering inside the door, Greg said: "Who is that girl in the unhappy brown hat, Chad? Something in me says Oxford, but I'm damned if I can fix her. She doesn't *look* Oxford."

I knew her at once. It was May Ingleby. All the misery of a year ago rushed back to reinforce the misery I had felt from the moment of reaching Manchester. I wished her to hell.

I told Greg who she was. "Go on. Be a knight," he said. "We can squeeze another in here."

Miss Ingleby, in a Manchester typist's workaday clothes, did not look the girl who had danced divinely the night through and then slept in a punt at my feet. But she wasn't bad-looking in her way, though now I didn't think she looked much like Rose Garland. She seemed pathetically glad when I invited her to our table. "Oh, Mr. Boothroyd, fancy meeting you here of all places! It's ever so good of you to ask me."

"Perhaps you're waiting for someone?" I optimistically inquired.

"Oh, no," she said, drawing off shabby gloves. "Actually, I've got very few friends."

She didn't remember Greg, but no encounter seemed to daunt her. If I had introduced her to Freud and Einstein, I am sure she would have said: "I'm ever so glad to meet you," and confidently assailed them with a shower of prattle.

There was an innocence in this, an unawareness that her own narrow world might be infinitely depressing that had touched me when I first met her, and that now gradually made me take a more favorable view of her. She was almost refreshing after some of the earnest bores of Somerville and Lady Margaret Hall. As she laid heartily into a plate of sausage and mash that Greg had ordered, I ventured to chip her on her invincible talkativeness.

"Oh, I always talk when I'm not dancing," she said. "I don't think you can talk and dance at the same time, not seriously, but there's nothing else you can't talk at the same time as."

Greg shot her a wicked look. "Nothing?" he asked.

It didn't ruffle her innocence. She didn't get it. "No," she said. "I can always talk. I expect it's all the experience I get at my mother's place. You meet all sorts there—plenty of give and take."

She didn't need much prodding to tell us about her mother's place, which was a house in Ackers Street, a caravanserai where the smaller fry of the theatrical profession alighted for a week and then passed on. "Of course, mother doesn't want me to stay in that sort of life, which is why she sent me to Oxford—well, not actually to Oxford, was it?— but she thought Oxford gave a girl good opportunities."

"I hope you made use of them, Miss Ingleby," Greg said.

"Well, one *does* meet *gentlemen*. Mr. Boothroyd was consideration itself."

Greg gave me a long pondering glance. "I have always thought Mr. Boothroyd's origins a little dubious," he said. "I once had great difficulty in getting him admitted to the membership of an Oxford society. Would you call him a gentleman?"

"Oh, definitely. Handsome is as handsome does. Well, I must fly. It's just on two, and the manager's ever so strict."

Her lack of curiosity—she had not asked what I was doing in Manchester—her engrossment in her own small concerns, were incredible, touching, leaving her vulnerable. She seemed to pass out of our lives the moment she passed through the door. She had that quality. I don't remember that either of us mentioned her again.

"D'you feel up to a five-mile walk?" Greg asked.

It was five miles of stony going, the pavements under our feet, the racket of the trams for accompaniment. Greg stopped when we reached the University. "There it is, Chad. Looks rather like the Bastille, don't you think? When the revolution comes, that's where they'll find me, chained by the leg to a ring in the floor, haggard and white-haired, surrounded by tattered remnants of Ricardo and John Stuart Mill, and scribbling with chalk on the pavement a refutation of Gossen's Law of Satiety. But, honestly, Chad, this is a hell of a life I've chosen, and a hell of a place to live it in."

He laughed, well content.

Things were better when we got to Fallowfield and Withington. There was a park, flat like everything else, its distances fading out in the afternoon's gray. There were sizable houses, gardens, trees. We trudged along as far as the Barlow Moor Road, turned left into it, and then turned right into a small side street. It was quiet. A few fine Lombardy poplars stood up over the rooftops. It was a short street, with a mission church on the corner. Greg stopped at a house on the right-hand side. The front garden was about two yards long and three wide. Nothing grew in it save a privet hedge and a laburnum tree. I wondered how Greg, who had known the spacious beauty of Wharfedale and the glory of Oxford, could shut himself up in this small box, itself shut up in the miles of Manchester. He was looking at the little house with satisfaction, the door key in his hand. He stroked the sooty trunk of the laburnum tree. "That was a grand sight in May," he said. "Come along in."

The passage was narrow. On the left was a small sitting room. "We feed in the kitchen," Greg explained. "It's cozy in the winter." Behind the sitting room was a room, equally small, looking out on to the arid back garden. To my surprise, the windows of this room were barred. I asked why. "So that Ronald can't climb out," Greg said. "This'll be his nursery."

We went upstairs. There were three rooms on that floor. "This is where you'll sleep," Greg explained, opening the door of one of them, "when you come to visit us." The second room also had bars to the windows, and I didn't need to ask about them now. It contained a cot, and a frieze of country scenes was pasted round the walls. This was Ronald's bedroom. "And this," said Greg, opening the door of the third, double-bedded, room, which was at the front of the house, "this is where His Nibs will get born."

"You've done everything," I said, "except arrange with the local authorities to put up the plaque on the front of the house."

"No cheek from you, Mutton-chops,' he said. "There'll be *two* plaques on this house. Come and see where the work's done."

So we climbed more stairs, for the house was tall and narrow. "There were two attics here," Greg explained. "I've had 'em knocked into one."

The result was the only sizable room in the house: **L**-shaped, low-ceilinged and comfortable. Bookcases covering the walls, a big writing table and two easy chairs, were all the furniture. One tiny window looked, across a few intervening yards of space, at the blank end of another house, and there was a second window that looked across the back garden at another back garden and then another house. I thought of my room in Smurthwaite, opening upon white limestone breaking through the turf of the fells like wave crests upon green water, and of my room in Pendeverel that was filled at night with a shell's sea murmur, and of my cozy Oxford den lapped round with eons of antiquity. I wondered how Greg could stand this. "It's snug enough," I said.

"Aye," he said. "This is where we spend most of our nights. In the winter you don't hear a sound, and when the fire's lit and the curtains are drawn, and Phoebe's sitting there at her work and I'm sitting here at mine—well, you can imagine."

Yes, I could imagine that this was something Greg had been cherishing in his thoughts time out of mind, and that he had no fault to find with any of it.

"Of course, next winter things'll be a bit different, with Ronald around. There are some good kindergartens about here."

"Enter him for Eton right now, and have done with it."

"Well, I don't know," he said seriously. "Phoebe and I have discussed schools, and we're rather gone on Winchester."

He had no difficulty in picking up his missing notes. His desk was neat, with a bank of labeled pigeonholes at the back of it, and with a system of folders in various colors to indicate this and that. He explained it all to me like a ship's engineer making clear how the vessel was kept on her course.

We went down to the kitchen-dining room and Greg put a kettle on the gas ring and made tea. There was a banging and hammering beyond the door that led into the back garden. "That's the carpenter," Greg explained. "Let's see how he's getting on."

The door opened on to stone steps that led into a patch of fruitless bitter-looking earth. On one side was a well down which further steps led to a door opening into a cellar beneath the house.

"That's the danger spot," Greg explained. "It's a damn-awful playground, but he'll have to use it such as it is, and a fall off these steps into that well wouldn't be too good. Look at it which way you will, a broken neck is a poor start to any career."

So there the carpenter was, boarding in the steps.

That evening, we took the train in to Manchester from Didsbury station and gave ourselves a good dinner before going on to the second house at the Hippodrome music hall. Afterward, I slept in the little house for the first time, and the next morning we returned to Bradford, ate our luncheon there, and then entrained for Smurthwaite. We had left our bicycles in the porter's room at the station there; and we wheeled them out and were mounting when Greg's father unexpectedly appeared in a trap. He jumped down, and we did not need to be told that something was wrong. "I didn't want thee to get home un-knowing, lad," he said to Greg. "Phoebe's lost the child, and she's very bad."

5

There had been a great affection between Phoebe and her father. No one knew the strength of it more than Greg did, for from boyhood he had been in and out of the Smurthwaite Rectory almost as though it had been his home. That is why he had concealed from Phoebe, and from his father and mother who might have blurted out the truth, the manner of Mr. Hawke's death. It had been bad enough to have to tell her that he was dead. He did not dare to go beyond that, seeing that she was carrying Ronald. She seemed to me to take the news quietly enough, but Greg knew better than I how hardly it had borne upon her. He had been doubtful about leaving her in order to bring his notes from Manchester, but Phoebe had—she was always to have—a sense that Greg's work was something not to be hindered, and she urged him to go.

Of course, it was futile to think that the facts would not reach her. They might have come in any of a score of ways: a newspaper paragraph, gossip that had reached a neighbor and been passed on, anything. The effect of Greg's poor thoughtless strategem was that the news reached her in the worst possible way and at the worst possible time: in a letter from my mother, and while Greg was not there to comfort her.

I suppose my mother did what she thought was the right thing. She could not be expected to know that Phoebe had not learned the truth. Thinking that the girl knew everything, she wrote in the hope of comforting her. Comforting herself, too, I imagine. She must have been desolate in the time between Mr. Hawke's death and the arrival of Uncle Arthur. To pour herself out to someone was natural enough; and, unhappily, she chose Phoebe.

The letter came while Greg and I were in the train between Smurthwaite and Bradford. Everything was in it: the news that had come from Rose, the fact that Rose was expecting a child, her fear that Rose and Eustace were not married, Mr. Hawke's suicide. It is impossible to imagine a worse blow being struck at Phoebe, situated as she was.

When the letter came, Phoebe was alone. Mr. Appleby was out in the fields; Mrs. Appleby was in the dairy. Phoebe took the letter into the garden to read it. She fell in a faint. It was not till some time later that Mrs. Appleby found her there. By then, Ronald was no more. Phoebe was in bed when she came to her senses and heard Mrs. Appleby telling her husband to send a telegram to Greg. "No—don't," she said. And so they didn't.

She got over it in time, and so did Greg; neither of them was a neurotic brooder. But from then on, it seemed to me, they treated life a little less as though it were a well-trained dog that could be whistled to heel or made to jump through hoops.

I did not see my mother before going back to Oxford. Uncle Arthur, who had not yet taken his summer holiday, decided to take it now, so that he might whisk his sister away to some new town where nothing would remind her of her tribulations. I think they went, of all places, to Redcar. I went back with the Michaelmas term before me: a prospect of fading autumn and nights lengthening to winter, no Greg, no Billy Pascoe, nothing to keep me from my resolve to apply myself to a play. I had now long been a member of the Oxford University Dramatic Society. I didn't act, but I did a lot of work behind the scenes, and built up some knowledge of what a playwright can do and can't do. I read an enormous number of plays, ancient and modern, and I never missed a chance to see a play acted, whether by the O.U.D.S. or anyone else, whether *The Trojan Women* or *What the Butler Saw*. I was furtive about all this. I never mentioned my preoccupation, which had become overwhelming, in my letters to Uncle Arthur or my mother. I said nothing to Greg about it. I still had a fear that my direction would seem trivial when placed against his absorption in economics and Billy's in physics. I was shy about it all with other people, but ruthless with myself. I did work hard that term, though my work was all what Uncle Arthur would have called extracurricular. I wrote a play and tore it up. I don't think the Lord Chamberlain would have approved it, anyway. It was about Queen Victoria's pathological longing for her dead Albert. I caused the gods to relent and return him to her. Then they had a devil of a life, for the old lady had become so used to authority that she couldn't bear opposition, even from Albert. He disliked Disraeli, especially his primroses, and backed everything that Gladstone wanted. He told her she had made a mess of the Prince of Wales and that it was high time that young man was learning something about his job. The climax was her prayer to the gods to relieve her of this disturbing interloper. They sent an embassy of three archangels to say that nothing could be done without her authority, whereupon she called in Disraeli to draft the appropriate mandate. Ruthlessly and triumphantly she signed *Victoria R.I.* "Dispatch that at once. How are the primroses at Hughenden?"

"They are graciously permitted, ma'am, to enter upon a convalescence. Is it your wish that the relics of the Prince be now removed from your apartments?"

"Certainly not, Lord Beaconsfield. The gods may fool you but not me. That man was not the Prince. He was nothing but a Radical impostor. I shall worship dear Albert till I die."

John Begg was the only person, except myself, who read the play. The O.U.D.S. put on a Greek play that winter, and Begg, who was on the London staff of the *Manchester Guardian,* came down to write about it. He had been an Exeter man himself in his day, and that gave us a point of contact. He came around to my rooms and we made a night of it. Begg was amused by some bits of the play, but he encouraged my opinion that it should go into the wastepaper basket. "Write it again in ten or fifteen years' time," he suggested blandly. What was to give my life an unexpected twist was this. Before going back to London, Begg said it seemed to him a good idea that someone, at the end of each university term, should write a brief account for the *Manchester Guardian* of what the undergraduates had been doing in drama. He asked if I would take on this small job, should his office approve. I agreed gladly, and in due course these end-of-term reports, signed C.B., began to appear in the august sheet. It gave me an enormous kick to see those initials in print, and, though I did not know it, this was the first step toward my marriage with May Ingleby.

6

In 1910 Miss Orlop who had been an A.R.A., became a Royal Academician. I had written to congratulate the old girl, saying nothing about Rose Garland but hoping that in her reply she would pass on a little news. However, she didn't. The letter she wrote was formal, but it ended with a sufficiently warm invitation to call upon her should I be in London. "I don't visit Oxford now," she said, "though I am occasionally in Cambridge." I took this to mean that she was still keeping an eye on Billy Pascoe. I hadn't seen him or heard from him since Rose had run away with Eustace Hawke.

Miss Orlop's invitation had been so imprecise that I took no notice of it till the following June, when I went up to London to see something of the coronation of King George V. It was altogether a restless moment for me. The Trinity term was all but over—my last term. Almost four years had passed since Rose and I had walked together near Mr. Hawke's vicarage and she had wished me luck at the University and had made it clear that I didn't amount to anything special in her consideration. I sat, as I had so often sat, in a willow-shaded punt, doing, as I had so often done, nothing in particular. So much, it seemed to me, had happened in those four years to everybody but me. Greg and Phoebe were married, and the window bars in their small house in Didsbury were finding a use, for, though there was no son to replace the missing Ronald, there was young Penelope Appleby; and Greg had already added another book to *Cook's Son, Duke's Son*. Rose and Eustace were I knew not where. Mr. Hawke was dead, and my mother was back at Smurthwaite, sharing Uncle Arthur's house. She was still only in her forties, but now, for the first time, I saw a fading of the youthful charm which, rather than any positive good looks, had made her attractive. It was nothing much—a mere streak of autumn foliage—but there it was. During the last vacation, I had been talking to her in her room at the top of the house, and noticed that a photograph had been framed and hung over the mantelpiece. I had not seen it before. It was of my father, hatless, careless-looking, on the beach at Pendeverel, that air of the irresponsible *gamin* that he had always worn fixed forever. There was no picture of Mr. Hawke. I said nothing, but it gave me something to think about.

To me alone, I thought, as my punt swayed to the passing of another, laden with obvious first-year men who made me feel old and cynical, to me alone nothing seemed to have happened. Billy Pascoe was purposefully burrowing along his groove. I had been talking to a physics man who had recently been to Cambridge and met him there. He was full of admiration. "He'll stay on with a research fellowship. Sure as houses. Nothing can stop him."

Sure as houses, I thought, I'll go down, for all my extra year, with a mediocre degree; and, after that, what? I got up, pushed the punt out from the bank, and poled along to the place where you could get honeycomb for tea, not seeing any answer.

I went up to London a few days before the coronation. At such a time it would have been impossible to get a room at any hotel, but the parents of a man I knew at Merton—the man I had seen, very tight, shooting with an airgun on the dance floor on that memorable night when I last saw Rose and first saw May Ingleby—had a flat in a street behind Park Lane. They had gone out of town, and he, being excessively studious despite his occasional divagations, was staying in Oxford. Hearing of my difficulty, he magnanimously handed over his parents' abode. "They won't mind. You'll find a couple of old buffers to look after you." He telephoned to the old buffers and gave me the address.

I had had no experience of London flats, and had always thought of them as poky makeshifts that I would never want to live in. However, I discovered that there are flats and flats. The one I occupied can only be called palatial, with old masters on the walls, furniture so splendid that it terrified me, spacious rooms, and a surprising quiet. The couple of old buffers turned out to be a butler and his wife who was the cook. A houseman had been too inconsiderable for young Margesson to mention. It was he who carried my bag to a room containing a bed which could hardly escape having been slept in by Queen Elizabeth.

All this, including a country house to which Margesson's parents had departed, was done, I knew, on the sale of a patent medicine. However, it was not for me to complain about that. There was a telephone by my bed, and I at once rang up Miss Orlop to arrange a suitable time for calling upon her.

She was not at home, said the servant who answered the call. At a chance, I asked if Mr. Pascoe were there. No, I was told, Mr. Pascoe had left that morning with Miss Orlop. They were gone into Cornwall, and it was not known when they would be back.

So that was that. I resigned myself to the splendid hospitality of the Margesson flat, ate a five-course dinner, went to a theater, and that night insulted the enormous Tudor bed by sleeping in it as casually and soundly as though it were my old shakedown at Exeter College. A pot of tea, offered with deference, awakened me to a memorable day.

It was June weather of the best. I strolled out in the middle of the morning, down the short street, across Park Lane, and into the park. I would have preferred London without the flapping gee-gaws that everywhere met my eye, but the park was green and cool, people everywhere were in a holiday mood, and I walked aimlessly about, well content. A girl was pushing a baby in a perambulator a little ahead of me, and I was attracted by her fine carriage, the swing of her skirt, a feeling of joy that seemed to flow out of her and make itself manifest even to one who could not see her face. It was a smiling face; I could tell that from the way she now and then gave a little run, stopped, and then bent with a sudden "Boo!" over the child. Then off she would go again, and I could hear the child crowing and see a small chubby fist waved excitedly.

It made such a pleasant picture that I followed, entranced: the sheep grazing, the trees in June leaf, the bowling clouds, the blue sky, and this young person so happily at play with a child. She looked a part of the day, as airy as one of the colored balloons that an old woman was selling near by.

It was because she spared a glance for the balloon woman that she did not see the child throw a small object out of the perambulator. She was off again when I picked up the coral toy, congratulating myself on the chance to see her face, her smile. But I had not time to overtake her before the child's howl told her of the loss. She turned just as I came up, the hat which I had whipped off in one hand, the coral in the other. And then I could not speak. I could only gaze at her, open-mouthed. She laughed at my discomfiture, showing white teeth and a red tongue. Her face was tanned, her eyes shone as incredibly blue as ever.

After a moment she held out her hand. "Well, Chad, what do you think of Henrietta?"

Henrietta seemed threatened with apoplexy. I dumbly held to her the coral bauble. She seized it with a swift possessive greed, began to suck it and to smile.

"Rose!" It was all I could say. My legs were trembling. I had thought the house in the Bayswater Road to be empty. There was no preparation for the encounter.

"I rang up Miss Orlop's house," I said stupidly. "She is gone to Cornwall with Billy Pascoe."

Rose smiled again as I pedantically presented this piece of news which she must well have known.

"Let us sit down," she said. "Here. This will keep Henrietta quiet for a moment." She turned to the balloon woman, bought a purple sphere, and tied the end of the string to the perambulator. With this bobbing above the child's head, she moved away. "Come. Sit down," she repeated.

I sat down, gazing at the child, thinking of Eustace Hawke. I dared not, then, mention his name. I dared not ask the question that was in my mind.

"I'm so glad we met, Chad," she said. "It's by the merest fluke. Henrietta's nurse has gone. She had the romantic idea that she must be married on Coronation Day. So I'm left with Henrietta on my hands. Otherwise, we'd have gone off to Cornwall with the others. As it is, I must find a nurse as soon as I can, and then follow. There's a galaxy of applicants to be interviewed this afternoon."

She chattered on, and I could still find little to say. I had a sense that she was chattering not as May Ingleby did, because she could do nothing else, but in order to fend me off from intimate conversation. She needn't have worried. I was incapable of it. But it must come. I would see to that.

"I don't know much about babies," I said. "What time does Henrietta go to bed?"

"At six o'clock. She'll be two next September, and she's as good as gold. Once she's put down at night we don't hear a squeak out of her."

"Then you can leave her. I suppose there are responsible people in the house?"

"Yes."

"You could come out and have dinner with me."

"Yes—I *could*."

"Will you?"

She considered for a moment, graver now, as though she, too, realized that there were things we must say sooner or later.

"Yes," she said at last.

8

"It was all right," Rose said, "till Henrietta was on the way." She looked round the drawing room of the Margesson flat. "Do you know, Chad, I haven't talked about this to anyone—not even to my mother. I find this de luxe setting excellent for confession. Do you think that really is a Breughel?"

"I don't know. The label says so, and as Mr. Margesson has made a fortune out of people who believe what the label says, he no doubt pays this one the compliment of taking it at its word."

It was still difficult to keep her on the track. She was dodging. We had dined early at the Café Royal and had returned here by ten o'clock.

"When did you get back to England?"

"A month ago."

It was extraordinary how padded this ornate room was. Hardly a sound came in from the street. The butler had accepted it as nothing out of the ordinary that I had brought a beautiful girl home with me. He put a tray containing brandy and cigars on a table near us. He watched me choose a cigar, pierced it and held a light, then went.

"How was Eustace when you left him?"

"I didn't leave him. He left me."

She was trying to be gay, to make it all sound light and of no great

166

consequence. I found this unbearable. She didn't belong to the type we later called hard-boiled.

"Did he marry you?"

"Eustace *marry*? You surely know him better than that, Chad."

I stubbed out the hardly started cigar, got up raging with an inner fury, and paced up and down the room.

"Something seems to have annoyed you," Rose said.

She was sitting in an eighteenth-century winged chair under the light of the chandelier. One of her legs was thrown across the other, and her full dress of crimson silk made light and shade with its small hills and valleys. Her hair was as black as coal, and as shining. I came to a stand before her and said vehemently: "I hate that man like poison. And so in your heart must you."

She got up then, with that identical slurring rustle of silk that I had heard when, a crying child, she had got up from her knees before the fireplace at Pentyrch, so long ago. She placed her hands on my shoulders, and it was all I could do to prevent my arms from going round her, my lips from falling upon the breast that the low-cut dress offered to my eyes.

"Do you hate him, Chad?" she asked gently. "Think now. *Do* you, really?"

I shook her off almost roughly, and paced the room again, thinking of Eustace Hawke: the boy who resented my mother, the pale rangy youth striding the rangy Yorkshire fells, talking to me, in a snowy night, about Keats, lying drunk and despairing under the hedge where Greg Appleby and I had found him.

"No," I said. "I'm not a good hater. But I hate what he's done to you."

She sat down again, her hands folded in her lap. I noticed that she was not wearing a wedding ring. She must have interpreted my look, for she held up her left hand for a moment, then let it fall lightly back. "An odd family, aren't we?" she said. "We don't seem to run to wedding rings. My mother, with a legitimate child, has never worn one, and I, with an illegitimate one, intend to make no pretenses. Don't be mistaken, Chad. I don't hate Eustace. Who could? He made me very happy. Any unhappiness I feel now is because it wasn't in me to keep him."

"No woman will keep him."

"No. We must be thankful that, for a time, we seemed to him to be whatever he's looking for."

"Oh, that's highfalutin stuff and nonsense," I burst out, my anger kindling afresh. "You're accepting the scamp's own excuses."

"No," she said gently. "I'm telling you how I see it. And I see it like that." After a moment's silence, she added: "If I were to marry

167

someone now, Chad, I wouldn't answer for the consequences if I met Eustace again."

It was beyond me. I came back to a prosaic question. "What did your mother say when you returned?"

Rose chuckled quietly. "Do you remember," she asked, "the day when I was abominable in the boat at Pendeverel?"

"I do, indeed."

"When we got back to your house, my mother had finished her painting and the pony cart was there waiting to take us to Pentyrch. My mother asked what sort of time I'd had and I said I'd been very sick. She just looked at me absent-mindedly and said: 'Oh, well . . .' and pushed me into the cart."

"I remember."

"Well, it was exactly like that. I hadn't told her I was coming, and there I was on the doorstep, Henrietta and all. She said: 'Ah, well. So you're back. Let me have a look at the child, and go and change that dreadful dress.' From that point we went on as though I'd come in from an untidy afternoon on the beach."

"She's an angel."

"Yes, and such a practical one. She said to me that night: 'I've just heard from my lawyers that that ghastly man I married is dead at last. Long overdue. He was costing me a pretty penny. I'd better settle his allowance on this child of yours.'"

Then she began to cry, and I could understand how this comic incident loosed her tears.

"Eustace and I would have starved without her," she said.

9

They had gone to Munich, and everything at first was wonderful. I don't say that cynically. For any woman life would be wonderful with Eustace Hawke in the morning of one of his revelations. And every new woman was a revelation to him, a glimpse of the perfect poem still cherished in the breast, still unwritten. But the writing had to come, however long it was fended off; and it was never the thing of the vision. When the ray touched the earth, it was full of mundane motes and smuts; and someday it would fall again from a new point in the heavens upon a new landscape.

"Phoebe knew it was coming," Rose said, "and she knew there was nothing she could do. She was so charming about it all, and she tried to make me see what was ahead. Go to it if you must, but don't go to it quite blind. That was how she looked at it. She warned me that Eustace drank too much. Which would you prefer, Chad, if you were a woman: a drunken archangel or a sober municipal official?"

168

From her talk that night, and on other nights I pieced together a picture of their life. It was simply a prolongation of those few exquisite days on the river at Oxford, except that they were now alone. "Sometimes we hadn't a roof over our heads for weeks on end." They wouldn't put up even the small tent they carried. They slept under haystacks and on beds of pine needles, and bathed in lakes, and cooked food like tramps by the roadside.

"He couldn't be bothered to shave. His beard was like the corn that was ripening everywhere."

He carried a guitar, and they hired boats and rowed on lakes and sang songs. In the evenings he would speak poetry to her. "He didn't need books. He could give me the whole *Golden Treasury* by heart. But he would never say any of his own verses. They were trash, he said, not fit for my ears. What he was going to write next—that was something I should hear."

Eustace was at a point in his life when he reeled from influence to influence. It had been Strindberg. Now it was Goethe, and that is why, when the winter ended their wanderings, they went to Weimar.

"We became pure Germans. We talked nothing but German, we read nothing but German, and we rented a little German house. We even had a maid named Gretchen."

And the snow! "Oh, you don't know what snow is, Chad!" They climbed the white hills, and they skied and skated, and came back through snow-dumbed streets to the little house and the porcelain stove and the long still evenings and the featherbed.

They went out one day when the snow was gone and the air was warm and the larches in the foothills were tender with emerald buds. Eustace was quiet and thoughtful, and she was aware of something stirring in him that she had not known before. They had taken food with them, and as they sat eating it, sitting on a rock with the gentle sun in their faces, he began suddenly to erupt. He talked of a poetic drama that had been simmering all the winter and that he would now begin to write. Their early weeks were to be repeated. They had been too long in Weimar. They must tear up their roots and wander again; but there would be this difference: he would be producing his own songs for her instead of speaking the songs of other people.

"But, my darling, we can't do that. I'm going to have a child."

She said: "He made no answer to that. Not so much as a word. But his silence was terrific. It was as though I had literally struck him dumb. He walked home in silence, we spent the night in silence, and the next day, without a word to me, he went off walking alone."

Then the weather worsened. The snow came back, not pure but harsh and sleety with bitter wind, and they were wrapped up together in the cozy little house that had suddenly become for her a torture chamber. If only he would work, do *something!* She asked him when he proposed to start on the drama. He said: "How can I start on the drama, how can I start on anything, if you destroy the conditions in which I can work?"

She said they never quarreled. She might have taken up that remark and made it the point of a tirade. "But what would have been the use?" she asked. "It would have done me no good, and it would have hurt him."

She knew now that the drama would never be written—not in *her* time with him, anyway—that she had ceased to give him the apple tree, the singing, and the gold. She had dropped suddenly to the status of hausfrau; and so she sacked the young Gretchen, and cooked, and reddened her hands with scrubbing. "Scrubbing is a wonderful sedative, Chad."

All that Phoebe had feared came true, except that he held off the drink. Outside Weimar there was a boys' boarding school, and in the spring he took a job there as English master. He slept in the school throughout the week and came home at the week ends. He remained morose and for the most part silent, saying only hurtful things as he put money on the table. "Here are the hack's wages." "A family man must earn his bread." "Here you are—pennies instead of poems."

She asked him once if he had ever read Hans Sachs, the Nuremberg cobbler-poet, whose boast it was that, for all his poems, he never made a shoe the less and raised a large family. "I can well understand that," he said, "if his boots were as bad as his poems."

I said to Rose: "I can't understand the man. What's wrong with having a baby?"

"I imagine," she said, "that for Eustace it meant that he couldn't be a boy any longer. I was his mother, among other things, and he didn't want anyone to share his privileges."

I threw up my hands, baffled. "I don't understand—not you, nor him."

"Dear Chad! Of course you don't."

Eustace began now the odd task, as it seemed to me, of translating the best of his own verses into German. A Hamburg publisher agreed to publish them, and in the August of that year Eustace went to Hamburg on this business. He never came back. "I met that publisher later," Rose said. "From what he told me, I gathered that the woman this time was his own secretary, very young, very fair, a regular fairy-tale goose-girl."

Henrietta was born the next month. Little Gretchen came back and stayed with Rose till she left for England.

"Why did you wait all that time?"

"Really, Chad! Don't you understand *anything?*"

"You would have taken him back?" I asked, abashed.

"Like a shot."

That summer of 1911 was torrid. There was hardly a sprinkle of rain anywhere in England throughout its months. I recall clearly the hot, used quality of the air as Rose and I, at midnight, left the Margesson flat. I said I'd see her as far as Park Lane and find her a cab there. "No, let's walk," she said.

Even at that late hour, the streets were full of coronation revelers, many of them tight, singing, strolling arm in arm, whirring rattles. The grass in the park was burned to the color of ripe hay and trodden smooth. But we didn't cross the park. We walked toward the Marble Arch, pushed about and jostled.

Rose said: "Take my arm, Chad."

I did so, feeling shy of her, because I didn't want to take her arm; I wanted to put my arms around her, and draw her into some dark entry and kiss her like a shop boy out with his girl. Nothing she had told me had diminished my longing for her. Rather, I had a childish wish to make up for what she had suffered, which jarred against my awakening adult understanding that she had suffered nothing. She had experienced, and the experience was in her and would remain in her, guarded and nursed as something precious.

Her long white glove lay upon my black sleeve. Her silks whispered over the hot pavement with the sound that had always been her sound to me, from the day I first heard it at Pentyrch.

"This makes me very sad," she said, "all this singing and thoughtless mirth. I wonder what will come of it?"

"Why," I said, surprised, "a coronation, a sweeping-up of the streets, a back-to-work, and then, I fear, a continuation of the heat wave."

"You Oxford men seem to know as much about life as novices in a nunnery. Why don't you spend your holidays abroad?"

"Because my mother and my uncle would hate it, and because I'm very fond of the West Riding dales."

"Poor Chad!"

It nettled me. I remember stopping on the pavement just after we had moved left by the Marble Arch and facing her as she came to a standstill, too.

"Why do you again and again call me Poor Old Chad?" I asked hotly. "What sort of a numbskull do you take me for?"

She was instantly contrite. "I'm sorry. But sometimes in Germany, especially when Eustace was gone and I was all alone, I was terrified. There are so many people there who hate us like poison."

She took my arm, and we moved on again. "It broke out even at the school where Eustace worked. Some of the parents raised an awful row and wanted him thrown out. A damned Englishman. Why should he have any part in the education of their sons? Fancy that, Chad. In a lovely place like Weimar! Fortunately, the headmaster was an intelligent person, one of our friends."

I laughed. "Rose, my dear, I'm sorry to think that you could be upset by a few hot-air merchants. Good lord! We have 'em here as well as over there. Look at this chap Lord Roberts—a dear old thing whose mentality belongs to the days of the Indian Mutiny. Stumping the country predicting death and damnation. Believe me, we don't sleep the less easily in our beds because of that sort of stuff."

"That's a pity," she said; and, as I made to intervene again: "No. Don't let's argue about it. But I lived in Germany long enough to know that the place isn't all Weimar and Goethe. Leave it at that."

We left it at that, and I walked with her as far as Miss Orlop's front door.

"There was a good maid among the batch I saw this afternoon," she said. "We shall be leaving for Pentyrch the day after tomorrow."

"Then what shall we do tomorrow—lunch or dinner?"

"Neither, I'm afraid. We shall be away for six weeks, and there's endless packing to do."

We stood irresolute for a moment. There was so much I wanted to say, but always, with Rose, I could not say it. I said lightly: "I'm terrified at the thought of your being out of my sight."

"Dear Chad," she said. Better than Poor Chad, anyway. She raised her face to be kissed, and I kissed her, but with dreadful shyness. She mounted the few steps, waved her hand, and went in.

CHAPTER SEVEN

1

IT IS a time-tattered emotion; it has been written about endlessly; and I endured it: that emotion when the bags are put into the cab, and the horse heads for the station, and you awake from the dream of Oxford. Nothing to come can be like it. There will be no other river like its river, no other bells like its bells, no other stones like its stones. But you can never go back except as a ghost.

Ten days had passed since I said good-by to Rose, and, in the train, I opened and read again the letter that had come yesterday from Miss Orlop. I still couldn't believe it. The pain of it threaded through the pain of leaving Oxford, and in the corner of a first-class compartment, which I had taken in order to be alone, I was close to tears.

DEAR CHAD:

Rose has been here a week now with her Henrietta, and from what she tells me I know that you are aware that Billy is with us, too. Would it be possible for you to join us? It is so long since you have been in Cornwall. I don't recall your returning once since leaving Pendeverel after your father's death. Now that you are done with Oxford, I expect you'll want to take a long holiday before deciding what to do with yourself. Your mother, and your dear uncle, to whom, please, give my best wishes, will no doubt, and rightly, want most of your company; but we shall all be glad if you will give us any time you can spare. What would be especially delightful would be if you could be here during the last week of August, when Billy and Rose will be married. It's a pity Rose didn't think of this two years and more ago; but there—I've been fool enough myself in my time, and have no talent for nagging about the folly of other people. Enough to say that I am very happy that this has at last happened. *Do* come.

Sincerely,

LUCY ORLOP

For all the sorrow of it, I should have liked to go at once. I should have liked to find out for myself what had happened to Rose in those ten days. It had seemed to me, during the few hours we spent together, that Eustace was as much in her heart as during the time I could never forget when we lived from morning to night on the river and I alone could not see the stroke of fate about to fall. Billy Pascoe, as much as myself, had had for her then no more substance than a ghost, nor had he seemed more significant when we talked in London.

I know now what happened. I know how your heart can be all but crushed and how you can, just the same, put a good face to the world, especially to such a nonpercipient fool as Chad Boothroyd. Having stayed for so long alone in Weimar, why should Rose suddenly run home unless home had been what she was crying for? You can love, and yet feel hell's own pangs of bitterness and resentment against the loved one, and hide them, and crave the warmth and comfort of common understanding. I know this now, because, so terribly soon, I was to find it out for myself.

Rose found at Pentyrch what she needed. I can well imagine now how the gruff affection of her mother would wrap her round, how the unadventurous safety of her life took the sting out of her anguish. In that lovely sunny year the sea would be ever kind and blue, and she and the child would play on the beach, and walk hand in hand over the rotting leaves of the sunken path where long ago we found my father pinned to the ground by a spike through his neck. Perhaps Rose would think of that, and of how she and I went up to the lawn and she covered me with blankets. But I was not there to share any tenderness such memories might arouse; and Billy Pascoe was there, always Miss Orlop's favorite, her creation, almost, and a favorite, too, I was to learn, with the child. So there they were, cooped away from the world, shut in by their woods and by the sea, and Rose would be shut in by a great understanding tenderness such as she had not known for years. She would be living in a mellow light, never intensified by the vivid lightning and the stormy sunsets that she had known with Eustace; but it could well be what she needed and valued above all at that moment. The sheer reaction of entering into this safety, perhaps of seizing it eagerly for the sake of the child, could account for the swift final step.

I stayed in London overnight and traveled the next day to Smurthwaite. Thence I wrote to Miss Orlop, thanking her for her invitation; and, twisting the knife in my wound, I said I would be glad to come.

2

Uncle Arthur had strolled down to the station to meet me, and was surprised to find I was not alone. Traveling up from London to Bradford, I had gone along to the dining car and there found John Begg, the young man whom I had met at Oxford on some business of the *Manchester Guardian*. My terminal reports about drama at Oxford had been few, for I began them too near the end of my university life; but I had done one or two other things for the paper: what they called "back-pagers," those agreeable trivia that, in those days, were printed daily in the first column of the back page. Occasionally a name of distinction was attached to them, permitting one the feeling of belonging to the élite; but mostly that was a column for the first flutter of nestlings' wings. Still, it was agreeable to be able, on so slender a basis, to call myself an author. I had bought a sumptuous folio of pages that were almost parchment, bound in dark green leather and with "C.B." embossed pridefully in gold on the cover. Therein my few sedate offerings trickled through wide snowy margins, enormously to the fortification of my spirit. Even now, I occasionally take up the book and look through one or two of them, and wonder how I ever could . . .

John Begg and I ate our lunch together and I found that he was bound for Yorkshire on a solitary tramping holiday. He had not been there before and had no plans. I sketched a route for him, and persuaded him to make Smurthwaite his starting point. When that was settled, we talked of this and that, and, finding that I had now come down from the University, he put the ever ready question: What was I going to do with myself? I gave him the ever ready answer that I hadn't the

174

faintest idea. He thought there was a lot to be said for journalism. Why didn't I give it a trial?

I said boastfully: "Journalism? But I want to *write!*"

And there, for the first time, I had said it, and knew that, come what might, I would stick to it.

Begg laughed. "What d'you think you'd do on the *Guardian*?" he asked. "You'd write or go out on your backside. After all, Masefield was on the staff, and there's Montague and Monkhouse and Mills, to name but a few. You'd *write*, my boy, or the Old Man would say a word or two."

We were back in a compartment. Begg had lit a pipe and was chuckling. "A leader writer," he said, "once wrote *from whence*. The Old Man wanted to know why the *from*, and the culprit brought the defense that George Meredith had more than once written *from whence*. 'Mr. Meredith would not have written *from whence* more than once in the *Manchester Guardian*,' the Old Man said. And that was that. When the Old Man says a thing, that, always, is that. Jehovah is nothing but his trembling understudy."

No more was said about the Old Man, but before Bradford was reached I had given a reluctant consent to Begg's raising "in the proper quarter" the question of my working for the paper.

3

Begg stayed with us in Smurthwaite overnight, and set off the next morning not as walkers do today with a ton on their backs and a hundredweight of hobnails on their boots, but shod in reasonable leather and carrying in a small haversack his mackintosh and shaving kit. I walked a few miles with him, then sat on a boulder and watched till he reached a bend in the white road, turned and waved his ash stick, and disappeared. I never saw again this young man who had so decisive an effect in my life. As I have said, he worked in the London office of the *Manchester Guardian*, and when I joined the staff of the paper it was at the Manchester end. Nothing took me to London in the three years that were left between those apparently cloudless days and the chaos that was to deepen throughout the rest of my life. When the breakdown came, Begg was in the army among the first. He survived till 1916, and then died in Delville Wood. You know, in those In Memoriam notices, "Their name liveth for Evermore," in the *Daily Telegraph*, commemorating men killed in war, on an August day, year by year, I still see this: "Begg, John, Major, M.C., died Delville Wood, 1916, aged 27. Never forgotten darling, Aimee." It is one of those small things that break the heart. If Begg were alive, he would be heading for seventy. I sometimes wonder who Aimee is and I am sure that what she still sees is something like the hatless youth I watched waving his stick on that sunny West Riding road.

Though no such thoughts as these were casting premonitory shadows, though already I had forgotten the few foreboding words that Rose had spoken, I walked back to Smurthwaite with a heavy heart. Greg was not at his father's farm. He and Phoebe had managed to dump their small Penelope somewhere and were gone to Austria. The days when Smurthwaite meant young companionship were gone. I should have liked nothing better than to be footing it with Begg for a week or ten days, but I owed it to my mother and Uncle Arthur to stay. I walked back past the new cemetery, looking not so new now, filling up nicely, and I could have wished that even Madeleine had survived. "What the hell's the matter with you?" I grumbled to myself, refusing to face the fact that down in Cornwall things were happening that would rob of its savor even a day in paradise.

I stayed in Smurthwaite for a week, restless and on edge, doing small household jobs for my mother, toddling about in the evenings with Uncle Arthur, even going to church on the Sunday, and marveling, as I looked at the pie-frilled choirboys, that I had ever been one of them. I felt at odds with the older generation, and had not yet come to terms with my own. I listened twenty times to Uncle Arthur's story of how he had organized Coronation Week in Smurthwaite and of how Sir Titus Newte had called round to congratulate him personally and to give him a box of cigars. I hated to tell him and my mother that I was staying for only a week, but at last I could stand no more of it and let out the secret. I did so at lunchtime on Saturday. "I'd better be off on Monday," I said.

As soon as the meal was over, Uncle Arthur said: "Chad, let us perambulate." His perambulations were becoming more and more restricted. He was putting on weight at all points of the compass, and occasionally talked of going to Bath or some German spa to endure what he called a *reductio ad absurdum*. But I knew that he would not do this: he was secretly proud of his massive appearance, which added to his air of benign dignity. "I doubt," he said, "whether a man of the greyhound cut can justly claim to have the qualifications for high municipal office. I imagine the Roman emperors were in the main men of substance. There is something treasonable about a refusal to accept the consequences of good roast beef and Yorkshire pudding."

We moved slowly up an acclivity that rose from the fields behind the house. It took us no more than half an hour to reach the limestone outcrops from which Uncle Arthur could take a bird's eye view of his municipality. I thought that day that it looked absurdly small: one sweep of the eye took it all in: but Uncle Arthur, leaning on his stick, surveyed it with a sort of complacent affection, as though he had with his own hands laid every stone of its buildings and out of his own loins begotten every man, woman and child within them. At last he sat down heavily in a scooped-out hollow of the limestone, a place that he called Arthur's Seat, and he said: "Well, Chad, I'm not surprised that you are anxious to leave us."

I thought I had concealed my feelings well enough, and I cried falsely: "Oh, Uncle Arthur, how could you think such a thing? I'm not *anxious*."

He patted the stone alongside the seat and smiled at me affectionately. "Sit down," he said. "Light your pipe."

I did so, and he took from a metal tube one of the cigars Sir Titus had given him. He carefully pierced and lit it, and said: "You can't bluff your old uncle, you know. D'you remember the day when you and Greg Appleby went after the grouse?" He chuckled. "Uncle Arthur had his eye on you. There's not much gets past Uncle Arthur."

"I haven't been to Pendeverel," I said, "since you brought me and my mother away from there. I have an invitation from Miss Orlop. I thought it would be agreeable to see the place again."

"And why not!" he asked. "When the young eagle has mewed his mighty youth, he must move off into the midday beam."

"It's very kind of you to say so, Uncle Arthur, but I feel more like a fledgling sparrow, wondering which way to fly."

"Fly, Chad, fly," he said, as though inviting me to take off over the Smurthwaite rooftops. Indeed, he waved his stout hand, with the cigar clasped between two fingers, comprehensively toward his municipality. "Take off. That is the thing. Embark. Obey the tug of the tides."

He took up his straw hat and fanned his perspiring face. His assault on the roast beef at lunch had been heroic, and he appeared to be paying for it. But I was becoming confused as to whether he wanted me to be a seaman or a seagull.

"Get on the road," he said, casting me now for Whittington. "Foot it, Chad. That is the thing. Be off somewhere. All roads lead home at last."

"Uncle Arthur," I said, "I shouldn't be at all surprised if you and mother were disappointed with me. You've done everything possible for me. You've showered me with bounty." I cried, warming up, "and it's no one's fault but my own if you're wondering what use I make of it all. Well, I want to write books or plays. I don't suppose it'll be easy. I'm not such a fool as to imagine that I can become either famous or prosperous overnight. But I'm determined about one thing: I'm not going to hang round your neck any longer. I think I could earn my living as a journalist while trying to do this other thing. That man

John Begg who stayed with us for a night is going to try to land me a job with the *Manchester Guardian*. If I get an offer, I'll take it."

"Why, Chad!" he cried. "That's the longest speech I've ever heard you make." And then, his mind overleaping all intermediate considerations: "Books, eh! Now that's something. A Dickens in the family! Well, Chad, if you can make me weep as old Charles can I shall feel that my money's well spent. Not that the money enters into it. I'm glad you said what you did, Chad, but let it be said once and for all. Why, what sort of Uncle should I have been," he cried. "If I hadn't done what I could?" And there, simply, he had said all that I felt in my heart about him.

We talked for a long time, and now we were on a different footing. All my vague dreams were already, for Uncle Arthur, achievements. He even proved to be the first of many people I have met in the course of my life anxious to supply me with what they call "plots." "Who among us, my dear Chad," he demanded, "has not at some time or other felt the urge to take up the pen? But time forbids and our plots lie in our minds unfertilized. Now an idea I have often pondered is this." And he gave it to me at length, adding: "Now Dickens, with all the time there was on his hands, could have made something of that, and something that would have done his reputation no harm."

I remember nothing of this outline except one sentence which Uncle Arthur spoke in tones almost of reverence: "And then came the night in Liverpool when, for her crippled brother's sake, Lois made the supreme sacrifice." He could hardly go on for the choke in his voice.

We had eaten so well at lunchtime that I could have done without tea. But Uncle Arthur couldn't. We went downhill in a happy mood, and he presented me to my mother as though I were someone she had never seen before. "My dear," he said, "this is our young author. The world is his oyster, and with his pen he will open it. The oyster, with a suitable hock, is not to be sneezed at. He begins with the advantage of a name that would grace any title page. I can imagine it attached to the world's greatest works. *David Copperfield,* by Chad Boothroyd. *Misunderstood,* by Chad Boothroyd. *The Sorrows of Satan,* by Chad Boothroyd. It would do. The name has a ring."

My mother was rather perplexed by it all, and took, I think, a more realistic view of the matter. "What is this all about, Chad?" she asked me in her room that evening.

I told her. "Well," she said, "I hope you will get somewhere in the long run. I'm glad you think of taking a job in the meantime."

I had never said anything to them about the "back-pagers" in the *Manchester Guardian,* but that night I produced my sumptuous volume for Uncle Arthur's inspection. We retired with it to his den, and there he put on his smoking cap and read from end to end the complete works of Chad Boothroyd. When he had done—and it didn't take long—he sat

178

for a moment with the closed folio on his knee, gazing into space. Presently he said: "You have it in you, Chad. Bring it out. These," he said, stroking the book, "are the buds. Cultivate them. As the most successful auricula grower and hybridizer in the North of England, and possibly further afield than that—speaking for the moment without prejudice, but bearing in mind certain jealousies in the Southern Counties—I know something about cultivation. You will do nothing, Chad, without cultivation. And cultivation means a year's work for a moment's perfection. Remember that, my boy. The Almighty Himself, who blesses the human eye with the sight of *tigridia*, natural order *Iridaceae*, for but one summer's day, works to that end throughout the other three hundred and sixty-four days of the year. Not that *tigridia* should be mentioned alongside *auricula*. Still, it is an illustration. Cultivate!"

"By Order, Arthur J. Geldersome, Town Clerk," I thought mischievously; but, after all, what would I have done without him?

4

I was so relieved to be in the train, speeding away from Smurthwaite, that I felt a sense of ingratitude, even of sin. Why I should feel relieved, when I knew too well what heartache I was rushing into, who can say? I was young and well; the wonderful summer had filled everything with ripeness. The cornfields of Shropshire and Herefordshire were golden lakes; already, here and there, the woods had taken flame; the orchard trees were bowed with apples; and soon I should be seeing Rose. In whatever circumstances, I should be seeing Rose. Oddly, that made me happy.

I should have arrived unpardonably late if I had made the journey in a day. I spent the night in Bristol, and the next afternoon the white hills of my childhood blazed under the sun and the train drew into the little place that had been to me then "our Town."

Outside the station modernity had struck: a taxicab stood there. But also standing there was that ramshackle victoria, and a fat white horse that may or may not have been the one I used to know, and in the driver's seat, wearing the same moth-eaten silk hat, was unquestionably the same driver, looking as incredibly old as his vehicle. He looked, indeed, like Time himself, ready to drive his crazy carriage for the last time over the edge of the world I had known.

Rose was sitting in the carriage.

She got down, and came toward me, smiling and holding out both hands. "The choice was not large," she said. "I thought you'd prefer this."

I looked at her, speechless for a moment. She was so beautiful. She had been living in the sun and the sea, and she glowed like the Shropshire fields, full-weighted with gold. She did not, as she had done when we parted in London, offer her face to be kissed.

"You did well," I said at last. "Do you know, you were riding in this when I first saw you? I was gathering blackberries, and I was so astounded that I spilled the basket. But don't flatter yourself that your beauty did that. It was because I recognized my Uncle Arthur."

Old Horsehair! It was a long time since I had heard him called that.

I tried to pass the moment off lightly, but I was intolerably affected.

"I remember," she said. "That was why I chose the victoria."

Unmoving, with the flies settling on his white horse and on his black hat, the reins languid in his gnarly hands, the old man sat there, looking straight ahead, not seeming to listen to a word we said, waiting, the short remnant of his time seemingly of no account. When we got in, he gave the reins an imperceptible shake, but it was enough, and the horse ambled forward. Broken springs jarred my behind; the axles groaned.

Are you trying, I wondered, to do the worst you can to me, to get it over right at the start?

Certainly, nothing could have been more calculated than that drive to stir the bitter lees that clouded my memory. Save the taxicab, there seemed nothing new in the world. I recognized every gate and tree, every cottage and coppice. Had there been clouds, I should have recognized them and the way they bowled across the void we call the sky.

"It was there," Rose said.

We were passing the gate on which I had sat. That, too, was unchanged: insecure, held to its post by a fag end of tattered rope.

"You met us both that day," I said, "and now you have chosen between us. I haven't congratulated you yet. Let me do so."

She looked at me from under the flopping corn-gold brim of her wide hat, placed a hand on mine. "Thank you, Chad," she said.

I wanted to say: "You don't sound very enthusiastic. What's it all about? Are you happy?" But how could I say any such thing? The horse's hoofs flopped on wearily through the white dust; the old man seemed to be dozing; we turned between the ball-topped granite pillars, and the gloom of the long drive swallowed us.

The sun had long declined from its zenith, and the house, set about closely with tall trees, was in shadow. But so hot had that summer been that the honey-yellow stone seemed to glow with stored light. The lawn was a vivid green. Where so much was burnt up, this, little shone upon each day, was fresh and eager. It had recently been cut: the smell of it was on the air.

I remember that: how the old man took his money with never a word and turned his horse and went, and how the house glowed and the grass was green, and fantail pigeons that I had not seen there before were tumbling through the air, fantastically white, and Henrietta, holding Billy Pascoe's hand in one of hers, was holding up a red apple with the other, in the delusive hope that the birds would alight upon it. Billy Pascoe was wearing cream-colored trousers, a white shirt open at the neck, and white shoes. It was a long time since I had seen him, and then he had not looked like this. He had had the pallor of a student driving himself too hard. Now he had not the superficial tan of a holiday-maker, but looked as though the sun had cooked him through to the bone. He was taller than I, dark and sinewy. I was intensely aware of him: the ragamuffin I had played with on the beach. He was full of eager, vivid life. A lot had been happening to Billy Pascoe, inside and out, I realized. I looked at him with a pang of jealous envy. He looked so damnably at home.

He loosed the child's hand and came across the lawn. "Well, Chad," he said. "It was good of you to come."

We shook hands, and he felt like a steel spring.

"Good?" I said. "Nonsense, Billy. Sheer self-indulgence."

A nurse came out of the house: the treasure Rose had found in London, I supposed. "Bedtime!" she called to Henrietta, and the child began to howl and toddled on fat legs to Billy, hiding her face in his creamy trousers. He took her up in both his hands and kissed her. She is Eustace's child, I thought.

"Tomorrow we will feed the pigeons," said Billy. "Then we will dig on the beach. Then we will swim. Then you shall bury me in sand." The child began to smile. "But *now*," said Billy firmly, "you will go with nurse, have your bath, and go to bed. When you are in bed, I shall come and sing to you, and when I have sung to you, you will go to sleep. That's the program." He handed her to the nurse, and she went away quietly.

"Pascoe the Lion-tamer," I said.

He didn't answer that, but took up my suitcase. "Let me show you to your room."

It looked out over the front porch, across the lawn toward the path that ran to the beach. It was the room from which Rose had looked down that night when my father and I had trespassed through the woods. Billy looked about, efficiently checking that this and that was in order. "Bathroom next door," he said. "Dinner at half-past seven." Yes, quite at home, the young master of the house.

"Thank you, Pascoe," I said.

He gave me a saturnine look and moved toward the door. There he paused and said: "By the way, Miss Orlop has cast you as best man." Then he went.

I stood for a moment at the window, sensing the invisible sea, watching the languid stir of the trees' topmost twigs. There was no bird song, nothing but a deepening silence, the whole world seeming exhausted by the unending heat. The lawn alone was cool, and Rose, still wearing her wide straw hat, was moving about slowly down there, gathering things that the child had scattered: a doll, the coral bauble, this and that. Billy came out of the house, took the things from her hands, and put them on a wicker table. My window was wide open, and I heard him say: "I've sung to Henrietta. Let's have a little walk before dinner."

"I shall have to change," she said. "There's not much time."

"You must never, never change," he said amorously. "That is something I could not bear."

He put his arm round her waist, and began to draw her toward the leafy tunnel that led to the beach. She looked round toward the house with an almost prudish glance, as if to see whether they were observed, and then went with him, as I thought, reluctantly.

5

I was fagged by the journey, and the heat, and the emotional disturbance of my arrival. I had a bath and changed from my tweeds into a lounge suit and strolled down to the garden. Passing through the hall, I noticed hanging there a picture that I had not seen before. It was of Billy Pascoe in a doctor's robes. The colors of the new paint glowed in the dusk. It seemed to me a good portrait. I remembered that Miss Orlop's father had once hung there, and wondered whether she had put him into the fire. Certainly, she would feel prouder of this: her own creation, subject and portrait alike.

The garden had a new feature. To the right of the path leading to the beach another, narrower, path had been cut through the trees. It went off at a tangent from the old path, and, following it, I found that here the ground, instead of falling away, rose slightly. It ended in a little rocky bluff, looking forward to the sea, giving an enfilading glance along the beach to the left, and on the right shut in, like so much else, by trees. Mesembryanthemum, the noon flower, that would blaze there at midday, had closed its thousand eyes, but the scent of thyme was heavy and gorse was afire. On the seaward edge of the bluff was a stout log cabin with large windows. As I stood looking with pleasure at this charming enclave, all wrapped in the quiet of the evening, with the glistering sea stretched away to the indigo of the horizon, the door of the cabin opened and Miss Orlop came out. Her halo shone white above an overall of lemon paint-plastered linen that shrouded her to the

182

feet like a fantastic nightgown. In one hand she held her palette, in the other a palette knife.

Seeing me, she gave a start, and said: "Chad! You've come! Good gracious, whatever can the time be?"

"Just on seven," I said.

She began then with the knife to scrape the palette, stropping the paint from the knife onto the jamb of the door. She must have been doing this off and on for months—perhaps years—for the door jamb was a marvelous palimpsest of color, like the door of a yacht builder's yard, where, through year after year, the green and yellow and black and scarlet are tried out before going forth to dance on the waves under the white or brick-red sails. When she had cleaned the palette, Miss Orlop said: "Come in, Chad," and I followed her into the studio where she completed her job with a few wipes of a turpentined cloth. Then she heaved the nightdress over her head, threw it onto a chair, and took me by the arm. "We must run," she said. She literally did so, banging the door behind her and taking to her heels, with me in tow. At intervals she panted: "Nice welcome, I must say." "Well, Chad, how are you?" "Won't take me a minute to change."

Certainly it took little longer, for as the gong boomed in the hall I saw her come majestically down the stairs arrayed in a flowing horror of magenta that looked as though she had flung it into the air, thrust her head and arms through it as it descended, and left the rest to God.

I was waiting in the hall for them to come down. Rose came first, wearing dark blue silk, with shoes of pale Cambridge blue. She said nothing to me as I hovered by the door of the dining room, but pressed my hand and went straight in. Billy came wearing a suit of light gray flannel, with a dark blue shirt and a pale blue tie. He had learned to wear his clothes well. At Oxford, though he had worn good clothes, he had worn them as carelessly as the magenta dress was worn by Miss Orlop, who now came charging down the stairs, sweeping me into the room with her arm through mine, and crying: "Am I in time? Am I in time?" Billy was waiting to pull out her chair.

Once she was settled, she was the courteous hostess, full of apologies for not having been at home to receive me. "It was so good of you to come, Chad, and I should have been here, and I do sincerely apologize. I went off intending to do no more than make a sketch, and then I thought of something and started to work, and—well, you know what it is. I expect you writers are just the same. I received a letter this morning from that unexpectedly delightful uncle of yours, telling me you're going to be a famous writer. How lovely! When I'm in town you must come down here and use the studio any time you like. Don't write. Just come. I'm sure you'll find it an inspiring place to work."

I didn't bless Uncle Arthur. He had delivered me naked to the curiosity of them all. Miss Orlop was vaguely enthusiastic. "You should go in for science fiction, Chad. Look at Mr. Wells. I met him once and thought him a most disagreeable man, but that's another matter. He's doing very well, but Billy tells me his stuff is only a child's dream to what science really has in store for us. I'm sure a few good long talks with Billy would give you material for books that would frighten people to death."

I said I would rather keep my readers alive, if any ever came my way; but I couldn't sidetrack this unwanted subject. "It's the atom," she said. "There was a book by Marie Corelli called *The Mighty Atom*. But I'm afraid she wasn't thinking of the sort of atoms Billy's concerned with. I had no idea how mighty they were till he began to talk to me about them. Every one a universe, with a sun and planets revolving round it. Imagine the sheer *energy* of that! Now what would happen if we could get hold of that energy and use it for our own purposes?"

"It would depend on the purposes," Rose said. "Chad, you haven't any red currant jelly." She passed it along.

"Everything," said Miss Orlop, "even red currant jelly, is made up of these atoms that are bristling with energy. Take this table," she said, giving the oak a hearty smack. "There it's been God knows how long. It was already an ancient thing when some Orlop acquired it from a monastery that Henry the Eighth had dissolved. You may remember, he had queer hobbies: dissolving monasteries and cutting women's heads off. I know nothing more about him, and don't want to. An unsavory person. Well, in this one table, through all those centuries, there has been this energy that nobody's known how to use. Think of the waste."

"Why is it wasted?" Rose asked. "It's been doing its job of holding a useful table together. Perhaps holding things together is the real business of atoms, not blowing them apart."

Billy let such talk slide. He wasn't even smiling the aloof smile of the expert, who listens to the chatter of the uninformed. He simply wasn't interested. He was eating a good meal, and enjoying it.

"Are atoms your specialty, Billy?" I asked.

"Yes."

"You wouldn't like to give me material for a few hair-raising books?"

"No."

Billy wasn't playing. "Is it true, Chad, that you're beginning to do a bit of writing?" he asked.

"Yes."

"Are you working along any particular line?"

"No."

We were like a couple of cats eying one another, I thought; and to ease the situation I became more expansive. "You must take what my uncle says as no more than a fond patron's exaggerations. The fact is, I've got no further than hoping for a start in journalism. I may go to the *Manchester Guardian*."

Then Billy became really alight for a second. "Manchester!" he said. "Ernest Rutherford is there!"

I remembered how, as a ragged urchin, he used to breathe the names of Davy and Faraday as though they were holy. The same light was in his eye now. "Gosh!" he said, "I'd give something to work under Rutherford!"

Miss Orlop said: "We'll drink our coffee in the lounge," and Billy sprang up to draw out her chair.

No lamps had been lit, and the lounge was full of a greenish twilight, almost dark. The door and windows were open, seeming to do no more than make the room warmer as the enervating heat rolled in from out of doors. There wasn't a stir to a curtain or a tremble in the petals of a flower. I looked at the bowl of tall white blooms standing in a vase on a table at the window. They were a carving in alabaster, motionless against the darkness. The sound of the sea came up, a tired whisper.

Rose was sitting in the part of the room farthest from me. Her dark blue was obliterated. The pale blue of her shoes, glimmering one above the other, for she was cross-legged, and the oval of her face, were all I could see. Billy Pascoe was pouring out the coffee, and Miss Orlop's magenta bulk was collapsed in a large chair. She had grown very stout since I last saw her.

We seemed to be shadows in the shadowy room. All at once, a deep sense of depression flooded me, as one might suddenly be overborne by an unexpected wave. Depression and foreboding. Nobody is really happy here, I thought, except Miss Orlop. The rest of us are putting a face onto a bad job.

I got up and said: "Don't bother about coffee for me, Billy. Miss Orlop, would you excuse me if I took a turn in the garden?"

She was immediately the concerned hostess. "Oh, Chad! Aren't you feeling well?"

"Well enough," I said. "It's this continuous uncanny heat. I've had hours in a stuffy railway compartment today, and it's taken it out of me. I shall be all right when I've had a breather."

"I'll see that coffee is kept hot for you."

"Don't bother, please."

"It's no bother. It shall be done." She was so determined a woman. Let there be coffee, and there was coffee. Let Rose marry Billy, and—what?

No, no. You're imagining things, I told myself, as I stumbled through the dark tunnel that led to the studio on the bluff. Here, it was almost midnight black. An owl was quavering in the trees, and a bat had swirled almost into my face as I was crossing the lawn. I went slowly—it was new territory to me—groping toward a pallor that showed the moon was rising. It rose as I sat on a rock of the bluff, dry and still warm from the day's heat. The scent of the thyme was strong as my feet crushed it, and the moon's gentle rays made the gorse luminous. Luminous, too, was the spreading skirt of the water on my left hand. A heron was moving above it, a gray ghost of a bird, fanning itself forward on gray ghostly wings. It passed from my sight beneath the bluff, and must have alighted there, for suddenly the quiet was torn by its hideous cry that seemed to belong to pterodactyl swamps in haggard woods rather than to this still, open night, shining and opalescent. I shuddered. It's the true voice of this place and of this moment, all the same, I thought. It's the horror behind the seeming-fair.

It was not that anyone *intended* ill. I was sure of that. The ill was in the absence of intention, the good-natured drift to rocks and shadows.

I don't know how long I sat there, but the moon was well up the sky, and I was watching a dinghy being rowed by some solitary, the soundless oars dripping sparks of phosphorescence, when the rustle of silk told me that Rose was behind me. She must have been into the studio, for she was carrying a cushion and an old plaid shawl that I had seen thrown over a stool there that afternoon. She sat down, drew the shawl about her shoulders, and looked out to sea, her fingers linked round her up-drawn knees.

"What is making you so unhappy, Chad?"

"Are *you* happy?"

"Why should I expect to be? Happiness is illusive, my dear. I know. I chased it once, frantically."

"Any port in a storm," I said with brutal resentment.

I had not looked at her, but now she looked at me, so compellingly that at last I was forced to turn my head. I saw no love for me in her eyes, but sorrow and pity. Without a word, her glance condemned what I had said. Before this, when I had looked at her eyes it had been only to admire, to love, their beauty. Now I saw in them a depth of knowledge, and, beyond all knowledge, of wisdom, that made me feel ashamed at having judged her. "I am very fond of you, Chad," she said; and with the words she put an arm about my shoulders and drew my head down upon her breast. My cheek lay upon the plaid shawl. I could hear the steady unexcited beat of her heart, as a mother's heart must sound to a child that is being comforted. I could feel the gall oozing from my mind.

At last, she put me away from her and got up. "I'm glad you came, Chad," she said. "It's very kind of you to help me at a difficult moment like this. Stay there now. Don't come in yet. Let me get in first, alone."

When at last I came out from the leafy tunnel, I stood spellbound, looking across the lawn to the house. The moon was high enough for the trees to be cleared by its light that lay pale gold on the pale gold stone, softening it and the big spheres of the hydrangea flowers at its foot almost to insubstantiality. There was not a whisper of sound, not a shiver of movement: nothing but the dreaming house and the flowers entranced about it. The slates of the roof were silver-wet; and at the beautiful vision all the foreboding rushed back and kicked my heart over. I remembered Manchester. I remembered that there were other things in the world than this.

6

It was the oddest wedding. If the banns had not called attention to it, I suppose the church would have been empty. No invitations were sent out. However, Billy Pascoe was a village boy. The boys and girls who had been at school with him and me were naturally inquisitive about his wedding to the heiress of Pentyrch, and a goodly crowd of them and of their parents turned up. What they made of the situation I don't know. The bride's mother was still Miss Orlop to them, and how Miss Orlop had come by this daughter she would be the last to explain. The daughter's daughter was another puzzle. At any rate, it all gave them what they wanted, and that was something to talk about: food for myth and legend. I have no doubt that on one point they were agreed: it was high time someone in that family went to church and contracted a Christian marriage.

There were no wedding garments. Billy and I walked in lounge suits across the fields to the church, taking turns to carry my suitcase through the blistering heat. We dumped it in the porch, and I saw that Miss Orlop's, brought by a gardener, was already there. Billy was silent, almost grim, all the way. I don't remember that we exchanged a word.

Miss Orlop had drawn up the timetable, so that everything went smoothly. Billy and I were hardly standing in our places, aware of the popping eyes of the villagers, when Rose began to walk up the aisle from the west door. Christine Darby, the charming girl she had engaged as Henrietta's nurse, was bridesmaid, but there was no train to be looked after, and Christine had nothing to do but walk behind Rose and Miss Orlop. Rose's hand rested on her mother's arm. She looked self-possessed. When she and Billy at last stood side by side and the service began, she turned and smiled at him. He did not return the smile. He was, I think, the only person in the church not at ease—or at any rate not able to assume an appearance of ease. As we were walking through the fields I was aware of his physical and mental rigidity. Every nerve and muscle in him, and every feeling, was at an intolerable tension. Since this had to be, I should be glad, for his sake, when it was over.

It was over soon enough. I felt, as I handed him the ring, that I was handing him my life. His hand was shaking as he took it.

That remains in my mind as the most poignant moment: the moment when Billy's shaking hand fumbled the ring onto Rose's finger, standing out from a hand that was steady and looked cool.

The parson's sermonic words were few. They gave me time, now that my part in the thing was done, to look about me, to savor the cool in this small stony casket, smelling of ferns and moss and rotting stone and mildewed fabrics. It was only when Rose and Billy, arm in arm, began to move toward the vestry that a sharp prod from Miss Orlop's elbow jerked me out of my dream, and, with her and Christine Darby, I followed.

When at last we stepped out of the shadowed porch into the burning caldron of the day, I saw the taxicab from our Town waiting beyond the lich gate at the end of the short path. This was in accordance with Miss Orlop's written schedule. Christine hurried away at once to the path through the fields that would take her back to Pentyrch and Henrietta. We others walked down the path, between the stone or slate slabs that were askew above the unremarkable dead, and under the lich gate I kissed Rose and shook Billy's hand. I was unable to speak a word to either. Miss Orlop kissed them both. Then she and I got into the taxicab in which our suitcases already lay, and off we went amid the village cheers for all the world as though we were the "happy couple" leaving for a honeymoon. This, too, was part of the program. She was bound for London; I for Smurthwaite. We would travel together as far as Plymouth. What better place than Pentyrch for Billy and Rose in that moment of their lives? Screwing my head round to look through the back window of the cab, I saw them standing side by side in the road, waving their handkerchiefs.

7

John Begg had lost no time. The day after my return to Smurthwaite a letter for me arrived from Manchester.

DEAR MR. BOOTHROYD:

I am told that journalism might interest you as a career. The pieces you have already written for this newspaper give hope that we might find a use for you if you cared to make a trial run with us. Could you make it convenient to be in Manchester next week? If so, would you call upon me here in the office at about 8 in the evening? Please let me know, beforehand, on which evening you will come.

Yours very truly,

C. P. SCOTT

It was written, not typed, and was in a firm legible hand.

There was also a letter from Greg Appleby, back in Manchester from Austria. The printed letterhead showed that he now had a telephone. I rang him up, and wangled an invitation to stay with him for a few days. I told him what it was all about, and to my surprise he said: "I'm playing tennis with the Old Man this afternoon. I'll put in a word for you. I'd better let him win first."

I thought this was one of Greg's jokes, but I learned in time that it was no joke at all. It was rather damping to learn how much one's friends were doing of which one knew nothing, and to find oneself towed along in their wake. What had happened was that, during the previous winter, Greg had delivered a series of lectures on economics, and the Old Man, after reading the report of the first one, had given orders that the others were to be reported more fully. Greg had then received a "Dear Mr. Appleby" letter from "Yours very truly," but now he was "Dear Appleby" and the Old Man was his "Sincerely." He had been asked to review, and had reviewed, any important books that came along on economics, and occasionally he wrote a leading article on some economic subject. He had now reached the distinction of being invited from time to time to play tennis on the lawn of The Firs, the Old Man's house in the Manchester suburb of Fallowfield.

He told me all this on the night of my arrival, as we sat smoking in his L-shaped book-lined room at the top of the house. "Of course," he said, "I have to tone myself down a bit. I say what I think, but, in the *Guardian*, it has to be pretty cautious. For a Liberal, the Old Man's prepared to go a long way, but not by a long chalk so far as I'd like."

There was nothing wrong with Greg's manner to me; he was the cheerful openhearted companion I had known for so long, but I had a sense of lagging, of being far behind in achievement, that the difference of a few years did not account for. There was the sound of a child crying, and Phoebe's voice called up the stairs, and Greg said: "Excuse me. Penelope's howling. I must go and calm the storm."

I was left alone in the cozy room, facing my own feeling of insufficiency. I got up and prowled about, looking at Greg's big writing table, the order, the work in progress, the work done in the shape of a few books lying there, and I thought of all that Greg had: this well-provisioned base, Phoebe, the child. From Greg my thoughts passed to Eustace who had walked Rose off under my very eyes; and to Billy Pascoe, alone with her now amid the leafy woods by the sea at Pendeverel. My three friends, the only three friends I had ever had: they seemed, almost without effort, to pick up and bear away from me what I would have given so much to possess. And, of course, it all meant Rose. If I had had Rose, I shouldn't have given a tinker's curse for what any of them had or did.

Phoebe came in. "Sorry about this, Chad," she said. "Whenever Greg's at home, Penelope expects him to tell her a story before she goes to sleep. He broke the rule tonight in order to be with you. But Penelope knows her mind."

"Stories?" I said. "I should have thought Greg would want to lull her with a few pages from John Stuart Mill or Thorold Rogers's *Economic Interpretation of History*."

"That shows how much you know about Greg. He makes up the loveliest stories. It's a serial, all about a boy and girl named Weg and Wog."

"God help us," I said. "I am adrift."

"Of course you are," she said. "Who wouldn't be after what's happened? And with this *Manchester Guardian* business still unsettled."

She came and sat on the arm of my chair, all comfortable maternity. Dear Phoebe! "After what's happened." She was the only one who seemed to understand that *anything* had happened. My mother and Uncle Arthur had taken it for granted that my visit to Pentyrch had been a bit of pleasant junketing. Greg had shown hardly any interest one way or another. Only Phoebe knew at once what was the matter with me, and she said no more than that. She didn't mention the thing again, but it was comforting to feel that she understood.

She sat with her arm round my shoulder and talked about my writing. She had read my bits and pieces in the *Guardian*, and strove to make them seem more than they were. And she did at last succeed in getting me talking, in taking me out of my obsession. "And don't worry about Old Man Scott," she concluded. "You're a bit afraid of him, aren't you?"

"I've heard rather terrifying stories."

"Take a leaf out of Greg's book," she advised me. "He's not afraid of anyone. He never was—not even of me. I tried hard," she said with an almost complacent smile, "to get the upper hand. But I know now who's the boss."

8

I survived the interview with the Old Man. I found that he had talked to John Begg about me as well as to Greg Appleby, and then there were the things I had written, which he was kind enough to call "slender but not unpromising." He said: "I don't think, Mr. Boothroyd, that your inclination runs at the moment to the political side. But I expect you will find your own way of being useful."

It didn't sound enthusiastic; he clearly was not under the impression that he was engaging a Montague or Hobhouse. Later, I received another of his neat hand-written letters, formally engaging me as a member of the staff, telling me that I would be paid five pounds a week, and asking me, in the undemanding way he had of giving an order, whether it would be "convenient" to me to report on the following Monday to the chief of the reporters' room.

I remained in Manchester for the next three years, and then left the town forever. In the office I was, through all that time, an odd man out. My status was never defined. I was everybody's dog's-body. I worked at times in the reporters' room, though I had never been appointed to the reporting staff. I was occasionally asked to write a short leader, though I was not on the "corridor," as we called the domain of those archangels who most closely surrounded the Throne and whose proper business leaders were. Each of them had his own snug room, with his own fire burning of a winter night. Their lot seemed to me enviable, though I knew in my heart it was one my talents and inclinations would never permit me to share. I reviewed books, and the lesser dregs of the theater, beneath the notice of greater men, were often mine to deal with. Occasionally, I obeyed with trembling an order to attend the Old Man at The Firs and do a stint as amanuensis. When I left the paper, I don't suppose that anyone noticed it. The only person to whom my departure mattered was my wife.

When the war broke out, I had been married to May Ingleby for a year. I had forgotten the girl's existence when I took up my job in Manchester. Greg and Phoebe were kind enough to ask me to share their little house, but I didn't want to do this. Oxford had given me a taste for rooms of my own. I stayed with them only until I found lodgings. In a little house in a street tucked away behind the main road in the suburb of Withington I found a sitting room and a bedroom in the house of an aged widow. She had no family. She had nothing to do but look to my wants, and that suited me, especially as a profound respect flowed from her because I worked for the *Manchester Guardian*. I was able even to persuade her to remove all unwanted furniture from my sitting room. I installed a few bits of my own, surrounded myself with my books, hung Miss Orlop's drawing of Rose above the fireplace, and thanked the stars for my luck. With the green curtains drawn of a winter night, and the fire going well, I was as snug as any man needs to be. Not that there were many nights like that, for most of my nights were spent at work, with a rattling ride home on the tram through deserted streets at midnight, or, in the summer, even at break of day.

Of these nights at work, there was one that I detested above all others. During my frequent turns as a buttress of the reporting staff there would sometimes come what was called night duty. It meant standing by in readiness for anything that might arise till the building vibrated with the news that the first edition was on the machines. One was supposed to be alert, conscientiously tapping the sources of possible news. At intervals one rang up the hospitals, the railway stations, the police. The men with news-hunting in their blood would even make rounds of calls in person. I rarely did this, but now and then I would noctambulate through the city, where the lights were going off, or had long since gone; and if the duty came on a Sunday night, when Manchester seemed wholly dead, and the back streets were given over to spewing dustbins, and prowling cats, and occasional couples dubiously clasped together in dark warehouse doorways, when one's own footsteps sounded nefarious on the stone setts, and the turn of any unlighted corner was made almost with apprehension: then I could work up a fine imagination of evil such as could not visit me on the widest midnight moor. From such a prelude one entered a police station prepared to receive news of stealthy knives and nocturnal arson, only to find a comfortable policeman sipping his tea and handing out the assurance that there was "nothing doing."

But on one of these dreary Sunday nights, when I had been with the paper for about a year, something was doing. The day before this had been my own. It was a Saturday, and there was no Sunday paper to think about. I took a train to Millersdale in Derbyshire, so as to beat the town out of my mind. It was a lovely day of late autumn, and I spent it afoot in the valleys and on the moors. The sky was unsullied, the heather was aflame; the pub where I ate cold meat and drank beer was a homely gray stone place with mountain ash trees standing about it, hung heavily with scarlet berries. It was all so much what I wanted that I felt more keenly than ever a sense that went with me whenever I took a walk like that, a sense of dissatisfaction with Manchester, an unexpressed question: What are you doing in the place? And what are you going to get out of it? St. Michael Pendeverel, Smurthwaite and Oxford had conspired to forbid me ever to be at home in that dense city of the plain.

I was back in the town by six o'clock. The evening had turned cold and my landlady had lit the fire in my room. This was better; Manchester was always better when you could shut it out. I ate my evening meal, lit my pipe, and said to myself that if ever I was to get out of Manchester I must *write* myself out of it. In the last year I had written, except for the paper, next to nothing. Now I thought of Miss Horniman's Gaiety Theater, there in the very midst of the city, a target if ever there was one. Manchester men were writing plays for it and fine players were acting them. I would write one myself.

It was a mood and a moment I had known before and was to know often again: the mood when a theme swells and swells in the imagination, like a balloon of finest skin, needing only the first prick of the pin to crumble it to nothing.

The little house was quiet. My landlady was gone and I knew she would not disturb me again till she brought a cup of coffee at ten. I felt buoyant. The fire purred, and the gaslight buzzed softly. At ten o'clock my landlady tiptoed in. I drank the coffee, threw what I had written into the fire, and went to bed. It was my worst defeat. I even thought, at that moment, that I might as well accept it as final. And, indeed, I did not again put pen to paper, except as a journalist, for years to come.

During the night the weather changed. I woke up to Manchester at its most damnable. It was Sunday. The traffic of a working day would have done something to mitigate the misery of the gray streets empty under weeping skies, but I was denied even that. The sense of failure, of being trapped in a town which at that moment I hated, is something I can laugh at now. I have learned that life affords no reason why youth should take its miseries so heavily or its joys so buoyantly as it does. But it's no good to tell this to the young, and it was no good telling it to me then. I had missed all the things I wanted in life: Rose, and success, some sort of distinction in my university career. I knew it. I knew I was a failure.

Inevitably then I thought of Greg. He was all that I wasn't. I decided to go and seek the comfort of his solidity. I would wangle an invitation to lunch, and spend the afternoon with him. I told my landlady that I would not be back till teatime, put on a mackintosh and went out into the rain. A tramcar would have taken me for more than half the way, but I was in a self-scourging mood—or so I thought: it was really a mood of disgusting self-pity: the last thing I wanted was to hurt my precious self—and so I trudged the mile or more to Greg's house. Dripping on the doorstep, I rang the bell.

There was no answer for a long time, then shuffling unhurried footsteps sounded within. The door was opened by Eustace Hawke.

When last I saw Eustace, it was in the great marquee at the Oxford ball, at a moment, for him, of triumph, for me of despair. He was looking then insolently handsome and successful. The man who confronted me now was haggard and forlorn. But it was the other man I was seeing: the man who had snatched Rose away, and abandoned her, leaving her, something done with, to be handed by her mother to Billy Pascoe.

I suppose this was in my eyes as I gazed at him. He smiled palely. "Don't stand there in the wet, Chad," he said. "You're not looking at a ghost. Come in. I'm afraid Greg and Phoebe are out. Lunching somewhere. I'm looking after Penelope."

He held out his hand, and I did not take it. I could not take it. At first he looked astonished, as though there was no reason why I should not rush to him, open-armed. Then he looked resentful. "After all," he said, "Phoebe is my sister. Are you coming in?"

I couldn't. I just remained planted there. I had not spoken a word. He shut the door quietly, and I heard his slippers flapping over the boards of the narrow passage.

I made the two steps that were all I needed to put me outside the little front garden; and there I stood in that Didsbury street, with the rain falling through a Sunday morning, and pain falling about my heart. To see Greg's door shutting in my face was as though friendship itself had withheld its hand. But it was my hand that had been withheld.

The back streets thereabout wind in and out till you come upon the Wilmslow Road. I followed them dully. I had told my landlady I would not be in to lunch, and now I obstinately held to this. I walked down the Wilmslow Road in the weeping weather, over the pavement slippery with fallen beech leaves, and so I came to the Cock Inn. I stayed there an hour, ate nothing, and drank too much beer.

Looking back on that day, I know that I did everything wrong. I could have taken Eustace's hand, gone into the house and chanced what might befall. If I had chosen not to do that, I could have gone back to my rooms, where my landlady would have found me something to eat, and then I could have gone to bed and slept off my misery. Even now, with two o'clock come, I could still have done this; but I was too deeply sunk in martyrdom to turn back. I went out of the inn resolved to deepen the mood of hopelessness, friendlessness and misery which was to stand me in such fatal stead that night.

I went into the fields through which the river Mersey flows, and rejoiced to see how dark and damnable they were, how turbid the river was, flowing swift and silent and sinister between banks that had been built up high to restrain its worst excesses. At Northenden I found that rowing boats could be hired, and amazed a man lounging there in charge of them by hiring one. He glanced at me oddly, his only customer that day, I'll be bound. "Keep away from the weir," he warned me. I may well have looked suicidal.

But I only wanted to show myself how miserably everything in this place compared with things I had known. This was not like the river at Oxford, where you could laze along, looking at the meadows, the fritillaries beyond Addison's Walk, the willows, the cattle, where you could disembark and in a garden share a honeycomb with a girl. Here you could see nothing but the banks rising steeply on either hand, so that you seemed to be moving through a deep grassy gulch, and the grass itself was nothing to write home about, coarse rubbishy stuff, I told myself, that a decent-minded sheep would turn from in disgust.

There was no one else on the river, no one on the paths that ran atop the banks. Why should there be on such a day, with a feeble but persistent rain continuing to fall out of the leaden sky? No one but a fool like me.

How much of a fool I had been that day I did not learn till later. There was someone whose need was as great as mine, and that was Eustace. There had been no one for him to go to save Phoebe when he came back to England that time. I could imagine with what tenderness she would receive him, and how Greg would receive him, too. When Greg had found him drunk in a ditch he had wrapped him up in blankets and cherished him. He would do something like that now. Eustace had never, till then, known the manner of his father's death, but that night they told him; and it was a Eustace with this bitter knowledge newly in his heart who had opened the door to me and held out his hand. It might have been better for us both if I had taken it and gone in. As it was, what a picture I must have seemed to him of the self-righteous disapproving world! Eustace would have felt that.

When I got back at teatime to my rooms, my landlady said that Mr. Appleby had called just after I had gone out that morning and had left a note. I read it as I sipped my tea by the fire.

DEAR CHAD:
Phoebe and I are lunching in Withington today. I write this in case you are out when I pass by. Eustace dropped in unexpectedly last night, and this is my invitation and Phoebe's to you to come along and share an evening meal with us tonight, if you are free. The old beggar is not in very good heart. We don't like leaving him alone in the house, but this lunch engagement is rather un-put-offable. Come if you can.

GREG

To hell with the old beggar, I thought. I'm not in very good heart, either. I tossed the note into the flames, glad that my night duty gave me a reason for not accepting the invitation.

9

The horror of a vast provincial town is cloaked by its weekday activities. It grins at you in the silence and emptiness of a Sunday. It grinned at me as the tram lurched and rattled over the steel rails that night. I was the only person on the upper deck. The rain had ceased to fall, but the atmosphere, the very buildings, grim, unoccupied and soot-stained, seemed saturated with moisture. A wind was beginning to moan through the streets. The lights came on. Under the black bulk of the sleeping Town Hall the statues gleamed, with no one to listen to whatever message they had for mankind. Beyond them was the uplifted façade of the teashop where Greg and I had stood a meal to May Ingleby on that day when I first visited this town with him. I wondered fragmentarily what had become of that young woman.

In the office life was at half-cock. The corridor men were at work, but the reporters' room was deadly dull. Saturday's affairs had already been written up, and not much happened on a Sunday. It was a fair-sized, disorderly and rather depressing room, with a cubicle opening off it, in which the chief reporter had his being, going through the offerings of his staff before passing them on to the subeditors. He was in there now, and in the room only one man was scribbling.

"Pretty postcard for you," he said without looking up.

The pretty postcard was stuck into the tapes crisscrossed on a board. I pulled it out without much interest and looked at a blue sea, a crumble of ruin on a hilltop, a few white villas edging the water. Underneath was the name of a village on the eastern shore of the Adriatic.

I wondered who was having a jolly time in such a desirable place while I was torturing myself by pulling a boat about on the Mersey in the rain. I turned it over. The signature was simply "Rose."

Since the wedding, I had not written to her or to Billy or to Lucy Orlop. They didn't know my address, but they knew I worked for the *Manchester Guardian*. And here it was. "We are all here: Henrietta, Mother, Christine Darby, and Billy." In that order. I know. I still have the postcard. "A lovely place. Hope you are prospering in Manchester. Rose."

Whatever reservations one may have about heaven, at all events it must look very nice from hell.

My colleague finished his work and got up. "Another jewel," he said. "Only twenty lines, but incomparable. Mills could do no better. I shall shoot myself if any impious hand takes out or alters one of these words."

"What's it about?" I asked.

"Nothing. That's the beauty of it."

He took it through to the chief reporter, came back and put on his overcoat.

"I think," he said persuasively, "a little sustentation for the stylists?"

We crossed the road to the Thatched House. A fire was burning and we lit our pipes. For an hour we stood one another round for round. At last he got up. "Back to my digs," he said. "I shall burn there with a hard gem-like flame."

"Are you writing something?"

He was a nice boy. He looked at me with laughter in his eyes. "My dear Boothroyd. From time to time you let fall solemn hints that you are engaged to a Muse. It should encourage you to know that you are not alone. I don't know which Muse you are engaged to, but you may take it from me that every one of the nine is engaged, if not adulterously married, to half a dozen men on the *Manchester Guardian*. This is the only newspaper in the world absent-mindedly produced by stylists in their time off from immortal dalliance."

"I should except the Old Man," I said.

"So should I. There is no Muse of Unitarian Ethics. Only a housekeeper, smelling of carbolic soap and plain cooking."

I watched him jump onto a moving tram, his coat blowing out like wings, and returned to the office. The light was out in the chief reporter's cubicle. The reporters' room was empty. It was nine o'clock and I made my round of calls on the telephone. Fruitlessly, as usual.

If there had been a fire in that room I should have stood up better to night duty on a Sunday. But there wasn't. I sat there reading through two all but lonely hours. Once the chief subeditor looked in, bobbing and bowing in a way he had, holding a sheet of copy in his hand. I saw that the writing was that of my colleague, who was now, with luck, burning with a hard gem-like flame. Seeing he was not there, the chief subeditor gave me good evening and bobbed at me, and went. I feared for the survival of the masterpiece. Once the Old Man sent for me on some trivial point. He was eating an apple and a glass of milk stood to his hand. He combed his beard with his fingers and fixed me with a glittering eye. "I sent for Mr. Boothroyd," he said.

I explained that I was the worm in question, feeling ashamed at having to recall his attention to a fact so mean. We collogued for a moment or two about something unimportant, and I escaped, vividly conscious that there was but a quarter of an hour to go before closing time.

I spent the quarter of an hour in the Thatched House; and the thought of returning to the dreary office was so intolerable that I resolved for once to make the eleven o'clock round of calls on my legs. That was how it began.

10

There was no rain now, but the wind that had begun to stir earlier in the evening had strengthened. I did not go straight along Cross Street to the Town Hall square and so to the police station tucked into an angle of the huge building. It was possible to tack and turn through a maze of narrow side streets, and at night I always did this, lured by their faint tinge and smell of evil. So I went that night, with the wind leaping upon me round corners and with a star or two twinkling remotely in the lanes of sky above these ebon canyons. I had been drinking a bit too much off and on since midday, and this induced the mood of fear and excitement that raised this nocturnal dandering and all that followed into something more than life-sized.

Filling myself up with notions of sunlight falling on the Adriatic, and comparing this with the plight of a poor devil condemned to wander through the back streets of Manchester on a Sunday midnight, I came at last to the police station, and there, to a sergeant sitting at a desk, I put my routine question: "Anything doing tonight?"

"A bit of a dust-up in Ackers Street," he said.

Something clicked in my foggy mind. "Ackers Street?"

"Yes. You know—where the theatrical digs are."

Then I had it. May Ingleby had prattled to me and Greg about the theatrical digs her mother kept in Ackers Street.

The sergeant produced some papers. "Here you are. Corney Blaine. He's one of these tenth-rate comedians. Bottom of the bill at the Hippodrome sort of touch. He's just been brought in. Crowned his landlady with a beer bottle. A Mrs. Ingleby. He'll be up tomorrow. Not *Guardian* stuff, I should say."

I took down the particulars, and there was nothing else I needed to do. Certainly, it was not *Guardian* stuff in anything more than the sense of three or four lines at the bottom of a column, if that. I was inclined to leave it there, but as I walked out of the station a late cruising taxi came by. I stopped it. "Drop me in Ackers Street," I said, and climbed in.

Was everything in my life to be determined by that night when Rose and Eustace, almost literally shining with love, fled from the ball? For that was what suddenly exploded in my mind; and I remembered how, when they were gone, I had danced and danced with May Ingleby, and in the dawn had spread rugs over her in a punt, and poled to a tea garden where we had eaten breakfast in the strengthening light. May Ingleby had done something for me that night. I owed it to the poor wretch to see what had happened to her now. And confused with such thoughts was the absurd notion of showing for once that I knew my business as a reporter. I was not the sort of man who merely wrote up a policeman's notes. Here I was on the way to the scene of the crime, the man who Followed Things Up.

And so, alas! what might have remained names on paper became a girl and a woman in a desperate moment.

The taxicab turned into Ackers Street. "What number?" the driver asked.

"I'll find it," I said and got out.

It is a miserable street at best. That Sunday midnight, with the wind blowing, it was a cold repulsive hell. Late though it was, a light still burned here and there behind a thin linen blind. The houses were all alike. The one I was seeking identified itself by a few slatterns gaping on the pavement. I pushed by them, walked through the pathetic few feet of sour and acid dirt that such houses have for a "front garden," and saw by a hanging thread of light that the front door was not shut. I leaned against it and went in.

The dingy smell, the oilclothed hall, the hat-and-umbrella stand of rickety bamboo, the worn red carpet climbing the narrow stairway, were what I expected to find. I had not expected to find Whitworth Rhodes coming down the stairs. But the night's doings had become so phantasmal that even this I accepted as in the nature of things. He saw me standing there under a gas flare buzzing in an oblong contraption of many-colored bits of glass. He merely said, "Hello, Boothroyd," as though he, too, was unsurprised, brushed past me, and entered the front room.

I followed him, to find an unexpected scene of domesticity. A large policeman, whose helmet stood on the wideboard, neatly centered between two plates, one containing oranges and the other apples, was sitting at a table, pouring out tea. In an easy chair on the rag mat by the empty fireplace May Ingleby was gracefully reclined. I had once thought she looked like Rose Garland, but she didn't now; nor did the scene look so domestic when I realized that she was in a dead faint.

"She passed out soon after you went upstairs, sir," the policeman explained to Whitworth Rhodes. "Thought a cuppa might bring her round. Found the kettle boiling in the kitchen. Lucky."

Whitworth Rhodes said: "Would it be in order for you to nip round to the Infirmary?"

"Yes, sir."

The policeman was promptly up and reaching for his helmet.

"Tell them I want an ambulance here at once. Emphasize that—at once."

"She hasn't come round so that I can take a statement, sir?"

"No. And she's not likely to if you don't hurry."

The policeman went. The Infirmary was round the corner, five minutes' walk away.

Rhodes bent over May Ingleby, held her wrist, turned up her eyelids. "Nothing much wrong with her," he said, and sat down at the table. There were two cups. The policeman had clearly intended to join the lady. Rhodes filled the cups. "Sugar?" he asked politely.

"No, thank you." He handed me a cup. It was scalding hot.

"What the devil are you doing here?" he asked.

I explained.

"So you've been in Manchester for a whole year?"

"Yes."

He looked at me over the saucer from which he was drinking the too hot tea. "Friendly bloke, aren't you? You might have given me a call."

"What's been happening here?" I asked.

It was quite simple. Before passing out, May Ingleby had explained it all. Mr. Corney Blaine always stayed here when in Manchester. He had arrived that afternoon, having solaced himself with bottle beer during a tedious Sunday railway journey. Having stowed his goods and eaten a meal, he had gone forth and spent some hours in a pub.

199

He came back, reeling and quarrelsome, demanding supper. When this was put before him, he drew two beer bottles from his pockets and stood them alongside his plate. Mrs. Ingleby chose this unfortunate moment to remind him that, after his last visit, he had gone away owing her thirty shillings. Mr. Blaine denied this, and bickering began. It soon blew into a quarrel, in the course of which Mrs. Ingleby told him to take his traps and get out. Mr. Blaine rose in wrath, a beer bottle in his hand. He struck Mrs. Ingleby twice on the head, and she fell to the floor. May was in the room throughout this time.

Mr. Blaine, somewhat sobered, said to her: "Get a doctor," and while she was running to Rhodes's surgery, not far away, he stayed there on his knees over the prostrate woman.

Alert neighbors were not long in letting a policeman know that something was amiss, and when Rhodes returned with May the law was in command.

"I had her carried up to her bedroom," Rhodes said, "and now we'll have to carry her down again. She'll have to get into the Infirmary for a thorough examination. She's worse than I thought at first. To put it in layman's language, I shouldn't be surprised if the skull isn't shattered and bone penetrating the brain."

We had neither of us noticed that May Ingleby had come out of her faint, but a penetrating shriek told us that she had heard these last words. Rhodes threw the dregs of his tea back into the pot and from a bag he had with him he poured something into the cup and gave it to May. "Drink this," he said, "and put your head back and close your eyes. We're doing all we can for your mother. There's nothing *you* can do. Sleep if you can."

He had a way with him. She lay back obediently, but she didn't sleep. She stared at us aghast. To me, she didn't speak. "I thought I was just imagining you there," she said to me later. "And that frightened me, sort of."

At this moment there was an unexpected interruption. The door opened and a most attractive woman came into the room.

"Oh, Nan," Rhodes said, "this is very wrong of you. You should have been in bed an hour ago. I've told you again and again not to follow me about."

She smiled at him.

"Well, so long as you're here, meet Chad Boothroyd," he said. "His mother married that parson I was curate to in Smurthwaite long ago. This is my wife, Boothroyd."

She shook my hand, but all her attention was for Whitworth Rhodes. "I didn't think you'd be so long," she said.

"I shall be longer. I have to take a patient to the Infirmary and stay while an examination's made. Now you get home, Nan, and go to bed. Parsons' wives should lay off being unofficial curates, and doctors' wives should keep clear of the practice."

"There's a message from Mrs. Smethick," she said. "They expect the baby any time."

"Oh, hell. They always expect the baby any time, usually three days before it's due. Anyway, the nurse will be there. I'll look in when I'm through with this lot. You can expect me home at about three, with luck."

"I was afraid so," she said. "I've brought some sandwiches."

"Thank you, Nan. Now get off to bed, you interfering angel." He looked at May Ingleby. "Oh," he said, "what about this girl? She can't stay here all night on her own. Miss Ingleby, would you like to go with my wife? You can spend the night at our house."

Nan Rhodes, to whom, I had an idea, such Samaritan proposals were customary, went across to May and took her by the hand. "Of course she'll come. Get your hat and coat, my dear."

Like her husband, she had a way. "It's awfully good of you," May said. She went off, still looking terribly dazed, with Mrs. Rhodes. "And you, Nan," Rhodes said, "remember henceforth that a good woman's place is the home."

As we watched them across the doorstep the policeman returned with the ambulance. I had my only glimpse of May Ingleby's mother as she was carried through the passage, an inert and horrible body on a stretcher. She was dead by the morning. "I must go with her, sir," the policeman said to Rhodes, "in case she recovers and makes a statement."

"Well—" Rhodes said: and in that one word I read the end of the matter. Before climbing into the ambulance, he turned to me. "Your breath stinks, Boothroyd. You've been drinking too much. Take my tip. Lay off it."

The vehicle moved silently away, and the few people still standing in the dark street dispersed. I pulled the front door to behind me. The bang echoed with finality through the empty house. It was one o'clock of another day.

II

I went back to the office and wrote my few lines, which were in time for the City Edition. I now felt cold and fearfully sobered. The Old Man had long since pedaled on his bicycle to Fallowfield; all the corridor men were gone; and even those late birds the subeditors were drifting away. The thought of boarding a night tram and clanging through desolation to Withington was nauseating. In the chief reporter's cubicle I made a pile of old newspapers, put down the chief's chair cushion for a pillow, and was asleep in no time. I had taken care to "indoctrinate" my landlady. If I was not at home, she would think some emergency had taken me out of town.

I slept long and deeply, and when I awoke in the grim light between six and seven, and let myself out into the streets, the inflow from the suburbs was already in its first dribblings. I walked to London Road station and had myself shaved in the barbershop there, then went on into the baths, and thence to the restaurant. Coffee and ham and eggs and toast soon made me a bright-eyed boy again, and I could look sanely at what had happened to me.

Now that I had rediscovered Whitworth Rhodes, I should have to make at any rate the pretense of keeping in touch with him. I walked back to the office and rang him up to inquire about May Ingleby.

"Pretty groggy," he said. "I've had to tell her that her mother is dead."

I had expected it, but there was nothing I could say. Rhodes broke the silence. "She tells me she knows you. I've just succeeded in convincing her that you were not a ghost. You were pretty cautious last night, weren't you?"

"Well," I said lamely, "it was a chance acquaintance. I've seen her only twice before in my life—once at Oxford, and once here in Manchester. Both accidental meetings."

"Anyway," he said, "it would be a Christian deed if you could see a bit of her now and then when this lot's done with. She seems to have nothing you could call a friend, and she's had a hell of a shock."

"I could take her out to lunch today," I said, with a fine feeling of generosity.

"Oh, no, you couldn't. She'll have to be at the police court when this basher comes up. Nan will go with her, and as soon as that's over she'll come back here and go to bed."

"You're very kind," I said, meaning it.

"The curate in me will out," he said, "but I prefer sense to incense. Well, I suppose this'll be a manslaughter charge, and that means this chap'll be committed, and then we'll have to wait for the Assizes. You'll have time between this and that to give me and Nan a hand."

"You're not keeping her all that time?"

"We'll see. Well, I must ring off. I'll have to be in court myself today."

It all gave me something to think about. I felt quite a pleasurable sense of being caught up in a humanitarian adventure. My brooding about my own loneliness and failure dissipated, and my mind occupied itself with small schemes for making May Ingleby's life endurable. Greg, my only real friend in Manchester, was also one of the most ambitious and one of the busiest men in the town. Through no fault of his own, he left me too much aware of my own deficiencies. It was time I broke my feeling of dependence.

All this sort of stuff floated airily in my mind that morning as I agreeably disposed of the few hours that passed before my reporting for duty at half-past twelve. I dawdled in the bookshops, visited the pictures in the City Art Gallery, smoked my pipe and drank a mid-morning coffee. The autumnal sun was shining, the streets were busy, and even the tram bells had a merry sound. There was no fear or evil in the side streets where the great horses stood patiently between shafts as the bolts of cotton cloth hurtled down from the top floors of warehouses to thud on the drays. This was a commercial city, actively and intelligently moving through a working day.

Meanwhile, in the police court, the chairman of magistrates was saying: "The witness may be seated" as May Ingleby sobbed through her sorry story; and Whitworth Rhodes, judicially weighing a beer bottle handed to him by a policeman, was saying that yes, this would have been sufficient to cause the injuries he had just described in a wonderful jargon. Mr. Corney Blaine contented himself with the assertion that Ma Ingleby was one of the best and 'e didn't mean to 'urt 'er, and he was committed to the Assizes, to be tried for man-slaughter. His sentence, when at last it came, was not heavy; and I am glad to be able to report that, after serving it, he went back to the music halls under another name, climbed to the top of the tree, made Queen Mary rock with mirth at a royal command performance, nar-rowly escaped a knighthood, never killed another woman with a beer bottle, and, when he died, left a considerable fortune to a home for actors' orphans.

CHAPTER EIGHT

I

I HAD twitted Greg some time before this autumn of 1912 about the plaque on the front of the small house at Didsbury that would commemorate his living there. Up to this year of 1953 in which I write there is no plaque on the house, and if one is ever affixed it will, I imagine, commemorate Eustace, not Greg. He stayed there during that autumn and winter, and wrote all the poems that appeared in *English Grass*. They were published in the summer of 1913, and they were May Ingleby's favorite reading. I say this not to sneer at them but to commend them. *English Grass* was one of the last books of poetry to be published in this country for the people—all the people. Poetry was soon to go as queer as many other things, but there was nothing queer about *English Grass*. It was more "traditional" than anything Eustace had done before. The sonnets, especially, were beautifully shaped. Soon they were being quoted everywhere. Everyone could understand them; everyone was deeply moved by them, and when the war came everyone felt something prophetic in them. For this book of praise to English beauty was then seen to be written by a man aware of praising what was in mortal danger. I felt this from the first. Eustace was saying in these elegiac lines what Rose had said to me under a London lamp post.

I dined with Greg and Phoebe three times during that autumn and winter, and Eustace was there each time, polite as an iceberg, talkative as a totem pole. What he was doing was never mentioned. Even Phoebe, I learned afterward, had known nothing, though her sympathies embraced Eustace so closely that she must have guessed a lot. In the afternoons, she told me, he would push Penelope in her perambulator to a small pleasance called the Marie Louise Gardens, and there it was, I imagine, that he wrote, or at any rate shaped in his mind, the work that was to be so famous.

2

However, this was still the late autumn of 1912, and I had promised Whitworth Rhodes to give him a hand in cheering up May Ingleby. There didn't seem much to be done at the moment: I could hardly rush the girl round in a whirl of gaiety while her mother's slayer was awaiting trial. Fortunately, the Assizes were at hand; and a few days after the case had been disposed of I called on Rhodes. As chance would have it, the reporting of the Assizes had fallen to me, and I had been interested to observe May's deportment in court. The horror-stricken and haggard look that had been on her under the shock of the moment was gone. She was self-possessed, and Mr. Blaine had a lot to thank her for. "Actually," she said, as his counsel played her like a trout, "I always liked Mr. Blaine when he was sober. He wasn't drunk so often as all that, and when he wasn't drunk he treated me and my mother as a gentleman should." She wasn't sure that Mr. Blaine owed her mother thirty shillings. Yes, she had heard her mother tell other lodgers that they owed her money from their last visit. Yes, she would be inclined to say that her mother sometimes started a quarrel. Yes, she felt that if Mr. Blaine had been left alone he would have gone quietly to bed and slept his beer off.

"Look here, Rhodes," I said, when I called on him, "do you get the impression that the girl isn't at all sorry to be quit of her mother?"

"I do," he said. "And it doesn't surprise me."

I sat down in the chair he pushed toward me. "Don't look so horror-stricken," he said. "I know a bit about this girl from my brother."

"It was he who palmed her off on me," I said brutally.

"Yes. He's teaching now out in Cheshire. When he saw this case reported he remembered the name and came over and had a talk with me. He told me about the night of the ball. In a way, you're as responsible as anybody for the poor creature's state of mind."

"Well, I like that!"

"Like it or lump it. Look at it this way. There she is, living with that ghastly mother. If May had known nothing else, it might have been better for her. But in the dim quarter that we will call by courtesy her mind, the crone is aware that Oxford is full of what she conceives to be glamorous, and, better still, wealthy young men. So she saves enough to pack the girl off to this commercial school. Undergraduates being what they are, she gets picked up by plenty of them, and she was lucky enough not to be picked up by a wrong 'un. One of them goes so far as to invite her to this ball, and then, no doubt, saw a fairer prospect and unloaded her onto my brother. He passed her on to you. Well, that's how it goes. Her memory seems to be stuffed with a wonderful night of dancing, and a wonderful time in a punt, and a wonderful breakfast."

"Just routine," I said.

"No doubt. I never thought otherwise. But the point is that, what with that night and other nights, the poor little devil had a taste of something that makes her mother and Ackers Street and the fag ends of the music hall profession seem pretty dreary. Now she thinks she's escaped. But I doubt it."

"None of it has anything to do with me. What's the girl doing?"

"She lost her job as a typist because this mess-up kept her away so long. You may think she was jaunty in court, but I tell you she's still suffering from a good deal of nervous shock. I've packed her off to a place by the seaside, where they look after cases like that. She'll be there a month."

"Always the saint."

"Not a bit of it. I loathe patching. I try to finish a job."

He got up. "Well, I'm off on my tour of the parish. Look in when you feel like it."

I promised to do that.

3

It was on a Monday night when winter was fully come that I called again on Rhodes. I liked Mondays, because the chief reporter had the notion that I did the music halls rather well, and, consequently, on that day my sole job, often enough, was to write about two of them. The halls, then, were still pretty earthy places, full of robust humor and huge frank personalities that gave me plenty to write about. Moreover, we were allowed to put our initials to that work, and I got a kick out of seeing "C.B." in the paper. The little bits and pieces were cut out and pasted up in the fat volume of my collected works.

That day I had been to the Hippodrome in the afternoon, and now I was on my way to the first house at the Ardwick Empire. It began at seven, and seeing that Rhodes's house was on the way, and that I owed him a visit, I set off early and rang his bell at six. May Ingleby came to the door.

"Oh, Mr. Boothroyd, come in! It is nice to see you."

What made me say what I did I shall never know. I said: "It's nice to see *you*, Miss Ingleby. I'm on my way to the Ardwick Empire, and I looked in to see if you'd care to come with me. I have a spare ticket."

She was looking quite attractive. The fugitive hint of Rose Garland was there again. Her holiday had put some color into her cheeks and her stay with Nan Rhodes had given her animation. But she was ever one for the small proprieties, and she said: "Oh, Mr. Boothroyd! Do you think I ought to, so soon after—what happened?"

"Of course you should," I assured her. "It's not so soon as all that. It'll do you good. Think of it as your medicine."

We were standing in the passageway, and Rhodes's voice came from the living room on the right. "That you, Boothroyd? Come in, if you're going to. I haven't much time. Surgery in ten minutes."

May and I went into the sitting room, where Rhodes and his wife were cozy by the fire. Nan Rhodes got up and shook my hand. "How d'you think she's looking?" she asked.

I had to say that she was looking fine, wondering how she would have looked if it had not been for these two.

"Well, she's on the mend," Nan admitted, gazing critically at May. "In about a week's time we'll have to start finding her a job. Poor child."

I looked at the poor child, and saw that she could take plenty of that sort of thing. "Mr. Boothroyd called," she said, "to ask if I'd go to the Ardwick Empire with him. Do you think I should?"

"Of course you should," Rhodes prescribed quickly. "Best thing in the world for you."

"Just what I've been telling her," I said.

"Well, if you all think so—?" May turned to Nan for a third opinion.

"Go and get your hat and coat," Nan said.

When May was gone, Nan went into the kitchen and Rhodes

said: "Sit down, Chad. This really is very good of you, you know. It's time the girl got out a bit. Nan has done what she could, but she can't provide the sort of liveliness that you can. Very good of you. Very good, indeed."

His approval inflated me. "I thought I'd take her on somewhere after the show to eat a bite of supper," I said.

"No, no. That's asking too much of you."

I cried magnanimously: "Not at all, my dear Rhodes. Between us, we'll soon have her as right as a trivet. I'll see she's not too late back."

He got up from his chair and patted me on the back as though I were a good dog. "Splendid! Well, I must amble into the surgery to take a look at the halt and blind."

I stood for a few moments on the hearthrug, warming my behind, troubled by an odd feeling of rectitude and regret. Deep down in my heart I knew that I no more wanted to take May Ingleby out than I wanted to visit the moon. But dammit, I thought, the girl's human and she needs a friendly hand. If it came to that, so did I. There was the teasing thought that it would be something to have a girl to take about.

4

It went on from there, slowly at first. That night, I said nothing to May about the bite of supper till the show was over and we were out in the dank rawness of nine o'clock on a winter's night on Ardwick Green. God knows, that should be an appetizer in itself, even a whip to drive one to warmth and cheer. The trams were banging townward, and I said what an agreeable end to our entertainment it would be if we boarded one and found a snug eating place. I had it all worked out. We would eat and drink; it would all be over by half-past ten; then I would put her into a taxi, give the driver Rhodes's address, pay him, and that would be that. I would go to the office and write a nice little "C.B." piece.

May thought otherwise. When I proposed supper she said: "Oh, do you think we ought to, Mr. Boothroyd—the very first time?"

The very first time. There was an undertone to that that I didn't like. I could have said: "Dr. Rhodes approves," but I wasn't having that. I wasn't going to present myself as a tonic that the doctor ordered. So, standing there with the mist pressing down over Ardwick Green, I said lightly: "Oh, come, Miss Ingleby. It's not the first time, you know. After all, you've spent a night with me, and then taken breakfast."

It was the wrong approach. I had often read of women "bridling" and wondered what exactly it meant. Now I knew. May Ingleby bridled.

"I don't think you should say a thing like that, Mr. Boothroyd. It might be misunderstood."

I was a bit taken aback, and yet felt a great pity for her forlorn foolishness. However, if she took things that way, there was no more to be said. I certainly had no intention of abducting her onto a two-decker Manchester tram and breathlessly carrying her struggling form over the threshold of a restaurant.

"All right," I said. "I'd better see you as far as Dr. Rhodes's. Thank you for coming out."

"Oh, no. Thank *you*. All the obligation is on my part."

We were walking toward Rhodes's house side by side. Crossing a wet road, I put my hand under her elbow. When we reached the pavement, I slipped it through her arm. She broke the arm loose. "Oh, Mr. Boothroyd, not the very first time."

I rang Rhodes's bell, called good-night to her, and left her there. I ran back to the main road and jumped onto a tram, shaking with laughter.

Even then, that might have been the end of it. So far as I was concerned, the spark that had flashed was quenched. But the devil himself seemed concerned in my contacts with May Ingleby and contrived another meeting a few weeks later. I had been careful on the intervening Mondays not to go near Rhodes, not to hint that there was a spare amusement ticket that might be used on the mental therapy of Nan's poor child. Then came a day when a disagreeable job fell to me. It was concerned with the Lancashire cotton trade, a matter that never stirred me to passionate interest. What I liked to write about, and consequently what I wrote about best, was something happening under my eyes; a play, a street procession, the show of tulips in a springtime park: anything that didn't involve that tiresome process called "inquiries." Even a train wreck would be better than that.

That day I was at a loose end in the office. The chief called me into his office and said that Sir Charles McCumber had just rung up and asked if a reporter could be sent round to see him. He had an important communication to make.

All I knew of Sir Charles McCumber was that he was a big name in the local trade and that he would involve me in technicalities that would leave me floored and floundering. However, there was nothing for it but to go, and I went, and things turned out better than I expected. Sir Charles's secretary, a young man, took me into a large room where Sir Charles sat, his eyes fixed in brooding satisfaction upon an immense flamboyant portrait of himself that filled half the wall opposite his desk. The desk was as big as a billiards table. Sir Charles, happily, was taking no chances with reporters. What he had to say had been typed. The secretary handed it to him as deferentially as a courtier handing to the monarch a speech to be read from the throne. Sir Charles could easily have passed it to me, but he was not to be denied the pleasure of reading it, which he did in a sonorous Scottish voice. It began: "Interviewed yesterday, Sir Charles McCumber, Bart., lucidly explained . . ." From time to time, a phrase would carry Sir Charles's eyes across the room to rest for a moment on the portrait, as if he were saying: "You put that well, old boy." I felt that he and his portrait dwelt together like twins who approved of one another very much.

When the reading was done, Sir Charles said: "Now, if there are any questions arising out of this, we can discuss them over a cup of tea."

His secretary pressed a bell. The signal had clearly been prearranged. The tea came in promptly, and it was May Ingleby who carried it. I should like to be able to write that she was so startled that she dropped the tray. She was, in fact, self-possessed. May always "knew her place." After the first glance, the first dawn of a smile that was instantly clouded by a businesslike austerity, she ignored me.

But she had not forgotten me. I had no questions to ask. I had finished my tea and was making my way down a long corridor toward the lift, when a door opened, and there was May.

"Oh, Mr. Boothroyd," she said. "Fancy seeing you *here!* You *have* been neglecting me!"

It was so direct that it shook me. "Oh, come!" I protested, but at the same time I was impressed by that innocence in May that I have spoken of before. She didn't see anything wrong in saying what she thought, and she seemed to think that some bond had linked us.

"I hope you didn't mind my not speaking to you in there," she said, nodding along the corridor. "It wouldn't have done."

I agreed that I didn't mind and that it wouldn't have done, and stood uneasily fingering the scroll that the secretary had tied up in red tape. It only needed a seal.

"Well—" I said vaguely.

A bell rang in the room behind her. "That means I must take away the tray," she said.

"Yes," I agreed, aware of the sparkle in my conversation.

She held out her hand. "Well, thanks awfully, Mr. Boothroyd, for sparing me a little of your time."

I watched her move off toward Sir Charles's door. She had a trim figure and neat ankles. I wondered if her last remark had been a bit of elementary irony, and decided that it hadn't. She was incapable of anything but direct statement. I remember how, after our marriage, I once teased her: "You only married me for my *Manchester Guardian* salary," an obvious bit of irony, I should have thought; and she answered gravely: "Oh, no, Chad. Indeed it wasn't that. I was attracted from the first by your gentlemanly manners."

Going down in the lift and walking back to the office, I felt guilty toward her. I hadn't even asked after her health, or where she was living now, or how she was enjoying her work. It was always like this with May. When I was with her, a sense of annoyance and frustration overcame me. When I was not with her, all that was to be said on the other side clamored for hearing. It did so now. After all, I said, turning into a teashop to reinforce Sir Charles's cup of tea, whether I liked it or not, circumstances had thrown the girl across my path at one or two desperate moments. She had always been, at the least, amiable in her fashion; and now that life had dealt her a heavy smacker, common decency required that I should give her the sort of helping hand that she, if unconsciously, had extended to me.

"Pregnant thought appears to oppress your brow, my dear Boothroyd," said the chief, who was given to hyperbolic speech. "An exposition by Sir Charles is not something I should have exposed you to so lightly."

"It was not exposited. It was simply read and handed to me."

"And you have been so long over that! Why, I should have expected you, in your relief, to bound homeward like a chamois."

He took up the portentous scroll and said: "Be it known to all men by these presents. Well, between you and me, my dear Boothroyd, I know no more about the cotton trade than you do. We will simply pass this on to the competent authority, and reserve ourselves for matters that call for limpid prose. You wrote yesterday *owing to the fact that*. Say it to yourself, my dear Boothroyd. Say it several times. What does it sound like? Nay, *feel* like? A mouthful of sand! I hope you noticed that I changed it to *because*."

"I did."

He got up and wound a white muffler round his neck. He put on a tight full-skirted overcoat and kid gloves. He took up his silver-knobbed Malacca cane. "Good, my dear Boothroyd. So long as you notice things like that, your prose will bloom like a garden in God's good time."

He was an actor. That was his exit line, and he moved off stage. It was a quarter to five. Perhaps May was still at Sir Charles's office. I rang up, and a woman answered. I said: "This is Mr. Boothroyd. Is it possible to speak to Miss Ingleby?"

The voice said: "Sorry. Personal calls are not permitted on the office telephone."

The line went dead. I was certain the voice was May's.

So far as I remember, I only once received a letter from May. Seeing one another often, we had no occasion to write. And that last sentence says quite enough about how things were between us. I can well imagine a relationship with a woman in which, the moment she had left me, I would sit down and, even though I knew I would see her again in a few hours' time, pour out on paper what my tongue had just said and would so soon be saying once more. It was never like that with me and May.

The letter was waiting for me in the office rack the next morning.

DEAR MR. BOOTHROYD:

You left your umbrella in Sir Charles's room this afternoon. I will hand it in at the *Manchester Guardian* office when I go out to lunch tomorrow, and I hope that in the meantime you will not be inconvenienced by its absence. We are having a fine bit of weather for the time of year. If you thought me abrupt when you rang up asking to speak to me last night, this signifies my apology. After all, orders are orders.

Yours sincerely,

MAY INGLEBY

When the chief reporter had given me my orders for the day, I went downstairs and loitered till May appeared. It was very cold. There had been hard frost in the night, and a winter sun was a small red ball that was up there from sheer habit, doing no sort of job, seeming related not at all to the midsummer swelterer. I remember that May turned up wrapped in a not impressive fur coat and with a round hat of fur snug over her forehead. The sting of the weather put color into her face and a brightness into the eyes peeping from under the eaves of fur. I took the umbrella.

"Thank you, May," I said. "Come and have lunch with me."

"Oh, Mr. Boothroyd! Should you call me May?"

I didn't know whether to laugh madly or to turn and run back upstairs, leaving the girl forever.

"Of course I shouldn't," I said. "I'm an ill-bred hound. You must take me in hand and teach me manners."

"Oh, no. I wouldn't presume to say that."

"Look, I'm hungry. Let's go and eat."

We set out along Cross Street. "Mind you," she said, "I *like* you calling me May. I just wondered . . ."

I was left wondering what she wondered, and I said to myself that the time had come to give her something to wonder about. When we reached Albert Square she began to turn left toward the teashop where Greg and I had seen her during my first visit to Manchester.

"No," I said, "we're not going in there," and I hurried her across the square. This was going to dent my salary, but to the devil with that for once.

The taxicabs and private cars were sliding up to the Midland Hotel entrance. I hustled her, wide-eyed, through the swing doors, handed my hat and umbrella to a commissionaire with a flourish, and swept her onward to a lounge. "Sit here. I have a telephone call to make. I'll join you in a moment."

There were plenty of elegant women in the lounge, waiting for escorts, and plenty of flourishing-looking men. May sank into a soft chair and drew off her gloves, looking apprehensive. "Shall I be all right?" she asked.

"Quite. You are impregnable."

I went to a telephone booth and rang up Sir Charles McCumber's office. I asked to speak to somebody in the department in which Miss Ingleby worked, and at last was in touch with an acid voice which announced itself as Head of the Female Clerical Staff.

"This is Dr. Whitworth Rhodes speaking," I said. "I'm Miss Ingleby's doctor. I chanced to meet her in Cross Street a few moments ago, and as she was speaking to me she came over very faint."

"Came over?"

"Yes. Came over very faint. I took her into a chemist's shop and prescribed a draft for her. Then I put her into a taxicab and sent her home. I shall see how she is this evening. I've no doubt she'll be fit for work in the morning, but I thought you'd better know she won't be back this afternoon."

"Thank you, doctor. I expect we shall manage."

"Now, May," I said, when I had bustled back into the lounge, "what about a snifter?"

May looked as if she had not moved an inch. She was sitting upright in the easy chair, her legs uncrossed, her knees pressed tight together. "Oh, I'm so glad to see you again, Mr. Boothroyd," she said, as though I had popped in from Kamchatka. "What is a snifter?"

"A snifter," I explained, beckoning to a waiter, "is a preliminary alcoholic stimulus to the serious business of eating. The range is infinite, the names are alluring, the accompaniments can be black olives, cheese straws, this and that."

"You *do* seem gay," she said. "But I never take alcoholic refreshment."

I told the waiter to bring a tomato juice and a dry Martini.

"You may remember, Mr. Boothroyd, that I drank nothing but orangeade all through that night when first we met. I shall always remember it. It was delicious."

"May," I said, "I see a number of heavy pewter tankards lying conveniently to my hand. Would you like me to bash you upon the head with one?"

"Oh, no, indeed I wouldn't."

"Then will you please desist from calling me Mr. Boothroyd?"

"What should I call you?"

"Anything you like but Mr. Boothroyd. I have been called in my time Angel-face, Pie-frill, and what not. I prefer Chad."

"Should I—so soon?"

"The sooner the better."

"Very well—Chad."

She had taken the plunge. I felt as proud as a dog trainer when the brute for the first time goes to heel at command.

Our drinks arrived. It was twenty past one. May looked up at the clock on the wall. "Oh, look how the time's getting on Mr.—Chad."

"I am not Mr. Chad."

"I don't want to be late back, Chad. They're terribly strict."

"Bless my soul," I said, "you can't take lunch at the Midland and expect to be back in an office at two o'clock. Good health, May."

She took up her tomato juice and sniffed it suspiciously.

"There is nothing in the smell of that stuff to suggest any reason why you should drink it," I told her. "Throw it back valiantly like medicine." She did so.

"And speaking of medicine," I said, "are you feeling any better now?"

"But Chad, why not? It's a beautiful day. I love cold weather."

"Then I've made a great mistake. When I left you here, I rang up your office and spoke to the Head of the Female Clerical Staff."

"Not to Miss Mytholmroyd!"

"If Miss Mytholmroyd is indeed the H.F.C.S. then indeed I spoke to no less a person. She sounded like a refreshing draft of prussic acid. I told her you would probably be quite well tomorrow."

I explained to her what I had done. I had wondered whether my announcement would be greeted by a burst of carefree laughter. It was not. If I had confessed to assassinating the Pope, the Archbishop of Canterbury, the President of the Wesleyan Conference and Sir Charles McCumber she could not have been more horrified. Sir Charles McCumber himself now came into the lounge, accompanied by his secretary.

"See what you have done!" May cried dramatically. "I am lost! Oh, Mr. Boothroyd, I shall never be able to lift up my head again!"

I reached across to a neighboring table, picked up an empty tankard that lay there, and placed it threateningly before her. "Chad," she said.

We went into the French restaurant. The lamps lit on the tables, the quiet service, the carpet underfoot, even the enormous document on which the day's fare was set out, impressed May and daunted her at the same time.

"You choose for me, Chad."

I chose for her, and for myself I chose a bottle of wine in which she would not share. Gradually, in her quiet way, she began to enjoy herself. She hadn't much to say, but she relished her food and from time to time she looked across the table at me with a shy smile. Once her foot touched mine, but clearly that was an accident. She withdrew it quickly. So then I sought her foot, and squeezed it between both mine. She withdrew it again, blushing as hotly as a virgin who has been indecently touched.

Presently she sighed. "It will seem so dull tomorrow," she said.

I think this was the only thing May ever said to me that touched me to the quick. It woke in me a sudden sense of guilt and shame. God knows, this was not my own idea of life. A little of this went a long way with me, and if I had to do without it altogether I should not think myself the poorer. But May's innocent words made me aware of her dull tomorrow, and of her so many dull tomorrows; not of this vapidly bright moment of contrast, to which, I feared, her thoughts would unprofitably recur, but of the continuous pattern of dreary toil to which she seemed doomed. I wondered whether even her mother's life, with its changing background of flash amusing people was not better than that, even with a knockout to end it.

I wished my silly whim had not brought May here at all. It was simply pique at her failure to live up to some notion my skull housed about what a girl should be, how she should joyfully accept such advances as I chose to make. I was going to dazzle her into a realization of what knowing Chad Boothroyd meant, and all I had done was disgust myself. I had done something cruel, and cruelty is the last indecency.

I should not have drunk a whole bottle of Liebfraumilch; and having done that, I should not now be drinking Armagnac with my coffee. And there had been two Martinis. It was fortunate, I reflected, that my sole job for the *Guardian* that day was to attend an amateur theatrical performance in Stockport at seven-thirty. I looked at May's hand lying on the table cloth. It was slender and the nails were well cared for. I took the fingers in my hand and fondled them. She had been relaxed, but instantly she was rigid. I felt the tremble run through her that one would expect in a colt that had never before been hand-led. But she did not withdraw her hand.

I said: "May, I hope you'll forgive me."

She looked at me, surprised. "Whatever for? You've given me a lovely time, Mr.—Chad. D'you mean for telling that lie to Miss Mytholmroyd?"

"I could lie myself blue in the face to Miss Mytholmroyd without a pang."

"I'm still worrying about it a bit," she said, as I went on stroking her fingers. I could feel some of the tension leaving her.

"Don't worry. We shall be able to deal with Miss Mytholmroyd. No. It's not that."

I couldn't put it into words.

"I don't see what else it can be," she said. "You *are* a funny boy, Chad. I thought so at Oxford. You seem to want to be with me, and as soon as you're with me you're somewhere else."

Well, that was fairly percipient.

"I'm very unhappy, May."

"Then let's stay and dance," she said.

I remembered that dancing was May's "thing." I looked at my watch. It was three o'clock. A tea dance began at half-past. "Very well; let's stay and dance."

A sense of her own brand of propriety came back to her. "I shouldn't have suggested it, Chad. It's not my place to do it. Besides, it's so soon after . . ."

"Forget that. Forget it," I said. "If you'd like to dance, we'll dance. But first let's take half an hour in the fresh air."

It is odd to remember that in those days there were no Treasury notes. I put golden money on top of the bill lying on its plate, and May opened her eyes wide at the amount. I wondered whether her service of Sir Charles brought her that much in a week.

"Let us watch the pigeons," she said as we walked out of the hotel.

A cheap and innocent amusement. We had only to cross a road, and there the pigeons were, in the stony patio behind which rose the façade of Central Station. Surely they must once, like other birds, have delighted in trees, as the wood pigeons still do? But they have forgotten all that, and certainly they look none the worse for it. Their delicate pink feet seemed at home on the cobbles; their eyes were rubies. Brown, speckled in black and white, slate-gray, all in common had necks whose fluent and changing color made me think of mackerel, fresh drawn from the Cornish sea, gasping on the floor boards of a dinghy. May had picked up some biscuits from the plate that had accompanied our cheese. She crumbled them and threw them to the pigeons. They crowded round her feet, ever new ones dropping from the soot-crusted ledges and cornices of the surrounding buildings.

"Have you ever been in Cornwall, May?"

"No."

There were pigeons on her extended hands and on her forearms. The keen air, becoming sharper now that the sun was due to go, and the excitement of her novel occupation, flushed her cheeks and brightened her eyes. She was attractive.

I told her about Cornwall. I told her about my father's brilliant scheme to make a salt-water pond in the garden, so that we could keep mackerel fresh. I told her about the beaches and the woods and the shining peaks of the clay hills, and of the fun I had had with Billy Pascoe and the other boys.

"I never knew boys," May said. "Mother would never let me play with boys. She said I must wait till I could meet proper young gentlemen."

She dusted the last of the crumbs from her fingers, and the inconstant pigeons strutted or flew away.

"May," I said, "let's not go in to dance. Let's go into the country. I've eaten too much, I've drunk too much, and fresh air will do me good. You, too."

"Oh, Chad, should I?"

"Well, for heaven's sake! Don't ask me. Make up your own mind. Would you *like* to do it?"

"Well, I do know you better now, don't I?" she asked doubtfully. "It wouldn't be like going with a stranger, and really I'd *love* to go."

We crossed the city and took train to Marple, which in those days could pass as rural. At all events, trees grew there, and one's eyes could rest on fields and on buildings of comely stone not too deeply corrupted by the city's satanic breath. Not that there was much to be seen that night. It was dark when we got there. But I knew my way about, for this was one of the places I went to if I wanted a breather in quick time. We walked, and we leaned on unmortared walls and looked down over sloping pastures to lights in homely windows, and upward to the sky full, now, of wintry stars. We could hear a stream tinkling over some unseen bed, and owls calling.

I didn't take her arm. I feared to startle her, aware that she was in some trepidation at what seemed to her the hardihood of her conduct. She once or twice spoke of her alarm at having seen Sir Charles and his secretary in the Midland Hotel.

"Well, they didn't see *you*," I assured her. And I was sure that was so. "As for Miss Mytholmroyd, she has your doctor's orders. Buy a bottle of smelling salts in the morning. Sniff them occasionally in the office, and look a little woebegone. Say that you're feeling a bit better and will soon be all right. You might even ask to leave an hour earlier than usual."

She laughed. "Really, Chad! You'll end up in the hands of the police!"

It wasn't much of a saying, but it was the first time she had ever said anything sprightly, and I was glad.

But we didn't say much. The cold deepened. It was clear that the night was in for another sharp frost. We walked briskly, making now

216

toward Stockport, where I had my small engagement to fulfill. We reached there in time for a bite before the show, and in contrast to our midday splendor we chose a tripe saloon. The flaccid slabs of pale honeycombed offal were washed down with scalding tea, and I twitted her, urging her to hurry, lest Sir Charles McCumber should appear for his evening snack. She smiled, looking startlingly the better for her day out of the office and her couple of hours in the air.

She went with me to the theater and enjoyed the show prodigiously. We took train back to Manchester, and in the yard outside the cold cavern of London Road station we stood for a moment saying our goodbys. She held out her hand, and I took it, and wondered whether I should kiss her. I should have liked to. She looked at that moment, her eyes shining with gratitude, a nice girl to kiss. But I felt I might spoil something for her. So I said: "Now, May, don't forget that bottle of smelling salts," and I called a taxi, put her in, and paid the driver. I waved her off, and walked to the office to write my piece.

6

Whitworth Rhodes and his Nan had made themselves May's guardians, and, though they said nothing about it, I imagined that May was not the only one. They had found her a bed-sitting room not far from their own house. May was immensely proud of it. "My little place," she called it. I never saw it, for she thought it "wouldn't be nice" for me to visit her in her bachelor quarters, but she talked as though it were sumptuous. All she meant, of course, was that she was enjoying what she took to be freedom. Her life had been spent in her mother's shadow, and that odd person, whom I never saw save as a corpse on a stretcher, had for May, if hardly for herself, a social code as rigid as that of an old-time mama seeing a girl through her first "season." May had never been out unchaperoned. Those dances that she attended, though she danced at them superbly, were not carefree. She was accompanied by an old crone who sat against the wall, glad to pick up sixpence a time and supper with Mrs. Ingleby when she returned the virgin unsullied.

Though up to this point Mrs. Ingleby could follow the highest social precedents, she couldn't go all the way. Oxford, with its galaxies of desirable young men, allured her imagination, and in Oxford May would have to take her chance for a year. I often wondered how deeply disappointed she was when May came home unmated and even unattached, having acquired nothing more than a rudimentary knowledge of shorthand and typewriting.

Except for her office hours, she remained in purdah. "Mother wouldn't

217

let me mix with the lodgers," she explained. "I wasn't supposed even to see them. It was only because of hearing the row that I went into the room that night."

And now May was free, rejoicing in her "little place," but she had been conditioned by the dead woman to a fear of "men" and a regard for "purity" that one would expect in an Irish girl whose brother was a priest and sister a nun. She did not willingly leave her "little place" once she had regained its sanctuary at night. It was her cell, and Rhodes and Nan were her spiritual overseers. She adored them.

The more I got to know about May the more I was surprised at having succeeded in bringing off that luncheon and afternoon and evening. It wouldn't have been possible without audacity; and I expected that what I took to be its success would act as the loosened stone that might undermine the wall of her resistance. In this I was mistaken. Knowing where May was accustomed to eat her midday meal, I waited outside the place the next day, and when she appeared I said: "Do we take lunch together again today? Not at the Midland. It doesn't run to that too often. Some nice little place."

"I'm used to *this* place," she said. "They expect me. The waitress smiles at me."

"Make a change. Let *me* smile at you."

She looked at me severely. "We did wrong yesterday. Miss Mytholmroyd has been ever so nice and understanding all the morning. I've felt ashamed."

A cold wind was blowing round the cold bronze and marble statues of Albert Square, chockablock with overcoated mufflered figures, waiting for trams, hurrying head down to restaurants. I didn't want to stand there arguing with the girl. "I apologize to your conscience," I said, "for giving it some unhappy moments."

"Oh, no, Mr. Boothroyd! Don't look at it like that. I enjoyed it all enormously, but now I see it shouldn't have happened in office hours."

As so often with May, I didn't know whether to hoot with laughter or write *finis* to the whole affair. I thought of all the outrageous things that *could* happen, but *should not* happen in office hours. Her eyes considered me gravely from beneath the fur of her casque.

"You really are an extraordinary creature," I said, meaning it.

"No. You mustn't think that. I just try to know my place, that's all. But look—this café is filling up. My waitress won't be able to keep my table."

She waved a furry hand and went, leaving me standing. I hadn't expected that, and I walked away fuming.

Chad Boothroyd didn't like so decisive a douche of cold water, slap in the face. He was six foot tall, fair, and passed for handsome. May Ingleby was a bit on the short side, and not much to look at. When she was at her best, "pleasant" was the word for her. Pleasant and comfortable. A comfortable armful. She could be that.

I didn't feel like eating now. I strolled to a cinema where there was a coffee room, and ordered coffee and biscuits. The place had a sprinkling of demiprostitutes who hoped to do a bit of quick lunch-time trade in the darkness. But these ladies had never appealed to me, nor their more robust sisters. Nevertheless, they and May between them set me thinking of women.

I didn't need to live the life of an anchorite. There were women easily to be met. If I cared to be at Greg's house more often, I would meet them there. It was his habit and Phoebe's to entertain under-graduates, and these were often girls. I recalled one in particular. It isn't difficult to know when you have made an impression, and this dark vivacious little thing left me in no doubt. Her way home and mine went together for a long way, and she chirruped all the time like a witty sparrow. At the corner where our roads parted we paused in the dark, and she said: "Well?" But I didn't give her the kiss her raised lips were waiting for, and I never saw her again. Anyway, now that Eustace was there, I was not much at Greg's.

Miss Orlop's picture of Rose Garland still hung over the mantel-piece in my sitting room. Rose Pascoe. I didn't like the name and I didn't like the idea. But like it or not, there it was: it had to be accepted. And since there couldn't be Rose there would be nobody. Or so I said to myself. And that, I suppose, is why I had not fol-lowed up any of the openings that offered themselves at Greg's. They were girls of some sense, some accomplishment or promise; once involved with one of them I might find myself in a serious affair from which there could be no withdrawal. And so, deeply interested in the companionship of women, yet fearing where these ones might lead me, I was drawn to dally with May Ingleby because, funda-mentally, she did not mean and could never mean anything to me at all. Looking fairly at the situation in that way, it seemed to me extraordinary. Now I know what a fool I was not to have realized at once that it was more full of danger than any of the other situations I had taken into account. For one thing, May had my fatal pity.

7

An evening at home was a luxury I didn't often enjoy in those days. When one came my way, my only thought was to spend it by the fire-side, worrying away with ink and paper. I had postponed trying to do anything of depth and compass, but I had not given up the idea that I would do it some day. I told myself fatalistically to leave it alone—not to worry it—to wait till it was there. I should know that visitor and how to deal with him when he came along. In the meantime, there were pleasant bits and pieces to tackle, especially *Manchester Guardian* "back-pagers" that added three guineas to the budget.

I was so engaged one night, the room fire-warmed, comfortably thick with tobacco fug, and a coffeepot at my elbow, when Whitworth Rhodes called. He came in bringing the wet night with him, glistening in his mackintosh that shone like metal in the firelight, and seeming to exude its vital pelting from his whole vigorous personality.

He shed hat and mackintosh into a corner, from which my landlady rescued them and carried them out, promising: "I'll bring in some hot coffee, Mr. Boothroyd, and another cup."

I put Rhodes into a comfortable chair by the fire and took one opposite him. He filled his pipe and stretched out his long legs, and his trouser ends steamed in the heat. He waited till the coffee was on the table between us and then came straight to the point.

"What are you up to," he asked, "playing about with my professional reputation?"

"Oh, come," I said. "I do nothing but praise it whenever the occasion offers."

"May Ingleby is ill. Not seriously. A bit of flu. Her landlady called me in this morning. I had a look at her and told her to stay in bed. I said: 'Don't worry. I'll ring up your office.' Does that mean anything to you?"

I must have looked rather sheepish. "I suppose May spilled the beans?"

"What else could she do? If I'd rung up without knowing about your monkey tricks, I could have blundered into an odd sort of misunderstanding—don't you think? And if I'd done that, and had had to say that it wasn't I who spoke to them the other day, where would May have been? Probably sacked."

"I'm sorry."

"Give me some more coffee, you crazy coot."

That told me he wasn't really angry. In fact, he began to laugh. "There was nothing for it," he said, "but to compound your felony. So I rang up and apologized for having to ring up *again*."

"Thank you. It was very silly of me."

"Well, so long as you understand that. I happened to be out this way, and thought I'd better drop in and read the riot act. How are you and May getting on?"

"How, exactly, do you mean?"

"Well, damn it all, Chad, looking at your offense as cheerfully as one may, it does seem rather a grave thing to have done without sufficient cause. You surely don't go lying to her office and taking my name in vain unless you feel a powerful urge to have her company?"

"It was a whim. I had a sudden impulse to give her a day out."

"Give yourself a day out, you mean."

"As you like."

We were becoming quietly angry with one another. He knocked his pipe out into the fender and took a cool one from his pocket. I pushed the tobacco jar toward him. He pushed it back and took out his pouch.

"If you were simply up to a lark for your private amusement," he said, "I'm not sure that I can leave the matter where it is. You had no right to use my name."

"Look, I've apologized. If any harm was done, it's done. It can't be undone. What can you do about it, anyway?"

"That is something to be considered," he said grimly.

This was impasse. We glared at one another. It was Rhodes who broke the tension. Literally. He got up and moved to the middle of the room, took a few deep breaths, reached his arms up high above his head, and stood as rigid as a steel bar. Then in one movement he allowed himself to collapse till he was like jelly. He smiled. "Try it, Chad. It eases the body and the mind."

I didn't try it, but I was glad the evil moment was passed.

"I'm truly sorry," I said, "that this has happened. All over again, if that does any good, I give you my apology."

He sat down, and I refilled his coffeecup. "My medical instinct has led me astray," he said. "I thought I detected a romance three months gone on the road to matrimony."

"Does May give you any reason to think that?"

"Well, Nan is my spy in that quarter. If you imagine May is indifferent to you, you're mistaken. I say no more than that. Except this. What with that mother, and the manner of that mother's death, and one thing and another, the girl's had as bad a time as I could wish my worst enemy. At the moment, so far as I can see, she hasn't a soul in the world except Nan and me and you. And, where you are concerned, I now see that she is mistaken. If I were you, I wouldn't give her any reason for persisting in the mistake."

I walked him to the front door and watched him mount his bicycle which was standing against the curb. "Be sensible about it, one way or the other," he said, pealed his bell unnecessarily, and moved off into the slanting silver of the rain.

8

For two days I did nothing about all this. Then I decided that a gesture of friendship could do no harm. I bought a basket of fruit, a fine richly colored display, and took it to the house where May had her room. Inside, I tucked a note, saying formally that I was sorry to hear of her illness and that I hoped she would soon be quite well again. I asked the woman who came to the door how May was, and she said: "Obstinate as a mule. Do what I would, I couldn't keep her in bed yesterday. Before the doctor appeared, she was up and off to that office of hers."

"Well," I said cheerfully, "she must have felt equal to it or she wouldn't have done it."

She looked at me, pitying my optimism, my assumption of sanity in human conduct. Her stretched bony face and sorrowful eyes didn't suggest that she had had much reason to accept either.

"Well," she said, "she asked for it and she's got it. What's that there?"

"Fruit. It'll do her good."

"How do you know? Give it to me." I handed her the basket. "I'll have to see what Dr. Rhodes says. Probably the worst thing in the world for her."

She looked at me as if the intentions of an especially toxic-minded Borgia were written on my face, and quietly closed the door without another word.

Later in the evening I rang up Rhodes. He said that May had pneumonia. "Why doesn't the little fool wear wool next to her skin?"

It seemed a pedantic point, one I couldn't discuss.

"I've done all I can for the time being," Rhodes said. "A nurse going in and so forth. Now we'll have to wait and see."

They sounded ominous words and they imposed a weight of guilt on my mind. It was absurd, but I couldn't shake off a sense of responsibility for May Ingleby. I realized that after the day I had spent with her, I had hoped for other such days; days perhaps of decreasing restraint that might end in a kiss or two, all of course with no significance, but not less acceptable—more acceptable—for that. I hadn't been thinking of May's reaction to a situation carried so far. I had been thinking simply of a feminine touch that my life needed in its loneliness and disappointment. And now the girl was dying.

She didn't die. I hadn't the nerve to ring up Rhodes again, fearing what he might have to tell me, but after what seemed to me an unendurable stretch of time he rang me up. "Well," he cried heartily, "we're over the worst."

I was amazed by the glow of relief that warmed me, and when Rhodes had given me fuller news I finished the work I was doing and went to my rooms feeling more buoyant than I had done for many a day. And the odd thing is this: that May well—or at any rate on the road to being well—immediately began to diminish as a theme of contemplation. I felt as though it were I, not she, who had, as they say, "passed the crisis." She would soon be as robust as ever; she would be able to look after herself; I need never see her again.

Except, perhaps, once. As a matter of decent manners, I would have to see her to say that I was pleased by her recovery.

There was always, in my relations with May, this fatal one other time. And, anyway, I had counted without Whitworth Rhodes.

Christmas came, and Rhodes rang me up and asked me to look in and eat one of Nan's mince pies and have a drink. I accepted, not knowing that I should meet May Ingleby. But she was there. These Samaritans had once more taken her under their roof. I arrived in the dingy quarter in a flurry of snow that a bitter wind blew vertically along the street. It was an infinitely sad region, and on such a night as that the colored paper chains that draped the windows, the Chinese lanterns glowing behind fanlights, the Christmas trees seen through parted curtains, all seemed valiant wasted smiles in face of an overwhelming futility.

Such reflections were not lightened when I met May Ingleby. Her face was desolate and wan. It seemed to me that if she was alive it was only just.

Rhodes answered my ring, shook the snow from my coat at the open door, and hung the coat on a peg. "Come in, come in, Chad." He took me firmly by the arm and led me into the sitting room. It was a cheerful firelit room, with decanters and glasses and fruit and cakes on the table. Only Nan and May were in it, and as Nan rose to greet me I saw that she was far gone with child. She looked radiant, but not her radiance nor the cozy domestic scene could weigh with me against the chill that May's appearance struck to my heart. I had in one or two fugitive moments seen in her face a likeness to Rose Garland's, and it was perhaps the very thought of this that now the more emphasized her fallen cheeks, her hollow eyes, the gray aura of a risen Lazarus that lay upon her like a pall.

She got up and shook my hand. She said: "I'm ever so glad to see you again, Mr. Boothroyd. Thank you for the fruit."

"Don't mention it," I said, not to be outdone in polite backchat. "I am delighted to see you up and about again."

Rhodes took her by the shoulder and gently put her back into her chair. "You sit down, May, and stay down," he ordered. "Anyway, it's your bedtime. You are allowed one drink with Chad, then off you go."

May had her drink, and then Nan said: "Come along now. I'll give you an arm upstairs and help you into bed." She was as weak as that.

When they were gone, I said to Rhodes: "May looks terrible."

"So would you if you'd been through what she has. It was the nearest squeak I've ever known. Fundamentally, the girl must be as tough as an old boot, or she wouldn't have come through it at all. You helped, too, of course."

"What on earth had I to do with it?"

"Well, you brought her that basket of fruit."

He filled my glass with the cheap wine that was his idea of joy-making. I drank and laughed heartily.

"It seems easy," I said. "Let me know when you have other patients at death's door."

"I'm not talking through my hat," he said crossly. "When you *want* to live, then you're on the way to living. Believe it or not, you gave May something to hang on to. She's still got the basket. It's at her bedside with a few odds and ends in it."

I was deeply disturbed by this. "Why, man, an act of common courtesy . . ."

"All right. I don't care how you look at it. It helped to do the trick. Of course, May's not out of the wood. You can see that for yourself. She'll have to get away for a time from this sulfurous corner of hell if she's to pull through."

"What about her job?"

"I'm not worrying about that. I expect you've noticed how Nan is. Well, when this infant appears we'll want someone here. Nan won't be able to go on as unofficial secretary and all the rest of it. What we have in mind is to send May into the country for a month or so, and then, if the idea appeals to her, she could stay on here."

I said I thought it an excellent idea.

"Where is she to go—now, or at any rate within the next week? I've written to the home that took her after that ghastly affair of her mother, but there's nothing doing. They're full up."

I didn't like the look in his eye. I felt that something was coming, and here it was. He filled his pipe thoughtfully. "What about the Yorkshire dales?" he asked.

"What about them?"

"Just the thing. Smokeless. Bracing. A few days of walking up there always makes me a Titan. What about Smurthwaite?"

"There's an excellent pub there."

"Can't afford it. We must find a Samaritan."

"If you'd remained in the Church, you'd have been irresistible."

"The Church reminds me. If old Hawke had still been there, he'd have done this like a shot. I don't know the new man. Dammit! I'd quite forgotten! Your mother is Mrs. Hawke, isn't she? She's still living in the place—didn't you tell me?"

I was sure he'd forgotten nothing. I looked at him cautiously. "What are you asking me to do?"

He smiled like a fisherman who feels the trout on the line and now

224

has only to play it. "Just back me up. I'm an expert at writing begging letters. You have to be, in this place, unless you're content to be a mere disher-out of pills. I'll write the letter, Chad. You just say you know the girl and can vouch for her. Will you do that?"

"It seems rather a nerve."

Nan came into the room. "Darling," Rhodes said, "Chad is going to help us. He will write to his mother."

"Oh, how good of you!" Nan said; and, then, what could I do but smile and say: "Oh, it's nothing. Nothing at all. I think my mother will agree."

She did. After all, Uncle Arthur could not be expected to have forgotten Mr. Hawke's curate. Indeed, he remembered him with affection and sent him hearty greetings. To me Uncle Arthur wrote on Town Hall paper:

December is, of course, a critical month for the Auricula, and I am engaged in one or two experiments that may leave exhibitors at next April's shows not unsurprised. But hospitality is the duty of an English Gentleman, and I have no doubt that between us your poor mother and I will find time to cheer up Whitworth Rhodes's patient and return her in excellent fettle.

P.S.—I now subscribe to the *Manchester Guardian* and read occasional reports of utterances by Gregory Appleby, who seems not to have outgrown his grouse-poaching days. I hope he will live to learn that so long as property is respected and municipal affairs are soundly administered this old country has little to fear.

9

In the first week of February, having earned one of those joyous occasions called a long week end, I traveled to Smurthwaite in order to bring May Ingleby back to Manchester. I had heard nothing from her during her month of absence, unless you count a picture postcard with a photograph of the imposing entrance to Uncle Arthur's municipal cemetery. The years had already played with it, turning it into what might be taken for a Roman triumphal arch, bowered in trees now well grown. But if I had not heard from May I had heard about her. My mother wrote to me every week, and thus I had news of May's continuous progress in health. "You won't know May Ingleby when you see her again," my mother wrote. "She was like death when she came, but good air and good food have worked wonders. She looks almost attractive. She makes herself useful in all sorts of ways, and seems a sensible girl enough. Your Uncle Arthur has taken quite a fancy to her, and says she's almost one of the family."

When I reached Smurthwaite, May was waiting for me at the

station, and she certainly was an advertisement for Smurthwaite as a health resort. The weather during her stay had been at its best: no rain, little snow, a succession of bracing sunny days, with a touch of night frost to put an edge on one's sense of being alive. So the dark girl who met me and walked with me under the bare sycamores to Uncle Arthur's house, with a blue sky over our heads and the familiar desirable wine of the air rinsing my lungs with every breath, was round-cheeked and rosy, and the eyes that always looked their best when peeping out from under the eaves of her fur hat had a brighter sparkle then I had seen in them before.

"Oh, Chad," were her first words as I joined her on the platform, "everyone's been so good to me!" And then, at once remembering her place, as she would have said: "Should I call you Chad?"

"I once threatened to drive the idea into your head with a pewter pot. If that is not enough, I'll have a document drawn up conferring upon you, your heirs, assigns and what not the inalienable right to Chad me to your heart's content *in saecula saeculorum*. My Uncle Arthur is a barrister and will do the job, finishing it off with a yard of red ribbon and a blob of sealing wax as big as a cartwheel. How are you, May?"

"Well—look at me! And think what I was."

And that was certainly all that needed to be said about that.

We met Uncle Arthur in the main street, contemplating a steam roller that moved to and fro, crushing down soil that had recently been disturbed. "I've been having my drains up," Uncle Arthur said somberly.

May looked at him with open admiration. "Mr. Geldersome has a finger in every pie," she said. "He ought to be knighted."

"I should expect to be knighted myself," I said, "if I carried my public spirit so far as to consider drains a pie."

"You know very well what May means, Chad," said Uncle Arthur. "Give me your arm, my dear. You must not presume on your slight improvement."

"Slight!" I could not help crying. "Why, if this is a slight improvement, when May is really well she'll be running round with that steam roller under her arm."

"Not without the consent of the Borough Engineer," said Uncle Arthur; and May, who was clearly still prepared to be, at command, an interesting figure, tucked her arm through his. "You had better rest when you get in," Uncle Arthur advised her. "I have ordered a sustaining dinner for tonight."

Smurthwaite seemed changeless, and seemed, alas! is the right word, for it is changed now. But then, as we walked home in the sharpening evening air, every tree was as I had known it, every shop window had a homely twinkle, the people who greeted us in the streets seemed not a day older, and Uncle Arthur, walking a little ahead of me with May's hand resting genteelly on his forearm, seemed unaltered from the robust reliable figure who had invaded us at St. Michael Pendeverel half my lifetime ago. In this place and these circumstances, May Ingleby looked at home. To know May as a junior typist in Manchester was one thing. To see her strolling along so familiarly with Uncle Arthur was another. I was not analyzing this situation at the time, but I see now that her presence there, so naturally accepted among my trees, and my strong gray homely buildings, and by my people, changed her focus; and on her part, too, there must have been, whether consciously or not, a readjustment of attitude. I was no longer the casually met stranger of Oxford who, by chance, had again intruded once or twice into her life: I was part of something which had accepted her and made her welcome.

So we tagged along fatefully to the crossroads where stood the solid Town Hall, which, if painted, I thought with a smile, would be an admirable portrait of Uncle Arthur, turned left and came to the house. Here, the very smell was unchanged: the beeswax with which the furniture was perpetually fed, the not offensive but unmistakable reminder of a thousand well-cooked meals, the smell of middle-class tradition in its rectitude and rigid limitation. May was at home in it. "Thank you, Mr. Geldersome," she said, releasing his arm. "I'll take my things straight up to my room."

My room!

"Yes, do," he told her. "And don't let us see you till dinnertime. I'll have a cup of tea sent up." She might have been his beloved daughter.

I stood for a moment contemplating the popeyed relic of poor Madeleine, one paw pathetically and perpetually upraised beneath her glass canopy on the hall table, then took up my bag.

"The old room, Uncle Arthur?"

"The old room, Chad. It's always there for you, dear boy. Your mother is having her afternoon nap. I insist on it. We'll all meet at dinner."

I went up to the familiar top story. In my bedroom, the paintwork, the curtains, the chintz-covered window seat, were as I had known them when first they were prepared for the small boy from Cornwall. A fire whispered in the grate. The day was dying, and, standing at the window, I watched the fells withdrawing into the darkness and a light spring up in a cottage window at their foot. Around me and beneath me was absolute quiet. The house seemed asleep. "If May Ingleby snores, I shall hear her," I thought. And that made me think how odd it was that May Ingleby was here, in this house, asleep in a bed. I pushed off my shoes, got down upon my own bed, and was soon asleep myself, lulled by the drowsy unapprehensive warmth of the room.

I was awakened by a sharp rat-tatting of knuckles on the door, and, hardly yet aware of where I was, called drowsily: "Come in."

The door opened a crack, and Greg Appleby's face looked through. I never knew Greg to be without a book or two in his pockets, and now he took one out and scored a bull with a calf-bound duodecimo upon my navel. There was still enough fire glow for us to see one another. He followed the book into the room and boisterously rolled me off the bed onto the floor. This put me into a good position to seize his legs, and I brought him crashing down on top of me. We began to pummel one another and the racket brought my mother running. "Whatever's going on here?" she cried.

Greg got to his feet. "The boys are home again, Mrs. Hawke," he grinned.

"Boys!" she cried. "You'll both be grandfathers before you know where you are, the way things are going."

"Why, Mrs. Hawke—how go things?"

"Well, I'm not blind. Chad, let's have a look at you."

Greg lit the two candles standing on the mantelpiece. My mother embraced me and kissed me. "Good heavens," she said. "I believe you're still growing. You should visit us more often. Then we wouldn't notice."

It was said in a slightly reproachful tone, and the reproof was not undeserved.

"Well," she commanded, "both of you be down in a quarter of an hour. Not a minute later. Your uncle doesn't like to have to hurry over his sherry, Chad."

She went, and I said to Greg: "What are you doing here?"

"I, and Phoebe who is below, are here by order of Arthur J. Geldersome, Town Clerk. Your uncle has a social sense that you lack. Your mother sounded to me a bit pained."

"I know I don't get here as often as she'd like me to."

"You don't get out to Didsbury as often as Phoebe and I would like you to. If you did, you'd know that we've been here over Christmas with my father. Your uncle took the occasion of your visit to arrange this reunion. We came on our bikes."

"He said nothing to me about it."

"No. He has a sense of drama. He said nothing to me about this Ingleby girl whom I met downstairs looking radiant as the queen of the May. What on earth is she doing here?"

I explained what had happened.

"So you've been seeing her in Manchester?"

"Now and then. Mainly by chance."

"She's not the girl I would have chosen for you."

"Nobody's asking you to choose a girl for me."

He looked at me sharply. "All right. All right. But I suppose this explains your having no time for Didsbury. Now let's go and sample Mr. Geldersome's good wine."

Uncle Arthur was standing with his back to the roaring fire in the dining room, glass in hand. Phoebe was wearing the tweeds she had cycled in. My mother and May had gone in for some sort of toilette. I forget what May was wearing, but she looked well in it under the quiet lamplight, and, so far as health goes, I had never seen her better. Phoebe shook my hand, saying briefly: "Hello, Chad. You're quite a stranger," and I thought: The old gang—Greg and Phoebe, myself, my mother and Uncle Arthur. And now May Ingleby, apparently quite at home among us. Eustace had never been at home among us. For whatever reason, he had seemed always a visitor, a bird in flight.

"How's Eustace?" I asked.

"Gone to London," Phoebe said. "He's been writing a lot this winter, and he's gone up to supervise publication."

"Is he coming back to you?"

Uncle Arthur filled glasses for me and Greg, and Greg answered. "Even if we were staying in Manchester, I don't suppose he would. Once he's on the wing, you just let him fly."

"But aren't you staying in Manchester?" I asked.

"You see, Phoebe," said Greg, "what this boy misses by neglecting his friends. He's hopelessly out of touch."

"Well, come on," I said, "what are you up to?"

Phoebe explained. "We're going to London in March. Greg's got a lectureship at the School of Economics."

The sustaining dinner that Uncle Arthur had promised began to appear. A maid wheeled in a trolley with a huge soup tureen and six warm plates. We sat. My mother was on one side of me and May on the other. Uncle Arthur gave himself to serious business; the rich fume of the tureen ascended into his face as he ladled, his nostrils dilated with unashamed greed.

"A little more sherry with your soup," he urged us. Greg and I alone accepted.

"It is a great pity," Uncle Arthur said, "that John Ruskin didn't marry Miss Domecq and go into his father's sherry business. Sherry is something you can understand." He poured sherry into his soup and urged May to do the same.

"Are you making a backhander at John's understandability, Mr. Geldersome?" Greg asked; and Uncle Arthur replied firmly: "In any crisis of life, I'd rather have one pint of the old man's sherry than Seven Lamps of the young man's Architecture."

"It is fortunate," said Greg, "that we don't have to choose. We can have both. Though, as an economist, I must say that when I read John I choose incidental beauties, stimulating hints, rather than anything else. I find no system in him."

To everyone's surprise, I am sure, May piped up nervously: "Do you understand *Sesame and Lilies*, Mr. Appleby? A young gentleman at Oxford gave me a copy to read. I couldn't make head or tail of it."

Greg laughed. "Speaking again as an economist," he said, "I would never give a young lady *Sesame and Lilies* to read. As an average sensual man, I should look with suspicion on any young gentleman of Oxford or elsewhere, who expected a young woman to live up to that book. I hope you never saw this young gentleman again?"

"No," said May, "I didn't. Not after I returned the book and said I didn't understand it."

"You're lucky," Greg assured her. "He's probably still searching round."

"Father gave me a copy for my fourteenth birthday," Phoebe said. "I loved it, every word of it, but only as a poem."

"Only?" Greg teased her. "You speak slightingly of poetry, young woman."

"Not a bit of it. It's the greatest thing in the world. But you mustn't expect it to give you a path in life."

"Then what do you expect of it?" Greg urged her; and she said: "I haven't the faintest idea. But I should wilt without it on any path."

"A wretched definition," Greg said, looking at her fondly, "but I can't supply a better."

I took no part in the chatter. I felt deeply depressed at the thought that Greg and Phoebe would be so far from me. Uncle Arthur was happy, officiously carving the saddle of mutton at the moment. "The St. Emilion is on the mantelpiece, decently *chambré*, I hope. Serve it, Chad, there's a good fellow."

I did so, and then Uncle Arthur was fussing about the red currant jelly, and whether the roast potatoes had become brown instead of remaining golden. "It is such points that distinguish *cuisine* from cookery."

At last all was to his satisfaction. He raised his glass. "Well, Greg— well, Phoebe—I've watched you both grow up, you know, not without apprehension at times, but on the whole I see no cause to complain. Let me wish you all success and all happiness in your new venture."

We drank to that; and I said: "But it's the very devil that you're going away. I'm deeply disappointed."

"You should have used us while we were on hand," Greg said, and I answered impetuously: "How could I, when Eustace was there?"

A look of complete surprise came over Greg, and he began: "What has Eustace got to do—?"

I could almost see the kick Phoebe gave him under the table. He stopped abruptly, and Phoebe said: "Make the most of us while we *are* there, Chad. We'll be back in Manchester soon, and we shan't be moving off for a month or two."

She looked at me and smiled, not just a social grin but a smile that took me confidently into her understanding and comforted me. She, if no one else, was aware of Rose and of the crosscurrents of my life. She, more than anyone else, looked at me and May with a wondering compassion.

At the sideboard Uncle Arthur, grave as a priest at an altar, stood above the blue flickering light of a spirit lamp, preparing *crêpes* into which dashes of liqueur fell from time to time. "I should not be able," he said, "to look Whitworth Rhodes in the face again if I did not send May back a different woman from what pills and potions could produce. Kitchen physic leaves the whole *British Pharmacopoeia* looking exceedingly silly. God send I do not live to see the day when lean automata subsist upon pellets." He had been drinking freely, not to say lavishly, and now broke into a hoarse laugh. "Ill fares the land," he quoted, and my mind went back to Pendeverel, "to countless ills a prey, where pellets accumulate and pullets decay."

My mother, more practically, asked May: "Are you a good cook, my dear?"

"Fair to middling, Mrs. Hawke, thank you," May answered.

Uncle Arthur had certainly put a benedictory touch upon the meal. When the *crêpes* had been consumed and highly commended the three women went up to my mother's sitting room. I wanted nothing more to eat, and joined Greg in a little brandy with my coffee. Uncle Arthur set before himself a large Stilton cheese, ruddy with port wine, and moreover he filled a glass with port. He looked at us pityingly. "The gastronome," he said, "never to be confused with the glutton, does not shirk the last fence. To turn from your port and Stilton is to build your cathedral without its cloud-brushing spire, to constitute a municipal body without a town clerk. All things must have their peak and culmination."

He finished his cheese and port. "Now I will join you in a little brandy."

Greg and I were sipping our brandy from thimbles. Uncle Arthur got up, with a dignity the more impressive for the difficulty with which it was sustained, relit the spirit lamp, passed a balloon glass expertly through the flames, and poured in his brandy. He sniffed, and announced: "It rises to greet you." He pierced and lit a cigar and sat down splodged abroad in his chair, the stem of the glass in one hand, the blue-spiraling cigar in the other. He beamed upon us. He had reached his goal. After a moment of profound meditation he said: "This is the point where we should sing a catch or troll a lay," but Greg, at that, was quickly on his feet. "We must be off, Mr. Geldersome. Phoebe and I have quite a ride before us," and, indeed, at that moment Phoebe herself looked round the door. "Time to be off, Greg."

Uncle Arthur prudently remained seated. He extended a hand. "Shake an old boy's fin," he said.

Phoebe did more than that. She kissed him. "Thank you. You're a dear," she said. "It was a lovely dinner."

"Well," said Uncle Arthur, "we do our best, you know. We needs must love the highest when we see it."

May Ingleby was in the hall to say good-night. My mother had not come down. "I've said good-night for you to Mrs. Hawke," Phoebe said to Greg.

Their bicycles were leaning against the front of the house. May and I watched them mount, called our good-bys, and stood side by side on the pavement till the red eyes on their back mudguards fell asleep.

May sighed. "Well, that's that," she said. "It was a lovely evening. I've never had a lovelier evening, Chad. You *do* have nice friends. That Phoebe doesn't say much, but I'm sure she's clever. I wish I was clever."

The street was as quiet as the grave. The air was cold and bracing and the moon was high and small.

I took May's arm and we walked a pace or two. "I wish I had friends like yours," she said.

"Rhodes and his wife are very good friends to you," I reminded her.

"I suppose so," she said reluctantly, and added with a flash of insight, "but they're so good to *everybody*. So it's not the same thing."

I had not drunk anything like so much as Uncle Arthur, but I was in a pleasantly relaxed state of being. I pressed May's arm. "Not the same as what?"

"Well—oh, I can't explain. I tell you I'm not clever." There was a catch in her voice. "I can't talk, I didn't like *Sesame and Lilies,* I can't cook—not really. . . ."

"Oh, what the hell does it matter whether you like *Sesame and Lilies* or not! Here—give us a kiss."

We were passing a gap between two houses and I pulled her into the darkness there. It was I who did the giving. I put my arms round her, pulled her to me, and felt the softness of her breasts against me. I kissed her again and again. She did not respond, but she did not resist. Only, when I stopped, she said: "Does that make you feel happy, Chad?"

"It makes me feel all sorts of things," I said hardily and truthfully.

"I am glad," she said innocently. "That's all right then."

CHAPTER NINE

I

IN JUNE of 1913 I married May Ingleby. One kiss led to another, and so it went. I kissed her in the train on the way back from Smurthwaite to Manchester. The holiday had done her good. Her skin was glowing, her eyes were bright. She was ripe for kissing, and having survived the shock on the night when we watched Phoebe and Greg ride away, she submitted to as much as I cared to administer. I liked it, and so I could have it, but she seemed always to wonder what there was to it that I liked. But one thing at a time. I ventured in the train to put a hand upon her breast. I felt the sharp instinctive recoil, the withdrawal of her whole body from me. "Don't, Chad," was all she said, and then there wasn't any more even of kissing for that time.

I got used to her. I got to like all that was likable about her. She was anxious to please me, and something protective in me rose up to avert from her even those desires in myself which I felt alarmed her. Throughout the winter and spring we were together as often as we could be. In the course of my work, I took her to theaters and music halls. She even, at times, sat with me through dreary speeches and lectures. The times when I was called in to do "corridor" work for the paper became fewer and fewer. I felt myself to be bedding down firmly into the reporting staff. I didn't mind that from one point of view, for the work had variety and often took me about the country; but, from another point of view, I was unhappy. After all, I had been engaged as a possible corridor man, and I was oppressed with a feeling of having failed. The Old Man's Jehovan eye had looked me over and found me wanting. I was not fish, flesh nor fowl: an unattached body drifting with no special allegiance.

Greg and Phoebe were gone, and that made matters worse. Yet another book by Greg was published—one of those books in which he discussed economic matters within a context of contemporary manners and conditions that made them marvelously readable; and Eustace's book of poems came at the same time, shooting him up like a rocket into popular esteem. As for Billy Pascoe, his was not work that either courted or met the public eye; but there was a word that Greg had dropped in my ear: "Billy? Well, yes, I hear about him from time to time. Don't ask me what he's up to. I'm not a physicist. But I gather he's unostentatiously undermining the universe. For myself, I'm rather nervous about these blind young Samsons."

It all left me feeling like the fool of the family of young men who had grown up together. Any one of those three would have been more worth Rose's time than I was.

There was consolation in this patient unpretentious little creature, so demurely determined to keep our courtship within the rules of good taste and impeccable conduct. She, at least, thought I was wonderful, if inclined to be naughty.

There was no doubt that it was courtship now, that May expected me to ask her to marry me. There had been nothing impetuous about it, but we drifted into a situation from which, as I am sure May would have put it, it would be dishonorable for me to withdraw.

The thing was clinched on a May evening. We had been for a walk through those Didsbury fields in which I had wandered desolate that day when Eustace softly shut the door in my face. It was an exceptionally warm evening for the time of year, and we sat on the grass of the river bank. The place was populated with lovers lying entwined, and I put an arm round May's waist and tried to draw her down beside me where I lay. She resisted. "Oh, Chad—no! Look, everybody's doing it. It's so common."

So I sat beside her and kissed her, decorously upright. She didn't mind that.

On the way home I said: "You've never seen the place where Greg and Phoebe used to live. Let's go that way."

We turned and twisted through the little back streets till we came to the house. The quietness there was enchanting. The beautiful symmetrical Lombardy poplars climbed above the rooftops, and in the front patch of what had been Greg's house the laburnum was festooned with golden chains. In those days there seemed never to be a "shortage" of houses. You would see them in the market for months on end, and in the window of this one was a bill: TO BE LET OR SOLD.

We looked at it—the fairy tree with its hair down, the manageable little house—and I could hear the thoughts in May's head.

"It would be almost like living in the country, Chad," she said. "It's as quiet as the country, and near the shops. The rent can't be much."

"Where would you like to go for your honeymoon?" I asked.

She said without hesitation: "Morecambe."

"Morecambe!"

"Yes, Chad. Don't you like it?"

"Well—but why? Why Morecambe?"

"I went there once for a holiday with my mother, and the tide goes out ever such a long way."

"I cannot think," I said, "of a higher commendation for a honeymoon place. We'll go to Morecambe."

2

Whether or not the girl you are you are going to marry is the girl you want to marry, there is a pleasurable excitement in the idea of marriage, unless it is something you have been forced into with a person who is repellent. May was not repellent, and since the woman I would have liked to marry was married and living far away in Cambridge, and since I was not made for chastity, though I had been chaste till now, I found my situation agreeable enough. I saw the house agents and began to pay my rent right away. The idea of living in a house once occupied by Greg and Phoebe pleased me. I remembered the attic rooms that Greg had knocked into one, and pictured myself there getting down at last to work which wouldn't make me feel so far behind the other men who had started out with me. As for May, her temperament never permitted her to boil over. She was quietly happy, so that the good looks she had brought back from Smurthwaite persisted. She busied herself with finding bits of secondhand furniture. She was a good haggler and, I am sure, saved me a lot of money. She always remembered, and did not mind, that I was a poor man; and if nothing she bought was what I would have liked to buy, I told myself that, like Greg, I would make the little house in Didsbury a perching place from which, before long, I would take off on wings of wealth and renown. Then I would do some furnishing to my heart's desire. The only things I bothered to buy for myself were a substantial writing table, with a chair, an ashtray, a pentray and an inkpot. These were all beautiful and expensive and have lasted me through life.

May was living with Rhodes and Nan and she had plenty to do in that busy household, but the Rhodeses never objected to her coming out with me. They were the sort of people who could not resist what they considered a romance, and I am sure Nan would have got down gladly to washing the baby and the medicine bottles and the kitchen floor if thereby she could give May another half-hour with me. The Rhodeses were the only people who knew that the marriage was to take place. I didn't reason about it at the time; I didn't ask myself why I said nothing to my mother and Uncle Arthur; but I can well understand now what deep but unacknowledged foreboding was causing me to keep the matter in the dark. Someday—and soon—everybody would have to be told, and I was pathetically reminded of this about a week before our wedding took place. The kitchen of our house was now furnished, as well as a bedroom, a sitting room, and, sketchily, what I called my study. For the time being, poverty forbade any more. On an evening in June May and I went out to have a look at the place.

"Let's call at my rooms first," I said. "I've packed some books and we'll take them along."

I looked round the room where I had so unprofitably passed my spare time thus far, and my eye fell on Miss Orlop's sketch of Rose over the mantelpiece. I unhooked it and said: "I'd better take this."

May took the picture from my hands and studied it. "Isn't she pretty? Who is it?"

"No one in particular. Just a picture."

"How *wild* she looks! My! She wouldn't half fly off the handle if she felt like it!"

I took the picture from her, wrapped it up, and put it in the suitcase with the books.

As we were wandering round our domain that evening, May showed me a few things she had been making. There was a set of what she called doilies.

"What are they for?" I asked.

"Oh, Chad! Where were you brought up? Haven't you ever heard of doilies? You put them under a cake on a plate."

"Why? Don't plates like the kiss of cake?"

She looked at me perplexed. "How do you mean? Nice people always use doilies. Don't you like them? I made them myself."

"Then I'm sure they're all that doilies should be. I'll give you a kiss for each one you've made."

"Oh, Chad! You and your kissing. Look—the curtains aren't up yet."

I kissed her all the same till she broke away and said: "Now, Chad, there are serious things to discuss. I want you to look at these—to see if you approve. They've just come from the printers. I'm paying for them myself."

It was a small packet of folded-over bits of paper. It was nice paper, stout and deckle-edged. The printing was in silver. It announced the wedding of Chad Boothroyd and May Ingleby. In the corner was a silver cupid, discreetly wearing a napkin, and a silver arrow from his bow had struck through the name of May Ingleby, expunging it for ever from the honorable company of virgins. May was looking at it over my shoulder, and I could feel that she was palpitating with pleasure. I wondered if she had ever seen Caravaggio's unnapkined painting of *Cupid Victorious,* and what she would make of it if she did.

"They've done an awfully nice job," she said. "I think they're sweet."

"What do we do with them?"

"Oh, really, Chad, I'm sure you're just pretending. You can't have a nice wedding without sending these out to your friends. It's bad enough being married in a registry office."

"Now, May. We've settled that."

"You settled it. I know I agreed."

"It was very kind of you, May."

"Well, I like to please you. You know that."

She did. Within her limitations, there was nothing she wouldn't do to please me. I knew it was a grief to her not to be married with church trimmings. And why I had decided that I didn't want to be married in church was another thing I didn't face at the time.

I lugged the books upstairs and put them into the shelves I had made. "Now, May, is there a hammer in the house?"

There wasn't. Surprising how many things a house needed.

"What do you want with a hammer?"

"I want to hang this picture over my writing table."

There was a nail in the wall over the fireplace. May pulled at it, and it came out. She slipped off a shoe. "Here," she said, "make do with these."

So with the heel of May's shoe I drove in the nail and hung the picture of Rose.

"I don't know why you want it there," May said. "She's no more than a child, but she looks capable of anything."

3

I believe that All Saints Church in Manchester was smashed during the Second World War and that the ruins have now been erased and the tombstones taken away and the place turned into a playground. It was, when I lived in Manchester, a deplorable testimony to the blight of industrial civilization. It stood on the main road that runs from the heart of the town to arrive at last in pleasant suburbs, but at this spot there was nothing pleasant. There was the church so filthy that it appeared to be carved out of charcoal, there was the churchyard surrounding it, full of dirty tombstones, some broken, some askew, and dirty grass and stunted grimed trees that in the spring remembered their youth, achieved an efflorescence that was miraculous, and then fell back upon the haglike existence that they maintained for nine months of the year. Alongside the churchyard was a urinal in cast iron, and in front of it was a cab rank where scrawny horses stood in the shafts, dejectedly awaiting a customer to awaken them to a few moments of shambling life. The cabmen all seemed as ancient as their horses, and it was one with red-rimmed rheumy eyes and a moth-eaten silk hat that I engaged to wait outside the registry office and drive me and May to the station.

Perhaps the registry office is still there, even now when the church is gone. I don't know. It stood behind the church, and all about it and around it were those heart-breaking utilitarian houses, row upon row, each like the next ten thousand, none with a tree, a garden, a flower, save such as peeped from window pots upon a world that their timid flames were not enough to cheer.

My three weeks' holiday began on my wedding day. It was a June day, with the promise that before it was ended the narrow streets would be broiling. I took what comfort I could from the thought that by then I should be in Morecambe.

I lounged in the street opposite the registry office waiting for May. The Rhodeses, who disapproved of a registry office wedding, came with her. They arrived in a four-wheeler cab, and as I crossed the road to join them my own cabman, who was to take us to the station, drove up, and proved to be not unmindful of the nature of this occasion. The old fellow, looking ripe rather for his own funeral than for someone else's wedding, wore a white carnation at his lapel, and had tied to his whip a bow of not altogether white ribbon. These proved to be the only concessions to poor May's repressed wishes for *éclat*.

However, as I was crossing the road and the old nag was slithering to a standstill, I became aware that in the church behind me someone was enjoying what I had denied to May. At this moment a bridegroom, with his best man at his side, was standing at the altar, and up the aisle was pacing, with her retinue, the girl he was waiting for. "Here comes the bride." As I joined May outside the door of the registry office and tucked my arm through hers, she, too, heard those familiar notes rising in the church. She paused, stiffened, and turned round, listening till the music ended. Then she gave me a look of infinite reproach and we walked into the office together. What happened in there I do not remember. It is one of those spots in my memory across which a sponge has passed, effacing the record. But memory returns with our coming back into the bright midsummer morning and with May instantly cocking an ear in the direction of the church. "Love divine, all love excelling." The organ sound came out into the warm day, and the voices of people with it, and May said: "Oh, Chad!" and with an arm linked in mine drew me willy-nilly almost running across the road and into the churchyard and between the soot-black tombstones to the door of the church. Because of the heat the door was wide open, and we could see the altar lights and the bride in white kneeling with her husband. We stood there till the hymn ended, alone, for the Rhodeses had left us.

238

> *Changed from glory into glory,*
> *Till in heaven we take our place,*
> *Till we cast our crowns before Thee,*
> *Lost in wonder, love, and praise!*

May listened, her lips parted, and tears began to run down her cheeks. I, too, was deeply moved, both on my own account, for that happens to be a hymn that always moves me, and because of poor May, so eager for the crumbs of someone else's feast and fulfillment. And in this tangle of emotion we looked at one another and knew, I am sure, that we were going to fail one another. We were crying unashamedly when we climbed into the cab. Our ancient didn't seem surprised. He looked old and used, and as though nothing of human joy or sorrow could touch him. Like a scarecrow animated by a hidden spring, he flicked his white-ribboned whip and trundled us off as though he didn't give a damn whether he was taking us to bed or to Bedlam.

4

If it wasn't much of a wedding, it was going to be a good honeymoon. I had made my mind up about that, and had even gone so far as to visit Morecambe in order to see and choose our room. No boardinghouse for me. I chose a small attractive hotel on the sea front, toward the Bare end of the town, and explained to the manager that my wife had been suffering from double pneumonia and wanted a place where she could have good food and pick up her strength. It was true enough, even if six months out-of-date. I didn't want us to be surrounded with the innuendo of the newly married. It was a large airy room, and it hadn't the sense, usual in an English hotel bedroom, of doing its damnedest to chase you out. It had a couch at the window and a writing table and a decent carpet on the floor. I hoped May would like it. The first thing she said was, "Oh, Chad! Can we afford it?"

It was on my tongue to say that it wasn't so expensive as a classy wedding, but I held this back, warned by the episode at the church door. May, I saw, was in an odd, apprehensive mood. During the train journey she had been extraordinarily quiet, even for her. I could sense that she was in a dither about what I might wish to do, thus early in our married life. I humored the feeling, and did not so much as kiss her. She read a woman's magazine that had been left on the seat, and I was aware of her relief when, halfway through the journey, some boisterous talkative fellow travelers to Morecambe got into the carriage.

As soon as we arrived, I asked to have tea sent to our room, and now here we were, with the tea disposed of, sitting on the couch at the window, looking toward the sea, which needed, at that state of the tide, a telescope for its inspection. A maid came up to take away the tea tray. I opened the door for her, and locked it behind her. I turned down the bedclothes, sat again at May's side, and slipped a hand inside her blouse. I began to kiss her. She was unresponsive. I opened all the buttons on her blouse and began to kiss her breasts. She turned and cast a look of terror toward the door.

"Don't worry about that, May," I said. "It's locked. There are three hours to dinnertime. Let's go to bed."

"Oh, Chad! I couldn't! Not in broad daylight!"

With trembling fingers she did up her blouse. "We haven't unpacked," she said. "We ought to get on with that."

So we unpacked, dodging every physical contact with one another, and when it was finished May said, giving me a wan smile: "There! I do like things to be done in order."

I could see that she was wondering what, in this business of doing things in order, I would consider to be next on the list.

"May," I said, "it's been a trying day for you. Have a good rest. Get into bed and sleep." I took up my hat. "I'll join you at dinnertime, and I'll warn them down below not to disturb you."

A quick look of gratitude lit her face. She even kissed me of her own free will. "Thank you, Chad," she said. "I really could do with a good sleep."

I promised myself at least the pleasure of watching her undress, perhaps of helping her. But she made no sign of beginning, and presently I went.

The sun was shining. The sands were thick with children building their castles, digging their moats, and with adults lying full stretched in blessed relaxation. On the promenade a band was playing. There were gardens blazing with flowers. The shops were gay. Awnings: red, white, yellow, green. Flannels, summery floating dresses, everyone laughing. Happy holidaytime. Release from Leeds and Bradford.

I felt like hell, and paid for a deck chair, and sat listening to the band. Or rather, aware of the band. I was not listening to the band, or anything. I was not seeing the children, or anything. I was a mash of anger and pity and frustration. I was not aware of the girl who had come and sat down in the chair next to mine. It was the cessation of noise that first made me aware of the noise. The bandsmen were packing up, gathering music sheets, shaking spit from trombones. Soon they were gone, and most of the people. The girl said: "You look sad, dear. Could I help you to amuse yourself?"

The question identified her profession, but she couldn't have had long professional experience. She was young—younger than myself, I guessed—with a dark vivacity in her face. She was well dressed. Her smile showed perfect teeth. "Do you like me?" she asked. And added: "I'm young enough to enjoy it. Not like some of them."

Nothing save her words identified her. We might have been two lovers having a pleasant chat. The passers-by took no notice of us. "I could give you a very good time," she said.

"No."

"Don't you like me?" she asked again.

"Well, you see, I'm on my honeymoon."

She laughed merrily. "Oh, well, that makes a difference, doesn't it? You'll have no energy to spare for me. Sorry to trouble you."

She twirled the parasol that sloped across her shoulder and looked at me with a roguish twinkle. "Well, back to your good work," she said. "Don't keep her waiting. I must be on my way."

She got up, and a waft of scent from her brushed me, and I was overcome by the thought of all that she would so willingly and gaily give me, and I said: "Just a moment. Don't go."

She stopped, looking at me with surprise breaking through her amusement, and a sudden tinge of seriousness in her face, a swift hint of mercenary calculation, chilled me more than May's reluctance had done, and, getting up, I strode away without a word, aware only of her shoulder lifted in a shrug that was all amusement again.

I don't remember much about the intervening hours except that I walked and walked, sent picture postcards of Cartmel Priory to everybody I could think of, and on the way to the hotel passed my little professional, arm in arm, as though determined to keep him now that she had him, with an enormous man who looked like something prosperous from the Bradford wool trade. She flashed me a triumphant wink as she went by.

May was up and dressed for dinner in a long affair of swishing yellow silk. She looked too well in it to sustain the part of a convalescent. "I had a wonderful sleep," she said. "What have you been doing, Chad?"

"Watching the tide coming in. The outriders appear now to be only ten miles off."

I kissed the back of her neck.

It was the very devil trying to make absurd conversation, feeling as I did.

I took off my coat and washed, reknotted my tie, and brushed my hair.

"Didn't you bring your dinner jacket?" May asked.

"No."

"Oh, what a pity! Some of the men are wearing them. I've been peeping down from the window. You can see them down there sitting on the chairs in the garden, having drinks before dinner."

She would dearly have loved to be joining in this urbane ritual. My own feelings were for something more Bacchic.

"You are so tall, Chad," she said. "If you were properly dressed, you'd look the most distinguished man here."

"I don't want to be properly dressed, May. I want to be most improperly dressed, which is to say I want to be naked and to have you naked, too."

She backed toward the window, alarmed. "Oh, Chad," she said. "I thought you'd love me in this dress."

"It would be complicated. May, do you love me?"

"Oh, Chad! How can you ask such a thing? On our wedding day!"

"Still, I ask it, May. Do you love me? And do you know what loving a man involves?"

A gong sent brazen sound vibrating through the hotel. May clutched at it. "There's the gong! Let's go down."

We went down, and the head waiter himself conducted us to our table, pulled out a chair for May, and hoped that madam would soon be completely recovered. May answered him with *savior-faire,* took up a napkin daintily, and looked about her as though wishing that Sir Charles McCumber could see her now.

"I think this is all very lovely, Chad," she said, as though nothing were between us save the small change of polite manners. "Thank you very much for bringing me here."

She even put a hand on mine and smiled at me.

"My chief reason for bringing you here," I said, determined to keep her to the point, "is that bed upstairs."

She looked round in wild alarm, and blushes rushed to her cheeks and neck. "Chad—really! You have such a penetrating voice."

There was nothing more to be said at the moment, for one waiter was putting soup before us and another was handing a basket of rolls. When they were gone, May took a spoonful of soup, and then said quietly, not lifting her eyes from her plate: "You know, Chad, I don't think we *should*—not on the very first night."

Well, that was that. I knew where I stood. All right, I thought. Have it your own way. I'm damned if I'll break into you like a burglar using a jimmy on a money box.

May took up the bill of fare. "I do wish," she said, "they wouldn't have all this French. What does *escalope de veau* mean, Chad?"

"Pigs' trotters," I said. "I don't recommend them. You'd find them very coarse."

"Well! Fancy having a dish like that in a place like this!"

We drank our coffee in the lounge, where the young men in dinner jackets inspected May with the eyes of house agents considering a desirable little property of more than usual charm.

"Shall we go dancing?" she asked. "You know how I love dancing, Chad. And we haven't danced since that night at Oxford."

Oh, my God, I thought. Do you know why women dance, and why they wear clothes of yellow silk that sigh and rustle? And why tonight of all nights do you remind me of *that* night?

"I'll get your cloak," I said.

"Thank you, my dear."

In the bedroom I stood at the window watching the western sky smolder. The cloak, of black silk lined with yellow, lay over my arm. Poor little devil, I thought. She's done herself well—probably blued every cent she ever saved on these honeymoon geegaws. I wondered about her mother—saw the pallid bandaged corpse jolting down the stairs on the stretcher. That, I was sure, was what lay between me and May. I could imagine all the years of guarding her "purity," warning her of some composite evil called Men, till purity itself became putrescent, a festering fear. I felt very adult and understanding, pleased with my percipience. I decided that I had been hasty with May, had not allowed enough for her need to be wooed. Well, now, she should have it her own way. I would wait for her to come to me. I went down and almost paternally put the cloak over her shoulders.

We trailed back to the hotel in the warm dark full of lovers. "It would have been just like Oxford, Chad, if you'd been wearing your dinner jacket."

"I wasn't wearing a dinner jacket. It was white tie and tails. And a carnation."

"Oh, you know what I mean."

In the lounge I said: "Now you run away to bed. I'll give myself a drink before I come up."

I knew she would want to undress alone. When I went up she was in bed and the light was out. I undressed in the dark and got into bed and spent a fevered night. Oddly, May slept like a top.

5

One of the advantages of Morecambe, as of many other places, is that it is easy to get out of. The Lakes are on the doorstep. Had this been ten years later, I suppose I should have whisked May to the Lakes in a two-seater car. As it was, we went in a horse-drawn brake, accompanied by girls in long skirts and tight lacquered waistbelts and flat straw hats, and by their young men in striped blazers and white flannel trousers. It was a lovely day, if a bit hard on the poor old horse. It was a day of culture, too. At Windermere we were joined by a clergyman wearing an impressive beard and a speckled straw hat, fastened to the lapel of a black alpaca coat by a string hooked to the hatbrim. His bicycle was leaning against a cottage wall. This clearly was his daily chore, and I suppose the people who owned the brake paid him a small fee. He climbed into the driver's seat and addressed us. He told us what we were going to see. The names of Wordsworth, Southey, Coleridge and Ruskin threaded his discourse. Rydal Mount. Dove Cottage. Brantwood. As Windermere lay on our left hand, he took off his speckled hat and recited "When on thy bosom, spacious Windermere," as an example of what we were to expect. Then he said to the driver: "All right, George," got onto his bicycle and pedaled slowly ahead of the brake.

After my sleepless night, I was annoyed with the clergyman. I was annoyed with the holy fervor of his recitations, always performed with hat pressed to the heart and eyes uplifted. I was annoyed with the insufficiency of his information. When he had finished his piece at Brantwood, I asked: "Wasn't Ruskin mad for a good deal of the time he was here, sir?"

He answered concisely: "I have said what I had to say about Ruskin. If it pleased God to afflict one of his prophets, that was between God and Ruskin. It is not a matter for us. Now—to the brake! To the brake! Ready, George!"

"Oh, Chad," May began, and it sounded so much like our clergyman beginning another poem that I burst out laughing.

I said: "Oh, Chad! How chaste the nuptial sheets can be, if you want her but she does not want thee!"

"I don't see anything to laugh about," May said.

"Nor do I."

"Was Mr. Ruskin mad?"

"He was mad himself, and the cause of madness in others. First, he drove his wife so mad because he wouldn't sleep with her that she had the sense to run away and marry a painter well on the make. Then a girl named Rose la Touche drove him mad because she would not sleep with him. One way and another, he spent a very sleepless life."

"You're making it up," May said.

The clergyman shouted. "To the brake, you laggards. We are all aboard but you."

His iron horse seemed to be pawing the ground. One felt it should have a nosebag full of steel filings. He leapt upon its back and drove down the pedals with the air of applying spurs.

It was altogether a rum day. I wanted to see a lot more of the Lakes, but I didn't want to see them in those conditions. At dinner I asked May: "Did you enjoy your day?"

"It was lovely," she said. "I thought the people were all so nice, and the clergyman was a dear old gentleman."

"I enjoyed the horse most," I said. "He had such a frank way now and then of expressing his contempt for all of us."

But it was no good saying things like that to May. She didn't know what I was talking about.

"It would be lovely," I said, "if we could be in the Lakes alone. Just tramping about. Walk when we like. Lie down when we like. No one with us. No one to recite to us. Take a night's lodging here and there, just where we found it." Excited by my own speculation, I said: "We could do it, you know. Buy rucksacks, and take only what we wanted. Send the rest of our things home by train. What about it, May?"

She looked at me aghast. "But you can't spend a *honeymoon* that way! And what about the bill here?"

"I think it's a first-rate way to spend a honeymoon. As for the bill, all they care about is that it should be paid. I can do that, and just have enough left for the other things."

Although it was still broad day, there was light in the golden silk shades on the tables. In this light, the cutlery gleamed and glass twinkled. There were flowers on the tables, too, and the penguin-waiters moved about noiselessly and efficiently. I could see May drinking it all in, weighing it all up. I knew my case was lost, and I said mischievously: "If we couldn't find a cottage, we could sleep in a barn, or even in the heather."

"Chad," May said, "I sometimes think you're stark staring mad. Talk about Ruskin!"

We danced again that night, and on the third night I possessed May. She had gone up before me, undressed and got into bed. When I came in, the room was dark. I switched on the bedside light, undressed and got into bed naked. May was wearing a long nightgown. I said: "Will you take this off, May?" She didn't answer, and she didn't take it off. She put out the light and turned toward me. She left the rest to me. When it was over, she pulled down the nightgown and lay with her back to me. I kissed her ear, and went to sleep.

She said nothing about it in the morning, and neither did I, but months later, when things were strained between us, she said: "I've always done my duty to you as a wife. You can't deny that." And I couldn't. But to poor May it was always a duty, and an unpleasant one at that—certainly nothing to be talked about in the morning.

6

During our second week in Morecambe I wrote:

DEAR MOTHER AND DEAR UNCLE ARTHUR:

I am here on my honeymoon, and I think it will not surprise you to know that my wife is May Ingleby. We were married on Monday of last week and shall be remaining here till next Saturday. May we then come on and spend the last week of my holiday with you?

I stopped there and chewed the end of my pen. How explain the impulse that had made me jib at asking them to a wedding which I felt at the time I was blundering into, and knew already that I should regret? "Explanations—if any!—" I wrote rather cockily, "when we meet. Meantime, all love, in which May joins me."

"My dear boy," Uncle Arthur wrote,

"This is for your eye alone. Your Mother is a little upset. I therefore take up the pen on her behalf. You are, so to speak, her one ewe lamb—though you are no more a ewe than I am—but you see what I mean. I need not expatiate. I leave it to your imagination, which I am sure is able to comprehend the sense of slight that on such an occasion must afflict a maternal heart. For me, inured to the shifts and chicanery of municipal affairs, this small private blow is no great matter, especially as I am sure May will make you an excellent wife. But I grieve on your Mother's behalf and wish you had acted differently. When another person is about to become dominant in his life—that is the moment when an English Gentleman cherishes with special consideration her who will be henceforth, and necessarily, the declining light. No woman takes happily to the role of Declining Light.

But hence, loathed melancholy. You must not think, dear boy, from any of these things that I am unhappily compelled to say, that there is nothing else to be said. There is, above all, this—that we love you and will love May for your sake. It will be a poor lookout if some sort of fatted calf does not meet a sorry end on Saturday night, to which we look forward with lively joy.

By the way, we had heard of the wedding in a letter from Whitworth Rhodes, but did not know where to communicate with you.

As ever, in all love, your

UNCLE ARTHUR

This letter, and especially the last sentence, plunged me into gloom. I damned Rhodes for his officious good will to all around him, and felt, so far as Uncle Arthur was concerned, that I wasn't fit to lick his boots.

May watched me reading the letter, and inevitably asked whom it was from. "Come on now, Chad. There are no secrets between married couples," she said brightly.

"It's from the plumber," I said, "the chap who's fitting the new gas stove."

"How on earth did he know where we are?"

"Oh, plumbers know everything. They're wonderful people."

"Now, Chad. You're holding something from me. There mustn't be any secrets between us."

"May," I said, "you might as well make up your mind from the beginning that I shall please myself whether or not I tell you what's in my private letters."

It was the first time I had spoken to her crossly and firmly.

"Well, that's not my idea of married life," she said, and looked sulky.

"I expect," I said, "that we shall find a number of points about married life on which our ideas differ. You must make the best of that, as I try to."

"I know what you're hinting at. I believe that's all you think about."

I left her sitting at the breakfast table and went out to the small garden in front of the hotel. The sea was in for once—I could never get over my surprise on seeing it at Morecambe—and I sat in a deck chair and watched its glitter and sparkle as a breeze played under the morning sun. It was a lively heartening day, and I felt as miserable as sin. One of the young gentlemen who wore dinner jackets in the evening came up to me and said: "Good morning, Mr. Boothroyd. We're getting up a little party and wondered whether you and Mrs. Boothroyd would care to join us?"

Now the last thing I wanted—the last thing I ever wanted—was a jolly day with strangers; but May came out in time to hear the invitation.

"What sort of party?" she asked.

"We've hired a small sailing boat. There are four of us. We could do with another two. Split the cost."

"Oh, I'd love it," May said. "I've never sailed. Do let's go, Chad."

"I'd make you all miserable," I said. "I'm a bad sailor. I'd be as sick as a dog."

It was a lie. At Pendeverel I had been on the sea in all weathers and had never been sick.

"Oh, it's such a wonderful chance," May said.

"Well, go," I urged her. "My absence needn't prevent you. Can you men handle a boat?"

"That'll be all right, Mr. Boothroyd. A fisherman's taking us. If you can come, Mrs. Boothroyd, tell the waiter to have sandwiches ready for you in half an hour. We shan't be back till teatime."

I walked down to the beach with them: two young men, two young women, and May. What with one thing and another, it was eleven o'clock before they were off. I turned then and went into a tearoom for my morning coffee. I sat in a quiet alcove window, and presently the young professional came in, saw me, and strolled across with a swaying mannequin's walk, and sat down at my table. She gave me a saucy smile. "Hallo, handsome," she said. "How's the honeymoon going? Still a dead loss to me?"

I went home with her, and learned what I had been missing. I was back just in time to have a bath and join May at tea.

My Uncle Arthur so naturally accepted me and May in our status as married people, and so easily conducted himself as though the fashion of our marriage was something only to be expected, that he greatly eased the situation at Smurthwaite. When I thanked him quietly toward the end of our stay, he brushed the thing off with a laugh. "The great Melbourne," he said, "however much he might resist what he didn't like, accepted it when it was there. There are several differences between me and Melbourne, dear boy, but we are alike in seeing the folly of making ourselves miserable about what can't be mended."

He never so much as referred to our wedding, except that on the Saturday evening of our arrival he drank our health at dinner and wished us long life and prosperity.

This casual treatment of the matter was the best possible thing for my mother. Twice now Uncle Arthur had come to her rescue in a distressing moment of her life. Her admiration for him grew, and I am pretty sure that by this time the family affection that had always been between them had deepened to a loving companionship. In most things she accepted his opinion as wisdom, and that was fortunate for me. She left me in no doubt that I had hurt her, but she was never the one to nurse a grievance, and she treated May as a daughter. Altogether, I am sure May left Smurthwaite at the end of the week with a good deal of regret that her time of rather special coddling and consideration was over, and that now she would have to face life as best she could with a husband whose tastes seemed to her more than a little reprehensible.

But there it was. Off we went, taking with us a handsome set of fish knives and forks that were Uncle Arthur's present, and on a breathlessly hot Saturday evening we arrived at the small house in Didsbury, with such glamour as the honeymoon had furnished at last behind us.

8

May was a good housekeeper. "I like things nice," she was forever saying. She was very good at making an apple pie, and when she had put her portion onto her plate I would say: "Give me the dish. I'll finish it up."

But she wouldn't. "It's not nice to eat out of the dish," she would say. "What does it matter? We're on our own."

"You should have as good manners when you're eating with me as if the Lord Mayor were here."

"Manners my foot. Think of the washing up you save."

"That's my affair. You never help with it."

"Why should I? I've got my own work to do."

"Eat your food, Chad, and don't bicker. It's not nice."

When the winter came, May rarely accompanied me to theater or music hall as she had been used to do. "I think my place is in the house," she objected when I urged her. "You like the place kept nice." I got sick to death of the word.

Our country walks ended, too; and I suppose that was my fault. We had walked a good deal after coming back from the honeymoon, and May was happy enough on the flat unadventurous roads of Cheshire. But one day I took her into Derbyshire and we climbed up onto the moors. The autumn had come. The bracken was rusting and the heather was in its purple glory. The sun was at its height when we sat down to eat our sandwiches miles from the possibility of intrusion from any direction. When we had eaten I pulled her toward me, and she had no doubt of my intention. She sprang to her feet. I sat up and looked at her. Often enough I had seen her pained, or resentful, or even sadly acquiescent. But now I saw her blazing with anger. "Oh," she cried, "how could you? *In the open air!*"

"Why, May, what's wrong with the open air? We are alone except for the skylarks."

She seemed really beside herself. "Oh, you want to be filthy everywhere."

The word was a smack in the face. Intentionally or not, she had said all that she felt and thought about what was to me the essence of a stable marriage.

She began with trembling fingers to put our things back into the knapsack. "My mother warned me what men were," she said.

I don't know whether any other man would have succeeded with May where I failed, but from then on I had a profound sense of insufficiency, as deep a humiliation as if I had been pronounced a eunuch. More and more, as the winter wore on, I tended, when I had any time at home, to shut myself up in the attic study, making the excuse of "work to do." But I did little enough—little enough writing anyway. For the most part I read and savored my privacy. May didn't seem in the least to mind this. Indeed, she seemed much happier now that I had given up being filthy, and she went blithely about the job of keeping everything nice. I don't think she had the faintest idea what she had done to me. She would have been shocked if I had suggested— as I never did—that she was not an admirable wife.

How this was all to end I had no idea. It had its absurd side. On

May's birthday I bought her a small present and handed it to her at the breakfast table. She was delighted with it, and came round the table and kissed me. "You really are a darling, Chad, the way you think of me. In the last couple of months you've become a better and better husband all the time."

From May's point of view, I'm sure I had.

But there were occasional rougher passages. One day in the winter the chief marked me in the diary for a job that would mean taking a railway journey and staying out of town for the night. I had to dash home, both to pick up my night kit and to let May know that I should not return till morning. The railway timetable showed me that I could just get to Didsbury and be back at Victoria Station in time for my train if I lost no time. Fearing that May might have nothing in the house for a quick scratch meal, I bought a plaice at our Didsbury fishmonger's and hurried home with it. I explained the urgency to May, ran upstairs and packed my things, and came down to find her frying the plaice in the kitchen.

"Lay the table, Chad," she said. "It'll save time."

I threw a small cloth over a corner of the kitchen table and opened the cutlery drawer. "I'll eat here," I said. "You can bring it straight from the pan to the table."

But May wouldn't have it. "No, Chad. I will not serve meals in the kitchen. It's not nice."

I swore, and carried the cutlery through to the dining room, and presently May came in with the fish on a plate.

"There," she said, putting it before me; and then: "Oh dear, Chad. Look what you've done. That's not a fish knife and fork."

"I don't care what it is. It'll cut fish. Let me get on."

But I couldn't get on, for she had snatched the knife and fork and hurried away. "Where did we put the case that Uncle Arthur gave us?" she called.

"Oh, May. Come along. I'm in a hurry. What the devil does it matter if I eat the damned fish with a buttonhook or knitting needles?" I looked at my watch. Time was running out.

Unfortunately, May returned empty-handed to the door to argue the point. "Now that's the sort of thing you must get out of, Chad. Fish means fish knives."

I knew that there was greaseproof paper in the sideboard drawer. I took out a few sheets, slabbed the plaice onto them and put the parcel on top of my pajamas. "Damn the fish knives," I said, running toward the front door. "I'll eat this somehow in the train."

May had the last, illogical word. "A nice way to treat your Uncle Arthur, I must say."

I recognized, with a sense of guilt, that occasions like this, when I was out of town for a night, or a few nights, or a week, brought a feeling of freedom, almost of happiness. What was worse, when I was back in town there was no eagerness to do what, if I had thought of marriage a few years ago, I should have imagined myself doing: that is to say, flying gladly to my nest as soon as duty released me.

I came back to Manchester in this way on a day in June that was the first anniversary of my marriage. I had been away for four or five days and I was in the town by teatime. There was nothing more for me to do that day. Here, if ever there was to be one, was the occasion when I should have rushed to Didsbury, embraced my wife, and proposed a celebration. But I felt, more acutely than I had ever felt before, a reluctance to go home at all. I went out with a couple of my colleagues and had tea, and then lingered, playing dominoes. A session for a drink or two was customary among the men who were at liberty, and I joined this at the Thatched House at six o'clock. I stayed longer than usual, and the thought of jolting out to Didsbury on an electric tram was repulsive. I decided to walk home. It was about five miles, not pleasant miles either. However, I had covered the more revolting part of the journey, and was on the stretch between the Infirmary on the one side of the road and Platt Fields on the other. I was not feeling any happier now, for the sight of the Infirmary filled my mind with thoughts of the night when all my troubles—as I now frankly called them—began: the night when I watched May's mother being bundled into the ambulance to be borne hither.

And then, on the other side of the street, I saw a young man walking, going in the same direction as myself, and I stopped dead, with a catch of the breath. He was tall and thin and bareheaded, wearing a tweed jacket and flannel trousers, and though I could not see his face I was certain that it was Billy Pascoe. I crossed the road, quickened my step, and overtook him. "Billy!" I said.

He turned. It *was* Billy. I had not seen him since his wedding at Pendeverel. That was not so long ago, but even in this short time there was a great change in him. He looked enormously more mature. It was one of my sorrows that I had no sense of maturity. Any middle-aged person made me feel distressingly young, and with a famous person, even one moderately distinguished, I was shy and tongue-tied. I can tell you all I felt about Billy in that moment by saying that he brought this feeling of inadequacy sharply upon me. His look had authority.

I can't say that he helped me. I don't think he meant to be aloof, but the point—which I can recognize now—simply was that we were creatures of entirely different tastes and habits, and that he, in his line, had already reached some distinction, while my own mind was still chaotic and hadn't begun to settle down to the exercise of its powers. Moreover, a year of marriage had shockingly undermined my self-esteem.

Billy held out his hand. "How are you, Boothroyd? I'm told you're still on the *Guardian.*"

We began to walk on toward Platt Fields. I noted that he was aware I was in the town and had made no effort to dig me out.

"Yes," I said. "What are *you* doing in Manchester?"

"Working with Rutherford at the University."

I had been in Manchester now long enough to know that Ernest Rutherford's name was among the foremost in physics.

"How long have you been here?"

"About a fortnight."

"You might have let me know."

"My dear Boothroyd—I'm up to the eyes."

"Will you be staying long?"

"Can't say exactly. They want me back in Cambridge. But I'm doing a paper for the British Association, and I wanted to check up a few things with Rutherford."

"I see."

My God! I thought. This is being a wonderful conversation with old Billy Pascoe.

We had reached the gates into Platt Fields. The sun was setting and a thin mist was rising over that grassy arena. Even the trees were beginning to look a bit insubstantial. Billy stopped at the gate and held out his hand. "Well," he said, "I'm going in here. I find it a good place. Come here most evenings. Featureless. No distractions."

I took his hand. "Is Rose with you?" I asked.

There was the slightest hesitation before he said: "No. Au revoir," and his lanky form paced away slowly into the mist.

I wandered on, feeling abominably depressed, till I came to the branching of the road at Withington. One branch takes the way to Cheadle and the South, and that is the one I followed, for I knew that a hundred yards or so along that road there was a cozy red-curtained pub.

I stayed in it for an hour. When at last I reached home, May heard my key in the lock and came to the door. She gave me one glance and said: "You've been drinking."

"I have, May. I have indeed."

She closed the door and faced me in the little passage. "Dr. Rhodes warned me about that," she said.

It was the last straw. "Your mother warned you about me," I said. "Rhodes warned you about me. You were lucky, weren't you? Why didn't someone warn me about you?"

"Oh, what a thing to say!" she flared. "And tonight of all nights! When I've cooked a special dinner and got everything nice for you!"

"Whatever sort of thing it is to say, consider it said. Good night. I'm going up to put the sword in the bed."

I suppose after that it would have had to end anyway. Two months later war was declared, and that gave me a way out.

CHAPTER TEN

I

IT IS difficult in these days to recapture what we felt then. It would be too much to say, even now, that war is within our daily expectation, but at least it is within our daily reckoning of what may come. Then, for most of us—and I was as thoughtless as the rest—it was unthinkable. We had been so lulled with the dream of progress, the good animal man walking, slowly maybe but certainly, toward the New Jerusalem come down from heaven, that right up to the brink of the chasm we went on with no real belief in our hearts that the gathering clouds would break. I remember how imperturbably we arranged our holiday dates in the office, and how no one saw much reason for abandoning or even postponing assemblies that had been decided upon.

There was, for example, a Liberal summer school at Oxford in the last week of July. The paper sent me to deal with this, and I was glad to go not only because an escape back to Oxford would be joyful in the circumstances of my life at that moment, but also because Gregory Appleby would be there. With a fine broad-mindedness the Liberals had asked Greg to give them the Labour view of their long achievement in office.

I was in Oxford for a week. That was an incredible summer. My memory is of a succession of peerless days, of much time spent on the river, some of it with Greg and Phoebe, and of a garden party on the Worcester lawns when, if there was any whisper of death in the air, it was drowned by the whisper of silks and the tinkle of teacups. It was at this party that I saw Eustace and Rose Garland, and the first thing I noticed about Rose was that she had the lit-up look that had frightened me on the night of the Commemoration Ball.

It was a charmingly civilized setting in which to receive a stab to the heart. Greg and Phoebe were somewhere about, but I had got separated from them, and I was sitting at a small table with a girl in a cloud of smoke-gray chiffon who was eating strawberries and cream, to make up, she said, for starvation in jail. I gathered that jail was accustomed to her, for she had a habit of knocking off policemen's helmets and breaking windows and setting fire to letters in pillar boxes. This was her contribution to bringing justice into the world through the medium of votes for women. "I tried hunger-striking last time," she said with a honeyed laugh, "but it didn't last long. I'm so greedy." She detained more strawberries and cream from a passing tray; and, meanwhile, a madrigal society was regaling us with airs of Byrd and those chaps.

And then Eustace and Rose passed by, near enough almost to brush my knees. But neither of them saw me. Eustace had the grave collected look I knew well, as though he were seeing nothing that we clods bothered with; and Rose, hanging on his arm—almost literally hanging, I saw with anguish, so that her blue-shod feet seemed only to brush the grass—had the air of dreaming awake. I remembered what she had said to me on a night in London: that if she should ever marry and then meet Eustace again, she would not answer for the consequences.

I couldn't sit there, merely looking dazed as a poleaxed steer. I turned to the girl and said: "That was Eustace Hawke." There was no need then to explain who Eustace Hawke was.

"Oh, I *am* glad to have seen him! I say all his poems to myself over and over again when I'm in jail. It's a wonderful help. Because really, you know, say what you will, being in jail isn't great fun. I wish I knew him—really knew him. But look at that girl! How can anyone compete with that? I suppose poets are lucky. They get the pick of the bunch."

It seemed rather a generalization to me, from what I had read about poets, but I let it go; and presently Greg strolled up and hailed my companion. "Hello, Daphne. Out of jug for the moment?"

"For the moment is the word," she said. "I must get back to town at once. I'm due to break Selfridge's window at eight-forty-five. See you when I'm out again. Au revoir." She blew away like a cloud.

Greg sat down. "What's wrong with you, Pie-frill?" he asked. "You look a bit disarranged. Has Daphne been boring you?"

"No."

"She's one of my girls at the School of Economics, in the odd moments when the Home Secretary can spare her. Ah, well. Those girls will have something else to think about soon. What are *you* going to do about it?"

"About what?"

"This war."

"What war?"

"Now, Chad, don't talk bloody nonsense. I shall join the West Yorks."

Phoebe was in time to hear the last words. She sat down between us. "If war comes," she said, "you must do what you think right. In the meantime, to please me, shut up about it."

I could see that she was deeply distressed. I could see that she *knew*. And in that instant I knew, too. The wool seemed to go suddenly off my eyes, and the thought rushed through my mind that by joining the army I would be quit of May. I didn't say to myself that a long absence might bring healing between me and May. I didn't want that now. I wanted to be done with it.

The grave thought of war, the glimpse of Rose and Eustace together, and this sudden insight into a dark ungenerous region of my own heart, combined to make the moment unbearable. The madrigal society had packed up. Some strings were giving us Handel's Water Music. The swishing dresses, the music, the happy voices—hiding who knew what dark foreboding?—got under my skin, and I said: "Let's get out of it. Let's have a quiet hour together on the river."

I didn't say it, but I thought they might read in my words: "It may be the last—at any rate for a long time."

We didn't bother to go back to dinner, but stayed on the river as long as light lasted. All three of us, I think, had hearts full of sad comparison. Here, where we had been gay and careless, we heard the forewhisper of age and care. The fading of the light, the lengthening of the shadows, that had been all beauty, were now all solemnity. I was poling the punt, not speaking, content to hear again, and in heightened significance, the drip from the pole, the slur of the bows through the water. Greg and Phoebe were sitting side by side, holding hands.

When the moon came up, we tied the punt to a tree root in the river bank. "I don't think I told you," I said, "that I met Billy Pascoe in Manchester a few weeks ago."

"No," said Greg, "you didn't. You don't tell us much. How is May getting along? How is life in our little Didsbury house?"

He now had his arm round Phoebe's shoulder. You could feel the sanity of their understanding like something palpable about them. I thought how small the chance seemed of anything happening in this world so satisfying as their love was to even the most unimaginative observer. Rose, Billy, Eustace, May, Chad: all at sea. I loved these two the more for showing that married love was not an illusion.

I said: "You don't know how lucky you are, Greg."

I can't say whether he realized all that was in that remark, but Phoebe saw it at once, so percipient beneath the open candor of her appearance. She said: "You change places with Chad, Greg," and when I was sitting at her side she put her arm round me with an almost maternal gesture. "Oh dear, Chad," she said, "it's a great mistake to marry just for the sake of marrying. Especially for you. Why," she said, softening the remark with a laugh, "if you married someone as beautiful as Helen and passionate as Cleopatra, you'd still be dreaming of Rose Garland."

"I suppose you're right," I said. "I suppose that's the whole trouble."

"How bad is the trouble?"

"Beyond repair," I said. "It's all over."

No one said anything for a time, and then I said: "When I met Billy in Manchester, Rose was not with him."

"No," Phoebe said, "Rose was not with him. I'm afraid that's all over, too."

Between them, they told me about it.

2

When Eustace had finished writing, in the house in Didsbury, the poems that had now made him so famous, he became restless. He no longer wanted to push the young Penelope about in her pram or to muse in the Marie Louise Gardens. There is—or was—a train that leaves Didsbury at about nine in the morning and lands you in the heart of the Peak district soon after ten. Eustace with a few sandwiches stuffed into one pocket and tobacco in the other—he was the only man I ever knew who kept tobacco loose in his pocket—often caught this train, got out at Millers Dale, and wandered all day through the dales and over the moors that must have reminded him of his boyhood in Wharfedale. He became lean and fit. Sometimes he would not return for a few days, "and of course," Phoebe said, "it was only a question of when he would decide not to return at all."

One day, when Greg was at work in his study, and Penelope had been put to bed, and Eustace was sitting by the fire with Phoebe, he asked: "What became of Rose?"

"I was frightened to death," Phoebe said to me, "that this would come. He hadn't mentioned Rose all the time he was with us. But no man could forget Rose."

She told him that Rose was married to Billy Pascoe.

"I think I have a right to see our child," he said. "Was it a boy?"

"No. It was a girl. They call her Henrietta."

"Could you give me Rose's address?"

Phoebe could have said: "I don't know it. We've lost touch with them." She could have lied in all sorts of ways; but, even had Phoebe been a liar, she would never have lied to Eustace. She said: "I could. But I don't intend to."

"Well," Eustace said reasonably. "I suppose I could find it for myself if I tried."

"If you must, you must. But don't expect any help from me. When you took her away from Oxford I did nothing to prevent you, though I could see what was going to happen. You can say if you like that I was so acquiescent as to be an accomplice. But this is another matter."

"Why?"

"Because you abandoned her, and for two pins you'd abandon her again."

Eustace smoked in silence for a time; then he said: "You seem to harbor hard thoughts about me."

"I am the last woman in the world," Phoebe protested, "to harbor hard thoughts about anybody, if by that you mean letting them fester without speaking them. I've always accepted you as you are, and all the time you've been with us here you've known what love is."

"Yes," he said simply. "That is true."

"You must do as you please. You've always done as you pleased. But this time I can't be an accomplice."

"Do you believe in marriage?"

"I'm not talking about marriage. I'm talking about faithfulness. You had her, and you abandoned her. If you hadn't done that, I wouldn't have cared whether you'd married her or not. Though, come to that, I would have preferred it if you had. For yes. I do believe in marriage. All that *Ann Veronica* stuff is childish."

Eustace got up from his chair, crossed over to her, and kissed her. "Thank you," he said. "I wouldn't want you any different."

Phoebe confessed that by this time her eyes were wet, though the hard tears wouldn't fall. "I *would* want *you* different, Eustace," she said. "I would want you faithful. But I shall not try to impose my wants on you or anyone else. There's work enough trying to let a bit of light into one's own basement."

Eustace said no more. He went out and wandered in the suburb till bedtime.

He went up to London to see his book through the press and he didn't return. When the book was a success, he was a gift to the interviewers and photographers. He was at the peak of his remarkable beauty—a word I hesitate to use about a man, though, in fact, more men are beautiful than women, especially in these days of painted blocks. Now, indeed, one might aptly say, as Uncle Arthur had said long ago, that Eustace would grace an Athenian thoroughfare. I remember that one day, when I was idly turning over the pages of the *Tatler* in a Manchester teashop, I came upon a full-page picture of him, with the most quoted of his sonnets printed beneath it, and I was moved almost to forgiveness of all that he had done.

Five weeks passed between the shooting of the heir to the Austrian throne and England's declaration of war. They were five weeks, as I have said, in which the truth would not inescapably present itself to minds unwilling to receive it, but the tension was there, growing and menacing, and it was especially in those five weeks that Eustace's poems, with their love of England, their praise of English things, became almost the voice of English hearts. You saw them wherever you went: in the bookshops, in the hands of people, quoted in the newspapers. It would have been surprising indeed if, then, Rose had not become aware of Eustace. Whether because of what Phoebe had said, who knows? But he made no move toward her. It was she who wrote to him, saying she had read the poems and thanking him for them.

He wrote to say that if she were in town at any time he would like to give her lunch or dinner; or, if she would prefer it, he would come to Cambridge.

She came to London, bringing Henrietta with her. The child was within a few weeks of being five years old. "She's with us at Hampstead now," Phoebe said.

"Oh, no! They can't have done that!"

"There's no can't about it where those two are concerned. And, after all, I am the child's aunt. She's a lovely little thing."

"But surely they hadn't the nerve to come to you and say, 'Look, we're going off together. Take care of this child.' "

But that, more or less, is just what they had done. Their meeting was as swiftly fatal as I should have expected it to be. It took them no time at all to decide that Rose would not go back to Cambridge.

"When you met Billy in Manchester," Greg said, "this hadn't happened. But I suppose he had realized by then that it was the sort of thing that might happen. Phoebe and I went down to Cambridge once or twice to stay with them, and I didn't feel that it was a very happy setup."

"The first thing in Rose's life," Phoebe said, "will always be a man, not a man's work. If the work robs her of the man—well, so much the worse for the man. Billy Pascoe doesn't even talk to her about his work. He didn't talk to us about it. Not that I would have understood a thing, even if he had done so. He didn't talk about anything. And I hated the feeling that my host's head was full of such great matter that I wasn't there at all."

I began to see it. I knew Rose well enough for that, and Eustace, too.

"Why on earth did she marry him?" I asked, even while thinking that I was a good one to be asking that. Poor me! Poor May!

"If we knew a bit more about Miss Orlop we might have an answer to that question," Greg said.

"What does Miss Orlop think about it all?"

Phoebe said: "I know no more than Rose told me—or hinted. I should think there was a dreadful scene. Rose went along with Henrietta, and I gather they were almost hustled out onto the pavement. It was the first time Rose had quarreled with her mother."

"You've got to admit," Greg said, philosophically puffing smoke into the moonlight, "that the old girl had plenty to annoy her. She put up with Rose's running away in the first place. She took her back, and Henrietta too, without blowing up. Then you've got to understand what she feels about Billy. Rose has talked to me from time to time about things her mother has told her. She seems to have loathed her father. She came to loathe her husband, and her brother was more or less an amiable nonentity, like the run of dead-end squires. Our sex was not very shining in eyes, Chad. She never had a son, but there was Billy Pascoe, ready to be worked on, so that she might show what *she* could do when it came to making a man. And, damn it all, he's something to be proud of in his way. It's not your way, and it's not mine, and from the little I know about it I can guess it's a way full of mystery with perhaps a glimpse or two of fear. I don't say that Billy's not going to miss Rose. Any man in his senses would, even if he'd never used more than a tenth of what's in her. And he'll feel deeply hurt and humiliated. But he'll get over it, because he's dedicated as I'm not and you're not. But perhaps Eustace is, in his fashion. And now you can change places, Chad. My wife has been cuddling you long enough."

I took up the pole, and we began to move back toward Oxford.

"What are they doing in Oxford?" I asked.

Greg explained. "That was just a fluke. Eustace had a long-standing engagement to give a reading from his poems. That's what brought him, and I suppose someone asked him along to the party. They'll be on the wing by morning, believe you me. And now, shut up. We've all talked too much, and I want to hear Phoebe's heart beating."

He lay down with his head on her breast. She pulled a rug over him and rumpled his hair. I smelled the river, and listened to its small night sounds, and felt desolate.

3

In this crisis your Country calls on all her young unmarried men to rally round the Flag and enlist in the ranks of her Army.

If you are unmarried and between 18 and 30 years old, will you answer your Country's Call and go to the nearest Recruiter?

I returned thoughtfully to the small house in Didsbury. "May, I've joined the army."

"Why, Chad, whatever for? We've only just got married."

May's resilience was extraordinary. About two months had passed since the night when I met Billy Pascoe and loitered too long in the pub and came home to say offensive things. She had not mentioned those things the next day, nor on any day thereafter. To her, our marriage still existed, seeing that I continued to use the house as a base from which I set out in the morning and to which I returned at night. She went placidly on with her job of keeping the base nice.

I sat down at the table and May brought our evening meal in from the kitchen. "You'd never guess what I've been up to today," she said.

"Something unbelievably dashing, I've no doubt."

"I've been to the sale in that big house near the Wesleyan chapel where the old man died. And I bought those two vases—there, on the mantelpiece. I don't think you even noticed them."

They were tall red glass affairs, with dingle-dangle lusters.

"They were very cheap. D'you think they look nice?"

"Very nice, May. But I shall not long be here to enjoy their beauty. I've joined the army."

"Oh, well," she said, "joining is one thing. Being called up is another. Especially as we're married. Married men will come last. And everybody says the war will be over by Christmas."

"I think," I said relentlessly, "that, when I am gone, you had better give notice to our landlord and find a room somewhere, as you had before we married. I've no doubt you'll get a job as easy as winking. There's bound to be an increasing demand for women's work as the men go. You could sell the furniture, except my writing things. I'll put those in store."

"Well—that's a fine way to talk. Look at those vases. D'you think I'm likely to sell them as soon as I've bought them? They were an absolute bargain."

I gave it up. "I'm going for a stroll," I said.

I strolled first to the end of the street, where there was a builder's yard. I knew the builder: he had done a bit of work for me in the house: and I arranged with him to collect my writing table and chair in the morning and store them in his loft. He said he would box my books, too, and look after them as well. There was nothing else I wanted to keep except the picture of Rose. I had decided to pack this up in the morning and leave it at the bank where I had what the humorous manager had once called a lively little account. It bobbed about, between five pounds to the good and five in the red.

When I left the builder I walked to the Mersey fields and wandered there for an hour, feeling a relief that amounted almost to exhilaration.

I had shed the few shackles that bound me, and now I had nothing to do but await orders and obey them. I drank a pint of beer at the Cock and went home in high spirits. "You seem to have pulled yourself together," May said. "I do hope we shan't hear any more of your nonsense."

4

So many novels and plays—including my own—and histories and memoirs have been written about the First World War that I shall not add to them in this autobiographical work. I shall write only of those moments of the war that touched my relations with the people you have met thus far. It was not till November that I was ordered to go to London and report at a depot. I had been worried about May because, little as I wanted ever to see her again, I did want to know that she wouldn't starve, and she had for a month obstinately refused to accept that she would soon have to rely on her own exertions, with the small help of a separation allowance. However, the facts gradually entered her mind, and when I got home from the office one night, after a day spent in gathering news about the doings in recruiting offices, she told me that she had been to see Whitworth Rhodes and his Nan.

"What have they warned you about this time?" I asked.

They had, I was glad to hear, advised her to seek a job without delay, and Rhodes had then and there rung up the fabulous Miss Mytholmroyd at Sir Charles McCumber's office and found that already men were leaving and that there was room for May. Rhodes had also backed my advice that the house should be given up and that May should find a room to live in. As was to be expected, indeed, he said he would find one for her. May began to work at once. She left our little house at eight o'clock, which was long before I did; and when I watched her go one morning, rather importantly hugging a dispatch case containing I don't know what, I had no idea that I should never see her again. The postman came with a few letters as I stood there at the door, and one of them instructed me to report to London at an early hour of the next morning.

I could have waited for her to return that evening and then taken the night train; and I certainly should have gone to the office, and told my chief what had happened, and said good-by to one or two people. But I was suddenly resolved to cut instantly all ties with Manchester: with May, whom I now felt no more for or against than if I had never met her; with the office in which I had failed to make any sort of impression. So I scribbled a note, and left it for May, and I wrote a letter and posted it to the chief. Then I threw my things into a bag and ran to the

Didsbury station where the London train stopped at about nine o'clock. I was in London by lunchtime.

I did not write to May throughout the war. Even to me, this seems callous; but I was terrified lest any smallest approach should lead on to something else, as it had done before our marriage. Despite all, she was capable, I felt sure, of letting bygones be bygones, as she would have said, and welcoming me back with a warm smile and a cold bed. None of my wartime leaves took me to Manchester. I spent some in Paris, some in London, some in Smurthwaite. When May divorced me after the war, it was on the ground of desertion. I do not know what became of her.

5

On that day of my arrival in London, I went out after lunch to Greg's house at Hampstead. Greg was at the School of Economics, Phoebe had just tucked Penelope up for her afternoon sleep, and she suggested that we should take a walk on the heath. There was a girl living in, so Penelope would be all right. "And it's a long time since we had a heart-to-heart, Chad. There always seems to be someone else about. Of course, you'll stay here tonight?"

I had brought my few things with me, and said I would be glad to do so. "How I thank God for this heath," Phoebe said when we were on it. "With a great deal of imagination, I can feel I'm in the country. I loathed Manchester. Didn't you?"

"Yes. I loved the office, though I failed to shine there, and I liked most of the men I worked with. But anyone who wants Manchester can have it, for me."

"I was happy enough," Phoebe assured me. "I could be happy enough in hell with Greg."

"The mind is its own place," I quoted sententiously.

"Not altogether, Chad. Not for me, anyway. I need another mind and another heart alongside my own."

"Well, you've got it."

"For how long, I wonder?"

There was no sob in her voice, no catch in her breath, but I knew Phoebe well enough to sense her deep distress and anxiety. It was not a day to cheer us up. The cobwebs on the hawthorns were gray with last night's dew that there had been no sunshine to absorb. The clouds were low and sag-bellied, and mists filled the hollows and hung in dirty unwavering chiffons over the ponds. The bright-eyed squirrels with cold paws were our most cheerful companions.

"I don't see why Greg should go," I said. "A married man with a child and an important job."

"He'll go because he wants to," Phoebe assured me, and I knew there was nothing more to be said about that.

She asked me: "How is May taking your departure?"

"She's got a job now. She won't get back till about six o'clock tonight, and she won't know about my departure till then." I told her what I had done.

"I'm sorry you did it that way, Chad. Were things really so terribly bad?"

Phoebe was not squeamish. I told her exactly what was the root of the trouble between me and May. "And even if she'd been normal about that, I don't think it could have lasted after the glamour had worn thin."

"The poor creature."

"My dear Phoebe, you can't conceive the impossibility of making her understand that life was a farce for both of us. Trying to enlighten her was like boring into a fog of cotton wool. We had been through a ceremony, we were living together, we ate together and even slept together, one on each side of the bed, and so we were a respectably married pair. She couldn't understand why I wasn't as happy as a lark. Well, there it is, and May isn't the only one to blame. I think she's to be pitied, for having the mother she did and the husband she did. Let's go in here and drink some tea. Will Penelope be all right?"

"Oh, yes. Our girl Alice is splendid with her."

It was a comfortable little teashop with a fire burning and no one in it but ourselves. We ordered tea and muffins, and when we had eaten I picked up a copy of the *Times* that was lying there. Set within a panel was a new sonnet by Eustace Hawke, with a line underneath saying that Eustace Hawke had joined the Artists Rifles.

I looked at Eustace Hawke's sister, wondering whether to show her this. She's got enough on her plate as it is, I thought. But there was no point in holding it back: it had to come: I passed the paper without a word across the table. She read it, and pulled on her long fur gloves, and said: "We'd better be getting back, Chad."

Not till we were halfway home did she make any comment. Then she said: "Poor Rose! What on earth will she do now?"

"Somehow," I said, "I can't imagine Eustace as a soldier."

"Can't you, Chad? I'm afraid I can. He wouldn't have joined the army unless all his emotions had been engaged. Now that he's in it, he'll be more bloody than you can imagine."

I was to see once again the Eustace I had known: the greyhound who had coursed over the Yorkshire fells, the beauty who would have graced an Athenian thoroughfare, and now with the added panache of fame.

263

Greg insisted that night on taking me and Phoebe to dinner in town. He wore a mask of high spirits, but I sensed beneath it the feeling: "Let's have this good night while we can. Who knows when we shall meet again?—if we shall meet again?"

We went to the Café Royal, and it was still early enough in the war for us to eat and drink magnificently, and magnificently Greg and I did both, though Phoebe was more restrained. We sat upstairs, looking down on to the floor where uniforms were plentiful at the tables. We toasted everybody we knew with a hail-and-farewell recklessness. We toasted Mr. Ashmole, who had been dead these three years and more. We toasted Sir Titus Newte and Uncle Arthur, and innumerable men we had known at Oxford. We even, in our mounting warmth, toasted "Poor old Billy, and to hell with his atoms," and at that moment Phoebe said quietly: "You can toast Billy's wife if you like. There she is."

I was getting a bit over the edge, but the words sobered me, and I looked down and saw Rose and Eustace following a waiter who was taking them to their table. She was in the crimson silk in which I liked her best, and Eustace was wearing full-fig evening clothes. They looked magnificent. The light was on in Rose's face, and Eustace—well, I could weep now to think how Eustace looked then. People were aware of them. That much-photographed face could not escape attention. We all three stared as if at something that did not belong to our own world. They did not look up; they did not see us. For myself I felt a wish to steal out as though I were overlooking something not intended for my eyes. We stayed long enough to see this: a flapper, dining with a young lieutenant near them, got up and went hesitantly to their table, and spoke to Eustace. He turned to Rose, as if asking her consent to something, and she nodded. Then he took the white carnation from his buttonhole and handed it to the girl. Perhaps some sixty-year-old dear even now occasionally looks at the carnation pressed between the pages of *English Grass,* and remembers that moment as clearly as I remember Greg dashing the dregs of the burgundy into our glasses and saying: "To Rose and Eustace. God bless 'em."

I said: "To Rose and Eustace. God bless 'em." And I think I meant it.

Phoebe said. "To Rose and Eustace. God help them."

6

We formed fours on the Horse Guards Parade the next morning: lounge suits, severe morning dress, blazers, tweeds and flannel bags, caps, bowlers, felt hats, straw hats: and with a band at our head we marched. We marched along Whitehall and the Strand and Farringdon

Street and then switched into Holborn, following the old route of felons from Newgate to Tyburn Tree. The sun came out, and Tyburn Tree didn't look so bad, transformed as it was into the Marble Arch. On we went down the Bayswater Road, and where we went after that I don't remember, for on the Bayswater Road was Miss Orlop's house, and I looked up to the first floor window and saw her standing there. Rose was standing at her side, and between them was a child, whom I took to be Henrietta.

After the march we were dismissed and told to report again the next morning. I rang up Miss Orlop and asked if it would be convenient for me to call upon her. She said she would have loved to ask me to lunch, but she had to go out. "However," she said, "why not come all the same? Rose is here. Perhaps she'd like to see you. And try to stay till I get back."

And so Rose and I took lunch together. This was not the Rose I had seen last night, open to rapture. She was closed and restrained and greeted me almost sadly. "Well, Chad, what years it seems since we've seen one another."

"Oh, no. I saw you at a garden party in Oxford a few months ago. And I saw you at the Café Royal last night."

"Last night," she said, as though that was years ago.

Presently she said: "So you know about Eustace and me."

"I seem always to have known about Eustace and you. I suppose I always shall."

"Well, he's gone now. That was our last splash."

"He'll be back," I said, with what heartiness I could muster. "We'll all begin to splash again when this lot's over. Phoebe and Greg were with me last night. We drank your health, and Eustace's."

"Thank you. Why didn't you come and speak to us?"

"You didn't look as though you wanted any other company."

"You're quite right. We didn't."

We had been sitting at the window where I had seen her standing during our march. Now we went in to lunch.

"Where has Eustace been pushed off to?"

"Oh, what does it matter, so long as he's not with me?"

I thought it was time to try and switch her mind from Eustace, so I said: "This is the second time I've seen you today, you know. You and Miss Orlop watched us marching past this morning."

Instantly she was all concern and contrition. "Oh, Chad! So you're in it, too! How horribly being in love sinks us to self-centered brutes! I think and act as though there were no one in the world but me and Eustace. Now tell me, my dear. Tell me all your news."

I told her all my news, including the news of May. "I feel," she said, "like those rich people who develop a sudden conscience about the poor.

They're prepared to give them the last pang of sympathy, but not a penny out of the pocket. That's how selfish loving Eustace has made me. I wouldn't part with a moment of what we've known together to mitigate all the sorrows of the world."

She was back to Eustace again: she would always be back to Eustace, I felt; and I said: "Some of the sorrows of the world are going to fall on Phoebe, too. Greg's enlisted, and is only waiting for his marching orders."

She said: "Poor Phoebe! She was so kind to Henrietta," and she told me, what I already knew, of how she had quarreled with her mother and taken the child to Greg's house. She gave a little laugh at the recollection. "I had to do something. Eustace was no help. I think he'd have been ready to throw her over an orphanage wall. Oh, I suppose he loves her, but her presence bores him. Can you understand that?"

I thought I could, and said so.

"And no sooner were Eustace and I out of the way than mother brought Henrietta back here. In the long run, mother can't get along without me. We're reconciled now. She was even reconciled to Eustace once he'd joined the army. She had him here to dinner." Rose jabbed viciously at a roll on her plate with her fork. "You see," she said, looking me straight in the eye, "she thinks there's a chance now of all the mischief ending by his being killed." Her voice rose sharply.

I was staggered into a moment's silence. Then I said: "Oh, Rose—! No!"

She began to cry, and she went on crying. I had never before seen Rose all to pieces. I went round the table and put an arm about her shoulder, but she shrugged me off. "Oh, don't touch me, don't touch me," she said. "I am contemptible. You should thank God you've never been in love. It's terrible, terrible, all mixed up with hate and malice." She was dabbing almost frenziedly at her face with a handkerchief.

"But I have been in love, Rose. I have been, and I am."

"Oh, don't. I know what you're going to say. Don't say it. Forgive me, please, and go now. Will you, Chad? Will you please go?"

I hated to leave her like that, trembling and distraught. But there was nothing I could do, and so I went.

.

7

Billy Pascoe did not join the army. That was the first war in which scientists, working at home, made their contribution. What Billy's contribution was I don't know, but when the war was over he became Sir William Pascoe, and I must assume, therefore, that it was something considerable.

Greg and I, till the war ended, sat eyes on one another only once after those few days I spent with him and Phoebe at Hampstead. We were both lucky, as things went in those days. He became a lieutenant colonel, D.S.O., M.C., and lost a finger of his left hand at Arras in 1917. I became a captain, a thing it was difficult to avoid doing as young officers were mown down in swathes on the Somme and in Flanders. It was in Flanders that I myself, leading a file along a moonlit road, felt suddenly as though one of the dead and decomposing mules lying thereabouts reared up and slammed me in the side. I remember saying: "Hey! What the hell!" and noticing with surprise that most of the file were plastered about the road. It was a long time before I noticed anything else. I did not notice stretcher bearers or field dressing station. My hands lying on a white sheet were the next thing I saw, and when I tried to lift one of them the pang in my side made me gasp. A nurse said: "Be as still as you can. Try not to move," and then I had another long stretch of nothingness.

Bits of the exploding shell had peppered me as small shot peppers a partridge. The ribs on my right side were almost all broken. In a hospital near London I had operation after operation for taking out pieces of bone and metal, and later for putting in bits of silver to join the gaps in my ribs. My heart to this day lives like a bird in a silver cage.

When I was well enough to receive visitors, Phoebe came often to see me, and once she brought Greg, who was on leave.

"Well, you're a grim-looking tyke," I said. He was. Thin as a lath, wearing a war-battered uniform, his eyes sunk in his head. He was a major then, and I a lieutenant.

He squeezed my hand, and hurt it. "You're nothing to write home about, come to that, Pie-frill," he said.

I was allowed by then to potter about on the hospital lawn, using two crutches. Not that my legs needed support, but the rests under my arms took the weight of my shattered casing. It was autumn, and I remember the red and umber of some buckthorns and the dahlias and Michaelmas daisies. The sky was blue and tender. Greg and Phoebe and I sat down on some garden seats, and all three of us were wrapped in the day's serene unbearable beauty. Greg's hand, with the finger gone, lay on his knee. Phoebe was absent-mindedly caressing it.

For no reason at all I said: "I remember you two riding like a couple of crazy coots barebacked round the paddock at the Rectory."

Greg said: "D'you know what, Chad? You and I and a lot of other people have reached the age when we begin to say, 'D'you remember?' It's a thought I don't like."

"And we're only in our twenties."

"Yes—and the lucky ones at that."

After that, there wasn't much said. It wasn't necessary to say anything. We were happy to sit there, so near to one another, so full of thoughts of one another, absorbing strength from one another, as friends will.

After a while Greg said: "D'you remember that funny little bit of smoke-gray fluff I found you talking to when the Liberals had their garden party—Daphne Dawson?"

"Yes."

"Would you believe it of a girl like that? She became a nurse, and the Boche bombed the hospital she was working in—a hospital in a damn-fool place as usual, right alongside the railway leading from Boulogne. Daphne worked like a trooper, taking wounded men into dugouts while the raid was on. Then she copped one. Blown to bits. I suppose, after this lot, women will be handed their votes on a silver salver greased with soft soap. I can imagine the bloody speeches."

He was getting angry, and Phoebe soothed him, massaging the maimed hand.

"I used to think," he said, "that history, allowing for certain ups and downs, was a fairly reasonable progressive business, but I'm beginning to wonder whether it's anything more than catastrophic kicks in the pants making us see a bit of common sense."

"Even if we see it then," I said. I added: "It was when I was talking to that girl that I saw Eustace and Rose. Do you hear from Eustace, Phoebe?"

"Not much more than other people hear."

"Well," Greg said with grim satisfaction, "Eustace certainly made 'em hear plenty in *Now, Soldiers, March!*"

It had come out in that summer, and as *English Grass* had met the mood of the early war days, so *Now, Soldiers, March!* was full of the somber, foreboding mood of 1917. Siegfried Sassoon, Wilfred Owen, Eustace Hawke: they were saying it all, and Eustace's book had a savagery of resentment that went beyond the other two. He wrote like a man betrayed. *Now, Soldiers, March!* had come out just before I was blown up, and a copy had been sent to me. I remember how I was reading it in a dugout, my legs curled up on an ammunition box to keep them out of the water, when an adjutant brought along a visiting general. They barged into the dugout before I could put the book down, and the general took it from my hand, gave it one glance, and threw it away in disgust. "D'you find that good for your morale?" he asked.

I said: "I'm reading it because I know the author, sir. The book was sent to me." I added smoothly: "So far as morale goes, I know it's not in the Bruce Bairnsfather or Ian Hay class."

The irony passed him by. "I should think not. The feller ought to be stopped. He's only a private, they tell me."

"Yes, sir."

Eustace would not take a commission. He remained a private to the end.

"When d'you go back, Greg?"

"The morning train. I'm taking Phoebe out to dinner and then to the *Bing Boys,* so we'd better be moving on."

"What frivolous tastes you professors have at heart."

He flipped me lightly across the face with his glove. "Cheese it, Pie-frill."

Phoebe kissed me, and they went.

8

When I was able to do without the crutches I wangled a move to Smurthwaite for rounding off my convalescence. Sir Titus Newte's castle had been lent to the Government as a place where these last stages could be gone through. I had written to my mother begging her and Uncle Arthur not to visit me in London. I didn't want them to see me hopping about on crutches, which made me look worse than I was. I told them it was a matter of waiting for a few fractured ribs to join up and that I'd see them as soon as I could. However, there was more in it than that. I had gone through plenty before that blast caught me, and the accumulated effect of it began to tell now that the need to go on was ended. My nerves were in a twitter, and I was visited with day-dreams of going into action again, and, looked at from this quiet lawn, with the consequences of action strewn about me, the prospect was more frightening than the experienced reality had been. Also, with so much time for thought, I thought of May Ingleby—May Boothroyd—and the temptation to write to her, which had been subdued till now, became troublesome. Fighting this temptation alone jangled my nerves horribly. If May had not written to me, it might have been easier, but the poor wretch had done so, frequently at first, then not so often. But still the letters came, now every month or six weeks. May had seen her duty, and did it. A good wife wrote to her husband at the wars, and so May wrote.

DEAR CHAD:

I am still awaiting a letter from you. I know what a terrible time you must be having and how difficult it must be for you to find time to write, but I am sure there is sometimes a lull in the dread conflict when you could pen me a line. The job I took when I left Sir Charles is quite satisfactory and well paid, on the welfare staff of the big munition factory whose location I must not reveal. Would you believe it, your little wife is now top but one of the whole welfare staff! Don't think I'm boasting, but I'm proud of this, and I think you should be proud of me, as I am proud of you doing your bit for King and Country. But I shall be proudest of all when this is over and I've got together a nice little home again where we can resume our married life. So pen a line when possible.

Your loving and dutiful wife,

MAY

That is the sort of thing I got from May, and I am sure she believed every word of it. I am sure she believed that we had experienced "married life," and that she was still a loving and dutiful creature. I had not realized how difficult it would be not to answer such letters. There were times when I loathed myself and thought how pleasant it would be to rid myself of the loathing by sending her something, if only a field postcard. But I knew I should loathe myself the more when I had done it, like a man who, fighting a secret vice, permits himself one "last" indulgence that leaves all to be done again.

And now, with so much time on my hands, this became an obsession; it kept my nerves on edge, and did more than anything else to delay my recovery, because it was a secret thing that I could not talk about. Again and again I began letters to May. When the plague was at its worst, I began five or six a day, and it seems a miracle to me now that none was posted. I wrote—or began to write—factual letters, and loving letters, and playful letters, letters explaining that this one was the first and the last because I did not want to see her again, and letters describing the bedtime joys of our reunion, written with the wicked intention of shocking her to the marrow. They would be such joys, I said, as I had experienced on that afternoon of our honeymoon when she had gone out sailing, and I told her about it in considerable detail.

The whole thing was like a disease long-suppressed, but now triumphantly in charge. It played the devil with my temperature chart and puzzled the doctors who saw no reason for it. Happily, Uncle Arthur, ignoring my request, turned up when things were at their worst. I knew what I needed, and that was simply to tell someone about the whole thing. But I hesitated to tell Uncle Arthur. I was afraid of shocking him. But the day after his arrival, when we were sitting on the hospital lawn, I found his hand on my knee as it had rested that day when I sat with him in the victoria and he was making his first stylish call at Pentyrch. It had been such a hushed day as this: an autumn day, with slivers of gold leaf spinning through the air; and suddenly I felt my jangled nerves steadying, and the two moments fused, and I was that boy, comfortable in a rocklike understanding presence.

His hand rose and fell gently on my knee and I let myself swing as if on a soothing tide. "Out with it, Chad. Out with it," he said.

And it was the easiest thing in the world to let it out. I told him of my love for Rose and of my recoil upon May Ingleby. I told him of the

270

farce of our honeymoon and even of the young prostitute I had visited. I told him of our married life, of my joy when the war ended it, and of my resolve never to try to mend it. I told him of May's letters and of the strange compulsion I now felt to write to her—to write anything to her, including filth.

He didn't budge all the time I was talking, and he was silent for a long time afterward. Then he said: "Write to her, Chad my dear. Write anything you like, pure as the driven snow, black as the pit. Don't frustrate yourself by not finishing what you start to say. Say it all. And when you've written, give the letters to me. I won't read them. I'll burn them. But you will have written them."

I did that, and it was odd how few I wrote now that I was at liberty to do it. And that was the end, the very end, of May. It was Uncle Arthur who killed her at a stroke.

9

I asked my uncle where he was staying, and he said: "On the Bayswater Road with Miss Orlop."

I had wangled a day off from the hospital. My errant temperature had steadied, my ribs were mending and I had got rid of the crutches. An understanding young doctor said: "Yes, push off by all means. It'll do you good to spend a day out of this hellhole."

So, escorted—almost carried—by Uncle Arthur, as solicitously as if I were a fragile egg, I went early to Paddington station and got onto the Oxford train with him. He had given me the choice, and that was where I wanted to go. Always Oxford. The crises of my life seemed to set themselves in that mellow frame. It is the saddest place in the world, the place perpetually alight with young hope doomed. I love it.

With the war on, it was not the Oxford I had known, but on the river, the very symbol of the place, flowing to the Thames, flowing to the sea, there was peace. I could not take the punt pole, but a small matter of that sort didn't daunt Uncle Arthur. "It would be an odd thing," he said, seizing the pole like an athlete about to toss the caber, "if a man who has steered the municipal affairs of Smurthwaite through the rapids could not steer this coracle along a mile or two of quiet water."

So I reclined on cushions, and watched him, like a hippopotamus on its hind legs, driving the pole vehemently into the river bed and hurling us hither and thither from bank to bank. His weight at the after end raised the bows out of the water like a speedboat's and formed a pivot for unpredictable rotation. He sweated. He groaned, he even swore. "My God, Chad," he said, "if an untutored Indian can drive a canoe with precision, shall it be said that these few planks of wood defeat such a man as I?" He drove the pole down again with force enough to spear the hide of an alligator.

I was lazy and content. I left it to him, and in time he found a knack of at least imparting a reasonable forward motion to the punt. It was then, as I was watching this happy subsiding of his gigantic efforts, that he answered my question.

"On the Bayswater Road with Miss Orlop."

I was twenty-eight. That meant that sixteen years had passed since these two oddities met for the first time. I suppose it was the oddity in each that attracted the other. They met rarely, but they seemed always to meet with gladness. I remembered the night when my mother and I, so long ago, arrived for the first time in Uncle Arthur's house, and she wept because of his whippet and his flowers, and told him he should find a wife. And I remembered the last time I was at home, during my first leave, and a letter from Miss Orlop was lying by Uncle Arthur's plate. He had not yet come down. My mother must have known the handwriting, for she said: "Miss Orlop! He thinks that woman's a wonder." There was a sharpness in her tone that made me look up anxiously, and I divined with a shock that my mother was jealous of Miss Orlop, even feared, perhaps, old as the pair were, that the friendship might turn out to her disadvantage. She was snug here, under Uncle Arthur's wing.

Few things have made me feel more miserable. I was a man—a wretchedly married man—and, too, I had come from a bloody experience, but my mother was my mother still, and to think her perfect was habitual. It was only a tiny peep behind the armor of another soul: and soon enough I was able to accept it; but it was a useful hint of time's subtle changes in us all. My mother became for me more of a human being and less of my childhood's remembered vision. I saw with a new sympathy the lines in her face, the gray in her hair.

"How is Miss Orlop?" I asked Uncle Arthur.

"Very unhappy, dear boy."

With pride, he succeeded in bringing the punt, at the cost of no more than a violent bump, alongside the bank. He tied the painter to a willow with a knot that would have raised the hair on a sailor's head, and took up a basket that he had carried from London.

"Very unhappy, but thoughtful as ever. Herein enshrined," he said, opening the basket, "are the mortal but serviceable remains of a cockerel from Pentyrch, cooked to a T. It arrived yesterday, and Miss Orlop insisted on having it prepared for my midday meal. For afters, there is an apple pie with Cornish cream, and the nectar is Clos Vougeot of a reputable year. It is the last of three bottles that Sir Titus gave me at

Christmas seven years ago. I brought it with me, thinking we might enjoy some such *fête champêtre* as we now have."

He held up the fowl by the leg and addressed it: "This is wartime, old friend, but *ruat coelum, fiat fiesta*."

We ate facing one another, with plates upon our knees. There was salad with the fowl. We ate the pie, every last crumb of it, and we drank Sir Titus's wine. When we had done, Uncle Arthur put everything back neatly into the basket and was about to close it when he exclaimed: "What's this? Why, it's a letter! For you, Chad. Bless my soul, I nearly forgot it. I shall now take my after-luncheon nap. Youth can do without such indulgence. Get out, Chad, and stretch your legs while old age pampers the digestive processes."

He no more wanted to sleep than I did. He wanted me to read the letter undisturbed by any sense of being overlooked. I humored his inclination. He stretched himself on the cushions and I put the rugs over him, for the day, though sunny, was none too warm. I walked a little way along the river bank, came to a gate, and leaned upon it. Farther up the river, just round a bend, I could see a spiral of smoke rising against the blue of the autumn sky. I couldn't see the cottage, but I knew that it was the one in whose garden I had given Rose a honeycomb, and I knew that the letter was from Rose. This was the first letter she had sent me.

DEAR CHAD:

I am asking your Uncle to give you this, so that it will reach you in Oxford. You once asked me to write to you while you were at Oxford, and I never did. I feel more and more ashamed about that as I realize how much this sorry world needs kindness. I am not given to writing letters, anyway, but here's some amends: a letter to Chad at Oxford.

I am sending it to ask your forgiveness for not calling to see you in hospital. I couldn't have stood it. Do you think that weak of me? Well, there it is. You and Greg and Eustace and my husband are the only four men I have known well, and three of them are in this. Perhaps it is because my imagination is sufficiently engaged that I shrink from the sight of a hospital. There are faces I would see on the pillows. And it's no good calling my attention to the heroic work of nurses at home and on all the battlefronts. I'm not much of a person, am I?

Well, now that I've written to you, what a letter I've sent! If there is time before you go home with your Uncle, would you call to see me and my mother? She would like that, and I could stand the sight of you now that you're well enough not to be a ghost-raiser. Don't wear any medal ribbons, or anything heroic. Come as Chad.

Yours ever,

ROSE

It didn't take long to read, but it took long to think about. "You and Greg and Eustace and my husband." Not Billy. And I knew whose face she feared to have called up on a pillow. "There are faces." No, Rose, there is a face. Still, it was a letter from Rose. I folded it and put it in my wallet, and strolled slowly back to the punt. As I expected, Uncle Arthur had not slept. I could tell that, because his cigar was smoked halfway through. However, he assured me that he had had a wonderful sleep. He did not ask about the letter and I said nothing to him except: "Do you think it would be a good idea if I looked up Miss Orlop before going north?" He thought it would be a very good idea indeed.

10

He called for me the next morning in a taxicab that had a vast bag of gas sagging on top of it. But if war time changed the appearance of a taxicab, that was no reaon why it should change the appearance of Uncle Arthur. He was going to take luncheon with a lady, and, though he was living in that lady's house, he would be returning to it with me in custody, and so in some sort would be presenting himself.

"Is that *The* Hat, Uncle?" I chipped him.

He took it off and rubbed the nap affectionately with a silk handkerchief. "It is, my dear boy. A Hat, properly groomed, should last a man a lifetime. This Hat has done more. Wearing it, my father led my dear mother to the altar. Or at any rate, arrived at the church door so to lead her. It thereafter served him on many memorable occasions and on innumerable lesser occasions such as Sunday morning service at the Wesleyan chapel. It has been a notable receptacle of gloves. Many a time I have watched my father place this Hat on the floor of the pew, withdraw his kid gloves, blow into them, and drop them into his Hat. Only when the seed of respectability had thus been planted in its appropriate flower pot would he bow his head in prayer. Yes, Chad. One may call this a Hat. In due course it will be passed on to you."

He was wearing a cutaway tailed coat and striped trousers. His Malacca cane was silver-headed. There was a white carnation at his buttonhole.

Using its own mysterious processes, the gas bag delivered us to the Bayswater Road. A small maid opened the door, and having dropped his gloves into the Hat, Uncle Arthur handed her the Hat and the cane as pompously as though they were being handed to a footman in white silk calves at a splendid reception.

But there was no voice to shout: "Mr. Arthur Geldersome and Mr. Chad Boothroyd." The house was quiet. And there was no ambassadorial stairway for us to mount. It was a rather dark and rather narrow stairway, and as we stood there a child came round the turn of it and began to walk slowly down. Her dark hair, her crimson silk, her gravity, made my heart bound. It might have been Rose Garland walking into my childhood. How old will she be now, I wondered? Seven. The child who had been born at Weimar.

She said: "Mother is in the drawing room. Will you go up, please? You know the way, Mr. Geldersome."

Three years had passed since I had seen Rose. She was sitting alone at the window whence she had watched the march of us recruits, and through that window I could see the tranced autumn trees of the park, the thin bright leaves waiting for no more than a puff, if that, to bring them down. When I had taken lunch, alone with Rose, after that march, I had seen her distraught. She had begged me to go. She was distraught by foreboding; but, seeing her now, I knew that something more than foreboding was in question. She seemed ruined, overthrown. She had not looked up as we entered the room, and if she knew we were there, we mattered no more to her than any of the strangers passing by on the pavement below.

I strode across to her and said gently: "Rose! Rose! What has happened?"

She looked up then and took me in, but did not seem to take in my question. "What has happened, Rose?" I repeated.

She said: "What was bound to happen."

She would—or could—say no more. I might as well have tried to get words from a corpse.

Uncle Arthur whispered to me: "I'll see if Miss Orlop is in the house."

He went, and I sat on the window seat at her side, holding her cold unresponsive hand.

Presently Uncle Arthur returned with Miss Orlop and beckoned me out. I shall not forget how, when I loosed Rose's hand, it fell into her lap like a stone.

Uncle Arthur, who seemed to know his way about the house, took me to Miss Orlop's studio, which had not changed since the only other time I had seen it, and that was when I was a child.

"Miss Orlop had to be out this morning," Uncle Arthur explained. "She was just returning when I went down. Well, my dear boy, it looks as though something bad has happened to young Hawke. We shall see. We shall see."

It was twelve o'clock, and it was not till one that Miss Orlop came in to us. "I've got her to bed," she said, "and was lucky enough to find the doctor in. He lives just along the road. He's given her some dope or other and now she's sleeping. We'd better go and eat something."

I was amazed at her practicality. She seemed even cool. Uncle Arthur's percipience was sharper than mine. He took her hand and bowed over it and kissed it. He didn't say a word, but everything had been said between them, and I saw then that a tear was trembling on the old woman's eyelashes. She dashed it away impatiently and said: "Come along."

Though we all made a pretense, not much was eaten, even by Uncle Arthur. Halfway through the meal Miss Orlop said: "I used to know a man who was once our ambassador at some pettifogging German court. That was when Victoria was on the throne, and with her mania for matchmaking she'd married off some sprig of a girl belonging to her family to the reigning prince. It was a ghastly failure, and there were such scandals about the doings in the royal menage that my old friend was called to Windsor to discuss the business with the Queen. He told me that after a long powwow, she said to him: 'I shall never arrange another marriage. It does no good.'"

Nothing was said till she herself added: "What disasters it takes to make us learn the simplest things."

A soft autumn sunlight was falling into the room, lighting up the white dandelion puff of her hair that had always fascinated me. She sat erect, eating nothing, and none of us said anything. A little ormolu clock on the mantelpiece ticked away merrily in the silence.

Presently Uncle Arthur said: "Would you care to tell us, Lucy, what has happened?"

"I don't know, Arthur. I don't know. She's all at sixes and sevens and incoherent. Phoebe is Eustace's nearest relative, and has had some news of him. She rang up to tell Rose as soon as I went out this morning. What it all comes to I don't know, except that he's not dead."

"Then Chad and I had better try and find out for you. You know Phoebe's address, Chad?"

I said that I did.

"Then let's be off."

We went by underground to Hampstead. Phoebe was not overthrown like Rose, but what it cost her to be erect I could guess. She took care not to talk much. It is talking that brings the catch to the breath, the tear to the eye. "You'd better read this," she said. "It's all I know up to the moment." Then she left us to ourselves. If she had to cry, she would do it alone.

All officers did not take the view of Eustace that my general had done. The lieutenant who had written to Phoebe clearly admired him beyond measure and wrote with sorrow of what had happened to a poet as well as to a man. There had been house-to-house fighting in the taking of a village, and Eustace had been buried in the ruins of a falling wall. Both his legs had been amputated to the thighs, and whether he would live or die was in doubt. As it turned out, he lived. He lost

276

more than his legs. What the lieutenant could not bring himself to say in that letter, even if he knew it, was that Eustace's sex had been destroyed.

11

I can say briefly what else remains to be said about the way that war affected us. I was back with my regiment in time for the German push toward Amiens in March of 1918. In July, when there were cheerful reasons for thinking that we had seen the turn of the tide, a sniper got me in the left arm. I wish I knew his name, for I would like to thank him. He did me a wondrous service. I found myself back in London again, and it was not till September that I was out of the doctors' hands. I was given indefinite leave, and said to Miss Orlop who had called to see me: "Do you remember telling me a long time ago that I could use your hut on the cliff at Pendeverel if I wanted to do a bit of writing?"

"No, Chad. An old chatterer like me, an old botcher of other people's lives, is always spilling the wind. No—I don't remember half I say; but all the same, use the place. Are you working at something?"

"Well, it's just an idea." I was shy about it. "Perhaps nothing will come of it, but there's something I do rather want to have a shot at." I couldn't tell her that it was something that was burning me up as no idea had done before.

"I think you'll be all right there," she said. "I've been only once since the war started. There's an old couple keeping down the dust. That's all it amounts to nowadays. I'll write to them this very afternoon and tell them to expect you. Stay in the house, Chad. You'll be more comfortable than camping in that hut. You'll be well fed at all events. They don't know what rationing means in Cornwall."

I thanked her, but made up my mind to live in the hut. The idea pleased me: up there on the bluff, with all my childhood's sea before me. I would even sleep in the hut, though I could eat in the house. My old sleeping bag . . . I was beginning to work things out.

"How are Rose and Eustace?" I asked.

She winced. She was looking old and haggard. "Oh, my dear," she said. "Don't ask me about that. Please don't." She managed a difficult smile. "I shall have enough to do," she said, "to answer to my God, without bothering about battered captains of infantry."

"I'm sorry. I beg your pardon."

I walked with her as far as the gate. "Happy writing," she said, and marched away.

It was happy and it was miserable, heaven and hell, as writing tends to be.

I waited for a day or two, so that Miss Orlop's letter might reach Pentyrch, and then set off, hoping that the War Office would perform one of its miracles of somnolence and forget all about me. It did. I traveled in tweeds and never put on uniform again. At our Town I was fortunate enough to find an old Pendeverel schoolfellow of mine on the platform. He was one of the boys who had delighted to chip me as I pushed the perambulator to the well, and, changed though I must have been, it was he who recognized me, not I him.

"Well, damme, it's Chad Boothroyd, isn't it?" he asked, advancing with a broad farmer's hand outstretched. He eyed my tweeds and grinned. "You dodged the ole army like me, eh, Chad? Bugger the army, I say. I been workin' on the ole man's farm, but I'll soon be off that when this lot's over. Bugger the farmin', I say. Still, mustn't grumble. Kep' me out o' the bloody army. 'Ave you come from upalong for a good feed? Plenty down 'ere."

He was a big raw-boned red-faced lout, stuffed with good living; and I thought of a white-faced undersized Cockney I had had in a platoon, as free as this one with his buggers and bloodies, but a man I had come to love. "Come ahn, you silly bugger. I can carry yer bloody rifle as well as my bloody own, cawn't I?"

I marveled at the mystery of the spirit of man, but was ready to use this oaf. He had come expecting to meet someone on the train, and, this visitor not appearing, he put my baggage into a gig and went out of his way to drop me at Pentyrch. He was full of idle questions— about Miss Orlop, about Billy Pascoe—and I answered him evasively.

Old Mr. and Mrs. Penhale, who were looking after the house, had been known to me vaguely since childhood; and they seemed glad to have someone to fuss about. They had a good meal ready for me and had prepared a bedroom. To please them, I slept in it that night. I went to bed at eight o'clock, feeling more tired by the journey than I had expected to be. It was already dark by then. The windows were open upon the whispering of the woods and the calling owls; the old familiar sigh and murmur of the sea drifted in. This, I thought, is the first time I have been alone—really alone—since 1914. I was thinking of my Cockney lance corporal, long since dead, and I began to see where he would fit in. It wasn't till ten the next morning that old Penhale came in to awaken me with a cup of tea and the explanation: "Miss Orlop said you was to have plenty of sleep, captain."

12

The Cockney fitted in as Bill Kent, and others began to fit in, too. I decided to call the play *I Don't Want to Die*.

278

I found the mornings the best time for work. Once I had made it clear to the Penhales that I would live in the studio, and that I was on no account to be disturbed there, they fell in with my wishes. After dinner each night I strolled back there with a thermos flask of coffee that Mrs. Penhale had prepared. I lit the fire and the oil lamp and I read till it was time to get into my sleeping bag. I stretched out in the warmth of the fire and slept well. The morning sunlight wakened me, and the morning was a blessed time: no newspapers, no letters, nothing to bring me either hopes or fears. My mind, without urging, began to inhabit the little world I was building up. I would go out onto the bluff and watch the sea mists weaving and dissolving and the tender autumn sunshine gaining strength, and I would go down to the yellow sand and walk there on the whispering edge of the tide, with the oyster catchers and turnstones running and twittering, and the curlews calling out of the mist, and sometimes with the swans majestically beating their great wings against the sky that was still more milky than blue. Then I would go back and light my fire and drink the thermos coffee. A handful of rusks and a few apples made my breakfast. I did not bother with shaving. Like a Nazarite, I let my beard grow till the vow was fulfilled.

At one o'clock I would go back to the house and eat my lunch, and after that I wandered in the woods and along the coast and sawed logs for my fire and carried them to the studio. When the afternoon was at its warmest I would have my daily swim. I kept away from the village, and throughout all my time down there I saw no one but a few chance-met strangers to whom I gave no more than a good-day. I didn't look at the daily newspaper that reached the house in the afternoon, and, save Miss Orlop and the Authorities, no one knew where I was. If the Authorities had dared to intervene at that moment, I think I should have used my father's old trick of evasion. As for Miss Orlop, when I later reproached her with not having once written, she said: "But I knew you were working. Don't be silly."

After tea, I loafed in the library till dinnertime, idly pulling out old musty books, reading a few pages, dozing by the fire. I had the companionship for that daily hour or two of a silver-blue Persian cat, the spit and image of the cat that Rose Garland had been stroking by the fireside that afternoon when first I set foot in this house. But by some unconscious operation of the will I did not allow myself to think of Rose, or of my mother, or of my father dying in the lane a few hundred yards away, or of Billy Pascoe, talking out his dreams on the beach as the gulls screamed over him. I had dreams enough of my own, and they were my only reality, bounded by the few square stinking yards of a dugout on the Western front, with a sackcloth doorway and girls from *La Vie Parisienne* pinned on the walls. Nothing made me happier throughout that time than the feeling, as I was eating my dinner, of being impatient to get through with it, of my little world condensing to an agonizing reality that I must run and enter. I would seize my thermos and be off, for now, toward the end of the enterprise, I was writing in the evening as well as the morning. As I threw the bolt of the door, curtained the windows, lit the lamp and the fire, there they would be: Bill Kent and Captain Chambers, the Padre, Lieutenant Stokes, and the rest of them—the men who didn't want to die. Bill Kent would say: "You been a bloody long time away, cock." "Ah well, here I am. Let's get on, shall we? Stokes, what was in that letter you got from Margaret this morning?" Stokes would probably reply: "What's it got to do with you? Find out, you nosy old bastard."

And I would proceed to do so, uplifted to have them all about me again. It was a wonderful feeling. It held all through. I have never had anything quite like it again. They say I am a one-play man, and maybe they're right. Certainly I've never since then written about people whom I loved as I loved that lot.

13

It took me a month to write *I Don't Want to Die*. I put down the pen in that mood of exultation and regret with which one finishes such a piece of work, feeling at once both empty and fulfilled. There was a huge thankfulness that this was done, and there seemed for the moment, nothing more in the world worth doing. It was about eleven at night, and I resisted the temptation to read the whole thing through at once. That could wait till the morning. I put the manuscript into a drawer and drank my morning coffee, seeing that there was nothing else to drink in celebration. Then I pulled on my overcoat and went out onto the bluff to look about me. Eastward, there was a blaze in the sky. It seemed to be in the heart of St. Michael Pendeverel. I went back toward the house, intending to by-pass it and walk through the woods to the highroad, whence I could easily run to the village. To my surprise, for the Penhales were early bedders, there was light still on, so I banged on the door and the old man appeared with a grin on his face. "It's over, Captain! It's over!" he cried, and indecorously seized me in his arms, as though about to whirl me in a dance.

"What's over?" I asked. "And what's on fire in the village?"

"It'll be that ole bonfire. It's over, Captain. The war's over."

I was so bemused by what I had been doing that I thought: "Thank God! Chambers is all right then."

And in a flash the mixture of dream and reality sorted itself out, and I remembered that Chambers was dead, that, in fact, if not in my fiction, every one of these men who didn't want to die was dead except Stokes, the only one of them all who wished to die daily.

I said: "Is there anything to drink in the house?"

"Yes, Captain. As a matter of fact, the news being what it is, Mrs. Penhale and I ventured to crack a bottle in the kitchen."

I ought to have joined them, but I couldn't face it. "Bring another into the library."

"Very good, Captain. You're going on afterward to the bonfire?"

"I think not."

"Would it be convenient if Mrs. Penhale and I went?"

"As you like."

He looked at me anxiously. "You all right, Captain?"

"I'm as right as rain," I said. "I feel madly pleased with life. Bring me something to drink."

CHAPTER ELEVEN

I

WHEN you were out of the trenches and footling about in back areas you came upon the oddest activities. I remember listening to John Drinkwater reading poetry to the troops and to a French colonel of gunners lecturing on "Ronsard, Du Bellay, *et* La Pléiade." But on the morning after I had finished writing the play, I especially remembered my meeting with Max Middlemass.

It was in December of 1916. The blessed mirage of Christmas leave had faded, but there was at all events the consolation of being out of the muck and in a township with reasonable opportunity for enjoyment. For one thing, I found that a scheme was afoot for putting on a pantomime, and my old passion for the theater roused up. The show was to be in a public hall that had been banged about a bit but was serviceable, and I used to stroll round there and watch the scene builders at work and the rehearsals in progress. Max Middlemass seemed to be running everything. He was a fat little sergeant of the R.E.'s, older than I was, and for a time I was content to watch him and weigh him up. I had done a lot behind the scenes for the O.U.D.S. and quickly recognized the professional touch. Max could slap paint

281

onto a flat, organize lighting, drill a chorus, and do a bit of acting himself. I suggested after a time that I should give a hand with the scenery, and he was kind enough to concede at the end of that day: "You're bloody good, sir."

In my billet that night I knocked out a fifteen-minute sketch, and the next day I took it to Max as nervously as I had taken essays to my tutor at Oxford. Max read it, and, like my tutor, said: "Pretty good— but," and proceeded to tear it to pieces. "Shall I rewrite it, or you?" he asked.

"I think you'll make the better job of it," I said, meaning it. He did, but was kind enough to give me credit for it on the program, the first program my name appeared on.

What impressed me about Max was that while all this was a lark to everybody else, it was for him a deadly serious matter. I found him in tears one day at a rehearsal. There was a love scene that he wanted played straight, but the sergeant major in a blonde wig who was playing the girl kept on fooling and breaking down in laughter.

"For Chrissake," Max shouted through his tears, "can't you *see* it? Can't you *feel* it? Can't you *yearn* toward him, as if you wanted him to give you a couple of kids?"

The sergeant major removed his wig and advanced, waving it threateningly, to the front of the stage. "Cheese it, Sarge," he said. "Let's keep this clean. Don't start putting ideas into people's heads."

Nevertheless, the sergeant major learned to play it straight. Max was like that. In the long run people did what he wanted.

I had some talks with Max, and asked him one day: "How long have you been at this game?"

He said: "From the Sunday afternoon when I was born in a train between Manchester and Macclesfield and shoved into a clothesbasket while they revived my mother with gin."

I don't think that was strictly true, but it became in time part of the Middlemass legend. But it wasn't far from the truth, either. His mother was a music hall soubrette, his father a conjuror, and what Max didn't know about the rough and tumble of theatrical life wasn't worth knowing. His mother died while he was a child; his father settled down as manager of a small theater in the Midlands, and the boy spent all his time when out of school playing about behind the scenes and absorbing gaslight and greasepaint. It was inevitable that he should go on the stage himself, and from the time of leaving school up to the outbreak of war he had been touring with third-rate companies.

Those were the banal facts of his life up to that moment, but I soon learned that Max's life was more than facts. He was a dreamer, and his dreams were stupendous. He was very humble about what he could do, but he was a megalomaniac about what he thought he could make other people do. "Give me the money, give me the play, and, Chris', I'll make history!" That was one of his humbler pronouncements.

Max and I took a fancy to one another. If he amused me, he also impressed me. On his part, he was not used to having his visions taken seriously, and to find someone who would listen to him was consoling. If few people had listened seriously to Max, it was because he didn't look as though he had anything that could be seriously listened to. He was squat, black and ugly, with a pushed-in nose sprouting hairs, as his ears abundantly did, too. As he talked, it was like listening to a toad conjuring up fairy palaces. Indeed, I remember strolling away, after one of his tirades, murmuring: "Which, like the toad, ugly and venomous, yet bears a precious jewel in its head."

Anyhow, when I saw what Max Middlemass made of that pantomime, working with amateur players all of one sex, and with bits and pieces of cloth and canvas scrounged up from God knows where, I did not abate the opinion I had been forming of him. Often enough, in the long boredom of the trenches, I thought of the years after the war and what I should do with them. There would be no going back to May, and there would be no going back, I now resolved, to the *Manchester Guardian* or to any other newspaper. That was as far as I got; but when our stay in that quiet area was ended and we prepared to move again I hunted up Max Middlemass and said, with an odd feeling of making an important decision: "Keep in touch with me, Sergeant. Let's know how you go on."

Max saluted as smartly as he knew how and said: "Very good, sir," and that was that.

2

And now, on this morning after the play was finished, I was thinking of Max Middlemass. He had not proved a formidable correspondent. I had heard from him twice. A week after we parted, he sent a sort of "duty" letter about nothing at all; and then a year or so later, he wrote he had been discharged from the army, "mucked up a bit by old Jerry." That was a Middlemass fantasy. He had, in fact, smashed his right foot by dropping a heavy weight upon it by accident, or, not improbably, by design. In either case, part of the foot had to be amputated, and, marching being impossible, his war was over. "This address will always find me," he wrote. "If I'm away, Ma will post anything on." The address was in Whitechapel.

I put it into my wallet, and now, on this fateful twelfth of November, 1918, I took it out and wrote a letter.

283

DEAR MAX MIDDLEMASS:

I ended the war down here, convalescing after a smashed left arm. I've been spending my time trying to write a play. It's finished now, such as it is, and I don't think it's bad. It's about the war, and what war does to men. I'd very much like to read it to you and have your advice about how to dispose of it, if you think there's anything in it. I'm leaving here at once, and shall be staying at my uncle's house in Yorkshire. Write to me % Mr. Arthur Geldersome, Smurthwaite, W. Yorks. I hope all goes well with you. Send me your news.

I wrote to the Authorities, giving them my change of address; wrote to Miss Orlop, thanking her for the holiday and telling her I was off; and the next day I set out for Smurthwaite. I stayed there, doing nothing, till I was summoned to my formal discharge from the army in March, 1919.

In the December before this a laconic letter came from Max.

DEAR MR. BOOTHROYD:

Thanks for your letter. Not a cat in hell chance of making a go with a play about the war. Still, as I shall be doing panto work in Bradford I'll run over next Sunday week and have a look-see at the thing. Cheerio till then.

MAXIMILIAN MIDDLEMASS

These few uncheerful lines filled the whole of a mauve sheet of quarto paper. The ink was green. The Maximilian was unfamiliar and ominous.

On a morning of bitter winter weather I took the well-known walk between the stripped sycamores to the station. Nothing had changed in Smurthwaite beyond the sudden death of Sir Titus Newte and a fall in the young male population. I was not in a cheerful mood. It had been impossible to hide any longer from my mother that my marriage was a wreck. When she learned in addition to this that I was not going back to the *Manchester Guardian* I found myself, for the first time in my life, openly at odds with her.

"I suppose you're not going back to Manchester because you're afraid of meeting that girl," she said. "I could have told you from the start that she was not the girl for you. But of course children know best in everything nowadays."

I hated above all things the idea of quarreling with my mother, and so I said nothing to such remarks; and that did not help. "All right. Be sullen. But fancy a man of your age living on his uncle!"

Well, there it was. I was a child defying his elders when she wanted it that way, and I was a man with no standards of conduct when that was how she wanted it. Altogether, it was an unhappy time—unhappiest of all because both she and Uncle Arthur were unhappy. He did his best. "Give Chad time, my dear. Give him time. War is a very unsettling experience. You'll live to be proud of him yet."

Even this was not very consoling, implying as it did that I wasn't much to be proud of at the moment. Nor was I.

I did not tell them about the play. The impulse that had carried me through the writing of it, my conviction, when it was finished, that I had done something worth while, faded out in the atmosphere of my mother's disapproval. I had nursed a foolish hope that nothing was necessary save to have the play read by the right people and fame and fortune would at once bow down to me. I began to see how misguided such thoughts were. With hope gone that, in this way, I could make my mother see me in a new light, with the bawdy, reliable and desperate companionship of wartime dissolved forever, I found myself, at thirty years old, as miserable as the child my mother called me would have been in a room of toys all suddenly broken. Max's letter put the tin hat on it. "Not a cat in hell chance."

I was not going to burden my uncle and my mother with Max for lunch: they would not have understood him: such an odd companion would have been another mark against me; so I said: "I'm meeting a man coming over from Bradford this morning. I'll lunch him at the pub, and then, if I may, I'll bring him on here for a chat. We can use my den at the top of the house."

Uncle Arthur looked at me sadly. "If you *may?* Really, my dear boy! I'll see that the fire is lit."

And so, with a north wind blowing my ears off, I walked down to the station. I would give Max his lunch, we would look at the play and have our talk, he would tell me again that there was not a cat in hell chance, and that would be that. Good-by, Max.

He was the only passenger to get out at Smurthwaite, and he looked as though he should have arrived in a stage coach a hundred years ago, to the blowing of postilions' horns. How he had come by his overcoat, I didn't know. Perhaps, like Uncle Arthur's Hat, it was an heirloom. It fell to his feet. It surged from his shoulders in overlapping wave upon wave of capes. Each of its immense bone buttons was a cameo of a stag's head, worthy of Landseer. On his head was a tweed earcap, the flaps down and tied beneath his chin with a tape. He looked heartier, healthier and uglier than when I had met him in France. He came forward with the limp he was never to overcome, his hand out. "Well, Mr. Boothroyd!"

I was better at once. I was glad to see Max for Max's sake, even though he thought the play hadn't a cat in hell chance.

"Chad to you, Max," I said. "How are you going?"

"Get me under cover, for Chrissake," he said. "That train's a white hell on wheels. I've got no nose and I've got no feet, and I'd have no ears if Sherlock Holmes hadn't left me this hat in his will."

I soon had him thawing out before the log fire in our notable pub. While I fiddled with a sherry he downed three beers. Unwrapped, he was revealed as corpulence bursting through bright blue tweeds enlivened by a scarlet tie, itself enlivened by a golden fox's mask.

"What are you doing in Bradford, Max?"

"Every bloody thing, from trying out the chorus girls' legs with sixpences between the calves and ankles to reconstructing the transformation scene from the ground up."

"You certainly did some good work that time in France."

"If you're edging cautiously toward this play you've written, edge off again," he said. "We'll talk about that when the time comes. What's to eat?"

I don't remember what there was, but I know I did him pretty well. Whatever my mother might say, if I was living on Uncle Arthur it was by his wish. I had my army "gratuity," and it was out of that that I fed Max.

"Now come on," he said at last. "Let's have a look-see at this masterpiece."

I helped to pack him up again. I even tied the tapes under his chin. We went out into the blast tearing through the skeleton trees. My heart began to beat fast. The compound of pride, doubt, and terror took hold of me once more. Never again would *I Don't Want to Die* be my very own. I was going to share it. "Look, Max, are you sure you want to hear this thing?"

"Don't worry. I'll stop you the moment I think it's sheer punk."

Uncle Arthur had lit the fire. It was good to be here in this room where Eustace had talked to me about Keats, where Greg and I had talked of heaven and earth. Beyond the window the world looked black with frost under the hectoring of the north wind. And now here was another in the room: this strange chance-met companion. I turned from the window to see him settling into one of the easy chairs, stuffing an enormous curved pipe with tobacco. It looked as though it would see him through a reading of the *Encyclopaedia Britannica*. I took the manuscript from the drawer in which I had locked it away and began to read.

It was three o'clock. I read on and on till half-past five, wondering at first when Max's voice would break in to tell me it was sheer punk; then forgetting even my audience of one, so pulled back I was both into the actuality on which this thing was based and into the fantasy that had been reared upon it.

When I had finished there was silence for a time; then Max said: "Well, for Chrissake! If you haven't written a play!"

286

He had brought his overcoat and cap upstairs with him, and began to pull them on. I was disappointed. I had expected an outburst of some sort, whether for or against.

"Got to catch my train," he said. "Work to do in Bradford tonight."

"Don't you like it?" I couldn't resist asking.

"Now, Chad, now. Don't try and rush the Old Man. He'll talk to you when he's chewed it over. Come to Bradford tomorrow. Come and have lunch with me."

"All right," I said.

"That's the boy. It'll be a chance for you to meet the missus."

I saw him off, watched the wind bowling him down the street, and then climbed back to my room feeling that what I had hoped would be a great occasion had ended rather flatly.

3

Max once said to me: "All I want to do, Chad, is give 'em the best. I'm a showman. Give me the best, and I'll know how to show it." But a lot had to happen before he was in a position to do that.

Happily for me, he had decided that my play was the best one ever likely to be written about the war. He told me so as we sat at lunch in his dingy Bradford lodgings. The missus was not present. "There'll be scores of 'em, Chad, but there'll be none better than that."

"So you think it's got a cat in hell chance?"

"Not at the moment I don't. In this game you've got to know the right moment. When that moment has come, I'll know. Trust the Old Man. But don't expect it inside five years. Everybody's fed up to the back teeth with the war, and the last thing they want is to see it all over again on the stage."

"Five years!" I was dismayed.

"At least," he said firmly. "Take the Old Man's tip and don't start showing it round. Some fool might choose the wrong moment, put it on, and pop goes the weasel."

"Look, Max, that's no good to me. What am I going to live on for five years?"

"Faith, hope and charity," he said. "And the greatest of these is charity, if you can find it. I never could."

I resisted, I argued, I became angry. Max remained unmoved and ate steadily. "I'm not stopping you. I'm just advising you. If you want to put it down the sink, now's the time." He drained his beer. "Here's the thing in a nutshell. You've got to live for five years. If you can't do that somehow, you're a bigger fool than I take you for. All the rest you leave to me. Could anything be simpler?"

It sounded fine. But who was Max Middlemass to put it like that? What reason was there to think he could work the miracles he talked about?—a chap who had done nothing but potter round at everything in the theater and became notable in nothing? A chap as short of pennies as I was myself. The odd thing was that he convinced me. There was something about his ugly mug that I liked and believed in.

"All right, Max. I'm on. Where's the missus you said I was to meet?"

"Gone off to Cumberland to see her father."

"And what are you really doing in this pantomime?"

"What d'you mean, doing? I told you. I'm running the whole damn thing."

I looked skeptically round the blear lodging room.

"All right, all right," he said. "I'm living on bread and dripping. The caviar's coming. I can wait. I'm on a payroll at the moment. When I've made my first thousand pounds we shall see."

"How does one make a thousand pounds, Max? I'd love to know."

"You've made it," he said confidently. "You've just got to wait to pick it up."

4

I never knew how Max came to meet his wife. You couldn't imagine a more oddly assorted pair. While he had been brought up amid the catchpenny fripperies of the theater, she came from generations of Cumberland farming stock, "statesmen" of the dales. There was something appropriate in her family's surname, which was Crag. I never once saw Bessie in a theater. All that Max did was foreign to her. All that he was was her life. In his heyday, when from reading of his doings in the newspapers you would think he was living in a world of glamorous excitement, he was, I know, living in a market whose merchandise of beauty and talent never meant so much to him as the moments he could spend with Bessie once the strings were arranged and the puppets assembled. She was a woman whose serenity was remarkable. She was plain, as a homemade loaf of bread is plain, without cellophane wrappings. Max's work gave him a lot of real and pretended temperament to put up with, and he had a good deal of both himself. There was nothing like Bessie to knit up his raveled sleeve. He said to me once: "A cup of tea with Bess is better than all the champagne I have to drink with my bitches." And that's how it was.

That Sunday afternoon when I said good-by to him in Bradford and traveled back to Smurthwaite through a snowstorm, Bessie was going to her father's house. One of his farm laborers was the greatest light of that time in the sport of Cumberland wrestling. He was in the prime of his strength and had never been thrown. It was on him that Max's career as an impresario was founded. Max preferred to say as a showman. He christened his mountain of Cumberland brawn the Great Gable, and began with him in village booths. All comers were invited to have a go at the Great Gable and the Great Gable had fun with them as a terrier has with the rats chivied out of a rick. Then they moved into halls in small towns and then into bigger towns, and the Great Gable ate up casually anything that came in his way. The gate money rose steadily all the time till Max had enough to challenge Vishnik, the Taurus Terror, to defend his world championship title in London. This was the big money at last, and when the two fleshy monsters had strained against one another for an hour or two to the equal delight of pimply clerks and society ladies, and the Great Gable had finally got his opponent's shoulders onto the mat, Max had had enough of that sort of thing. It had taken him two years.

After that, he staged two or three other spectacles before settling down to the series of incomparable revues that are chiefly associated with his name. It was not till 1925 that Rose said to me: "Here's Max Middlemass on the telephone, Chad," and Max said: "I think we might get down to some preliminary talk about that play of yours."

5

"If you can't live somehow for five years you're a bigger fool than I take you for," Max had said that day in Bradford. The remark stuck in my gullet, challenged me to get out from under Uncle Arthur's wing, and I took myself straightaway to London. I rented two rooms on the third floor of a house in Bloomsbury, and allowed full play to a mood of recklessness. I'm damned, I thought, if I shall be the conventional literary hack, starving in squalor. If I'm to starve, let me starve in a pleasant place, and so I spent my gratuity in making myself comfortable. The windows of the rooms looked onto back gardens where some green things grew, and a splendid plane tree was opening its leaves before my eyes. In the sunset dusk there was beauty. I had my writing furniture, books and bookcases sent from Manchester. I had the rooms pleasantly decorated, hung the picture of Rose over the mantelpiece, and bought some decent Medici prints. I put down carpets and lavishly acquired a small fourposter bed from Heal's. I found my gold velvet curtains and pelmets on a lucky day at a saleroom. I loathe electric fires and gas fires, but you can have what you pay for. I paid my landlady to carry up coals and dump them in an oak chest on the landing. In the daytime I wrote with my legs wrapped in a shawl and reserved the luxury of a fire for the evenings, when I read.

It was hard going, but I survived. After that first war the newspapers were not reduced to the shivering skeletons that they became after the second. There was space, and I set out to fill it. I continued to write back-pagers for the *Manchester Guardian*. I occasionally landed a jingle on *Punch*. Short stories found a home in the magazines that then proliferated, and it was not for me to despise *Tidbits* and its like. I wrote for anything and anybody who would pay, kept body and soul together, and occasionally added a bit of luxury to my surroundings. In a suburban junkshop I picked up a Rowlandson water color for a few shillings and a fine Royal Copenhagen figure for a few pounds. But for a long time I had to go very easy indeed where a few pounds were concerned. Max and I wrote regularly to one another, and just before the fight of the Great Gable and Vishnik something happened that touched me deeply. Max wrote to say that he was "in the money," and he went on: "Don't think I've forgotten your play, Chad. I haven't, and when that goes on you, I still think, will be in the money also. But what about the meantime? Do you want a bit in advance? Don't be la-di-da and up in the air about it. If you want money say so. Could you use a hundred pounds—strictly in advance and to be knocked off royalties?"

I could indeed use a hundred pounds, but I told Max that I was in clover, a member of the Athenaeum Club and the Heythrop Hunt, with an Indian nautch girl—"and they come expensive"—as my mistress. I could laugh it off, but I never forgot that offer from Max.

The disadvantage of this sort of life is that, to survive, you must be forever occupied with trifles. There is not much time for serious work. I was tempted again and again to find some breadwinning job that would pay my rent, so that my evenings might be given to writing. But I liked free evenings: free to read, free to go out and mingle with the crowds, free to wander along the ever fascinating reaches of the river, or to visit the few friends I had. Few, indeed. Greg was the chief of them, and Greg was a busy man. He was now well in his stride to being the *éminence grise* of the Labour Party that had always been his ambition. For parliamentary work he had no liking, but by his writing and his talking he had made himself a name hated outside his party and loved within it. He could write and talk with most effective rudeness, and did. His stupendous industry made me blush. His books chased from the press one on the heels of the other, and when he pulled my leg about my odd and pointless life I could only yearn for the day when Max Middlemass would be in action, and think: "You'll see, you'll see."

The worst of making an unexpected call on Greg at Hampstead was that you never knew what you'd blunder upon. I once broke into a dinner party of Greg and Phoebe, Ramsay MacDonald and Mrs. Philip Snowden. I was scared out of my wits and refused to stay. It was useless for Greg to urge me as he saw me off. "Why don't you stay, Chad? For God's sake try and get some *savoir-faire*. Meet people. Learn to talk. It'd do you all the good in the world to listen to me briefing Ramsay Mac against the day he's Prime Minister."

I fled into the night. The very idea of the sort of political conversation that would make an H. G. Wells novel filled me with horror.

So it was a comfort when Phoebe rang me up one day in 1923 and said: "Can you come to dinner tonight, Chad?"

I asked cautiously: "Who's going to be there?"

She laughed. "Nothing to frighten you, my dear. Only the ghosts of your youth. You and I, Greg and Billy Pascoe."

I said I'd go, though I was not too happy about Billy Pascoe—Sir William. I could not think of Billy without thinking of Rose. And I could not think of Rose without thinking of the Divorce Court. I had been through it myself by now; but that Billy Pascoe should pull Rose through it! Yet what could the poor devil do? Both cases were undefended. Mine wasn't worth one line to the press: I was nobody. But Sir William Pascoe was somebody, and so was the corespondent, the wreck of the man who wrote *English Grass*. There was plenty there for the jackals. It had all been over for a year, but I didn't like the idea of meeting Billy Pascoe again. I hadn't seen him since that casual meeting in a Manchester street long ago.

6

Since coming to London I had not called on Miss Orlop, I had not seen Rose, or given them any hint of my whereabouts. I had a morbid feeling about my mediocrity. Heaven send soon the day when that play would go on! Then I'd see them. And so, a few months after Rose's divorce case had been heard, I was surprised to feel a hand laid on my shoulder and to hear a voice saying: "Well, so we had to leave the meeting to chance? I wondered how it would come about."

I was browsing in Hatchard's bookshop in Piccadilly and turned with a start to see Rose at my side. The girl with her clearly was Henrietta, Eustace's daughter. She was fourteen then—a grave self-possessed child.

I said: "Let's go and walk in the Green Park."

Henrietta said: "May I stay, Mummy? I want to have a look about. I can find my way home."

"Are you sure you'll be all right, darling?"

"Oh, yes. You needn't worry about me. But I expect I'll want some money."

Rose gave her a pound note, and we went out into the hot midsummer racket of Piccadilly. Odd, I thought: Rose, little Rose of Pentyrch, having a daughter old enough to wander alone in London! It made me, at thirty-four, feel patriarchal.

"I suppose I was bound to bump into you sooner or later," Rose said.

"How did you know I was in London?"

"How shouldn't I know? Your uncle writes reams to my mother. I sometimes see Greg and Phoebe. They know, so I know. I even know your address."

She was wearing the clothes of the time—the most hideous clothes that fool fashion ever imposed on woman. She looked adorable. We found some chairs in the Green Park and sat down.

"Why didn't you look me up?" I asked.

She laughed. "It was your business to do the looking up. But since you didn't, I understood you must have some good reason for wanting to be left undisturbed."

I told her why that was, and not only that: I suddenly told her everything. I told her about the play that I had sworn to Max to mention to nobody. I told her about my marriage and divorce, about all the shabby messes and wild hopes of my life. I felt very happy that someone shared things I hadn't shared with my mother or Uncle Arthur, with Phoebe or Greg.

She said: "It's not good for you to be so lonely, Chad."

It was very hot. Men and women were flaked out on the grass, dozing in the chairs; the sun burned down; and the rushing hum of Piccadilly filled every crack of every moment.

"How is Eustace?" I asked.

She got up. "That child!" she said. "I really shouldn't have left her alone. I must get back and see if she's still about." She almost ran away, and I knew she did not want me to follow.

It was too soon to talk of Eustace.

7

I received a letter from her the next day.

Dear Chad:

I wonder if you can guess how glad I was to see you this afternoon—how I have longed to see you ever since I knew you were in London. I am lonely, you know. My mother has her work, and though she loves me and is ready to give me all the time I ask, still, I puzzle her. There is only the love between us, not understanding. It isn't true, as so many people think, that love includes understanding. People who love one another can quarrel dreadfully, and she and I could easily make a nice little hell if I talked to her about my unlaid ghosts. Henrietta is a comfort when she's here, but that is only when she's on holiday from school. And tomorrow she's leaving me. She and her grandmother are off to Pentyrch. I am not going, because I must see Eustace every week.

Who else is there? Greg? Phoebe? I hate intruding on Greg. He's so busy and important. Phoebe comes with me each week to see Eustace, and somehow this gives us not only a link but a cause of separation. Meeting like that in abnormal conditions makes it impossible, when we meet at other times, to forget the tragedy of her brother and my husband. I cannot think of Eustace as anything else.

Well, then—there is you. Why did you leave me alone for so long? You would have left me alone for longer if I hadn't met you by chance. When we met, you used me as a vessel to pour your troubles into. I was glad to listen, if listening helped. But did you never think, all this time, how *I* might have been helped?

Of course, when I saw you in Hatchard's this afternoon, I could have stolen quietly away, left you in the private world you cherish. But I was overcome on seeing a friend, and I wonder whether you can understand that there are times when one longs for friendship more than for love? Seeing you there, I thought of what seems, fairly young though I am, the already long and painful way I have come. It's not that I want someone with whom to *talk* about all that, but you are a friend who *knows* about all that. We haven't met often, but we've met almost from the beginning, and always on the same road. We know all about each other. I now know even about your May Ingleby! I almost feel jealous of her. If you and I *had* to have loveless marriages, it would have been better if there had only been one, and we had had it together. It mightn't have been a hopeless mess. Most marriages are loveless, and those concerned usually get on without disaster if without exaltation.

However, here I am, wandering off into speculation and nonsense, while there are practical things to be done. I must see to Henrietta's packing. I hope you liked the little you saw of her. She's a darling child. She swims like a duck. She'll have plenty of that at Pentyrch. My mother is reviving the place, spending a lot of money on it. I see them off tomorrow on the Riviera Express.

Ever,

Rose

A wonderful day followed for me, and I hope it wasn't too bad for Rose. I went to Paddington station and waited till the majestic train drew out and Rose came back through the barrier.

"I thought you'd be here," she said. "I've been praying that you would. It's horrible parting with Henrietta like that. She kept on saying: 'Why aren't *you* coming, Mummy?' and that made my mother glum and silent."

We stood for a while in the jostle of the station, pushed about by young hearties with mountainous rucksacks on their backs, and by mothers, tickets nipped between their teeth, holding prams with one hand and excited children with the other; we dodged luggage barrows and people coming from the restaurant with slopping cups of tea. The tobacco kiosks, the gaudy newspaper stalls, the guards' whistles and the slow, spaced coughing of departing trains: it all added up to a heartening moment in which I stood there looking at Rose's sad face and thinking: "Well, here I am. Billy Pascoe let you down, Eustace let you down, walked out on you at Weimar, you find dear old Greg too excitingly clever, so now you turn to me: not a famous poet, not a famous scientist, not a famous economist: Chad Boothroyd, dumb cluck. Well, here I am, on any terms—friend or anything else you like."

I was enormously happy. I said: "Let's find a taxi and go to Bond Street. I know a good place there for morning coffee."

Rose said: "I'd rather walk."

So we walked. The sun shone down on the dirty streets about the station, and on the gathering respectability of the region, and at last on the splendor of the West End. We didn't talk, but everything pleased me or excited me or amused me, even the chemist's shop with the fine word CHYMYST on the fascia board. It sounded as though, inside, one could buy love potions in an aroma of dried crocodile and bats' wings. Not that I needed any potion. And when you came to think of it, ninety per cent of what these shops sold today was the modern equivalent of love potions. If there wasn't much to stimulate the male, there was plenty to make the female alluring: scents and sweat cures, paint, powder, eyeshade; eyelashes, even, like sweeping brushes; dyes for the talons of fingers and toes, tan for the skin, shine for the hair, nourishment to make breasts as firm as apples. Oh, yes, the "chymyst" was still earning his keep, and slipping in the wherewithal to pip old mother nature on the post, so that there could be wench without tears.

But, dear me, these are nice thoughts to be visiting a man on a sunny London morning! Where will such thoughts get you, Chad Boothroyd? It is not thus that one becomes a famous scientist or economist. Well, they are the sort of dithering thoughts that come to me, so let them stay, nesting in my hair like birds in a tree.

"What are you thinking about, Chad?"

I told her, and she laughed. She stopped dead still to laugh. "We're a bright lot, we women," she said. It was good to see the laughter in her blue eyes.

"There should be a law about it," I said. "If you fake merchandise you can be prosecuted. If you fake a personality you can get away with it. Sir Thomas More was an honest man."

"And what did he do except start the sorry fashion in Utopias and have his block knocked off?"

"Well, there was a suitor for one of his daughters, and Sir Thomas took him along to where the girl was sleeping naked, stripped off the bedclothes, and said, 'You'd better see what you're getting, chum,' or words to that effect."

"Go on talking nonsense to me," she said. "It's years since anyone talked nonsense to me."

"It's not nonsense. It's one of the world's most pressing problems. I attended a first night of a film last week—*world première* to you—and I found myself in the foyer cheek by jowl with a woman star. I had a maniacal wish to throw her over my shoulder, rush her to a bath, then put her through the wringer and see what came out."

"There is something wrong with your subconscious. Still, it would have been one way to achieve fame. Go on talking nonsense."

"At the moment, we're *walking* nonsense. Did you ever see such nonsense as this street? I love it. Here's our coffee shop. Let us go in, and have the privilege of paying twice over for our coffee because we drink it here."

We went in, and the quiet was carpeted in green that dumbed our steps, and the acolytes were clad in green linen, mystic, wonderful, and the rattle of a spoon on china was an insult to the holy silence. "I dare not," I whispered, "go on talking nonsense in this shrine. I might make you laugh, and then Negroes with bangles and muslin trousers would rush upon us and throw us over a bridge into the Bosphorus."

"I wonder if the sugar will dissolve *silently*, without our stirring it? Try and make me laugh."

So I told her about our Cockney lance corporal who was asked when he came back from leave what sort of time he had had. He said: "I spent every day in St. Paul's, praying for strength to get through the night. I've come back an atheist."

"I don't believe it. It's too elliptical for a Cockney lance corporal."

"Well, that's how I've put it in my play. I couldn't use his more than Chaucerian idiom."

"You must read your play to me."

"When?"

"Tonight, if you like."

"Why should we spoil a perfect day?"

"Now you *are* talking nonsense. You're dying to read it to me."

"Yes. But I'm a good man and I try to say good things."

"It wasn't so good as all that. And what do you mean—a perfect day? The day's hardly started. It's half-past eleven. The Riviera Express will be just passing through Reading."

"Are you always thinking about Henrietta?"

"More or less. I shan't be happy till I read tomorrow's paper and find that the Riviera Express is not reported to be wrecked."

"It must be wonderful to have someone thinking about you like that."

"I suppose so. But I'm not sure it's good for the thinker. I've done too much of it in my time."

The shadow was coming over her face again. I didn't want that. I paid the bill and whisked her out into Bond Street. We loafed along, window-shopping as far as the Piccadilly end, crossing the road from time to time. We bought, in this inexpensive way, an enormous ham, a hat for her and a pair of riding boots for me, handfuls of Jensen silver, a tiara from Asprey's, a superb Princess and the Pea in Copenhagen porcelain, and a nice Boudin of children on the seashore. "That'll do for today," I said. "I don't like spending more than five thousand pounds in a morning, and, with the coffee, it's a bit over that today."

"But we're being very selfish," Rose protested. "We've spent it all on ourselves. What about your uncle?"

So we bought Uncle Arthur a box of beautiful quarto parchment paper, a dozen quill pens, and a case of sealing wax in alluring colors: gold and lime green, primrose yellow, cerise and magenta. And this time I *did* buy it, and as I gave my uncle's address and paid the bill it passed through my mind that this was the first time in my life that I had spent a penny on him in return for all that he had done for me. It was a shaming thought, especially as the gift sprang from nothing but the bravado excited by Rose's presence.

"We'd better curb this expensive conduct now, and do something cheap," I said. "What about the Green Park? That is handy for the Ritz. Have you ever drunk a cocktail there?"

"No."

"Then you shall drink one with me, and after that we'll have lunch there, and you'll hear pages singing out, 'Mr. Chad Boothroyd, Mr. Chad Boothroyd,' and I'll hurry to the telephone and tell my brokers that they'd better sell one or two of my railways. Then, if you see me looking furtively into my wallet, you'll know I'm calculating whether I can pay for the lunch."

We turned into the park.

"Poor Chad! Are you so very hard up?"

" 'In dreams a king, but, waking, no such matter.' However, tell me about your taste in wine. What shall we drink with our lunch?"

"It will depend on what we eat."

"Yes. But talk to me about wine. I love to hear people talk about wine. To me, it's something I drink. Some I like, some I don't like so much. But to them it's a *mystique*. They sniff it, and turn it on their tongues, and look immensely wise, and wonder if this has passed its prime, if that shouldn't have been kept till next Tuesday week, was '35 as good as '39, and do you remember the really great year of St. Estephe?"

"Well, I suppose it's a *thing* like any other—like being a great expert on samplers or china dogs. What are you going to do with me after lunch?"

"Are you so utterly in my hands?"

She gave me a sidelong glance. "Well, within reason."

"Ah, reason! Limiting and frustrating reason! Then I shall take you to Westminster, and we'll go on the river."

"What a one you are for water transport! One of my first memories of you is that you made me violently sick in a dinghy."

"Nonsense. You made yourself sick. You said, 'I am going to be sick,' and you were sick."

"And you took me on the river at Oxford."

"I shall never forget it. I gave you honey for tea."

"And now again—the river. Well, I shall love it. I've never been on our river."

"Neither have I. So it will be a day Old Thames will have reason to remember."

"Yes. But let us have our cocktail. I'm tired of walking."

I didn't sell any railways during lunch, but I was as happy as if I'd sold the G.W.R. for twice what I'd given for it. I spent as much as my food would cost me for a week, and there's dinner to come yet, I told myself, if I know anything. I'd be broke tomorrow, and I'd get an advance from an editor I knew, and, altogether, this was the life!

We went as far as the Nore, and the sun-burnished gray water was Cornish blue to me, and had the heaving chunks of flotsam that we pushed aside turned to dolphins, each one a mount for an Arion, I should not have been much surprised.

It was a wonderful afternoon, but when we were back at Westminster landing stage and I said: "Now, what shall we do till dinnertime?" she said: "Oh, no, Chad. I really am tired and I must rest."

I must have looked down in the mouth, for she said, laying a hand on my arm: "I promised to hear your play. Shall I do that? Shall I call on you, or would you like to bring the play to my mother's house?"

"No. Come to me—will you. You've never seen my rooms."

"I'd love to see them. I have the address. Half-past eight."

She left me at once, sped across the road, and got into a taxi before I could follow. She seemed suddenly distraught, anxious to fly, and I stood there watching her speaking urgently to the driver, and at him nodding as urgently. He leapt to his seat and shot away full tilt. Thank you, I thought bitterly. That saves the cost of two expensive dinners. I needn't call on my editor for an advance. I can just live through till a check comes along. I took a taxi to my rooms and slept for an hour, suddenly as tired as she said she was, and deflated. Never before had I spent so long a time alone with her. Is every day with you, Rose, to end in this sense of deflation?

The room was evening-dusky when she came, and I turned on the lamps and drew the curtains across the window. I thought the place looked charming in its sparse way, and Rose did, too, or said she did. But she sounded merely polite, and her eyes had a desperate look. She sat in an easy chair and said: "Now, Chad."

"Are you all right? Would you like something to drink? I have some sherry."

"No, thank you. Let's hear the play."

Rather wearily—wearily both because of this unsatisfying end to the day and because I was, by now, sick of this years-old play and had no belief in it—I began to read, not looking at her; and I was halfway through the first act, at a passage of what I hoped was humorous relief, when she began to cry. I dropped the typescript and went over to her and fell on my knees before her chair, and the crying increased till it shook her like a storm. I had never seen a woman weep like that, as though she would be torn to pieces if something couldn't stop it; and I could think of nothing to do but take her hands and say: "Rose! Rose, my darling. What is it? What can I do for you?"

She tore away from me and went into the bedroom. I did not follow. I pulled the curtain away from the window and stood looking out over the now heat-crinkled leaves of the plane tree and over the slates and chimney pots to the quivering sky above the West End, and I listened to the crying. At last I heard the sound of water running in the bedroom and knew that she was soothing her burnt eyes. No need to tell me what had happened. When she came out, pale but in charge of herself once more, I asked: "Eustace?"

She nodded, and said: "Could you make me some tea?"

I laid the tea before her and put a match to the fire. Hot though the day had been, she looked as though during her weeping she had been among ice. Even now, when she was firmly taking herself in hand, shudders rippled through her body. As the sticks began to crackle she stretched her hands to the warmth and said: "Thank you, my dear."

"Would it help you," I asked, "if you told me about things? Would you like to tell me where you went to when we landed at Westminster? I couldn't help seeing that you made your mind up suddenly about something."

"I went to see Eustace."

"Where is he?"

She told me the name of the orthopedic hospital. "A wonderful place for the doctors," she said bitterly. "The things they must learn! They've got all the last deplorable wrecks there, the final bits and pieces, all the Humpty Dumpties that they'll never put together again, try as they will."

She trembled, but I did not touch her or speak. Let her go on now she's started, I thought. If she keeps this poison to herself it will be the end of her at last.

"You should see them, staggering about with their new legs flying out at all angles, trying to work their machine-made fingers, trying to smile as though it's all a marvelous joke. That's the hell of it, seeing them smile. And seeing them *not* smile when they think no one is looking at them."

I refilled her teacup and slipped a drop of brandy into it. "Do you smoke?" I still didn't know these small things about her.

"No. I have no vices, except Eustace."

"Why do you go there, torturing yourself?"

"You ask that, knowing nothing. If you saw the place! I'm glad you haven't seen it."

I said: "The greatest line, the most terrible line, that came out of the war is in three words by Wilfred Owen: 'Death's extreme decrepitude.' I have seen that."

"Oh, death! Death is nothing."

"Is it?"

She hadn't been looking at me. She had been looking at the fire, her cold hands still outstretched. On that question, she looked at me, as though seeing me anew, and she cried: "Oh, Chad, I know, my dear. I know what you have suffered. It's terrible how all one's love and all one's hate can concentrate and exclude the rest of the world. All I've been doing today is using you. I feel ashamed."

"Go on using me. I won't interrupt any more. Tell me anything that you want to."

She had said that she wasn't going to Cornwall with her mother because she must see Eustace every week. But this was becoming more and more difficult. For a long time Eustace had welcomed her visits—at first almost hysterically; but for the last month or two a change had come over him. He would fall silent and look at her askance. "Sometimes he looked as though he hated me." He began to say things that disturbed her. "Do you think you ought to be wasting your time on me?" "I shall never walk, you know. I don't want their bloody clever legs. They've made a mess of me, and they can put up with the mess." And one day he said, quite reasonably: "You do me no good coming here. It distresses me. You look so appallingly alive." The week before this night when she sat in my room the dam finally burst. She had in the beginning seen him legless. She had seen him swaying about on artificial legs, and now he was legless again. A doctor told her, before

299

she saw Eustace, that he was being troublesome. He had announced that he would never wear the bloody legs again. "I wonder," the doctor asked, "if your visits disturb him too much?"

She had been staggered. "What! Eustace disturbed by me! He loves me as he loves nothing else on earth."

The doctor said: "Perhaps that's the root of his trouble." He was a young doctor, terribly nervous and diffident. "You see," he said, "the thought of what has been, and what can never be again, may be what is pulling him to pieces."

"What did he mean by that?" I asked.

She told me. I had not known till then. I had thought he had only lost his legs. I was appalled, and speechless.

"Well," she said. "I told him I wanted to see Eustace all the same."

And Eustace told her to clear out. They took her to him in a garden, with a path going round a circular lawn. He was in a carriage that he propelled with his hands, but it was not moving when she arrived. Eustace just sat there, his head on his chest. As soon as he saw her coming with the doctor across the lawn he started up the machine, whizzing it along as fast as he could make it go, and shouting: "Get out! Get out! Leave me alone."

The young doctor laid a hand on her arm. "You see. Hadn't we better leave him?"

But she broke away, crying "No! Oh, no! Eustace!" And she ran at a tangent across the lawn to cut him off. He stopped and glowered at her. "Will you get out?" he said. "I don't want you. Not now. Not ever. Will you *get out*?"

His voice was rising madly. The doctor took her away, gave her a sedative, and put her into a taxicab.

"Did you tell your mother?"

"No. Nobody knows about it. Not even Phoebe. She wasn't able to go that day."

"Why didn't you go down into Cornwall with the others?"

"Because I wanted to see Eustace. And then, there you were, at Paddington, and I used you all day. I thought: Give it a miss for this one week, and go next week. Perhaps by then he'll have settled down again. I couldn't have done it without you. I wanted you to occupy me all day. And then, when we got back to Westminster, I couldn't do it after all. There was still time if I hurried."

"And what happened?"

"They wouldn't let me see him." She added with a finality of bitterness. "They pointed out that I wasn't even a relative. And, of course, I'm not."

The fire had died down. The teapot was cold. The typescript lay scattered on the carpet where it had fallen when I got up, hearing her weep.

"I shall go down to Cornwall tomorrow," she said.

"I was looking forward to seeing something of you—at last."

"No, no, my dear, don't bother about me."

"I agree it would be better for you to go to Cornwall."

We went down and found a taxi, and I got in with her and saw her safely home. She sat with her arm through mine, and on her doorstep she said: "You look so woebegone. Please don't bother about me."

She gave me a swift kiss and ran in.

8

I went to Paddington the next morning, and did all the things: put up her suitcase, bought the sort of papers I hoped she'd like, reserved a seat in the dining car, talked cheerfully till the whistle blew and the green flag was waved. Nothing was said about yesterday except a joking exchange. She was hatless, and I said: "I love that hat. I knew it was *you* as soon as we saw it in Bond Street."

She said: "Yes. And those riding boots are wonderful. But is this the time and place for them?"

And we said nothing about tomorrow. It was an uneasy moment, which we thankfully allowed our small inanities to fill. It was unbearable. I was almost glad when she was gone and I could go out into the cruelly perfect day where my heart could be miserable alone.

I hoped she would write to me. I was always hoping she would write to me. She didn't. It was a wretched time from which Max Middlemass helped to deliver me. As I was turning in at the front door of my house an open two-seater car pulled up, and Max shouted: "Hop in, Chad." He looked as darkly ugly as ever, and prosperous in a tussore silk suit, Panama hat, and generously tumbling dark blue bow tie.

"Hop in, indeed!" I said, my heart rejoicing to see him. "You pluto-crats forget that a man has to earn a living."

"You'll never want for a living so long as you know me. You should learn your place. Join the queue. Scores of 'em, all waiting to say, 'Yes, Mr. Middlemass.'"

I said: "Yes, Mr. Middlemass," and got in.

It was a new car, full of glittering gadgets. Max's hand, plentifully adorned with monkey fur, lay lightly on the ivory wheel. "How does it feel to be rich, Max?"

"You'll know."

He pressed a button, and a honey-throated gurgle of music announced that we were off.

"Where are we going to?"

"Oh, anywhere. Far from the madding, etc."

"How's Bessie?"

"Up to the eyes making Cumberland rum butter. I ask her: 'Why can't I buy the damn stuff? We're rich, aren't we?' 'All right,' she says. 'Fair do's. You be rich, and let me make rum butter.' There's a pound of it for you somewhere in the dickey, wrapped up in cabbage."

We went out along the Great West Road, and somewhere near Maidenhead Max turned in between two lodges on to a tree-shaded drive. We came to an old gray mansion, a lawn, and beyond the lawn the Thames sliding between willows. It could have been beautiful and peaceful, and was not bad even with the bedizenments that broke it to pieces. The lawn was littered with deck chairs in flaming colors, inflated mattresses, little colored tables with striped umbrellas over them. Gay electric light bulbs threaded among the branches of trees and festooned the front of the house. A few girls and youths in sun-bathing suits were drinking cocktails. I could not but notice how they all eyed Max hungrily.

He shouted: "Roddy! Find Bill for me, will you?"

"Yes, Mr. Middlemass."

"You see," said Max. " 'Yes, Mr. Middlemass.' They're all pros and all resting."

It was a riverside club, used mostly by theatrical people.

"Won't you join us, Mr. Middlemass?"

"No, thank you, Effie."

We sat at a small table near the water, and Bill came to take our orders. "When I was a kid," Max said, "that man was one of the best pantomime dames you could set eyes on. Look at him now." Bill, in his white linen jacket, was shuffling back to the house on broken arches. "He made pots in his time. The B.F.'s *won't* save. Look at those kids. They can't afford to belong to a place like this, but they *will* do it. Think all they have to do is lie around showing all they've got and have a cheerio with someone like me. B.F.'s. I could find better-looking meat in Smithfield."

We drank sidecars and watched the swans sail by, and I thought: I suppose the Riviera Express is going through Somerset. She'll be looking at Athelney and Glastonbury Tor. The waiters will be shouting: "Take your places for the second lunch." That's the one I'd ordered.

"Well, there's one good thing about it," Max was saying, "the place is going bust hand over fist. Never caught on with the right people. Too many of these small-time bits and pieces who are behind with their subscriptions. It keeps the others out. Well, roll on the Official Receiver. I intend to buy it up. Nice and quiet for Bessie when all this muck is swept up. Effie! Tell Bill we'd like the same again."

"Yes, Mr. Middlemass."

Three girls leapt up, but Effie won.

Max looked pleased. "You see?"

Effie herself brought the drinks. "Anything else I can do for you, Mr. Middlemass?"

"Thank you, my dear. No. There's nothing else."

"You know, Chad, for a languishing female, I could get more out of the old sergeant major than out of that one. Remember?"

I remembered; and inevitably we talked of old days, till Mac said: "Let's see what's to eat."

He wasn't pleased with it when he got it. "Ah, well, Chad. The worse the better, so far as I'm concerned. It's that much nearer to the sell-up." He amused himself by furnishing the room as it would be when it was his. Let him go on, I thought. He'll come to it in time. I can't imagine he's spending one of his busy days on showing me this just for the fun of it.

"Now, let's get into a punt, Chad. That is, if you'll do the work. And keep an eye on those girls. You'll see things."

The ladies had changed into bathing suits and sat on the landing stage, dabbling their toes with shrill screams as we embarked. Effie went so far as to get wet. She swam alongside us with a creditable trudgeon stroke. "That's very bad for you," Max warned her. "You shouldn't go into the water so soon after a meal. You'll be having a really serious illness just when someone wants you for a big part."

However, I soon left Effie behind. The river was peaceful without its week-end crush, and Max settled himself on cushions with a cigar pointing like an aimed rocket at the sky, one black-strapped white shoe cocked over a knee. Dapper is the only word for him. "Max," I asked, "where did you get those beautiful clothes from that you wore when you came over to Smurthwaite from Bradford? Remember? The coat with four capes and all the rest of it?"

"They belonged to my old man. He once played a highwayman, and I suppose he thought that was how a highwayman looked, God help him. Anyway, I was glad of 'em. They were all I had." He didn't say it, but I could hear it: And look at me now.

He took a wad of dirty creased paper out of a pocket and smoothed one or two sheets. "Funny what a lot of muck follows you about in your journey through life," he said sententiously. "Guess what this is."

I gave it up. "It's that sketch you wrote for our pantomime in France."

"*You* wrote, you mean. You tore my stuff to bits and wrote it yourself, Max."

"But the ideas were yours, Chad, and they were damned funny.

Give me more ideas like this, and I'd be thankful. Anyway, you've done things since then. Maybe no one would have to tear you up."

"What are you getting at?"

"My next revue. I could do with some sketches. Three of 'em. Not more than ten minutes each. Have a go at it."

It sounded dazzling. A Max Middlemass revue was not just a revue like any other. It was the king of all birthday cakes against bread pudding. Music, lighting, dancing, fabrics: I had seen it all and been stunned by his insistence on perfection. I recalled how I had been present at one of his first nights, and had gone behind afterward to tell him there was no flaw in it, and had found him raving mad with everybody. It seemed that the show was flawed from end to end, though I hadn't known it. His leading lady was in tears, and so was he, for that matter, and a famous comic actor, tight-lipped and white, was saying: "Well, what the hell, Mr. Middlemass! We're only human beings. We're not God Almighty's archangels."

"What have the bloody archangels got to do with it?" Max shouted. "It's news to me if they're employed to make people laugh. They're trumpeters, boy, celestial trumpeters. That's all. It's easy."

I didn't talk to Max that night. I stole out and left them to it.

"It's all very well, Max," I said, "and thank you for thinking of me. But aren't you picking the wrong man?"

At that he sat up and glared at me, and I wondered for a moment if an explosion was coming. He relaxed and lay back again. "I came out," he said, "to have a few hours' peace, and I won't let you taunt me into not having them. But don't say that again, Chad. Let me tell you two things. One: I don't choose the wrong men or the wrong women. I can buy anything that's going, and I only buy the best. Two: you were the only officer who ever treated Sergeant Middlemass as a human being. Mind you, a good many of 'em were all right. I'm not complaining. But there was just the something extra about you. And it's always the something extra that gets me. See?"

"All right, Max. You can put a sock in all that. I'll have a go at it for you. When are you going to put on that play of mine?"

He thought for a moment, then said: "This is June, 1923. I had thought of November, 1924. But, all things considered, I should say November, 1925."

"Good God, Max! D'you want the author brought on for his curtain with his beard entangled in the wheels of his bathchair?"

"If you get a curtain," he said placidly. "Leave it to the Old Man."

He said no more of that, and we doodled about for the rest of the afternoon among the swans and the wild roses and the fields of sorrel and dog daisies. It was while we were having tea in a cottage that he said: "If I find anybody in my theater who isn't connected with the show, I kick him out. I won't have unattached odds and sods loafing round. If you're going to make the theater your business, you'd better learn something *about* the theater. Writing plays is all very well, but there's a hell of a sight more to it than that. So now you'll have a standing, and you can come and keep your eyes open."

"When I was at Oxford I did a lot with the O.U.D.S."

"That's a good line," he said. "Use it some time. But don't make me laugh."

9

Max was trying to put a bit of bread and butter in my way; but he did more than that. He helped me over the hellish weeks that followed my seeing Rose off to Cornwall. A temptation was on me to throw up everything and go down there myself; for, if she felt anything of what I was feeling, she must be in desperate need. I had known that things were bad, but I had imagined that there was at least the consolation of Eustace's misfortune having drawn the two of them closer together. To discover how appalling the misfortune was, and to know that so far from drawing them together it might drive them forever apart: this left me baffled and distraught. Rose was in need, but I doubted whether she needed me. And what finally made me decide to stay out of Cornwall was that such contacts as I had had with her always came about of themselves. She had never invited me; I had never pursued her. Leave it alone, I thought. See what happens. Rose was like one of those problems that make the mind at night a hell of unsolved conflict and perplexity. You go to bed and sleep, and in the morning the answer is there, smiling on the pillow.

So I comforted myself, and filled my days with work, till Phoebe rang up to ask me to dine with Billy Pascoe. I said I would, though my reluctance was as intense as it was unfair. Half of me said: To hell with Billy Pascoe. He had been handed a treasure, and had not known how to keep it. If he had been half a man, Rose would have been with him still, and there would have been no problem at all. And the rest of me said: Poor devil! What a hopeless job with Eustace on the loose!

Well, we had the dinner, but what I most remember is Billy's call on me in the afternoon. Usually, I did not work in the afternoon, but I was seized that day with an idea for the last of the three sketches I was to do for Max. I ate some sandwiches and drank a glass of beer at a pub near my room and then returned, full of virtuous feeling. I went through the odd preliminary stages without which I cannot write at all. I filled and lit a pipe and walked up and down the room. Not knowing I was doing it, I put a picture straight that was probably straight before, pushed a book an inch back in the bookcase and pulled another an inch forward. At some time or other I was sitting down, putting the tobacco jar a bit to the left, the ashtray a bit to the right, shaking down the sheets of quarto paper till not one overlapped another by a millimeter. So the little game went, and I would soon have started to write when my doorbell buzzed. Annoyed, I got up to see who it was. It was Billy Pascoe.

"Hello, Billy! Come in," I said.

He came in, and was quick in the uptake. The curtain was drawn across my window, for looking out of a window kills for me the private world within. The lamp was burning on my writing table.

"This is too bad," Billy said. "I've interrupted your work. Greg said you didn't work in the afternoons."

"I don't as a rule, and this can wait."

I let in the light and switched off the table lamp.

"I came up to town early," he said. "I had a call or two to make this morning. And then Greg gave me lunch. We meet at his place tonight, I understand."

"Yes."

"I was at a loose end. He suggested I should drop in. You don't mind?"

"Good lord, no."

I wondered: What has he come for? I said: "You're looking well, Billy."

He looked anything but the popular idea of the absent-minded professor. He was dressed with unobtrusive care: gray suit, white collar, dark blue tie. He was lithe and dark, and he looked ten years older than I was. We were about the same age.

It was no good trying to hide it: there was a constraint between us. I decided to butt right at it. "Well, it's good to see you again, Billy, after all this time. What a long time it is! D'you remember? I ran into you in Manchester. You were bloody rude to me."

"I'm surprised to hear that, Chad, and I'm sorry. What did I do?"

"You were walking near Platt Fields, and you turned in to meditate upon profundities. You hardly bothered to give me a good-night."

"I don't remember that," he said. "I remember meeting you, but I don't remember being rude. I really am sorry. It was a difficult time for me. I was in Manchester to see Rutherford. I had a ticklish problem on my mind. I found I was right, but I expect I was worrying about it that night. And then there was Rose."

I wanted to get up, to say: "Look, let's keep Rose out of this. I won't discuss Rose with you," but there was something about Billy that stopped the words on my lips. I saw, with a sudden clear insight, that I had been building up a Billy who didn't exist, a fantasy, a scapegoat for my own hurt at never having had Rose myself. This Billy, sitting here now, with the sketch of Rose looking down at him from over the fireplace, was speaking to me sincerely.

"Chad," he said, "it was Greg's idea that I should come and have a talk to you. He thinks we've rather drifted apart. Well, so we have. There's not much anyone can do about a thing like that. But I don't see why Greg should think we need to pour out oil, so that he won't have a couple of Kilkenny cats spitting across the table tonight."

"Billy," I said, "have I any right, do you think, to ask you to give me your confidence?"

"No. I don't think anyone has a right to ask another person for his confidence. Whether I choose to give it to you is another matter."

"All right then. Put it that way. You've known me pushing the pram to the well at Pendeverel. I've known you cleaning the shoes and knives at Pentyrch. I thought it might still mean something."

"I am not the boy who cleaned the knives. I am what that boy became. You are what you became. You can't go back and back like that unless there are links of the chain all the way through. There aren't, Chad. That's the pity, so far as we go."

"Oh, damn it all, Sir William," I said, "you are Billy Pascoe to me, and always will be; and if I'm not Chad Boothroyd to you then, as you say, that's a pity. I'm not going to chop logic with you. Why did you marry Rose?"

That's what I had always wanted to know. It was out, and now he could make what he liked of it. "As for links in the chain, Billy, I was your best man."

"I didn't ask you to be," he said.

"No."

"Who did?"

"Miss Orlop. If I remember, you passed on her message."

When I had said that, Billy gave me such a look that I felt everything had been answered.

Billy said nothing for a time, and then he said an astonishing thing. "I hardly knew I *was* getting married. There was so much else to be thinking about at that time that it was no more than putting a clean handkerchief into one's pocket. Just a routine action that you do without noticing."

This was fantastic. "You don't casually put a girl into your pocket twice a day."

He frowned as if he were trying to clear up something that baffled him. "For years, I knew that Miss Orlop wanted me to marry Rose, and let's be frank about it: I was flattered. Even in the last few years things have changed enormously, socially. But think of Pendeverel as it was when we were growing up there. Damn it, Chad, the place was feudal, every stick and stone owned by the Orlops, as it had been for centuries. I remember your father. He was an odd type and a stranger to the region. I expect, what with him and one thing and another, the impact of Pentyrch and the Orlops wasn't so strong on you. But most people, including my own, had lived there for generations. The Orlops were Lord God Almighty, with all his angels and archangels thrown in. Already, I can begin to laugh at such a notion being held about a family of disintegrating backwoods squires of less than average intelligence. But the feeling was almost as strong as ever when I was a boy, and I tell you I was flattered when Miss Orlop began to take notice of me."

"I should have been surprised, Billy, if it hadn't been like that."

"I was just beginning to get worked up about things. I already had a few ideas buzzing in my head. You remember I used to spout about them to you on the beach—just before you went away to Yorkshire. I came into the Town to see you off. You said you'd write to me, and you never sent your address. I had my letters ready. I wrote a long one every week, and after a time I tore them up."

And he wanted me to believe he was not the boy of Pendeverel! The little Billy was in his eyes and his voice.

I said: "I'm sorry about that, Billy. Everything was so strange. I was dumped suddenly into an exciting new sort of life."

"So was I," he said. "It was very sudden. Just when we were getting to know one another. Some odd notions jumped together, and I knew I wasn't like the other boys."

"I knew that."

"Yes," he harped on it, "and you left me with no one. D'you remember that lot? Opie and Sara and Jose Johns and Trewince? No good to me."

He looked for a moment at his beautifully polished shoes. "Well," he said, "that's where Miss Orlop came in."

It sounded like a play. "Pascoe, polishing the knives, looks up. Enter Miss Orlop L. He gets to his feet."

She said: "What's that you're reading, Billy?" and he showed her the book, standing there in the kitchen in his green baize apron.

"I've forgotten what the book was," he said, "some elementary mathematical stuff, and she asked, 'Do you understand this?' and I said, 'Oh, yes.' She said, 'I should have thought it was beyond you,' and I said, 'Oh, no.' That's how it began. I was grateful, as well as flattered. There was no one else. My mother drowned herself. The boys were oafs. You were not writing."

Is this, I wondered, how our omissions as well as our deeds, write our horoscopes?

"Writing! Damn it, Billy, I was only a kid."

"So was I. A lonely one."

His loneliness became enfolded by Miss Orlop. It worked well enough for a time, but as his mind matured resentment now and then peeped out. I had seen that for myself at Oxford.

"I was always asking myself," he said, "whether I could have done it without her. I think I could. But it would have been hard, and whether I could have done it without her or not, the fact remains that I did it with her. She threw in all the extras that I couldn't have got for myself—foreign travel and all that. Out of term, she and Rose and I were always pottering about the Continent."

"Yes—Rose. I asked you: Why did you marry Rose?"

"Because Miss Orlop wanted me to," he said. "I didn't see it so simply as that, but that's what it comes to, I suppose. When a wish broods over your life for years, the dearest wish of someone to whom you owe a lot—well, it conditions your reflexes."

"I should have thought her elopement with Eustace Hawke would have done some conditioning, too."

"It was all a side line," he said, surprisingly. "In my heart, I didn't want to marry anyone. So what did it matter whether she'd run off with him or not? I was bitterly hurt when it happened, but that was years before we married."

I couldn't believe this. I looked at the picture of Rose, and it was impossible for me to imagine that anyone could take marriage with her in that casual way. He must have understood what I was thinking, for he said: "They say, 'What you've never had you never miss,' and as usual they are wrong. I should say it works rather the other way about. I remember that picture of Rose in your room at Smurthwaite. I remember it at Oxford. And now here it is. And every year Rose is getting less and less like the picture. But that doesn't matter. When you look at it, you think 'Rose,' you think of something you've wanted for years, and because you've never had it you miss it terribly. I had her for years as a companion, for some years as a wife. I don't miss her at all."

"If Rose married me," I said, "and something parted us, I'd miss her and she'd miss me. There can have been nothing between you." I knew this because there had been nothing between me and May Ingleby. I didn't miss May.

"No," he said, "nothing, I'm afraid." And then he added surprisingly: "Have you ever considered the marriage of Charles Dickens?"

"I didn't know fiction was in your line, Billy."

"It's not. But biography is. And I'm using this to try and show you what happened between me and Rose."

"Go on, then."

"Well. You know, Chad, everything that happens to a great man is a consequence of something that happens *once,* and once only. The rest is just a follow-up. This very sensitive and observant boy and young man discovered with extraordinary suddenness that he could put it all into fiction. One moment, there he is hacking away as an overworked reporter. The very next, he has a book published, he's working simultaneously on two more and has signed a contract for another. Can you imagine the boiling of his mind? Do you think anything *really* mattered to him except that? Read the letters he was writing to his girl at that time. They amount to little more than 'Keep off. I'm up to the eyes, and this comes first.' Still, he was engaged to marry the girl, and so he married her, more or less to have the thing out of the way of what he wanted to do."

"Everyone knows he should have married her sister."

"*He* didn't know it. If he'd married the sister, it's she who would have had the babies and become the obstructive feature about the house."

"Well, where do we go on to from that?"

Billy thought for a time, then he said: "I, too, had been a fairly observant boy and youth, but I wasn't observing Dickens's things—if observing is the word—I think it's too self-conscious—'soaking in' is perhaps better—you hardly know the thing's happened to you—but all of a sudden you know that it has. You've *got it.*"

He paused, looking confused. "Do you know what I'm talking about? If not, it's no good going on."

"Yes, Billy. It's happened to me—not tremendously, but enough to tell me what you're trying to say."

"Well, that summer Miss Orlop hauled me and Rose and Henrietta off to Pentyrch. I had been working hard and was badly in need of a rest. I was alone a good deal. I used to wander about on the sand and in the woods, and one day when I was sitting on a rock throwing pebbles into the sea, everything I'd ever thought, and worked at, and guessed, all through my life suddenly rushed together into one point, so simple that I wrote it down there and then in a few words and equations on half a sheet of paper, but so stupendous that nothing else will matter as long as I live. That was my one moment. Everything else will go on from there."

This was beyond my imagination. I just had to accept it. I said nothing.

"Well," Billy went on, "there was, of course, normal life going on round me. We met at meals, we talked, Rose and the child and I bathed together and played on the sands. I was doing my best to make things happy for Rose. Remember, I knew her as you never did. We had been friends for years, going everywhere together, and neither she nor I had any doubt that nothing would have pleased Miss Orlop better than to see us married. We liked one another well enough on a certain level. But with me there was my work, and with her there was, all of a sudden, Eustace Hawke."

I thought of what Rose had told me about Eustace. I thought of Rose, now, at this moment when we were sitting here, weeping at Pentyrch for what life had done to Eustace and Eustace had done to her.

"I was terribly upset by that elopement," Billy said. "There was never any engagement between me and Rose, but she had become something I was accustomed to, we were easy together, and when I found that he had not married her, and later that she had a child, and then that he had deserted her, I was torn to bits with pity. Since this is an inquest, Chad, put that in as evidence."

I was beginning to understand Billy better and to like him more.

His pity did not abate when Rose and the child came home and they all went down to Pentyrch. I had often wondered about Rose's part in the affair; but it became clearer as Billy told me of how Miss Orlop's anger had changed to a brooding melancholy, a disapproval that could not help welling over in look and gesture and occasional speech. Billy's pity, expressing itself in an unusual attention to her and Henrietta, would have been, at that moment, something for Rose to overprize, something that looked as though it might be counted on for always. At worst, it was an escape from a situation that was becoming intolerable.

"One hot night after dinner," Billy said, "when Henrietta was in bed, we three strolled down to the sea. We were standing on that little headland where the studio is, and Miss Orlop suddenly said in that gruff way she has: 'I've been thinking it would be an excellent thing if you two married.'"

"She was never one for beating about the bush."

"No. I was not surprised when she said that, and I'm sure Rose wasn't, either. The idea was so familiar to us that, once Miss Orlop had spoken, nothing more was said that night."

Billy didn't often smile, but he smiled then. "D'you know what settled it?" he asked. "A row I had with Miss Orlop! The only row I ever had with the old dear. Oh, I was annoyed with her often enough. The sense she radiated at times that here was this little bit of nothing that she'd nursed into the up-and-coming William Pascoe—it used to make me hopping mad. But there was just that grain of truth in it that kept me from shouting at her. However, that morning she went over the limit. She was going into the Town to do some shopping, and I said I'd go with her. There were a few things I wanted to buy. A gardener drove us in and we separated, she to her shops, I to mine. She said: 'Let's meet in the church.' You know the church. It always fascinated me, and that morning it was especially sentimental: dim light falling through the stained glass, someone practicing on the organ—all that sort of thing. I wandered into the Orlop chapel, and there they were, all lying round about under tombs and plaques."

"It was like that in Smurthwaite, Billy, where the Newtes are buried. Greg called it the Glorious Company of Marmoreal Newtes."

He smiled again. "Yes. That's just how it was: the Glorious Company of Marmoreal Orlops; and to read what was said of them you'd think that every man Jack had been born of the Holy Ghost and had lived without a sin to his record. I knew better. The Orlops produced some pretty tough boys, and some slippery ones. I was sitting down, giving my thoughts a free rein about them, when Miss Orlop came in and sat at my side. 'That one,' she said, pointing, *"Matthew Orlop, Captain, R.N., best of husbands, most provident of fathers, good neighbor and loving friend,"* wasn't an Orlop at all. He was Matthew Frome. The Orlop of that time had no son, and it's a thing with the Orlops that, in that case, whoever marries the eldest girl takes the family name and inherits the estate. It's happened several times.' She added, trying to make it as light as possible: 'How would you like being an Orlop, Billy?'"

It was my turn to smile now. I remembered the Billy Pascoe of boyhood, almost insanely proud on the beach when he had scarcely a backside to his pants, and I could imagine what Miss Orlop's words would do to him. Even now, telling me about it, he looked outraged.

"What did you say, Billy?"

He looked at the toes of his shoes. "I hardly like to tell you. I feel rather ashamed of it."

"Go on."

"I said, 'Bugger the Orlops. If Rose marries me, she'll marry William Pascoe.'"

"Bravo!" I was liking Billy more than ever.

He looked apologetic. "D'you think I should have said it? Sometimes I wish I hadn't. But it was the sum of all those feelings in her that had worried me for years. 'Look what I've created. And now, as a crown, I make it an Orlop.' No, Chad, I couldn't stand for that."

Miss Orlop was stunned. The light was still shining through the stained glass. The organist was still rumbling his subdued notes into the air; but Billy's fearful words were all she seemed to hear, and presently she got up and left him sitting there. After a moment or two he followed and found her wandering forlornly in the churchyard. He said: "If I said that too grossly, I apologize. What I mean to say is, it's important to me to be *one person*, just myself, not one of a line, especially a bogus one, grafted on. I'd rather be an ancestor than a posterior—if that's the right word."

She smiled, and he knew he had won. "It's not the right word, Billy," she said, "but I must say it sounds apt. You mean you'd rather be a beginning than an *end*."

In this odd way Miss Orlop arrived at the point that she had tenaciously headed for through so many years.

"The thing was becoming a nuisance," Billy said. "I thought I might as well have it settled and done with. It seemed to me that there might even be some advantages in it. I'd have a place where I could go and be quiet, for one thing." He looked at me inquiringly. "I suppose there are plenty of marriages like that, aren't there, Chad? They're not all, are they, the consequence of what's called falling in love? Frankly, I know nothing about that. I've never had that feeling about anybody, and I don't think I ever shall."

"I imagine, Billy, that it's present at the beginning in most marriages and that it lasts throughout life with about one couple in a hundred. With about twenty-five per cent of the rest something remains durable and valuable enough to make it worth while to hold the thing together. Twenty-five per cent of the others break it up. Those who are left endure to the end."

"Thank you," he said, as though I had given him some important information instead of a rough and rather cynical summary. "I don't know about these matters."

"Tell me, Billy, what was Rose's reaction to all this?"

"Honestly, Chad, I don't know. You mustn't forget what I told you just now. This was the moment when all I shall ever know was made clear. Believe me, I wasn't thinking much about Rose."

This seemed to me incredible, and I said so.

"I'm sorry, Chad. But I'm telling you the truth. Moralists think telling a lie is sinful. I think it's just damned silly. What's the good to us of anything but the truth? And this is the truth I'm telling you. If you want my *guess* about Rose you can have it."

"It would interest me."

"All right, then. It stands to reason that in the years that followed I often wondered why Rose had married me. She was after a time so unhappy that I had to ask myself the question. Well, then: before she went off with Eustace Hawke she was aware of his reputation. I happen to know that. Whether she thought he was going to marry her I *don't* know. But when it was obvious that he *didn't* intend to marry her, you can imagine the edge it put to their relationship—a dangerous and exciting edge, with the question always in her mind: Can it go on? Can I do what other women have failed to do? That means tension, too much tension. There must be a certain tension in everything that's really alive, but that's overdoing it. Don't you think so?"

"Go on," I said. "For someone who says he knows nothing about these matters, you're not bad."

"Well, there's not much more to say, is there? When the crash came, and she at last came home, she was emotionally exhausted. She seemed reasonably bright down there at Pentyrch, but psychologically she must have been a wreck. What she wanted was Hawke, but knowing him as she did, she must have been aware that, with him, the end of one woman was the beginning of another, and he was out. And so, subconsciously, I suppose, she turned from what she wanted to what she needed—and that was peace. Well, her mother didn't help. I'm sorry to have to say that, but there it is. She was disapproval incarnate. And I was on the spot: the well-known, the unexciting, the roof over the head, the buoy that you tie up to when you come in out of the storm. She'd tried poetry and it had knocked her endways. It's hardly surprising that she decided to try a bit of prose."

Poor Billy! Poor Rose! She may have been tied up to the buoy, and the canvas may have been furled, but how little had been needed in the long run to make her shake it out and head again for the dangerous tensions of the sea!

Billy got up and stretched his legs and I made some tea. We sat down in a more relaxed mood. "Did you ever know any happiness with her, Billy?" I asked.

He said: "I don't think I was made for what people call happiness. I don't really know what they have in mind when they use the word. I get enormous satisfaction, as well as shocking disappointments, out of my work, but you can always have another go at it, and that's my life. Rose and I were cozy enough together for a time, if that's what you mean. We had a little house. After a time I began to miss my rooms in college. I was glad when it was all over."

I had never heard anyone talk so frankly about these things as Billy did that afternoon. It seemed a bit inhuman, but it had the supreme human virtue of honesty.

"Well," he said, "I'm glad we've had this talk at long last, Chad. And now that's enough about me. How are *you* getting on?"

To my surprise, I found myself telling him everything, even about the play that I had promised Max not to mention to a soul. I had a feeling that things were safe with Billy, and I never heard of his spreading the news. Perhaps it didn't interest him enough. I never heard of his seeing the play, either.

"You must come down to Cambridge sometime," he said. "I'd like to show you something of what we're trying to do. Of course, there are things I mustn't show you."

"You're peeping and prying into pretty dangerous things, I understand."

He looked at me with surprise. "Dangerous? Good lord, Chad! The

314

dangerous thing is to sit on your backside and not find out what's there, waiting to be known."

He stayed for the afternoon, and we traveled together out to Greg's where, as usual, I contributed little more than a listening ear. Certainly, when they got going, Greg and Billy were worth listening to.

CHAPTER TWELVE

I

MAX liked my three sketches. They were tinkered with a bit, but not substantially altered, and off my own bat I wrote a few lyrics, too. He paid me extravagantly, as I thought, for these things, and I didn't have to worry so much about whether a trifling bit of work found an editor. Indeed, had I but known it, my worrying days were over—so far as money went, anyway. Max had taken me firmly under his wing. By the autumn he had bought the house that had been a club at Maidenhead, and he said to me one day, while giving me lunch at Kettner's: "Chad, I want you to do a good turn for the Old Man. Can you drive a car?"

"Yes."

"All right. I'll buy you one—or at any rate one for you to use. I want you to go down and live at Menin Gate."

This was the appalling name he had chosen for the Maidenhead house. I suppose it enshrined some memory.

"I'm not going in there till next spring," he said, "and I want you to get it shipshape. I could do it myself better than the next man, but I just haven't the time to bother with it. I'll be down from time to time, and if you're making any mistakes I'll fire you. Anyway, I'll give you a general plan to work to. The car's for running up and down to town. You'll have to keep in touch with furniture people, decorators, and so forth. Choose yourself a bedroom and sitting room. They can stay till the last—till your job's finished. I've put a gardener into the lodge, and his wife will do your cooking. That's all you'll need."

"Yes, Mr. Middlemass," I said. "What does Mr. Boothroyd do for money?"

"With ten pounds a week and all found, Mr. Boothroyd will be better off than I imagine him to be now. And what's more, he'll have a quiet place where he can get down to a new play during the winter evenings. Time you were thinking about that, Chad. You'd better have something ready to follow *I Don't Want to Die.*"

It suited me, and so the picture of Rose that had been in Smurthwaite and Oxford and Manchester and London came to Maidenhead, and my familiar writing furniture came, too, and from my room on the first floor I looked out at the lawn, lovely now that it was swept clean of nonsense, at the willows drooping their shoulders in the evening light, and the river running—the same river that I had taken Rose on at Oxford, that we had journeyed on as far as the Nore. The smoldering torches of the chrysanthemums and dahlias were extinguished as the sun went down; and I drew my curtains, lit my fire of logs, and pondered on the odd consequences of meeting by chance in a back area of France a sergeant named Middlemass. Anything might happen from any trivial contact. It had always seemed to me one of the strangest things about human life. You walked through the millions of London, and if you kept your mouth shut not one of them was anything to you. But one word could plunge you right into another life, with consequences impossible to foresee. My father had said to my mother: "Could you lend me half a crown?" and the consequence was Chad Boothroyd with all his perplexities. You might say to a man: "Could you oblige me with a match?"

I wrote in my notebook: "Could you oblige me with a match?" and that was the title of a novel I worked on throughout the winter.

2

It was a pleasant winter: as pleasant, at all events, as it could be with no word from Rose. She had not written from Cornwall and I had kept my resolve to do nothing that would seem pursuit. I itched to send her a letter about my writing for Max, about my odd job here in this house at Maidenhead, about the novel that I was working on, but I sent her nothing. I went up to town two or three times a week, attending sales, buying in antique shops, ordering carpets and wallpapers. When I didn't go to town I superintended the workmen inside and out. Outside, the chief job was the boathouse, and, Max being his grandiose self, this wasn't a shed for a punt of two. The garden was cut away to admit the river into a basin that would house a thirty-foot motor launch, and over this the boathouse was built. It was of Elizabethan brick that I had bought for next to nothing when a few cottages were pulled down to widen a road, and it was roofed with Cotswold slate. On a fortunately sunny day of February Max himself, wearing a yachting cap, navigated his white launch from the builder's yard at Rotherhithe to her winter quarters in the boathouse. She was gleaming with brass, and her cabin was upholstered with green watered silk and had primrose yellow curtains at the windows. A bevy of Max's beauties, furred like Arctic explorers, was aboard, but Bessie wasn't, though the sumptuous vessel bore her humble name. The dining room was finished. Its paneled walls were painted lime-green, with touches of gold leaf. There were three pictures, each with its own lighting: ballet scenes by Degas. The cost of them had frightened me, and for once I had consulted Max before spending his money. He had been gaily careless. "Damn it, Chad, I'll tell you when I'm broke." It would have surprised me and given me enormous pleasure if I had known that day how near to being broke Max would find himself, and how triumphantly *I Don't Want to Die* would float him again to high water.

But nothing of that was in our minds as we sat down with the lovelies at the long Sheraton table under the icicles of the chandelier. Two waiters from the Berkeley had made the trip, bringing a luncheon in hampers, and at three o'clock cars arrived from London to carry the party home. "Thank you, Chad," Max said, "you're doing well. Don't buy that fourposter bed. Bessie says if she finds such a damn thing in her bedroom she'll sleep on the hearthmat. How d'you like the launch?"

"I prefer a punt."

"Well, if you can condescend to my level and feel like taking a run in her, you have my permission. In any case, see that the engine's turned over now and then."

"Yes, Mr. Middlemass."

"Have a cigar."

"I prefer a pipe."

"You bloody pleb."

"That'll do, sergeant," I said, and watched him climb in among the famous beauties, and thought what a rum, amusing thing life was.

3

When they were gone, I took a walk along the country roads, and ran into that peculiarly English spectacle, a crocodile of schoolgirls. They looked atrocious in their brown hats and brown uniform dresses. The procession was geometrical, tapering down from a few tall lasses in the lead to toddlers tagging at the tail. A grim-looking teacher walked ahead and a more winsome one closed the file, carrying some sprays of hazel catkin, destined, I guessed, for a botany lesson. On my walks, I had seen such crocodiles several times. I knew the school they came from, housed in a mansion with extensive lovely grounds. A costly place, I imagined. What I had not seen before was Eustace Hawke's daughter, Rose's daughter.

How often had I seen her? I could remember only a few times: a child who threw a coral bauble out of a perambulator, and I had picked it up and run with it to give it to Rose, pretending I had not recognized her; an older child whom Uncle Arthur and I saw briefly on the day when we called at the house on the Bayswater Road and Rose had gone to pieces; and a self-possessed young person who was with Rose in Hatchard's bookshop not so long ago. Henrietta. She would be fifteen in September. I know enough of Rose's story to be able to make that calculation.

It was three o'clock. The sun was shining, but already its heat was all but gone and a sharpness of the air predicted frost for the night. It was of this nip that I was aware rather than of the sun. The girls went by, taking no notice of the stranger; and that Rose's daughter should thus pass on, with not so much as the glance she would have given to a good-looking dog, left me feeling a chilled outsider. Eustace had begotten her but never known her. Billy Pascoe had lived under the same roof with her but had never, I supposed, had any use for her. She would be another thing distracting his mind from immensities. I, who would have loved her because Rose was part of her, was a stranger who chanced to be passing on a country road. There didn't seem to be any sense in the way things were turning out.

I walked into Maidenhead and took my tea there, and then back to Menin Gate. I was, usually, glad to be there, working in my firelit room. Aloneness in the great house didn't disturb me. It was a house with a happy aura. In the course of its long history men and women must have died there, but their ghosts didn't walk—not for me, at any rate. That night, my log box was well stored, my table light invited, no sound intruded save the quavering of owls, and that was always more delight than intrusion. But I couldn't work. With the curtains pulled back, I stood at the window and looked out onto the moonlight, frosty on the lawn, silver on the boathouse roof. Everyone, I falsely said to myself, seemed to be getting what he wanted out of life—everyone but I. Max had his beautiful bevies, and his costly boat, and this house, and his endearing Bessie. I couldn't have even what other men threw away. Eustace, Billy—what had they given to Rose compared with what I could have given? And what they had to give they had not given for long. But most dreadful was that I knew that I was deceiving myself. I knew, even then, that I had nothing to give to Rose that she would think worth tuppence if she weighed it in one hand against what the mere memory of Eustace could give her in the other. The memory had been there when she married Billy Pascoe. It would be there if she married me. But I wouldn't admit this ugly intruding thought. I kicked it back to its dungeon as soon as it poked its head up through the mind's trapdoor. I smoked and watched the logs smolder to a handful of ashes, and then went to bed with a promising thought. Schools had such things as half-term holidays, when parents came to visit their young. They took them out, fed them in the teashops. Very well, then . . .

4

And so there was no sense of pursuit. It seemed by nothing but a happy accident that I was at tea when Rose and Henrietta came in. It had been easy to find the teashop. I had only to observe which one the parents and their children were making for and to go in with them. I was sure—and with what joy!—that Rose was glad to see me. When I got up from my chair she halted, surprised, then said: "Chad!" and came on swiftly, holding out her hand, gloved with white lace. A short lace veil did not dim the brilliance of her blue eyes.

She introduced the girl. "Darling, this is Mr. Chad Boothroyd, a very old friend of mine. I don't think you've met him."

Henrietta said: "Oh, yes, I have. He was in the bookshop that day you left me alone there. And I saw him a week or two ago when we were out walking. He didn't seem to remember me."

"I'm sorry," I lied. "You must forgive me. I'm afraid that when twenty girls are all dressed alike in a rather depressing uniform the eye doesn't take in individuals."

"I agree it's a dreary outfit," Henrietta conceded. "I don't know why mother ever sent me to the place. It's all hockey and horses. I loathe both."

"You mustn't judge after only one term, darling," Rose said. "You'll get used to it in time."

"That's just what I'm afraid of," Henrietta said wisely.

She was rather roly-poly, but she looked as though she would become a handsome woman. That was all I noticed about Henrietta at the time. My eyes had other occupation.

"Are you living in this district now, Chad?" Rose asked.

I told her about Menin Gate and my job there, and about the launch and the lovely girls, and about the novel I was writing and Max's hopes of putting on my play before I was a centenarian. She told me of her own life at her mother's house, which sounded vague and aimless. "But there are holidays and half-terms," she said.

It was only of these things that we could talk there in the teashop, full of brown uniforms and pigtails, shrill young voices and rather terrifying mammas.

"What time," I asked, "does Henrietta have to be handed back to the hockey and horses?"

"Not a moment after six," Henrietta answered for her mother. "I have

319

to make up for the play tonight. I'm Juliet. That's Romeo over there."

Romeo, with flaxen hair and blue staring eyes, was tucking into cream buns. She looked more Rapunzel to me, and I said so. "Oh, she's not bad in tights and a black wig," Henrietta assured me. And she surprised me by adding: "Would you care to come? I'd like you to see me. I'm pretty good. I think you could squeeze in, but it'll be an awful jam."

"I'm not invited," I said. "Surely these things are by invitation?"

Rose said: "That'll be all right, Chad, if it would amuse you. I accepted an invitation for two. My mother hoped to come, but some important person in Sussex, whose portrait she's to paint, suddenly decided that he can now spare a little of his precious time. She's gone down to stay there for a day or two. I could pick you up at six-thirty at this Menin Gate."

I don't need to say anything about the performance of *Romeo and Juliet*: it was what these school plays usually are. I was longing for it to end, and when it did we had to wait for Juliet to wash her face and come to receive our congratulations and kiss her mother good-night. It was nearly ten o'clock before we were sitting in Rose's two-seater and winding slowly through the twists of the long school drive.

"What now?" I asked as we came out into the road.

"Now? Back to the Bayswater Road, and here again tomorrow for the second day's fun and games."

"You haven't time to stop for a moment and have a look at Max's house? It's pretty well finished now, and it's quite a show-place."

"Could I bring Henrietta over tomorrow afternoon? She'd love to see it."

"You could, if you'd prefer that. Would you?"

I wanted to be more explicit. I wanted her to stop the car, and for me to put my arm round and say: "You're so unhappy. I've been watching you. You've been a proud mamma with all the rest. But I've known you too long to be deceived. You're unhappy and unfulfilled, and you never can have the fulfillment you're longing for. Take what I can give. There's nothing else now." But this was more than I could say.

She was a long time answering. Perhaps my voice had said it all. Then: "Very well, Chad. Let's see it now."

Anyone could have burgled Menin Gate. The gardener and his wife were sound asleep in the lodge when the car turned into the drive.

We didn't explore the show-place. We went straight up to my room and I put a match to the fire. She dropped her fur coat and hat and gloves onto a chair, sat on the couch drawn up to the fire and stretched her long legs to the blaze, kicking off her shoes. My heart was troublesome, but I did my best to be calm, putting a small table before her, with cigarettes on it and sherry and biscuits. There was no light but the firelight. It gleamed in her eyes and on her black hair. She had not followed the fashion of bobbing that came in after the war. Her hair was in luxuriant piles on her head. I went behind the couch and began to pull out hairpins. She stretched up her arms lazily and completed the job. Then I came round and knelt before her, laying my head in the hair that showered upon her lap. She stroked my curls till I looked up and saw that she was smiling at me: a lazy, compassionate, almost maternal smile. "What an odd sort of host you are, Chad," she said. "You bring the sherry and then introduce this distraction."

She pressed my head back onto her lap, and we stayed like that for a long time, the fire warming us. She said: "I intended to be back in London tonight. I've brought no nightthings."

"You have all the nightthings I shall require," I said; and at that small sally I could feel her shaking with laughter. She was never solemn about these things—always gay. I loved her the more for that.

5

I went to sleep thinking: "I shall awake to find Rose's hair on the pillow." I had never awakened to find a woman's hair on the pillow. May Ingleby was not the one to loll. She was always up before me, bustling, efficient, seeing that everything was nice in the dining room by the time her man appeared. Apart from her, there had been only the young professional in Morecambe. I was sometimes surprised by my own chastity. Naturally, my sleep was often disturbed by dreams of women. Usually, they were anonymous—just women. If they became personal, they were Rose.

When I awoke she was gone. We had lit the bedroom fire the night before. Poor May! Why did I always think of her with derogation? I remembered how, more than once when feeling amorous, I had suggested that we should light the fire in our bedroom, but she would never have it. "No, Chad. It seems like *dwelling* on things, making an *occasion* of them." Lying at Rose's side last night, tired and happy, I had loved the fantastic play of the flames upon the ceiling. They were banners of triumph.

Now the ashes were gray in the grate and the day was gray against the window panes. While I was shaving and bathing the winter sun appeared, and I went out onto the gravel sweep in front of the house, full of well-being, to greet the frosty morning. The willows were shaking the cobwebs from their hair, and a robin tinkled his son. Rose's car swept in from the drive and pulled up at the front door.

She got out, looking as I felt—radiant. She kissed me. "I'm as hungry as a hunter," she said. "I hope you can give me some breakfast."

We did ourselves well at Menin Gate. Max had been known to appear even for breakfast, and we were bounteously prepared. I went in and told the gardener's wife, my cook, that one of Mr. Middlemass's young ladies had arrived and would be staying to breakfast, and a quarter of an hour later Rose and I were sitting down to our liver and bacon, our toast and coffee.

"You are a strategist," I praised her.

"Please don't think, Chad," she said seriously, "that I'm practiced in these arts. We weren't thinking of much last night, except one another. But when I woke up I got a fright. I know nothing of the routine here, and I was terrified lest some housekeeper should come barging in with your morning tea. And it wouldn't have done, either, for a strange car to be found at the front door. So I dressed and went, and found a cup of coffee at a roadside café, and here I am. After breakfast, I must motor to the school, as though I'd come on an early start from London."

She was looking beautiful and distressed.

"So many people to deceive," I said. "You still haven't thought of the servants in Bayswater. They were expecting you last night."

"I rang them up from a call box and said I'd met a friend and stayed the night."

"How true. But am I only a friend? Now?"

The distress was still in her eyes. "I hope I haven't promised you too much, darling?" she asked.

"Promised! Why, all my life seems to have been one damned weary Israelitish trudge to the Promised Land, and last night I was there."

"You've been very faithful to me, Chad. I've always known that. And you've made so few demands on me."

"So, as a reward for twenty years of faithful service, you handed me a superb bonus. Was that all it meant to you?"

She seemed shattered when I put it like that: "Oh, no, Chad! I love you. You must believe that."

"You love me, but you're not *in love* with me. I've heard that subtle get-out before. I don't accept it. Perhaps I'm old-fashioned, but, with me, what happened last night couldn't happen except with a woman I wanted to marry. Does this seem an odd way to propose? Does it seem an odd moment to propose? Very well. I'm proposing to you. I'm asking you: Will you be my wife? I'm sick to death of being the faithful Dobbin, calling the cab, handing the cloak, for his lady to go off and meet someone else. I watched you run away with Eustace. I even—by God, what a joke!—stood best man to Billy Pascoe. They're both good men, and I've hated their very guts, but not now. I love them next to Greg Appleby. But, so far as you're concerned, you've done with 'em. Do you want to be done with me, too?"

I had got up and walked to the fireplace, and stood there haranguing her as she sat at the table with her head bowed. I was horrified at what had welled up in me and poured out of me; and when I had said it I felt drained and flaccid and done-for. Done-for in every sense of the word. This is the end of it, I thought. What is left for her now but to go?

She said: "For years, Chad, I have done you great wrong," and hearing that, so humbly said, I shouted: "No, no. What else could you have done? It's just the damned way circumstances have snared us both. There seems no road out of it."

I strode to the window and watched the blackbirds hopping on the lawn, leaving tracks in the rime, and at the winter sun red and round and smoky, and she came and joined me there and put an arm through mine and said: "I never knew you loved me so much."

At that, I was near to tears. "So much?" I said. "Why, my dear, I should go on loving you if all your life was a treason against me."

"Kiss me," she said.

I kissed her, and she seemed to hang on to me in desperation. "I wonder if you know," she asked, "how much I *need* a love like yours?"

"We have wasted so many years."

But she wouldn't have that. "No. Nothing is wasted. It's all in us, darling—in both of us. There's that much more to give to one another."

"Are you saying Yes?"

She nodded; and I said: "Very well, then. Let's have another cup of coffee before it gets cold." I was so happy I could have babbled any idiocy.

We finished breakfast, and I asked: "How are we to spend this day?"

"I have a daughter and I must go to her."

"Come and see Max's motor launch."

We went down to the boathouse and stepped aboard and laughed at Max's rich tastes, and even as we laughed we turned suddenly serious, and I took hold of her and kissed her and fondled her. She trembled from head to foot, and at last said: "Not here, darling. Let's wait."

"Very well. But not too long. And now let me tell you what we're going to do today. Max has given me permission to use the launch, and this is a lovely day. Go and get hold of your Juliet, and bring Romeo, too, if you like. Bring the whole tribe of Montagues and Capulets, if no doting parents want them, and let's make a day of it."

We were back on the lawn, and she was laughing, as they say, fit to burst. "Oh, Chad! You beautifully predictable Chad! Will you ever, in your great moments, want to do anything with me but hustle me onto the nearest strip of water? You're a regular Neptune, and take me for a dryad."

"Your mythology's all mixed up," I said, happy beyond measure. "Neptune belongs to the salt seas and dryads to pleasant rivers. And what I shall want to do with you in my great moments is something you have forbidden my imagination to dwell on for the time being."

In the grass, under a forsythia whose twigs were strung with buds, a few aconites wore their yellow frills, and a few snowdrops dangled green-streaked alabaster. The sunlight fell upon Rose's teeth and tongue as she laughed, and all my life surged up in me as though I had never been alive before. I said "Rose!" as if I were beholding a miracle.

And all the day had the quality of miracle. The weather remained miraculous for the time of year, and the girls we scooped up and took on the river were angels. The sunshine was a benediction upon the meadows; the hazels were trembling with the pollen of catkins, and under them water buttercups were brave gold. I suppose it was just a usual river day in unseasonably lovely weather. I suppose the swans on the water and the cows in the fields were swans and cows, and that the luncheon we ate in an old pub was not, in fact, the bread of heaven that memory recalls. But there must have been something about it, something that put a shining into Rose's face and mine; for when we had taken the girls back to school and driven in the dusk to Menin Gate, Max, pacing up and down on the gravel, took the cigar from his mouth and looked at us silently for a long time. Then he said: "Where have you two come from—Sinai?"

Max had just arrived. I was glad he had not a bevy with him. He had only Bessie. She had not seen the house before. Now it was finished, and Max had brought her down proudly to see what he had made of it. "She's inside," he said. "We'll sleep here tonight and tomorrow she'll give the place a proper go-over. I feel like some poor playwright, Chad, trembling as he awaits a producer's verdict."

It was strange to introduce Rose as "Mrs. Pascoe." I said: "We're engaged to be married, Max," and I hoped he would not come back with some ribald crack. I did him wrong even to think he might. He simply said: "I thought so as soon as I saw you. Bessie is very fond of you, Chad, and she'll be glad about this. So am I."

Then he shook hands with Rose and said: "Will you join us at dinner, Mrs. Pascoe?" but Rose said she must get back to town.

"Then at all events you must come in and meet my wife."

We found Bessie sitting in a winged chair, embroidered in petit point, looking with calm appraisal round her drawing room. She seemed more amused than perturbed. However, she was not the one to comment to other people upon Max's vagaries, whatever she might think of them herself. He was Max, and this was how Max behaved, and she accepted it.

When told our news, she kissed me and she kissed Rose, and then sherry was brought and our healths were drunk. It was all charming and civilized, but it hadn't the rapture of the day till then. Max took care not to come out when Rose went. It took us a long time to say good-by, and during the evening I was going over every yard of her homeward journey in my head. I was so obviously absent that at last Bessie said: "I reckon she should be there by now, Chad. You'd better ring her up to make sure she hasn't killed herself on the way."

I was about to lift the telephone when it rang. It was Rose. "I just wanted to let you know I'm back safely, darling." After that, I was able to talk sensibly to Max and Bessie.

6

Rose and I were married in the Savoy Chapel in June of that year. There were few people present: my mother and Uncle Arthur, Miss Orlop, my best man Greg, and Phoebe. Phoebe and another girl, whom I had not seen before and did not see again, were bridesmaids. Max, who was there with Bessie, always claimed that she was a stage property, supplied for the occasion out of his chorus—"a trivial part of the Middlemass service, Chad"—and that may well have been so. Anyway, the whole business pleased my mother, who had never got over the furtive marriage with Miss Ingleby, and it gave Uncle Arthur one of his last occasions for wearing the Hat and all the rest of the outfit that had solemnized his first call upon Miss Orlop so long ago. We went back in taxicabs to Miss Orlop's house, and the old girl drew me aside and whispered urgently: "For God's sake help her to make a do of it this time, Chad. You've wanted her long enough. I've known that. Well, see that you keep her now that you've got her."

"I'll do my best," I promised her.

"You'll have this place to live in," she said. "I've made it over jointly to you and Rose. I've taken a small flat, which is all I shall need for the time I intend to spend in London from now on. I want to get back to Pentyrch."

She bustled off before I could thank her, and I went into the dining room where a meal was spread and Uncle Arthur was pouring sherry. He looked suddenly a good deal older than I had ever known him. He was sixty-four, and I wondered what he would be doing in a year's time when retiring age would have come. He had given up growing auriculas. "The pangs of the flesh, Chad," he had said to me the night before, "gain upon me. The Auricula is not a flower to trifle with. It is as demanding as a woman. To brace myself on a winter night in Yorkshire to make even the small journey to the greenhouse is something from which I occasionally shrink, and a few days' neglect can mean total disaster. That is, considered from the highest standpoint. I might still produce Auriculas of a sort, but that would never do for one with my reputation in the Auricula World. My association with the Auricula has always been on the basis, '*Aut Caesar aut nullus*,' and the time has come, alas! when I must resign the purple. Still, I have made my contribution. I think I can say that. The Geldersome Green will live."

I had not realized then that his town clerkship was nearing its end, and I said: "Still, Uncle Arthur, you'll have your municipality to keep you busy for many a day."

"No, Chad," he said. "Our little clerkships have their day, they have their day and cease to be. *Sunt lacrimae rerum*, but so it is, for the greatest of us as for the least. Time calls the count, and on the dreaded Ten we don't get up again, lump it or like it. Still, I don't envy the man who will be called upon to follow *me*."

However, he seemed reasonably cheerful now, and it was soon clear that nothing could deflect him from applying all the trimmings to what he called, when he rose to speak, "this auspicious nuptial occasion. That Chad should marry Rose," he said, "is, if I may so put it, a piece of inspired poaching upon Miss Orlop's preserves in the best family tradition of the Boothroyds. Chad's father set the example, knocking off many a pheasant, as Miss Orlop has informed me, and like father like son. Except that the son aimed higher, and did not content himself with a mere bird from the woods. He possessed himself of the dearest treasure of a mother's heart. I, perhaps, am not without responsibility, for it was I who introduced this young serpent into the Eden of Pentyrch."

He was off now, and nothing could stop him. He gave us the story of that long-ago visit, and of how Rose had appeared with vine leaves in her hair at a bend of the path—"a wild woodland vision that has dwelt in Chad's heart from that day to this. And who shall wonder? My own odd and antiquated collection of auricles and ventricles beats the faster as I recall the moment. You may depend, it was my avuncular duty to make Chad fit for so high a destiny. It was no easy task."

The saga moved north. "Death's fell hand smote Chad's father in the very purlieus and precincts of his diurnal occupation," Uncle Arthur assured us, and, whether from the champagne or from emotion recollected, his eyes were damp. "*In loco parentis* there was much to be done. The hereditary tendency to poaching, coupled with evil company, might easily have led him astray. A boy who shall be nameless, but who is now not a hundred miles from my left elbow, a boy since become celebrated for many a learned tome expounding the doctrine of economic poaching on a national scale, was then mewing his mighty youth upon an odd grouse or two acquired from the estates of my old friend Sir Titus Newte."

My exploit with Greg was fully accounted for; and if the unlooked-for bridesmaid was by now a little confused and confounded no one could wonder at that. I refilled her glass to help her through to the end, which came at last. "And so as Destiny's humble instrument in what I take to be a sound piece of work, I invite you to raise your foaming glasses and drink the simple toast—to Rose, to Chad. God bless you, my dears."

Uncle Arthur, happily, was the only one who attempted oratory, and it wasn't long, once he had finished, before Rose and I were in her two-seater with me at the wheel and the luggage in the boot. "Where are we going to, darling?" she asked.

"That's your husband's secret. You've left all the honeymoon arrangements to him. How d'you like being your husband's wife?"

"At the moment, very much. Ask me again in a few years' time."

I drove on and on for miles into the country, glad to be rid of everybody—even of Uncle Arthur, even of my mother. Even of Eustace Hawke, I said to myself. We were purring along a road cut into a Berkshire hillside. The hood was down, and the evening air was cool on our faces. Below us the shadows of tall trees were falling eastward.

"What became of Eustace?" I asked.

"I don't know. I suppose you can't *compel* a man to stay in a hospital. He went. They couldn't tell me where. Phoebe doesn't know."

I wished I hadn't asked. I found extraordinarily disturbing the thought of that bright spirit vanished into thin air. Oddly, I felt as though I were doing him a wrong.

Rose said: "Don't think about Eustace, darling. Think about me. I need to be loved. I always have done. I always shall do. It's a big job, Chad," she added with a rather sad smile. "You'll find it a full-timer."

I said: "I love you so much, darling, there will never be time enough."

I stopped the car and kissed her. We remained there for long, embraced, and then I drove back to London. I had booked a room at the Savoy for the night, and when the porter had dumped our luggage and gone we stood at the window, looking down on the river.

"The river," Rose said. "Why always the river, Chad? Do my sins need so much cleansing?"

"We'll come up after dinner," I said. "By then it will be dark. The lights will be on out there. It will be very lovely. It's one of the loveliest sights in the world."

She locked the door, turned on the bedside light, and drew the curtains across the window. "I don't want any dinner," she said. "Do you?"

"No."

"Very well, then. Undress me."

7

The next day we took the car oversea to France and for a month went wherever fancy led. We ended the honeymoon in Holland and crossed from the Hook to Harwich. To Rose, it was accustomed, but I had never been able to afford foreign travel, and foreign travel in such a heyday of the blood brought me back feeling capable of pushing the world over. It was time I did it, I thought. It was all very well for Rose to call my scruples childish, but I didn't like the idea that the ravishing holiday had been paid for out of her pocket.

"Why should you dislike taking this from me? I don't object to taking it from my mother." Miss Orlop allowed her a thousand a year. It didn't help me to be reminded that in the long run the money came from Miss Orlop. She had given us this Bayswater house and was paying us to live in it. It made me feel too much like Billy Pascoe. I took some comfort from the fact that the novel I had written at Menin Gate, and which was published a week before our marriage, was selling well enough, though not well enough to subdue my impatience. It was high time, I thought, that Max did something about the play.

However, all these were irritations beneath the surface. We were very happy, and we had plenty to do. We accounted it lucky that Miss Orlop had a magpie's fondness for possessions. Here in this house had been the accumulation of all her life from the time when she walked out of Pentyrch on the death of her mother. There was little of it that she could bear to part with, and during our month's absence most of it had been packed and taken to Pentyrch. What was left we shamelessly sold, resolved to begin anew. For one thing, I thought this would be good for Rose, psychologically. The place had too much of memory. And so it was my job at Menin Gate all over again, except that I hadn't lavish money to play with. We modernized the kitchen, turned the front room on the first floor into a study, and furnished a bedroom. The rest would have to wait. For the time being, the study was sitting room as well, when I wasn't working in it. When I was, which was every morning, Rose used the bedroom as a boudoir. An easy chair and a writing desk justified her use of the word. So we waited, in what we called our camp, for Max to sound the trumpet.

228

It was on a beautiful September morning that Rose put her head round the study door and said that Max Middlemass was on the telephone. "Chad," he said, "could you scrape me up some lunch today? I want to come and talk to you about your play."

"A bit early, isn't it, Max? I thought it was going on in November of next year? Aren't your hands full with your new revue?"

"Will you keep to what I'm talking about?" he snarled.

"Certainly, Max."

"Very well, then. One o'clock."

I told Rose of these brief emphatic words, and we looked at one another perplexed. "Something wrong," she said.

"Wrong! He sounded like a wolf with one leg in a trap."

"We must feed him well," she said practically. "I'll make some soup. There's a cold chicken. I'll prepare salad. Then cheese and fruit and coffee. We have some sherry. Go and buy a bottle of Château Yquem."

Our modernized kitchen was rather like an operating theater in a hospital, with its gleaming gadgets and its floor of linoleum in black and white squares. However, the table looked hospitable, covered by a cloth checkered in green and white and spread with shining glass and silver. A low Lalique bowl full of autumn leaves and a few white roses stood in the middle, and a tall window gave a view of our garden strip surrounded by whitewashed walls.

"I hope you won't mind eating in the kitchen, Mr. Middlemass?" Rose asked when he arrived.

"I am lucky to eat at all," he said morosely; and she and I exchanged sad glances over his head.

I took him up to the study where the sherry was, leaving Rose to look after the meal, and while sipping his drink he gazed gloomily out of the window as though the prospect, fair enough on that morning of early autumn, had been infernal. He said nothing, and I was glad when Rose came to tell us that lunch was ready. She put an arm through his and asked: "May I call you Max?"

"Of course you may."

"Very well then, Max," she said, leading him down to the kitchen, "try not to look so much like the condemned man going to his last breakfast. It's no compliment to my cooking, which isn't to be sneezed at."

It worked. "I'll tell you when I've eaten it," he said. "But I'll bet you in advance that your cooking's not so good as Bessie's."

"How much do you bet?" she challenged him.

"Well, that's where I've got to be careful. That's what I want to talk about to Chad. Finance. Say half a crown."

"You're keeping it within my means at all events," she said, serving the soup.

She chaffed him into a happier mood, but it took him a long time to come to the point, and when he came to it I couldn't pretend to understand more than the bleak fact of it. The byways and sidetracks of finance have never been clear to me, but what did emerge was that Max had been spending a lot of money—so much that he couldn't, as he had done till then, finance out of his own pocket a new revue. He had hoped to put it on that winter, and now the long and the short of it was that he couldn't afford to do it, what with Menin Gate and one thing and another. "I daresay I could borrow the money, Chad. My reputation's good enough for that, but I just am damn well not going to risk it. I've always been my own financier till now. What if it was a flop? There's always the chance. Where should I be then?"

Rose edged in gently: "You said you wanted to talk about Chad's play, Max."

"So I do."

"Go back to the study. I'll bring up some coffee."

Max and I went upstairs. He was in a better mood and gave himself what looked like a millionaire's cigar. "You know, Chad," he said, "you've got yourself a good girl there."

"Well, I waited for her long enough. Even longer than for you to put my play on. And that's saying something."

"It will go on in two months' time. It will go on on November 11. That's a symbolic day."

"It's a symbolic day to me all right. It was on November 11 that I finished it—six years ago. I've almost forgotten what it's all about."

"I haven't. I've read it two or three times every year, and I've got my ideas about what to do with it. If you've forgotten it, you're going to have a sharp reminder, and so are a good many other people. I think they're ready for it now. I think they can stand something better than funny music hall stuff with an all-male chorus."

Rose brought in the coffee, put it down, and was discreetly sneaking out when Max caught her by the arm and said: "You'd better stay, Rose. This is a Moment, and it concerns you. Give Chad a kiss and wish him luck."

She did so.

"Now you can give me one. I shall need some luck, too."

She kissed him, and sat down and poured out the coffee.

"It's a lovely day for having a Moment," she said. "Look at the trees."

I hoped she was seeing only the trees. You have seen too much from

330

this window, I thought. It was along the street out there that I marched with a mob of recruits in civilian clothes. It was at this window that Uncle Arthur and I found you when Phoebe had rung up with disastrous news of Eustace. Billy Pascoe must often have sat at this window with you and your mother.

I said: "Max, I remember marching along that road, one of a bunch of rookies, with a band at our head. We were wearing our civvies, and we tried to stick out our chests, and I think there was some good in us. I suppose some of us were running away from wives, and some from boring jobs, and some from debt collectors. But most of us had a spark of something else. It was brighter in some than in others. I saw it here blown into a flame, and there blown out altogether. That's what I wrote about, and it seemed marvelous when I'd done it. But I can't believe it means a thing now. Look at the people going by. Those are the soldiers and the nurses and the W.A.A.C.'s. Do they look as if they give a damn for that old story?"

Max said: "Those are the soldiers and the nurses and the W.A.A.C.'s, and there are tens of thousands of them, and it's my bet that they won't mind being reminded of what they were. When the war ended, civvy life was glorious. They wanted nothing but to forget. Now they've had time to find out how glorious it is, and I think they'll want to remember."

"How can you be so sure about a thing like that, Max?"

"I went to a music hall last night. There was one of those sketches that have been tooling round ever since the war ended—you know: ferocious sergeant major and a daft recruit who's always dropping his rifle and getting mixed up with his equipment. There were two chaps sitting next to me, and in the middle of it one said to the other: 'Christ! Come an' 'ave a drink.' I followed them into the bar. 'Christ!' this same chap said, 'fancy that sort of punk still staggering round! Remember what it was like? Remember old Dusty at Noove Chapelle?' They went on and on about old Dusty and old Mich, and Noove Chapelle and Bourlon Wood till I could almost hear your play being recited. 'Remember old Fat Arse?' 'Wot—the pore bastard who copped one with 'is name on it the night 'e came back from bein' married?' 'Aye, that was the night Jerry was usin' gas.' That's how it went, Chad. Those boys *wanted* to remember. That's when I made up my mind that the time had come."

"I thought it was because you couldn't afford to put on your revue?"

"That helped," he agreed. "I can't sit on my behind and do nothing. I can *afford* to put on your play. Buying a few old uniforms and tin hats is one thing. Dressing a hundred floozies is another. Buying a few bits of timber and sackcloth is one thing. Paying a top-notch designer to make half a dozen different scenes is another. With you, I can think

331

in hundreds, not thousands, so get off the high horse, Chad, and thank your stars that these two things have fallen fortunately for you. Now then, let's get down to business. We'll have to draw up a contract. Who's your agent?"

"I haven't an agent."

He looked at me aghast. "You poor ruddy lamb! The wolves will devour you! And when it comes to wolfing I'm in a class of my own. You'd better get in touch tomorrow with Tommy Cannock. He's the toughest nut I know. He's fought me to a standstill over one-half of one per cent."

So it went, and it was five o'clock before Max left us. He had arrived lamenting what he couldn't do. He went having talked himself into a flame of enthusiasm for what he was sure he could do superbly at a tenth of the cost. "My first straight play, Chad! Well, we must meet tonight. The Café Royal. Eight o'clock. Just the three of us and Bessie. She loathes eating out. But she'll come this time if I have to carry her in a hamper."

9

I Don't Want to Die is a matter of theatrical history. It is nearly thirty years ago since I sat in the box at the first night in the Parthenon Theatre, with Rose, and my mother and Uncle Arthur, and Miss Orlop and Henrietta, and watched the slow swing down of the curtain on the final scene. It showed my Cockney corporal and a few men standing-to at dawn, their shapes barely outlined against the pallid light. *All right, chaps. That'll do. Another bloody day.* Then he sits beneath the parapet, and as the curtain sweeps down is playing softly on his mouthorgan

> *Oh my! I don't want to die;*
> *I want to go home.*

I remember how Rose squeezed my hand, and I sat there listening to Henrietta sobbing, and my stomach felt sick at the utter silence in the house. And then as the house lights came on I saw that there was no customary move to go, that what was holding people silent was the spell that every playwright dreams of putting upon them—a spell which, when it breaks, releases the torrent. So it was that night, and it uplifted me till I felt I could fly, and it scared me till I wanted to run out of the theater. I'd have done it, too, if Max had not come into the box, seized my arm, dragged me by tortuous ways to the wings, and pushed me onto the stage with a hand between the shoulder blades. I was more frightened than if a Very light had shown me up crawling across no-man's-land, and I did nothing but scuttle like a rabbit from one wing to another, waving a hand to the audience as I went.

I don't remember much else till I found myself in a private room at the Savoy that Max had booked. Bessie was there, bless her heart. She had come to that play though she would go to no other. Max had fed her with tales about my being "good" to him in France, and she never forgot anyone who had been "good" to Max when he was no one. Phoebe was there with Greg who was slapping my back and shouting: "What price Pie-frill now?" and the players were there, quiet men who seemed glad that a trying moment was over. Everybody I wanted to see was there, Uncle Arthur solemn, as though he couldn't believe it, Henrietta wearing her first grown-up dress. I often wondered what was passing in that beautiful child's head. It isn't easy to be a stepfather; but I wasn't worrying that night; Henrietta seemed to want nothing but to keep close to me and to look at me as though I were something wonderful.

Everyone was there except Max. I suppose it was characteristic of him to wait till we were all assembled, so that a tension could work up for his entry. Certainly, so far as the actors were concerned, it was soon evident that they were sipping their sherry and nibbling their olives with growing anxiety; and when at last Max came, an opera hat in one hand, a cane in the other, a cloak flowing loosely round him, everybody stopped talking. He looked at us all for a moment with an ominous frown on his face, and then the frown changed to his cheeky ugly grin. "Stand at ease," he said. "Fall out." And to a waiter: "Serve the supper."

We sat at the table, all talking again, all happy again because Max, our barometer, was so obviously happy. He got up at last and said: "We don't want a lot of talk tonight. It's high time you were all in bed. I'm ready for mine, anyway. But before we part, I give you one toast. 'To the thousand-and-one nights of Chad's play.' If it doesn't make that I'll eat my hat."

Henrietta went off with Miss Orlop to her flat. It was one o'clock when I opened the door of the Bayswater house. In the passageway Rose said: "Well, I suppose that, too, was what Max would call a Moment. Am I allowed to be proud of you, darling?"

I took her in my arms. "During the last six years I've occasionally boosted myself up a bit by thinking of what this First Night would be like, if it ever came off. I was vain enough to see it just as, in fact, it has turned out to be. Except for one thing. I never saw *you* in the picture. You *are* in it, and you say it makes you proud. Well, that's what makes *me* proud. That, more than anything. And now I think we'd better follow Max's advice. It's high time we were in bed."

She smiled invitingly. "You have such intelligent friends," she said.

CHAPTER THIRTEEN

I

YOU could make money in those days. Taxation was becoming steep, but it hadn't yet ruined the will to work, and before *I Don't Want to Die* was done with I was a rich man. While the play was still running in London, Max sent a company with it to New York, another company took it through the English provinces, and two companies were playing it in the Dominions. A film was made of it, and my publisher induced me against my will to write it all over again as a novel. I have never done any job that bored me so much as that, but even the novel sold, the poor dead thing, and, what is more, Tom Cannock, my agent, got rid of the serial rights to an evening newspaper at a price that astounded me. For five years my name was Midas, but never again.

We sold the house in Bayswater. I had never liked living there. It was too full, for me and for Rose, of a past we wanted to kill. Once the play was rolling along its course we had time on our hands. It was as though I had touched a button that had set a machine to work for us—a machine that was eager to pour into our laps everything we wanted. Fortunately for us, Tom Cannock was more than my money collector. He was a lantern-jawed Scot with eyebrows like rooks' nests and sad deep-set eyes. He was the most unillusioned man I have known. "One of these days, Chad," he said to me, "people will talk about Boothroyd—'You know,' they'll say, 'the chap who once wrote *I Don't Want to Die*.' I've seen plenty of that, and I expect to see plenty more. Heydays and holidays are nice things, Chad, but they don't last. You leave your money with me. Let me invest it."

These were early days, when I didn't know what was happening to me. "I wondered if you could let me have a fiver," I said humbly.

Even Cannock laughed at that. At any rate, his eyebrows performed the extraordinary antics that you took to mean that he was laughing. "Yes," he said, "we could go to that. We could go to twenty, I should say."

He was sitting in his office in Shaftesbury Avenue, with a large earthenware teapot on the table. From time to time he poured himself a cup of tea that looked stone-cold. He was a teetotaler and he didn't smoke, but he was a lion in combat for his clients. Max had said to me: "If Tommy offers to look after your money, let him. I wish he'd look after mine."

And so it was that if Rose and I wished to do something that seemed extravagant we asked Tom Cannock's permission. Sometimes he would give it, and sometimes he wouldn't. He allowed us to buy Chalk Hill in Hertfordshire. It was in the spring, when the play had been running for six months, that we found it. We were doing a lot of motoring, just for the love of being together with fancy free. We would take our nightclothes, so that we needn't go back to London unless we felt like it. It was a prolongation of our honeymoon, with the added joy to me that I wasn't honeymooning on Rose's money. If we came to some lovely village with a good pub, I could say: "D'you think Tom Cannock would allow me to spend a night here with a woman?" and Rose would say: "Chance it, darling, and ask him afterward."

"D'you think Tom Cannock . . . ?" was becoming our leitmotiv.

So it was when we saw Chalk Hill, but that time we asked it seriously. The house was on the outskirts of a Hertfordshire village. All we saw at first were wide white gates opening into a drive bordered with rhododendrons in bloom. A notice saying that the place was for sale was tacked to a pole. I stopped the car and looked through the gates, and as there was nothing to see but a twist in the drive I started up again, when Rose said: "I think we ought to have a look at that place."

"What place? I can't see any place."

"Neither can I. But I've got a feeling about it."

So we took a note of the house agent's name, drove into the neighboring township where his office was, and, after lunching, returned with the house keys.

It was a simple house, simple in the Georgian way. It had a little pillared porch. There were three sash windows on either side of the porch, and the windows of the upper story repeated those of the ground floor. It was stuccoed and painted white. That was all, but it had elegance and proportion, a well-bred rejection of fuss.

We stood on the broad gravel sweep in front of it, looking at the gentle spring light falling upon it, and upon the land rising above it, and upon the newly green beech trees growing on the hill that shut out the north. Rooks were clamoring over the trees and nestling among them was a small white domed pavilion.

It was not a place that excited you. It was a place that contented you. We turned to one another after a moment not with exclamations of rapture but with smiles. "It's lovely," Rose said. "Let's climb up to that little building among the trees. It should give a lovely view."

It did. Inside was a curved bench of teak, and the walls were painted light blue. We sat down and looked over the roof of the house and over the village beyond it to a panorama of fields and coppices, plow and pasture, fading in a gentle lilac haze.

"I believe this is it," I said.

"If the inside's as good as the outside, it certainly is."

The inside was all right, and we began to spend money on it. We decided which bedroom could become a second bathroom and how the kitchen should be gutted and renewed. We apportioned the rooms and got on with the decoration.

"D'you think Tom Cannock will mind?"

"This time," Rose said, "he'll have a woman to deal with."

We went out and locked the door behind us. "Let's have a look at the stables before we go."

The stables stood a little way off from the house. They were of narrow rosy brick and belonged to a time when stables were as well proportioned as the house they served. A clock stood above them. The yard that surrounded them was paved with brick and round its edges daffodils and scillas were a brave show. The clock struck four.

"It goes!" Rose said, pleased as a child. "We'll have to make this very nice. It could be turned into the most delightful little house. Somewhere to put a very special visitor."

2

The stables had been long neglected. The roofs were none too good; a clutter of wooden sheds had been built against the walls, and inside had been stored the rubbish of years. Old bicycles, an old perambulator, children's toys and mildewed books filled the place. There were even hens, cared for by no one, but well able to look after themselves, nesting in the mangers. All this ground floor was paved with cobblestones.

It was high summer now. Rose and I had taken a room in the village inn as a base for our campaign. She was, at the moment, up at the house, superintending the work on the kitchen quarters. The reconstruction of the stables had been left to me, and I was giving them a good look-over. All these cobblestones would have to come up and a hardwood floor go down. I climbed the shaky ladder that led to a trapdoor in the ceiling. Up here, the space was divided by wooden walls into two large rooms, with only skylights to let in the day. They could become dormer windows, and there would be plenty of space for a bathroom. I climbed upon a box and pushed up one of the creaking skylights to let in some air. I stuck my head through the opening and saw a young man in gray tweeds looking at the house. I took no notice of him. All sorts of people were turning up, concerned in one way or another with the work in hand.

To begin with, I said, there would have to be an almighty bonfire. I went down the ladder with the intention of starting a clearance at once. I took hold of the perambulator and pushed it through the door into the yard. The young man was standing there. "I can remember," he said, "being pushed about in that."

"In a perambulator?"

"In *that* perambulator."

He was fair, tall and thin. Too thin. He had a suitcase with him, and that was thin, too: thin cardboard, with the corners worn to fluff. His gray tweeds were fortified with leather wherever that would help to hold them together.

"You know this place?"

"I lived here. I was born here. D'you mind if I have a peep inside?"

"Oh, no. Come in."

He came in shyly. He seemed altogether a shy person. He had a charming deprecating smile.

There was a box full of tattered books. I had glanced through them and seen nothing that I wanted to keep. He pulled out a copy of Marryat's *Children of the New Forest*. "Good Lord!" he said. "Fancy this still knocking round! I used to like this."

He showed me the flyleaf: "Adrian Wybird, from Father. Christmas, 1912."

"I was fifteen," he said. "A bit old for Marryat—don't you think? Father always thought I was a kid. Still, two years later, at seventeen, I wasn't too old to be a second lieutenant."

"You went through that lot, did you?"

"Oh, rather!"

I looked at the blue veins in his thin wrists as he ruffled the pages, and at the whiskers fraying his shirt cuffs. The heels of his shoes were turned over. I felt sick.

"Would you like to keep that?" I asked. "Or any other books?"

"Oh, no. Souvenirs are not in my line. Forgive my intruding. I had no idea anybody'd be around."

"Would you care to look over the house?"

"No, thank you."

"My wife and I will be going down to the village for lunch in a moment. Would you join us?"

"No, thank you."

"Well, is there anything—?"

"Would you mind if I took a stroll up as far as the pavilion?"

"Of course not. It's a wonderful lookout."

"Yes. It was our favorite place—my sister and I."

"You have a sister?"

"I had. She was bumped off in France."

He took up the suitcase, started off, then said: "I'll leave this here. May I? I can pick it up on the way out."

337

There were white pigeons crooling as they strutted along the ridge of the stable roof, and there was the full drone of summer vibrating in the air. I sat on the ruins of a Chippendale chair and pulled book after book out of the box. Hall's *Algebra. De amicitia. Gulliver's Travels.* Some were signed, some not. One was signed, "Adrian Wybird. Rugby School."

The strong midday sun fell through the open door, showing up the frayed edges of the suitcase. I couldn't help it. I felt a burning shame as I did it, but I couldn't help it. I opened the filmsy lock, threw back the lid. There was what I expected: buttons, studs, tie pins, tape, knitting needles, notepaper and envelopes. I snapped the lock angrily and rushed to the house. "Give it a rest," I said to Rose. "Give it a rest. For God's sake let's go and eat."

She looked at me, surprised, but passed it over. "Look," she said, "through this window. You can see him up there. I watched him climbing up just now. There he is, sitting in the pavilion. Should we go and see who it is, and what he's up to?"

"No, let's go and eat. If some poor devil wants to rest his weary bones for a moment, that does us no harm."

I wanted to keep him from Rose. I didn't like the idea of her knowing that some poor Adam, pushed out of his native Eden, had been prowling round, peeping, remembering. I took care that she was not present when I questioned the pubkeeper about the Wybirds. He and old Wybird were of an age. He remembered him succeeding his father, "and bless you, Mr. Boothroyd, I remember being one of a gang that pulled him and his missus up to the house in a carriage when he brought her home after the marriage." A scholar, he was, a proper old bookworm, always writing, and worse than ever after his missus had died. That was when Mr. Adrian was born. Miss Jessie was a year older, killed in the war she was. They hadn't had any money, the Wybirds, not for a long time. Everyone knew that. And the old man was the last to know how to make it. "Moneylenders was the end of him, so they say. But whoever it was had the pinch on him, they closed in pretty quick when he died. That was in the last year of the war. Cleaned up everything—books, pictures, furniture, and put the place in the market. Well, it's nice to see someone back there at last."

"What happened to the old man's son?"

"What could happen to him, Mr. Boothroyd? We saw him about on leave once or twice, but after the old man died and all the stuff was carried out there was nowhere for him to come back to, was there?"

"No, I suppose not."

"I'm sorry for that sort. Nothing but schoolboys when the trouble started. Not properly trained to do a thing. Aye, it beats me, Mr. Boothroyd, what that sort can do in a bloody world like it is today."

338

The stables had completed their transformation by August. The bonfire had done its work, but I did not burn the books. I have a horror of burning books in any case, and there was something special about these books. I could not rationally explain my feeling about them, but I knew I had to keep them. There was, for example, a copy of *Little Women,* with a child's scribble on the flyleaf: "Jessie Wybird. Aged 12 years, three months and twenty days." Could I burn that? No. On the contrary, I took every care to conserve them. I had them laid out in the sunshine to chase away the damp and mildew. Some that were far gone I had restitched and rebound. There was a craftsman in the village, a genius with wood, whom I was employing a lot at that time. I got him to make a special bookcase for what I called the Wybird Collection. I tried to be facetious about it, to cover my deeply disturbed feelings. The thought of the young man wouldn't leave my mind.

There was another relic of the Wybirds. The ghouls who had closed in and cleaned up on the old man's death had overlooked it. I suppose they gave no more than one glance at the stable junk and then left it for someone else to clear up. What I found was a picture leaning against the wall in one of the upper rooms. No wonder it hadn't been noticed. A few planks hid it, and a pile of rotten harness was in front of the planks. There was a horse collar, with the straw extruding from the mildewed leather. Mice were nesting in the straw, and there was a strip of brass on the collar with a name engraved on it. Tiny Tim. A pony, I imagined, that had pulled the children about in a trap or jingle. Oh, yes. The stables were a reminiscent place. It was the picture that interested me—a portrait of a man. It was in a shocking condition, but, from what I could make out, the rig seemed to be eighteenth century. Miss Orlop was at her London flat, so I motored to town the next day and showed it to her. She was greatly excited. "Hogarth!" she said. "I'll bet you tuppence, Chad, it's a Hogarth. We must have it cleaned. I know an excellent man. And then we'll get an expert's opinion on the painter. How's Rose?"

"Very well, but hopping about more than I like, seeing that she's in the family way."

"She's not!"

"Oh, yes, she is. I should know. The Boothroyds are a virile race."

It was a nice little flat, but she looked out of place in it. She was aging visibly of late. Her eyes had become strangely hooded. She looked like a tattered old eagle in this neat box.

"Well," she said, "you've been a long time giving me your news, but now that you've condescended to do it, I'll give you mine. Your uncle's coming to live with me."

I couldn't help it. I sat back in my chair and rocked with laughter. "Oh, Miss Orlop," I said, "if it had been Lancelot I could have understood it. But Arthur! Cornwall will rock with scandal from end to end."

She did not reprove me, as I deserved to be reproved. It was a hot day. The white muslin of the curtains stirred in a small breeze, and there was a blessed glimpse of a tall tree's foliage. She was enveloped rather than dressed in some shimmer of Liberty stuff, and on a finger of one of her gnarled hands a ring held a vast cabochon emerald. She looked old and noble and sad.

"Did you know," she asked, "that he once asked me to marry him?"

"Yes."

"Well, I never wanted to, and I had reason enough for not doing so. But I'm very fond of him, and he's very fond of me. I suppose we have something in common, being figures of fun."

I saw that this was something real and serious, and I had nothing to say.

"He's a bit of an old woman," she said, "and I'm a bit of a man. We should get on. Why on earth shouldn't we? We shall be good for one another. Pentyrch is a big house—plenty of room for both of us; and if anyone, down there or up here, thinks there's cause for scandal, well, let 'em think and be damned. I haven't worried so far about what stupid noodles think, and I'm not going to start now. Anyway, your mother will be about the place."

"Oh, no," I said. "Now that Uncle Arthur's finished in Smurthwaite, I'm asking my mother to live with me. Rose agrees. Mother can either have the little house we're making out of the stables or she can live in Chalk Hill. Whichever she likes. It's time I did something for her. I haven't been much of a son."

Miss Orlop said frankly: "No, you haven't. And if your mother would like that, so much the better. I'd rather have Arthur to myself."

I got up to go. "Bless you, my children," I said lightly; but all the same I found something moving in the thought of those two oddities coming together at last.

4

A low semicircle of brick wall shut in the yard that stood in front of the stables and had now been cleaned up. A white gate led into the yard. Under the wall, inside, autumn flowers were approaching their blooming time. The little building had been repointed and retiled. The rotting window frames had been torn out and replaced with sash windows. There were two on either side of the door, and in the roof were two dormers. A small kitchen had been built below, with a bathroom next to it. When you went through the door you faced a staircase that had taken the place of the old ladder. On the left was the main sitting room. The floor was oak blocks. The ceiling was raftered. The new fireplace was a simple arch of brick containing a cradle grate. A settee and two easy chairs were covered with rosy chintz. Above the fireplace was the Hogarth. Miss Orlop had been right. It was the only picture in the room. Between two electric light sconces, its color glowed. To one side of the fireplace stood the bookcase containing the Wybird Collection. It was a lovely room. I was proud of it. But my mother never lived in it, or in Chalk Hill. When, last November, she had come up to London for the first night of my play, I had seen a change in her. She tired easily, and I was aware of Uncle Arthur's anxious solicitude. He confided to me that the doctor had warned her against overexertion, and he was taking the doctor's orders so strictly that he fussed if she carried so much as an umbrella. It had been arranged that he and she should travel to London together and that he should bring her on to Chalk Hill and spend a week with us before going down to St. Michael Pendeverel. But first of all there was a great to-do at the house in Smurthwaite. They had to decide what was to be sold, what my mother should have sent to us, and what Uncle Arthur should send to Pentyrch.

It was a long time before Uncle Arthur found himself able to tell me of the absurdity of my mother's death. It must have been at least a year later, and even then he could not speak of it without tears in his eyes. I have written before of being aware that a jealousy of Miss Orlop troubled her, and even he could not fail to discover this when he told her of his decision to live at Pentyrch. Not much was said, but there was a tiresome atmosphere, with little flames of bickering spurting up now and then. I suppose there was something in her point of view. She had faithfully kept house for him for more than twenty years. "It's too absurd," she said, "such a drastic change at our time of life. There's no reason whatever why you should go to Pentyrch or why I should be imposed on Chad and his wife. Whether your job's ended or not, it would be common sense to remain in this house. We're Yorkshire people, and I'm happy in Yorkshire. All this nonsense tires me out."

She began to palpitate, and that frightened him. He insisted on her going to bed.

And there was argument about what should be taken and what left. Uncle Arthur wanted to take with him the by now rather revolting remains of Madeleine. She was molting badly, but he had disguised this by dressing her in one of the yellow coats that he liked to see on her.

341

My mother laughed at the idea of Madeleine making the journey to Cornwall, and Uncle Arthur said: "Very well, Edie, if it would please you to see poor Madeleine remain here to fall into the hands of strangers, she shall remain."

At last a small van came to take Uncle Arthur's things away. It was a very hot day, and when all was stowed and the tailboard had gone up my mother came downstairs and looked at the glass case containing Madeleine standing on the hall table. She said: "You're not letting them leave that behind? You'll never forgive yourself if you do."

Uncle Arthur made no reply. He walked into the den where he had been accustomed to wear his tasseled smoking cap, and the van moved off through the sultry noon.

A fatal compunction must have smitten my mother as she watched that bowed back moving from her. She put both arms round the case, picked it up, and ran into the street. The van was some way off, and she pursued it, shouting as she ran: "Stop! Stop! You must take this!"

The driver heard her at last, checked the horse, and looked back. She never overtook him. He saw her fall, and when she was picked up she was dead, and amid the broken glass the brittle bones of Madeleine, which, at best, had never been more than a chicken's, were finally shattered beyond hope of reshaping.

But of what had led to this strange tragicomic end of my mother's life I heard nothing when I went to Smurthwaite to stand by Uncle Arthur's side at the grave in Geldersome's Four Acre. "Beyond this point horses must proceed at a walking pace. By Order, Arthur J. Geldersome, Town Clerk," a notice said at the entrance. As he passed that spot he took off his hat as though for the last time saluting his municipal eminence. All he said to me about his sister was: "When she was fifteen, Chad, I brought her to Smurthwaite for a birthday outing. This cemetery was a field. We ate our sandwiches in it. How strange are the ways of Providence."

5

Simon Boothroyd was born on the first of September, 1925. On September the second I was standing in the bedroom watching Rose suckling the child. Astonishing creatures, women. Last night all seemed to me agony and terror. I couldn't stay in the house. I climbed up to the pavilion among the beech trees and looked dumbly at our bedroom window which faced that way. How soothing beech trees are! They are my favorites of all noble trees, with their serene gray trunks and clouds of whispering leaves. But they didn't soothe me that night, and the leaves didn't whisper. Everything seemed tranced, expecting this advent. A full moon flooded the roofs of the house with silver, and beyond the house the countryside was breathing out a quiet mist that shone opal.

It must have been nearly midnight when I went down and found Bessie Middlemass in the hall. "It's a boy," she said. "Eight pounds seven ounces."

"That doesn't sound much."

"Well, it's only a beginning," she said reasonably. "You'd better give yourself a drink."

I did, and then I was allowed a moment's glimpse of Rose, sleeping soundly, and of the child, who gave me an odd sort of conspiratorial wink, as though we had managed something pretty good between us.

Bessie led me firmly out of the bedroom. I thanked her for the kindness she had shown. She had been running the house for a week, and there was a battle light about her suggesting that she would be there for another week yet. She brushed off the thanks, and told me to go to bed, which I did.

And now, with only half a day behind us, all this fear and sweat seemed remote, and there was Rose, cool and beautiful, feeding the child, and I was standing with my back to the bed, looking up at the pavilion. I could see Henrietta there, reading a book. Rose said: "September the first seems my favorite day for having babies, darling. That was Henrietta's birthday, too."

Henrietta—Weimar—1909!

"Good lord!" I cried. "I wish you'd told me. I knew she was a September child, but I didn't know the day. I hope she won't feel slighted."

I turned to the entrancing picture on the bed. Rose's hair was down. One pink nipple peeped through. The child's fuzzy head was laid greedily over the other. I had never seen anything more beautiful. But she looked a little sad.

"I'm sorry about Henrietta," she said. "I should have told you about the birthday. I had bought her Rupert Brooke's poems. She adores them. And then, yesterday, I felt like nothing on earth, and she went out of my mind."

"Well," I said gallantly. "You still look like nothing on earth. You look like something heavenly. May I share with my son?"

I bent down and kissed the warm disengaged breast.

But she didn't smile. She said: "Henrietta hasn't been to see me today. Take my book to her, will you, darling, and try to make things right with her. It's in that drawer."

I took the book, glanced at the author's face reproduced as a frontispiece, and looked again toward the white pavilion. Sitting there in the mild sunshine, with the leaves turning autumn gold about her, Henrietta looked lonely and aloof. She wasn't reading. A book lay in her lap. Her eyes were wandering.

I made to go, and as I was at the door Rose said: "Darling."

I turned to her, and she was smiling now. She plucked the child from her breast and held him up. "Thank you, Chad," she said.

I grinned at her. "Don't mention it, Mrs. Boothroyd. It's a pleasure."

So it was with a mixture of elation and melancholy that I crossed the field behind the house, climbed the rise, and came upon Henrietta. She gave me no time for small talk. She said at once: "Do you think I could go back to school?"

"But I thought you hated it, Henrietta—the hockey and the horses and all of it?"

"No, no. Not all of it. There's a lot besides the hockey and the horses. I think, perhaps, I'd better put up with them for the sake of other things."

She had a grave adult way of speaking that delighted me. I had never tried to talk down to Henrietta, and since she had seemed glad to leave school I had been glad, too, to have her with us. And she *had* been glad. On her first visit to Chalk Hill she had wandered everywhere, delighted, and had asked: "Is it really necessary, Mother, for me to remain at that boring school? I wouldn't waste my time here. I'm rather good at self-cultivation. Don't think me a prig, but I really am. And I wouldn't be a nuisance to you and Uncle Chad."

That is what she had settled down to calling me, after several false starts.

"Why, darling," Rose asked her, "what's so exciting about this place? You were never gone on Pentyrch, which has so much more to offer."

"Oh, I like Pentyrch, but, frankly, I *don't* like being with Grandmamma. She rather terrifies me. I don't think she altogether approves of my being illegitimate."

Well, that startled me and Rose; we decided that if there were ghosts in the girl's mind she had better stay with us; especially as she added: "Of course, the girls at school don't know that I'm illegitimate, but they *do* know that Flo Burbage is, and it's not pleasant. Silly little fools. Flo's father is Lord Birstall, and I'd rather have him than any of the dreary old bores who drift along at half-term."

So, I noted, she was ready to risk something that was "not pleasant" rather than stay here with us.

"What are you reading?" I asked, playing for time. I took the book from her lap. *English Grass,* by Eustace Hawke. On the flyleaf was written, "My book—Henrietta Hawke."

I had seen the book with her before, but I had not seen that inscription.

I said: "You wrote that yesterday, didn't you?"

344

"Yes."

"Why?"

We looked at one another, and her face flushed. She hesitated for a moment before saying: "Well, it *is* my name, isn't it?"

"No."

Henrietta looked embarrassed at that frankness. She was always called Henrietta Orlop. In that name she had been entered at school, and Rose, wearing Billy's wedding ring, had passed as Mrs. Orlop. But Rose had been candid with Henrietta. As soon as the girl had been old enough to be told such things, she had been told of her parentage. I should have liked to take her hand and so pass some comfort into her from my own love for her. But she was like a nervous filly that would bolt at a touch.

"Do you remember your father?"

"I don't remember anybody who called himself my father. But I remember Mother and a man taking me to Mrs. Appleby's house at Hampstead and leaving me there. I am sure that was my father. He was very beautiful."

I remembered Rose and Eustace at the Café Royal that night when Greg and Phoebe and I dined there to say good-by to our youth, and, for ought we knew, to one another. Yes, Eustace was very beautiful then.

Rather forlornly, Henrietta took the book from my hands and opened it at the frontispiece portrait of Eustace. She showed it to me without speaking.

"Yes," I said, "that is your father. I knew him well. His father married my mother."

At that, to my delight, the dawn of a smile trembled over her unbearable young solemnity. "What a mess!" she said. "You old people do make things complicated for us young ones, don't you?"

"I'm afraid we do, Henrietta. You must try to forgive us."

"This is my father, who is your mother's stepson. But I mustn't have my father's name. And there was Sir William Pascoe, whose name I mustn't have. And there's you, whose name I mustn't have. I don't seem to belong to anybody, do I?"

"My dear," I said. "You belong to everybody who loves you. May I be one of them?"

She said nothing, but put her hand in mine.

"And your mother loves you. She loves you all the more because she loved your father so much. Even though you can't have his name because they never married."

She nodded.

"And if you love your father, so much the better. He was a father worth having. So far as names go, that's just a matter of convenience.

345

Your mother is Rose Boothroyd. I am Chad Boothroyd. If you would like to be Henrietta Boothroyd, we can fix that legally."

"Would you like me to be Henrietta Boothroyd?"

"Very much."

"Then I will be."

"I didn't wish you many happy returns yesterday because I didn't know it was your birthday. Your mother remembered you and bought you a present, but then she was in great pain and forgot—not you, but everything except her pain. She has asked me to give it to you, and to say that she loves you."

I gave her the book, and she read what was written on the flyleaf: "To Henrietta, my first-born darling. With Mother's love."

Her smile was now full-blown. "I am so happy," she said.

I told her proudly: "We shall call the new baby Simon. Your half-brother."

She got up and was frankly laughing. "Well, with a whole mother and half a brother I should be able to make out. When may I see them?"

"Mere husbands and fathers are not allowed to answer such questions. You must ask the nurse. What I suggest is that we now have a good walk. We'll walk to St. Aspen's, have our morning coffee at that place you like, and walk back. Then, after lunch, you can make your bow to mother and child."

And that is what we did, walking through the golden weather, kicking the rustling leaves and admiring the polished mahogany of the fallen conkers. The hedges were full of the bright berries of bryony, and blackberries were ripening. "Long, long ago," I said to Henrietta, "on a day such as this, I was gathering blackberries near Pentyrch. I had a basketful and was sitting on a gate when along came an old white horse drawing a broken-down carriage. And in the carriage was a beautiful girl, younger than you. I suppose she'd be about twelve. I gaped at her and dropped the basket, and the blackberries rolled in the dust."

"And her name was Rose," said Henrietta.

"How on earth do you know?"

"Because when you tell me about the beautiful little girl you look just as you look when you're gazing at Mother."

"You've spoiled my story. But never mind. You've given me a good testimonial."

6

Sometimes Greg and Phoebe came down to Chalk Hill for a week end, and sometimes Max and Bessie. If Greg and Phoebe, they brought

Penelope. Henrietta was her mother all over again, as they say, so far as coloring went, but she promised to be taller. She was already as tall as Rose, and in her graver moments, which came often, she looked more than her sixteen years. The contrast between her and Penelope was almost ludicrous, for Greg's girl was short and fat, with the flaxen curls and round light-blue eyes of a German doll. With the hand from which the finger was missing Greg would stroke the mustache that he had kept since the war and watch the girls setting off together, pushing Simon in his pram, and he would say: "I don't know where Penelope gets all that fat from. Look at me and Phoebe—we're not fat. And that Nordic coloring. I suppose that's the Hawke strain. Eustace was as fair as they come."

I remember the day he said this. It was in the summer after Simon's birth. Rose was with us. She said: "Why don't you send her away to school, Greg? Do you think it's a good idea to keep her at home?"

"We talked it over, Phoebe and I, and decided it was the best thing to do. She's a bit dumb, you know."

"Oh, no!" Rose protested. "She's a charming girl."

"If you mean her manners are passable and so forth, all right," Greg said. "But she doesn't seem to have anything to think with. That's one reason why we kept her at home. She goes to a day school, and when she's in the house she's got us to talk to and to keep an eye on her. And there are all sorts of interesting and intelligent people for her to meet." He shook his head. "But, dammit, Ah doan't know. Talk abaht water off a duck's back!"

I smiled at Greg's lapse into reight Smurthwaite lingo, but I wondered if this was a smiling matter. How long ago it seemed—before the war—when he and I had taken the journey to Manchester and he had shown me the small house at Didsbury. I had chaffed him about the municipal plaque that would go up on the wall, and he had said there would be two: one for him and one for his son. I had looked into the son's bedroom, and had watched the carpenter building a fence to keep the son from falling down the area steps. And there had been no son. How deep did that sort of thing go? Did Greg still remember? Had he foredoomed Penelope? She was not a brilliant child, but she wasn't a bad little dumpling.

Rose had moved off by the time Greg had come out of a brooding fit and exclaimed: "Ah, well! I don't suppose there was ever a father on God's earth who wasn't plagued at the beginning with the notion that his children would do something better than he did. They're such attractive little devils to start with. We live and learn."

"Penelope," I said, "will have one claim to immortality. She was Eustace's sedative while he was writing *English Grass*. I remember your

347

telling me how he would park himself with the pram in the Marie Louise Gardens. Does Phoebe ever hear from him?"

"Not a word. So far as I know, nobody does. *English Grass* still sells, and Phoebe asked the publisher where he sent the royalties to. Another blank. The publisher knows no more than you or I. Eustace just managed to get out of that hospital, and from there on he doesn't exist."

"Poor devil."

"He's a devil all right—in his satanic pride, anyhow. Can you imagine anyone more in need of what we could give him, or more quick to say: 'To hell with their pity'?"

"He'd be poor material for the paternal state you long to give us."

"He certainly would," Greg readily admitted.

7

My study was on the first floor of the house. It had once been the principal bedroom, and a cozy dressing room opened out of it. This became the office of my tall and beautiful secretary, Henrietta Boothroyd—now formally and officially entitled to that name. In November of 1927, when she was eighteen years old, I was standing at the window, looking down at the lawn gray with frost. The fire was purring. A distant squall from Simon broke the quiet, which then settled down again. It was a good place for working, was Chalk Hill, and I had not been idle. Since coming down here, I had written two novels that had had moderate success; I had finished a new play that I had shown to nobody but Henrietta, who typed it; and the unclothed skeletons of two more were in my notebooks. Henrietta loved her work and earned her pay. She went through my morning post and soon developed a flair for dealing with it. She knew, impeccably, what to drop into the wastepaper basket, what to answer herself without troubling me, and what to bring me for personal attention. It was rather more than two years now since she had made her rather pathetic little boast that she was good at self-cultivation. She certainly was. Rose and I were very happy about her, and, for herself, she was gaining all the assurance and poise that came from doing a job well, and knowing it.

She came through from her room now with a letter in her hand. "I think you'd better deal with this yourself," she said. "It's from Max Middlemass. I don't know whether you'll call it good news or not."

I stood with my back to the fire, over which hung two pictures: Miss Orlop's painting of Rose, and one of the Degas pictures I had brought from Menin Gate. Max had insisted on our taking it as a wedding present.

I read his letter, and was aware of Henrietta studying my face anxiously. Max said that he had decided, rather abruptly, to take off *I Don't Want to Die* in London. "On the eleventh, which is in eight days' time, it will have completed its third year. A good moment, I think, to end, before a certain slight falling off in public interest becomes pronounced. When are you coming to town? I expect you have something up your sleeve, and, anyway, it's time we had a get-together about this and that."

I smiled, chiefly in order to relieve the tension in Henrietta.

"Well, it had to end," I said, "and how many playwrights have the luck to take a child to a first night and see her grow into a handsome young woman before the last one? I don't suppose I'll ever have such a stroke again, but we'll get along. See if you can get hold of Max now."

He was in, but we arranged to meet at one o'clock at the Garrick Club, of which we were both members. I motored to town, and after lunch Max and I lingered for a long time, talking of this and that, and then I went to see Tom Cannock. We had tea together, and then there was just time to look up the man who published my novels. What with one thing and another, it was later than I had hoped before I was at liberty to start for Chalk Hill.

My publisher's place was in Essex Street, and I came out of his office into the gray of the November evening at about half-past five. It was but a moment's walk to the Embankment, and I decided to stretch my absence by a few more minutes in order to watch a sight that always fascinated me: the daily retreat of London's great army over the bridges.

On the Embankment the wind was cold and cutting, rustling the last sere leaves of the plane trees and ruffling the water as tide and wind found themselves at odds. On foot, on bicycles, in cars and busses, the people streamed south over the bridges. I was halfway between Blackfriars and Waterloo, and over against me, near Cleopatra's Needle, a bearded pavement artist was packing up for the day. It was a bitter night even for those who could move, and I pitied the poor devil nailed to his pitch with the wind agitating his long unkempt beard and hair. He was nailed to the pitch by something more than the need to earn the coppers which I watched him slip into his pocket, for he was legless and nailed to the crude wooden platform on which he squatted. He lifted his pictures away from the wall, tied them together, and looked about him, as though expecting someone.

He was a fair way off, for I was standing in the Victoria Gardens with a wide roadway of traffic swirling between me and him, but even from this distant view I formed the impression of nobility. The way he sat, upright despite his fearful disablement, looking about him with serenity in the wind that had a sting of sleet, moved me deeply. I didn't doubt that the war had brought him there, though he was not following the fashion of decorating his chest with medals. But he was decorated with more than medals. He seemed adorned and ennobled by man's superb ability to take the worst that could come and sit among the ruins, almost contemptuous. The beard and hair gave him a dash of Lear on the heath, but without madness. He looked as though winter wind and man's ingratitude alike were things he didn't give a damn for. I ceased to notice that he had no legs. Upright like that on his wheeled truck, he might have been a bearded squatting Buddha, far removed from the rush and dither, the hoot of motors, the iron clang of tramwheels, the treading of impatient feet, that encompassed but did not touch him.

I felt moved to cross the road and speak to him, but I did not do so, for at that moment, on the pavement outside the garden, waiting for a break in the traffic so that he might cross over to the river side, I saw young Adrian Wybird. More than two years had passed since his brief appearance at Chalk Hill, and a glance was enough to show that the two years had not been kind to him. He carried the same sort of tattered cardboard case. His gloveless hands were thin and blue, and I guessed that beneath the inadequate shabby raincoat his clothes were as thin as his hands. He made me think of a far-gone building which will have to be repaired if the corrosion of neglect is not altogether to destroy it, and that soon.

And then I was sitting on one of the seats in the garden, my elbows on my knees, my head in my hands, trying to steady a world that was oddly vibrant and unstable.

I had remembered a day when Uncle Arthur took me from the hospital to the house in Bayswater and we found Rose in pieces. Phoebe had rung up to tell her of a letter that had come with bad news of Eustace. Uncle Arthur and I had gone to Hampstead to see what, in fact, this letter said. It was from one of Eustace's officers, and I recalled the beautiful spirit of it, for it had understood what Eustace was and what his loss would be. What shook me now was to recall that the writer's name was Adrian Wybird. It was Eustace I was thinking of on that far-off day, and of Rose and Phoebe, not of the letter writer. The name didn't stick and the years had erased it. But after the young man had come to Chalk Hill and told me his name, something uneasily stirred. More years passed, and it slept again, but suddenly I literally *saw* it, saw the handwriting on the page, read what was written there. "Believe me when I say in all sincerity that I am not making an official report. I am telling you, from the depth of my heart, that in a very special way I share this sorrow with you. Yours sincerely, Adrian Wybird."

I knew that as Adrian Wybird stood there, watching for a break in the traffic, he was about to cross over to meet Eustace. It was a long time before I could bring myself to stand on shaking knees. When I did, and looked across the road, they were gone.

8

Driving home, I loathed myself. Shock had given place to exultation. How fortunate, I was telling myself, that I had *not* crossed the road and spoken to Eustace. I would not have recognized him, even face to face: I was sure of that. He looked an old man. But he could not have failed to recognize me. It did not occur to me that, though recognizing me, he might have chosen to say nothing, to act the stranger, and to take care that henceforth the chances of an encounter should cease. But, ten to one, that is what he would have done. However, I didn't think of that. I was thinking what a narrow shave I had had. Eustace might have come back into my life, and I didn't want him to. I was afraid of him. I was afraid of what he might do to me and Rose. He was a wreck, robbed of his manhood, but I remembered the day when I took Rose on the river as far as the Nore, and suddenly she fled from me when we had got back and landed at Westminster. She had fled to Eustace, as incapacitated then as now, but she had fled to him because she loved him. And so I was afraid of him, and I hoped I had seen the last of him; and I was riven as this hope collided in my mind with a sense of the baseness that gave it birth.

It takes little more than an hour to motor from London to Chalk Hill, and I pray that life will not afford me many hours like that one. Such companions were with me: my fear, my self-loathing, my sense of life's unfair rewards: Eustace on his square yard of planking with the sleety wind tousling his hair and beard and I in this swift warm padded comfort. That boy Wybird looking chilled to the bone in soul as well as body, crossing the road to wheel Eustace to who knows what lair while I was bowling along to dinner and fireside in the home that so lately was his. Three soldiers: Hawke, Wybird and Boothroyd; and one of them, for a month's work, plucks great fortune and some fame out of the disaster, and here he is—Look at him! I said to myself—dashing away like hell lest the other two, or either of them, should put a finger into his pie and pull out a plum.

"How did it go, darling?" Rose asked.

"Oh, well enough. But it was a filthy day in town—bitterly cold."

"Had you better go up and have a hot bath?"

"I don't think so."

"Well, you must get some food into you. Dinner's ready any time you like. Go up and kiss Simon. He won't sleep till he's seen you."

"Still love me, darling?"

"As much as ever."

"How much is that?"

She gave me a light kiss. "Don't keep Simon waiting."

9

The play that I had finished was called *Armed Neutrality*. I had mentioned it to Max at lunch and explained to him the general run of its idea, and he had commanded me to give it a final brush-up and send him a copy. After dinner, I said to Henrietta: "Let's take the new play down to the stables and have a look through it."

We still called the little house the stables, chiefly, I think, so that the word might pridefully emphasize the change that had taken place. The electric fires were occasionally turned on to air the bedrooms, and now and then Henrietta and I would work in the sitting room with the log fire blazing. There was just that added touch of remoteness, self-contained serenity, about the place that we both liked. The trees that clustered behind it were a favorite place for hooting owls.

I switched on the light, put a match to the fire, and Henrietta drew the curtains. The friendly room leapt to life, seemed to open its arms to receive us.

"I like to think," Henrietta said, "that only so little time ago there were mangers against the wall, and beasts happily munching their hay, and straw on the floor. I know it's all gone, and this is rather sophisticated, but I can recall it, shut my eyes and see it. It was the sort of place Jesus could have been born in."

"You don't sound in a mood for work," I said with a smile, and I was glad, for I was not in a mood for work myself. I had brought her here to talk about things so important that I was at a loss how to begin.

I lit my pipe, and changed my shoes for the slippers I kept there. The fire took hold of the logs, and I put out the lamp. Ruddy light and black shadow danced a changing flickering dance, and Henrietta sank into a chair and lay back with her eyes closed. The bookcase containing the Wybird Collection was at her hand.

"I often wonder," she said, "when I sit in here, about the people who were here before us. I turn over these books and read what's on the title pages, and take note of the bits that have been underlined. Adrian Wybird and Jessie Wybird. I think Jessie must have been a serious girl. She always underlined the serious bits in her books. In her Milton she underlined 'He for God only, she for God in him.' I know so little about Jessie Wybird. I sometimes wonder whether she underlined that because she was annoyed and thought it belittled women, or whether she was madly in love with someone and would have wanted to approach even her God under his direction. Perhaps she married him," Henrietta mused.

"No. She didn't marry anyone. She was killed in the war."

Henrietta sat up sharply. "You knew her?"

"No. But I've heard things about her. I have a bad habit of loitering in village pubs and talking to landlords. I don't know whether I should recommend it to a young lady like you, but our landlord is a good type. I've heard him swear like a trooper, and he plays the organ in church on Sundays."

"Never mind the landlord. Tell me something about the Wybirds."

I looked up at the Hogarth over the mantelpiece. "That, I imagine, is one of them."

"You are most annoying. I can read you like a book, you know."

"I'm not surprised. I'm transparently honest."

"There was something conspiratorial about you when you asked me to come here this evening. You didn't want to talk about the play. You have something to tell me. I expect Mother noticed it. And now that we're here, you talk about the village landlord and an eighteenth-century Wybird."

"Well, it's the Wybirds I want to talk about. Jessie, I know, is dead. The boy, Adrian, is alive. I've met him, twice."

"Is he a nice boy?"

"When I say boy I'm a bit wide of the mark. I suppose he's about thirty, and he's been through a lot—the war, and then an unhappy time after the war. I saw him today. I think he was starving."

Henrietta looked shocked, and asked practically: "Did you feed him?"

"I don't think he would have liked me to. And, anyway, I didn't speak to him."

I knocked out my pipe and put on more logs. For a time we said nothing; then Henrietta got up from her chair and came and sat on a pouf by my knees. She took my hand and said: "You're worried about something, aren't you, darling? Tell me."

"I *am* worried about something. I'm worried about you. How much do you know about Eustace—about your father?"

"Not much—not much about him *as my father*. I know a lot about him from reading his books. I adore him. But about him and Mother, I don't know. I just guess, and I don't think that's good for me."

"Have you asked her to tell you?"

"Yes. She says, 'One of these days.' And you know what that **means.**

Never. I can feel at times that she's longing to tell me, but she can't bring herself to do it."

"Do you think she would mind if I did?"

"She'd probably be glad."

"You say you guess things. What do you guess?"

"I know some things and I guess others. I know that I was born in Weimar. I can remember a few things out of that time. I can remember the blue designs on some white tiles of a porcelain stove. I remember sitting by that stove when it was snowing outside, and I had a doll with blue eyes and flaxen hair, like Penelope Appleby. But there's no father in the picture, and I guess he'd deserted my mother."

"Yes."

"I don't remember a thing about the journey back to England, but I remember how odd everything seemed when I got there, and how terrified I was of Miss Orlop, and how sad my mother was. She became *dim* to me, not bright. Do you understand?"

"Yes."

"Then there was Pentyrch, and I met Sir William Pascoe. He wasn't Sir William then. Miss Orlop and my mother called him Billy, and so I called him Billy, too! Imagine that! I remember how one day Miss Orlop told me that Billy was going to be my father, and I asked 'Why?' which annoyed her. Then there was the wedding. I've been told since that you were there, but I don't remember. You didn't exist till I met you one day in Hatchard's bookshop.

"There was Cambridge, and oh, it was dull! I went to a day school, and my memory of all that time is just a long brown blur. Except one day toward the end of it. A man came to the house, and now I am guessing again. I guess it was my father. There was talk about spending a day on the river, going up to Grantchester, and child as I was, I could feel how madly excited my mother was. She said: 'We'll take Henrietta,' and the man said 'No,' and I remember how my heart sank into my boots. It was a Saturday—no school. I should have loved to go on the river with that exciting man, but when he said 'No' I knew my mother would not insist. I was not first. She kissed me, and they hurried off together, and I spent a miserable day. Uncle Pascoe, as I was calling him then, was away for the week end.

"They came back sooner than I had expected, and—I'm guessing again now—they had decided in a great hurry to go away together. Some of my clothes were bundled into a suitcase, and the day became absolutely hectic for a child whose last few years had been lived like a long funeral. It ended up by my being left with Mr. and Mrs. Appleby.

"Well, then there was the war, and my mother came back to me; and there was the end of the war. And there was the divorce and all that mess. By then I was beginning to be old enough to understand something about what was happening. My mother told me that Eustace Hawke was my father, and that he was terribly wounded. It was a most unhappy time, and I didn't know where I was. I asked if I should see my father again, and she said, with a terrible sort of earnestness, 'Oh, yes. Oh, yes. It must be, darling. Whatever happens, it must be.' And then, soon after we met you at Hatchard's, she came down to Pentyrch, and one day there she told me that neither of us would see my father again."

There was a long silence, and then I asked: "Would you like to see your father again?"

"Oh, yes," she said without hesitation. "He's nothing but a specter to me, but such a beautiful specter. I read and read again all his books, and I remember his face and know his picture. He is so lovely. I am proud that he is my father."

I said: "Do you want to know *all* about him, or just treasure a few bright images?"

She answered sagely: "Who can know all about anyone? I expect he's very unhappy, wherever he is."

"You are right, my dear, in saying that I can't know all about Eustace. There were things about him that I loved. There were things I hated. Do you think you should know them?"

"Tell me anything you like. I hate being in the dark."

"Well, let me say a few things, without comment. He abandoned your mother and you in Germany quite thoughtlessly. He had abandoned other women before, and abandoned others afterward. He abandoned you again when he took your mother away from her husband. After the war, your mother showed an extraordinary devotion to him. Do you know the consequence of his wounds?"

"No."

I told her: "His manhood was destroyed. He could never be a husband again, except insofar as a ceremony can make a man a husband, which isn't far. Despite that, your mother wanted him back, married or not. He abandoned her again, and terrible though her life with him would have been, I think that was the basest abandonment of all. It was throwing God's own mercy back into her teeth. She was angelic even to dream of doing it."

I felt Henrietta's fist clench on my knee, and then she said: "I should still like to know him. How splendid they are—my father and my mother."

What to say to that I did not know. And then Rose came in. "It's time you two were back," she said. "Anyway, you don't seem to be doing any work."

I got up and put her down into my chair. "I was just about to do

355

the hardest job of my life," I said. "I'm glad you're here as I do it. I was going to tell Henrietta that I know where her father is. I ran into Eustace this afternoon."

10

Henrietta stood up when her mother came into the room. Now she sat down again on the pouf at Rose's feet and held her hand as she had held mine. I looked at them sitting there, and suddenly I was extraordinarily happy. An intuition that all was well flooded me. It was an assurance that had come to me a few times in my life—the last time when I got up in the studio at Pentyrch after finishing the play and knew, with a vivid certainty, that, whatever might happen to it, it was good. I had never, till now, had this certainty about Rose. Our marriage had been happy. My long, long dream, coming true, had not brought disillusion. But my happiness had had a quality almost of anguish at times, because of Eustace; and now this was gone. I bent down and kissed Rose, and she smiled at me and said: "Sit here." I sat on the rug at her feet.

"What have you been telling Henrietta?" she asked.

"Everything, so far as I know it."

"I don't think you have," she said quietly. "I am sure you haven't told her how good you have been to me—how patient, and willing to accept whatever I did. If Henrietta is being told things, let her be told that."

Henrietta said: "Tell Mother about the Wybirds."

Here was another thing that had suddenly become unknotted. I remembered the day when Adrian Wybird had turned up here and had strolled to the pavilion and Rose had pointed him out to me, asked who he was, what he was up to. I hadn't told her. From that day to this I had said nothing about him. I had nursed in my mind almost a sense of guilt, of being an interloper; and pictures had from time to time visited me of that boy's dark lot set against my own brighter faring. I hoped, in my bad moods, that I should never see him again; and now I had seen him, desperately worse, and I was glad. I knew that this, too, was part of my sudden happiness.

"Do you remember," I said to Rose, whose hand was warm on my head, "while we were moving in here, you saw a young man in the pavilion and asked me who it was?"

"I don't remember whether he was young or old. I remember a man."

"That was Adrian Wybird."

I told them of what had passed between me and Adrian that day and of my conversation with the pubkeeper.

"I saw Adrian again today."

I told them of that, too, and of Eustace, and of my sudden understanding of the relationship between the two. I painted the picture in low tones. I said nothing of the sleety wind or of Eustace's strange prophetic air. I merely said: "I can't get Eustace's face out of my mind. Despite what I've told you, it was a happy face. It's hard to believe, but he's happy. I'm sure of it."

Well, now they knew it all. I was glad to be rid of the burden, or at any rate to be sharing it. I wondered if I had done the right thing. Driving back from London, I had told myself that I would do anything to keep Rose from meeting Eustace again. Now I had put the whole thing into her lap, for her to look at it and decide.

So there we sat, with the fire sunk to a glow of embers, and one of Rose's arms was round my neck and one round Henrietta's. It was as though she were a medium, bringing us three into a current of love. I felt for the first time that she was not only a beautiful woman but a spiritually strong one. I wondered how much of it she had absorbed from Eustace and from her love for him. I had more than once seen her shattered by a crisis, but in this crisis, whatever she felt, she was in control. Leaning against her, I was reassured.

At last she said: "Do you remember, Chad, when we were fitting out this place, we said we'd keep it for a visitor—'Perhaps some very special visitor,' I said. I wonder whether that's going to be so, in a way we didn't know?" She got up. "Well, it's getting late. We'd better be off to bed."

In bed, I said, "Well?"

She said: "There are loves and loves, darling. And there are things that only a fool would break. There's Simon, and, believe it or not, there's you."

She put her arms around me.

11

No one who knew Eustace would think it possible for me to go up to him and say: "Well, Eustace, here we are again. Let's talk things over." There would have to be something different from that. I decided to be at the pitch early, and to tackle Adrian when he had left Eustace installed for the day.

This worked well enough. I saw them come, saw the pictures propped against the wall, and saw Adrian set out. I watched the way he took, made a detour, running, came round a corner and bumped into him. It was a nice bit of acting, so effective that I knocked the flimsy cardboard case out of his hand. It burst open, and the contents spilled onto the filthy pavement. It was all lace, of various sorts and colors. My shoes crushed a lot of it into the mire. The weather had been wet for some days.

Adrian said: "Damn you, you clumsy oaf! Can't you look where you're going?" He seemed on the edge of tears.

"I'm sorry, Mr. Wybird."

He had not been looking at me. His eyes were on the frisky bits of frilling stamped into the mud, and his mind, no doubt, was on his lost earnings. He glanced up, and at first my face meant nothing to him. Then he remembered me.

"Mr. Boothroyd."

"Yes."

To see someone he knew, even so remotely, seemed for a moment to cheer him. His thin face brightened, but quickly went dark again.

I picked up the damaged stuff, wrung water from some that had been in the gutter, and was about to drop it back into the case, when he stayed my hand. "No. Don't spoil what's left. It's a day's work thrown away already to pay for what's ruined."

"It was my fault. Let me pay for it. Damn it," I said, overcome by shame and anger, "let me pay for the whole bloody issue, good and bad. Take a day off and get some grub into your guts."

He looked as if he were about to explode into wrath, to say: "To hell with you and your charity," but he choked it back and said quietly: "Very well. Thank you," and that told me, more than a thousand words could do, how far he was gone.

We were near Blackfriars Bridge. I stuffed all those bits of whorish frippery back into the pitiable ruptured cardboard bag, took it in my hand and crossed the road to the river wall, he tagging at my heels. The tide was a high brown swirl, and I swung the wretched case up and out, smack into the water. "To hell with that as a way of making a living," I said.

"You're very high and mighty."

"I'm nothing of the sort. I'm crawling in abasement at the feet of people like you and Eustace Hawke. God damn those who let you do this."

"They're not so bad," he said. "The only thing I bar is wearing medals. I pin 'em on when I call at the warehouse to stock up, and put 'em in my pocket when I'm on the rounds. A woman at Ealing said to me the other day: 'Weren't you in the army?' I said: 'No,' and she said: 'You ought to be ashamed of yourself—a great lout like you.' At the warehouse they call that losing a prospect, so they expect us to wear medals. A lot of the chaps buy 'em. Our outfit's very distinguished: eight V.C.'s—one genuine."

We walked up Blackfriars Street to the Strand, and in a coffeehouse there I gave him breakfast which he ate with a gusto suggesting that if this was his second breakfast of the day the first had not overblown him. I kept him company with a cup of coffee, and then we went out and I called a taxi. "I say," he said, "this is being quite a day—a remarkable saving in shoe leather. That's quite an item, believe me."

His shoes looked as though they were made of the waste products from the cardboard factory that had made his bag.

The car dropped us at Tom Cannock's office in Shaftesbury Avenue. I had planned this day carefully, and had decided not to take Adrian to my club, where he would have felt self-conscious. I asked Cannock if he had a cubbyhole to which I could take a man for a long talk, and he said: "Use my room, Chad. I shan't be there till the afternoon." So in Tom's untidy but comfortable lair, walled with pigeonholes stuffed with plays that would never see the rise of a curtain, Adrian and I sat down and faced one another. He pulled off an inadequate raincoat and dropped it on the carpet. His clothes were threadbare, but he was at least warmed by a pullover of startling magenta wool.

"How do you like it?" he asked, seeing my eyes upon it. "Eustace knitted it. These socks, too. He does a lot of knitting on the Embankment."

"You assume that I know Eustace," I said.

"I don't assume it. I know it. We've been together now for about a year, and in that time I've learned far more about you than I expect you know about me."

I said: "I saw Eustace on the Embankment the other day. As days go, it was the end. Bitter. And obviously he'd been sitting there in that weather for hours. Yet he looked happy. Is he happy?"

"Oh, yes. So am I in a way, oddly enough. Happier than I ever expected to be again."

"What is there to make you happy?"

"Why, Eustace."

"And what makes him happy?"

"His faith."

There were two good leather chairs in Tom's room. I took Adrian off the hardwood kitchen chair that Tom sadistically kept for unwanted callers and put him into a more comfortable one. I sat in the other chair and lit my pipe. The fire was burning. I said: "Please yourself, but would you like to tell me what you know about me?"

He said that on that day when he had turned up at Chalk Hill he went away not knowing who I was. "But I saw your photograph in a newspaper some months after that, and recognized you. I was glad someone like you had got Chalk Hill, since it had to go. It's a nice little place."

Yes, I said, it was a nice little place.

359

"I was glad you were there, because I'd got a gallery seat one night and seen your play. I liked it. I thought: 'Here's a chap who knows what it was all about.'"

"That's the last thing I know," I told him. "I know what it was *like,* but what it was all about God only knows."

Well, he said, he hadn't thought much more about that. He didn't suppose he'd see me again, and as for Chalk Hill, he wanted to forget he'd ever known what that sort of life was like.

"It wasn't difficult to forget," he said. "There were plenty of pressing personal problems.

"The devil of it was, I went straight into the army from school. Even at school, I was pretty dud, and as for learning to *do* anything—well, it never came my way. So I drifted into what you found me doing. I knew it was absolutely the end, and I kept trying to break out of it. I took a few jobs where I thought there was a ray of hope, but I was unlucky. Sometimes need to reduce staff. Sometimes sacked for inefficiency. After each experience of that sort something's gone. That's how I found it, anyway. A bit less eager to try the new thing. And there was always this job to fall back on, where, if you more or less starved, at any rate starvation came along in easy stages."

There was nothing new in all this. It was a terribly familiar story. You could see it being played out before your eyes in every suburban street. I looked at him pityingly, and he looked back from under his rather long eyelashes. "I suppose you think I'm a feeble type," he said. "You think there's *something* I ought to have got my teeth into. But you try it. My father dead. My sister blown to bits. My house sold over my head."

His voice had taken an edge. "There's no need for you to justify yourself," I said. "I'm not blaming you. Now let me tell you something. When Eustace was wounded, you wrote a letter to his sister. She's a very dear friend of mine. My mother, when a widow, married her father. That's how I came to see the letter. It was a very beautiful letter, and it gave great comfort to me and Eustace's sister. When you came out to Chalk Hill, you told me your name. It's only recently that I remembered it was the name of the man who wrote that letter. So you needn't tell me anything about how you came to know Eustace or what you felt about him. I know all that. How did you meet him again?"

Miss Miles, Tom Cannock's plain spinster secretary, came in with a large brown pot of tea and a couple of Tom's chipped disreputable teacups. "Tell Mr. Cannock," I warned her, "that I drink from these microbe-haunted vessels under protest. Considering what he makes out of me alone, I'd expect a silver pot and Rockingham china."

"I'm always telling him, Mr. Boothroyd, but he says we mustn't have an air of affluence. It gives authors wrong ideas. As a matter of fact, I use a Rockingham cup myself. It belonged to my grandmother. Would I bring it in for you?"

"I'll content myself with a factory reject. Bring the Rockingham for Mr. Wybird. This is a rather special day for him."

When she had brought the Rockingham cup and saucer and was gone, Adrian said: "This rings a bell. We always used the Rockingham on special days at Chalk Hill. Are you psychic or something?"

"If I am, this is the first I've heard of it."

"It's odd how small things can please or pain a man. I was peddling round St. John's Wood some time ago, and a woman said to me, 'You look very cold, young man. Come in and have a cup of tea.' She took me into a drawing room where tea had just been served. There was the loveliest china on the table. Looked like old Worcester. Some of the cups hadn't been used, and she took one up and then changed her mind. She went out and came back with a chipped kitchen cup. That made me feel more of a pariah than if she'd kicked me in the backside on the doorstep and shooed me off the mat. Odd, isn't it?"

"Perhaps she's tried it before, and some hungry type munched the side out of an heirloom. However, tell me how you met Eustace again."

It was a year ago, Adrian said. He had a room in Stepney, and was going back there after a grueling day's trudging when he saw a truck, like the one Eustace used on the Embankment, trundling down a mean street in front of him. The man sitting on the truck was sending it along by the simple means of pressing upon the pavement with a block of wood in each hand. "He'd become quite an expert at the game, because he could steer by using now the port block and now the starboard. It was fascinating to watch him scooting along, but I held back to give him a chance to get out of my sight. It makes me rather sick to look at extreme disablement."

Then a dog, chased by a boy, dashed round a corner, and, swerving to dodge the creature, the cripple drove his chariot over the pavement's edge. He was thrown out and, to use Adrian's words, rolled like a barrel into the road. A street lamp lit up his struggle to right himself in the mud.

"Naturally, I hadn't the foggiest idea that it was Eustace. He was already wearing that beard, and he looked about sixty. What amazed me was that he wasn't damning the dog or the boy. He was laughing, and apologized to me for needing help. I pulled the truck to the middle of the pavement and somehow got him onto it. The blocks were still in his hands. He had straps on them that his fingers passed through. He tried to push off, winced, and said: 'Sorry. Can't do it.' He'd sprained a wrist. I was looking at him rather helplessly when he produced a bit of rope and asked me to tie it to a hook in the front of the contraption.

'Things sometimes go wrong like this,' he said. 'My life's full of occupational hazard. I have to ask for help, and I find people astonishingly kind. Will you be an astonishingly kind person, Mr. Wybird?' You could have knocked me down with a feather. You see, I still didn't get him. I said: 'Who are you?' and he said: 'Charley Martin. Just heave and I'll give you the direction.' "

So Adrian dragged Eustace round a corner or two of the bedraggled neighborhood, through the blear bedraggled winter night, and at last came to a cul-de-sac, ending in a high wall and lighted by a single lamp fixed to the wall on a bracket. He said: "My God, Mr. Martin, this is worse even than my place."

Mr. Martin said: "It took me a long time to find it. It is a most desirable place, with the two conveniences that I require. No traffic can pass through, and so it is quiet. The houses have no doorsteps. You wouldn't believe, Mr. Wybird, how few houses there are so unpretentious as to have no doorsteps."

He pulled a string in a front door, pushed it open, and said: "You see. Street and entrance passage all on one floor. Push me in."

Adrian pushed him in, and through a door into the front room. "Light the gas," Mr. Martin said. Adrian did so, and Mr. Martin took a stick and flicked the curtain across the window. He trundled himself to a gas fire and lit it, then rolled himself off the chariot onto a mattress against the wall.

Adrian looked about him. Everything was on the floor: a gas ring, a frying pan, boxes containing food, boxes containing books. The gas fire warmed the room. It began to seem a more possible place. Mr. Martin watched Adrian's exploring eyes, smiling. "There's something to be said," he remarked, "for living literally on the ground level. You learn to shed the unnecessary. You get rid of ambition. You are not tempted to run about with the crowd, chasing the crowd's illusions. You have little to look at except yourself, and the inwardness of yourself. I don't even read much nowadays. My life, more and more, is contemplation, free of things. I'm a bit of a Buddha. Years ago my greatest illusion was that I could capture beauty, especially the beauty of women. But when you capture a thing, it's gone. Never try to capture things, Mr. Wybird. If a thing's worshipful, worship it. If it isn't, pass it by. Fry a few sausages and make some tea."

Adrian said: "Hadn't I better do something to that wrist? What about a cold-water compress, at any rate?"

"Do that, if you would like to, Mr. Wybird, but I shall tell it to get well, and it will get well. I can do that with troubles that aren't organic. I can't do it yet for other people, but I can do it for myself. I shall be all right in the morning. I can't grow a new pair of legs. I don't think I would if I could. I might be tempted back into the old gallop."

Sitting there in Tom Cannock's room, Adrian said: "The odd thing was, I believed all he said. He fairly mesmerized me. However, I decided I'd better do something about the wrist. Among the stuff I was peddling at the time were first-aid outfits. He told me where to find a tap, and I took a wad of lint and soaked it, and I was walking back with this in one hand and a bandage in the other when I suddenly knew who he was. Don't ask me how. Perhaps the voice, perhaps the whole impact of a man I had known very well, believe me."

"Tell me," I said, "how did you come to know him so well? He was a private. You were an officer. I was an officer myself. I could get to know the men in a sort of way, but not in the intimate way you seem to have known him."

"It was in the first Battle of the Somme. Do you remember the bombardment before that?—day after day, night after night. I don't suppose anyone on God's earth ever heard a noise like that before. It terrified me, and when the time came to go over, I felt as though I were going into *that*—not into something that *that* was supposed to clear for us. I was trembling as I stood with the watch in my hand, waiting for the second. I was only a youngster. Then I was aware of a chap leaning on me. I could feel his body against mine. I looked sideways at him. It was Eustace, and he smiled at me. 'It's all right, sir,' he said in a whisper. 'Take it easy now. We're both coming back, you and I.' The effect on me was extraordinary. He so obviously wasn't afraid of a damn thing on earth, and something did flow out of him to me. Well, I got over my funks in time, like the rest of them, but I never forgot that, and I was always glad when Eustace was around. That day, he got the only wound he ever received till the last one. It wasn't a wound—just a deep graze from a flying splinter, but I knew it had left a scar on his right wrist. I remembered it as I walked in with the compress. I rolled back his sleeve, and looked at the scar and looked at him, he grinned and said: 'It's a fair cop, Adrian. I'll come quietly.' "

I asked Adrian how Eustace had been living, and he said: "D'you know that Sherlock Holmes story 'The Man with the Twisted Lip'? He was a thoroughly healthy type who used to make up as a cripple, sit around the streets, and keep his family on the takings. Well, it wasn't quite like that with Eustace, but he did manage not to starve on the coppers and odd shillings that came his way. He wanted so little. When we began to live together in that room of his I found that he wasn't drawing his pension or applying to his publisher for royalties, though his books were still selling pretty well. He said he'd die rather than approach 'Authorities,' and he wouldn't write to his publisher because he had a mania for concealment. That explained the beard, of course. But fundamentally it all added up to doing without *things*. Sometimes he sold a picture."

"He never drew or painted when I knew him."

"He draws in pastel on board. I don't know whether they're any good, but they keep him happy. Anyway, I thank God for the day I ran into him. There's something to go home to now at nights. The nights used to be my worst time. Sometimes I thought I'd go crackers. I'm not much of a reader, and I never had any use for what are called the pleasures of the town. So you can imagine . . ."

"How do you and Eustace spend your evenings?"

"In the summer we mostly sit out in the parks. He feeds the birds. In the winter—well, I've got quite attached to that room that looked so ghastly when I first saw it. The old girl who runs the place isn't so bad. Eustace knows how to talk to her and she adores him in her way. I do the cooking and cleaning, and he does his drawing and knitting. We don't talk much, but there doesn't seem to be much need to. When my day's dingdonging about the streets is over, you wouldn't believe the joy I feel when I'm back with Eustace again and we set off for home."

"I told you," I reminded him, "that Eustace's father married my mother. So you see Eustace and I know a lot about one another. Did he ever speak about me?"

Young Wybird gave me a long look from under the thick fair eyelashes. "I know all about it," he said at last.

He told me that one day he had been talking to Eustace about his old life at Chalk Hill, and said: "The place has been bought now by Chad Boothroyd, the man who wrote *I Don't Want to Die*."

Nothing seemed to surprise Eustace in these days. He took this calmly, saying: "I know Chad Boothroyd well. I see from the papers that he's married now. I suppose my daughter will be living with them. Chad married her mother."

A day or two later he said: "Adrian, I want you to be my father confessor. I don't want you to give me or deny me absolution. No one can do either. But it will do me no harm to unbutton my soul."

Thereupon, he told Adrian of his life: of the women, of Rose, of Billy Pascoe, of Henrietta, of myself. He said: "If I had come back from the war fit to marry, I would have married Rose. But do you know, there are times when I am glad that I didn't. There are men who must find their peace in the world, but I am not one of them. I tried it long enough. I know."

I asked Adrian what he thought of all this, and he said surprisingly: "It seemed a beautiful idea to me that Eustace's daughter was living at Chalk Hill. How old is she?"

"Eighteen."

There wasn't much more to be said, and this talk had left me in a mood which didn't chime with meeting Tom Cannock; so I took Adrian

364

out to lunch. He was very quiet until the meal was over and we had walked down to Leicester Square. We sat in the garden amid the stripped planes, not very comfortable in the winter-gray weather, and he said: "What does it all add up to, Mr. Boothroyd? There seems something—well, rather intentional about this long talk."

"You took it in very good part. I hope I haven't seemed too pressing and inquisitive."

"Well, it wasn't altogether unexpected. Eustace said to me last night: 'There's something brewing. Something important. I can feel my antennae quivering.' "

"Oh," I said impatiently, "that's all hooey."

For the first time that day, he was offended. "Oh, no," he said. "I know what I'm talking about. Ten to one, when I meet Eustace tonight, he'll say, 'Well?' and give me a look. Incidentally, I shall meet him without my bag. That'll take some explaining. What am I to tell him?"

"Tell him," I said, "everything that's happened today. Tell him that I love him, and that Rose and Henrietta love him, and that we want him to come and live with us at Chalk Hill. If you want to come, too, there's plenty of room. I'd like to have you."

He said nothing for a moment, but sat there twisting his thin fingers together. Then he got up, and I could see that he was about to burst into tears. That was something I couldn't put up with, so I marched away quickly, leaving him standing there, staring after me.

CHAPTER FOURTEEN

I

IT WAS a week later that I brought Eustace and Adrian to Chalk Hill. Rose was in her room when they arrived, and stayed there. I took them straight to the stables, and Adrian and I carried Eustace in. Henrietta was in the living room, and she silently watched us as we put down the bearded bundle on a contraption that I had had made by my friend the village carpenter. It was a half-length mattress, with a padded back that could be leaned against. Henrietta had put a few late pale roses into a vase, and she was paler herself than I had seen her for a long time. I knew that for her, more than for any of us, this was an ordeal. Rose and I had seen what was left of Eustace. Henrietta had nothing to go on except a memory of the beautiful man who had arrived impetuously at Cambridge and the portrait frontispiece of the poems. The classic profile of the youth was an odd preparation for this bulky torso surmounted by a head of gray hair and a long prophetic beard. Eustace's body had grown fat, and his arms had an appearance of great strength.

When Adrian and I had put him down on the couch by the fire, he looked at her and smiled and said: "You are Henrietta."

He held out his arms to her, and he must have been aware, as I was, of a moment's hesitation. Then she knelt down by the couch and he put his arms around her. They did not kiss. She got up and said: "Be happy, Father," and, turning to me, said rather formally: "Introduce me to this gentleman."

I introduced her to Adrian Wybird, and she told him she hoped he would be comfortable, and went.

I showed them what had been done for their convenience. A table had been made with short legs that straddled Eustace's couch. He could use it for eating, writing, or anything else. He could sleep here in this room. Adrian could have one of the bedrooms upstairs. Fortunately, it had been found convenient, when we made the bathroom, to have it on the ground floor.

Adrian was at the bookshelf, pulling out the volumes that I had had rebound. "I don't know why you have done all this, Mr. Boothroyd," he said in a tight voice. He looked about the cheerful little room. "It was such a pigsty."

Eustace asked: "Where is Rose?"

I took Wybird's arm and said: "Come and see if you approve of what we've done to your old house." I had to get him out of the way. Rose wouldn't want him there, or me either, when she met Eustace.

I left Adrian in the drawing room and went upstairs. Rose was putting Simon to bed. "Leave his lordship to me," I said. "They've arrived."

"Oh, have they?" she asked casually.

"Yes. Young Wybird is here in the house. Eustace is parked in the stables. I thought you might like a word with him."

"Yes," she said, keeping the casual tone. "I suppose I'd better see him."

She gave her hair a pat before the mirror and said: "I won't be long." I could guess at the beating of her heart.

I popped Simon into bed, invented a tale for him, and droned on till he was asleep. Then I went down and found Adrian loafing uncomfortably where I had left him. I had thought that perhaps Henrietta would have turned up to take him in hand, but he was alone, not looking happy, conscious, it seemed, of his down-at-heel shoes and seedy clothes. Well, I thought, I suppose this experiment will turn out all right in the long run. We're all a bit on edge at the moment, but use and wont will smooth things down. I felt on edge myself at his overdeferential air. Years of being humble, with his pack open on suburban doorsteps, had taken something out of him. I did my best to put him at ease, checked the too frequent Mr. Boothroyd and told him to call me Chad, and was glad when Rose returned. I introduced Wybird to her, and when she had welcomed him she said to me: "Have you explained the kitchen arrangement to Adrian?"

So, seeing that she wanted him to be off, I took him to the kitchen. I had bought containers for keeping food hot, and it would be his job to carry his meals and Eustace's down to the stables. "You'll find cutlery and crockery there, and you should be able to manage your own bit of washing up."

He accepted this chore, and I watched him trot off with the evening meal.

Rose was sitting by the drawing room fire. "Well," I said. "How did it go?"

She reached out and took my hand and drew me toward her. I sat on the arm of the chair and caressed the hair on the nape of her neck. "Tell me, darling," she said, "how did Henrietta take it?"

"It's difficult to say, but I think it was more than a bit of a shock. God knows what she was expecting, but certainly not Eustace as he is."

"He is so—pitiable."

"I don't think so."

"I know what you mean. He's got something that he never had before. He's serene. I don't think anything will excite him or fluster him again. He's utterly unconscious of the—the wreckage. It doesn't seem to disconcert him in the least."

"I'm sure of that."

"He talked to me," she said, "as if we were two old buddies. I must say it put me wonderfully at my ease."

"But you didn't find what you hoped?"

"I didn't find what I feared," she said.

2

Everybody wanted to help Eustace, but Eustace didn't seem to want anybody's help. What was done for him he accepted with smiling thanks, but he made it clear, without rudely saying so, that the best thing you could do for him was to leave him alone. I sometimes wondered why he had consented to come to Chalk Hill at all, and I got my answer in the casual way in which all my contacts with him now seemed to be made.

Greg and Phoebe and Penelope came over to spend a week end soon after Eustace and Adrian were installed. The reaction of the three was interesting. Phoebe, who had been in the habit of going to the hospital with Rose when Eustace was there, could not have been surprised by his condition, but she seemed brokenhearted. She had last seen him a young enough looking man, clean-shaven, vehement and rebellious. And here was this bearded sage, this squatting Buddha, a creature of mere acceptance, with all his fires dead, as she seemed to think. It wasn't any Eustace she had ever known. He had moved outside her comprehension, and though during that visit she spent more time with him than any of us, she got no nearer to him.

As for Penelope, she saw him only once. I took her along to the stables one afternoon, and we found Eustace squatted with the window's light falling over his shoulder, working on a pastel. They were odd pictures that he drew, crowded with creatures of his imagination such as never were on land or sea. They were certainly, if I am any judge, no good as works of art, but they seemed to express something in him— something he never talked about. He didn't keep them. It was one of Adrian's jobs to clean the boards so that he might use them anew.

He put down the work and looked at Penelope, and said: "I used to push you about in a perambulator in Manchester. You were a placid little thing."

He surveyed her with a smile of half-amusement on his face, the rather stout, rather self-satisfied, blue-eyed girl. There was always, when Eustace met a new person, this sense of assessment. Penelope didn't stand it well. She shuffled from foot to foot, and found nothing to say except: "Of course, I was too young to remember anything about that, Uncle Eustace." And then, almost like royalty remembering what is due to the plebs: "Are you quite comfortable here?"

The half-smile turned to a relishing grin. "As well as can be expected, ma'am, in the circumstances."

It was clear that he could get along very well without Penelope, and I took her away. Outside, she said: "How frightening," and that was all I heard her say about Eustace during that visit. He had brought with him the truck that he had used for pushing himself through the London streets, and to see him in this, moving about like a hairy monster, terrified her. She kept her distance.

Greg was practical. He and I, during that week end, were up in the pavilion whence we saw Eustace moving about "like a damn great water boatman," Greg said.

"We'll have to do something better than that. You leave it to me. Look at him down there. You see, he's confined to the flat. He can't make that small gradient. And another thing, Chad. What are you doing about that chap Wybird?"

I said some nonsense about feeling him on my conscience because I'd ousted him from Chalk Hill, and anyhow he and Eustace were used to one another, and someone had to look after Eustace.

"Take my tip," Greg said. "Find him some work, or you're going to land yourself with a problem. He hasn't got all that much to do for Eustace, and he's loafing about eating his head off. He had a hard time. All right. So did you. But you didn't go about selling bootlaces. He strikes me as a pretty feckless customer. His hard time helped, but there was something there, if you ask me, for it to get started on. Now that his hard time's ended, what's he doing? Is he training himself for anything, so that he can take himself off your hands?"

"I don't think so."

"Neither do I. I've had a few talks with him. He's got a well-developed sense of grievance against society, but all it adds up to is a feeling that society ought never to have pushed his family out of a cushy groove. I don't see that it's up to you to keep the groove comfortably oiled for him, but that's what he expects. Well, that's enough of that. Let's go down and have a word with Eustace."

What Greg did about Eustace was to send him a sort of Bath chair, electrically driven. I should have thought of it myself. It transformed his life, so far as its physical side went. He could get up hills, and he ventured outside the grounds of Chalk Hill, and he didn't so much want Adrian.

On a June day in the following year I found him in this chair parked in a lane a mile or so from the house. He was just sitting there, apparently doing nothing. But I knew him well enough to be aware that he was in communion with all that was about him: the small stream that tinkled under the hedge, the magpies that went over clacking like rattles at a football match, the foxgloves and bluebells that raised their spires and sprays of blossom along the bank.

He smiled when he saw me, and I sat down on the grass and asked: "Why do you never want to *express* it all now, Eustace?"

"But I do, my dear boy," he said. "Am I such a washout that you don't realize that?"

I knew what he meant. "Perhaps express it was the wrong word. I mean *communicate* it to others."

He didn't bother to answer. I sat there, watching the goldfinches flirting about over the hedge and the wild roses, white or blushed with carmine, lifted against the blue sky.

After a time he said: "How is it working out, Chad?"

"If it's all right for you, it's all right for me and Rose. We are happier now than before you came."

"I feel that myself. That is why I came. I was all right in London. I shouldn't have minded going on there as I was. When you turned up and asked me to come here, I was in two minds about it. But I owed it to Rose to come. To you, too. It would have been a bad thing for you to have an enigma, an unknown quantity, hovering outside your marriage. There is no *question* to be nagging at Rose's mind now. She knows where she is, and she accepts it."

"Well, so long as you're happy," I said rather lightly; and added more seriously: "Are you happy? It seems so odd for you, of all people, to be—well, just existing from day to day."

He looked at me with his considering smile, and then his stout torso was shaken by chuckles, as though I had said something childishly amusing.

"What does anyone do," he asked after a moment, "save exist from day to day? The only question is what have we to give our existence a meaning? It seems to me that most people do little but fill in time with trivial stupidities. I used to watch them when I sat on the Embankment, marching to and fro on the bridges at morning and night, most of them harassed and anxious and hurried, looking as though they were without God or hope in the world. It became a mania with me to watch for lovely women's faces and happy men's. I didn't see one in a week. Greed, pride, vacuity and vice. Sometimes, when they looked at me, a stirring of pity. That's the average lot, Chad. Busy? Oh, yes, they're busy enough. But do you think their existence from day to day has more meaning than mine?"

We were interrupted by the arrival of Adrian Wybird. He was not the pale thin young man with whom I had talked in Tom Cannock's office. He was still slight, but it was the slightness of his natural build. His face was tanned and he looked as fit as a fiddle. He was wearing flannel bags and brown brogues and a cream-colored shirt, open-necked. The sleeves were rolled up, showing sunburned arms.

I'm afraid I didn't look very welcoming. A few doubts about Adrian were stirring in my mind. He had settled down among us with remarkable assurance, and it was no good for me to tell myself that that was as it should be, and that I should be thankful for it. I couldn't look at it that way. At first I couldn't stand the overdeferential "Yes, Mr. Boothroyd." It reminded me too much of "Yes, Mr. Middlemass." He was Chadding me now right and left, and that didn't please me, either. There was a day when Simon, who was now running about like a colt, had been given a scooter. I had to go up to town and I was taking Henrietta with me. Rose was going to lunch with a neighbor. I said: "Adrian, keep an eye on Simon now and then. He's a bit overenthusiastic, and I don't want him to break his neck with that thing."

Adrian said coolly: "Well, I've got rather a handful with Eustace, you know, Chad. I can hardly play nursemaid to both of them."

It made me so hopping mad that I said: "Play? You're not playing—you're working for a wage."

He put on a hurt look. "Well, of course, if I'm to be reminded of my dependence . . ."

"Aren't we all dependent?" I said. "Henrietta gets a wage. I am dependent on being able to please people."

"Very well," he said; and when I got back that night Simon proudly displayed a skinned knee and said: "That Adrian man said he'd clip my ear if I did that again."

"And did you do it again?"

"Twice times," he told me with satisfaction.

"And did he clip your ear?"

"Yes. Twice times."

That was one thing. And there was the affair of the rhododendrons. They were thick on the drive that led from the road up toward the house, and they were all of the *ponticum* breed that would produce nothing but the magenta flowers that I didn't think inspiring. They extended for about a hundred yards on either side of the drive, and I decided to have the lot out. I would replant with better sorts and not so many of them. I would intersperse with forsythia and cherry and lilac and laburnum, and have a regiment of daffodils on parade to border them. I put the job into the hands of a gardener in the neighboring town, and he sent out a few men to do the preliminary clearing. The morning is my worktime, and Rose knew that interruption, except for some mighty reason, was forbidden. I was surprised when she tapped at the door and put her head round: "Darling, I'm sorry to interrupt, but there's a bit of a schemozzle."

My surprise was not lessened when Adrian followed her into the room. She turned on him reproachfully. "Adrian, I told you to stay where you were. Really . . ."

He was hot and excited. "This is important," he said. "Do you know what they're doing to the drive, Chad?"

I was coldly furious. "Of course I know what they're doing to the drive. Would they be doing it if I hadn't told them to?"

"I just wondered," he said foolishly.

Rose said: "I'm so sorry, darling. But seeing you've been disturbed, would you tell the man it's all right?"

"What man?"

"One of the gardeners. Adrian brought him up to the house to speak to you."

I went down and found the man on the doormat. "Sorry, sir," he said, "but Mr. Wybird told us not to go on till he'd seen you."

"Of course you're to go on. Weren't my orders clear enough on the point?"

"Yes, sir. But Mr. Adrian told us to stop. And seeing it's a Wybird place . . ."

"This is not a Wybird place. It's my place. Carry on with the job, and if Mr. Wybird gives you any further orders, take no notice of them or him."

Adrian and Rose had come down after me. I turned and saw that Henrietta had followed them. She must have heard what I said. I didn't want to berate him in front of them, so, work being now out of the question, I hooked a hand through his arm and drew him away. "Now," I said. "In the first place get this. You know, as everyone knows in this house, that the morning is my worktime. That you should interrupt in that way was a piece of damned impertinence that I won't tolerate a second time. In the second place, perhaps you'll tell me what all this is about."

He had gone white and miserable-looking. I felt sorry for him, but the time had clearly come to cut at any queer notions he had got into his head.

"Those rhododendrons have *always* been there," he said, "as long as I can remember anything. I thought if you knew . . . Or if you'd only told me what you were going to do . . . You don't think I take it easy seeing the place messed about?"

"The place is not being messed about. It's being enormously improved. But whether it's being messed about or improved is nothing whatever to do with you. If I should level the house to the ground and build a roadhouse blazing with neon lights, that would have nothing to do with you."

"I know I had no right to interfere, but . . ."

"If you know you had no right to interfere there's no but about it. And, above all, don't interfere with my work. I know there are supermen who can write in buses and trains, unaware of any riot going on. I'm not one of them."

He was looking miserably apologetic now, and that didn't help me to like him any the more. But I decided to send him away on a happier note. "When that job's finished," I said, "I think you'll like it. We'll have a bit of color as we come up to the house. And it'll want looking after. Shrubs have to be pruned, for one thing. That's something you could do." I warmed to the thought. "And then there are vegetables. We buy everything we eat in this place. There's an excellent vegetable garden—or was. It's gone to pot. You could take that in hand. There's no reason why we shouldn't have a cow and plenty of poultry."

Perhaps I was overdoing it. He didn't look as though he was taking to the idea enthusiastically. "I don't know a thing about shrubs," he said, "or vegetables or cows or poultry."

"But, damn it, Adrian, you could learn, couldn't you? There are such things as books in the world."

"Oh, books! Of course, if I've got to wear my eyesight out on books—!"

I turned on my heel and left him. I couldn't trust myself to speak, but any guilty feelings I may have had about dispossessing the Wybirds began to fade.

Since it was impossible now to pick up the work I had been doing, I went back to my study to write a few letters. I had hardly settled to this when Henrietta came out of her little office. "I suppose you can't get on now," she said, "so I'm not interrupting anything serious?"

"No. Come in, my dear."

She hovered for a moment, looking unsure of herself, then plunged. "Adrian is having a very unhappy time," she said. "I think he should be gently handled."

"What have I done now?"

"I couldn't help hearing what you said to the gardener—that if Adrian gave any orders he was to take no notice of them or him."

"Well?"

"Put like that, it sounds a bit brutal, darling. It couldn't but make Adrian feel very small. I don't know what the row was about, but that was publicly telling him he didn't amount to tuppence."

"How much does he amount to?"

"That's a quibble, Uncle Chad. The question is what *could* he amount to? He'll never amount to much if he's made to feel inferior in front of us all. He's been through a lot. He needs to be bucked up."

I told her that there was just a fear that he was making the most of the lot he had been through.

"Oh, no," she said earnestly. "I'm sure that does him a wrong."

"And one way to buck him up," I persisted, "is to make him feel that he's really doing a job here in our small community." I told her of what I had said to him about finding a few chores and of his reaction to it.

"I'm sorry he took it like that," she said. "Perhaps he was still smarting under your dressing down. If I put it to him, he may take to it more kindly."

She went back to her room, and now I couldn't write so much as a letter. I didn't like the sound of this at all.

However, a slight movement came out of it. There was no cow. It was Rose who sensibly squashed that. "My dear, have you ever thought that a cow *must* be milked twice a day? You can neglect anything else occasionally, but a cow no. They're the most demanding creatures God ever made. Sunday and weekdays alike, someone's *got* to be there, and nothing could ever be proposed in this house without the question coming up: Who'll milk the cow?"

But a few hens began to run about the place, and in the kitchen garden a bit of disorderly work scarred the earth here and there amid the old wilderness. It was all ramshackle, spades left sticking in the ground to rust, rakes lying teeth up on the paths, so that an incautious step might give you a slap in the eye with the handle. I occasionally walked that way to take a breath of air before settling down to my morning's work. Adrian was never at work so desperately early as nine o'clock, and there was a chance to look about me and sardonically reflect that this untidy pile of rubbish was theoretically a compost heap, and that this boot-trodden bed was oddly unlike a bed in a seedsman's catalogue. Henrietta joined me as I stood thus one morning, and she could have no doubt of my feelings. She put an arm through mine as we walked back to the house, and said: "Give him time. This is only a beginning. And we *did* have our own eggs for breakfast."

"Damn it," I said crossly. "I bought the hens, and the hens laid the eggs. Where does Adrian come into it? He hasn't cleaned the dropping boards since the creatures arrived."

3

Even Uncle Arthur couldn't make a gardener of Adrian. I had heard from him occasionally since he settled at Pentyrch, and settled is the word. Any doubts I may have had about that experiment were soon at rest. "With Miss Orlop's approval," he wrote, "I have constituted myself estate manager here. It would be an odd thing indeed, my dear Chad, if one who had controlled the municipal affairs of Smurthwaite could not handle a few hundred Cornish acres." He was seventy years old now, but this did not prevent him from being a practical as well as a theoretical gardener, and he wrote as proudly of cabbages and kale as he had once talked of auriculas. And so I was not surprised that the kitchen garden was his first concern when he came to spend a week with us. Miss Orlop was in London, and her one-bedroomed flat was no place for the two of them. He was an impressive figure in gray-blue tweeds and a tweed hat decorated with fishing flies, though he had never been known to take a rod in his hands. He and I perambulated my few acres, and he talked of swedes and turnips, arable and pasture, the rotation of crops, as though he were Cobbett, Arthur Young and Coke of Holkham rolled into one and surveying a county. I approached the walled kitchen garden feeling as though I were about to submit to the judgment of Solon the first dim essay of an Athenian schoolboy. Indeed, I said so to him, preparing him for the worst, and he replied: "During the Megarian War, my dear Chad, the sarcasms of Solon's stirring Tyrtaean verse induced the desponding Athenians to continue the struggle. I cannot promise you Tyrtaean verse, whatever that may have been, but if sarcasm will prevail it shall not be wanting. Believe me, a man whose cauliflowers have struck dumb the professionals at St. Austell will not fail to do his duty by agriculture."

It was a June day, and, as I had expected, we did not find Adrian toiling. We had the place to ourselves. In silence we walked along the paths between the beds. Occasionally Uncle Arthur would take up a handful of soil and crumble it in his fingers. He took off his coat, rolled up a sleeve, and plunged his arm to the elbow into a compost heap. None of these performances appeared to give him joy. I felt like a subaltern on the Western front, trailing behind an inspecting brass hat whose gorge can be seen rising through the back of his neck. He spoke only once, and that was to say in a hollow voice "Canker" after a profound stare at a row of espalier apple trees. I said that I was afraid our apples were not such as would have caused the fall in Eden, and he did not deign to answer the levity. He tore a shallot from the earth, tossed it to the path, and trampled it underfoot.

Not till we were outside and I had shut the door did he speak. "Why do you close that door, Chad?"

"To keep out the rabbits."

"Let them in, my dear boy. Let them see the poverty of the land, and in a few days' time you won't find a self-respecting rabbit between here and Abinger Hammer."

"So you think things are pretty bad?"

He gave a sepulchral laugh and swished his walking stick in a circle through the air. "If I were the Caliph of Bagdad," he said, "an office that, in its extraconjugal aspect, at any rate, would put no strain upon my resources, and this were my scimitar, your gardener's head would now be lying at your feet."

I could not wish that even for Adrian, so I suggested that Uncle Arthur should spend some part of his stay with us in instructing the young man, and he gladly consented to do this. But it all came to nothing, for Uncle Arthur had become mazed by the theories of Rudolf Steiner. I suspect that his own practice was robust and walked right through the theories, but Adrian had to learn the importance of occult influences on crops: to sow his seed at this phase of the moon and reap at another. He became desperate and at last rebellious. I chanced to be in the kitchen garden when the crisis came. Uncle Arthur, wearing a green baize apron, with mustaches of bast peeping from the patch pocket, and with hobnailed boots on his feet, was looking as dangerous as a bull about to charge. But Adrian would not stay to be charged. He walked out of the garden shouting: "I'm damned if I'll cast the horoscope of a horseradish to please you or anyone else!"

I felt some sympathy with him.

4

Adrian was mowing the tennis lawn on that morning when Uncle Arthur figuratively laid his head in the desert sand. It was a handsome head enough: the face fair, blue-eyed, lean and well-bred. Leaving Uncle Arthur to amble toward the stables, where, as he told me with obvious relish for the daring modernity of his speech, he had a "date" with Eustace. I walked toward the whirr of the motor mower and the smell of new-cut grass. Adrian was just finishing the job, and I reminded him to see that the clippings were wheeled away and scattered over the roots of the new shrubs in the drive.

"Yes, yes," he said impatiently, as though thinking that I reminded him too much to do this and that. But it was necessary all the same. The grass would stay there if he wasn't told to take it away. I must say, though, that the tennis lawn was one thing he kept in order. It was weedless and perfectly shaved. The nets were never left taut when not in use, and the lines were a triumph of whitewashery.

"Can you help to make up a four this afternoon, Chad?" he asked.

"I can, but we'll still be one down. Rose is driving into town with Uncle Arthur."

"That will be all right. Penelope is coming. She rang up to invite herself just after you'd set out to view my horticultural triumphs. With you and me and Henrietta, we should have some real play. Rose isn't terribly good."

Why did it so deeply rile me to hear him say even that in disparagement of Rose? It was true. She played occasionally "to oblige," as she said, but she wasn't interested. "She's good enough for me," I said shortly. "All right. I'll make up the four."

I wandered into the house, feeling rootless and loose-ended, as I always did when I had no work on hand. Henrietta was arranging flowers in the drawing room. "So the old man's got to sweat again," I said. "I understand we're playing tennis this afternoon."

"But Mother's going out. Who's making the four?"

"Penelope's coming over. Adrian says she rang up this morning."

Standing by the big window of the room, silhouetted against the blaze of sunshine without, her arms full of flowers, she was tall and slender in pale blue linen.

"So that's what Adrian was hanging about the house for—a telephone call," she said. "I think Penelope rings at prearranged times. Ah, well," she added, turning again to her task, "I suppose it'll give her a chance to show off a new pair of pants." The short divided skirt and the pants that Penelope wore for tennis were notorious.

I took my morning coffee up to the welcome cool of my study, and there read again the letter that had come that morning from Greg. He and Phoebe were in the United States. He had begun with a lecture tour, had then spent three months going about the country on what he called a fact-finding expedition, and was now settled down to do a year's stint as Professor of Social Science and Economics at a Midwestern university. He and Phoebe had spent a week end with us before they set out. "It'll be an excellent thing for Penelope," I said.

"We're not taking her," Greg answered. "What with the lectures and the bumbling round on my own and then a year in a university, we'll be away for the best part of eighteen months, and I want her to stay on at London University and take her B.S. I think she's got quite a flair for mathematics."

I suppose I showed surprise, for Greg gave me a rather sad look and added: "Well, I *hope* she has."

I said nothing to that. We smoked in silence for a time; then he asked suddenly: "What do you make of the girl, Chad?"

It rather knocked me aback. I couldn't say: "I think she's frivolous and irresponsible." I thought of the son whose room Greg had shown me in Manchester: the son whose illustrious achievements would cause a plaque to go up on the house. I said: "If I were you, I'd take her."

He bit hard on the stem of his pipe and said nothing for a time. Then he said: "I'm damned if I will. It's time Phoebe had a holiday from her."

Well, this was at all events startlingly honest, a coming-to-the-point with a vengeance. I tried to laugh it off. "Holiday! I can see Phoebe having a holiday, rushing around the States with you!"

He didn't take it up, and I asked: "What are you doing with Penelope?"

"She can't stay alone in the house," he said, "so I'm letting that for eighteen months. She'll board with old Crothers, the archaeology man. He's got a nice wife and no children. I hope you'll let her come out here when she feels like it."

"But of course we shall! What does she think of the arrangement?"

"She's all for it. And, of course, she promises to work like a horse. Keep an eye on her, Chad, so far as you can."

I said that I would, and I had had opportunity to do so, for Penelope had made a habit of buzzing along to us in her open scarlet two-seater. She often stayed for the week end. She was an excellent tennis player, and she was eighteen years old.

5

From the hill behind the house a trickle of water flowed into my bit of land and thence into a ditch along the road outside. Even in the dryest weather it didn't disappear. I had had a swimming pool dug—a hole three feet deep tapering down to six feet, fifty feet long and twenty wide, lined with concrete. It was a pleasant place. Where the stream fell toward it the grass was extra green with a few willows and alders enjoying the moisture. Water mint grew there, and, in the spring, kingcups and abundant cuckoo flowers. Along the course of the water after it had spilled from the shallow end Rose had planted candelabra primulas and other water-loving plants. There were two white-painted sheds for bathers to change in, and between them ran a long table—solid oak planks resting on balks of oak sunk in the ground. It was a favorite teatime place in summer.

Soon after Rose had left us that day Penelope arrived like a bomb as usual. Her small scarlet car was braked violently in front of the house and she shouted: "Hello! Anyone in?" as if we might, though expecting her, have all departed for Timbuctu. Adrian showed promptly that he was in. He ran out and relieved her of three rackets, a net of tennis balls and a handbag. I strolled after him to welcome her. As she got out of the car she pulled off a light dust coat and revealed herself in the garments that Henrietta had predicted. Adrian gave her a cigarette and lit it for her. She puffed at it with the greedy avidity that marked all her doings, flicking off ash that had not yet appeared. "Hallo, Uncle Chad," she said. "There's a frock in that bag. I hope you'll let me stay over Sunday. London is positively the end on a Sunday, especially *chez* Crothers. Have you ever dined *en famille* with a septuagenarian archaeologist and his wife?"

I said that I hadn't. "Don't," she advised me. "Who was it said, 'Can these dry bones live?' He must have known the Crothers. Dead from the neck up and the loins down."

I thought it a horrid thing for a young girl to say, especially as Crothers, whatever his loins might be now, had had two admirable sons, both killed on the Western front. But I said nothing. Penelope was not my pigeon, or poule, or whatever she was. I left her chattering with an obviously enchanted Adrian, and took her bag indoors.

Henrietta was in the hall. Eying my burden, she asked: "Does that mean she's staying?"

"I'm afraid so."

"Oh, damn."

"Exactly, my dear."

I put the bag into the spare bedroom, and when I came down Adrian and Penelope had moved off toward the tennis court. Henrietta was still in the hall.

"Why are you waiting?"

"To give you a pep talk before we join them," she said. "You're a lazy player, you know. You'd better not be today. I want to knock hell out of them."

I managed a laugh, but was anxiously aware that something un happy was behind Henrietta's fierce dark face. When we arrived on the court Adrian was showing off by jumping over the net. It was this more than anything that tightened me up to accept Henrietta's challenge to play my best. It was such a masculine, almost sexual, display of agility and virility that I thought: Very well, my lad, I may be forty to your twenty-nine, but you're going to work harder this afternoon than ever you did in the kitchen garden.

We didn't knock hell out of them, but we just beat them. Henrietta played with a tense fury that had something to do with more than tennis, and Penelope, sensing this, I think, used all she had. She was roly-poly to look at, but she had the resilient energy of a puma, and she made the mistake of being so anxious to win that she wouldn't trust her partner. She occasionally dived for a ball that was obviously Adrian's, and this confused him. There came a moment when he wasn't certain whether to take a ball or leave it to her. The second's hesitation gave us the set, and I said to Henrietta: "If Emily Brontë had ever played with someone whose guts she loathed, that's how she would have played."

Henrietta was panting hard, but she managed to give me a grin that was almost malicious. "Don't be too obvious, darling," I warned her.

Penelope didn't take it well. She was frowning, and already shouting: "Come on, Henrietta! Ladies' singles."

"For Pete's sake, Penelope, take it easy," I said. "Come and have a breather and a glass of lemonade."

In singles, I knew that Henrietta had never beaten Penelope, and I knew, too, that she was out to murder her today. But I made them sit at the table, with cloaks around them, for ten minutes, sipping lemonade through straws. Then Penelope bounded to her side of the net and Henrietta walked to hers with a grim look on her face. She served first, and with an energy that was almost shocking in its obvious intent. There was no need for a second service. For all her cat's eyes and cat's agility, Penelope had no more chance with that first ball than a cat in hell. But it taught her what was coming, and thereafter they fought for every point with unsmiling ferocity. They kept up rallies of astonishing length and speed, dipping like wind-blown willows and leaping like greyhounds. But it wasn't play. It was naked battle, and I was glad when it was over. "Game and set," Henrietta said quietly, when the fight was hers, and she came toward me and Adrian almost exhausted. She handed me her racket as though its weight were too much for her, and sat down.

Neither she nor I cared whether we played any more after that, but we stayed for a few desultory games. I gave Penelope the pleasure of beating me, and Adrian beat Henrietta, but I think they must have felt, as we did, that the real battle was over and that this was mimic warfare. What had it decided? Nothing, so far as I could see, but Henrietta was now relaxed and pleased, so I took it she had exorcised some devil. We strolled away and left the court to them, and when we came back Uncle Arthur was sitting on the bench near the swimming pool, which adjoined the tennis court, and Eustace had drawn himself up alongside in his Bath chair.

He had recently been a nine-days wonder, or hardly that. Nine days is a long time for a wonder to live in a modern newspaper. His identity, and his presence with us, had been discovered. I suspected Penelope, though she denied having given him away, but I knew that George Crothers' nephew was editor of the paper that ferreted Eustace out, and Penelope herself had mentioned him as being from time to time at his uncle's house. Be that as it may, the first thing that Eustace knew about it was that, as he sat one day in his chair in the lane where he liked to meditate, a flash bulb attached to a camera exploded a few yards away, and the photographer scurried off. He was not such a fool as to be unaware of what this meant or to be surprised, when he was steering his machine through the gates, to be hailed by a smooth young man as Mr. Hawke. He admitted that he was Mr. Hawke, and even invited the man to see the cottage where he lived. But he would say nothing about his life since his disappearance or in answer to such questions as: "What are your intentions for the future, Mr. Hawke?"

Nevertheless, the paper made a splash. There was a headline, "Look on this picture and on that," with the snapshot of the bearded cripple on one side and the famous profile on the other. There was also a full account of Eustace's hidden life in London, with credit given to Mr. Adrian Wybird for his loving care—"Mr. Wybird whose family, by an odd coincidence, occupied for some hundreds of years the house where Mr. Hawke is now sheltered." The two, the paper said, had come to know one another during the war, when Captain Wybird had befriended Private Hawke and encouraged his poetic genius.

I had no doubt where this had come from. I happened to stroll down to the stables just as Eustace was courteously bidding the reporter good-by and regretting that he had nothing to say—nothing at all. I saw the man go, and I saw Adrian go with him. It was half an hour before he came back.

Seeing that Eustace was unperturbed by it all, I considered it nothing but a nuisance. For a few days other papers rang up or sent reporters, and one offered a large sum for an article on *My Hidden Years*. Once more, when the man who came with this offer went away with a flat refusal, Adrian went with him. I followed them, drew Adrian aside and said: "Next to a signed article by Eustace, the best thing would be a signed article by you *about* Eustace. Don't do anything silly, will you?"

He blushed and stammered and shouted to the man who had gone ahead: "Well, good-by. I must be getting back."

When Henrietta and I joined Eustace and Uncle Arthur that afternoon of the tennis match, Penelope and Adrian were still on the court, playing not seriously, and presently Adrian shouted: "Penelope wants to have a look at my vegetable garden. We'll join you at tea."

He loosened the net; they left their rackets with us and went off together. Eustace was looking at his daughter. I often noticed him doing so. It was not with the fond look of a doting parent, or even, I should say, with love. It was the look of benevolence that Eustace now turned on most people, but when it rested on Henrietta it had a profundity that seemed to wrap her round. He took her hand and said: "I shouldn't worry about him if I were you, my dear."

She gave him a startled look. Like most young people, she imagined herself to be unreadable. I said to Uncle Arthur: "Let's go and help to carry out the tea."

However, teatime was half an hour away, and we sat in the cool drawing room. Uncle Arthur said: "Yes, Chad. It's a good idea to leave them together. Eustace is rather worried about her."

"So am I. I hope Eustace won't tell her too heavily what a feeble reed that boy is. She's the sort of girl who might take it as a challenge. There are women like that. They think they can teach any lame dog to leap over stiles like a greyhound."

"No one will teach him so much as to grow a carrot fit to look a bit of boiled beef in the face. Do you know, Chad, he has talked to me about his *rights* here. I shouldn't be surprised if he thinks of you as his agent, keeping the estate in order."

"Neither should I. And yet there must be some good in him. He looked after Eustace when nobody else did."

"I'm not sure of that. In the last few days I've seen a lot of Eustace. I didn't think I was going to like it. I didn't think I was going to like *him*. You know, my dear boy, a chap who takes to drink in his teens and who lets it get the upper hand of him, a chap who plays fast and loose with women, especially," said Uncle Arthur without boggling at the words, "with the daughter of the woman I love, well, that's not the sort of chap I expected to get on with."

He paused and looked at the glow of a cigar he had lit rather unseasonably. Then he pronounced: "Well, I've come to the conclusion that a saint can absorb a lot of sin and somehow be cleaner than most of us."

I asked him: "Has Eustace been talking to you about Adrian?"

"Only to praise him, and to regret that he hasn't been able to do more for him. He blames himself for all Adrian's weaknesses. But when you say Adrian looked after him when nobody else did, I must say I see it the other way round. A bit of ivy doesn't look after an oak, even one," said Uncle Arthur, producing a startling simile, "that has been rather severely lopped."

I heard the tea trolley being pushed from the kitchen and went to take charge of it. I pampered my taste for useful gadgets, and this one had been made for me by my village craftsman. It had handles like a perambulator's, and balloon tires that would not injure the lawns. Uncle Arthur regarded the contraption benevolently. "You have inherited a certain ingenuity from your dear father," he said. "Do you remember the perambulator we pushed to the well on the auspicious occasion of our first meeting?"

"Don't remind me," I said with a shudder.

"Then permit me to remind myself. You were afraid of the boys, and they might indeed have involved us in what is vulgarly called a rather sticky moment if dear Miss Orlop had not come out of the village shop and invited us to tea. That was the first time I saw her, Chad. Old Horsehair will never forget that moment."

"Uncle Arthur!" I protested with a blush. "You never heard me call you that!"

"No. It was your dear father. I remember that we met young Pascoe that night. How is Sir William?"

"I don't see much of him, or hear much from him, but we shall be putting that right next week. He's coming to spend a week end here."

"The Fellowship of the Rose," Uncle Arthur murmured.

"I beg your pardon?"

"Did you never read *Westward, Ho?*"

"No."

"Ah, well."

Adrian and Penelope were back from their horticultural exploration. They both ate like hungry horses. There were raspberries and cream, and honey, and cake, and bread-and-butter. The day was still hot, and as soon as he had finished eating Adrian went to the edge of the pool and said: "Let's swim!"

"For goodness sake give yourself a rest, Adrian," I said. "It's bad for you to swim so soon after a meal."

He turned his head and looked at me mockingly. "Old wives' tale," he said; and Penelope, who had joined him, said: "I'm sure it is. Oh, it looks divinely enticing! Let's get our swim suits. Coming, Henrietta?"

Henrietta shook her head, and the pair raced off to the house, highly excited. They came back dangling their bathing suits, with towels round their necks, and ran into the changing huts. Adrian came out first, wearing a navy-blue loin slip. He had been doing a lot of sun-bathing and was golden. "Sure you won't change your mind, Henrietta?" he asked.

Henrietta shook her head again, and then Penelope came, leaving nothing to the imagination in a skin-fitting suit of yellow. She walked to the edge of the pool and stood there for a moment with her bare arm laid on Adrian's bare shoulder.

"You ought to put up a diving platform, Chad," Adrian said. "It's silly flopping in off the edge."

"I'm sorry," I said. "I'll bear it in mind. And send me a note about any other suggested improvements."

Penelope slapped his shoulder. "See," she said. "Now you've offended Uncle Chad. You really are the limit."

She pushed him into the pool and dived after him, and they struggled for a moment in the water.

"I'll take the trolley back to the house," I said, and as I walked away, Henrietta walked with me. She didn't say a word and went straight up to her office, which she used also as her boudoir.

6

Rose's journey to town that day was to see her mother. She would be spending the night with Max and Bessie at Menin Gate. And so only four of us sat down to dinner: Henrietta and Penelope, Uncle Arthur and I. Adrian took his meal, as usual, with Eustace in the stables. The dining room was on the east side of the house. Dusk reached it early, and when we sat down at eight o'clock it was with tall candles burning on the table round a bowl of crimson roses. Penelope had changed into a blue silk dress and Henrietta was wearing her favorite red. It was a pleasant civilized scene, with the candlelight winking in the topaz wine.

"What a pity Adrian isn't here!" Penelope said. "He so appreciates this sort of setting."

I explained: "We shouldn't at all mind having him, Penelope, but, you see, your uncle Eustace—naturally enough, I think—doesn't like dining in company. For myself, I shouldn't mind if he had his table in here, and I suggested once that he should. He laughed and said: 'You'd never be able to resist throwing your bones down to me, Chad. Leave me where I am.' He prefers it that way."

Penelope was squinting at the candlelight through her wine. "It's Adrian I was asking about," she said.

"Well, we can't leave Eustace alone, you know. Now and then I go down there and eat with him, and sometimes Rose does, so as to give Adrian a change. He comes and eats here."

"I *think*," she said judicially, "he's getting rather tired of it all. Mind you, I don't want to butt in on what's not my affair, but isn't he rather wasting himself? After all, he's more or less a servant, isn't he—a valet?"

"Yes," I said, "that's about what it comes to. I wish he were a better one."

"Now, Uncle Chad," she said coyly, as Henrietta looked at her murderously, "I've offended you again. I'm afraid I'm rather a tactless little thing."

Henrietta said: "I, too, don't want to butt in, but this wouldn't have arisen unless my father were concerned. I don't like my father's affairs being discussed in this way by a stranger."

"Oh, but darling, I'm *not* a stranger. He's my uncle."

"Well," said Henrietta, "he's done some foolish things in his time, but that, at any rate, is something he couldn't help."

It was obvious that Penelope was delighted to have piqued her. With her round blue eyes, her platinum hair cut like a page's, she sat there demurely as a kitten licking its paws.

Uncle Arthur said: "This sole *bonne femme* reminds me, Chad, of an extraordinary happening at a banquet of municipal officials soon after my appointment to Smurthwaite. . . ." He droned on and on, and even succeeded in being occasionally very funny. Gratefully, I left it to him.

7

On the Monday morning I motored to town early, taking Uncle Arthur with me. He was to join Miss Orlop on the Riviera Express for their return to Cornwall. Penelope started at the same time, setting a fine dashing pace, thinking, it seemed, that I would enjoy trying to race her to London. I slowed down to thirty to let her get away, and once she was out of sight we didn't see her again.

Uncle Arthur said: "I feel sorry for that child, and for Greg Appleby, too. An only child is a great risk."

"I was an only child," I reminded him; and he said: "You had the advantage of growing up in Smurthwaite under my wing. London in these days is a pesthouse, especially if your father is such a great man that he's got no time to spare from his own greatness. Greg has never relaxed among auriculas."

However, now that Penelope was out of my house and out of my sight I was content to put her out of my mind, too, for the time. It was going to be another hot day, but now the air was cool, and in the fields the cheerful racket of the haymakers' machines was breaking out. The sky was full of the song of larks, and I was content to dawdle along and enjoy the serenity of the moment. I was happy. I had rung up Rose at Menin Gate, and she said Max was bringing her in to see her mother off, and that then he wanted the two of us to go back with him to Maidenhead.

When I arrived with Uncle Arthur they were already on the platform walking up and down with Miss Orlop. "Dear lady," Uncle Arthur said, and bowed over Miss Orlop's hand and kissed it.

"Well, Arthur," she said. "Have you had a good week?"

"Yes, so far as such a thing is possible when I am away from you. And how are you, Lucy?"

"In the pink," she said briskly, "and there's no need for you to fuss. Mr. Middlemass has done everything—luncheon tickets, newspapers, even a copy of *Vogue*. Could chivalry go farther than to suggest that I am the sort of woman that *Vogue* would appeal to? I ask you—look at me!"

We looked at her, standing among the luggage trolleys, and the boys shouting their newspapers, cigarettes and chocolates, and the jostling crowd, with the huge span of the roof over her, echoing the deep coughs of a parting train and clouded with mushrooms of steam. She looked as ever, a striking creature amid the universal commonplace: hatless, white-aureoled, draped in a thin dark cloak. From the time I had known her as a boy who rather feared her, her eyes had had a hooded look. Now the lids seemed to be made of thin creased leather, like a wise old bird's.

Suddenly Rose, seeming to be deeply moved, ran to her and kissed her. "Now get in, mother. There's only one minute to go, and you know you think it's unlucky if we watch the train go out."

"Very well, then. Good-by, all of you." She kissed Rose, and unexpectedly, me. She shook hands with Max, and Uncle Arthur handed her up the step. A moment later, the two old heads leaned out of the window, side by side. Their hands waved, and we went. The whistle blew and the engine groaned to its start as we passed the barrier.

Rose came into my car and Max drove, alone, ahead of us. Rose was subdued. She didn't speak all the way to Menin Gate, except once when I asked if she had been having a good time. "So-so," she said. And as we were turning into the drive she said: "Darling, try and get away from Max. I'd like to spend the day on the river."

However, it wasn't so easy as that. Max, as usual, was brimming with hospitality, and Bessie, who was knitting socks on a deck chair by the river's edge, seemed hurt when it was suggested that we should not be staying to lunch. I looked at Rose, and she gave a slight nod, and we said that, of course, we'd be delighted to stay, but who could be near that beautiful river without wishing to be on it? So might we, after lunch—?

"Please yourselves," Max said. "I've got some scripts to go through. I'm not like you playwrights—three months' work and eighteen months' rest. Take the launch and be back in time for dinner."

He could never understand that I preferred a punt to his showy launch, or to any launch; but we had our way and were on the river at two o'clock. Bessie put a tea hamper aboard.

It was a burning day. The wild roses were over, but there was still a field or two of uncut grass with the red spires of sorrel standing up among the pale moon faces of the dog daisies; and flashing over the water were huge green-scaled dragonflies, and smaller ones that were like frail tubes of blue grass, winged. It was not a day for hard work, and presently I pushed the punt into a backwater that was little more than a green tunnel with a watery floor, filled with the heavy smell of elderberry flowers that grew in creamy bosses overhead. I tied the punt to a root and lay down on the cushions alongside Rose. She put her arms round me and pulled me close to her and kissed me.

"How I've missed you," she said.

I laughed into the deep blue eyes so close to mine. "You've been away for only two days."

She said: "An eternity, as it happens. Love me."

Then she went to sleep, lying in my arms, and I listened to the lazy cluck of the water, and to the silence of which it seemed the voice. All the songbirds were asleep. Soon I slept myself, and when at last I woke again I saw that tears were forcing themselves through Rose's shut lids. I kissed the lids that, with no chemist's help, were blue as scabious, and she opened her eyes and presently sat up.

I said: "You were crying in your sleep, darling. What's the matter?"

She threw off the rug that had been over us and rearranged her clothes. "Let's get into the sunshine. I don't want to talk about it here. Those elderflowers smell deathy."

When we were out again on the flowing sparkle, amid the yellow lilies and the diving red-billed moorhens and white-blazed coots, she said: "Mother wanted to see me about arranging her affairs. When Uncle Arthur asked how she was, and she said: 'In the pink,' I could have cried there on that crowded platform. She's dying."

I was not poling the punt. I was sitting facing Rose, dawdling along with the paddle. The news was so unexpected that I stopped paddling and let the punt drift. "But she *looks* in the pink!"

"I know, darling. That doesn't make it any easier, does it? She's got about six months. That's why she came up to London: to see if Harley Street confirmed the opinion of her local doctor. It does."

"Who knows, besides us?"

"No one. She says she'll tell Arthur in her own time."

We ate our tea in a field, with the sun blazing on us, and Rose said: "I've slept hardly a wink for two nights. I shall sleep now."

I put a rug under her and covered her with another, and she dropped a handkerchief over her eyes. She was asleep almost as soon as she lay down. I took the tea things to the river and swilled them, and then wandered restlessly about the fields. It was so bright a day that dark news was unbearable. A kingfisher flashed from his nest in a rotten stump. Cows were standing knee-deep in the water. In a field beyond the river a man was whistling to a dog that bounded to him across the pasture, exuberantly alive. They will be somewhere on the Devonshire coast, I was thinking, the train shuttling in and out of the short tunnels through the red rocks, with glimpses of sun-glistered water in between.

Perhaps with a hand beneath her elbow, Uncle Arthur would be taking her along the lurching corridor to the tearoom. He would be joyous: his Lucy with him again in that odd half-realized union that both seemed to find comforting, speeding back to routine, tranquillity; and so soon, now, all that would be ended for them. There would be another burial in the church where Billy Pascoe had rudely and rebelliously said: "Bugger the Orlops," and that would be the last of the tribe.

Rose was still sleeping when I got back. I sat down and smoked, waiting for her to awake, and at last I had to awaken her. I lifted the handkerchief from her eyes, and she opened them but did not sit up. I took her hand and she pressed it to her breast and smiled at me. She said: "I can stand it now, darling. It was terrible till you came." After a moment she added: "My mother said to me: 'What with your nonsense and my own, your life began with a pretty mess, didn't it? Well, thank God, that's one worry off my shoulders. Give Chad my love.'"

This moved me very much. "Would you call that an honest report?"

She had no words for answer, but pressed my hand more firmly to her breast. Then she stood up and said: "We must go back. If you *can* get out of accepting Max's invitation to dinner, please do so. I'd like to go straight home."

We met Max before we had gone far. Wearing a tussore suit and a yachting cap, he was at the wheel of *Bessie,* and a youth who looked to be in his middle twenties was standing alongside him. His face seemed familiar to me. Max slowed down and said: "Put out the ladder, Martin."

Rose and I went aboard and I tied the punt astern. Max introduced his companion as Martin Napier, and then I remembered him. He was an actor whose work I had watched and liked. We didn't see much of him that time. Max turned the launch round and headed for home. I asked him to forgive me if I took Rose away. "Well, I do want Martin to myself," he said. "He turned up unexpectedly, but as it happens at the right moment. Would it surprise you if I told you that you'll prob-ably be seeing more of him?"

"It would be a pleasant surprise," I said sincerely. I liked the young man.

And as I drove Rose home she said that she liked Martin, too. "I wonder what Max has up his sleeve now?"

"My guess is that he wants Napier for Peter Rosslyn in my new play."

The guess turned out to be right.

8

The hot weather lasted all that week, and the hay was got in, and then the rain started. Billy Pascoe came down on the Saturday morning, and the rain went on all the time he was with us. I had hoped for an outdoor week end, a time of excursions, but we were bottled up in the house. Thus I learned more about Billy than I should have learned, in other conditions, in a month.

It was an odd experience, having under one roof three men who had lived with Rose. Billy was perfectly at ease with her and with me and Eustace, but I think we all had the feeling—Henrietta told me that she had it, too—that trying to get into touch with him was like rambling outside the walls of a fortified city. I do not think that once during the two days he was with us he began a conversation. If one of us did so, and directly addressed him, he would answer, and his answers showed him to be remarkably well informed about many things. But he would drop out of it as soon as he politely could, like an adult who had been discussing a problem in toy bridge-building with children. Eustace alone had the daring to chaff him, and he would listen to the chaff as politely as to anything else. We had hauled Eustace into the drawing room one evening. He was squatting on cushions on the floor, smoking his pipe, and Henrietta, as I noticed she often did, had thrown a rug over his lower parts, so that anyone who didn't know of his infirmity would see nothing but a man who had chosen to squat: a remarkable man at that, with an impressive mane of iron-gray hair, piercing blue eyes, and a clean-shaven face beautifully chiseled. Rose and Billy, Henrietta and I, were on chairs in a half-circle before him, like novices in presence of a sage. The night was so wet and cheerless that I had lit the fire. A standard lamp behind Eustace drew a halo round his head and filled the hollows of his face with shadow.

I looked at him, and I looked at Sir William Pascoe, more than ever like a tall, dark, grave Spaniard, neatly dressed. It occurred to me that though, by his own wish, Eustace had slipped outside the knowledge of "the public" that once adored him, and though Billy's work was of a sort that the "public" was not likely to hear about, here were two of the most remarkable men in England. I wondered what on earth Rose had ever seen in me.

I said: "Is there any point where physics and metaphysics touch?"

Eustace blew out a cloud of smoke and laughed. "Any point?" he cried. "Why, Chad, there's no point where they don't touch. Didn't you know that that is why religion has had its day? Don't you agree, Sir William?"

Billy said: "I see what you mean. But go on. I'd like to hear your view."

Eustace said: "You know why Chad asked that?"

"Oh, yes," Billy replied. "He thinks I represent nothing but matter, and you nothing but spirit."

"Yes," Eustace went on. "Oddly enough, when you look at the pair

388

of us, he takes you for Caliban and me for Prospero. What poor Chad doesn't see—and how should he when his writings represent nothing but the surface of action?—is that Caliban and Prospero are two faces of the same person. That's what the theologians don't see, either. They've tied themselves up in knots splitting the human atom into body and spirit. The body, poor devil, is born in sin and iniquity and can't do anything right. Some Roman got nearer to it when he talked about *mens sana in corpore sano*, but even he maintained the difference and could think of nothing better than a sort of peaceful coexistence for Caliban and Prospero. It took Jesus—no theologian, goodness knows—to put it clearly. 'I and my Father are one.' And when you think how the All-Father works, through whirling flame and spinning gas and invading seas and falling mountains, through volcano, hurricane and earthquake, as well as through summer corn and April rain—well, then you begin to get the hang of the idea. So when Chad asks whether physics and metaphysics touch, I say they don't touch; they at last reach the point where each dissolves into the other and they become one thing. If thing is the word."

Eustace looked at Rose. "I don't know," he said, "who first talked of Rosa Mundi—the Rose of the World. I suppose, like Keats, he meant beauty. Everything—all seeming differences—are reconciled in beauty, and become one. The rejection of beauty is the sin against the Holy Ghost."

Billy said: "Yes. Keats said Beauty is Truth. It is also Power, and Power can be terrible."

"Beauty is always terrible," Eustace said, "in whatever form it appears. Did you ever hear of the girl who said: 'Well, actually, I'm rather partial to beauty'? Poor little soul. Still, I suppose she was on the right track, though she had a long way to go. Beauty is the most terrible thing in life, which is why men fall down and worship its passing manifestations —in a cathedral, a picture, a woman. At last we get beyond the manifestations and catch a glimpse of what is manifested."

Adrian Wybird came in and said without preamble: "Eustace, isn't it time I put you to bed? I'm rather tired."

"All right, my dear. Roll me home," Eustace said. " 'Unarm, Eros; the long day's task is done, and we must sleep.' "

Billy said: "May I roll you home for once, Eustace? Lend me a mackintosh, Chad."

He rolled him out into the still falling rain. "Stay here awhile," I said to Adrian.

It was not till an hour later that Billy returned and went straight to bed. What those two had been talking about goodness knows.

CHAPTER FIFTEEN

I

MISS ORLOP died sooner than we expected, and in circumstances that called for an inquest. The jury returned an open verdict—that death was caused by an overdose of sleeping pills but that there was no evidence to show whether they were intentionally or accidentally taken. This was in September of the year when she had said good-by to me and Rose at Paddington. We went down to the funeral in the church of what had once seemed to me our great Town, and as we were walking out into the autumn sunshine with Uncle Arthur, Billy Pascoe got up from a back pew and joined us. We had managed fairly well till then, but seeing, to the surprise of all of us, I am sure, that his eyes were wet, we were overcome, and we sat down again, speechless, struggling with our emotions. It was Uncle Arthur who at last raspingly cleared his throat, took Rose by the arm, and led her out into the churchyard. We stood for a moment talking among the graves. Rose asked Billy if he would care to stay at Pentyrch for the night, but he said No—he was taking a train back to London. "But I felt I ought to come. You don't mind? You don't think it an intrusion?"

Rose looked at him with her moist eyes and shook her head dumbly.

A man wearing corduroy trousers tied round the ankles with string was hacking at the long coarse grass between the graves.

Billy said: "Do you remember him, Chad?"

I looked at the man and said I did not remember him.

"He was at school with us," Billy told me.

He shook hands and hurried away; and I knew what he was thinking. "There, but for the grace of God and Lucy Orlop, goes Billy Pascoe." He had paid his tribute. It was odd to think that she had been his mother-in-law and mine.

We drove back to Pentyrch in a taxicab over roads that no longer raised a white dust; but once we had turned in among the trees of the wood through which the drive twisted all was unchanged. The rotting leaves of years hushed our approach, and when we swung out on to the gravel sweep before the house, time had stood still. All around us the blue and white and pink hydrangeas were blooming, and the honey-colored stone seemed merely to have sponged up the sunshine of another eleven summers since I was last here writing *I Don't Want to Die*.

It was after a melancholy evening meal that Uncle Arthur told us what I think we both expected to hear. He had come in one day from his work among the vegetables to find her in great pain. She told him what she had kept to herself till then. "Now that this has started, Arthur," she said, "it will get worse and worse, and there is nothing to be done about it. There is no cure—there is simply more and worse pain. If you want me to, I will put up with it. But is there any sense in suffering what you wouldn't permit a dog or a horse to suffer?"

He went out and walked for hours in the woods and on the seashore. "It was such a beautiful evening," he said. "It had been raining for days, and that day suddenly everything was bright. I had come in from work feeling as happy as a sandboy. All the apples here are bad—old overworked trees. I had a scheme for taking out ten a year and replacing them with decent stuff. It would have taken me about five years. You see what a fool I am? Five years! And it was a question of five days—perhaps five minutes."

He was overcome and could not go on. Rose said gently: "You agreed to let her do as she wished?"

He nodded and buried his face in his hands. She went to him and tenderly took away his hands and kissed him. "Thank you," she said. "Go to bed now. You've had enough."

He said: "My dear, I've had more than I ever deserved. So much more."

Then he went off, weeping.

He did not go with us the next day to the lawyer's office in the Town, where we sat among deed boxes, with dusty rays of sunshine falling upon pigeonholes stuffed with bundles tied in red tape, and received condolences and drank sherry and listened to the solicitor reading the will. Miss Orlop was a richer woman than I had imagined. There were only four beneficiaries. Uncle Arthur and Sir William Pascoe each received for life the interest on ten thousand pounds, the capital sum to revert, upon their deaths, in the case of Uncle Arthur to Rose, in the case of Sir William to Henrietta. Henrietta received also an outright sum of five thousand pounds. The residue went to Rose, and as the total estate was not far short of a hundred thousand pounds, this would be a lot of money, even when death duties had been paid.

The solicitor, a spruce young man far removed from the family lawyer of fiction, assured us briskly that it was a fine morning, that he was due in court and must run away at once, and shook our hands vigorously. "I'm glad to see you're not wearing mourning," he said, smiling, with a nice touch of modernity.

We strolled to a café for our morning coffee, and then walked about the Town. "We might as well talk this over and have done with it," Rose said. "The question is: What are we to do with Pentyrch? I don't want it, that's certain. Do you?"

I said that I preferred Chalk Hill. It was not too big. It gave us the quiet we needed, and one could motor to London in an hour.

"I have no sentiment about the place," Rose said. "Many of my most miserable hours were spent in it, and I think that was true of my mother and, from what I've heard, of her mother before her. And yet I don't want to sell it. Not yet, anyhow. I'll try to let it, furnished, and perhaps I'll sell it later."

There is no reason to go deeply into all this. I need only say that she did let it to a man who had retired from a life profitably devoted to making soap and shaving cream, but Rose had a sentimental feeling about the studio on the knoll in which her mother had worked and in which I had written my first play. We'll tinker it up," she said, "and if we want a Cornish holiday it will be there." The tinkering turned the studio into a living room. Two bedrooms, a bathroom and a kitchen were added. It was an expensive bit of tinkering before it was done with; but I was glad she did it. When it was finished and we went down to inspect it, I said: "I can walk out of the front door and look along the bay and see all that I want to remember of my childhood."

"What do you want to remember?" she asked.

"My father and mother lying on the beach with their hands linked, and little Billy Pascoe fervently damning a woman who had insulted Michael Faraday, and a small girl being sick in a dinghy.'

"How long do gulls live?" she demanded.

"Good lord! How should I know?"

"Look at them," she said. "I was wondering. Perhaps they were alive that day and were watching the small girl. What a little bitch she seems to have been."

"She's improved no end. Let's go in now and see if the new beds are comfortable."

2

When we went back to Chalk Hill after Miss Orlop's funeral, Uncle Arthur came with us. The old boy was badly shaken. He was ten years older than my mother, which made him about seventy. I drove the car easily and took two days on the journey. We stayed in a pleasant village pub for the night, and when he and I took a turn up and down the ancient street after dinner he said to me: "Chad, my dear, I want to say, and have done with it, thank you, and thank Rose, for offering me a home. I can accept it only on one condition."

"And what is that?"

"That you give me a job to do. Sack that young waster Wybird. I'll make your vegetable garden blossom as the rose, and I can look after Eustace, too. If you think you're going to turn Arthur J. Geldersome out to grass like an old horse you're much mistaken."

"A rest will do you no harm," I assured him.

"It will do me all the harm in the world. I have always been a restful man because I've had a job. The most restless people I've met are the poor devils with nothing to do."

I told him I'd think it over. I knew that Adrian Wybird ought to go, but I am temperamentally unable to be harsh with anybody. No doubt it would have been better for Adrian if I had been firmer with him. To this day I blame myself for letting him slide. But there it was, and as we drove through the second day of our journey my mind was fretted at the thought of meeting him again. I need not have worried. Henrietta, who came out to meet us, said that he was gone.

Uncle Arthur said briefly: "It was meant."

3

We had been away for six days, and Adrian disappeared on the first of them. "It wasn't the moment to bother you with the affair," Henrietta said. And to help us to put two and two together she said: "Mr. Crothers rang up yesterday to ask if Penelope was here with us." When that had sunk in, she gave us a further piece of information. "That Hogarth portrait of a Wybird has vanished, too."

So there it was: the boy—if you could call him a boy at twenty-nine —the girl, and the wherewithal.

I said: "Well, we're all pretty tired. Let it rest for the night."

Uncle Arthur had his suitcase carried to the stables, and I walked down there with him. We found Eustace squatting in front of the fire reading St. Teresa's *Life*. I apologized to him for having left him so long unattended. He was not worrying. "My dear Chad," he said, "I got on very well before Adrian came along, and I shall get along now in these much more comfortable quarters. I wonder if they're good for me? You spoiled the pair of us. Perhaps I'll run away next."

"Not while I am here to prevent it," Uncle Arthur said firmly. "Henceforth, you and the vegetables are my concern."

"You can count me in with the vegetables," Eustace assured him. "I sometimes fail to see wherein I differ from a garden marrow."

Uncle Arthur went upstairs to inspect his bedroom, and I explained the new arrangement. "I could get along very well on my own," Eustace said, "but I think it will be a help to the old man to be here. We shall get on. I like him. Do you remember the days when we lived together in his house at Smurthwaite? I'm afraid I gave him a lot to put up with."

"He was proud of you, you know. He once said to me that you'd grace an Athenian thoroughfare."

Eustace chewed that over in silence for a moment, and then said:

"Well, I suppose I would have done. They were heady days. Believe me, Chad, that was an experience." He looked at where his legs should have been and said: "This is an experience, too. All this love and forgiveness. You and Rose. Even Billy Pascoe. And now Mr. Geldersome."

"You'll have to learn to call him Uncle Arthur," I said, to laugh it off.

"I'll try," he promised.

"I'm very worried about young Wybird and Penelope."

"I don't see that you can do much," he said, "except not prosecute him for pinching your picture. But leave all that now. How is Rose? Ask her to come and see me. She must have had an unhappy time."

I told him of the funeral, and of Billy Pascoe's brief appearance. "Poor Billy!" he said. "Even when he was a boy, he never knew whether to love her or hate her. I suppose every first-rate pot loathes the thought of the potter now and then."

We heard Uncle Arthur's heavy footstep on the stairs, and Eustace said: "Uncle Arthur, come and sit down now. You must be tired from your journey. Put a match to the fire and let's have a talk."

I left them to it.

Rose spent that evening in the stable with them, and Henrietta said to me: "Do you feel like work? There's rather an accumulation of letters."

"Well, let's look at them, anyway," I said, sensing that what she wanted was the chance of a talk. It was always to the cozy study that she led me on such occasions. I ran through the letters and put aside those to be dealt with in the morning, and said: "This is the first of October. Let's celebrate with a fire."

We settled down alongside it, and I lit my pipe and said: "Well now, my favorite daughter, how have things been going?"

"Is it heartless if I say 'Very well'? I was glad when he went."

"If that's the truth, say it. I'm not sorry myself. I don't know whether I let him down or he let me down, but the experiment failed, for whatever reason. He'd been here about two years. There wasn't much more I could do for him."

"I was eighteen when he came."

"Yes. I was getting a bit worried about you. I want you to have a wonderful marriage like my own. I couldn't see it coming. How far had it gone?"

"One or two kisses. I suppose from such a handsome man that's too many or too few at nineteen."

She stretched her hands to the flames, and presently went on: "He was never taken with me as I was with him. And we had our quarrels. Mainly about you. He loathed working for you, especially in what he always called his own house. I'd try to make him see it differently, and

394

then he'd sulk for days. 'You're against me, like the rest of them!' he'd say. Even before Penelope took to popping in, I began to be utterly miserable. I knew he was as weak as ditchwater, and that I was a fool, and I cursed myself for liking him, but I couldn't help it."

"He was the first marriageable man you'd had anything to do with."

"There's something in that, but I did have very powerful feelings about him, and I suffered a lot of misery." She asked with a little laugh: "Is misery a fair measure of love?"

"In my time," I told her, "I had more than most; but then I never had a sense that I was in love with ditchwater."

"As soon as Penelope came along I knew it was finished. He helped me in a way, because his feelings about her made him more and more discontented with being here, and his grumbles made me like him less and less. I had to listen to outrageous things about you. . . ."

"Let's take them for granted. I can imagine them."

"All right. By the middle of this summer I was almost loathing the pair of them. You remember the day last June when we beat them at tennis?"

"My dear, shall I ever forget it! I wondered what devil had entered into you."

"He came to the house that day and asked: 'Has Penelope rung up yet?' I was sick of the pair of them and said: 'Oh, to hell with Penelope,' and walked out of the room. He followed me and took me by the arm. He quite hurt me. He was livid and said: 'Compared with Penelope, you're . . .' I didn't want to hear that, so I shook him off and walked away again. He came after me and said: 'Penelope understands me. She'll know how to value me. I'm sick of the way I'm treated in this place, nothing but a valet to a loathsome wreck.' "

I took her hand. "Why didn't you tell me about this, my dear? I'd have turned him out of the house on the spot."

"It hurt me, but I'm sure he had forgotten that he was talking about my father. Relationships are a bit odd here, aren't they? And, anyway, I didn't think he meant what he was saying. So far as he *can* have feeling, he had a good feeling for Eustace. But one's own insufficiencies can be a terrible plague, and to account for them and excuse them we turn and rend other people, often our best friends."

I listened to the beautiful young philosopher, who added with a smile: "But I didn't have such lovely thoughts then. Lovely thoughts are like so many things: they rarely turn up when they're wanted. I just felt flaming mad with the pair of them. I wanted to kill them."

"And did you?"

"I think so. They haven't worried me since."

"Good. What do you think I ought to do about it all?"

"Hand it over to where it belongs."

"You mean poor old Greg?"

"Yes. I like many things about him, but I don't like the way he and Aunt Phoebe have brought up that girl. We occasionally had talks together, you know, Penelope and I. She loathes her parents."

This was news to me. I had known Greg and Phoebe for so long and admired them so much that I was not prepared to find a fault in them. I had been thinking of nothing but original sin in Penelope.

"Do I surprise you?" Henrietta asked.

I threw some logs onto the fire and knocked out my pipe. "Very much," I said. I stood before the fire, filling a cool pipe, looking down at her sitting on a stool alongside my chair. She was very carefully dressed, and I noticed for the first time what a woman she was developing into and that she had put on a little lipstick that was becoming. The sense of talking to a girl from an adult height deserted me. After all, when I came to think of it, Henrietta had had a life calculated to mature an intelligent person, and she certainly was that. And now she had had even her first brush with sexual disturbance. I looked at her with respect tingeing my affection.

"Don't think I *like* Penelope," she said. "I don't. I'm only trying to say what can be said for her. She wanted to be a musician—a pianist. If she's to be believed, she was pretty good. However, her constant practicing disturbed her father, and she had long understood that what disturbed her father was frowned upon. Never forbidden. They are good modern parents and forbid nothing. But when you are practicing on the piano, and Father comes in and says: 'Will you be much longer, darling?' and Mother is at his shoulder looking worried—well, you begin to think. Anyway, she says that's why she gave up the piano."

"Greg used to talk to me about the wonderful things his son would do."

"And Penelope once said to me: 'I'm glad I'm not a boy. I think they wanted one.'"

We were silent for a moment, and then Henrietta said: "I'm afraid this is being a very sad conversation for you. There's only one other of her remarks that I ought to recall, and the thing is that she said it with glee: 'I've got my parents absolutely beat. They're worrying no end about me.'"

"That was not so good. I think you're right. I shall have to ring up Greg."

"That reminds me. You must ring up Mr. Middlemass, too. He came through first thing this morning and I said you'd be back tonight. He'd like you to ring tomorrow morning. Well, good-night, darling. I'm off to bed."

She kissed me and went, and I sat there till Rose came back from the stables. "You have a very beautiful and very intelligent daughter, my dear," I said.

"I know that. I'm glad the Wybird has flown."

"I don't think you need have worried. She handled it herself very well. It was the lightest brush as Eros flew by."

"So much the better. I stayed to watch Uncle Arthur put Eustace to bed and then trundle off himself. I'm happy about that, darling. I think it's going to work out."

"So do I."

And so it did.

4

A telephone call is not a good medium for what I had to say to Greg; so I spent the next morning writing him a long letter that I sent by air mail. Then I put the call through. He managed to get a month's leave, and he and Phoebe came to England. I shall tell of that presently. I had rung up Max Middlemass before writing to Greg. He said: "Chad, you remember young Martin Napier? I'm bringing him over to see you. Could you give us dinner and beds for the night?"

I suppose Martin was about twenty-five at that time, a dark spare youth, quiet and grave. I might as well say here what I came to know about him later. His father had kept a small greengrocer's shop in a London suburb. He died when Martin was ten, which was the year in which the First World War broke out. "I remember him pretty well," Martin said to me, "a big hearty chap. I always see him in color, with a background of white cauliflowers and red carrots, and green spring cabbage. We had some good times. As soon as I could crawl he used to drive me in with him on Saturday mornings to Covent Garden. It was great fun: the foggy light, and the stamping horses, and especially the color of everything. We used to feed in little cafés where you could draw your name with your finger in the steam on the window. I was always doing it. My first playbills," he said with a grin.

On Saturdays he worked in the shop—"polishing the apples—only the top ones"—and toting baskets of stuff round to customers. "We kept open till eleven on Saturday nights, and I'd be sleeping on my feet. But I didn't mind that. I loved it all. When the shutters were up, we'd have pea soup in the room behind the shop. Extraordinary!"

And then his father died, and his mother slaved, driving the pony to Covent Garden, while the small boy prepared breakfast against her return, and dashed off to school when they had eaten it. "She's a great woman, Mr. Boothroyd. You must meet her," he said. And I liked the light in his face when he spoke of her. "She didn't object," he said with a laugh, "even when I wanted to go on the stage. There's a woman for you!"

"Why did you want to go on the stage?"

"It was just one of those things. I never wanted to do anything else. I was always saving up coppers for a seat in the gallery, and then there was Mr. Burridge. Now he had it in the blood. Not acting—just the theater. So far as I could make out, Burridges had been callboys, electricians, dressers, stage carpenters and painters as long as there had been theaters and Burridges in the world. Our Mr. Burridge was a stage carpenter."

Mr. Burridge was a bachelor, a neighbor of the Napiers, and he used to look in for a chat and to join them over their inevitable supper of pea soup. "I think he'd have proposed to my mother," Martin said, "but she didn't give him any encouragement. However, he wangled my first job for me. I was a crocodile in *Peter Pan*. It didn't call for much personality. I just ponderously creaked. Extraordinary!"

So it began, and it went on with bits like that till someone took a fancy to him for a child's part in a straight play. He was sent along to Miss Conti for a brushing up, "and that's the only training I ever had," he said. "For the rest, I seemed to nourish myself automatically on the smell of greasepaint."

All the time, his mother kept the shop going, and he lived with her except when he was with a touring company and during two years when he was with a repertory theater in the North. "Wretched pay but wonderful work," he said. "I managed to send her home about a pound a week."

By an odd chance, it was when he was acting in one of my plays for the repertory theater that a visiting London manager saw him and marked him for a part in a play he was casting. "So you see, Mr. Boothroyd, I feel I owe a lot to you. And now this Peter Rosslyn part in *Unarm, Eros*. Gosh! I can hardly believe it."

The greengrocer's shop was sold when he found his feet in London, and now he and his mother were living in a flat in Knightsbridge. "Time the old dear took the weight off her feet," he said. "I motor her into the country every week end."

Well, this is something, I thought. This is no Adrian Wybird. And why did I think of Adrian Wybird? Because, I realized, I was thinking of the girl I called my favorite daughter. But be fair, I said to myself. This boy hadn't a war to go through.

5

However, I knew nothing of this when Max and Martin arrived that evening. Henrietta and I happened to be standing on the gravel outside the front door, watching the October sun going down in a mauve smother. We saw Uncle Arthur enter the stables and a moment later smoke rose from the chimney. "He's lit the fire," Henrietta said. "He treats Eustace like an old hen fussing over a chick. Astonishing how they seem to have taken to one another in a single day."

"They've got something to go on," I reminded her. "They remember days when Eustace was young and Uncle Arthur was not so old as all that. Though I must say that, even then, he seemed to me as old as the hills."

Then, with a toot of the horn, Max swept the car round the curve from the drive. A moment later he was presenting Martin Napier to Henrietta. It is a little scene that is photographed forever on my mind: those two shaking hands, with the white columns of the porch rising beyond them, and the beds under the windows flaming in the last of the evening light with wine-red dahlias and Michaelmas daisies.

Martin said: "Mr. Middlemass has been telling me about you. You are Eustace Hawke's daughter. When we set out, I had no idea of that. I didn't know Eustace Hawke lived here." He looked about him and said: "This is very beautiful. To meet him would crown it all."

Henrietta was obviously pleased, but she said with a smile: "He loathes fans, you know."

"Oh, I know all about fans," Martin said. "They are tiresome, but not without their value. I promise you I won't burst in on your father with a blush and an autograph book."

"You shall see him tomorrow," she promised gravely; and then Rose came to the door to welcome her guests, and we went in.

After dinner I took Max and Martin up to the study and we talked theater till midnight. Martin was the first to go to bed, and when we were alone Max asked: "Well, what d'you think of him?"

"He seems very modest, which is a refreshing change."

"He'll grow out of that," Max laughed. "He's young and still ready to listen to his elders and betters. He doesn't think he knows it all. He'll never make a Lear or Macbeth, but he's going to be hard to beat in polite comedy. He's got lovely hands and knows how to use 'em, and a lovely voice. Oddly enough, he still respects authors. He's not forever suggesting changes in his lines."

"Clearly a man of discernment," I agreed. "In time he may even consent to an author's name appearing on the playbill in something more than half-inch type. He seems to have heard of Eustace Hawke."

Max grinned. "Yes. That is something again. He's an actor who reads. He nearly jumped out of his skin when I said Eustace Hawke lived down here. He can recite Eustace by the yard. He gave me a bellyful on the last half-hour of our drive."

"I hope he won't do that to Eustace, who says he's forgotten he was ever a poet. 'That was the cocoon,' he says. 'I've shrugged it off. Now I'm a butterfly.'"

Max got up and yawned. "Some butterfly! You'll be telling me next your Uncle Arthur's another. I'm for bed."

The next day was one of autumn's best. The sky was milky-blue, and the beeches that sheltered the pavilion draped themselves in motionless umber wings. I walked up, as I often did before breakfast, and found Martin already there, looking across the wide plain where the yellow of wheat stubble and the green of pasture were disengaging from the mists. "Extraordinary!" he said as I joined him.

"You seem to find a lot of things extraordinary."

"Well, they really are, you know. I never seem to get over it. Look at all that color coming out. And a couple of hours ago it wasn't there. There was no gold, there was no green. Where was it? How has it come? Look at the red of this girl's dress, coming up the path toward us now. What a note it puts into the picture."

"That's Henrietta. She'd put a note into any picture, whatever she was wearing."

I left him and gave her good morning as I passed her on the path. She did not turn back with me, but went on and joined him in the lookout. We were halfway through breakfast before they came in.

I had no work on hand and walked to the stables to greet Eustace. He was in high spirits. "Ha, Chad!" he cried. "You have arrived in time to deliver me from this tyrant." He grinned at Uncle Arthur who was sturdily making his way through a plateful of ham and eggs. "Wybird chastised me with whips, and this monster proposes scorpions."

"My dear Eustace," Uncle Arthur said, "on this plate is the flesh of hogs and the produce of a hen's misguided endeavors to perpetuate her species without the assistance of a cockerel." He held up a piece of bread. "And here is wheat—maltreated, I admit, in the name of purification—but some residue of wheat remains, the fruit of sunshine blazing on a field of Canada or maybe the Ukraine. It matters not. All these substances are energy incarnate in one form or another, and the metabolism of the human body transfers that energy to us—to you and to me. I am ashamed to add the obvious corollary that this energy, if it is not to waste, leaving us a pair of mere clods, must find an outlet in action. In short, I must walk. In that way I shall dissipate the energy, which is God's far-seeing method of making me ready to do justice to another meal. I merely propose that, instead of propelling yourself in your machine to some near-by spot where you will sit and stodge, you should come far afield with me and enlarge the circle of your cognition. Thus, you mentally and I physically, will throw our energy overboard, so to speak, and come back ready to reload with a good dinner."

Eustace was rocking with laughter. "You must save me, Chad. He is determined to drag me out of the skies and plant me in mud, like one of his cabbages."

"I wish," said Uncle Arthur, evidently approving his own phrase, "to do no more than enlarge the circle of your cognition."

"Once we were on the road, I'd leave you standing. That machine of mine can move."

"So, adequately to my needs, can I. And you would not, my dear Eustace, leave me standing. It's you who would do the standing—you, the hare who would shoot along and wait, while I, the tortoise, plodded. I am prepared to lay you three-and-ninepence that you will not shake me off."

"It is my experience," I said, "that nothing can shake off Uncle Arthur when he is in Arthurian mood, as he clearly is now. You'd better go quietly, Eustace. And I think it would do you good."

"So that is that," said Uncle Arthur, lifting another egg and a few more rashers from the chafing dish. "Since it is now agreed that energy is to be dissipated, let me make sure that it is there to dissipate. This is a moment for deeds, not words."

Eustace threw up his hands in a gesture of surrender, and I used the occasion to tell them about Martin Napier. "He seems to know your work inside out, Eustace, and I can assure you he's modest and won't be a bore. Take him with you. I'm sure it's something he'd enjoy and remember. He and Max don't return to town till after tea."

They went, and Henrietta went with them, and when they got back Uncle Arthur said: "The result of the race is: Eustace Hawke first; Arthur J. Geldersome second; Henrietta Boothroyd and Martin Napier, a dead-heat third. They came in a long way behind the others. And would you believe it, Chad, they had the impudence to look as flushed as though they were victors. Napier was wearing a bryony vine, the leaves and berries, in his hair."

I wondered if his memory was as good as mine, whether he recalled a day like this, a nut-brown autumn day when we rounded a curve of the drive at Pentyrch, and standing among the trees was a nut-brown girl with vines in her hair. I found that memory of Rose sweet and painful. I was not surprised that these two young things had looked flushed, "as though they were the victors."

6

It was typical of Adrian Wybird and Penelope that they began their life together with an expensive splash. A letter came from Penelope a few days after Max and Martin had left us. I did not show it to Henrietta: I merely told her the essence—that they were married and honeymooning in the south of France. Rose and I read it together.

DEAR UNCLE CHAD:

All sorts of apologies are due to you, and here they are, from me and Adrian. As you see from the address, we are in Cannes. Whenever I thought of a honeymoon—as, believe you me, I often did!—I pictured myself sunning on a Riviera beach, and to be doing just that with Adrian beside me is sheer heaven. We are married, so don't think we are being naughty. And now comes the rather difficult part of this explanation. You may think it a bit fishy, but actually everything Adrian did was straight and above-board. It was no more than a temporary borrowing. You see, we *had* to have money. You *must* admit that. The question was how to get it. Then in a moment of inspiration, Adrian thought of the Hogarth picture. He explained it all very clearly to me—that it was undoubtedly a part of his family's property and that it should never have been left behind in whatever place it was that you found it before having it cleaned. So my mind was not troubled on that score. However, I was a bit dubious about the next step. We wanted to go at once, and you can't pay your way with a picture, and the question was ready money, because it might be some time before the picture was sold. Then Adrian had another idea, and though, as I say, I didn't much fancy it at first, I am sure you will agree, on thinking it over, that it was a simple businesslike method of solving a difficulty. Adrian said he was sure you would have advanced him £500 on his picture, the sum to be returned to you immediately the picture was disposed of in a sale-room. Adrian said it would fetch at least £1,000. But the £500 was our immediate problem, and then Adrian thought of your checkbook which he says you leave about—forgive the word!—in a "criminal" fashion! The only thing that troubled me was that he'd have to sign your name on the check, but I'm sure you will agree that, in the circumstances, it was what he calls a "matter of formality." So I consented, and he made the check out for £500, which you will receive in due course, and here we are! Actually, looking back on it, it was all, as Adrian says, divinely simple.

Well, we're both in the pink, and please excuse more, as we're off to the swimming pool, and moving on tomorrow to some other place. Adrian hasn't told me where. He loves giving me little surprises. He's awfully considerate. Our love to you all, especially dear Henrietta, not forgetting our thanks to you for what old Micawber in *David Copperfield* would have called the temporary accommodation.

                                                                PENELOPE

Rose said: "Have you looked at your checkbook?"

"Yes. The check's gone all right."

"Poor Greg!"

"Poor Penelope! The little fool doesn't know what's coming to her. I imagine her addled head really does not see that wrong has been done."

"Do you think you'll see your money again?"

"Possibly. But a forged signature is not the best way of starting a marriage."

(I did receive the £500 six months later, but I lost on the deal. The Hogarth sold for £1,250.)

I put the letter into the grate and set fire to it. "Now," I said to Rose, "when Greg and Phoebe turn up, we can truthfully say that unfortunately we didn't keep the letter. I don't want them to know anything about this."

"Is that wise? Should they be kept in the dark?"

"It's a bit too late to be wise now. But you needn't worry. I shall manage to let Greg understand the sort of son-in-law he has acquired. I only hope that this divinely simple bit of roguery does not start a train of thought in Mr. Wybird's head. Eustace isn't a talebearer, as you know, but from some of his hints I gather that Adrian's about the weakest bit of stuff God ever made."

"And yet," she reminded me, "there was his love of Eustace and of Eustace's work. There was that lovely letter he wrote to Phoebe when Eustace was smashed."

We sat in silence, pondering the oddity of human make-up.

"There was good in him," Rose said, "but it wasn't enough to survive the wrong that was done to him. Don't tell Eustace about the check. He worries already over the thought that in some way he failed a disciple."

"I remember hearing a sermon once on the text 'Judas Iscariot, who also betrayed Him.' The parson dealt only with the word 'also.' What were the other things, he asked, that 'also' suggested? He ended up by making me see Judas as the prince of disciples with one small kink. All right. Nothing of this to Eustace. The letter's burnt. You and I will keep it to ourselves."

When she was gone, I stood at the window looking out at the misty blue and gold of the day. A David Cox landscape. And suddenly I remembered that it was Mr. Hawke who had delivered that sermon, when Eustace was beginning to trouble him, and I was sitting with the boys in the choir, an angelic child, and Greg was grinning at me— Greg who came to church only to see Phoebe—and when we came out he punched me in the ribs and said: "You looked gorgeous, Pie-frill. Halfway to heaven."

I could have wept at what life had done to all of us.

7

When Greg and Phoebe came, there wasn't much that they could do. They could have melodramatically set about the job of saving their daughter from a seducer if Penelope were not married. But she was. However, her letter telling us so didn't arrive till her parents were on the Atlantic. They couldn't verify her story, for they didn't know where the marriage had taken place. Greg rang up the hotel in Cannes from which the letter had come, and asked for the address to which they had gone on, but they hadn't left one. I was in a difficulty. I couldn't suggest to Greg that he had treated Penelope unwisely, for, as to that, I had nothing to go on save Penelope's own chitchat to Henrietta. It was the unhappiest time I had ever spent with Greg. I was aware of a feeling in his mind that I had been a careless shepherd, and in my mind was this doubt about his own wisdom. Nothing was said on either side, but once or twice we found ourselves bickering about irrelevant matters. The worst outbreak was at the breakfast table one morning. Fortunately, Rose, Phoebe and Henrietta had finished their meal and gone. He and I lit our pipes over a last cup of coffee, flicking through the newspapers, and at last Greg got up, threw down his paper, and looked about him with a sort of desperation. He said: "My God, Chad, what a life you live here! Idling along from day to day! I shall go mad soon if I don't get back where I can do a bit of work."

Now, steady, I told myself. You know what's the matter with him. It's himself he wants to kick, not you; and I said huffily: "We do our best. I'm sorry if we're letting you down, Greg. There's work I want to do, too, but I've been putting it off, doing my best to play the pleasant host."

"Don't let me stop you," Greg said. "I can look after myself. I've got a fairly self-sufficient mind."

"Perhaps that's the trouble with you. Well, if you'll excuse me, I think I *will* take a morning off from idling and get on with my banalities."

I went up to my study and sat down with my head in my hands, damning Adrian Wybird. It was all bluff: I had no work to do. Presently Henrietta came in.

"Uncle Greg says you're working. Is there anything you want me to do? I thought this was a clear day and that we had some scheme for a picnic?"

"So we had," I said. "You four go, and leave me out of it."

She looked at me for a long time, and then walked to the window and considered the morning. She turned, and, with her hands behind her resting on the window sill, said: "I feel the same as you do. It's worse for you, I know, because you and Uncle Greg are so close. But it'll blow over. I don't think Penelope is important enough to cause anything more than nettle rash. No bones will be broken—you'll see."

She was a comforting thing to have about. She came across from the window and kissed me on the forehead. "Shall I tell you," she asked, "of a very wicked thought that I can't get out of my head?"

"It would greatly surprise me if you had one."

"Oh, but I have! I think the real reason why Uncle Greg is in this mood is because he can't forgive himself for being glad that she's gone.

Perhaps he's not fully aware of his own thought, but I'm sure it's there, worrying him, and that's why he tends to smack out at other people."

"It's quite a theory."

She laughed. "Yes, isn't it? If Uncle Greg paid a psychoanalyst a lot of money to tell him just that, it would do him all the good in the world. Still, he's a sensible man. He'll tumble to it in time without spending a penny. I can't say I approve of fathers who wish they'd never had a daughter to take their minds off their own desperately important affairs, but if ever there was one it's Uncle Greg, and once he gets round to seeing it the better for all of you."

And, as it happened, when Greg was back in the States he wrote: "It's odd, Chad, how little I think of Penelope now. Phoebe is still deeply upset by the affair, but, after all, what reason is there to assume that this marriage will turn out unhappily? I am old enough to have seen the most promising marriages come to ruin and the most doubtful ones enduring. Anyhow, I'm so full of work that for days on end I don't give the matter a thought. There are at least three books that I shall have to write about these States when I am back. . . ." And so on. Not another word about Penelope.

CHAPTER SIXTEEN

I

WHEN I was a boy and I was allowed to sit up to hear the bells ring in the new year, I used to think: "That's another year gone," and the thought was not disturbing. There seemed so many years to come. Nowadays, when I go to bed, I often say, "Another day over!" It seems a mere flash, a wink of time's eye, since I was at the mirror shaving; and here it is: that day irrevocably ticked off; and a day is an important stretch of time. But when you sit down to write you can carelessly deal with the years, ruffling them over like the pages of a book, and say, "Four years later, when Simon was eight, we took him off to school."

Rose and I often wished that near Chalk Hill was some such school as Greg and I had attended in Smurthwaite, some such master as Mr. Ashmole; but there wasn't, and so Simon was waiting down there in the hall, wearing an important-looking school outfit, with an array of trunks and boxes about him. Rose gave a last flick to her hair and put on her hat. "The place will seem empty," she said. "It was bad enough when Henrietta went."

For a long time before she went it had been obvious that she would go, and, since go she must, we couldn't have wished her a happier going. Her brush with Adrian Wybird had thrown her into the arms of Martin Napier, and now, two years after their marriage, we still felt nothing but joy that it had happened like that. Martin's mother had died, and the young people were living in the Knightsbridge flat. They came down to us almost every week end. I greatly missed Henrietta from the little room next to my study, and the thought of bringing in a stranger horrified me. It was Eustace who suggested a solution. "Send a typewriter down to the stables," he said. "I guarantee to be pretty good in a month." And so he was. With the machine on his low table he labored away, and now he was fully efficient. I dealt with letters myself, and Eustace typed my manuscripts.

We could hear Simon down below whistling to keep his pecker up. "Let's go," Rose said. "I don't want him brooding there on his own."

This would be a severe break for the boy. He hadn't been even to a day school. For the last three years Uncle Arthur and Eustace had been his tutors. Eustace was not in it at the beginning, but when he was, I was moved to see the deepening of his affection for Rose's son and mine, just as I myself had been enchanted by Rose's daughter and his. But it began with a suggestion from Uncle Arthur. I found him one day kicking the mud off his boots at the kitchen door before taking some vegetables in to our cook-housekeeper. Occasionally I had seen Adrian Wybird doing this, clumsily carrying a few cabbages with muddy roots and infested with slugs and snails. But that wouldn't do for our new gardener. His offerings came as if to a show bench. Carrots and parsnips washed, trimmed and tied into bundles with raffia; cauliflowers as big as footballs and rich as cream; Brussels sprouts firm and rounded: all these came in trugs; and in their season came white chip baskets of strawberries and raspberries, currants red, white and black, or, neatly assembled, mouth-watering stalks of asparagus.

Having delivered his offering that morning, he made off to his kitchen garden again, and I went with him. Like an inspecting officer he surveyed his orderly platoons, and suddenly said: "Now that all this is reduced from chaos to creation, my dear Chad, I find a lot of time on my hands. I think I should take over Simon's education. He is five years old."

"*You*, Uncle Arthur?"

He bridled. "And why not I? If a Master of Arts and a Barrister-at-Law who for years controlled the affairs of a municipality is unable to teach the rudiments to one small boy, then there is something extremely cockeyed in the state of Venice. Alternatively, since the moment has arrived when the State insists on education, you could send him to the village school."

"Rose would hate that."

"Very well then. If such a man as Ashmole could lick even you into the rough semblance of an educated being, you need have no hesitation in entrusting your cub to such a man as I."

"What do you propose to teach him?"

"Reading, writing, and the rudiments of mathematics and Latin."

"Why Latin? It was driven into me. I dropped it as soon as I could, and I haven't opened a book in Latin from that day to this."

"That was my experience, too; but you have lived in vain, my dear boy, if you have not discovered that I am a Conformist. I have my surprisingly novel ideas on many subjects, but I keep them under my Hat. My Hat has always been the symbol of my Conformity. I take it Simon will go in time to a public school?"

"Probably."

"Well, then. The public school requires Latin; the boy requires the public school; therefore the boy must learn Latin. Which means, God help me," he said with a sigh, "that in his seventies Arthur J. Geldersome will have to learn it all over again."

I told Rose of this proposal, and it appealed to her at once. "The only education I ever had," she said, "was by absorption—going about with my mother and young Billy Pascoe and meeting all sorts of odd people that my mother knew. The more time Simon spends in the stables the better I shall be pleased."

Uncle Arthur began by giving Simon a slice of the kitchen garden and his own tools, which had to be kept spotless, and this was certainly a wiser start than setting him down at a desk with a book. The boy loved it, and they spent hours together every day, having, I should imagine, some rum conversations. At the end of a month I asked Uncle Arthur when the lessons were going to begin, and he said: "Well, it's early days, Chad. He knows his alphabet. That's not bad in a month."

"But when do you teach him? He spends all his time in the garden?"

"Simon and I have discovered the educational value of seedsmen's packets. An A is not a mere tiresome symbol: it is the first letter of Aubrietia, which Simon has growing in his plot. At the other end of the scale he has sown some seeds of Zinnia, and we have considered everything in between and planted or sown a lot of it. When Simon's garden is mature it may be a shade surprising horticulturally, but it will be a triumph of mind over vegetable matter. X rather foxed me, but happily I discovered the Xeranthemum, which you perhaps call the immortelle or everlasting flower."

"Can he write the alphabet?"

"Oh, yes, we have our blackboard in the garden—the door, in short.

You should have a look at it some day—a palimpsest of enormous interest to any right-minded horticulturalist."

"Well," I said, "I suppose the method's all right if it works."

"Oh, it works. When we came to V, which of course was Violet, I said: 'Violets dim, but sweeter than the lids of Juno's eyes.' Do you know what he said?"

"I couldn't guess," I answered, looking with an oddly chastened feeling at the old man, standing there with one boot on the spade.

"He said: 'Those are like Mummy's eyes. Who was Juno?'"

Now that line, as it happens, strikes me as perhaps the most beautiful sensual line ever written. I can never recall it without a tingle of tears behind my own eyes. That is what beauty always does to me. A beautiful picture, a beautiful line spoken beautifully in a play, a beautiful come-and-gone flash in a film, a beautiful passage in music, and my eyes swim. They swam now, to think that Simon had said that—so truly—of my darling's eyes. I walked away a few paces, rubbed off a tear, and came back to ask casually: "And what did you tell him?"

"I said: 'Now that's something you should ask your Uncle Eustace.' You see, I want Eustace to take a hand in this."

I suppose it was from this point that Eustace began, and a word must be said about Eustace and Simon. Few children are not revolted by deformity. Certainly Simon was. There was a day just before her marriage when Henrietta went to take tea in the stables with her father. "Would you like to come, Simon?" she asked. The boy ran and put his arms round my waist and sank his face into my stomach. He wouldn't answer, and Henrietta went off alone. Then Simon said: "I don't like my uncle Eustace."

"Why not?"

He said nothing, because, I suppose, there was nothing he could say. His dislike was instinctive. I told him about the war, and what things war could do to men, and what war had done to Eustace. But this obviously didn't weigh against a sense of horror. Eustace, to him, was a scuttling beetle, and he would run on his approach. I imagine that, at that time, he had never seen Eustace's face. He had seen nothing but a generalized figure whose abnormality frightened him. Now Eustace's face was becoming more and more beautiful. The almost arrogant beauty of his young manhood was gone, and gone was the wild beard in which for a time he had disguised himself. His hair was white, his mouth full and tender, and his blue eyes were wonderful pools in which his reflective life appeared. Simon saw this face for the first time in this way. He had been riding up and down the drive on his first bicycle, and, probably in one of those moments of panic when a new cyclist thinks about what he is doing instead of just doing it, he lost control and fell. His head smacked into the low wall that held up the bank where my shrubs grew, and he lay there unconscious. Eustace, returning from a ride in his electric carriage, saw him. His arms were very strong. He leaned out and lifted the boy and sat him on his knees—or where his knees would have been if he had had any. Presently Simon came to himself, and, looking up, saw Eustace for the first time. Eustace, who had been aware of the boy's aversion, said to me: "I knew it was all right. He grinned at me."

Eustace said: "You've had a nasty bump, Simon. How d'you feel? Could you ride home now?"

Simon said simply: "You ride me," and Eustace brought him up to the house. And then the boy wouldn't go in. "Another ride!" he shouted, and Eustace took him down to the gates and back. "You'd better go and have that head seen to now, Simon, and any time you want a ride let me know."

There was no trouble after that. Simon often waylaid Eustace for a ride, and sometimes they went off with the boy on the bicycle riding alongside the man in the carriage. They would take a meal and stay out for hours; and Uncle Arthur, accepting with reasonable grace this decline in his overlordship of both, said: "Well, it leaves me more time for the cabbages." And so, when Uncle Arthur told Simon to ask Eustace who Juno was, it was with no misgivings that the boy went to the stables and Eustace began to make his own contribution to the schooling.

2

Simon was an excellent swimmer. Henrietta accustomed him to the pool almost as soon as he could crawl, and when Henrietta was gone Rose and I, who used the pool almost every day in the summer, had him with us whenever he was not away on his own occasions. He was a fair, curly-haired boy, who took after me rather than Rose, and it was a joy to see him, a naked cupid, sporting among the willows that I had planted round the pool. In the July of that year when we saw him off to school Sir William Pascoe came down for a week end. I said to him on the Sunday afternoon: "Are you joining us in a swim, Billy?"

Billy thought not. "I'm apt to get cramp," he said rather primly.

"Oh, come along," I urged him. "How many hours have you and I spent in the sea at St. Michael Pendeverel?"

"Probably not so many as your imagination recalls," he said. "I remember you as an excellent swimmer. I was always a rotten one, and you did on at least one occasion haul me out when I was cramped."

"I knew my duty to posterity, Billy. But the water in our pool will be just about boiling, and you couldn't drown there if you tried."

Simon said: "I will look after you, Sir William," and at that Billy had to give in. He grinned at the boy and said: "Very well, Simon. My life is in your hands."

I had told Eustace on the Saturday that we would be at the pool at three o'clock the next day, and he said: "I shall join you."

"What!" I cried. "In the water?"

"In the water. For two reasons, Chad. I'm sure I can still swim, but I want to prove it to myself. And there's another thing. Do you realize how much I love Simon?"

"What's that got to do with it?"

"We're getting on fine, Simon and I. I don't want any reservations. I want him to see me as I am."

Only Eustace could have had such an idea, but there was one thing about it that shocked me. "Rose will be there," I said.

I think it was the first time a word had passed between us acknowledging that Rose and Eustace had once had a profound acquaintance with one another's bodies. "She would be deeply upset," I said. "She has become used to seeing you as you appear day by day. This would be something different."

We looked at one another for a long time in a thoughtful silence that seemed to survey the long years and all that had been between him and me and Billy and Rose.

He said at last: "I love her still, you know, Chad. Do you mind my saying that?"

I didn't answer him. I found it too deep a question to deal with off-hand.

"And I love you and Simon, too," he went on. "Anything could have happened to her. I'm glad that what happened was you and Simon. Well, you're right, of course. I was thoughtless. Call it off."

But at breakfast on the Sunday morning Rose said: "I'm afraid we arranged Billy's visit rather thoughtlessly, darling. We forgot Annie would be away. I shall be up to the eyes cooking the lunch and cutting up the tea. You'll have to take charge of the entertaining."

Annie was our cook-housekeeper who went up to London on one Sunday in each month to see her sister. On such an occasion as this she was always ready to say: "Oh, yes, mum, I'll stay if you're in a pinch," but experience had taught us that we should pay with a week's sulks and ill-temper. So after breakfast I motored Annie to the station and came back to tell Eustace: "All right. Swim if you want to. Rose won't be at the pool."

That afternoon, as Simon walked with me and Billy to the bathing place, I told them of Eustace's scheme. I didn't want either to be shocked by coming unexpectedly upon what even I thought would be gruesome. For Simon's benefit, I played up Eustace's old prowess as a swimmer. I told him of the tarn, the cold, lonely pool on the moors near Smurthwaite, reputed to be without measurable depth, and of how Eustace and I would go there on summer days to swim. "And once," I said, the occasion coming back to me vividly, "he saved my life when we both played the fool. We were there on a winter day. It happened to be wonderful weather—no wind, the sun shining. Eustace challenged me to swim with him. I would have funked it, but in those days I was terribly afraid of him as a superior being, and so I said 'All right.' We dived in, naked. The water was so cold that when my head hit it I felt stunned. I was for climbing out at once, but Eustace had swum toward the middle, and in sheer bravado I followed. Then I got so cold that I panicked and would have been done for if Eustace hadn't chanced to be treading water and looking back at me. He saw what was up, and he came toward me like a torpedo, with a terrific trudgeon stroke. He said: 'Lie on your back and keep quiet. It's child's play.' He went over onto his own back, took me under the arms and lashed out with his feet. He had me ashore in no time. 'You see,' he said, 'if you've got a good pair of legs lifesaving is nothing.' He slapped me and rubbed me till I could stand, and then we ran and ran till we were as warm as toast. So you see," I said to Simon, "it's not surprising that a man who once used to swim like that misses it and wants to see what his form is now."

Simon, a thoroughgoing Eustace worshiper by this time, said: "I bet he'll swim all right. Don't you, Sir William?"

"I think it more than likely," Sir William agreed.

Eustace and Uncle Arthur were at the pool when we arrived. Eustace was squatting on the edge, his robust torso very white, his arms immense. Each of his legs had enough stump left to pass through bathing slips. Simon, who was encouraged to wander about naked in the summer weather, at once went and stood by his side. "Let's dive in together, Uncle Eustace," he said. He eyed the excoriated stumps oddly, but did not flinch.

Eustace laughed. "Dive!" he said. "Whatever I may do, I certainly shall not dive. I shall roll in like a stranded porpoise falling back into the sea. And then anything may happen, for I am not a porpoise. However, here goes."

And roll he did, clumsily, into the six-foot end. He came up and lay on his back and then finned himself along with his hands. Then he rolled over onto his belly and used a breast stroke. To a looker-on, it was nothing to write home about. In the absence of a leg stroke, he seemed to be almost clawing his way through the water. But Simon was madly pleased and excited, and I saw with pleasure that when he was in the pool he didn't show off any of his fancy stuff. With a modest breast stroke, he trundled along side by side with Eustace.

Having thus literally made the plunge, Eustace found the pool a great distraction. He was in it most days, and Simon soon took the stumps for granted. But Eustace always told me when he was going to swim. For one thing, I had to be there to haul him out; and, for another, I was able to warn Rose to keep away from the pool.

3

The school we were taking Simon to was called Graingers. It was in the high heath-and-pine part of Surrey. I had been down there earlier in the year to look at the place, and liked it. An old country house was the main block, and half a dozen houses had been built in the grounds. When I had finished talking to Maxwell, the headmaster, in his study, and things were more or less settled, he said: "Perhaps you'd like to walk down to the Junior School House and see Rhodes, who is in charge there."

"A good old North Country name," I said.

"Yes. So is Boothroyd. You were in the North yourself, weren't you, for a time?"

"On the *Manchester Guardian*. Before that I lived in Yorkshire."

"I think Rhodes knows you. We were talking about your plays, and he said you were up at Oxford together."

"Good lord! *That* Rhodes!"

Memory rushed at me with a whirl of wings. Whitworth Rhodes's brother Bob, the Honorable Clogger who had palmed May Ingleby onto me at the Commemoration Ball.

> *And they are gone: aye, ages long ago*
> *These lovers fled away into the storm.*

We were out of the house. The afternoon was full of the warm healthy smell of the pines. The color of a bank of rhododendrons in bloom wavered before my eyes. And there the lovers were: Eustace, who had exulted in oceans, falling like a log into a concrete pool; Rose, whose glow that night had been unearthly, burning now with her quiet, reassuring domestic light. Maxwell took my arm as I stumbled. "These pine roots are tricky. You have to watch your step."

Maxwell said to Bob Rhodes with a smile: "Do you know this man?"

I looked at Rhodes, a man of about my own age, in his middle forties. I had the advantage of knowing who he was. But for that, I don't think I should have recognized him. My memory was of a stout youth, dark, spectacled, with rather flat spreading nostrils. He had put on fat, and under the nostrils was a black mustache. The spectacles now had pebble lenses. He peered at me through them for a time, then held out his

412

hand. "Well!" he said, "Chad Boothroyd! You haven't changed much. I'm afraid I have." He looked down ruefully at his corpulence.

"I'll leave you two," Maxwell said. "I'll be in if you want to see me before you go, Mr. Boothroyd."

"Come up to my den," Rhodes invited. I followed him to a small room on the first floor. His house was admirably placed on a ridge. I looked across an intervening valley to the wooded land rising on the other side. The room was a typical shabby schoolmaster's den, roughly comfortable. "I'm sending my boy Simon here," I explained. "He's eight. Look after him for me, Bob."

I was sure he would. He was an ugly beggar, but his heavy face had a tired kindliness. I remembered how, when I was about to go up to Oxford, Whitworth Rhodes had asked me to keep an eye on his young brother Bob. "How is Whitworth?" I asked. "Still slaving like a Good Samaritan in Manchester?"

He looked at me queerly. "You *are* out of touch," he said.

He pointed with the stem of his pipe to a photograph standing on the mantelpiece. I got up and walked over to look at it. Whitworth Rhodes, as I had known him, not changed by the years as Bob and I were. As I had known him except that he was in military uniform, wearing an R.A.M.C. badge. I knew what was coming: "He was killed in 1917."

I had heard it so often—killed in 1914, 1915, 1916, 1917, 1918.

"I'm sorry," I said. "I didn't know. I lost touch with everybody in Manchester."

"Ah, well, Chad, it's a long time ago. I was in it myself. I'm a pacifist now. That's the only thing Maxwell and I ever squabble about. He says we'll have it all over again and that we'd better be ready for it. But not for me."

We sat for a time in uneasy silence, listening to distant drums, and then Bob heaved himself up and said: "God! How I hate carting this belly of mine about! I must make you some tea. My wife's out. I expect you knew her—Nan, Whitworth's widow."

He lumbered out, and left me chewing that over. I had not come to Graingers expecting to find it so heavy with reminiscence; but here it was again: I was back in the *Manchester Guardian* office on a dreary Sunday night, and a policeman told me of a row in Ackers Street, and there I found May and Whitworth Rhodes, and Nan came in with his supper. A handsome woman, younger than Whitworth. She would be nearer to Bob in age. I remembered that they had a child. May Ingleby had stayed with them to look after it.

"Any children?" I asked when Bob came back with a tray.

"None of our own. I took over Whitworth's daughter with Nan. She's twenty now, studying medicine."

413

We drank our tea, and I asked him: "Can you ever get a week end off in term time?"

"It can be wangled occasionally."

"Come over with your wife and stay with us. It would be a good idea if you could meet Simon on his home ground. It's not difficult by road. Have you a car?"

"A schoolmaster's tin liz is all it runs to. I'd like to come. And you could send the boy to us for a week end."

These visits had been paid, and as Rose and I set off with Simon that morning we were happy in the thought that he wasn't being dropped too coldly into the unknown. Indeed, during his week end with Bob Rhodes he had met one Tubby Chambers, a little older than himself and invested with all the authority of having been a year at school. We had heard a lot about Tubby who had showered upon Simon a remarkable series of picture postcards. One showed a handsome young mammal in bed, stretching her arms above her head under the caption: "I'm longing for you to visit Blackpool." Another was of Highland cattle, and another of Amiens Cathedral. Obviously, to Tubby, a postcard was a postcard. Simon pinned them all onto the wall of his bedroom. At the pool one day he said: "Tubby Chambers can't swim. I've promised to teach him." He sent Tubby a postcard which was a reproduction of a Picasso lady with two noses and three eyes, one of them hanging from her chin by a thread. It looked like being an interesting friendship.

We met Tubby, who was a round, owlish, untidy chap with incredibly innocent blue eyes. He shook hands with Simon and said: "How are you, Boothroyd?" and Simon said: "Very well, Chambers. Thank you for the postcards."

Tubby said: "Don't mention it, Boothroyd. It was nothing," as though his prowess with postcards had a lot in reserve. "Well," he added, "you'd better come along to the washeries."

We carefully abstained from kissing Simon, who waved with a pathetic assumption of the grownup, and watched the two toddle into the house.

4

We lunched with Maxwell and his wife, and were away by two o'clock. "There's time," Rose said, "to look up the Wybirds, if you'd like to."

"I wouldn't like to, but I suppose we'd better."

It was four years since that pair had married on the strength of my Hogarth. Nothing was heard of them until a few months after Greg had returned from his assignment in the States. A letter reached him from Newcastle-on-Tyne, saying that Adrian had a job, but that it was difficult to make ends meet on his pay. What the job was remained undisclosed. Greg sent them a check—the first of many. He never heard from them unless they were in need, and they found themselves in need in a succession of towns that bespoke a vagrant life: Glasgow and Whitehaven, Hull, Leeds and Cardiff. Six months seemed about the limit of Adrian's ability to hold down a job, until the last one. News of it had come to Rose about a year ago in the first letter Penelope had written to her. The letter was on expensive notepaper headed "Heatherington Golf Club." It was the sort of club where the pro is a retired world champion who charges wealthy merchants and stockbrokers, their wives and daughters, fantastic fees for tuition; the sort of club where stylish dances are held in the winter and where the bar profits would be considerable. Under the embossed name of the club was printed: "Secretary: Major Adrian Wybird, M.C."

"My darling Aunt Rose," Penelope wrote, and if Rose had been capable of snorting, she would have snorted at that.

Here we are, in port at last! I always knew Adrian's talents would find their reward, and now you see how my faith has been justified. It has been a dreary time, with the poor darling working his fingers to the bone, earning a pittance from people not fit to black his boots. However, you must forgive me if I draw a veil over all that. Goodness knows how long it would have lasted if an extraordinary stroke of luck hadn't come our way. When Adrian *did* have any money ["from poor old Greg," Rose intervened] he treated me like a princess, and one evening he'd taken me to the best cocktail lounge in Cardiff. Who should come along but a man who had been one of his fellow officers in the army. They got talking together, and it turned out that this Captain Patterson, as he was, is now Sir Oscar Patterson, a tremendous person in the City of London and with a great house in Surrey. He had just been doing some business deal in Cardiff. Of course, Adrian was not so silly as to say what *he* was doing—in fact, he'd just resigned. He made out that he had enough to live on and had been visiting relatives in South Wales. Well, to cut a long story short, Sir Oscar, who is a remarkably nice person, chaffed him about his idleness, and said: "Why don't you make him take a job, Mrs. Wybird, just to keep him out of mischief? As a matter of fact, I've got a job in my pocket now, but I must find the right man." Well, of course, Adrian played him very cleverly, pretending he wasn't keen, and Sir Oscar said the job was secretary of the Heatherington Golf Club. "I'm chairman of the Committee of Management," he said. "If I drop a word the thing's as good as done." Well, he insisted on paying for all the drinks and ordered some more, and then we went in and had dinner with him. It was a real Old Comrades reunion. It was only at the last moment, as we were wishing him good-by, that Adrian said casually: "Well, I might consider settling down if Penelope could put up with ending our travels."

Sir Oscar said: "We're a happy bunch. Penelope would be an asset to us."
I thought him most kind, and I said: "Well, I'm rather tired of being always on the move. Hotel life isn't a home, after all," and so the thing was settled, and as you see from the heading, here we are. If you and Chad ever feel like honoring us with a visit we'll be glad to see you. We have a dear little bungalow near the course, and we meet an awfully nice set of people. I always keep it dark that I am an Appleby! I'm afraid poor Father's name would be no recommendation in these circles! And yet the dear does what he can for us. Adrian's salary doesn't amount to all that, and, living among the Heatherington people, we have to keep up appearances. So Father has assigned to me the copyright in two of his books which he says will go on selling for some time yet and should bring in about three hundred pounds a year between them. Pretty decent of him, I thought. But, after all, a parent has a duty toward a child.

Well, I'll expect to hear your car tooting at the door any day now. It *does* seem a long time since we met.

We were in no hurry to toot at the door, and when Rose had sent such answer as she thought fit, we more or less forgot the Wybirds. Now, about a year later, we found ourselves in their territory, and I headed the car toward Heatherington. It was a district of new, rich-looking houses, each in its own large garden. It was a "desirable residential area" of the highest order, with everything that makes such an area attractive, and everything that would have smothered me in a month. We skirted the golf links with their beautifully green undulating fairways, well-planted hazards, golden blobs of bunker.

"I suppose," said Rose, "if one played golf, one wouldn't dare here to carry one's own clubs?"

"It would be a black mark, and I imagine that even the caddies would revolt if the bag were not on wheels."

The bungalow stood on a little rise of land grown with pine trees. The ground was too rocky for a garden, but the paved path wound through aboriginal heather, now aflame. It was a well-shaped wooden house with a tiled roof blotched with red and orange lichen. A small two-seater car was drawn up at the gate, and on a white seat among the pines Phoebe was sitting with Penelope. Their backs were to us. When we reached them we found ourselves looking down on a wide valley through which the railway ran. The bungalow was quite half a mile from any other house. The Wybirds had come to rest in a better place than I had expected.

Penelope's fair skin never tanned, but she was looking remarkably well: plump and healthy. She was wearing a light blue linen suit. I didn't remember what her hair had been like, but felt that its style of dressing was new: quite childish, a pile of rollicking golden curls. When the formalities were over, and her squeaks of delight at seeing us had died away, I congratulated her on the luck of having such a charming little house. It was like a Swiss chalet.

"Yes," she said, "it *is* rather sweet. We were so lucky to get it. It belongs to Sir Oscar. He's a bachelor, positively rolling in money. He thinks the world of Adrian, and lets us have the place rent free. I expect you passed his house—the big one with the white gates."

"Big ones with white gates have haunted our progress," I said.

Penelope laughed and tossed her curls. "You couldn't miss Sir Oscar's. It's the biggest of all. Now do come in and have tea."

We wandered toward the house. "How's Greg?" I asked Phoebe.

"Very well, Chad. As busy as ever. He's away for the next four days. A Labour conference in Grimsby."

I shuddered. "He pays a high price for his fame."

"Oh, you needn't pity him. He enjoys it no end. Still gets an enormous kick out of it."

"You *used* to, Phoebe."

She looked at me sidelong. "A hint, Chad?"

Rose and Penelope had gone in. Phoebe and I stood on the stone slabs of the path, slippery with pine needles. We watched a gray squirrel doing sensational aerial leaps. I took Phoebe's hand and kissed it. "The first time I ever called on your father at Smurthwaite, I looked out of a window and saw you and Greg riding bareback on a pony. You looked as gay as that chap up there in the branches."

She took her hand gently from mine and said: "My dear! Neither we nor our joys are immortal. Believe me, everything fundamental remains. Let's go in."

Penelope was saying: "I'm sorry you won't meet Adrian. He'll be terribly disappointed now that you *have* turned up after all this time. He'd have loved to do the honors. He's in London for the day. He has to go up now and then on the club's affairs."

The sitting room was small but attractive in a chintzy way. The upholstery of the chairs was rose chintz. So were the curtains at the diamond-leaded windows. There was rather too much Birmingham brassware about: toasting forks that obviously were never used for toasting, horse collar ornaments, and things of that sort. The prints on the walls were excellent sporting scenes by Alken. Seeing my interest, Penelope asked: "Do you like them, Uncle Chad?"

"Yes. They're very good."

"Sir Oscar's hobby," she explained. "He's a great print collector. He thought the place looked rather bleak and insisted that we should have these. He's been a real friend in need."

The friend in need, she said, as we ate her cakes and drank her tea, had introduced her and Adrian to all sorts of nice people. "Nearly everybody about here has a tennis lawn and, of course, tennis is my game. I get ever so many invitations, and to bridge parties, too. Never a dull moment. Of course, they're all rather golf-mad. I suppose I shall have to learn soon. But the pro's fees are a bit steep and I'd hate to take lessons with anything but the best. Still," she said with a gay smile, "when the time comes, I imagine one hint to Sir Oscar will do the trick."

The profound silence which followed this remark at last recorded itself on her mind. She glanced from one to another of us, and addressed Phoebe: "Have I said something terrible, Mother?"

Phoebe looked at her sadly. "Do you really think it would be a good idea to speak to Sir Oscar Patterson about such a thing?"

"Oh, I didn't say speak! Naturally one doesn't go up to a man and say: 'What about paying for some golf lessons?' You don't understand the situation. Adrian and I owe everything to Sir Oscar, and we like to please him, and we know that nothing pleases him so much as helping us along in all sorts of ways. When he heard that I was fond of the piano, he actually wanted to buy me one! Of course, we couldn't allow that! Adrian says it would be too much. But I play at Sir Oscar's house when he has a party. I feel that's the least I can do for a real friend."

The last words were rather defiant. Penelope's little-girl look suffered a setback. There was a hard glint in her eyes. I knew that Phoebe felt herself on weak ground. If what Penelope had told Henrietta, and Henrietta had told me, was true: that Penelope's piano playing had been gently squashed out of existence at home: then Phoebe had been given a knock. I looked without affection at Penelope, and even wondered whether, sensing a general disapproval of her chatter about Sir Oscar, she had invented his offer of a piano as a knife to stick into her mother. "You and Father stopped my playing. Still, there are some who like it." Was she saying that?

"Well, we must be off, Penelope," I said. "Tell Adrian how sorry we were to miss him."

Phoebe said she must be off, too. She started ahead of us in her little car, and when we were well away from the bungalow I overhauled her and signaled her to stop. "Ask her to stay with us while Greg's away," I said to Rose.

Phoebe seemed glad enough to accept. "I can give you all the night things you'll need," Rose said.

So off we went again, with me in the lead this time. Presently, as though sensing my thoughts, Rose said: "I don't think the little fool would chatter so much about him if there were anything in it."

"Perhaps you're right," I said; and added unchivalrously: "Still, it's early days."

"When Greg's away, he rings me up every evening," Phoebe said as soon as we reached Chalk Hill. "I'd better get through to his hotel and give them this number."

She did that, and later on Greg came through and they had a long talk. This comforted me. It seemed to show that, as Phoebe had said, the fundamentals were all right. What had I expected? We were all getting beyond the age for frisking like ponies in a paddock. It had been a bit of a shock to me when a bright youth, writing about my latest play in a London evening paper, mingling gossip with his criticism, spoke of Martin's performance and reminded his readers: "He is the son-in-law of the veteran author." It wasn't accurate; Henrietta wasn't my daughter; but damn it all, I thought, me a veteran? It stuck in my gullet.

Still, taking a look round the dinner table that night, I was aware of the years grinning at me. On special occasions, Eustace made the effort of dining with us, and he did so now that his sister had come. I had had a chair made that could be levered up by a jack, raising him to the table level. There he was now, sitting between Phoebe and Rose. I was at the head of the table, facing down toward Uncle Arthur. My uncle's face was beginning to sag like heated wax. Pouches drooped under his eyes, his cheeks were pendulous, and beneath his chin flaccid folds trembled. His hair remained dark, but it was sparse and cunningly distributed to hide his pate. I looked at Eustace: a lovely face, but grave in repose, wise with the wisdom of more than years. It was like the face of a judge who has seen too much iniquity. In the light that fell upon the table his hair was a silver casque. Phoebe's hair was gray, and if you caught her off guard her face was anxious. Still, at the moment she had something to be anxious about.

And Rose. Could I look at Rose impartially? I'm afraid not. Perhaps Augustus John could do so. He had painted her a year ago, and there the picture was, over the mantelpiece, shining beneath its lighting strip. I thought she looked more woman than any woman I had known. If John had seen any thought in her face, he had left it out in order to concentrate on the essential: all impulse and instinct. He had given her an outdoor setting. Wearing flowing crimson, with a fringed and flowered black silk shawl flung round her shoulders, she stood at the entrance to a woodland path. She was caught in an extraordinary attitude of suspense, as though one step would take her among the trees and she would be gone for ever. It seemed to me a work of pure divination, as though the artist had fastened onto the present woman a moment of the past, which he had apprehended if not understood.

I came to, to hear Uncle Arthur saying: "Pheasant and straw potatoes, my dear Chad, are worthy of more concentration than you are bestowing upon them. So is my conversation. Did you hear the proposal I made?"

I apologized, and said that I had not.

"We are none of us getting younger," he said, as though he had guessed my thoughts, "and for me at all events the time has come when I say apropos of this or that, 'You won't do *that* again, Arthur.' But there's one thing I want to do again before I quit this mortal scene, and that is see dear old Smurthwaite. What I was proposing was a reassembly of Old Smurthwaitians: myself, and you and Rose, who at any rate has some passing acquaintance with the place, and Greg and Phoebe, and Eustace, and, if we can root him out from among his atoms, Billy Pascoe. I ventured to look into the kitchen before dinner. There is crème caramel to follow. I for one am anxious to lay into it."

"I'm sorry to keep you all waiting," I said, and demolished the pheasant.

I knew that Uncle Arthur had not sold his house in Smurthwaite. He had taken some bits of his stuff to Pentyrch, but the place was still adequately furnished and had been let. He told us now that his tenants had written to say that they were leaving Smurthwaite in the coming May; "and my proposal is," he said, "that we all move in for a June holiday. We'll treat ourselves," he said cheerily, "to a good old sentimental wallow, and then the place may as well be sold. I'd like to see if the roast is as good as ever at the Dragon. They have an excellent Pommery, too. And I think I should give an eye to my graveyard."

We discussed the matter, not very seriously, during the rest of the meal, and when Eustace and Uncle Arthur were gone back to the stables, Rose and Phoebe and I sat round the fire and talked. Inevitably, we talked about Penelope and Adrian Wybird.

"Today's visit wasn't my first," Phoebe said. "I've even had the pleasure of meeting Sir Oscar Patterson."

"Tell us about him," Rose invited her. "We had a letter from Penelope about their first meeting in Cardiff. He didn't strike me as a knight of the Round Table."

"He strolled in one day when I was taking tea with Penelope and Adrian. Strolled in as if he owned the place, as indeed he does. He's a big blond fleshy man, with wet-looking red lips and a small fair mustache. I should think he was an excellent soldier. He was very polite to me, but a bit on the gushing side. We shook hands, and his hands were moist and plump."

I asked Phoebe: "What does he do?"

"It's difficult to know. I've had several talks about him with Adrian, but there's not much to be got out of him. He obviously knows nothing himself. He just adores the man and leaves it at that. If we said he was a tricky financier I think we'd be near the mark."

I said at a venture: "You should get Greg to meet him. I'd like to hear his opinion."

"Oh, Greg doesn't go out there. I make my visits when Greg's away."

Rose asked bluntly: "Why?"

I thought Phoebe a little evasive. "I don't want to bother him," she said. "He's got plenty to think about without adding this to it."

Rose took Phoebe up to her bedroom, and I strolled down to the stables where I found Eustace playing patience on his low table, and Uncle Arthur reading *Gentlemen Prefer Blondes* by the fireside.

I twitted him: "Not an English Gentleman, I hope?"

"It takes all sorts to make a world, my dear Chad. It would be utterly irresponsible of me if I did not keep in touch with the vagaries of foreign races."

I sat down and said: "Eustace, can you recall a chap named Oscar Patterson who was with your mob in the war?"

He thought for a moment. "Yes. A fleshy hulk. He was a major. I don't know much about him. Remember, I was a private. I didn't brush shoulders with the upper classes."

"Still, I expect he made some impression on you. And don't be rude about the upper classes. I was one of them myself at that time."

Eustace lit his pipe and thought back. "Yes. I can see him now. We rude mechanicals called him Porky-boy. What base minds the troops had, God bless 'em! I remember Porky going on Paris leave, and the speculation about what he'd be doing at a given moment. Terrifyingly detailed. One chap said wistfully: 'Well, I bet old Porky-boy can afford the best—black lace knickers. I have to do with calico.' "

"He was the sort of man who gave rise to such guesses?"

"He certainly was," Eustace said emphatically. "Another thing I remember about him is his voice. It was always full blast. He went past me one day when I was on a firing step, and bellowed to another officer: 'Well, it'll mean a bloody heavy butcher's bill.' We knew there was something in the wind, and we had a lot of raw chaps with us, just out from training camps. The poor little devils were terrified. But why the questions? What's Porky-boy to you, or you to Porky-boy?"

"I ran across him with a friend of mine. Somehow it came out that he'd been with your mob."

"Ah, well. I'm willing to forget him. Uncle Arthur, come and tuck me up."

6

Perhaps it was because Uncle Arthur spent so much time with him; but, for whatever reason, Eustace became the most enthusiastic supporter of the Smurthwaite holiday scheme. "Lord, Chad! But I was happy there!"

"I wonder. It's the same with everybody, isn't it? We look back and we see a land where it never rained during holidays, where the snow never turned to slush, and every twilight was holy. But I'll bet at that very time most of us were full of dreams in which all the beauty was in the word tomorrow. Happiness is always fore or aft—never here, amidships."

He passed that by. "We mustn't miss the tarn," he said. "I used to think it the loveliest and loneliest place in the world. I can't remember ever being there with you or with anyone else. Yes; I was with you there once; but, as a rule, if I saw that someone was there before me I'd sheer off and leave it alone."

"It was a good place," I agreed.

"You could lie for hours on the heather listening to the larks and to the waterfall. Do you know Baudelaire?"

"Pretty well."

'It was by the fall into the tarn that I first came on

. . . les cascades
Qui se jettent sans peur dans les gouffres sans fond.

I thought at the time it was a most wonderful line. It is, too."

"Oh," I said, "if Uncle Arthur's wildcat scheme comes to anything, I expect we'll find a car park by the tarn, and a coffee stall, and cigarette packets on the heather, and a diving raft moored on a few fathoms of chain in the *gouffre sans fond*. They find the depth of everything nowadays. No more mystery."

"Perhaps you're right," he said. "Perhaps the *gouffre sans fond*, like everything else, is within us. Still, we'll go and see."

We did; but before that came about there were other things to occupy our minds. It was on a December morning that Rose, who was looking through the paper at the breakfast table, said: "Oh, my God! Here it is!"

She handed the paper to me. The headlines said:

BRUTAL AND MEANINGLESS ASSAULT
Golf Club Secretary Imprisoned

It was a long report. A few days ago Sir Oscar Patterson had walked into the office of the secretary at the Heatherington Golf Club. It was the room in which the meetings of the committee were held, and on the table was a gavel for the chairman's use. No sooner had Sir Oscar appeared than the secretary—"an ex-army officer named Adrian Wybird" —took up the gavel and began to belabor Sir Oscar's skull. "Fortunately," I read, "Sir Oscar is of powerful build and was able to disarm his assailant, but not before he had received injuries that necessitated hospital treatment."

The reason for what the chairman of magistrates called "this brutal and meaningless assault" was not disclosed. The accused man declined to make any comment. Sir Oscar could offer no explanation. He said that he had been responsible for Major Wybird's appointment and that he had gone out of his way to show him friendliness. He had known Major Wybird as a fellow officer during the war, and could only assume that some wartime neurosis had been latent and had suddenly manifested itself.

A doctor gave evidence, describing Sir Oscar's injuries and adding that had the blows been an inch or two to the right the prisoner might have been facing a more serious charge.

The chairman of magistrates said it would be a sorry thing for the country if everybody who indulged in an outburst of berserk vindictiveness were allowed to get away with it on the plea that the cause was service in a war now happily passed almost out of memory. Not that the prisoner had made such a plea. It had come from Sir Oscar, and it was creditable to him that he had suggested some exculpation of this wanton assault.

Indeed, Sir Oscar's attitude throughout had been generous. However, society had to be protected from men of Wybird's sort, and he must go to prison for six months.

The newspaper, one of those that loathed Greg and all that he stood for, added: "Major Wybird is married to the only child of Mr. Gregory Appleby."

"Well?" Rose asked.

"It is good of the chairman to protect society," I said "What's the betting that he's a member of the Heatherington Golf Club and knows what's been going on?"

"Very likely. But Sir Oscar has committed no legal offense. It's all in order to play on the vanity and cupidity of a little fool like Penelope."

"I never thought I'd find something to admire in Adrian. At least he had the decency to leave her name out of it. I imagine the smacker he took at Patterson was on the spur of the moment. He saw red and he saw the gavel at the same moment. He's not the sort of man who could *decide* on an attack and then carry it out. But when he'd done it, he had time to think, and he decided to spare Penelope."

"It looks like it."

"I admire him as much for that as for taking the smacker. Two good marks for Mr. Wybird."

"And one more headache for Greg and Phoebe."

Uncle Arthur came in. "I suppose you've seen the papers?"

We said that we had.

"Eustace would be obliged if you could go along and have a word with him."

423

"I expect he's terribly upset," I said.

"No, Chad. He is concerned, but not upset. Eustace is never upset."

"Well, what are we to do about this?" Eustace asked when we went to see him.

"What can we do," I said, "except try to comfort Greg and Phoebe?"

"When I went to Cambridge," he said, "and took Rose away from Billy Pascoe, we carried Henrietta along with us."

He had never before spoken in Rose's presence of those days: the days of *English Grass,* of his immense fame, the heydays of his romantic ardor and of her voluptuous abandonment to her desires. I wondered what was passing in her mind, but there was nothing to tell me. Her face was impassive, and his voice was impassive, as though he were recalling some old sad tale that had not concerned him.

"We took Henrietta to Greg's house in Hampstead," he said, "and we left her there as casually as a grocer's boy leaves a pound of cheese. Greg and Phoebe cared for her as long as their care was needed."

He looked up at us from his squatting place on the floor. "Nowadays I have a lot of time for thinking, and that is one of the things I think about. My whole life has been a piling up of debts that I have never repaid. To my father, and to Greg and Phoebe, to Henrietta, to you, Chad, and to Rose. And to Penelope and Adrian Wybird."

He stuffed his pipe and lit it, and we waited in silence for him to go on.

"You may wonder," he said, "why it is, if I feel like this about it, that I can talk calmly of these things. Well, that is because I have faced it and acknowledged it. So far as a man can find forgiveness by seeing his sins and knowing them for what they are, I have found it."

I tried to jerk him out of this mood. "Be all that as it may," I said, "I don't see that you owe much to Penelope and Adrian."

He looked at me with a sad kindliness. "I expect you know," he said, "how I wrote *English Grass* in a Manchester municipal garden. I used to push my sister's child out in the perambulator and sit on a seat under a tree. She was a good child. Most of the time she slept, and I would look at her mouth and the curve of her cheek. Sometimes I would stroke her cheek with my finger, and she would open her eyes and smile at me. Her eyes were blue. And this child, and the trees and flowers and birds and lawns in that little park, were the England I was writing about. In this child, all the past of my country and all its future seemed to meet; and in the autumn weather, with the leaves falling sometimes onto the page as I wrote, there was all England's loveliness. That is what I owe to Penelope."

He went on after a moment: "What I owe to Adrian Wybird is sometimes difficult for me to understand myself. But, you know, our debts are not always to strong and noble people. Adrian was as weak as water, but he loved me, and, whether you know it or not, he loved this place passionately. I remember when I was in hospital with this"—and he slapped the lower parts of his body—"he came one day to see me and he wept at my bedside. He said: 'You musn't die! You mustn't!' I said to cheer him up: 'Don't worry, sir. It'll take more than this to finish me off.' He'd got a copy of *English Grass* in his pocket—he never liked the other savage poems—and he asked me to sign it. I did, and he said: 'Every poem in it reminds me of Chalk Hill, my father's place.' Then he went on about Chalk Hill for a long time, and said: 'You must see it. I'll take you there some day.' Odd, wasn't it?"

I agreed that it was very odd, and marveled at the things Eustace kept under his hat.

"So long as he was down and out, I could help Adrian. We got on famously together in the East End. But as soon as he came here he began to go to pieces. He was mad to come, but the conditions on which he came were more than he could put up with. After that row with you about digging out the rhododendrons he almost cried on my shoulder. That was one side of it, and another was that you gave him some sort of security. The more he felt independent, the less he wanted me. I could feel the hold I had had on him in London slipping away. And that, of course, was my fault. Obviously, I failed him. I don't quite know how."

"Neither do I," I said. "You worry too much, Eustace, about what you owe to other people."

"I don't worry at all. What would make me worry would be to discover that I was thinking of no one but myself. God knows, I've done enough of that in my time."

Rose asked: "What do you want to do, Eustace?"

He said with a laugh: "As usual, I don't want to do anything. I want someone else to do it. So far as Adrian goes, there's not much to be done at the moment, but later on I'd like you to arrange for me to visit him in prison. I'm sure Uncle Arthur would agree that an English Gentleman should return a visit, and Adrian visited me in hospital. As for Penelope, go and bring her here."

"I don't know that she'd want to come," Rose said. "Wouldn't she be happier with her parents?"

"I think not," Eustace said. "Go and have a try."

I said: "Eustace, have you made any guess about why Adrian took a whack at Sir Oscar Patterson? You know, he's the Porky-boy we talked about the other night."

"I thought so. Does he come into it, apart from being the victim?"

"The chances are," I said, "that he's the villain rather than the victim." I told him what we knew about Sir Oscar, and what we suspected.

"All the more reason," he said, "why you should go to her quickly."

"Perhaps," I said bluntly, "Sir Oscar has gone to her already. We may not find her there."

"I think you will," he said. "She is a silly little sheep, but you misjudge her if you think she is capable at the moment of a grand passion, or a passion of any sort. She may be later."

7

Eustace was right. Penelope was at home. We had set off as soon as our talk with Eustace ended, and were at Heatherington by lunchtime. The bungalow didn't look as inviting as when we saw it in the autumn. Rain had been falling all day. The heather was rusty, and a melancholy wind shook the water out of the darkness of the pines onto the roof. As Rose and I stepped from the car, a young man came toward us, coat collar up to the ears, brim of black felt hat sloped down over the nose.

"You're Mr. Chad Boothroyd, aren't you?"

"No. I'm Abraham Lincoln, and this is Joan of Arc."

"Look. I've got my living to earn the same as you."

"All right. I've just given you the scoop of the century."

We went cautiously over the slippery pavement, and I banged the knocker. One of the windows was a bay, giving a view of the door. The curtain was drawn back a little and Penelope's face peeped through. In a moment we were inside. The poor wretch was white, tear-stained and starved-looking. I said: "Go and do something to your face, then pack your nightthings and get a coat on."

I guessed she hadn't eaten since yesterday. She looked resentful at being ordered about. Rose kissed her and took her arm. "Come with me," she said. "Where's your bedroom?"

While they were away, I went into the kitchen, saw at once that it had never been a strong point in this establishment, and made a pot of tea. I carried it, with some biscuits, into the sitting room, and when they came back I said: "We're taking you out to lunch, Penelope. You'd better drink this before we start."

She asked, as nervously as though the Devil himself were in question: "Is that man still out there?"

"Yes. But don't let him worry you. Drink your tea."

Rose had made a job of her, and she looked more human when, ten minutes later, I had them in the car. The young man had one more go at earning his living. He shoved his head through the door before I had banged it. "Mr. Boothroyd—"

"Lincoln," I reminded him. "See you much later at Washington," and started the car.

Penelope now looked almost cheerful, sitting back, as I could see in the mirror, with Rose's arm about her. She said, in words the young man might have envied: "I've spent a night of terror."

"Let it keep," I advised her. "You'll have plenty of time to talk."

When she did talk, she told a commonplace shabby little story that seemed to match her shabby commonplace little being. I took them to the nearest town and gave them luncheon in a hotel. In that midwinter season the lounge was empty, and Rose and I spent an hour there sitting by the fire, listening to Penelope.

It was about a month ago, it seemed, that she found Sir Oscar was not a disinterested philanthropist. He had invited her and Adrian to one of his parties at the biggest house with the biggest white gates, and when the day came Adrian was laid up with influenza. In the afternoon Sir Oscar made one of his routine calls as a kind neighbor, and Penelope told him she would have to stay at home in the evening to look after Adrian. It was Adrian himself who said: "No, no. I shall be all right. There's nothing to be done but stay in bed and sweat it out, and I can do that without assistance."

The cunning Sir Oscar backed Penelope up and said that obviously her place was with Adrian. It would be a disappointment to everybody, but they'd have to put up with it, and he'd send his own doctor along in the morning to give Adrian a look-over.

It was only when Adrian became vehement, declaring that he wanted neither company that night nor a doctor in the morning, that Sir Oscar laughed and said: "All right, Adrian. I'll meet you halfway. I'll come myself with the car for Penelope and bring her back after the show if you'll agree to have the doctor in the morning."

That's how it was done, and the party was as splendid as usual, and of course Sir Oscar had to wait to say good-by to all his guests before he could take Penelope home.

And so, when she had heard the last car door bang, and there was no one in the house but Sir Oscar and herself and the servants, he came back to where she was waiting with her cloak on and said perhaps one for the road was in order. He put the drinks on a low table by the fire, turned off all save one discreet light, and lifted her cloak from her shoulders as she sat down. He raised his glass, said: "Well, here's to us," seated himself on the couch close enough for his arm to go round her.

If the man in the black hat had searched for a month, that is all he would have discovered of impropriety between Penelope and Sir Oscar. Unfortunately, she made a lot of it. She was wearing a very low-cut dress, and his hand touched her breast. She was up like a shot. She berated him, and he in turn became furious. "Well, by God," he said, "you've been hinting at it long enough," and she seems to have been sincerely surprised that such a man as Sir Oscar Patterson should put that interpretation on her silly flutterings and fussings round him.

He in turn acted as stupidly as Penelope had done. Instead of taking her home, stealing a kiss on the doorstep, and calling it a lost trick, he said, perhaps in the bellow that Eustace remembered from the war days: "Well, you can damn well find your own way home," and that is what Penelope did. She had only about a mile and a half to go, but it was a winter midnight, with dirty roads, no lighting, and tottery evening shoes. There was plenty of time for Penelope to build up an incident into a sensational adventure. An intelligent woman would have said nothing. She said a lot, and to a man with a temperature that didn't lessen his impression of evil. As soon as she got in he said: "I've been lying awake, darling, listening for the car. I didn't hear it." That was Penelope's cue, and I could imagine how she spoke her lines. Poor Adrian must have thought that she had escaped rape by a hairbreadth after a desperate struggle.

Porky-boy sent his doctor in the morning, as promised, and a few days later, when Adrian was on the mend, called in to tell him to take things easy. Evidently, so far as he was concerned, the affair was all in the day's work and need not break up their association. Adrian said: "I will trouble you to leave my house."

Porky laughed, still unwilling to take things tragically. "No trouble, my dear boy," he said, "but let me remind you that it's not your house. It's mine."

"That's right," Adrian said angrily, "don't let me forget that I'm your servant."

"Now look, old boy—"

"Get out! Your fat face makes me sick."

Then Sir Oscar did get angry. "Look, Wybird, I've been trying to do you a good turn. You're a damned rotten secretary, and I've covered up for you again and again with the committee. You can't be trusted to add up a column or to write an intelligible minute. You were always the same. You always had to hang on to someone. During the war you nauseated everybody by hanging on to that bloody subversive poet. It was a pretty pansy affair, if you ask me. . . ."

Adrian said: "You shouldn't discuss poets or gentlemen. You are not qualified, Porky-boy."

I don't know whether, after that, the situation could have been patched up. Perhaps not. But Penelope took care that it wasn't. The more she talked about it—even now, as she talked to *us* about it, we could see this—the more she dramatized herself as a sweet Lucrece who had been lucky enough to beat off the assault of a determined Tarquin. By the time Adrian returned to his duties his mind must have been so inflamed that every look at Patterson made him want to land the blows that at last inevitably came.

I was surprised that he had gone back at all, knowing his readiness to throw up jobs on lesser provocation than this. I said so, as gently as possible.

"He wouldn't have dreamed of staying," Penelope said, "if we hadn't been rather in debt. This is an expensive district if you want to keep in the swim."

Even so, I said, I would have expected Porky-boy to tell him to go.

"Oh, he did. And I must say he was ever so nice about that. You mustn't think he's altogether bad. He came to see me privately," she said, trying to look like a *femme fatale*. "He said that for my sake he wasn't going to have Adrian sacked, but that he thought he should look for another job. Then he could hand in his notice and get a good reference. He might be able to help him to something better than this."

"I'm surprised you didn't ask him to stay to tea."

"Well, I couldn't very well *not*, could I?"

"And what did Adrian say to that?"

"Not much. There wasn't time, poor dear. It was just the day before he hit Sir Oscar."

She went out to make up her face, and Rose and I looked at one another ruefully. "Well?" she asked.

It was a sigh rather than a question, and indeed, a sigh seemed to me the only appropriate comment. "We'd better be off home with her," I said, "but first I must ring up Phoebe."

I rang up from the hotel and spoke to Greg. There was no telephone at the Wybirds', or Phoebe might have saved herself a journey. She had motored to Heatherington, "and she's just rung up from a callbox to say the place is empty," Greg said. "She's on the way back now, rather comforted, I hope, for a young man snooping round the house told her that Mrs. Wybird had gone off with Mr. Chad Boothroyd in a motorcar. She says he made it sound sinister."

I was glad that Greg could get a laugh out of that. "Not so sinister as it'll sound in his paper next Sunday," I said.

I explained what had happened, and that we were about to set out for Chalk Hill. He thanked me, and I told him to thank Eustace. "Phoebe and I will come out as soon as we can," he said. It was rather a restrained conversation, and I was glad to ring off.

8

I forget on what day in 1934 Adrian joined us at Chalk Hill. I know he had some remission of sentence for good conduct. But however long it was that he was away, throughout that time Penelope lived in the stables with her Uncle Eustace. When we got her home on that December night, we found that Uncle Arthur had removed his things into the visitor's bedroom that we had expected Penelope to use. "Eustace's orders," he said.

He himself took Penelope to the stables and showed her where she was to sleep. She went as obediently as a child from a "free" school, glad to be told for once how to occupy itself. When dinnertime came he took her to the kitchen and explained the business of carrying the meals out in the containers. We did not see her again that night.

In the morning I waited until I had seen Penelope leave the stables and go down the drive toward the highway. Then I went to give Eustace a report of what we had done and heard yesterday. He thanked me for bringing her and apologized for what he called turning my domestic arrangements upside down. But as soon as I began on Penelope he stopped me. "My dear Chad," he said, "before she went off with Adrian, Penelope was about the place a good deal. She didn't bother me much with her company, but I am not an unobservant man. My opinion of Penelope was formed long ago, and this latest piece of nonsense adds nothing to it. I'd rather you didn't talk about it."

"Greg and Phoebe will be coming down soon," I said. "Perhaps that'll relieve the tension a bit."

"On the contrary," he said, "it might produce just that extra bit of tension that is undesirable at the moment. I shall write to Phoebe and ask her not to come unless I invite her. I find that Penelope is able to ride a bicycle. Do you think you could have one sent here? Small lady's size."

I said that I would, and asked: "Are you sure there's nothing—?"

"No, no. Nothing at all. Except the bicycle. Penelope's walking all of four miles to and from my tobacconist's for my special brand of tobacco. It would be better for her to ride. And she'll be able to get about with me, too, when I use my machine."

I began to see his drift. "Keeping her close to your side—fully occupied, eh?"

"Leave it to me, Chad," he said. "Hand me my tobacco jar, will you?"

I did so, lifted the lid, and peeped inside. "You've got about half a pound," I told him. He looked at me severely and said: "That's enough from you, Pie-frill."

I went back to the house and Rose came up to my study with the morning letters. "How is she?" she asked.

"It's rather soon to say, darling. But we have one comfort: she doesn't seem likely to worry us much."

Rose looked at me gravely. "I feel rather ashamed," she said. "I've been thinking that too—that she won't worry us much. Are we becoming a bit smug and self-centered? You know—*damn you, Bill. I'm all right.* Wasn't that a saying during the war?"

"It was, but, believe me, it wasn't acted on very much. It was one of those jokes that take on by their very absurdity. What's upsetting you?"

"I'm not upset. But I'm wondering whether that's been the snag for Penelope all the time. *Nobody* wanted to be worried by her, ever. It would make you feel very small, wouldn't it? And you'd tend to do anything to make yourself seem important."

"Such as magnifying this absurd episode with Patterson."

"Yes. Even when she was telling us about it, you could feel her blowing it up into an importance that wasn't there."

"I don't see that *you* need feel ashamed about it."

"Well, I am. Eustace has passed judgment on us. He knew that we weren't fit to deal with her."

"What sort of a job is he likely to make of it?"

"I can't say. But he's a remarkable person. I should know that. There's nothing so satisfying to the ego as the feeling that someone is dependent on you. Forgive me, darling, for going back to something I'd rather forget. But can't. When Eustace walked out on me in Weimar, the most shocking thing I had to put up with was knowing that he could do without me. It was not myself, my loneliness. It was just that he didn't need me. It nearly destroyed me. Eustace is dependent on no one. But I shouldn't be surprised if he makes Penelope overlook that."

"One thing especially struck me as we were talking to Penelope. It was when Porky-boy said something slighting about Eustace that Adrian came back with an insult that put paid to the whole thing."

"One doesn't forget Eustace in a hurry," she said, and went out.

9

Before the spring holidays in 1934 Simon wrote to ask whether Tubby Chambers could spend them with us at Chalk Hill. Tubby had no home in England. His father was a British administrator in some out-landish part, which I was pleased to picture in my mind. I could see the dusky postmen trotting along the tracks, enlivening the journey by Tubby's postcards: Helvellyn, kittens in baskets, Notre Dame, girls in lingerie, the Statue of Liberty. Tubby shared Mr. G. B. Shaw's passion for this means of brief communication, but Mr. Shaw, to his detriment, did not share Tubby's addiction to pictorial effects. Whence the boy obtained the card that I received I cannot guess. It was glossy, with a picture of Phyllis Dare looking about eighteen. Tubby wrote: "Dear Mr. Boothroyd: My grateful acknowledgment of your invitation. I'll be seeing you. Love. T. Chambers." His name, I believe, was Theophilus.

I drove over to bring the boys, and we set off on the return journey

431

accompanied by some remarkable impedimenta. Tubby, it seemed, had an eye on the future. I have met few people with a clearer determination about how their lives should be conducted. He was to be an explorer, and this holiday was to be a rehearsal of some of his future achievements. "We're going to find the source of our river," Simon explained. I was wise enough not to ask what river, for there could be none other than our trickle through the musk and mint. I let them run on, and discovered that the swimming pool, in a pretty compliment to myself, was Lake Chad, and that, starting from there, they would set out into regions where anything might happen. The car contained, somehow, a tent, sleeping bags, binoculars, an airgun (so that they might live off the land, which, Tubby explained, was something every worthy explorer did), a primus stove, two solar topees that I guessed would block out the view of a whole herd of buffalo, and various odds and ends such as tin plates, a combination knife, fork and spoon, a compass, a folding canvas table and a canvas bath. "A fellow must keep his body decent," Tubby said, looking at me through his spectacles like a small wise owl. I wanted to ask, but dared not, whether they were taking their dinner jackets. There was an assortment of biscuit tins containing "hard tack" and biltong. The biltong gave me some anxiety. It was aromatic, but Simon assured me that Tubby had studied the Choctaw Indian method of preparing this comestible and that it was good for longer than this holiday would endure. They had been secreting chunks of meat down the fronts of their trousers during dinnertimes, and then drying them, cut into strips, over a fire of leaves. "The thing is to know the right leaves to use. Tubby does." Tubby shut his mouth hard, as though no conceivable torture from natives would wring the secret from him. Finally, in this clattering assortment, there was one of those pipes that bonhomous Germans are represented as smoking: an immense curved thing with a porcelain bowl and silver lid. This was for passing round at the campfire, and, true to Tubby's pictorial addiction, the porcelain was painted with a picture of some Gretchen in blond pigtails peering out of a bower of roses. To remind the explorers of home and beauty, perhaps.

We saw little enough of them during the holidays. They "cached" the biltong, explaining that it was a reserve in case, on their return journey, they should be foodless, and I thought this a bit specious, for, even to them, the stuff was stinking. Each morning they would come to the kitchen and stock up with a day's supplies, and march away with the solar topees over their ears, a diminutive pair in khaki shirts and shorts. Fortunately, the weather was fine, and they dwelt happily enough in their tent at nights, with a fire lit in front of it to keep off wild beasts. Geography suffered some rough handling, as I saw one day from a peep at the map they were preparing. Out of Lake Chad tumbled the

Victoria Nyanza Falls, and the pavilion to the north was the ruins of Palmyra. Between the two was an area marked: "Here be cannibals," and in the rough scrubland beyond the pavilion I learned that "okapi and hearty beasts abound."

I kept only the remotest supervisory eye upon them, always from afar. One morning I climbed up to the pavilion and strolled past it into the scrubland, and through my glasses saw the tent about half a mile away with the Union Jack flying from a pole before it. In the middle distance was a small running figure whom I saw to be Simon. I waited for him to come up, which he did panting heavily. He snatched a message from a cleft stick that was sloped over his shoulder and handed it to me. "Take this to the mission station," he gasped, and at once pounded back the way he had come.

I was not surprised to find that the message was on a picture postcard, portraying a red-nosed fellow holding a tankard as he leant upon a bar beneath the words: "All ale, from Skegness." On the other side I read: "For God's sake send bandages and morfia. We have many dead, but are holding out. The impis are closing in. Speed, speed, for God's sake. Captain Marmaduke Carruthers."

I strolled back toward the pavilion, wondering how I could deal with this crisis without debasing myself in the eyes of the beleaguered garrison. In the pavilion I found Penelope. "Is that the message?" she asked.

She snatched the card from my hand, read it, and began tearing an old white petticoat into strips.

"What is all this?" I demanded.

"I am the missionary's wife," she explained. "Captain Carruthers happens to be in love with me, and the least I can do for him is to tear up my petticoat in a crisis. The morphia's another matter."

She rummaged through a small basket and found an eyedropper. "This'll have to do. I'll drop water into his eye."

I asked with a grin: "How are you going to fight your way through the impis?"

She produced a toy pistol from her pocket. "I am a valiant woman," she said, "and love will find a way."

Then she began running toward the tent, taking the basket with her.

I gave her a quarter of an hour and followed. Simon was marching gravely up and down in front of the tent. There wasn't a Zulu in sight. I pushed through and found Carruthers lying on a sleeping bag with his arm in a sling and a red-blotched bandage round his head. His eyes were closed, and the missionary's wife was kneeling at his side, holding his hand. "Thank God you were in time, darling," he said

"I shall always find you through thick and thin," she breathed.

"We must keep this from your husband."

"Yes, yes. He has gone to convert the Umzimvubu."

Tubby looked as though he hoped the Umzimvubu would put up a memorable sales resistance, but conceded: "He is a good man. Perhaps he will give his life among the cannibals. I can think of no worthier end."

Perhaps encouraged by this hopeful thought, Carruthers made a remarkable recovery, declaring himself famished by conflict. I was permitted to light the primus stove and boil up some Oxo cubes. We drank this and ate biscuits, and then Penelope shook Tubby's hand and said: "I must be back to the station, Captain. I will see that your gallant stand is made known in responsible quarters."

Tubby saluted and said: "It was nothing. Maitland!"

Simon sprang to attention. "Order the camp to be struck at once," Carruthers said. "We must push on into the unknown."

As the canvas began to fall about our ears, Penelope and I strolled back toward the pavilion. Her eyes were sparkling. "I love those kids," she said, "and so does Uncle Eustace."

"Is Eustace seeing anything of them? I hoped this stunt was keeping them out of his way."

"Am I giving away secrets? They come sneaking down to the stables at nine every night. I fry sausages for them. They have an astonishing capacity for sausages. Then they listen to the latest verses of the saga, and after that they go back to the tent, finding their way by the stars, Carruthers says, but in fact with the help of pocket torches."

"What's this saga?"

"Uncle Eustace's saga. They tell him every night what they're going to do the next day, and he has it ready for them in verse, as prompt as the evening paper. I should think he hasn't enjoyed himself so much for a long time. He invented their names, Carruthers and Maitland. Sometimes, after his own saga, he reads William Morris sagas. They like those. Uncle Eustace is in the saga, too. He's the Bard who was mangled in battles long ago. They worship him, because they know that part's true."

We sat down in the pavilion, looking at the new green of spring surging over the land below us. "Why does everyone worship him?" she asked. "Adrian did, you know."

I let that go. "How do *you* get on with him?" I shouldn't have been surprised if she'd said: "He makes me feel rather small."

She said: "He makes me feel so big! I came here loathing everybody, including you and Aunt Rose. I don't know. But even yet, I've never properly thanked you for bringing me."

"No, you haven't."

"Well, thank you and Aunt Rose. And I mean that."

"What do you and Eustace do with yourselves all day long?"

434

"Well, we just live sensibly together. He seems to make things have meaning. He was reading the Bible one night, and he started chuckling. I said: 'Is there anything funny in the Bible?' 'Well,' he said, 'not funny, but extraordinarily human. Human things always make me smile. I'm reading a letter that St. Paul sent to his young friend Timothy. They'd laid the old boy by the heels and thrown him into jail. He talks here about his first defense, so I suppose he'd been up once and got remanded. He's asking this boy to come and visit him in jail. He was lonely and bored and cold, and so he wanted someone to talk to, and to have something to read, and something to keep the rheumatics out of his old bones. He asks Timothy to bring a cloak that he'd left at a place called Troas and to bring some books. He says: "Especially the parchments." I wonder what they were? They could have been the comedies of Aristophanes. Anyhow, it makes up a marvelous human scene. You do get cold in jail, and you'd give your ears for a decent book. I should know.'

"I said: 'You've never been in jail,' and he laughed again and said: 'Don't you believe it. All the saints get into jail sooner or later—or should do.' And he said he'd been in jail more than once, but wouldn't say what for. Well, that's how he is. Everything he talks about is fascinating, and he treats you as though you could understand *anything*."

"I notice you go about with him a lot."

"Yes. Now that the weather's fine we get away most days. I ride the bike, and he goes in his chair. We park anywhere, and read and talk, or he writes the saga, or we just doze in the sun."

"You're looking all the better for it, Penelope."

She got up, and I looked at her, and I saw in her face a tranquillity I hadn't seen there before. "I'm feeling fine," she said. "What time do you and Aunt Rose have morning coffee?"

"Right now. I'm going down."

"May I join you? Uncle Eustace has gone off on his own till lunch-time."

"Yes. Come by all means." It was the first time she had sought our company. "It's extraordinary," she said, as we went down the hill together, "what things interest Uncle Eustace. From St. Paul to those kids playing at explorers. I know where he's gone this morning. There's a blackcap's nest full of fledglings, and he wants to see them make their first take-off. Not so long ago I didn't know a blackcap from a cassowary."

"And now you do?"

"I'm getting on."

Later on that day I said to Eustace: "So you've been in jail?"

He looked puzzled for a moment, then laughed. "Oh, that! It's one of those half-truths, Chad. When I was a soldier I was pretty difficult at first. I remember writing from France to a friend giving a few pen portraits of officers and N.C.O.'s. Not very flattering. Of course the letter was read and they had me on the carpet and sent me to clink. There were other times rather like that. Does clink count as jail?"

"Could do at a pinch."

"Well, don't give Penelope this innocent explanation. She was worrying a lot about the 'slur' on Adrian's character. I don't see anything very shaming in going to jail for socking Porky Patterson. It amounts almost to a public service. I wanted her to feel that the best people are apt to land in quod sooner or later. They're doing it at this moment all over the world."

"How do you find Adrian when you go to see him?"

"Reasonably cheerful. He's looking forward to joining the Smurthwaite expedition in June. It should brace him up before we decide what we'd better do about him. You don't mind his coming?"

"It's not my outing. You'd better consult Uncle Arthur."

"I've done so, and he agrees, though they're not Old Smurthwaitians. That'll make nine: you and Rose, Greg and Phoebe, Billy Pascoe, Adrian and Penelope, and Uncle Arthur and I."

"Some of you'll be sleeping on sofas."

"Don't worry. I'm used to sleeping nearer the ground than that."

"Thank you for looking after those boys so well. Shall I pay for the sausages?"

"I'm doing my best," he said with a twinkle. "But I'll have to keep my eyes skinned if Adrian isn't to find himself confronted with a bigamous marriage between Carruthers and the missionary's wife. Penelope adores that little oddity, and he, poor child, is suffering the penalties of Empire. His mother died out there, you know, and he hasn't seen his father for years. He's got no relatives over here. He's good for Penelope."

"Do you think of everything in its relation to Penelope?"

He considered it gravely. "Yes," he said, "I think that at the moment I do. I know a bit about women, Chad. Penelope's good value. I hope I haven't made the discovery too late."

10

We went to Smurthwaite about a month after Simon and Tubby Chambers had gone back to school. I took them and their gear by road, and as the car stood waiting at the front door Penelope and Eustace came to say good-by. Eustace gave each of them a typed copy of the saga and Penelope gave them packets of sandwiches. They certainly would not need food before getting back to school, but Penelope knew that, with boys, need and food have nothing to do with one another. Carruthers gave her a stone ax that he had made by lashing a flint to a hickory shaft, and Simon gave her the map of the exploration. They kept stiff upper lips, saluted, and climbed into the car. As we moved off I noticed a tear squeezing itself out of Penelope's eye, and it seemed to me a pearl of price.

I was back in time for lunch. Rose said to me as soon as I arrived: "This is a world of miracles, darling. I like Penelope. She had a good old-fashioned cry after they were gone."

"Where is she now?"

"She asked permission of me and Eustace to go up to London. She rode her bike to the station, and she's spending the day with her mother. I rang Phoebe up to say she was coming."

I was glad to hear this, for I had feared that the Smurthwaite holiday would be ruined if Penelope and her parents were unreconciled. Eustace had said that he would invite Phoebe and Greg to Chalk Hill when he thought the right moment had come. He had never done so, and now I saw why.

"Eustace is a wonderful reconciler," I said. "It's better that Penelope should make the first move. Did he suggest this?"

"Not in so many words, I imagine. But you know what Eustace is."

It was a pleasant month, warm enough for the swimming pool to come into use, and Eustace flopped about there almost every day. He was always delighted to find some way of defeating his disabilities. Greg and Phoebe came down during the week ends, and postcards from Carruthers to the missionary's wife kept up an even flow.

Uncle Arthur sold his Smurthwaite house. The new owner would move in when our holiday was over. "So this will be *nunc dimittis*, my dear Chad. None of us will have much cause to go back after this. Greg's father and mother are dead. Your poor mother is dead. Sir Titus Newte is dead, and so is dear old Ashmole. I say nothing of Madeleine, but if animals are immortal then that wisp of beauty will add to my joy in the Elysian fields. We were such a contrast: we complemented one another's qualities. Well, there it is. I am grass like the rest of you," he said, surveying his immense rotundities with complacency, "but a spark of animation lingers in me, which urges me to look once more on the municipality I guided through difficult years, and to say Hail and Farewell."

Adrian Wybird was with us for a week before our caravan left for the North. For that week, we arranged that Uncle Arthur should return to the stables, and Penelope and her husband use the visitor's bedroom. I had not visited Adrian in prison, and I dreaded his coming. We had miraculously assimilated Penelope into our company, and I feared disruption. I had never liked the boy. My pity for him, and my wish to provide company and help for Eustace, had brought him to

Chalk Hill, but there had never been more than that. I need not have feared. He was not a gay member of the party, but his old attitude of ownership and consequent grievance was gone. He was subdued. He gave me almost a sense that he was frightened. We were all most careful never to mention prison or Sir Oscar or any other matter that might disturb his mind; but there was little chance to mention anything, for he shunned all company save that of Penelope and Eustace. When we took him up to his bedroom, he asked diffidently: "Don't I go back to the stables?"

We explained the arrangement we had made, and he said: "If it wouldn't be upsetting everybody too terribly, could I be with Eustace? There's plenty of room for Penelope, too, in the stable bedroom."

So everything was switched round again, and Adrian trotted to and fro with the food containers. Wherever Eustace went, there Adrian was like his shadow, indoors and out. This almost abject dependence, this fear of coming out from under Eustace's wing, disturbed me. I hoped it would end soon. When the holiday was over Adrian would have to go. He would have to find a footing in the world somehow for himself and Penelope. However, as things turned out, I need not have worried.

11

We set out very early in the morning on the first of June, so as to get the journey over in one day. Billy Pascoe was attending some scientific jamboree in Leeds and would join us when that was over. Greg had Phoebe and the Wybirds in his car. In mine, Uncle Arthur sat next to me, and Rose and Eustace were in the back seats. Eustace's carriage had been sent ahead by rail. Eustace didn't like the idea of being carried into a hotel, so we took food with us. At one o'clock I stopped in a pleasant place, and we got out to stretch our legs and eat. Greg's car drew up behind us. Eustace remained in my car and we handed food in to him. I could see Adrian was worrying his guts out about something, and when the meal was over he took me aside and said: "You'd better break 'em up and get 'em out of sight. Then come back and help me to lift Eustace out of the car. He'll want a piddle."

"I hadn't thought of that," I said.

"I don't suppose you had," he said rudely. "I don't suppose you've ever been able to put yourself in Eustace's place and realize that all sorts of unpleasant things have to be done for him. You left it to me, and then to Mr. Geldersome, and then to Penelope."

I could have hit him; but he was right. I'd never thought of it.

I dispersed the company. Then we lifted Eustace into the privacy of some bushes.

"You can push off now," Adrian said.

Eustace winked at me. "Leave me to my squire, Chad," he said. "Be back in five minutes."

I did so, and Adrian and I heaved Eustace back into the car. Adrian got in beside him, and asked stiffly: "May I stay here for the rest of the journey?"

Eustace gave me a nod, and I said: "Certainly, Adrian, I'd be glad if you'd take over." We continued the journey with Uncle Arthur in Greg's car and Rose beside me. Through the mirror I saw that Eustace was asleep, with Adrian holding his hand.

The cars drew up in front of Uncle Arthur's house in the evening, and this fact that we arrived in cars seemed to me the key to all the change we found. For, as I supposed we should have expected, we did not find Smurthwaite. As we rolled through the main street in the evening quiet we saw at once that this was not what we had come for. The cozy shop windows had given place to cold staring sheets of plate glass and the names of the citizens we had known as their owners— Sugden and Birtwistle, Feather, Hinchcliffe and Barraclough—to fascias emblazoned with the names of multiple stores. I went at a snail's pace, sorrowfully watching Uncle Arthur. At the entrance to the street he had stopped Greg's car, saying: "I'd like to walk home from here." I let him go ahead, past the lavatory-tiled front of a cinema that stood where the Assembly Rooms had been. There were no sycamores to shade his progress. They had been rooted out. Outside the Dragon he came to a standstill. It was still called the Dragon. A new sign of a ramping green beast left no doubt of that, and beneath the sign was a board saying: "Stop at this olde Englysshe inn. Char-à-banc parties catered for. Quaff a Stoup where men have drunk since 1554." The old Dragon hadn't cared a damn when it was founded. I think Uncle Arthur would have forgiven even all this if he had been able to recognize the face of his pub. But the face was gone, ripped out to make room for something more recognizably Tudor; and the less said about that the better.

Uncle Arthur walked slowly on, his hands clasped behind his back, looking up sharply now and then into the faces of passers-by like an old hound anxious for a friendly word. No one spoke to him, for no one knew him. The Town Hall was unchanged, islanded in the town center. He looked up at it, and at the unchanged Grammar School over against it, as though here at last was something of sanity in a crazy world. Then he turned left into the street where his house was. It had been a short street, with everything in it built solidly of the gray local stone roofed with stone shingles. Now we looked down its continuation, stretching out of sight: stucco, red brick, fancy tiles of green and gold, little white fragile gates sporting Chez Nous, Kozy Kot, Dun

439

Romin and We Two. From the other side of the road, he inspected with satisfaction the sturdy façade of his own house. He took the big old-fashioned key from his pocket, crossed over, and turned it in the lock. We gathered round him on the pavement. He looked very tired. He said: "I apologize. This would not have happened had I been permitted to remain at my post. I am glad Madeleine did not live to see this day." He seemed unaware that some of them had never heard of Madeleine and didn't know what he was talking about. "I had hoped," he said, "to invite you all to dine with me at the Dragon tonight. But please forgive me. We must take pot luck."

I left them to sort themselves out. Adrian and Penelope were fussing over Eustace, and seeing that he would be well looked after I carried the bags up to the room I had used as a boy. It had become shabby and was smaller than I remembered, but it was comfortable enough. I threw open the window, and Rose and I stood there looking out. From here, you might believe that nothing had happened to Smurthwaite or to any of us. In the evening light, the lean flanks of the fells undulated to the skyline, and I remembered how I used to stand here and watch the cloud shadows in windy weather racing till the fells themselves seemed to move and the whole landscape had a stretched-out greyhound's urgent ripple. Rose put her arm round me and asked: "Where's the tarn?"

"You can't see it. It's away over there." I pointed west.

"I was there only once," she said. "Greg and Phoebe, you and I and Billy Pascoe. Billy and Greg had a fight."

"Yes, I remember. You said something that seemed to flatter Greg and Billy didn't like it."

"He was so uncertain of himself in those days. My mother and I had a dreadful job with him. Odd to think that he has become the cold and utterly self-possessed person that he is. Invincible as God."

"I wonder." I was fumbling in the luggage for the sketch of Rose that Miss Orlop had painted so long ago. I carried it with me wherever I went. I found it and hung it on the nail where it had hung when I was a boy. Rose looked at it indifferently. Then she smiled in a way that I had learned to interpret. "Why bother with that far-off shadow," she said, "when you have the reality? It's been a sad weary day, darling, and I need reassurance. Is there time?"

I said there was time and locked the door.

12

Before breakfast I was out in the street, breathing again the stimulating northern air. It tingled through me, the most reminiscent thing

I had found in Smurthwaite, resurrecting as nothing else could have done the boy walking the short distance to school or church and noting the difference of this air from the drugged and lulling air of Cornwall where his lassitude had been, as his father said, chronic and constitutional. Greg and Phoebe joined me on the pavement. "We're going to have a look at the Rectory," Greg said.

"So you're one of the search party, too," I chaffed him, noting in my mind as I said it: A good title—*The Search Party*. "You won't find him," I said.

"Who?"

"The lost young man."

"Phoebe, my dear," Greg said, "what is this fiddler with words talking about?"

"A poem by Housman, I imagine," she answered, and left it at that.

"If you mean we're all grown up, that's obvious," Greg said. "Come on. D'you remember riding the pony bareback in the paddock?"

I strolled along with them, for I, too, had an interest in the Rectory. At one of its windows I had stood, surrounded by Mr. Hawke's ramshackle "collections," and watched my mother and the Rector come out from among the apple trees, his arm round her waist.

The Rectory was gone. A tidy little building stood on its site, appropriate to a modern parson's needs, and on the paddock bungalows had spawned like autumn mushrooms.

We crossed the road to Geldersome's Four Acre. It no longer had the raw repulsive look of a new cemetery in which the ghosts would yawn their heads off with boredom. The trees were noble, the population and its identity tags, as Greg called the gravestones, were plentiful. I chanced upon the grave of our Mrs. Ramsden and her gravedigger, with whom she had lived both in sin and sanctity. Now you wouldn't know the difference. The couple were among the oldest inhabitants; their gray stone had an air of respectable antiquity. Well, they had been a good earthy pair and were appropriately housed. Greg looked down at their stone and said, with a frown and a lapse into the Doric: "Damn it, Chad. Ah didn't recognize a face in t'street last night. Ah'm more at home here. Ah seem to know more dead 'uns than live 'uns."

The great wrought-iron gates were gone from Sir Titus Newte's castle, and the castle road was tar-macadamed. A notice board said that the building was a county isolation hospital. We didn't go in. "I couldn't stand it," Greg said.

"But damn it, boy," I chaffed him, "surely it rejoices your heart to see the mansions of the rich switched round to the service of the honest toilers?"

He looked at me fiercely. "Sir Titus was a good old cock," he said. "He did his duty according to the lights of his time and class. And if you knew what a job it is to make the honest toilers realize that they'll make a balls of this country unless that word duty sinks into their thick skulls—well, if you don't know that, you don't know much. You're the same woolly-minded Pie-frill as ever."

Phoebe took his arm. "Let's go and see what's for breakfast," she said. "Rose, Penelope and I are the cooks and housekeepers of this party. It may be a sentimental holiday for you men, but we've got to keep you fed and decently housed."

And that, more or less, is how it turned out. There was no service in the house save what those three could provide, and shopping, cooking and cleaning kept them busy while we men enjoyed ourselves. And we did enjoy ourselves; it was not all unfulfillment. In the cars we were soon clear of damaged Smurthwaite and out into the landscape of our youth. That Yorkshire dale and fell country would take a bit of damaging. The weather held, and the days' routine was much of a muchness. The women would pack our luncheon and off we would go with no especial destination. When we found a place that enchanted us, we would stop and lie in the sun and talk and smoke till lunchtime. After lunch Greg and I would take our sticks and set off on one of those long aimless walks that had filled so many summer afternoons of our boyhood. Uncle Arthur would take his stick and declare his intention to walk with us. But always some impeccable reason arose for his not doing it on that particular afternoon. We would reassemble in time to be back at Smurthwaite for dinner, and then we men washed up and left the women free for an evening drive.

Greg and I often pointed out to Adrian that he could safely leave Eustace in Uncle Arthur's company and join our walk, but only once could he be persuaded to give up his post as faithful watchdog. It was pathetic, and, I thought, a bit disturbing. During our walks, Greg and I often discussed the situation between Adrian and Penelope. "You know, Chad," Greg said, as we sat one day looking down on the fields that his father had farmed, "it was down there, in that farmyard, that Phoebe had her miscarriage. We were both set on a boy, as you know, and Penelope was damned from that moment. What Eustace has made of her in a few months shows me what could have been made of her in all these years, and there are times when I could die with shame to think of it."

I couldn't take Greg by the hand: there was too much virile companionship between us: but I felt like doing it, and if I had done so I am sure I would have had a crying man alongside me. I said: "I don't think you need bother. She's on the right track."

"Will it last?" he asked. "She's like a convert under the spell of a missioner. What happens when she's back with Adrian?"

I said: "She will be back with you and Phoebe, too. That should help. And Adrian has had the jar of his life. I think he'll have a sterner go at things now."

"I'm sure he will. But let me be frank with you, Chad. My only feeling for the poor little devil is pity. He'll want to have a go, but is there anything *there* for him to have a go with?"

This was so much my own despairing feeling that I could only murmur: "Well, we shall have to see. We must all keep a closer eye on them in future."

Then came the day when Adrian surrendered his post to Uncle Arthur and walked with us. I could see that he had something on his mind, and when at last it came pouring out, it was what I had expected. His thanks to me and Rose for all we had done for him and Penelope. His thanks to Greg and Phoebe for having, as he said, forgiven him; his sense of inadequacy and his intention to be a different man. Above all, Eustace, Eustace, Eustace. He was sure that, when he had to leave Eustace, the very thought of him would enable him to tackle life differently. It was all heartrendingly sincere and heartrendingly woolly. Looking to the future, he hadn't one practical thought in his head. As we walked back to join Eustace and Uncle Arthur, the song of the larks in the sky and the smell of the thyme underfoot should have raised me to heaven; but I was sunk in a hell of foreboding and despondency.

13

We decided to keep the tarn for our culmination. We would wait till Billy Pascoe arrived, and he had written to say that this, after all, could not be till our last week at Smurthwaite. When he came, he cut a strange figure among us. Three weeks in the sun had tanned us till we looked like farm laborers at harvesttime. Billy was haggard and apathetic. On the morning after his arrival we were in the cars at the door, waiting to set off, when a young man turned up from our weekly, The Smurthwaite *Sentinel*, no longer owned by old Hey, whose grandfather had founded it, but absorbed into a group operated from London. Somehow, the news of Sir William's presence had become known, and this young man, putting his head through the car window, said: "Sir William, will you have time today to make a statement on the Leeds conference?"

The Leeds conference had been private, but no doubt the newspapers had smelled its significance, for all those present were physicists known to specialize in nuclear research.

Billy said coldly: "No. The less said about it the better."

This reporter was an alert young man. He seized at once on these few suggestive words. "May I quote you as saying that, Sir William?"

"No, no," Billy said testily. "Please say nothing at all. I could say nothing that your readers would understand."

All his words were what that young man would doubtless have called jam. They were telegraphed to the *Morning Chronicle* in London, and the next day an article appeared, "By our Scientific Correspondent." Not many people at that time had heard of nuclear fission, and the few who had were not deeply aware of what it might portend. "Our Scientific Correspondent" thought it was time this secrecy was ended. Was it good enough, he wanted to know, naming no names, that one of the three most prominent nuclear physicists in Europe should tell an interviewer that "the less said the better"? Didn't this suggest a notion in his own mind that scientists were fiddling with something that they feared at least as much as they understood? And if the subject was so dark that the man in the street would not understand it, wasn't it time that light was shed on a matter that might be of fearful concern to everybody before another decade had passed?

Billy read this at the breakfast table the next morning. He said nothing, but his lean jaw pulsed with annoyance.

Uncle Arthur had read the article, and apologized to Billy. He could not rid himself of the notion that he was responsible for everything that happened in Smurthwaite, even now when he was of no more consequence than the Town Hall doormat. He had made a ceremonial visit to the Town Hall, wearing his frock coat and Hat, and his reception must have disconcerted him. He took it out on the doormat. "The mats were fit to wipe a king's boots on in my day," he declared.

He applied marmalade generously to his toast and poured himself another cup of coffee. "My dear Sir William," he said, "I know nothing of these new forces that you scientists are tapping, but I know something of the need for human courtesy. I blush to think what old William Hey would have thought if a youth in his employ had telegraphed to London the words of a man enjoying the hospitality of this borough —words which were specifically stated to be private. This municipality is not what it was; but on its behalf, even such as it is, I offer you apologies."

Billy said: "Thank you, Mr. Geldersome. But all the same, there's something in what this fellow says. It's time people woke up."

"Let us at any rate slumber for this day," Uncle Arthur said.

Billy, for once, smiled, and a grim smile it was. "That may yet be the epitaph of civilization, Mr. Geldersome," he said; but Uncle Arthur was not to be daunted. "I fail to see," he said, "that we shall be the less civilized for leaving this sixpenny bazaar of a town and getting out under the sky. We shall slumber in the sun by the tarn. It is the last time some of us will see it, and I hope, Rose my dear, that you cooks will worthily provide for what promises to be a memorable occasion."

444

"Chicken, ham and tongue sandwiches," Rose said. "Salad and cheese. Fruit."

"We shall make do. I demeaned myself yesterday by entering for the first time an establishment having what is called, I believe, a grocer's license. A few bottles purporting to contain Barsac are in the car. We shall chill them in the bottomless tarn. Some of our wilder spirits have expressed a determination to bathe. Though at the tender age of fifteen I won the hundred yards overarm at the Bradford municipal baths, I am today *hors concours*. I shall be a stranded leviathan."

"So far as I know," I said, "Greg and I are the only ones to be reckoned wilder spirits. Unless you're going in, Billy?"

"I have made no provision," he said in his precise way.

Adrian volunteered: "You can use my suit, Sir William. I don't suppose I shall swim, for Eustace doesn't intend to."

"Good!" I said. "That makes three. You *must* join us, Billy, for old Pendeverel's sake."

"We shall see," he said.

Eustace was very quiet. I knew that he was looking forward to this day. The tarn meant more to him than to any of us. He had been born with that water within reach of his walking legs. It was his secret and sacred resort. In summer heats and when the fells were white with snow, the tarn had drawn him like a fascination. All that surprised me now was that he should consent to go there with a crowd. He had loved the wild loneliness of the place. But now he could not get there unhelped. As we set out I determined that somehow or other I would contrive an hour when he and his tarn could be at one together for perhaps the last time.

Nothing was changed there, and, save ourselves, not a soul was in sight. We bumped the cars over the rocky soil almost to the edge of the water, and, for some odd premonitory reason, there was upon us as we sat down on the grass a gravity that the splendor of the day and scene deepened rather than dispelled. From the high lip where the moor ended the water thundered down, but, except at the point where the fall struck it, the tarn had the mysterious immobility, the air of profundity and menace, that was one of the dark enchantments of the place. I lay on my back and let it all soak into me: the smell of the thyme carpet and warm rock, the sound of everlasting water falling, the sight of two hawks hovering on the blue air; and memory overwhelmed me with a rush. We had come in a trap drawn by Phoebe's white pony, and Greg and Phoebe had leapt upon him and careered madly among the rocks, whooping with youth and joy. This recollection enhanced the silence that was upon us now. It was, save for the sounds of nature, so quiet that you could almost hear the sunlight pouring down.

When at last I looked up, Uncle Arthur alone was stirring, charac-

445

teristically employed. He had tied string round the necks of his wine bottles and attached the loose end to a gorse root growing on the very edge of the tarn. He sank the bottles carefully into the water.

I stood for a moment watching him, and looking at the fall's spray and at the ferns growing into the limestone crevices that were never dry, and this, I decided, is the moment when we had better scatter and leave Eustace alone. "They'll be chilled by lunchtime," I said to Uncle Arthur. "There's just about an hour. Let's take a walk till then."

The others sat up as my voice broke the silence. "Did you say a walk?" Greg asked. "Come on, then. Let's make it quick. We'll be back in time for our swim before lunch." His bathing things and mine and Adrian's were lying there among our gear.

Adrian said: "I shan't walk. I shall stay here with Eustace."

Eustace said: "My dear boy, I should be quite safe and happy here alone, but I should be glad if Billy would stay. You get along, Adrian, and have your walk. Do you mind staying, Billy?"

Billy sat down at his side, and the rest of us moved away, Adrian lagging with many a lingering look.

Only Billy was able to tell us what happened then. "What did he talk about?" I asked him later. It was a surprising answer. "About atomic energy, and about how happy he had been at Chalk Hill, with Rose in and out of his place now and then. "I don't think," Billy said, and I saw tears in his eyes, "that anyone loved Rose as he did. He was so happy, mangled as he was, to be living in her shadow."

"Why didn't you wait for us? Why did you go into the water?"

He seemed to find it difficult to answer, but at last said: "I was so ashamed of my body. You and Greg were looking so brown and fit, and I was so white and skinny. I didn't want to bathe at all, but I decided to do it out of bravado. I thought I'd get it over before you came back."

You could depend on Billy to tell you the facts as he knew them, and this moment's shame of his body was the exact fact that killed Eustace and Adrian.

Billy undressed and put on Adrian's bathing slip and stood on the edge of the tarn. There was no shallow end in that place. It was deep throughout. Eustace said: "Don't go in, Billy, unless you feel like it. I warn you that water's damned cold even at midsummer. I once went in on a Christmas Day out of bravado. I nearly killed myself. Bravado's a poor reason for anything."

This gentle warning had no effect. "I dived," Billy said, "and I came up terrified. I'm in pretty poor shape. My heart was thumping. But I made up my mind to swim across and climb out at the other side. Halfway across I knew I couldn't do it. I felt paralayzed, and I let out a shout. Eustace rolled himself over the edge like a log and swam toward me."

All of us heard Billy's shout: a wild despairing cry that chilled us. We were on the way back and began to run. Soon we could see the tarn. Adrian cried: "Eustace is gone!" and was ahead of me and Greg like a hare. I could see Eustace now, out in the middle, on his back, with his hands under Billy's armpits. But, having no legs to kick with, he was immobile, utterly helpless. I saw Adrian shoot over the edge, yelling: "I'm coming, Eustace! I'm coming!" and at that very moment Eustace and Billy disappeared beneath the surface.

"I think," Billy said to me, "he died suddenly. He was panting hard and saying: 'I can do nothing for you, Billy, but hold you up till the others come. Lie quite still and don't struggle, there's a good chap," and then all of a sudden he shook with a convulsion. His hands gripped me tighter, and he went down, taking me with him. I made a terrific struggle to break loose, and I knew nothing more till you had me on the bank."

By the time Greg and I reached the edge, Billy had floated to the surface and Adrian was swimming in the middle. Billy might have been a corpse for all the notice Adrian took of him. He was shouting: "Eustace! Eustace!" and dived.

Greg said: "Get Billy. I'll get Adrian," and in we went. The water was shockingly cold, and the long run I had had made my heart pound. Billy was sinking again as I got hold of him. I lugged him to the side, where by now Uncle Arthur had arrived. "Pump the water out of him," I said, and turned to see how Greg was faring. He looked toward me and shouted: "Adrian's vanished!"

"Then come out—come out, Greg! There's nothing you can do."

But he dived, and was under water so long that my heart sickened, and I plunged in again and swam toward where he had disappeared. He came up gasping, shaking the water from his hair and eyes.

Adrian had dived again and again. "I couldn't stop him," Greg panted. "I caught hold of him and told him it was no good. He glared at me like a lunatic, and landed me one. Look!" Blood was oozing from his lip.

"Come out," I said. "Come out! It's all over."

Uncle Arthur had pushed and pummeled water out of Billy Pascoe, and was now dribbling brandy from a pocket flask between his pallid lips. Greg and I drank, too; then we rolled Billy in a couple of car rugs and put him into one of the cars. Uncle Arthur got in, and I saw him lift Billy's frail body as though it were a child's, settle him on his knees, and put his arms around him. Greg said: "I'll drive. You stay here, Chad, and get your clothes off. Dry them in the sun and rub yourself down. We don't want a pneumonia case as well."

"What about you?"

He didn't answer. I watched the car bump over the uneven ground and through a gate, and gather speed in the lane.

And then I was alone with the tarn, as Eustace had so often been, and the quiet was terrifying in its influence, as though the sudden shocking end of two lives meant no more than the fall of two stones into the water. I stood there with the wine bottles, and the luncheon things, and Billy Pascoe's clothes, at my feet, and my own clothes began steaming on me, so that I stood in a little cloud, listening to the fall of the water and the sad crying of curlews.

I shed my clothes and spread them on the hot stones, and rubbed some warmth into my body that was shivering with more than cold.

Life came back into me from the shine of the sun at its zenith, and I sat naked on a rock with many things stirring in my mind. I remembered the *Idylls of the King* that Uncle Arthur had sent me after his first visit to Pendeverel, and how, when I had come to Smurthwaite and read them there many times, it was this tarn that I thought of as the place of Arthur's passing; it was upon this tarn that my boyhood's fancy saw the dark barge come, "dense with stately forms." And as I thought of these things, there happened what I never told to Rose or anyone, lest they should think hallucination had furnished what I swear I saw. I had got up again and was scanning the water lest, even so late, some sight of the bodies should appear, when through the surface, in the very middle, a hand slowly broke, and rose till the arm was revealed to the shoulder. It was Eustace's arm. I knew it by the stuff of his coat, and, more than that, there was this. He had had the affectation of wearing a splendid ring set with a diamond. While I watched, the arm revolved, as the body beneath it must have been revolving, and the sunlight flashed upon the jewel. For ten or fifteen seconds the arm turned and the jewel flashed. Then, as slowly as it had risen, it sank, turning still, and the spark was extinguished.

I lay in the sun then, thankful that amid so much disaster I had at least had the comfort of that heliographed Hail and Farewell; and presently I heard the distant sound of a car. I pulled on my shirt and trousers and walked toward the gate leading from the lane. The thin rock earth, padded with thyme, was warm beneath my bare feet; and as I gave Rose a hand out of the car she looked at my feet and said: "He loved to walk barefoot."

She put her arms round me and rested her head on my shoulder and cried. I said nothing to her but let her head lie there as the tears flowed, and indeed there was much for tears. He had loved to walk barefoot as he had loved all sensual feelings; but her words must have made her think how many weary years it was since he had had feet to walk with, and how splendidly, growing in stature before our eyes, he had borne his grief. And you will be thinking, I said to myself, of the years before that, when he padded with you through German forests and the pine needles were a warmth on your bare feet and his. I was glad she had that. There was no envy in my heart for what they had shared. I let her weep and remember for a long time; and when at last she stood away from me and I looked at her face, unashamedly haggard and ravaged under the burning sun, I said: "Shall we go to the tarn?"

"No," she said. "I didn't come for that. I came to take you home. Are you dry and warm?"

These commonplace words fell on my heart like a blessing. We got into the car, and I let her do the driving, because I knew she wished to show her tenderness by doing something, and that was all there was to do.

CHAPTER SEVENTEEN

I

THE industrialist who had rented Pentyrch from Rose had taken a fancy to livelier company than Pendeverel provided and had bought himself a villa at Cap Ferrat. It would make a better background for the sprightly and picturesque young women whose presence he increasingly delighted in as his age advanced. He departed in the ominous summer of 1939, and Rose and I went down in that June, taking Uncle Arthur with us. I was doubtful about imposing the rigors of the journey on him, but he brushed my objections aside. "My dear Chad, at eighty a man is either dead or he has taken on a new lease of life which may be the despair of his younger years but is consoling to himself. I have no intention of solving the Great Enigma for another decade or two. A little asthma, an occasional twinge of gout, and a touch of rheumatics when the wind is NNE, are not, I assure you, matters to raise your hopes unduly."

We lived in the house, not in the studio and other buildings that we had gradually added to it. We spent a week with all the doors and windows open most of the time so that the winds might disperse the smell of the cosmetics department of a London store. Till that was gone, Rose complained that she felt like the madam of a dubious establishment. "And the way the kitchen garden has been neglected!" Uncle Arthur grumbled.

"I imagine," I told him, "that cabbages were not high on the list of necessaries. They lived on grapes and nectarines, flown in from exclusive vineyards and orchards."

"The man's knowledge of vineyards was negligible, my dear Chad. I

449

could excuse the silk stockings and empty champagne bottles that I found in my wardrobe if the champagne had not been of an excessively vulgar brand. Even a departure from propriety should be conducted with gentlemanly taste."

The place was straight again toward the end of July when I left them in order to bring Penelope and Simon and Tubby Chambers. Six years had passed since Tubby made his exploration of Chalk Hill. He was fifteen, Simon fourteen, and Tubby was now fatherless as well as motherless. It was in the year after Eustace and Adrian had died that I met Tubby's father at the school. I had gone to bring Simon home for the holidays, and Tubby, with a thin leathery-looking man in tow, came up to me and said: "Mr. Boothroyd, this is my father."

Mr. Reginald Chambers was obviously anxious to get rid of the boy, so I paired him off with Simon, and Chambers said: "I'd be glad if you'd lunch with me, Mr. Boothroyd. Could you manage that?"

We went in my car to a hotel, and I found him a tongue-tied difficult fellow. This was easier to understand when he suddenly blurted out: "I've been using this leave to have a medical overhaul. I've had my death warrant."

He filled his glass from the wine bottle on the table and drank as though glad to have that off his chest. There's not much you can say to a thing like that, coming from a stranger. I muttered hopes that the diagnosis was mistaken, but he shut me up. "No chance of that," he said. "And frankly it doesn't worry me. But there's no one—no one whatever—to look after the boy."

He gave me to understand that by no one he meant me. He and Tubby were the fag end of a family, "and I've never had the art of making friends. No chance, either, come to that. All my life among blacks. Just saw a few chaps at the club during leaves. Not very helpful."

He looked at the wine in the glass he was twirling. "Of course, I shan't go back now. If I died out there it'd make things difficult."

A man of conscience, but awkward, and a long time coming to the point, I thought.

When it came, it all hinged on the holiday Tubby had spent at Chalk Hill. Chambers was well informed about it. There must have been something more than postcards. "Well, no one else has ever done a hand's turn for the boy. Till then, spent his holidays mooning about in the school. There's this boy of yours, and this young woman—a Mrs. Wybird, isn't it? He seems very fond of them."

I had to put it to him frankly at last. "What are you asking me to do?"

It was very simple. When he died—"any time in the next six months" —there wouldn't be much money. What he had saved and what came from insurance might add up to five or six thousand pounds. The interest on that wouldn't pay Tubby's school fees. They would have to be paid out of capital, and then when the boy had finished with school there should be a bit left to set him up in a job. "All I want is a trustee to take that on," he said, looking at me with painful anxiety. "Just to keep an eye on him—give him a holiday now and then."

"I like Tubby, Mr. Chambers," I said, "and I'd do this for him gladly if I didn't think there was someone who would do it even better."

"And who's that?"

"This Mrs. Wybird that you speak of. Let me have a word with her. Please don't let the thing worry you. I think she'll do it. And if she won't, I'll do it myself."

2

When Eustace died, Phoebe wept for a brother and Rose for one who had been more truly and beautifully husband to her than most men are to their women. She wept, too, for Henrietta's father. Penelope did not weep. She was dry-eyed and tight-lipped, white as chalk. She said to me: "I can't believe it. I can't believe he's dead." She was not talking of her husband. What would have happened if Wybird had not died I don't know, but I am sure Penelope could not have lived with him. Eustace had done her the bitter service of diminishing Adrian to a complete inadequacy.

Whenever I thought of those days, I was almost appalled at the way in which poor Adrian ceased to be, as soon as he was dead. Even the manner of his death, which had an apparent virtue, did not redeem him. "Greater love hath no man than this, that a man lay down his life for a friend." The coroner said that, and in the coroner's courtroom I harbored the thought—harsh but true enough—that Adrian had not been trying to save his friend so much as trying to preserve for himself the stability without which his life was a wretched and worthless thing. It was as though a starving man had sought to save his life by jumping into a stream that was bearing his dinner away, and died in the attempt.

The three women would not be concerned in the inquest, so Greg and I persuaded them to go back at once to Chalk Hill and await us there. The police dredged the bodies up, and they were buried side by side in Uncle Arthur's cemetery.

When we got back to Chalk Hill, life had to go on. Simon and Tubby had to be fetched from school, for their holiday had now begun, and Greg had to leave for a congress of Socialists in Sweden. He and Phoebe tried to persuade Penelope to go with them, but she would not. She asked me and Rose if she might remain with us as long as the holidays lasted. "I'd like to be with the boys," she said. "They'll miss Eustace." She was a disciple, set on continuing the work of the dead master. Eustace had given meaning to her life, in a way that neither Greg nor Adrian had done. I was delighted with her, and she stayed. We took her and the boys down to Pendeverel that year, and I noticed that for Simon and Tubby she passed through the stages of being Aunt Penelope and Aunt Penny to Miss Pennorth.

When she had put them to bed one night, she came to me where I was sitting on a rock looking out to sea and asked: "Uncle Chad, how do you think I could earn a living? I shall have to do something when this holiday is over."

"What can you do?"

"I can use a typewriter, and I'm learning shorthand. I've more or less mastered the theory, and now I'm working up a bit of speed. Tubby dictates letters to me, and I take them down."

"Where does he find the letters?"

"He makes them up. I've got some here."

She produced a notebook from her handbag, and said: "We had these today in intervals of building a Crusaders' Castle on the beach." She read:

To the Curator, the London Zoo
DEAR SIR:
I am sending you herewith in the care of my secretary several wild beasts, viz., a lion taken in the act of consuming a native, a rhinoceros with horn unfortunately damaged by a shot from my elephant gun, and several assorted creatures such as leopards, gnus and hyenas. There is no need to acknowledge. Treat the beasts well, and accept them with my affectionate regards.
Ever yours,
MARMADUKE CARRUTHERS, *Major*

To the Secretary, the Royal Geographical Society, London
SIR:
In reply to yours of the 1st ult., the lecture I shall give to your members on my return from the present expedition will include many startling revelations. The course of the Zambezi in its upper reaches has been diverted by a landslide, and the river must dig itself a new bed, with dire consequences. Moreover, an earthquake has devastated the Matoppos. Neither of these events has yet been recorded, so please keep them under your hat. I assure you your members will have something to think about.
With best wishes to you and yours,
MAJOR CARRUTHERS

P.S. A letter will find me at the Zimbabwe Mission Station, where I am recovering from a painful affliction of the feet, caused by jiggers under the toenails.

"Well," I said, "your transcriptions of these should stand you in good stead if you apply for something in Threadneedle Street."

"Oh, it's the speed that matters," she said, "not the words. He reels this stuff off at a great rate, and I can read most of it back."

I asked her to leave it to me, and when the holiday was over I saw Max Middlemass and told him Penelope's story from beginning to end. He put on his hard-boiled look and said: "I could use her if she's any good. Not otherwise. Send her along for a week's trial."

"What will you pay her?" I asked brutally.

"You mind your own business, Chad Boothroyd. And tell her," he added, twinkling, "that if she can put up with a surfeit of Cumberland rum butter, she can live with me and Bessie. What a damned thing it is not to have children!" His grin broadened. "God knows Bessie and I go on trying. Well, send her along. Maybe we'll give her a week end now and then at Menin Gate."

The arrangement was made, and there was no cause for anyone to regret it. Except perhaps Bessie, who was sad when Penelope was earning enough to set herself up in a flat of her own. She occasionally wangled a week end's leave from school for Tubby, and showed him the sights of the town, or took him down to Menin Gate where Max fell in love with the boy's oddity and the motor launch explored uncharted waters, with Max gaily cast as a rum-soaked planter. And so, when Tubby's doomed father put his case to me, what else was there for it save to carry the case to Penelope? Anything else, I knew, would have deeply hurt her.

3

Mr. Chambers had been dead now for some years, and Penelope's regard for Tubby had hardened into something almost jealously possessive. She had a flat on a top floor in Holland Park, with a view of rooftops and Lombardy poplars—a two-bedroomed place so that Tubby could live with her during his holidays. For the last two years they had not spent the summer holiday with us. They had gone off on their own, once to France and once to Italy. I knew that Penelope saved like a miser to make these holidays memorable for him. One day I had gone up to town to screw some money out of Tom Cannock, my agent, and he said to me as we drank his stewed tea: "This Mrs. Wybird that Max has got hold of is a bit of a hellcat, Chad. Some sort of relative of yours, isn't she?"

"No, Tom—the daughter of one of my two oldest friends. What's she up to?"

"Well, Max was never an easy man to screw a bargain out of. He seems to have taught her all he ever knew, and I get the impression that there's a bit extra that she adds on her own."

"If she's a tigress, it's because she's got a very attractive cub to feed."

"She'd steal the dinner out of an orphan's mouth."

"You interest me, Tom. I must look her up."

I went straight around there as soon as I left Tom. Middlemass Productions had the ground floor of a house in Bedford Square. I hadn't set foot in the place since I took Penelope there to meet Max nearly three years ago and saw her introduced to a secretary whose dog's-body she was to be. I remembered how that day she did something that was unusual with her: she kissed me. She walked with me to the entrance hall, paved in a chessboard of marble, and she said: "Thank you, Uncle Chad. I like this place. I intend to stay here." She was flushed and excited-looking, and I noticed that she had a resolute jaw. Then she kissed me and said: "That's for lots of things, and chiefly for dumping me on my own feet. You think I've been pretty poor value, don't you?"

As I didn't answer, she said: "Well, so I have. But you'll see."

And I saw well enough when I called on that summer morning. A secretary told me that Mr. Middlemass was out and that Mrs. Wybird was engaged. Would I wait for a few moments?

When the few moments were up ten minutes later, a secretary clutching a notebook and pencil came out as I went in. It was a small but lovely room. Those eighteenth-century people know how to do it, and it was Max's opinion that the last thing his office should look like was an office. Penelope was sitting at a beautiful desk and behind her a tall window, giving a view of a mulberry tree, was curtained with old rose brocade. Everything else was in keeping: the Adam fireplace, the few charming pictures, the embroidered fire screen. The walls were painted flesh-pink, the ceiling was gull-gray, and the woodwork white.

Penelope got up to greet me. She didn't look the hellcat that Tom Cannock's wry imagination had asked me to expect. In that awful summer, which was her nadir, when Greg had abandoned her to go to America and she had so disastrously met Adrian Wybird, she had looked a fat petulant overgrown child. She was still short, but her fat was gone, and she had learned to dress for a tall effect. She was in becoming black, with a couple of chunky gold bracelets on her left wrist. The blue of her eyes was brilliant, and her face had what I had never seen in it before: maturity and the confidence that comes from success.

We looked at one another for a silent moment, then she smiled and asked: "A tour of inspection, Chad?"

She had never called me plain Chad before. The word came naturally. For the first time we were talking as adult to adult. She gave me sherry and took a glass herself, and I said, though the idea had only just come to me: "I looked in to see if you'd join me at lunch, Penelope."

"Sorry, darling," she said, "I'm due at the Hags' Corner in the Ivy."

"You don't look as though you fed from a caldron on witches' brew."

"No. But Max likes me to appear there now and then. He says I am the flowers at the funeral."

"Happy?"

"In heaven," she said simply, and seemed to mean it.

"How is Tubby?"

"Very well. I wish you and Rose had accepted for tonight. Tubby will be here."

"Is it too late to change our minds?"

"Could you? Do say you will! We shall be awfully late and I expect you'll want to stay in town overnight. Shall I have rooms booked for you? My flat's no use—hardly bigger than a mousetrap."

"All right. Do that."

She took up a telephone and said: "Reserve a room at the Savoy for tonight for Mr. and Mrs. Chad Boothroyd. Leave a note on my desk to say it's done. I'm going out now and shall be back about three; but don't make any engagements for me for this afternoon. Call up a taxi."

I grinned at her. "The air of one accustomed to command," I said.

"It's the only way. That's one of the first things I learned."

4

The party in Max's office was one of the notable annual events in theatrical London. I knew that Henrietta and Martin Napier would be there, and that would have taken me and Rose along had it not been that they were coming to us in a day or two. Then they were leaving for Hollywood where Martin had his first engagement. We both disliked parties, and Max's began very late, as so many of his guests had to come on after the fall of the curtain. I changed my mind because I had never seen Penelope in that setup. The attraction was stronger as Tubby Chambers was to be there, too.

I hadn't met Tubby for a long time. When Rose and I arrived at eleven o'clock he was talking to Henrietta and Martin. I wouldn't have known the Major Carruthers with whom I had become so familiar. He was fifteen now, and for the last year he had not been at school. He had been in London in the company of Penelope or Martin, who had taken a great fancy for him, or at Menin Gate with Max and Bessie. He had learned to lunch out and dine out in adult company. He was still called Tubby, but he had grown rather tall, and he no longer wore the spectacles that he had used for some childhood defect of vision. He would be going to Marlborough in the autumn. This couldn't have been done on the money that Reginald Chambers left, which was much less than had been expected. There were debts that not only absorbed his savings but ate into the insurance money, and the question was whether Tubby could stay at school at all. I had some talks about this with Penelope, who wasn't earning much at that time. "Don't haggle," she said sharply. "He'll stay." He did, but Marlborough was another matter, even with Penelope's rise in the world. She could have done it, but it would have left her rather short. Henrietta told me privately that Martin was finding the money. He could well afford to. He was never without profitable work, and he and Henrietta had no children of their own. It was pleasing to see how Tubby had finally reconciled Henrietta and Penelope. One week end, when they were both at Chalk Hill, Penelope said: "Shall we play tennis this afternoon, Henrietta?" They looked at one another. Both, I think, suddenly remembered that they had not played since that far-off afternoon when their feelings about Adrian lay between them. After a moment they burst out laughing, and I felt that poor dead Adrian was now buried deep indeed.

Well, then, as we went into the party, Tubby, wearing what I took to be his first dinner jacket, detached himself from Henrietta and Martin, who came to greet us. Martin, who was thirty-five, was prematurely gray at the temples, and wisely did nothing to conceal it. It became him. He looked rather worried and drew me aside, insofar as one could be drawn aside in that shrieking assembly. The connecting doors between rooms were flung open, and look where one would the cream of theatrical society, as it was annually called in the gossip columns, was clotted on chairs and couches and surged over all the spaces in between. Finally, Martin took me out into the marble-floored vestibule. He wanted to tell me that "that handsome bitch over there," indicating an actress whom I would have given my ears to have in one of my plays, and whom I privately loathed, had swum up to him fluting, so that all might hear: "Martin, darling, what a *fortunate* moment for you to be going to Hollywood! You *enviable* creature! I thought it was only novelists who had the courage to hurl themselves into the dangers of American civilization at such a moment."

"The devil of it is," Martin said, "that she touched something that I *have* been worrying about. Things couldn't be lousier than they are. So far as I can see, war's a certainty. Should I cancel this thing?"

I could see through the open door Rose and Henrietta and Penelope sitting on a couch, and Tubby standing before them with a tray of drinks and sandwiches. And then I could see only Rose—Rose in the moving bloom of youth, floating at Eustace's side through the garden of an Oxford college. I was eating strawberries and cream with a girl in smoke-gray chiffon, who was soon to die, and an orchestra was playing Handel's Water Music.

"Is the situation so bad as all that?" I said to Martin. And I knew how dishonest I was being, for it was as bad as bad could be. Why did these moments always come to me with their anguish heightened by gay airs and social graces? "Let's get into the street, Martin."

It was nearly midnight, but the breath of the hot day lingered among London stones. We walked up and down, hatless, and the moon was full over the square.

"You're right, Martin. It's coming all over again, and this time it'll be worse. Does Henrietta ever talk to you about Sir William Pascoe? She should know something about him."

"Well, I suppose everyone knows he's a big shot in atomic science."

"I ran into him in town a week ago and we had lunch together. He was in a shocking mood of depression. He can see like the rest of us the way things are moving, and he said: 'War always pushes science into doing in a few years what otherwise it would do in a few decades. The thought of that compulsion applied to atomic research frightens me, Chad.' He'd never before breathed a word to me about his work, and so you can believe it made me think. When we were saying good-by he began talking about that horrible affair at Smurthwaite. He said: 'If one of us had to die, why should it have been Eustace?' I said: 'Eustace's work was finished, Billy.' And to that he said: 'I wish to God mine had never been begun.' "

A policeman passed us. "Lovely night," he said.

We walked up and down in the lovely night, and presently I asked: "What does Henrietta think of it?"

"She thinks I ought to fulfill my contract."

"So do I. This is your first Hollywood job, and to back out of it would make a bad impression. There's the legal side, too. Take Henrietta's advice."

"And have all the bitches in London talking like that one?"

"Do what you will, Martin, stay or go, bitchery will out."

5

We smelt the sulfur, but the gust passed. Mr. Neville Chamberlain came back with what he hoped was peace in our time; and it was in the following year that I left Rose and Uncle Arthur at Pentyrch and went to collect Penelope, and Tubby who had now been for a year at Marlborough, and Simon who had finished with his first school and would be joining Tubby at Marlborough when the holiday was over. Henrietta and Martin were still in Hollywood.

It was a rather broken-up holiday. Tubby's year as a man about town, followed by his year at Marlborough, had made a breach in his relationship with Simon. That didn't worry me; they would find a

457

ground of meeting again; but for the moment they were apart. During some of the holidays they had spent together, Penelope and Tubby had done a bit of sailing, and they wanted to do more now. There was no harbor at Pendeverel, but a couple of miles west along the coast was a creek where a few boats were moored, and Penelope hired one for the holiday. They would go off in her car every morning after breakfast, and we didn't expect to see them again till dinnertime. That left Simon on Rose's hands till lunchtime, for I had been churning over an idea for some weeks, and the moment had come to start work on it. I didn't like this: I preferred a holiday to be a holiday: but I had learned from experience to respect a monitory voice when it said "Now!" And so, when Penelope and Tubby were gone, I would go, too, making my way to the studio, and I would work for a few hours on *Halfway to Heaven*.

I was so engaged one morning when, to my amazement, Simon knocked and entered. He had been brought up to respect his father's workroom, and I said rather sharply: "Well, Simon?"

They were harmless words enough, but I suppose the tone hurt him. I saw suddenly how forlorn he looked. He was wearing nothing but a bathing slip and rubber shoes. He was as brown as a biscuit, but there was grief in his eyes. "So you don't want me, either," he said.

Worktime was nearly over, anyway, so I packed up and walked out onto the knoll. "Of course I want you, you silly little coot," I chided him. "I have to work, you know. That's got nothing to do with whether I want you or not."

Out at sea there was a sail, and we knew it was the boat that contained Penelope and Tubby. The patch of brighter red on the tan told us that. "Tubby thinks far more of Auntie Pennorth than he does of me," Simon said, and began to hurl pebbles over the edge. "He never asks me to sail with them."

"I expect he's not very good at sailing yet," I said. "He wouldn't like you to see him doing something unless he could do it well."

He lay down on the nibbled grass in the sunshine. "I don't think that explains it," he said. "He just wants to be alone with her. He thinks she's angelic. He keeps her photograph in our bedroom."

I looked down at him, startled. Had his innocence tumbled to something that all our sophistication had missed? I put the thought away. I couldn't entertain it.

"Oh," he said, "I forgot to say you're wanted at the house. That's why I butted in. Mother sent me with the message. There are some people she wants you to meet. I suppose it's important, or she wouldn't have disturbed your work."

An important-looking car was at the front door, and on the hall table were two black felt hats and two copies of the *Times*. Flaming as the weather was, two rolled umbrellas leaned against the table's edge. Tweedledum and Tweedledee. I began to picture them. I felt I could write their obituary notices.

They were talking to Rose in the drawing room. I was not surprised to find that they wore black coats and striped trousers. Rose handed me their cards, which lay on the table. Men from the Ministry.

Of course, the older one explained, nothing might come of it. The visit was purely formal, but there it was. No one could ignore the dangers of the present situation, although up to the last moment one was entitled to hope that there would not be war. Still, things were fairly Stygian, he was sure Mr. Boothroyd would agree?

Mr. Boothroyd agreed, and produced sherry, more for his sake and Rose's than for theirs.

Well, it was pretty obvious that, if it came, London wouldn't escape arrangements—purely tentative—had to be made for housing certain as lightly as it did in the last lot; and, as a mere reasonable precaution, departments, or sections of them; and common sense suggested—don't you agree, Mr. Boothroyd?—that the farther from London the better. And if you wanted to house some especially—shall I say hush-hush work?—well, a place like Pentyrch, literally hidden by trees from air observation—well, the place seemed made for such a purpose—you must see that, Mrs. Boothroyd?

Mrs. Boothroyd saw that, and looked sick to the teeth.

Formal papers would follow in due course—only, needless to say, if the Ministry approved and the need arose; but in the meantime, if they could personally inspect the accommodation and have a look over the estate, in case temporary buildings had to be put up. . . ?

This was the first whisper of the Pentyrch atomic research station, of which Sir William Pascoe was put in charge.

6

This was in August. In September Penelope said good-by to us—on Monday, the fourth, the day after war had been declared. She was deeply upset at something that had happened on the Saturday. She went sailing with Tubby as usual that day, and when she had moored the boat in the creek and was rowing toward the shore in the dinghy, Tubby said: "Looks like quite a reception committee for us, Miss Pennorth."

She glanced over her shoulder and saw that the owner of the boat, a few men and women, the local policeman and a couple of young oafs were assembled on the beach. Tubby jumped out, pulled up the dinghy, and gave her a hand ashore. Then he started to heave the dinghy higher up the beach. The owner, who had been pleasant enough all through the holiday, said: "You needn't sweat your guts out. She won't hurt. The tide's falling. Don't you know a thing like that?"

Tubby blushed at this slur upon his knowledge of how things should be done, and said: "Sorry."

Then one of the women chipped in. "So you ought to be sorry. And you'll be sorrier yet. What have you been up to this last fortnight? That's what we want to know."

The words touched off a feeling of hostility that Penelope had been aware of, and there were mutterings from the group. "Aye, that's it." "What have you been spying out?" "Nobody knows you round here."

"And then I saw what the trouble was," Penelope said to me. "The threat of war had been getting on the poor wretches' nerves. They didn't know us, and therefore we were suspect foreigners. But what there was to spy out around that bit of coast except a few lobster pots, God knows."

The situation seemed so absurd that she began to laugh. That was a mistake. Suspicion flamed into anger, and one of the women made a grab at Penelope. The policeman intervened. "None o' that," he said. "Let's do this thing properly. I'll have to trouble you for that camera, miss, and that book. Looks like a sketchbook to me."

Penelope handed him the camera and the book. He flipped over the pages, with an eager committee of inspection gathered round him. "See! That's our church! What did I tell you?" "That's the way into the creek!" "You ought to arrest her, Mr. Opie." "Aye, the pair of 'em."

The policeman said: "I'll have to keep these for the time being, miss. I'd like your name and address, please."

She gave him her London address. "Where are you staying round here?"

"Pentyrch."

"Don't you believe her, Mr. Opie! Pentyrch! That was old Miss Orlop's place. Daft as a coot that one, but she wouldn't hold with German spies."

Penelope said: "May I go now?"

The policeman told her: "Aye. Push off. And don't leave Pentyrch till you hear from me."

Penelope and Tubby began to crunch up the shingle toward the road where the car was. One of the young oafs shouted: "You didn't oughter let 'er out o' sight, Mr. Opie. Come on! Let's stab her tires!"

He snatched a small marlin spike from the dinghy and began to run toward the car. But Tubby ran faster. He waited by the car till the big gangling lout came up; then, without a word, he socked him under the chin and sent him reeling. He threw open the car door and said: "Get in, Miss Pennorth."

But Tubby's blow had set the pack in cry, and they closed round the car before Penelope was aboard. "God!" Penelope said, "how I hate these thick-headed yokels! I don't know what we'd have done if the bobby hadn't come up and taken charge. 'Now, I'm warning you all,' he said. 'I told these two to go, and if any of you try to stop 'em you'll reckon with me. As for you, Franky Chard, you got what you were asking for, and glad I am to see it.' Then we got away; but I ask you, Chad, don't these b.f.'s fill your heart with sorrow? What a way for Tubby's holiday to end! I so wanted him to enjoy it up to the last minute."

"I expect he did," I said. "To deliver a perfect sock to the jaw is as pleasing as to hit a boundary at cricket or to send a golf ball out of sight down the fairway. To say nothing," I added, "of the satisfaction a knight-errant gets from defending his lady."

She gave me an odd look. I thought she was about to make some comment, but she walked away.

Late that evening the bobby rode on his bicycle to Pentyrch. I was talking to Tubby outside the front door when we saw him coming. "I expect he's going to arrest me," Tubby said, and I could almost see him offering his hands to the manacles.

"No such joy, Tubby," I said. "Run away now. Better luck next time."

As it happened, I knew the bobby. I had met him during one of my walks, cycling contemplatively about the countryside, making me wonder whether a rural constable's life wasn't one of the best in the world. We had sat under a hedge and talked, and he did a bit of bird-watching through binoculars. I saw him enter in a book: "Aug. 14. Nuthatch. Thomas's fallow acre." He confided his ambition to write a book about what he called, knowing me to be a man of letters, avian activity in Cornwall.

It didn't take me long to show him the rights of Penelope's case. He handed over her sketchbook and camera, came in and drank a pint of beer, and told me that he thought there was a pair of white owls in the woods. Then he rode away, whistling, with Penelope and Tubby safely expunged from criminal record. Altogether an absurd episode, but it left me with something of Penelope's disquiet. It was an example, in its small way, of the bestial things war can do to the human mind.

7

When Penelope went, she took Simon and Tubby with her. She was to drop them at Marlborough. The world became very quiet: Rose, myself, Uncle Arthur. The curlews weeping and the first leaves beginning to drop from the flushed trees. I finished the play and rang up Max's office to tell him so. Max wasn't there and I was put through to Penelope. She said that when she was bidding Tubby good-by, he remarked casually: "I'm fifteen. If this is a long war I can get into it. I reckon a chap ought to be able to do something at eighteen."

"Not if I can prevent it," Penelope told me grimly.

"How are things in town?"

"Dreary in the daytime, damnable at night. I loathe groping in darkness."

"Cheer up, child," I said. "We've all got a lot of that in front of us. Any other news?"

"I expect you've heard about my father?"

I noted that Penelope didn't say "about Father." *About my father* had a cold sound. I wondered if that breach would ever heal. There was no longer the brash resentment, but the polite formality of Penelope's present relation with her parents seemed to me almost as distressing.

"I haven't heard. What's he up to?"

"Some Government job. I expect he'll end up with a knighthood. He's chairman of something. Board of economic co-operation with the Allies. Some tosh like that. Any news of Henrietta?"

"She and Martin are sailing from New York next week. We had a cable yesterday."

"The poor darling! If I know Martin, he'll plunge in up to the neck as soon as he lands."

The remark echoed my own fears, and I didn't pass it on to Rose. The days drooped by as September changed into October. Nothing seemed to be happening in our little world or in the world of the war. It was as though we were living in a fog, and it was bad for us. The melancholy of the season got into Rose's bones and mine. I knew what she was thinking about, because I was thinking about the same thing: about what I called *my* war. Exactly half my life ago. I was twenty-five then: fifty now. For many years I had not thought of May Ingleby. She haunted my memory at this moment. I remembered how she liked everything to be nice, and how I had walked out on her from our little Manchester house without the faintest prick of conscience. I recalled the absurd episode of the fish knives, and I said to Uncle Arthur: "Do you remember giving me fish knives when I married for the first time?"

"No. Did I do that, Chad? How banal! I hope you have long ago forgiven me." He looked at me keenly. "These are memory-searching days—eh?"

Rose would have more exciting memories than these. "Do you remember, Greg," my memory was saying, as I wandered alone in the sad

September woods, "how you and I and Phoebe went to the Café Royal and saw Rose and Eustace come in? My God, Greg, they were on top of the world that night!"

I wondered, not for the first time, what I had been able to give to Rose that could even faintly compare with the heady joys that had flowed from Eustace; and there she was, coming along a ride in the woods, as I had seen the small Rose Garland come, and she took my arm and kissed me and said: "Chad, darling!"

Just that, and I was happy again; and we walked toward the house whose chimneys were plumed with the blue smoke of a wood fire, and once more in the path she stopped me and kissed me and said: "What with my memories and what with this appalling waiting, I felt I couldn't go on, my darling, without you."

"That's a nice way for a woman of fifty to talk!"

"Oh," she said, "it gets worse and worse. Wait till I'm a hundred. You'll find me shockingly embarrassing."

8

Billy Pascoe rang up from a hotel in the Town and asked if he might come over to see us at Pentyrch. "Why, damn it all, Billy," I said, "why didn't you come straight here? You know this place is bursting with spare rooms."

"I didn't care to intrude." The cold formal voice of Sir William.

What a rum do life is! I thought. Billy Pascoe, who had known this house all his days, who had cleaned the boots and knives here and read the books in the library that no one else ever opened; Billy Pascoe, whom Miss Orlop and I, rushing away to London after the wedding, had left here with Rose for their honeymoon; Billy Pascoe, whom I had dragged, more dead than alive, and white as a shark's belly, out of the tarn. "I didn't care to intrude."

"Well, Sir William," I said, "I'm rather a busy man, you know. Hold on a moment. I'll ask my secretary to see how I'm fixed. I think it just possible that I can fit you in from three till three-five, or even three-six, tomorrow afternoon."

That drew what passed for a laugh with Billy. "All right, Chad. I'll cancel my room here and come right over."

I told Rose. She said: "Why not? I rather like Billy. He's not a bad old thing in his rather stuffy way." It was odd how those two could meet without a trace of embarrassment or self-consciousness. Whatever had been between them was as dead as the ashes you might find in an ancient burial mound.

Billy stayed for three days, and spent them mooning about the estate.

On the last day he invited me to walk with him. "You must have guessed, Chad," he said, "that I'm here as a spy."

"I thought it might be so, Billy."

"I feel very bad about it, because I'm afraid the place is perfect for our purposes. It'll have to be requisitioned."

"I love that word, Billy. It's the bureaucrat's equivalent of the old highwayman's cry: 'Stand and deliver!' With a pistol to back him up."

"Yes, it is. But I don't see what we can do about it," he said, bleakly. "I'm sorry it had to be Pentyrch."

"The irony of it is," I reminded him, "that it was once in your pocket, and might still have been all yours. Now it becomes yours anyway."

"Not exactly mine," he defended himself. "Certainly I have to report that it is suitable from my point of view: plenty of accommodation for the staff in the house, and good sites for what we'll have to build. But the property will remain Rose's."

"It must be a great consolation to a bird to be thrown out of its nest on its ear and told, 'The nest is still yours.' "

He looked uncomfortable and very obstinate. He said sententiously: "Needs must when the devil drives."

"Is this drive of yours so devilish?"

He stopped in the path, round about that very spot where, years ago, I had idiotically said: "Thank you, Pascoe," after he had carried the lantern for me and Uncle Arthur. I remembered how he had laughed about that, and how he had boasted that some day he'd give the world good cause to say: "Thank you, Pascoe." Well, as he stopped and looked at me, very sadly, I felt for a moment that we were nearer than we had been since those days to a confidential moment; but then the different directions of our lives that had been sweeping us apart all through so many years could not be denied, and Billy's look that had seemed a link suddenly snapped and he said: "What will be done here is, of course, something I shall not discuss." I could not restrain myself from using the old boyhood gag for the last time. "Thank you, Pascoe," I said; but it wakened nothing in him. I think he had forgotten it all.

We walked back toward the house, and past it, and down the path that led to the studio and the ramshackle buildings we had added to it, and we stood on the knoll and looked along the beach of our childhood. Down there Billy's mother had ended her haggard life. The day was drawing to its close as we stood side by side. The woods inland were misty, and an opal mist washed over the sea that was as still as glass. There was not a sound save the tired lisp of the water and the crying of the gulls.

I said: "I suppose Rose and I and our friends will be able to go on using these shacks at holidaytime?"

"I'm afraid not. As I see it, there'll be a lot of barbed wire about the place. It will have to be pretty heavily guarded. These huts would make good guardrooms on the seaward side."

We walked back toward the house, and I said: "I'm sorry we'll be pushed out from the huts, but don't worry about the house, Billy. Rose never felt much affection for it. It's been let for years. We preferred the huts. We've even slept out on the thyme in sleeping bags. But I suppose we're getting a bit beyond youthful larks. We fancied a bed this time. Still, Rose would have sold the place sooner or later."

"I'm glad it won't be too much of a wrench. I don't want to say good-by to Rose. She already has too many reasons for loathing me. I'll leave my car ready tonight and slip away first thing in the morning. I can get breakfast in the Town. Do you mind that, Chad? Will you explain to Rose, and give her my apologies?"

"Don't be so damned furtive," I said almost angrily. "There's no need to run away from Rose like that. She rather likes you."

"Since I untied the knot," he said with his bleak grin, "she has at least one good reason for doing so."

In the morning he vanished as he had threatened to do.

9

When Henrietta and Martin landed, they went to Chalk Hill to await us. We motored there a day or two after Billy had left, and that was the last long journey I made by car until the war was over. If I wanted to go to London, I drove to our nearest station, a couple of miles away, left the car there, and went by train.

Henrietta and Martin were looking very well. Martin had been a success, and thus they were happy. Happy so far as that went. But you could feel the cloud hanging over them. Not much was said about the war that first night, because there didn't seem to be a war. Here, as at Pentyrch, there was nothing but the sense of being shut up in a box, a fragile box, and waiting for a thunderbolt to smash it to pieces. After breakfast the next morning Martin walked with me to the pavilion, which had become a kind of confessional. I noticed that everybody who wanted confidential talk strolled up there. We passed Uncle Arthur, looking professionally agricultural, and he detained us to expound his intentions. The kitchen garden was to be exploited on a more intensive basis than ever before. Runner ducks were to be added to our few hens. In the summer there would be bees, and at once there would be goats. "Goats' milk, my dear boys, has a high nutritive content, if a somewhat repellent flavor. Goats have eaten up every civilization into which they have intruded. But this time they will learn a lesson: there will be no intrusion. The goat has yet to be born that could get the better of me."

We left him making for the swimming pool. He said he wished to investigate its possibilities as a stewpond. "Milk and honey, fruit and vegetables, eggs, an occasional duck in the pot and a carp from the pool —we shall not starve," he shouted.

" 'Fair round belly with good capon lined,' " Martin quoted with a smile. "You are lucky to have someone about who is so sensitive to food."

"Yes. Before this lot's over, we shall probably have a vineyard here, with the bottling of Château Geldersome in full swing." We sat down in the pavilion. "Well, what about it?"

"R.N.V.R."

"Have you done anything yet?"

"No. I'm going up to town tomorrow."

"You needn't worry about Henrietta. She can stay here as long as the war lasts."

"You don't know much about Henrietta, do you? She says she has two fathers: Eustace Hawke and you. Both her fathers were rather heavily involved last time, weren't they?"

"That's got nothing to do with her."

"She seems to think it has. I wouldn't try to dissuade her if I were you; but if you want to, here she is. And who's the admiral with her?"

They were climbing up from the house, the "admiral" making rather heavy weather of it; and when they were a bit nearer I said: "Well, look at that! It's Max!"

I got up, and when he reached us, saluted.

"Stand easy," he said. "How d'you like it?"

It was magnificent: a brand-new yachting cap, a reefer jacket, white trousers and natty black shoes. *Bessie* was emblazoned on the pocket of the coat. His tie was navy-blue.

Max said: "I have put my vessel at the disposal of the Admiralty." He sounded like Napoleon announcing that he had thrown in the decisive reserves.

"I hope my Lords Commissioners have suitably responded?"

"The sods haven't even answered. I beg your pardon, Henrietta. But I go to the trouble of bringing *Bessie* round to Hammersmith, cleaning out all the fal-de-lals and making her battleworthy, providing a crew of two at my own expense, and when I notify this to my Lords Commissioners of Admiralty, they don't bother to answer. No wonder we lose our wars."

"But, oddly enough, we don't, Max."

"Well, we damn well ought to," he said decisively.

"I expect there's a certain amount of confusion in Whitehall at the moment," I consoled him. "They'll come round to you in time."

"They'd better," he said, "or I shall offer my services to the French."

He did, too—to the French coast, at all events. None of us guessed, when we shook hands with Max that afternoon, that we should never see him again. But there came a night when the *Bessie*, with Max at the wheel and her crew of two, slipped out of the Thames and reported at Dover, and was directed to Dunkirk. To and fro she went, Dover-Dunkirk, Dunkirk-Dover, splashed with blood, packed with tattered remnants of England's expeditionary force. The pretty boat that had frivoled up and down from Maidenhead, adorned with Max's pretty girls, became a battered trull, spewed over and bled upon, until the night when the bombs that had rained about her got tired of her persistence and finished her off. Max was never seen again. One of his men swam to another boat. I had a talk with him later, and found him as dumb as most of his kind. "Well, we just kept going to and fro till we copped it." To some it might be an epic, but that's what it was to him. He could give me nothing that would help me to understand what it had been to Max.

10

I called up the stairs: "Come on, Corporal," and Uncle Arthur came running down. We were living in a world of wonders. I had never expected to see Uncle Arthur run, and I had never expected to see him in khaki. In the hall he saluted and said: "Ready, sir." He was a punctilious soldier. I picked up a shotgun and we set off together. We had both been in it from the beginning: from the days when there were no uniforms and we wore round our arms a brassard labeled "L.D.V." Now the Local Defense Volunteers had become the Home Guard; we had what seemed to me a sloppy sort of uniform, with a blouse instead of a tunic, trousers that had no puttees, and a forage cap that threatened to fall off the side of the head. There was one stripe on Uncle Arthur's sleeve, one pip on my shoulder. We still had one shotgun between us.

It was a bitter winter night with a full moon shining, and Simon and Tubby Chambers should long ago have been asleep. But we heard a tapping at their bedroom window, and there they were, waving us good-by. They would stay awake half the night looking southeast toward London. They would want to see the fires painting the sky and hear the thud of guns. Tubby was disappointed that he was not in it. If he had been staying with Miss Pennorth he would have been. But she was gone. She was a lieutenant of the W.R.A.F., and Henrietta was an officer of the W.R.N.S., both in distant stations. For this winter holiday Tubby had to put up with us.

Uncle Arthur was whistling, and I noticed that all his songs belonged to the Boer War. He whistled "Soldiers of the Queen" and "Dolly Grey." I didn't whistle, but if songs came into my head they were "Tipperary"

467

and "A Long, Long Trail" and "Oh My! I Don't Want to Die." Not that we were likely to die. But what a pair of has-beens we are, I thought. For the first time in my life I felt a contemporary of Uncle Arthur.

The frosty road rang under our boots. My nose tingled with the keen air. It would be another ghastly night for London: moonlight on the river, the fateful illuminated road to the city's heart. We began to hear the first thuds, and the customary sense of impotence made me writhe. I felt a fool, masquerading here as a soldier while tens of thousands of simple men and women were tasting a bitter reality. There had been altogether too much: a continent overrun by the enemy, London an all but defenseless sprawl, battered night after night, poor Max's death, Martin on the high seas, the girls gone.

"Don't whistle," I snarled. "Haven't you been taught to go about your duties quietly?"

Uncle Arthur said: "Yes, sir," and stopped whistling.

We walked on in silence, and presently I said: "The fact is you're too old for this nonsense. You should be in bed."

"I am little older than Mr. Churchill, sir."

"You're pretty well two decades older."

We walked again in silence, and then he suddenly burst out: "And another thing, I'm not having any snotty-nosed nephew telling *me* whether I'm too old for this, that or the other. I shall stay in this Home Guard if I drop dead in my tracks some night on patrol."

The naked rebellion cut the knots in my mind. I began to laugh. I said: "When I first went to Smurthwaite you checked me if I called you 'sir.' You said Uncle Arthur would do. Well, Chad'll do now."

"Smurthwaite!" he snorted contemptuously. "That pettifogging little borough! Don't remind me of my salad days. Let me be a man!"

We came to the guardroom, which was a shaky wooden shed draped over with branches and bracken. The platoon fell in on the moonlit road. I called the roll, apportioned the few miserable weapons. My men were a solicitor and a thatcher, a shepherd and an innkeeper, the sexton and curate to represent the church militant, and a few other odds and ends. There they were, standing in the moonlight under the hedge, and suddenly I felt proud of them and wanted to say so, but they would have wondered what I was getting at. Most of them had been youngsters in *my* war, and no doubt their hearts, like my own, were listening bitterly to the surge of time that had swept them into this half-farcical, half-heroic endeavor. Vimy Ridge, Menin Gate, Wipers and Armentières: it was all there for them, as for me. My heart warmed with something of the brotherly love I had known then, but had long forgotten.

"Corporal Geldersome."

"Sir!"

"Take your half-section to the bridge. You will be relieved at midnight."

"Yes, sir. Come on. Fall in now."

I watched them go; gave the others their duties, and went into the hut, lit by an oil lamp and warmed by an oil stove.

"Cold night, sir. I got a cup o' char ready."

I thought of the tens of thousands of cups o' char that batmen had produced at such moments as this. "Is it true," I asked, "that the British army marches on its bladder?"

The yokel looked at me, puzzled. "I don't understand, sir."

I felt I was back in the army all right.

II

That was near Christmas of 1940; and in August of 1941 I was thousands of miles away. I was standing above the huge stern guns of the *Prince of Wales*, looking down on the quarter-deck. A congregation of sailors with bare bowed heads stood with their backs to me, and facing me, grouped within the semicircle of the ship's stern rail, were the Prime Minister of England and the President of the United States, each with his entourage behind him. Autumnal sunlight fell on the sea, which was as still as sleep, and on the bleak Newfoundland shore, and on the cruisers and destroyers idle as painted ships. A few seaplanes were in the air, but their noise did not disturb the hush in which everyone stood.

O Eternal Lord God, Who alone spreadest out the heavens and rulest the raging of the sea; Who hast encompassed the waters with bounds until day and night come to an end; be pleased to receive into Thy Almighty and Most Gracious protection the persons of us Thy servants, and the Fleet in which we serve. Preserve us from the dangers of the sea, and from the violence of the enemy; that we may be a security for such as pass upon the seas upon their lawful occasions; that the peoples of the Empire may in peace and quietness serve Thee, our God; and that we may return in safety to enjoy the blessings of the land, with the fruits of our labors, and with a thankful remembrance of Thy mercies to praise and glorify Thy Holy Name; through Jesus Christ our Lord.

Beautiful vain words. The protection of God was not for all of these. A few months later many of them, and the great ship herself, had done with their warfare. But they were words that searched the marrow when listened to on that Sunday morning; and I was not surprised, when I clambered down to join the crowd dispersing from the quarter-deck, to find that Martin's eyes were wet. I was glad of that. I am not at home with the hard-boiled.

I had seen little of him during the voyage. Some freakish thought of the Ministry of Information that this Atlantic meeting might be recorded in words had brought me aboard a battleship for the first time in my life, and the occasion was so secret that it was not till I was climbing the ladder of the *Prince of Wales* in Scapa Flow that I knew that this ship in which Martin was serving was to be my home for a fortnight. I was lost in the illustrious concourse that came aboard with the Prime Minister: army and navy and air force chiefs, scientists, diplomats, civil servants, secretaries and detectives; and a chaplain took me in hand, introduced himself, and said: "I'll find an officer who'll show you your cabin, sir." He tapped a young officer on the shoulder, and Martin, wearing two wavy gold rings on his cuff, turned round.

Seeing me, he was as flabbergasted as I had been on seeing that the vast hulk towering like a cathedral above me was the *Prince of Wales*. In common with everyone else aboard, he had had no notion what was portended by the secret incursion they had been told to expect. We shook hands as though we had never met before, and he said: "Come this way, sir."

He led me through mystifying steel labyrinths and at last opened a door in a steel corridor, and stood aside for me to enter a steel cell. One glance showed me that it was his own cabin. Three photographs stood on a cabinet: an old woman whom I guessed to be the mother who had brought him up on pea soup, Max Middlemass, and Henrietta, wearing her W.R.N.S. uniform.

"Look, my boy," I said, "this is your own cabin. I can't turn you out."

"Can't you?" he said with a grin. "You do as you're told in this ship. Don't worry about me. I'll get my swede down somewhere." A marine put his head round the door. "This is Thomas," Martin explained. "He's your servant for the voyage."

"Can I get you a cup o' char, sir?" Thomas asked.

"Not for the moment, thank you," I said, but I felt I was going to be at home. After all, a marine is a soldier, not a sailor.

"What's it all about?" Martin asked.

"I know no more than you do, my dear boy. I was briefed to make a journey. I was not told whether it was to be by land, sea, or air. Now at least we know it's by sea and that the P.M. is in it. I still await further news."

"Well, the ship's like a summer boardinghouse. The landlady sleeps in the best bedroom all winter through. Then come the hordes, and she's lucky if she can crawl into a coal scuttle o' nights."

"I'm sorry. I hope I'm not being too much of a nuisance."

"Don't worry," he repeated. "I learned to make do with a hammock when I was an ordinary seaman. Well, I must run. I suppose we'll be getting under way."

I unpacked my few belongings, and presently the vast steel shell began to vibrate, and when I made my way onto the deck we were sliding westward. Away on the port bow a vast loom of land, darker than the deepening dusk, was Cape Wrath, mighty and ominous name. I stood watching it fade, thinking how inhospitable it looked, when a youth with one ring who had been standing at my side turned inboard with a sigh. "My home is there," he said, "almost on the point."

He began to talk to me about his garden, and his lazy gardener, and his fear of the neglect he would find when the war was over. I often thought about him after the tragedy had befallen, and wondered whether, as destruction flamed down off Singapore, his thoughts were turned back to a garden on that bleak height, which now was vanished astern as the ship began to bore her mighty shoulders into the gathering strength of the sea.

12

It was strange in mid-Atlantic, in that ship freighted with a moment of history so profound, to see Max's ugly mug looking at me whenever I entered the cabin. I had been walking the quarter-deck, with the weather freshening, and even leviathan shuddering at the sea's punches, and with the destroyers of the escort rearing up and plunging down, smothered and obliterated. The sun was gone, all was gray: sky, sea, and the ships themselves: and clearly the weather would worsen as the night went on. "Darken ship!" The loudspeakers shouted the order, and every porthole, every chink and cranny, was blanketed. We plunged forward, through dark night on the Atlantic and through a dark night of destiny, and I opened the cabin door, and there was Max who had died on an adventure so improbable. He seemed to link our two wars, and, looking at him, I was overwhelmed with despair that within the space of one short life a man should be permitted twice to see so complete a breakdown of human decency. We are like this ship, I thought. We climb to a crest apparently for no other purpose than to plunge into a gulf.

The cabin door opened and Martin came in, wearing his oldest clothes, his trousers tucked into sea boots, a muffler swathing his neck. He looked tired and overworked, as indeed he was and must be. He sat down in a chair and his eyes moved at once to the picture of Henrietta.

"How goes it?" I asked.

"Not bad. But thank God I'm not captain of this ship. I should feel

471

like a bank messenger carrying a million through streets full of thugs."

"What are you two going to do when this lot's over?" I asked him.

He gave me a look unbearably charged with foreboding, and twisted the picture in his long fingers.

"Over? Why, we've hardly started." And as if to emphasize his words, to remind me of what was happening outside this lighted steel cell, the ship shuddered, seemed to stay poised for a moment, then plunged.

"So much depends on this or that," Martin said, and I understood this or that to mean life or death. "For one thing, old Max's death has changed so much, hasn't it?"

"Yes."

"He was a father to me," Martin said simply. "D'you know, he never forgot that when he was a sergeant, or whatever he was, and you were a major, you were reasonably decent to him. Odd, isn't it, how a small thing like that can go on living forever. Or is it? Perhaps we underestimate the consequences of lovingkindness. Certainly the consequences of its absence are apparent today."

I had not known Martin before in so serious a mood, but there was cause for it.

"I shouldn't have got to the top so quick without him. How things will go now that he's not there I can't say. I have a notion that I shall go back to Hollywood, and perhaps stay there. They liked my work, you know."

"Yes, I know that."

He put the photograph down and rose. "Well, roll on our return to Scapa Flow. I should pick up a packet of letters from Henrietta. What about a quick one before dinner? Your dinner, that is. I'm due to glue myself to the radar."

We climbed up to the anteroom of the wardroom. The officers were clustered round the bar, a few, who had duties in hand, clad like Martin in their oldest rags; but most were in their Number Ones, with stiff-winged collars and black bow ties. Threading the gold rings on their cuffs were the colors denoting their callings: the surgeons' red, the paymasters' white, the engineers' purple, the schoolmasters' blue. A congregation of specialists. It looked almost sophisticated, but over their heads was a jagged hole torn in the steel, and they knew what that meant. It reminded them that this room was recently awash with blood and water, that from the deck above they had committed their dead to the sea, for that hole had been torn by a shell from the *Bismarck,* and when the ship was refitted it was left there, a *memento mori,* the skull on a philosopher's desk, to remind him that all flesh is as grass. It grinned down as we drank behind the double scuttles with the black curtains drawn before them. Then we went in to dinner, and after dinner the Prime Minister and all the other mighty ones joined us in viewing a film. The performers were Laurel and Hardy, and I couldn't help wondering what Napoleon—or Nelson, for that matter—would have said to that.

CHAPTER EIGHTEEN

I

HOW old are you now, Greg?" I asked.

"Sixty."

"That's a hell of an age to be. I'm only fifty-six."

"Sixty," said Uncle Arthur, "is a bagatelle. I am eighty-six. Now that the war is over, I propose to devote my mature years to some new interest. Music, perhaps."

"Are you thinking of composing?" Greg asked.

"No. I recognize my limitations. I am not a creator. I shall take up some instrument. Almost certainly the theorbo."

"I've never heard of it."

"Few people have. But that will be put right when I am seriously in my stride."

It was August, 1945, and we were sitting in the pavilion. We looked down on the back of the house. The *magnolia grandiflora* that I had planted as a sprig when I took the place was a tree. It makes you feel very old to be sitting under your own vine and figtree, I thought.

"Anyway, Uncle Arthur," Greg said, "the war isn't ended, you know. It has merely ceased to be in the open. It might have been ended if it hadn't been for that bomb on Hiroshima. The bombed of today always wants to be the bomber of tomorrow. We shall settle down now to prepare for that tomorrow. Whether it comes soon or late, we shall all be frightened to death of one another. Fear and peace don't go hand in hand. It's astonishing how full the Bible is of exhortations not to be afraid. Fear not, neither be thou dismayed. That sort of thing. But, you know, not to be afraid of what the other chap's got up his sleeve is the most difficult thing in the world."

"I was talking to our parson about it the other day," I said. "His view is that peace was never nearer, because fear of the consequences of breaking the peace will be so widespread."

"I've no doubt," Greg said, "that that will be the general parsonic line. Odd, when you come to think of it. The world that was to be saved by love must now be saved by hate, which is the psychological expression of fear. But what else is there for the poor chaps to say?"

"I should like," said Uncle Arthur, "to have Sir William Pascoe's view."

"Isn't it appalling," I said, "to think of things like this being cooked up at Pentyrch?"

"Yes, indeed," said Uncle Arthur. "I don't know what my dear lady would have said about it all. It was a place of such peace."

"You mustn't idealize it," I told him. "For one thing, your dear lady had a lot to do with creating Sir William Pascoe. For another, it wasn't a place of peace. Miss Orlop in her childhood knew misery there in beholding the misery of her mother. Rose was unhappy there. My father was brutally killed there, and in its shadow Billy Pascoe's mother ended an unendurable existence."

But Uncle Arthur defended Pentyrch stoutly. "No land," he said, "ever grew finer broccoli."

"Penelope's coming," Greg said. "I must go and give her a hand."

"Stay where you are, Greg," Uncle Arthur commanded him. "She has a more desirable hand than yours."

But Penelope shouted: "Hey! Father!" And Greg got up and ran down the hill to meet her. It stirred me, as I was rarely stirred, to see his eagerness. Uncle Arthur said quietly: "*And when he was yet a great way off his father saw him and ran . . .* Did it ever occur to you, Chad, that *ran* is the wonderful word in that passage?"

Tubby Chambers stepped aside as Greg came up, and it was with Greg's hand under her elbow that Penelope finished the climb. She sat down with a sigh of relief. A bomb on an A.A. gun site had shattered a bone in her foot. It would soon be right, but now it gave Tubby and Greg a chance to coddle her. She was pleased to have the pair of them treating her like an injured queen.

It was on this spot, not so long ago as it seemed—but how these little bits of not so long ago add up!—that I had watched her tearing a white petticoat into strips to make bandages for the grievously wounded Carruthers. In the days of Eustace and the Saga. Eustace, Max, Tubby, and the war: all had had a hand in making this Penelope in whom I could not but rejoice. "Good Yorkshire stuff will out," Greg had boasted. "She's a regular Clogger!" and when he said that, the old word from our Oxford days was more than I could bear. I remembered the night when Eustace brought Greta Lund to the club, and it seemed fantastic that so many years should be no more than a dream between a sleep and a waking.

"Where's Simon?" Tubby asked.

I looked at my watch. "There's ten minutes to go yet," I said. "They'll all be here."

Tubby was twenty-one. We had given him a birthday party last night. He had shot up into a slender reed of a boy with a homely face

474

whose plainness was redeemed by the candid blue eyes. He had had one year in the army, but had not been overseas. Science and mathematics, not exploration, had turned out to be his line. I had a nodding acquaintance with Sir Ernest Brotherston, a director of a great chemical combine, whose hobby was financing good plays that were tottering. He had a genuine love of the theater and lost a lot of money cheerfully. We were both members of the Garrick Club, and at lunch there one day I introduced Tubby to him. He took to the boy, and in September Tubby was to start with International Chemicals in some subordinate job. He had another tie with Brotherston, through Greg. It was amusing to me that Greg, who had spent his life in expounding the villainies of "capitalism," was now in the enemy's camp. The interallied economic job which had kept him busy throughout the war was ended, and he didn't want to go back to his professorship. It was then that International Chemicals decided to employ an economic adviser. He was offered the post, and took it at a lordly salary. "It will be like advising a nationalized industry," he explained, and I left him with this solacing thought. It wouldn't do Tubby any harm, and that was important.

When Tubby was replying to the toast of his health the night before, he rambled into a long discourse concerning Carruthers and the missionary's wife. "I am glad to tell you all," he ended, "that the missionary was eaten by cannibals last year, and, a decent period of mourning having passed, his wife has now consented to marry me."

He sat down so coolly that we wondered whether this was an odd joke, but Penelope, who was sitting next to him, leaned toward him and kissed him with so frank an avowal that we were left in no doubt. I noticed, as she now sat by my side, that she was wearing an engagement ring.

I wondered how she would take to West Africa, for that was Tubby's destination. International Chemicals had mines there, and I had heard whispers that uranium had been found in them. Uranium was a word very much of the moment—a word whose significance Billy Pascoe would understand better than I did. I had no doubt that uranium had occupied his mind at Site Y. Where that was I had but the vaguest idea, and I should have had no idea at all. I had heard of it in the most extraordinary way just before the bomb was dropped on Hiroshima. I had been asked to go to a camp in the West of England to talk to the soldiers there, and, more to relieve the tedium of my own existence than in hopes of doing them any good, I accepted. I wanted to have a day to myself before the lecture, in new country, so I traveled from Paddington on a night train. Just before we started, a young man carrying a brief case got in. The usual wartime collection of military and naval officers snored through the night in the slow-moving darkened coach. They left the train here and there, and by the time Plymouth was reached only the young man and I remained of those who set out from Paddington. He muttered, "Stretch my legs for a moment," and got out, leaving the brief case on his seat.

The platform at Plymouth was crowded with sailors, and sailors had no respect, in wartime, for first-class travelers. They stormed the train and soon my compartment seethed with sailors and kitbags. One of the matelots was grasping a beer bottle, and had clearly emptied many others. He applied to the brief case the only adjective at his command, and, as he wanted that corner seat, he picked the case up and hurled it through the window.

I was filled with an inexplicable sense of alarm. I had heard stories enough of what brief cases in wartime might contain, and of the criminally careless way in which they were sometimes lost, to fall into the wrong hands. I jumped out of the train, leaving my own bag behind me, and was then aware of two things: the train was starting, and the man in charge of the brief case was running along the platform.

I was annoyed at the thought of my night things and lecture notes speeding away, and I said roughly, stopping him: "Here it is. You ought to be damned well ashamed of yourself."

He was as white as a sheet as he looked hopelessly at the guard's van now sliding past us. He seemed inclined to try and leap upon it. I put a restraining hand on his arm and said: "Don't be silly. D'you want to kill yourself?"

He said: "Oh, my God! They'll be furious with me. These papers should have been there first thing in the morning."

"Who'll be furious with you?"

He said: "The people at Pentyrch," and then looked as though even to say that had been to say too much.

"If I know anything of Billy Pascoe's cold fury," I said, "you'll certainly be grilled."

Again an answer jerked out of him: "He's not there."

Then he took the bag from my hand, looked at me with eyes full of suspicion, and said: "Thank you for rescuing this. I must wait for another train or try and find a taxi. Good night."

"Good night," I said. "Let's see if we can find a drink."

We found a shrouded tearoom full of noisy singing sailors, and drank tea, and wandered out into the gray first light amid the shambles that had been Plymouth. I didn't mention Pentyrch or Billy Pascoe again for a long time. I let him get used to me. I told him of my own errand, and he had recovered enough to say that the soldiers in the camp had had a lucky escape.

The sun came up over Plymouth, and we held our breath as it indifferently showed us a city pounded to garbage. We sat down on a pile of rubble, the brief case tucked securely under the young man's arm. "Christ!" he said, "this is what bombs can do—even the ones we have now!"

We walked back to the station in time for his next train. For me, I decided to wait till the ruins awoke and see if I could find breakfast somewhere among them. Then I would go on by bus. I shook hands with the young man, whose name I never learned, and said: "Well, when Billy Pascoe gets back to Pentyrch give him my greetings. Don't forget the name—Chad Boothroyd."

"All right," he said. "But heaven knows when he'll be back. He's at Site Y."

"Where the devil is Site Y?" I asked.

He looked round apprehensively, as though there were danger in my even speaking the name.

"I have no idea," he said. "And I'm quite sure that, when he set out, Sir William had no idea either. All we know is that it's in the United States, and they cover a lot of ground."

I have learned since that Site Y was the hush-hush name for Los Alamos in the New Mexican desert, where American and European scientists worked together to produce the bombs that fell on Hiroshima and Nagasaki.

2

You begin to feel a bit out of the main current when you have a daughter of thirty-six, and I had long regarded Henrietta as in some sense my daughter. After all, she had borne my name for a good many years before she took the name of Napier. Martin was forty-one. They came up the hill arm in arm, and she still had the look of wanting never to let his arm go again. The time was so long when she had believed him dead. I had not discussed Hiroshima with Martin. Perhaps his view of the bombs would have been conditioned by memory of the Japanese bombs raining upon the *Prince of Wales.* He got ashore, and the jungle swallowed him for two years. They were two years of guerrilla fighting, accompanied sometimes by a few wandering Englishmen, sometimes by a few natives, a hard starving bitter life, which, he knew, was achieving nothing more than mosquito bites at the enemy, but that was enough to keep him alive and give him purpose. All the time, he was on the move, by land on his feet, and by sea in any sort of craft he could find. From the eastern tip of Java he dodged northward through the Macassar Strait to the Celebes Sea, and it was there, alone in an open boat with a homemade sail, that he was at last picked up by an American destroyer, two years to the day from the time his ship went

477

down. The destroyer put in to the Philippines and thence he was flown to the United States. Henrietta was at Chalk Hill on leave when the news came. She said brightly: "Really, it's too good to be true," got up from the lunch table, and went out. Rose made to follow her, but Uncle Arthur said: "Leave her alone, Rose," and she faced it by herself. She did not return till teatime, and then she was in an odd mood, like someone who had been communing with ghosts and angels. She said: "I think I'll go to bed, Mother," and she slept through that night and through the next day, as though there was much waking to be made up for.

Martin's work at Hollywood had not been forgotten. His name was news, and his odyssey, added to the name, made the news "front page." He met a number of the people he had known in Hollywood; and it was by influential invitation that he was about to return there, taking Henrietta with him.

I hadn't known, though I might have guessed, that when Tubby went to Africa Penelope would go with him. It was because of his departure, and that of Martin and Henrietta, that we were assembling in the pavilion for the photographs to be taken. The end of the war looked like robbing us of all the young life that had grown up alongside our own. Only Simon would be left. I could see him now leaving the house with Phoebe and Rose. He had just finished his first year at Oxford and was wearing the blazer of my own college, Exeter: a handsome boy whose character betrayed no particular trend or promise.

Of my contemporaries four were missing, and that is something to expect when you are heading for sixty. So far as Eustace and Max are concerned, nothing is here for tears, I told myself. Adrian? I had no tears for him, either, though for other reasons. Poor ineffective Adrian! He was a man I had found it impossible either to hate or to love. And how could one go on expending upon a memory nothing but pity?

Billy Pascoe? Indeed, I could weep for Billy, but I had to weep alone. When Martin returned from the United States, he brought me a letter. I did not know the handwriting; in all the course of our lives I had never before received a letter from Billy. That was my fault. A lonely little boy years ago had walked from St. Michael Pendeverel into our Town to see me off when I left with my mother and Uncle Arthur for Smurthwaite. "Write to me, Chad." I had never written, and so I had never seen Billy's handwriting. When I read the letter, it was of that moment on the railway platform that I thought, and then indeed I could have wept. I could have wept for the loneliness that, too late, I heard sobbing through those few words *Write to me*, the loneliness of the little boy, of whom neither my mother nor Uncle Arthur took any notice, of whom in the way of callous childhood I felt rather ashamed, for his backside was ragged and he had a starving look. The lonely boy, who would go back to the worst cottage in the village, to the feckless mother who did not know what she had brought into the world; the boy who then had not found Miss Orlop's powerful alliance and who would put on his green baize apron and shine her knives and clean her boots, while his brain was already stirring with intimations puzzling and profound. Was it any wonder, I asked myself, that Sir William Pascoe had a reputation for keeping people at arm's length with an icy self-sufficiency? How he used to curse that wretched Mrs. Apreece who had not understood Michael Faraday! How he must have cursed Chad Boothroyd and a thousand like him who had left Billy Pascoe in the lurch!

"I was asked," Martin said, "to give this letter to you. I was billeted in a hotel, and a chap called and said he understood I had married Henrietta Boothroyd. So I must know Chad. Would I oblige? A mysterious cove. Extraordinary! Wouldn't even give me his name. Well, I've fulfilled my promise. I hope it's not a begging letter."

We were all so excited by Martin's return that I did not read the letter at once. I put it in my pocket and found it there late that night when I had gone to my study to have a few moments of quiet.

3

MY DEAR CHAD:

Do you realize that I am one of the most important men in the world? I didn't know this myself till I was given a bodyguard, which is to say I was put under arrest, for I suspect that the purpose of my bodyguard is not so much to see that nobody gets at me as to see that I get at nobody else. I'm not the only one. Where I work, all the important people have body-guards. Mine is an amiable husky chap, and he carries a revolver. A gun, he calls it.

I am so important that you mustn't even know where my work is done. There are a lot of us swept together there—Italians, Danes, Germans, Americans, English—and we are shut up inside a barbed-wire fence, a genuine League of Nations, working in perfect understanding to give the nations something to thank us for. After *your* war, peoples were offered another sort of League of Nations. They didn't seem to want it. At any rate, they didn't want it enough to make it more than a gasworks; so now they must put up with our smaller and wonderfully elite League and with what it hands out to them.

If I can't tell you anything more than this about the place of our enchanting preoccupations, I think I may venture to say that I am at the moment in New York. There were one or two matters to be discussed with people in Columbia University. Being here, I couldn't help seeing from the newspapers that Henrietta's husband was in town. Everything—every last stitch of information—has been stripped from him. One would think he was an important person who had done important things. He is blazed abroad, while the people who are doing things that will make humanity look up are under lock and key, behind barbed wire, bodyguarded. Still, my dear Chad, that is how "democracy" works. That is how the people achieve life, liberty, and the pursuit of happiness.

Reading the bosh about this doubtless worthy film actor's adventures among the bamboos and the coral islands, I couldn't help feeling a stir in the region where my heart is supposed to be. The names cropped up. Henrietta. I could see her toddling about the house in Cambridge. She was a pretty little thing, but I never had any use for her, or for any children. God help me, I had my work to do. And Rose. She has come into it, too. Some of the papers have discovered that Henrietta is the illegitimate daughter of Rose and Eustace Hawke—"whose poems were, during the first World War. . . ." etc. And now this Rose is the wife of Mr. Chad Boothroyd, whose plays "so charmingly recorded the comedy of the English social scene between the wars."

So, you see, my brief time out of jail—though not out of the company of my bodyguard—has thrown me into a welter of reminiscence. I have breathed another air, as some wretch might on parole from a forced labor camp. And I suddenly find that this air belongs to a world which, for all its idiocies, trivialities and sentimental emotions, is worthy and desirable in a way that mine is not. It is a world that I have never lived in; but I have wandered along its fringes, and there have been times, especially when Rose was with me, when I longed passionately to enter into it. If I have never experienced its meaning, I have apprehended it; and now I know that what distinguishes it from my world is that, for all its tragic failures, it has within it the germ of life. And what I want to say to you, Chad, is this: that if the warm, bungling humanity of the life you know does not realize its responsibility to take hold of the life I represent and say: "Drop your bodyguards; come out from behind your barbed wire; let us know what you are doing, and let us judge whether you are to go on doing it, for *we* are the masters here, it is *our* lives and *our* future that you playing with in your icy solitude"—if you don't say that, and mean that, and do that, and do it *soon*—then the worse for you. Even now, it may be too late. Indeed, it *is* too late to prevent at any rate a puny demonstration of what, though it will fill the same world with horror, will be no more than the first mewling of a new-born giant who will stride among you, laughing at your boundaries, your nationalities, your pleasant delusion that you can order him to do your own little bit of dirty work, leaving you in happy immunity. Don't be a fool, Chad. If people say you can do that, you have it from me that you will be talking to half-witted morons.

Another thing I want you to know, Chad, is that the people who are doing this are in no way remarkable, in no way qualified to have so decisive a say in the affairs of the world. I have spent my life among them, and I know. They will tell you—most of them—that their business is discovery, and that what is done with the thing discovered is not their concern. That, in itself, is an admission of spiritual idiocy, of utter baseness, that makes them lower than the run of men and women, not greater, for who, with a grain of moral perception, would go on handing poison to a known murderer or manufacturing plates for a forger? But who am I to talk? My perception comes late. The only ray of light I see is that, even among my colleagues, there are some who are afraid.

However, for me, I have done with it. When I return behind the barbed wire I shall pretentiously potter and make no further contribution; and when I am back at Pentyrch, to carry forward the good work in England's green and pleasant land, I shall do the same. I shall be glad to be back at Pentyrch. My addiction to a morning swim is well known there. It's a wonderfully safe beach. The only danger is cramp, to which I am unfortunately addicted. That is why I always keep within my depth. In these last few months, I have been getting *out* of my depth in all sorts of ways. I must try—don't you think?—not to do that when I swim at Pentyrch.

Well, I should like to send lots of messages, Chad, but no one must know of this letter, so I can send none at all. I can't even ask you to let me have a line in reply. Not that it matters. Letter-writing always bored you, didn't it? But if you think of me sometimes, think back a long, long way.

Yours ever,

BILLY

4

Andy Miller, I supposed, would be the last. When your children are growing up, young people of one sort and another drift in and out of your consciousness; some of them, like Tubby, remain; most of them are no more than the guests of a night to an innkeeper. Andy Miller, Rhodes scholar from America, was Simon's latest, and after that, I supposed, the flow would stop.

I said so to Rose, and she said: "Nonsense, darling. Simon will marry, won't he, and have children?"

"Even supposing he does," I said, "I can't pretend that children interest me much till they begin to be recognizably human. That is never till they are ten—with luck. Allow three years for Simon to marry and produce, and that means another thirteen years. I shall have doddered well into my seventies, if I'm alive at all."

"Look at Greg," she said.

"What's so wonderful about him?"

"He's older than you are, and he's off on an entirely new line."

"He's not. He's simply selling the same dope to new customers. I was wondering about this pool."

We had strolled out through a most sweet spring day. The chestnut trees were lit up, and the trickle that flowed into the swimming pool was bordered by musk and mint and cuckoo flowers in lilac millions. But ever since the war began the place had been neglected. The channel of the stream had been allowed to silt up, and the water had diverted its course. It made a pool no more, and the concrete basin was dry save for rainwater that lay sodden among a deposit of leaves and mud. The paint had scaled off the dressing huts. They were dry planks that rattled in the wind. And the tennis lawn wasn't fit for a decent game. "I don't know whether it's worth while bringing this back into condition again," I said to Rose, "and once Simon is gone, as he soon will be, whether married or not, you may find this place altogether more than you need."

"Sit down," Rose said.

I sat down on one of the plank seats, and it collapsed beneath me. "You see what I mean?"

"What I see," Rose said, "is that that seat needs mending, or, better still, replacing."

Uncle Arthur, who had been coming toward us, quickened his step on seeing me upon the ground.

"I'm sorry, Chad," he said. "I should have mended that seat weeks ago. I've had it on my mind for a long time. And not only the seat. This whole area. Something must be done about it."

A cuckoo began to call, and some early swallows were flying high in the blue.

Rose said: "Chad is feeling a bit senile. He thinks we ought to give up Chalk Hill."

"It's what my mother called the spring sickness," Uncle Arthur said. "She used to give us children brimstone and treacle. If that didn't work, we had boiled raisins in senna tea."

I was not to be joked out of it. I had been thinking of Eustace and Max and of the mysterious death by drowning of Sir William Pascoe.

Rose said: "We've been here for nearly thirty years," and Simon, who had strolled up with Andy Miller, said: "And I've been here always. The first thing I can remember is the Adrian man smacking me across the head when I fell off my scooter."

Andy Miller said: "It's a good place to be, and this could be a good pool. I guess you and I could do something about it, Simon. We don't end our vacation for another fortnight. What do you say, Mr. Booth-royd?"

What could I say? "Go ahead," I said. "I'll give you a hand."

"The place used to be lovely," Simon said. "It could be as good as ever for next summer holiday. There's a girl at Somerville—Margaret Kingsley—she's a great admirer of your plays, Dad, and a first-rate swimmer."

Andy grinned at me out of a lean attractive face. "Now he's breaking the news, Mr. Boothroyd. I know Margaret."

Rose looked at me, and then she looked at Simon and said: "There's a place up the river at Oxford where one used to get honeycomb for tea. Is it still there?"

"I think I know where you mean," Simon said. "Why?"

Rose said: "I'm a great believer in tradition."

"Well, that's settled then," said Uncle Arthur. "Could we have an early breakfast, and all be on the job at eight-thirty?"

We left him and the boys discussing the job, sticking knives into planks to test their soundness. Rose took my arm, and as we walked back to the house I was well content. "Why on earth," I said, "should it give me such joy that you remember our honey tea? There doesn't seem much reason why, in such a world, so small a thing should matter."

"What's wrong with the world?"

"Why, Rose—"

"Yes, I know. I could name as easily as you could all the bits that make up the chaos the war has left, and all the foreboding that the bomb has cast upon the future. And do you think those boys don't know it, too? It concerns them far more than it does us. We've had our lives and theirs are to come. Alas, regardless of their doom, the little victims play. You can quote that if you like, and the answer is that the little victims grow up to play and to work and to live and to love because there's nothing else they can do."

She switched the direction of our walk, and we reached the pavilion, and she said: "I know, my darling, that the biggest lion ever lies across the path ahead, and it may be—it *may* be—that this one won't act according to precedent and nimbly leap out of the way as we approach. We can't know one way or the other. But we must go on. Life is life. It's got to be lived, and even if I knew I had to be blown to smithereens tomorrow I shouldn't call that any reason for not living as happily and intelligently and industriously today as I know how. I should still want to remember, and be thankful for, all the happy and beautiful moments I had known. And that includes a honey tea on the river at Oxford, because that was the day when I first knew—really *knew*—that you loved me. Although, poor darling, it was a long time before I realized that I loved you, too."

We stood arm in arm between the white pillars, looking down on the rushing glory of the spring.

Rose suddenly laughed. "Do you know, Chad, I think Uncle Arthur wants us to keep this place in order so that he may inherit it when we are dead. Look at the man! He's taking his coat off! He can't wait for tomorrow."

FALMOUTH
    December 2, 1953
    April 17, 1955